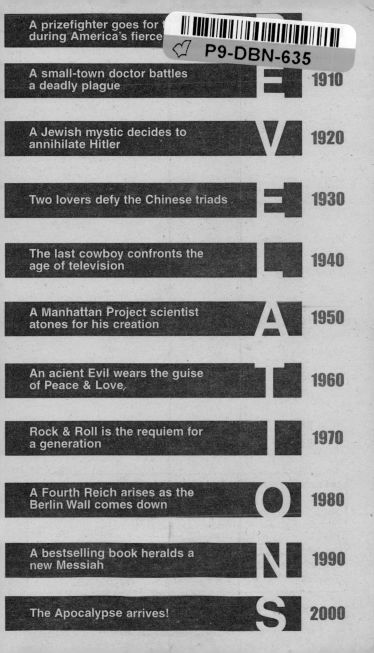

A prizefighter goes for during America's fierce

A small-town doctor battles a deadly plague — 1910

A Jewish mystic decides to annihilate Hitler — 1920

Two lovers defy the Chinese triads — 1930

The last cowboy confronts the age of television — 1940

A Manhattan Project scientist atones for his creation — 1950

An acient Evil wears the guise of Peace & Love, — 1960

Rock & Roll is the requiem for a generation — 1970

A Fourth Reich arises as the Berlin Wall comes down — 1980

A bestselling book heralds a new Messiah — 1990

The Apocalypse arrives! — 2000

P9-DBN-635

REVELATIONS

EDITED BY

DOUGLAS E. WINTER

HarperPrism
A Division of HarperCollinsPublishers

HarperPrism
A Division of HarperCollins*Publishers*
10 East 53rd Street, New York, N.Y. 10022-5299

Individual story copyrights appear on pages 649–650

Permissions appear on page 651

ISBN 0-06-105643-X

HarperCollins®, 🔥®, HarperPrism®
are trademarks of HarperCollins*Publishers*, Inc.

Cover illustration by Thomas Canty

A hardcover edition of the book was published
in 1997 by HarperPrism.

First paperback printing: January 1998

Printed in the United States of America

Visit HarperPrism on the World Wide Web at
http://www.harperprism.com

❖ 10 9 8 7 6 5 4 3 2 1

For Howard Morhaim
the long road home

TABLE OF CONTENTS

∞   "CHILIAD: A MEDITATION—MEN AND SIN"
       BY CLIVE BARKER   1

1900   "THE BIG BLOW"
       BY JOE R. LANSDALE   29

1910   "IF I SHOULD DIE BEFORE I WAKE"
       BY DAVID MORRELL   97

1920   "ARYANS AND ABSINTHE"
       BY F. PAUL WILSON   151

1930   "TRIADS"
       BY POPPY Z. BRITE AND CHRISTA FAUST   201

1940   "RIDING THE BLACK"
       BY CHARLES GRANT   301

1950   "THE OPEN DOORS"
       BY WHITLEY STRIEBER   337

1960   "FIXTURES OF MATCHSTICK MEN AND JOO"
       BY ELIZABETH MASSIE   389

1970   "WHATEVER"
       BY RICHARD CHRISTIAN MATHESON   447

1980   "DISMANTLING FORTRESS ARCHITECTURE"
       BY DAVID J. SCHOW AND CRAIG SPECTOR   495

1990   "THE WORD"
       BY RAMSEY CAMPBELL   551

∞   "CHILIAD: A MEDITATION—
A MOMENT AT THE RIVER'S HEART"
       BY CLIVE BARKER   595

Ω   "THE END" (AN AFTERWORD)
       BY DOUGLAS E. WINTER   633

REVELATIONS

For the movements of a man's life are in spirals: we go back whence we came, ever returning on our former traces, only upon a higher level, on the next upward coil of the spiral, so that it is a going back and a going forward ever and both at once.

—George MacDonald
England's Antiphon

CHILIAD: A MEDITATION

CLIVE BARKER

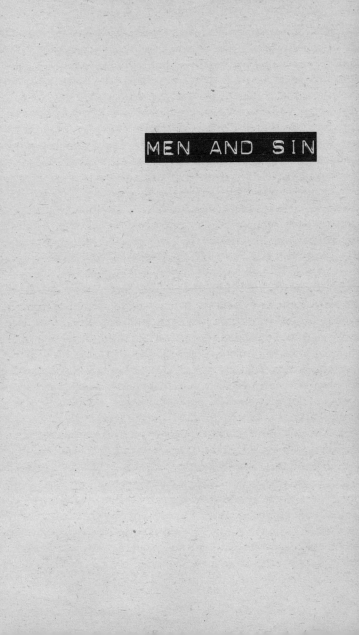

MEN AND SIN

In my mind, the river flows both ways. Out toward the sea, toward futurity; to death, of course; to revelation, perhaps; perhaps to both. And back the way it came, at least at those places where the currents are most perverse; where vortexes appear, and the waters are like foamy skirts on the hips of the rocks. I have made my spying places at those spots. Rough hides on the muddy banks, sometimes nests of sticks and blankets in the embrace of branches, from which vantage points I can surreptitiously study the river as it contradicts itself, setting the details down in my notebook for subsequent analysis. On occasion I have even ventured into the tumult: once intentionally, once by accident (a branch broke beneath me and I almost drowned, knocked back and forth between the rocks like a shuttlecock). It was far from pleasant, believe me. Don't trust what you may hear from shamans, who tell you, with puffy eyes, how fine it is to bathe in the river. They have their mutability to keep them from harm. The rest of us are much more brittle; more likely to bruise and break in the flood. It is, in truth, vile to be in the midst of such a commanding torrent: not to know if you will be carried back to the womb—to the ease of the mother's waters—or out into cold father death. To hope one moment, and be in extremis the next; and not to know, half the time, which of the prospects comforts and which arouses fear.

But as long as I am safe on the bank, merely a witness, it

is a fine place to meditate. And sometimes the proximity of
the waters—perhaps their spray, which mists the air, perhaps
their roar, which makes the heart tremble—induces visions.

Once, for instance, sitting in my hide spying on the river,
I imagined myself abruptly removed to a hillside. The scene
before me was that of a patchwork of fields in which men and
women labored. There was much about the sight that put me
in mind of a medieval illumination. The backbreaking work
of the peasants, the absence of any sign of modernity—a vehicle, a telegraph pole—but more than these, a flatness about
the whole panorama that made the cerulean sky and the
rolling horizon and all that was laid between my hillside and
that horizon—hedgerows, paths, fields, and cottages—appear
to lie in the same plane of vision; all in perfect focus, and in
perfect relation to one another. It seemed to me that this world
existed somewhere between actuality and design. It was part
document, part decoration.

My gaze became fixed upon a plowman who was working a little distance from me. He was digging up corpses, I
saw; the motion of his spade uncovering the dead, one by
one. Was this a cemetery? I wondered. I could see that there
were markers in the ground, but they did not resemble grave-
stones; they were simply stripped twigs, driven into the earth
to show the whereabouts of the cadavers, which had been
buried at regular intervals all across the field.

And then I realized my error. There was *movement* among
these corpses. They were turning over in their wormy beds so
as to look at the sky, stretching their pale, naked limbs like
sleepers stirred from slumber. Some were sitting up; standing
now, still doubting the reliability of their limbs. They were
most of them old: faces wizened, breasts empty, eyes blind, or
rheumy. And yet they were happy in their condition. They
capered as they grew to trust their legs and their good fortune,
greeting one another with toothless smiles. Then they proceeded to make their way down the much-rutted road to the

cluster of huts that lay a little distance from their field, their gait growing steadier as they went. I saw the doors of the huts flung wide, and the dead welcomed over the thresholds as though they were expected. Fires were lit to warm them; stew, bread, and wine were set before them. They ate, they dressed, then they sat and listened to their hosts' children, who talked to them with great gravity, as children do.

After a time, they began to live; to get about the duties of men and women who have purpose and appetite. And as they did so—as they thatched and fished and prayed and sat contemplating the sky—I saw the toll of years steadily removed. I saw their hair thicken, and their flesh grow ruddier; I saw the women's breasts become lush, and their haggard faces become smooth; I saw the men strengthen, and their gums get teeth, and the sexes turn glittering eyes on one another, and marry.

I understood the vision more clearly now. These were people who were born from the grave, and were living backwards toward the womb. No wonder they'd listened so attentively to the infants when they'd first returned; they were attending to the wisdom of their elders.

I longed to hear what passed between them: to ask them, if we had a tongue in common, what it felt like to be born from the grave. But that was not to be. The crop of couples I'd seen unearthed by the man in the field was by now reduced to treasured childhood, the oldest of them carried as babes-in-arms, shrinking still, until they were little more than red worms in the palms of their protectors, in which state they were taken back to the ground from which they'd come, and with great irreverence—much laughter, much drinking— buried. Several of the women stripped naked and danced a stamping dance on the earth to pack it tight upon the heads of these seeds. Then the crowd returned to the village. There it waited for sun, rain, and the goodness of God Almighty to raise another generation.

That was my vision, had on the riverbank. I've been warned more than once about looking for significance in these dreams. They come, many people say, simply to distract us from the simple verities of a life lived for pragmatic purpose. But I don't believe this, at least not entirely. Though I cannot myself see the meaning of this vision, or any other I may tell, that is not to say it cannot be profitably trawled for wisdom.

ii

In my mind the river flows both ways. Forward, to the explanation of things; to a destination which will justify the agonies of travel. And back, back to a time when the river was real, and those who wandered along its banks had little interest in visions.

This man, for instance, coming between the trees now, his boots dusting the frost off the grass, his eyes on the bank, and on the waters: he hasn't come here looking for revelation. He only wants sight of the woman with whom he has shared his filthy shack, some half a mile upstream of this spot, for the last four years. Her name is Agnes. His name is Martin, but she, for some reason he does not remember, dubbed him Shank, and Shank he is. He is also, let it be said, the ugliest man in this shire of England; his face a mass of lumps and tics, his beard, which he seldom trims, matted.

It is a day short of a thousand years since the year zero, and most of the God-fearing men and women who live along the river have gathered at the church in the village of Tress to give thanks for their Redeemer. But Shank has only one hope of redemption: his Agnes, who dared his ugliness and his violent soul to share her life with him; his Agnes, who went out in the early dawn saying she had to make water, and did not come back to their bed beside the hearth; his Agnes, who told him once that she did not believe in paradise, but that to share eternity in a common grave with him, to molder side by side, would be quite sufficient. He had not let her see how much it had moved him to hear this. Only later, alone by the river, had he heard an animal sound close by and realized that it was the growl of his own grateful tears.

Agnes is no more loved by those who live along the river than Shank. Though she is bighearted and wide-hipped, her body is strangely made between her legs; she has something of a man's anatomy there and something of a woman's, oddly configured. Shank doesn't care; in truth he takes comfort in the fact that for all the sheen of her black, black hair and the fierceness of her eyes, no man would take her to wife. So what if she can never give him children; he hates children. He hates everything, except Agnes and the river.

It is not a life that could ever be called civilized. They do not speak endearments to one another. They do not pray. They do not converse about anything abstract: they talk only of food, fire, and the roof over their heads. They fuck sometimes, though neither has a great appetite for it. Sometimes, alone in the woods, Shank masturbates. Occasionally, he violates an animal. But they live in a kind of marriage, nevertheless; a marriage stripped, to be sure, of every superfice of civilization; but bound to one another as surely as any couple who had spoken vows at an altar.

But now Agnes has gone, and Shank is filled with fear. These are lawless times; it is not unheard of for women here along the river to be attacked and raped by men who come down from the hills, and then, their crime committed, return there, leaving little chance for retribution. And stranger things than this he's heard. Men who were not quite men, but took at certain times the forms of animals, who carried off children and devoured them. One man, only the previous summer, found outside his own house, glutted on blood and baby flesh, and the cradle inside empty, the swaddling clothes shredded. This creature, at least, was hanged, and at the tree had claimed that the Old One had come into him, and told him: *At the passing of a thousand years the Son of God will come back into the living world, and my power over men will be passed, so I must do my worst.*

Shank did not believe this story when he heard it, but now he wonders if it could be true; there is something strange about the day, something he cannot name. He takes out his hunting knife and carries it at his side as he proceeds. He will be ready for whatever comes his way: man, beast, or the two in one.

iii

In my forty-fourth year a malaise crept upon me, and took me in its jaws, as Shank fears the wolfman will take him. But I had no knife. I had gone without caution into my middle years, and was unprepared for what felled me. My limbs turned to lead, my chest ached with the weary duty of breath, all I had made in my life, and all I had sought to make, seemed worthless. I was thrown by this beast into a chasm so deep and so dark I could not see the sky. And there—my body useless, my mind stupid with its own circlings—I lay. On good days, I felt enough to weep.

The conventional solutions were proffered by those who cared for me: I was simply enduring the familiar crisis of a middle-aged man, they said; I had lost faith with my purpose in life, and would have to find another. I had run out of joy, run out of certainty, was reduced, in the midst of popularity and plenty, to despair.

This despair was the reason I forsook all the places I called my own in happier times (they reminded me too much of what I had lost; of who I no longer was) and found myself a new place to sit. I went to the river. I had been there before, once or twice. But I'd never made a study of its motion the way I did now, never watched the waters so closely, or let my mind go with them, upstream and down.

Inevitably, a story came into my head. Tales had kept coming, even in the chasm, like invitations to parties I could not bear to attend, cracked and disfigured as I was. This one, however, seemed to speak to me more tenderly than the others. This one was not like the stories I had told in my younger days: it was not so certain of itself, nor of its purpose. It and I had much in common. I liked the way it curled upon itself, like the waters in the river, how it offered to fold itself into my grief, and lie there a while if necessary, until I could find a way to speak. I liked its lack of sentiment. I liked its lack of morality.

I think it was the presence of this tale that induced the first vision: that graveyard, and the souls that were born out of it. I set the vision down; and once my hand began to move over the paper, I felt the lethargy relieved a little, as though the very motion was soothing me with its familiarity. The words began to come. I saw Shank along the river; poor, deserted Shank. I found, in my dictionary, a title I liked. *Chiliad*: the period of a thousand years. Also *Chiliasm*, a doctrine which postulates Christ's reappearance on Earth, in visible form, and the establishing of a theocratic kingdom. I did not know, when I began to write, if Christ would come into my story. I still don't know. Perhaps, in the end, this will be a story of the anti-Chiliasm: of a time when Christ does *not* come, when the doors of Heaven are not thrown wide, and in lieu of God's infinite beatitudes we have only the comfort of our own inventions; a time when the lights seen in the sky are only the reflections of starlight off the sickened stratosphere, and the miracles of healing that occur in holy places turn out to be merely force of will, and are reversed when the witnesses look the other way; when the mathematicians tell us that on further reflection their calculations were wrong, and that nothing knits us together, nothing connects, nothing shows the least sign of elegance or sublimity.

There is in our natures a calamitous hunger for consummation. Having begun, without a choice in the matter, we want to be sure we have some hand in the conclusion. We want to mark it, on the calendar of the ages. *There we began. Here we end.* And if at our demise there is a universal ending, would that be so bad? If we leave only filth and dead seas to those who come after us, would that be so bad?

Mark me, though this wretched appetite is only confessed by hysterics—by the maverick messiah who leads his shabby flock onto the mountain in readiness, counting down the hours to his Armageddon (which is postponed by their prayers)—it is a universal desire. We all count the hours. We all look for completion, even if we fear it. We long to be consumed. I long to be consumed. If I were to meet Shank along the river I would be hard-pressed not to put myself in the way of his knife.

iv

And now he sees her. There she is, in the mud, facedown in the mud. She is not naked, but her dress has been pushed up by the waters that lap against her, exposing her buttocks. Her flesh is voluptuous, even in the flat December light, its paleness vivid against the dark mud. The first thing Shank does when he gets to the body is to pull the coarse, sodden fabric back down over her nakedness, so that the sky and the river will not see her this way. Only then does he pull her face out of the mud and roll her over. The wounds that took her life are at her neck, but there are many other, smaller cuts on her arms and hands, where she attempted to fight off her murderer, and a few on her breasts, which hurts only become apparent when Shank washes her face and upper body with handfuls of icy water from the river. There is very little blood; most of it has been washed away; the wounds are just flaps of skin from which pinkish fluid oozes. Her eyes are closed. Her mouth is open a little; her lips are bluish. At last, he brings himself to look between her legs, and finds that the strange formations of her sex have been horribly cut and dug out, so that her groin, which more than once he doted on while she slept, is an unrecognizable mass of tattered flesh. He does not hope for much, but he hopes she was dead when this was done.

Back to the river he goes, wading in a few yards to be sure he has the clearest water to wash her with, and tenderly, more tenderly even than the bathing of her face, he bathes her groin. Oh now he weeps; he weeps and weeps; and perhaps a poet would say he adds his tears to the waters with which he washes her sex; and if tears could heal, as sometimes in poems they do, if grief could perform miracles, as sometimes in fiction it must, then she would be returned with this devotion into her strange wholeness. But of course she is not. And finally he can weep no more.

He lifts her up and carries her into the trees, laying her weight down on pretty pillows of frosted grass. Then he thinks: *If I take time to attend to her any longer, the man who did this will certainly be gone, back to the hills. I can bury her later. But I can only catch him now. And whatever she suffered, he will suffer so much worse, so much worse. However loudly she cried, and begged him to stop, her murderer will cry out more loudly.*

He becomes—in this moment—another thing: he becomes death-in-life, the man whose knife is his only expression. He is not angry now; knives are not angry. He is not tearful now; knives are not tearful. He is simply sharp and keen and inevitable.

Do not be comforted by this, though it's hard, I know, not to enjoy the momentum he owns as he weaves between the trees; hard not to take pleasure in the simplicity of what he has become.

Two miles away, in the church at Tress, the priest, Father Michael, having served his congregation a healthy slice of sermonizing, and seen them from his door, retires to his tiny cottage and drinks a glass of sour wine. He has an iron constitution, though he looks old for his thirty-two years. He hopes he will not live long, however; they will have a new priest very soon, these people who sit gob-eyed in his pews, barely comprehending a word he says. Somebody who loves them better than he.

He pours himself another glass of wine, and thumbing a hole in the frost-flowered window, looks out on the church-yard. God help him, he does not want to be buried here; nor does he even deserve it. The bodies locked in the frozen dirt outside are those of men and women too ignorant to know the true meaning of sin, whereas he has no such defense. He does not deserve to lie at peace among them. The question is: what *does* he deserve?

He turns from the window, drinks his wine, and muses on this a little while. What punishment does Hell have in mind for him? He studied the tenets of his faith under a man who could recite the architecture of the Pit by rote: the spits, the vats, the wastes. Each had its purpose, created to remind the sinner of the sin for the span of his punishment. This same tutor, now a bishop, also reminded his students often that however terrible these torments might seem, they were insignificant beside that of the soul's loneliness if separated from God. Michael tried to believe this, but he never could. It was a theological pretension. Why, the merest sting of a bee, or a cut on the thumb, could make him cry out: bodily suffering on the scale that his tutor had described surely surpassed *any* loneliness. He was lonely now, Godless now, and it was bearable. Wine took the hurt away, if it was imbibed regularly enough.

So, what agony awaited him? Some terrible device, designed for him and him alone? Some private rack which would deliver upon his person torments a thousandfold worse than any he could suffer in this world?

Well, the longer he stayed out of its embrace, the better. Perhaps, after all, he wouldn't die young. He would pickle himself in bad wine and outlive Methuselah; deny the Devil the pleasure of his pain a few decades, and maybe, just maybe, find himself salvation in the meantime.

I pity Father Michael, in his cups. I would like to send Christ to him, right now. I would like to describe how—as Michael poured himself another glass of wine—he heard the sound of doves in the churchyard oaks and set his glass down and went to the door and saw his Redeemer there, sitting beneath the trees, which had miraculously blossomed. Michael would drop his glass, stumble out into the wintry light, fall to his knees and repent his sins. And Jesus would lay a bloodied palm upon his head, and softly tell him that he need not fear the Pit, for he was saved.

But I cannot find the Man of Sorrows today. Last night, sitting at my desk planning the day's work, I thought I might have Christ close enough to describe. But there is too much fog today; I cannot see the Son; so how can I deliver Him in that song-sweet place beneath the oaks? Oh, you say, invent Him; that's what writers do. Sometimes indeed that's true; but not here, not now. This morning, I have a clear vision of Father Michael, meditating on the terrors of Hell while he swills his wine; but his Redeemer is nowhere to be seen.

The doctor tells me my depression has made me anhedonic; in other words I cannot experience pleasure in things. This is particularly acute in the business at hand: writing. He asks me how long I've felt like this, and I tell him I don't know. Have I ever felt *pleasure* in the exercising of my craft? There's some small sensual thrill in the motion of pen over paper, I suppose, some puritanical satisfaction to be taken in seeing the pile of filled pages climb. But pleasure? As in the act of love, or of eating chocolate? No.

Which leads me to wonder if my work has not been all these years a form of self-castigation; if I am not like Father Michael in his cell, looking out through the tiny hole he made to see the world through, and then, despairing of the sight, returning to his meditations on suffering.

(Later, I think: why should I even *expect* pleasure from the work I do? Pleasure is a reward, given to the human system by evolution in return for services rendered to the preservation and increase of the species. I serve nothing natural in the business of making stories. It does not advance the race a jot that a writer tells tales of doubt and darkness and revelation. Why should I be rewarded with pleasure? I think the truest evidence of the divine in our dealings is the fact that our imaginations are indulged at all, that we are not simply breeding machines, programmed to procreate. The queer in his sterile heat, the anchorite in her sealed cell, the scientist measuring the distance between unreachable galaxies, and the poet agonizing for want of a syllable, are all living lives that serve no evolutionary purpose. Is the divine not most visible in our lack of practical application? Our dreaminess, our resistance to the imperatives of egg and sperm and family?)

V

There is a man called Oswald, who lives with his family on the edge of the woods, within sight of the village. He is the only man in the vicinity who has any regular dealings with Shank. A thick-necked, bald, and willful man, Oswald likes to laugh, especially when news is bad. His neighbors find this disconcerting, and on occasion wonder behind their hands if Oswald's entirely sane, but there is in him a kind of common sense that's hard to gainsay. When the most productive of his four cows died, and he was found laughing beside the corpse, he could only remark that she looked funny with her stiff legs akimbo, and what was he to do about it anyway: he couldn't resurrect her, so why weep?

Today Shank finds Oswald outside his hut, sitting on a log. His wife has thrown him out, he says, until he stops annoying her with stupid games. Shank tells him what happened to Agnes, and for once Oswald does not laugh.

"There's been three hillmen through here," he tells Shank. "Only an hour since. I spoke to them myself, and one of them was a bad fellow to be sure."

Shank asks him what this villain looked like, and Oswald tells him: small man, red hair, with the face of a shaved pig. This makes Oswald laugh.

"Shall I come with you, to take him?" he says.

Shank says no, this is his work and his alone. Oswald tells him he'll gladly hang the man; he's done it before, when justice required it, and he likes the duty, especially when they kick; that always wins his laughter.

Finally, as Shank leaves, he offers to bury Agnes. Again, Shank tells him no.

"At least let me fetch the body to your house," Oswald offers, "or else some animal may take her."

Shank conveys his gratitude, as best his lumpen vocabulary allows, and tells him yes, he'd like Oswald to take Agnes's body to the house. Then he leaves, in pursuit of the shaved pig.

———

I need not tell you much about this man, whose blade allegedly worked such terrible work upon Agnes. You need only know that he is innocent, at least of the crime he is soon to die for. He has committed other acts, almost as terrible (Oswald is not wrong to see malice in him); so perhaps there is some justice in what he is about to receive. But being—at least today—a man who does not expect to be stalked, and keeping the company of two other men (one his half brother) who are feeling equally blameless this late afternoon, the man makes no attempt to cover his tracks. Shank finds evidence of the trio quickly enough, and soon begins to close on them. Once he is near enough to see them, however—which is at dusk—he hangs back and waits. The trio have made a little fire among the trees, and are cooking a rabbit one of them caught; they will go no farther tonight. Shank can afford to squat on his haunches against a tree, and watch the stars come out above, until the men sleep. Then he will take them, one by one. There is no question in his head as to whether he should spare the killer's companions: their proximity condemns them. All three will die for the crime of one.

In Tress, the congregation returns for the evening service, and files into the little church to give thanks for another day lived without harm; but though Father Michael's flock waits for its priest to appear, it waits in vain. At last, somebody gets up and looks for Father Michael. He is not to be found.

(No, that's not true. I can find him for you. He's sitting high, high in the branches of the largest of the oaks in the churchyard. Though it's night, his form is discernible as an absence of stars. Nobody thinks to look up as they file out, shaking their heads at the strangeness of all this. Why would they? Nobody expects to see their priest perched in a tree.)

Oswald, meanwhile, has gone to fetch Agnes's body to a place of safety. He is not, by the standards of his age, a particularly superstitious man. If a creature half-man and half-wolf were to lope past him now, he would certainly believe the evidence of his eyes, but he does not anticipate such a horror appearing. He doesn't mutter prayers or old rhymes to himself as he goes, to keep evil from crossing his path; he doesn't have a talisman in his pocket, or a cross. But as he makes his way along the riverbank to the spot that Shank described where he will find the body, an uneasiness creeps over him. It is nothing to do with the grisly prospect before him; he's seen the worst that the world can do to human flesh in his time. What makes him slow down and study the trees a little more carefully is the strange fullness of feeling that has arisen in him. He wants to weep, and he does not know why. His eyes sting, and his nose runs, and for a moment he has to stop and wipe the snot from his moustache and the tears from his cheeks. When he has done so, and he raises his head, he sees a sight that will be the most peculiar of his long life. A little distance from him, a man has appeared on the banks of the river. He has his back to Oswald, but it seems the stranger is carrying some kind of light, because his figure is delineated by a pale glow. There is something calming about the sight. The light is as pretty as the light of a spring moon, and as steady. Though the wind has risen since Oswald began his journey here, the lamp the man carries does not so much as flicker. Nor is there anything about the silhouette that gives Oswald reason to think the man is dangerous to him. Indeed there seems to be something almost insubstantial about him; the clearer Oswald's gaze becomes, the more it seems to him the light the man carries seeps through his body here and there, as though he were only half-solid.

Oswald knows what the dead are reported to look like when they are glimpsed by the living: how they strive for corporeality, and fail. Is this, then, a dead man he sees? If so, why does Oswald feel such serenity? Why does he want to approach the man and see him better?

He does not analyze his instincts for more than a heartbeat, but follows them, approaching the ghost without any attempt at concealment. And as he gets closer, the mystery of the man's appearance deepens. He is dressed in clothes quite foreign to Oswald's eye: sleek, pale clothes that might befit a nobleman from some unknown country. He carries no weapon that Oswald can see, nor is there any sign that he has companions. He is simply standing there among the trees, bathed in and pierced by the light he carries.

Only as he comes within a stone's throw of the man does Oswald see what lies at the fellow's feet: Agnes's body.

Oswald stops, his thoughts suddenly chaotic. Is this Agnes's slaughterer; some phantom she encountered by the river, who took her life and then came back to gloat over the body? If so, Shank will revenge himself upon the wrong man, which in other circumstances might make Oswald laugh—he's taken pleasure in the absurdity of misplaced murder before—but gives him no such pleasure now. He is of half a mind to turn back and try to intercept Shank on his mission, but in the moment of indecision the phantom senses his presence and turns to look at him. *And oh, the face Oswald sees between the trees—the look in the spirit's eyes, the mournful expression—takes all hope of laughter from him.* After this moment, Oswald will not laugh again—not ever. He will grow old, very old by the standards of the time, but it will be a life lived in a state of sorrow.

The phantom speaks. *This is not my wife,* he says. And then, after a long time, *Who is she?*

Oswald doesn't want to exchange words with the spirit. The less contact he makes, he reasons, the better. Let the ghost quiz some other wanderer who comes here.

He starts to retreat, step by stumbling step, keeping his eyes on the dead as he does so.

Who is she? the phantom demands again, his voice as ragged as his substance.

Oswald finds it hard to resist replying, the face of the ghost is so pitiful. But he wills himself to look away from it, and lays his eyes upon the light in the man's hands. It is not, he sees, a lamp; no, nor any kind of light Oswald recognizes. It is as if the man is carrying a nugget of the moon itself, steady and serene. It is the light that calms him, he knows; and perhaps it is a fatal calm, a calm that will make his heart quit beating if he doesn't turn from it now, quickly, quickly, while he still can. Clammy and gasping, he comes at last to his hut; to the stump where he was sitting when Shank came along. He sits upon it, and does his best to compose himself. He doesn't want to frighten his children. At last, the door opens and his wife appears, asks him where he got to, and what did he bring back with him? He went nowhere, he says; he brought back nothing. She doesn't believe him, of course. She knows him too well. (Or at least so she thinks. After tonight, she will not know him as well as she had. Her laughing husband is gone from her, and somebody she cannot love so well has taken his place. She will die two winters hence and on her deathbed ask him what she dare not ask now, because now she sees the look in his eyes: she will ask him what happened to him. And he will try to tell her, and while he stumbles over the words, she will pass away.)

vi

And now to Shank, who has watched his quarry for many hours, waiting patiently for a chance to do his worst. The hillmen have three times stoked the fire, so that it burned bright as they drank and talked and drank again. But their ale has taken its toll, and they have laid their heads down to sleep, letting the fire burn low. It's only embers now, and by its fitful light Shank can make out the faces of the three men, inert beneath their tatty furs.

He has his plan: he will take the one closest to him first, who is also the biggest, and therefore the most dangerous to him. Or so he assumes. In fact Shank is just moving from his hiding place when the third man (not the giant, not the murderer) rises groggily and, with much grunting and throat-clearing, staggers a little way from the camp. Shank assumes the man is going to piss, which suits his purposes. He will kill the man while he's occupied emptying his bladder. He moves quickly and quietly around the edge of the camp to the darkness into which the man staggered, and comes upon him suddenly, no more than a body's length from him, squatting with his back against a tree, taking a shit. He's constipated; he grunts and swears. Shank is upon the man before he knows it, and deftly cuts the fellow's throat from ear to ear. The hillman's last breath whistles out of his throat and he sits down in his own excrement, slumped against the tree.

Shank looks back toward the other two men. Neither has stirred from their stupefied sleep. He doesn't give the dead man a second look, but moves quickly back to the fireside so as to stab the second of the killer's companions. He's quick. The knife is raised, and down it comes, straight into the man's chest. But there is a greater thickness of fur on the body than Shank thought, and it keeps the blade from doing its fatal duty. The man rises, roaring, with his fur pinned to his chest by Shank's blade. He throws Shank toward the fire, but unlike his victim Shank is not the worse for ale, and he's back at the man in a heartbeat, pulling the knife out of the hillman's flesh. The fur falls away. The man looks down at his chest, to see blood coursing. In that moment Shank takes him again, this time driving his knife into the man's belly and drawing it up and up, dividing flab and muscle and meat. When he pulls his knife out the contents of the man's belly come with it: his innards, his dinner, his ale. The man looses a sobbing sound, and falls down on the fur. Shank doesn't wait to watch him die. He is after the man Oswald called a shaved pig, the man he will make suffer over and over for the death of Agnes.

The third man is awake, of course, and up from the ground. But he has no intention of fighting; his best defense, he has decided, is to run. Shank has the benefit of his frenzy however. His lungs draw in heroic drafts of air, his limbs are swollen and throbbing with the passion of the moment; he feels an exhilaration that he cannot ever remember feeling before. He catches hold of the pig by the hair, puts the gutting knife to the man's neck, and cuts him there, a finger-length cut, no more, but enough, enough that the man knows he's dead if he attempts to struggle. Then Shank hauls him to the fire and pushes the man's face down toward the flames that here and there spring from the embers.

"You killed my woman," he says, close to the man's ear.

Despite his terror, the pig protests: no, no, no, he says, he did nothing. One of the others maybe, but not him. He swears, on Christ's holy blood, he did nothing.

Shank pushes his captive's face closer to the fire. The curls of the hillman's ragged beard catch fire, and go up, quick and bright. He says again that he's blameless, but with every word of protest he's pushed closer to the heat. His beard is on fire now; the hair around his ears is withering, his fringe and eyelashes the same. He starts to panic; struggles to shake free of Shank. His words of denial have become yells. He flails, and some of the embers fly, but he cannot free himself from his tormentor, who suddenly tires of torture and pushes the man's face down into the remnants of the fire. Oh, the pig squeals, and fueled by agony his flailings redouble, growing strong enough to throw Shank off. He pulls his face from the embers, his beard and hair alight, and, getting to his feet, he reels around, screaming. Shank is momentarily frozen, fascinated by the spectacle before him. He wishes he had somebody here to share it with, Oswald perhaps; yes, Oswald would be laughing until tears ran.

Then, suddenly, the man is off, still burning, staggering away between the trees. Shank picks up his knife, which he dropped in the struggle, and follows him. The quarry's not hard to find: his head is a bright ball weaving through the darkness.

And then, Shank hears the river. The hillman's led him to the river. He can see the waters glistening ahead; he can even see his quarry staggering into the foamy flood, throwing himself down to extinguish his agonies. The flames go out, but Shank is wading across the frozen mud now; he can still see his victim quite clearly. He throws himself into the water in pursuit, and catches hold of the man, roaring over the roar of the river. They have come into the river where the flood runs fast and white, and in their exhausted, wounded states they are neither of them the equal of the current. Shank's victim is first to be thrown off his feet, and Shank takes advantage of the fact, pushing the man's head under the water. He will not drown the man, he's decided; simply weaken him sufficiently to make him compliant. Then he'll drag him back onto the bank, and start to cut him, and cut him, and keep cutting him for as long as his sobs last. Only then, when the man has no more sounds of suffering to make, will he stab him through the eyes and consider Agnes's death revenged.

But first he has to get the man out of the water, and that's proving difficult. Though the pig's head has been down a while, he still claws at Shank's face, plowing his cheek. Shank pulls the man to the surface—getting a glimpse in the moonlight of the way the fire blistered him—then beats at the red-raw face with his fist. Still the man won't give up the fight. He reaches for Shank's neck and pulls him down into the water. This time it's Shank whose legs are swept out from under him by the current. Locked together, they are carried away downstream, thrown against rocks in places, caught in a raft of detritus (the boughs of trees, excrement, a dead goat) in another.

Shank has the breath beaten out of him by the violence of their passage, but he will not relinquish his hold on his quarry. It is a doggedness that will undo him. The man's body gets heavier, it seems, and as he sinks he pulls Shank with him. Shank inhales water, sputters, spits, inhales another draft, then sinks below the surface.

Only now does he realize that the man who seems to have such murderous purpose is already drowned. It's simply a trick of the hillman's constricted muscles that makes him hold on to Shank the way he does. The rest—the motion of his body, the way he seems to willfully drag Shank down with him—is all the river's work. It's too late, however, to give up his struggle. He could not now disengage himself even if he wanted to: the water and its dead agent have him fast. Down and down he goes, the last of his breath escaping him in a shoal of silvery bubbles.

Much later, a trick of the eddying water separates the bodies. Shank's victim is carried out to sea, but Shank himself is washed up close to the mouth of the river. The mud here is thick, and though a few people come wading through it in the next few days, searching for crabs, even dead fish, to supplement their meager supplies of food, Shank's body goes unnoticed. The crabs, however, are not so careless of his presence. They come to the corpse like pilgrims, sidling over its mounds, crawling into his clothes, into his mouth, into his belly cavity, to have every edible shred of him. His bones go into the mud; and the sun never shines on him again.

vii

In my mind, the river comes at last into the hut where Agnes and Shank lived together. It takes four years—four years in which nobody goes near the place, out of superstition—but one February a sudden spell of warm weather melts the heavy snow, which so swells the waters that they rise higher than they have in living memory, and the river comes into the hut. It is like an uninvited guest, throwing open the door and turning the place upside down. It beats the few pitiful pieces of furniture to splinters; it sluices the last of the ashes out of the hearth; it takes the skulls of animals Shank had collected, and the smooth, creamy pebbles Agnes used to bring in now and again from the riverbank, and called her children; it takes some wooden cups, a flask, a knife or two, the rotted furs under which they slept; takes it all and washes it away.

The walls of the hut itself survive another season, but in the heat of the following summer the place suddenly collapses upon itself. The next winter, when the flood comes again, it carries the remnants away, and in spring grass grows where the hut had stood.

viii

Nothing of significance will change here for almost a thousand years. The river will flow on, year after year, sometimes coming close to freezing in the bitterest winters, in the hottest summers reduced to a muddy stream, but essentially unaltered. Oh, it's carving a fresh path for itself, to be sure, eating away at one bank and depositing silt upon another. But these changes are so subtle the passing of a chiliad is not enough to make them visible.

The trees along the banks grow lusher, of course. They cast down their seeds, and when the parent trees perish of disease or antiquity, those seeds are sustained by the warm rot of timber and leaf, and they flourish. Some years the undergrowth is virtually impenetrable; then there's a small fire, which clears the dead wood, and a new cycle of growth begins.

I can tell you very little about the human stories that unfold here. No doubt there are countless goings-on in such a place: acts of seduction and devotion; little kindnesses, little cruelties. Nothing of note, however, except for this: In the summer of 1850, the painter John Everett Millais comes here, looking for a river scene that he can use in a painting he has planned. The subject is to be that of the drowned Ophelia, floating away with her garland of flowers. Millais stays for a day studying the curves of the river. But after a time he rejects it. He wants to find a place that better matches the details of Shakespeare's text; this river has no willows. He finally chooses the Hogsmill River, in Surrey, and paints his masterpiece there the following year.

It is not until 1940—with the end of the millennium approaching—that the landscape undergoes any significant change. In September of that year a lone Luftwaffe bomber, crippled by antiaircraft fire as it crosses the English coast, drops a full payload of bombs intended for London, and several fall in the vicinity of the river. One of them fails to explode, and—lost in the undergrowth—will not be discovered for another seventy years or so. A second explodes just north of the village, killing some cattle. It is the third bomb that concerns us, for it blows the church at Tress to smithereens, evacuating from their graves the many good Christians who were laid there in the belief that they would not see the sky again until Judgment Day.

When, after the war is over, the church is rebuilt, an artist who first came to the river because he was a devotee of Millais, and erroneously thought this was where the Ophelia painting had been made (and who so fell in love with the tranquillity of the place he moved his family there the following spring) is commissioned to design four stained-glass windows. Only three of the four designs are delivered and executed. They are glorious; the triumphs of his career. One depicts John the Baptist, standing in a river, with a congregation of happy acolytes waiting to be blessed. A second shows Christopher, bearing the child Jesus on his shoulders across another river, this one wilder than that in which John stands. The third is of Christ the Redeemer, walking on the waters, while fish leap around His wounded feet. In case anyone should think these waters were Galilee's, the artist made certain the fish were river trout.

The fourth window was reputed to depict the Second Coming, when the river would flow back against itself, and the sun, moon, and stars all shine at the same hour, and Christ, and the frightened soul who carried Him, and the shaman who baptized Him, would come together in glory to forgive the sinners and share with them the secret of bliss. But the artist dies of a heart attack before he finishes his great work, and the fourth window is instead made of plain glass, through which the congregation sees only sky.

1900
1901
1902
1903
1904
1905
1906
1907
1908
1909

THE BIG BLOW

BY JOE R. LANSDALE

—For Norman Partridge

The inhabitants of those islands we now call the West Indies, at least once a year, found their paradise subject to a horrible god that brought savage wind and rain, and finally devastation. They called their terrible god Hurakan.

Telegraphed Message from Washington, D.C., Weather Bureau, Central Office, to Issac Cline, Galveston, Texas, Weather Bureau:

Tropical storm disturbance moving northward over Cuba.

6:38 P.M.

On an afternoon hotter than two rats fucking in a wool sock, John McBride, six-foot one-and-a-half inches, 220 pounds, ham-handed, built like a wild boar and of similar disposition, arrived by ferry from mainland Texas to Galveston Island, a six-gun under his coat and a razor in his shoe.

As the ferry docked, McBride set his suitcase down, removed his bowler, took a crisp white handkerchief from inside his coat, wiped the bowler's sweatband with it, used it to mop his forehead, ran it over his thinning black hair, and put the hat back on.

An old Chinese guy in San Francisco told him he was losing his hair because he always wore hats, and McBride decided maybe he was right, but now he wore the hats to hide his baldness. At thirty he felt he was too young to lose his hair. The Chinaman had given him a tonic for his problem at a considerable sum. McBride used it religiously, rubbed it into his scalp. So far, all he could see it had done was shine his bald spot. He ever got back to Frisco, he was gonna look that Chinaman up, maybe knock a few knots on his head.

As McBride picked up his suitcase and stepped off the ferry with the others, he observed the sky. It appeared green as a pool-table cloth. As the sun dipped down to drink from the Gulf, McBride almost expected to see steam rise up from beyond the island. He took in a deep breath of sea air and thought it tasted all right. It made him hungry. That was why he was here. He was hungry. First on the menu was a woman, then a steak, then some rest before the final meal—the thing he had come for. To whip a nigger.

He hired a buggy to take him to a poke house he had been told about by his employers, the fellows who had paid his way from Chicago. According to what they said, there was a redhead there so good and tight she'd make you sing soprano. Way he felt, if she was redheaded, female, and ready, he'd be all right, and to hell with the song. It was on another's tab anyway.

As the coach trotted along, McBride took in Galveston. It was a Southerner's version of New York, with a touch of the tropics. Houses were upraised on stilts—thick support posts actually—against the washing of storm waters, and in the city proper the houses looked to be fresh off Deep South plantations.

City Hall had apparently been designed by an architect with a Moorish background. It was ripe with domes and spirals. The style collided with a magnificent clock housed in the building's highest point, a peaked tower. The clock was like a miniature Big Ben. England meets the Middle East.

Electric streetcars hissed along the streets, and there were a large number of bicycles, carriages, buggies, and pedestrians. McBride even saw one automobile.

The streets themselves were made of buried wooden

blocks that McBride identified as ships' ballast. Some of the side streets were made of white shell, and some were hardened sand. He liked what he saw, thought: Maybe, after I do in the nigger, I'll stick around a while. Take in the sun at the beach. Find a way to get my fingers in a little solid graft of some sort.

When McBride finally got to the whorehouse, it was full dark. He gave the black driver a big tip, cocked his bowler, grabbed his suitcase, went through the ornate iron gate, up the steps, and inside to get his tumblers clicked right.

After giving his name to the plump madam, who looked as if she could still grind out a customer or two herself, he was given the royalty treatment. The madam herself took him upstairs, undressed him, bathed him, fondled him a bit.

When he was clean, she dried him off, nestled him in bed, kissed him on the forehead as if he were her little boy, then toddled off. The moment she left, he climbed out of bed, got in front of the mirror on the dresser and combed his hair, trying to push as much as possible over the bald spot. He had just gotten it arranged and gone back to bed when the redhead entered.

She was green-eyed and a little thick-waisted, but not bad to look at. She had fire red hair on her head and a darker fire between her legs, which were white as sheets and smooth as a newborn pig.

He started off by hurting her a little, tweaking her nipples, just to show her who was boss. She pretended to like it. Kind of money his employers were paying, he figured she'd dip a turd in gravel and push it around the floor with her nose and pretend to like it.

McBride roughed her bottom some, then got in the saddle and bucked a few. Later on, when she got a little slow about doing what he wanted, he blacked one of her eyes.

When the representatives of the Galveston Sporting Club showed up, he was lying in bed with the redhead, uncovered, letting a hot wind blow through the open windows and dry his and the redhead's juices.

The madam let the club members in and went away. There were four of them, all dressed in evening wear with top hats in their hands. Two were gray-haired and gray-whiskered. The other two were younger men. One was large, had a face that looked as if it regularly stopped cannonballs. Both eyes were black from a recent encounter. His nose was flat and strayed to the left of his face. He did his breathing through his mouth. He didn't have any top front teeth.

The other young man was slight and a dandy. This, McBride assumed, would be Ronald Beems, the man who had written him on behalf of the Sporting Club.

Everything about Beems annoyed McBride. His suit, unlike the wrinkled and drooping suits of the others, looked fresh-pressed, unresponsive to the afternoon's humidity. He smelled faintly of mothballs and naphtha, and some sort of hair tonic that had ginger as a base. He wore a thin little moustache and the sort of hair McBride wished he had. Black, full, and longish, with muttonchop sideburns. He had perfect features. No fist had ever touched him. He stood stiff, as if he had a hoe handle up his ass.

Beems, like the others, looked at McBride and the redhead with more than a little astonishment. McBride lay with his legs spread and his back propped against a pillow. He looked very big there. His legs and shoulders and arms were thick and twisted with muscle and glazed in sweat. His stomach protruded a bit, but it was hard-looking.

The whore, sweaty, eye blacked, legs spread, breasts slouching from the heat, looked more embarrassed than

McBride. She wanted to cover, but she didn't move. Fresh in her memory was that punch to the eye.

"For heaven's sake, man," Beems said. "Cover yourself."

"What the hell you think we've been doin' here?" McBride said. "Playin' checkers?"

"There's no need to be open about it. A man's pleasure is taken in private."

"Certainly you've seen balls before," McBride said, reaching for a cigar that lay on the table next to his revolver and a box of matches. Then he smiled and studied Beems. "Then maybe you ain't ... And then again, maybe, well, you've seen plenty and close up. You look to me the sort that would rather hear a fat boy fart than a pretty girl sing."

"You disgusting brute," Beems said.

"That's telling me," McBride said. "Now I'm hurt. Cut to the goddamn core." McBride patted the redhead's inner thigh. "You recognize this business, don't you? You don't, I got to tell you about it. We men call it a woman, and that thing between her legs is the ole red snapper."

"We'll not conduct our affairs in this fashion," Beems said.

McBride smiled, took a match from the box, and lit the cigar. He puffed, said, "You dressed up pieces of dirt brought me all the way down here from Chicago. I didn't ask to come. You offered me a job, and I took it, and I can untake it, it suits me. I got round-trip money from you already. You sent for me, and I came, and you set me up with a paid hair hole, and you're here for a meeting at a whorehouse, and now you're gonna tell me you're too special to look at my balls. Too prudish to look at pussy. Go on out, let me finish what I really want to finish. I'll be out of here come tomorrow, and you can whip your own nigger."

There was a moment of foot shuffling, and one of the elderly men leaned over and whispered to Beems. Beems breathed once, like a fish out of water, said, "Very well. There's not that much needs to be said. We want this nigger whipped, and we want him whipped bad. We understand in your last bout, the man died."

"Yeah," McBride said. "I killed him and dipped my wick in his old lady. Same night."

This was a lie, but McBride liked the sound of it. He liked the way their faces looked when he told it. The woman had actually been the man's half sister, and the man had died three days later from the beating.

"And this was a white man?" Beems said.

"White as snow. Dead as a stone. Talk money."

"We've explained our financial offer."

"Talk it again. I like the sound of money."

"Hundred dollars before you get in the ring with the nigger. Two hundred more if you beat him. A bonus of five hundred if you kill him. This is a short fight. Not forty-five rounds. No prizefighter makes money like that for so little work. Not even John L. Sullivan."

"This must be one hated nigger. Why? He mountin' your dog?"

"That's our business."

"All right. But I'll take half of that money now."

"That wasn't our deal."

"Now it is. And I'll be runnin' me a tab while I'm here, too. Pick it up."

More foot shuffling. Finally, the two elderly men got their heads together, pulled out their wallets. They pooled their money, gave it to Beems. "These gentlemen are our backers," Beems said. "This is Mr.—"

"I don't care who they are," McBride said. "Give me the money."

Beems tossed it on the foot of the bed.

"Pick it up and bring it here," McBride said to Beems.

"I will not."

"Yes, you will, 'cause you want me to beat this nigger. You want me to do it bad. And another reason is this: You don't, I'll get up and whip your dainty little ass all over this room."

Beems shook a little. "But why?"

"Because I can."

Beems, his face red as infection, gathered the bills from the bed, carried them around to McBride. He thrust them at McBride. McBride, fast as a duck on a june bug, grabbed Beems's wrist and pulled him forward, causing him to let go of the money and drop it onto McBride's chest. McBride pulled the cigar from his mouth with his free hand, stuck it against the back of Beems's thumb. Beems let out a squeal, said, "Forrest!"

The big man with no teeth and black eyes started around the bed toward McBride. McBride said, "Step back, Charlie, or you'll have to hire someone to yank this fella out of your ass."

Forrest hesitated, looked as if he might keep coming, then stepped back and hung his head.

McBride pulled Beems's captured hand between his legs and rubbed it over his sweaty balls a few times, then pushed him away. Beems stood with his mouth open, stared at his hand.

"I'm bull of the woods here," McBride said, "and it stays that way from here on out. You treat me with respect. I say, hold my rope while I pee, you hold it. I say, hold my sacks off the sheet while I get a piece, you hold 'em."

Beems said, "You bastard. I could have you killed."

"Then do it. I hate your type. I hate someone I think's your type. I hate someone who likes your type or wants to be your type. I'd kill a dog liked to be with you. I hate all of you expensive bastards with money and no guts. I hate you 'cause

you can't whip your own nigger, and I'm glad you can't,
'cause I can. And you'll pay me. So go ahead, send your
killers around. See where it gets them. Where it gets you.
And I hate your goddamn hair, Beems."

"When this is over," Beems said, "you leave immediately!"

"I will, but not because of you. Because I can't stand you
or your little pack of turds."

The big man with missing teeth raised his head, glared at
McBride. McBride said, "Nigger whipped your ass, didn't
he, Forrest?"

Forrest didn't say anything, but his face said a lot.
McBride said, "You can't whip the nigger, so your boss sent
for me. I can whip the nigger. So don't think for a moment
you can whip me."

"Come on," Beems said. "Let's leave. The man makes me
sick."

Beems joined the others, his hand held out to his side. The
elderly gentlemen looked as if they had just realized they
were lost in the forest. They organized themselves enough to
start out the door. Beems followed, turned before exiting,
glared at McBride.

McBride said, "Don't wash that hand, Beems. You can
say, 'Shake the hand of the man who shook the balls of John
McBride.'"

"You go to hell," Beems said.

"Keep me posted," McBride said. Beems left. McBride
yelled after him and his crowd, "And gentlemen, enjoyed
doing business with you."

9:12 P.M.

Later in the night the redhead displeased him and McBride
popped her other eye, stretched her out, lay across her, and
slept. While he slept, he dreamed he had a head of hair like
Mr. Ronald Beems.

Outside, the wind picked up slightly, blew hot, brine-scented air down Galveston's streets and through the whore-house window.

9:34 P.M.

Bill Cooper was working outside on the second-floor deck he was building. He had it completed except for a bit of trim work. It had gone dark on him sometime back, and he was trying to finish by lantern light. He was hammering a side-wall board into place when he felt a drop of rain. He stopped hammering and looked up. The night sky had a peculiar appearance, and for a moment it gave him pause. He studied the heavens a moment longer, decided it didn't look all that bad. It was just the starlight that gave it that look. No more drops fell on him.

Bill tossed the hammer on the deck, leaving the nail only partially driven, picked up the lantern, and went inside the house to be with his wife and baby son. He'd had enough for one day.

11:01 P.M.

The waves came in loud against the beach and the air was surprisingly heavy for so late at night. It lay hot and sweaty on "Lil" Arthur John Johnson's bare chest. He breathed in the air and blew it out, pounded the railroad tie with all his might for the hundredth time. His right fist struck it, and the tie moved in the sand. He hooked it with a left, jammed it with a straight right, putting his entire six-foot, two-hundred-pound frame into it. The tie went backwards, came out of the sand, and hit the beach.

Arthur stepped back and held out his broad, black hands and examined them in the moonlight. They were scuffed, but essentially sound. He walked down to the water and squatted and stuck his hands in, let the surf roll over them. The salt didn't even burn. His hands were like leather. He rubbed them together, being sure to coat them completely with seawater. He cupped water in his palms, rubbed it on his face, over his shaved, bullet head.

Along with a number of other pounding exercises, he had been doing this for months, conditioning his hands and face with work and brine. Rumor was, this man he was to fight, this McBride, had fists like razors, fists that cut right through the gloves and tore the flesh.

"Lil" Arthur took another breath, and this one was filled not only with the smell of saltwater and dead fish, but of raw sewage, which was regularly dumped offshore in the Gulf.

He took his shovel and redug the hole in the sand and dropped the tie back in, patted it down, went back to work. This time, two socks and it came up. He repeated the washing of his hands and face, then picked up the tie, placed it on a broad shoulder and began to run down the beach. When he had gone a good distance, he switched shoulders and ran back. He didn't even feel winded.

He collected his shovel, and with the tie on one shoulder, started toward his family's shack in the Flats, also known as Nigger Town.

"Lil" Arthur left the tie in front of the shack and put the shovel on the sagging porch. He was about to go inside when he saw a man start across the little excuse of a yard. The man was white. He was wearing dress clothes and a top hat.

When he was near the front porch, he stopped, took off his hat. It was Forrest Thomas, the man "Lil" Arthur had beaten unconscious three weeks back. It had taken only till the middle of the third round.

Even in the cloud-hazy moonlight, "Lil" Arthur could see Forrest looked rough. For a moment, a fleeting moment, he almost felt bad about inflicting so much damage. But then he began to wonder if the man had a gun.

"Arthur," Forrest said. "I come to talk a minute, if'n it's all right."

This was certainly different from the night "Lil" Arthur had climbed into the ring with him. Then, Forrest Thomas had been conceited and full of piss and vinegar and wore the word nigger on his lips as firmly as a mole. He was angry he had been reduced by his employer to fighting a black man. To hear him tell it, he deserved no less than John L. Sullivan, who refused to fight a Negro, considering it a debasement to the heavyweight title.

"Yeah," "Lil" Arthur said. "What you want?"

"I ain't got nothing against you," Forrest said.

"Don't matter you do," "Lil" Arthur said.

"You whupped me fair and square."

"I know, and I can do it again."

"I didn't think so before, but I know you can now."

"That's what you come to say? You got all dressed up, just to come talk to a nigger that whupped you?"

"I come to say more."

"Say it. I'm tired."

"McBride's come in."

"That ain't tellin' me nothin'. I reckoned he'd come in sometime. How'm I gonna fight him, he don't come in?"

"You don't know anything about McBride. Not really. He killed a man in the ring, his last fight in Chicago. That's why Beems brought him in, to kill you. Beems and his bunch want you dead 'cause you whipped a white man. They don't care you whipped me. They care you whipped a white man. Beems figures it's an insult to the white race, a white man being beat by a colored. This McBride, he's got a shot at the Championship of the World. He's that good."

"You tellin' me you concerned for me?"

"I'm tellin' you Beems and the members of the Sportin' Club can't take it. They lost a lot of money on bets, too. They got to set it right, see. I ain't no friend of yours, but I figure I owe you that. I come to warn you this McBride is a killer."

"Lil" Arthur listened to the crickets saw their legs a moment, then said, "If that worried me, this man being a killer, and I didn't fight him, that would look pretty good for your boss, wouldn't it? Beems could say the bad nigger didn't show up. That he was scared of a white man."

"You fight this McBride, there's a good chance he'll kill you or cripple you. Boxing bein' against the law, there won't be nobody there legal to keep check on things. Not really. Audience gonna be there ain't gonna say nothin'. They ain't supposed to be there anyway. You died, got hurt bad, you'd end up out there in the Gulf with a block of granite tied to your dick, and that'd be that."

"Sayin' I should run?"

"You run, it gives Beems face, and you don't take a beatin', maybe get killed. You figure it."

"You ain't doin' nothin' for me. You're just pimpin' for Beems. You tryin' to beat me with your mouth. Well, I ain't gonna take no beatin'. White. Colored. Striped. It don't matter. McBride gets in the ring, I'll knock him down. You go on back to Beems. Tell him I ain't scared, and I ain't gonna run. And ain't none of this workin'."

Forrest put his hat on. "Have it your way, nigger." He turned and walked away.

"Lil" Arthur started inside the house, but before he could open the door, his father, Henry, came out. He dragged his left leg behind him as he came, leaned on his cane. He wore a ragged undershirt and work pants. He was sweaty. Tired. Gray. Grayer yet in the muted moonlight.

"'You ought not talk to a white man that way," Henry said. "Them Ku Kluxers'll come 'round."

"I ain't afraid of no Ku Kluxers."

"Yeah, well I am, and we be seein' what you say when you swingin' from a rope, a peckerwood cuttin' off yo balls. You ain't lived none yet. You ain't nothin' but twenty-two years. Sit down, boy."

"Papa, you ain't me. I ain't got no bad leg. I ain't scared of nobody."

"I ain't always had no bad leg. Sit down."

"Lil" Arthur sat down beside his father. Henry said, "A colored man, he got to play the game, to win the game. You hear me?"

"I ain't seen you winnin' much."

Henry slapped "Lil" Arthur quickly. It was fast, and "Lil" Arthur realized where he had inherited his hand speed. "You shut yo face," Henry said. "Don't talk to your papa like that."

"Lil" Arthur reached up and touched his cheek, not because it hurt, but because he was still a little amazed. Henry said, "For a colored man, winnin' is stayin' alive to live out the time God give you."

"But how you spend what time you got, Papa, that ain't up to God. I'm gonna be the Heavyweight Champion of the World someday. You'll see."

"There ain't never gonna be no colored Champion of the World, 'Lil' Arthur. And there ain't no talkin' to you. You a fool. I'm gonna be cuttin' you down from a tree some morning, yo neck all stretched out. Help me up. I'm goin' to bed."

"Lil" Arthur helped his father up, and the old man, balanced on his cane, dragged himself inside the shack.

A moment later, "Lil" Arthur's mother, Tina, came out. She was a broad-faced woman, short and stocky, nearly twenty years younger than her husband.

"You don't need talk yo papa that way," she said.

"He don't do nothin', and he don't want me to do nothin'," "Lil" Arthur said.

"He know what he been through, Arthur. He born a slave. He made to fight for white mens like he was some kinda fightin' rooster, and he got his leg paralyzed cause he had to fight for them Rebels in the war. You think on that. He in one hell of a fix. Him a colored man out there shootin' at Yankees, 'cause if he don't, they gonna shoot him, and them Rebels gonna shoot him he don't fight the Yankees."

"I ain't all that fond of Yankees myself. They ain't likin' niggers any more than anyone else."

"That's true. But, yo papa, he right about one thing. You ain't lived enough to know nothin' about nothin'. You want to be a white man so bad it hurt you. You is African, boy. You is born of slaves come from slaves come from Africa."

"You sayin' what he's sayin'?"

"Naw, I ain't. I'm sayin', you whup this fella, and you whup him good. Remember when them bullies used to chase you home, and I tell you, you come back without fightin', I'm gonna whup you harder than them?"

"Yes, ma'am."

"And you got so you whupped 'em good, just so I wouldn't whup yo ass?"

"Yes ma'am."

"Well, these here white men hire out this man against you, threaten you, they're bullies. You go in there, and you whup this fella, and you use what God give you in them hands, and you make your way. But you remember, you ain't gonna have nothin' easy. Only way a white man gonna get respect for you is you knock him down, you hear? And you can knock him down in that ring better than out here, 'cause then you just a bad nigger they gonna hang. But you don't talk to yo papa that way. He better than most. He got him a steady job, and he hold this family together."

"He's a janitor."

"That's more than you is."

"And you hold this family together."

"It a two-person job, son."

"Yes, ma'am."

"Good night, son."

"Lil" Arthur hugged her, kissed her cheek, and she went inside. He followed, but the smallness of the two-room house, all those bodies on pallets—his parents, three sisters, two brothers, and a brother-in-law—made him feel crowded. And the pigeons sickened him. Always the pigeons. They had found a hole in the roof—the one that had been covered with tar paper—and now they were roosting inside on the rafters. Tomorrow, half the house would be covered in bird shit. He needed to get up there and put some fresh tar paper on the roof. He kept meaning to. Papa couldn't do it, and he spent his own time training. He had to do more for the family besides bring in a few dollars from fighting.

"Lil" Arthur got the stick they kept by the door for just such an occasion, used it to rout the pigeons by poking at them. In the long run, it wouldn't matter. They would fly as high as the roof, then gradually creep back down to roost. But the explosion of bird wings, their rise to the sky through the hole in the roof, lifted his spirits.

His brother-in-law, Clement, rose up on an elbow from his pallet, and his wife, "Lil" Arthur's sister Lucy, stirred and rolled over, stretched her arm across Clement's chest, but didn't wake up.

"What you doin', Arthur?" Clement whispered. "You don't know a man's got to sleep? I got work to do 'morrow. Ain't all of us sleep all day."

"Sleep then. And stay out of my sister. Lucy don't need no kids now. We got a house full a folks."

"She my wife. We supposed to do that. And multiply."

"Then get your own place and multiply. We packed tight as turds here."

"You crazy, Arthur."

Arthur cocked the pigeon stick. "Lay down and shut up."

Clement lay down, and Arthur put the stick back and gathered up his pallet and went outside. He inspected the pallet for bird shit, found none, stretched out on the porch, and tried to sleep. He thought about getting his guitar, going back to the beach to strum it, but he was too tired for that. Too tired to do anything, too awake to sleep.

His mother had told him time and again that when he was a baby, an old Negro lady with the second sight had picked up his little hand and said, "This child gonna eat his bread in many countries."

It was something that had always sustained him. But now, he began to wonder. Except for trying to leave Galveston by train once, falling asleep in the boxcar, only to discover it had been making circles in the train yard all night as supplies were unloaded, he'd had no adventures, and was still eating his bread in Galveston.

All night he fought mosquitoes, the heat, and his own ambition. By morning he was exhausted.

WEDNESDAY, SEPTEMBER 5, 10:20 A.M.

Telegraphed Message from Washington, D.C., Weather Bureau, Central Office, to Issac Cline, Galveston, Texas, Weather Bureau, Central Office:

Disturbance center near Key West moving northwest. Vessels bound for Florida and Cuban ports should exercise caution. Storm likely to become dangerous.

10:23 A.M.

McBride awoke, fucked the redhead, sat up in bed, and cracked his knuckles, said, "I'm going to eat and train, Red.

You have your ass here when I get back, and put it on the Sportin' Club's bill. And wash yourself, for heaven's sake."

"Yes sir, Mr. McBride," she said.

McBride got up, poured water into a washbasin, washed his dick, under his arms, splashed water on his face. Then he sat at the dresser in front of the mirror and spent twenty minutes putting on the Chinaman's remedy and combing his hair. As soon as he had it just right, he put on a cap.

He got dressed in loose pants, a short-sleeved shirt, soft shoes, wrapped his knuckles with gauze, put a little notebook and pencil in his back pocket, then pulled on soft leather gloves. When the redhead wasn't looking, he wrapped his revolver and razor in a washrag, stuffed them between his shirt and his stomach.

Downstairs, making sure no one was about, he removed the rag containing his revolver and razor, stuck them into the drooping greenness of a potted plant, then went away.

He strolled down the street to a café and ordered steak and eggs and lots of coffee. He ate with his gloves and hat on. He paid for the meal, but got a receipt.

Comfortably full, he went out to train.

He began at the docks. There were a number of men hard at work. They were loading bags of cottonseed onto a ship. He stood with his hands behind his back and watched. The scent of the sea was strong. The water lapped at the pilings enthusiastically, and the air was as heavy as a cotton sack.

After a while, he strolled over to a large bald man with arms and legs like plantation columns. The man wore faded overalls without a shirt, and his chest was as hairy as a bear's ass. He had on heavy work boots with the sides burst out. McBride could see his bare feet through the openings. McBride hated a man that didn't keep up his appearance, even when he was working. Pride was like a dog. You didn't feed it regularly, it died.

McBride said, "What's your name?"

The man, a bag of cottonseed under each arm, stopped and looked at him, taken aback. "Ketchum," he said. "Warner Ketchum."

"Yeah," McBride said. "Thought so. So, you're the one."

The man glared at him. "One what?"

The other men stopped working, turned to look.

"I just wanted to see you," McBride said. "Yeah, you fit the description. I just never thought there was a white man would stoop to such a thing. Fact is, hard to imagine any man stooping to such a thing."

"What are you talkin' about, fella?"

"Well, word is, Warner Ketchum that works at the dock has been known to suck a little nigger dick in his time."

Ketchum dropped the cottonseed bags. "Who the hell are you? Where you hear that?"

McBride put his gloved hands behind his back and held them. "They say, on a good night, you can do more with a nigger's dick than a cat can with a ball of twine."

The man was fuming. "You got me mixed up with some-body else, you Yankee-talkin' sonofabitch."

"Naw, I ain't got you mixed up. Your name's Warner Ketchum. You look how you was described to me by the nig-ger whose stick you slicked."

Warner stepped forward with his right foot and swung a right punch so looped it looked like a sickle blade. McBride ducked it without removing his hands from behind his back, slipped inside and twisted his hips as he brought a right uppercut into Warner's midsection.

Warner's air exploded and he wobbled back, and McBride was in again, a left hook to the ribs, a straight right to the solar plexus. Warner doubled and went to his knees.

McBride leaned over and kissed him on the ear, said, "Tell me. Them nigger dicks taste like licorice?"

Warner came up then, and he was wild. He threw a right, then a left. McBride bobbed beneath them. Warner kicked at him. McBride turned sideways, let the kick go by, unloaded a left hand that caught Warner on the jaw, followed it with a right that struck with a sound like the impact of an artillery shell.

Warner dropped to one knee. McBride grabbed him by the head and swung his knee into Warner's face, busting his nose all over the dock. Warner fell face forward, caught himself on his hands, almost got up. Then, very slowly, he collapsed, lay down, and didn't move.

McBride looked at the men who were watching him. He said, "He didn't suck no nigger dicks. I made that up." He got out his paper pad and pencil and wrote: Owed me. Price of one sparring partner, FIVE DOLLARS.

He put the pad and pencil away. Got five dollars out of his wallet, folded it, put it in the man's back pocket. He turned to the other men who stood staring at him as if he were one of Jesus' miracles.

"Frankly, I think you're all a bunch of sorry assholes, and I think, one at a time, I can lick every goddamn one of you Southern white trash pieces of shit. Any takers?"

"Not likely," said a stocky man at the front of the crowd. "You're a ringer." He picked up a sack of cottonseed he had put down, started toward the ship. The other men did the same.

McBride said, "Okay," and walked away.

He thought, maybe, on down the docks he might find another sparring partner.

5:23 P.M.

By the end of the day, near dark, McBride checked his notepad for expenses, saw the Sporting Club owed him forty-five dollars in sparring partners, and a new pair of gloves, as well as breakfast and dinner to come. He added money for a shoeshine. A clumsy sonofabitch had scuffed one of his shoes.

He got the shoeshine and ate a steak, flexed his muscles as he arrived at the whorehouse. He felt loose still, like he could take on another two or three yokels.

He went inside, got his goods out of the potted plant, and climbed the stairs.

THURSDAY, SEPTEMBER 6, 6:00 P.M.

Telegraphed Message from Washington, D.C., Weather Bureau, Central Office, to Issac Cline, Galveston, Texas, Weather Bureau:

Storm center just northwest of Key West.

7:30 P.M.

"Lil" Arthur ran down to the Sporting Club that night and stood in front of it, his hands in his pants pockets. The wind was brisk, and the air was just plain sour.

Saturday, he was going to fight a heavyweight crown contender, and though it would not be listed as an official bout, and McBride was just in it to pick up some money, "Lil" Arthur was glad to have the chance to fight a man who might fight for the championship someday. And if he could beat him, even if it didn't affect McBride's record, "Lil" Arthur knew he'd have that; he would have beaten a contender for the Heavyweight Championship of the World.

It was a far cry from the Battle Royales he had first participated in. There was a time when he looked upon those degrading events with favor.

He remembered his first Battle Royale. His friend Ernest had talked him into it. Once a month, sometimes more often, white "sporting men" liked to get a bunch of colored boys and men to come down to the club for a free-for-all. They'd put nine or ten of them in a ring, sometimes make them strip naked and wear Sambo masks. He'd done that once himself.

While the coloreds fought, the whites would toss money and yell for them to kill one another. Sometimes they'd tie two coloreds together by the ankles, let them go at it. Blood flowed thick as molasses on flapjacks. Bones were broken. Muscles torn. For the whites, it was great fun, watching a couple of coons knock each other about.

"Lil" Arthur found he was good at all that fighting, and even knocked Ernest out, effectively ending their friendship. He couldn't help himself. He got in there, got the battling blood up, he would hit whoever came near him.

He started boxing regularly, gained some skill. No more Battle Royales. He got a reputation with the colored boxers, and in time that spread to the whites.

The Sporting Club, plumb out of new white contenders for their champion, Forrest Thomas, gave "Lil" Arthur twenty-five dollars to mix it up with their man, thinking a colored and a white would be a novelty, and the superiority of the white race would be proved in a match of skill and timing.

Right before the fight, "Lil" Arthur said his prayers, and then considering he was going to be fighting in front of a bunch of angry, mean-spirited whites, and for the first time, white women—sporting women, but women who wanted to see a black man knocked to jelly, he took gauze and wrapped his dick. He wrapped it so that it was as thick as a blackjack. He figured he'd give them white folks something to look at. The thing they feared the most. A black as coal stud nigger.

He whipped Forrest Thomas like he was a redheaded stepchild; whipped him so badly, they stopped the fight so no one would see a colored man knock a white man out.

Against their wishes, the Sporting Club was forced to hand the championship over to "Lil" Arthur John Johnson, and the fact that a colored now held the club's precious boxing crown was like a chicken bone in the club's throat. Primarily Beems's throat. As the current president of the Sporting Club, the match had been Beems's idea, and Forrest Thomas had been Beems's man.

Enter McBride. Beems, on the side, talked a couple of the Sporting Club's more wealthy members into financing a fight. One where a true contender to the heavyweight crown would whip "Lil" Arthur and return the local championship to a white man, even if that white man relinquished the crown when he returned to Chicago, leaving it vacant. In that case, "Lil" Arthur was certain he'd never get another shot at the Sporting Club championship. They wanted him out, by hook or crook.

"Lil" Arthur had never seen McBride. Didn't know how he fought. He'd just heard he was as tough as stone and had balls like a brass monkey. He liked to think he was the same way. He didn't intend to give the championship up. Saturday, he'd find out if he had to.

9:00 P.M.

The redhead, nursing a fat lip, two black eyes, and a bruise on her belly, rolled over gingerly and put her arm across McBride's hairy chest. "You had enough?"

"I'll say when I've had enough."

"I was just thinking, I might go downstairs and get something to eat. Come back in a few minutes."

"You had time to eat before I got back. You didn't eat, you just messed up. I'm paying for this. Or rather the Sportin' Club is."

"An engine's got to have coal, if you want that engine to go."

"Yeah?"

"Yeah." The redhead reached up and ran her fingers through McBride's hair.

McBride reached across his chest and slapped the redhead.

"Don't touch my hair. Stay out of my hair. And shut up. I don't care you want to fuck or not. I want to fuck, we fuck. Got it?"

"Yes, sir."

"Listen here, I'm gonna take a shit. I get back, I want you to wash that goddamn nasty hole of yours. You think I like stickin' my wick in that, it not being clean? You got to get clean."

"It's so hot. I sweat. And you're just gonna mess me up again."

"I don't care. You wash that thing. I went around with my johnson like that, it'd fall off. I get a disease, girl, I'll come back here, kick your ass so hard your butthole will swap places with your cunt."

"I ain't got no disease, Mr. McBride."

"Good."

"Why you got to be so mean?" the redhead asked suddenly, then couldn't believe it had come out of her mouth. She realized, not only would a remark like that anger McBride, but the question was stupid. It was like asking a chicken why it pecked shit. It just did. McBride was mean because he was, and that was that.

But even as the redhead flinched, McBride turned philosophical. "It isn't a matter of mean. It's because I can do what I want, and others can't. You got that, sister?"

"Sure. I didn't mean nothing by it."

"Someone can do to me what I do to them, then all right, that's how it is. Isn't a man, woman, or animal on earth that's worth a damn. You know that?"

"Sure. You're right."

"You bet I am. Only thing pure in this world is a baby. Human or animal, a baby is born hungry and innocent. It can't do a thing for itself. Then it grows up and gets just like everyone else. A baby is all right until it's about two. Then, it ought to just be smothered and save the world the room. My sister, she was all right till she was about two, then it wasn't nothing

but her wanting stuff and my mother giving it to her. Later on,
Mama didn't have nothing to do with her either, same as me.
She got over two years old, she was just trouble. Like I was.
Like everybody else is."

"Sure," the redhead said.

"Oh, shut up, you don't know your ass from a pig track."

McBride got up and went to the john. He took his revolver
and his wallet and his razor with him. He didn't trust a
whore—any woman for that matter—far as he could hurl one.

While he was in the can trying out the new flush toilet, the
redhead eased out of bed wearing only a sheet. She slipped
out the door, went downstairs and outside, into the streets. She
flagged down a man in a buggy, talked him into a ride, for a
ride, then she was out of there, destination unimportant.

9:49 P.M.

Later, pissed at the redhead, McBride used the madam herself, blacked both her eyes when she suggested that a lot of
sex before a fight might not be a good idea for an athlete.

The madam, lying in bed with McBride's muscular arm
across her ample breasts, sighed and watched the glow of the
gas streetlights play on the ceiling.

Well, she thought, *it's a living.*

FRIDAY, SEPTEMBER 7, 10:35 A.M.

Telegraphed Message from Washington, D.C., Weather Bureau,
Central Office, to Issac Cline, Galveston, Texas, Weather Bureau:

Storm warning. Galveston, Texas. Take precautions.

Issac Cline, head of the Galveston Weather Bureau, sat at his
desk on the third floor of the Levy Building and read the
telegram. He went downstairs and outside for a look-see.

The weather was certainly in a stormy mood, but it didn't look like serious hurricane weather. He had been with the Weather Bureau for eight years, and he thought he ought to know a hurricane by now, and this wasn't it. The sky wasn't the right color.

He walked until he got to the beach. By then the wind was picking up, and the sea was swelling. The clouds were like wads of duck down ripped from a pillow. He walked a little farther down the beach, found a turtle wrapped in seaweed, poked it with a stick. It was dead as a stone.

Issac returned to the Levy Building, and by the time he made his way back, the wind had picked up considerably. He climbed the stairs to the roof. The roof barometer was dropping quickly, and the wind was serious. He revised his opinion on how much he knew about storms. He estimated the wind to be blowing at twenty miles an hour, and growing. He pushed against it, made his way to the weather pole, hoisted two flags. The top flag was actually a white pennant. It whipped in the wind like a gossip's tongue. Anyone who saw it knew it meant the wind was coming from the northwest. Beneath it was a red flag with a black center; this flag meant the wind was coming ass over teakettle, and that a seriously violent storm was expected within hours.

The air smelled dank and fishy. For a moment, Cline thought perhaps he had actually touched the dead turtle and brought its stink back with him. But no, it was the wind.

At about this same time, the steamship *Pensacola*, commanded by Captain James Slater, left the port of Galveston from Pier 34, destination Pensacola, Florida.

Slater had read the hurricane reports of the day before, and though the wind was picking up and was oddly steamy, the sky failed to show what he was watching for. A dusty, brick red color, a sure sign of a hurricane. He felt the whole

Weather Bureau business was about as much guess and luck as it was anything else. He figured he could do that and be as accurate.

He gave orders to ease the *Pensacola* into the Gulf.

1:06 P.M.

The pigeons fluttered through the opening in the Johnson's roof. Tar paper lifted, tore, blew away, tumbled through the sky as if they were little black pieces of the structure's soul.

"It's them birds again," his mother said.

"Lil" Arthur stopped doing push-ups, looked to the ceiling. Pigeons were thick on the rafters. So was pigeon shit. The sky was very visible through the roof. And very black. It looked venomous.

"Shit," "Lil" Arthur said.

"It's okay," she said. "Leave 'em be. They scared. So am I."

"Lil" Arthur stood up, said, "Ain't nothin' be scared of. We been through all kinda storms. We're on a rise here. Water don't never get this high."

"I ain't never liked no storm. I be glad when yo daddy and the young'uns gets home."

"Papa's got an old tarp I might can put over that hole. Keep out the rain."

"You think you can, go on."

"I already should'a," "Lil" Arthur said.

"Lil" Arthur went outside, crawled under the upraised porch, and got hold of the old tarp. It was pretty rotten, but it might serve his purpose, at least temporarily. He dragged it into the yard, crawled back under, tugged out the creaking ladder and a rusty hammer. He was about to go inside and get the nails when he heard a kind of odd roaring. He stopped, listened, recognized it.

It was the surf. He had certainly heard it before, but not

this loud and this far from the beach. He got the nails and put the ladder against the side of the house and carried the tarp onto the roof. The tarp nearly took to the air when he spread it, almost carried him with it. With considerable effort he got it nailed over the hole, trapping what pigeons didn't flee inside the house.

2:30 P.M.

Inside the whorehouse, the madam, a fat lip added to her black eyes, watched from the bed as McBride, naked, seated in a chair before the dresser mirror, carefully oiled and combed his hair over his bald spot. The windows were closed, and the wind rattled them like dice in a gambler's fist. The air inside the whorehouse was as stuffy as a minister's wife.

"What's that smell?" she asked.

It was the tonic the Chinaman had given him. He said, "You don't want your tits pinched, shut the fuck up."

"All right," she said.

The windows rattled again. Pops of rain flecked the glass.

McBride went to the window, his limp dick resting on the windowsill, almost touching the glass, like a large, wrinkled grub looking for a way out.

"Storm coming," he said.

The madam thought: *No shit*.

McBride opened the window. The wind blew a comb and hairbrush off the dresser. A man, walking along the sandy street, one hand on his hat to save it from the wind, glanced up at McBride. McBride took hold of his dick and wagged it at him. The man turned his head and picked up his pace.

McBride said, "Spread those fat legs, honey-ass, 'cause I'm sailing into port, and I'm ready to drop anchor."

Sighing, the madam rolled onto her back, and McBride mounted her. "Don't mess up my hair this time," he said.

The study smelled of stale cigar smoke and sweat, and faintly of baby oil. The grandfather clock chimed four-thirty. The air was humid and sticky as it shoved through the open windows and fluttered the dark curtains. The sunlight, which was tinted with a green cloud haze, flashed in and out, giving brightness to the false eyes and the yellowed teeth of a dozen mounted animal heads on the walls. Bears. Boar. Deer. Even a wolf.

Beems, the source of much of the sweat smell, thought: It's at least another hour before my wife gets home. Good.

Forrest drove him so hard Beems's forehead slammed into the wall, rocking the head of the wild boar that was mounted there, causing the boar to look as if it had turned its head in response to a distant sound, a peculiar sight.

"It's not because I'm one of them kind I do this," Beems said. "It's just, oh yeah, honey . . . The wife, you know, she don't do nothing for me. I mean, you got to get a little pleasure where you can. A man's got to get his pleasure, don't you think . . . Oh, yes. That's it . . . A man, he's got to get his pleasure, right? Even if there's nothing funny about him?"

Forrest rested his hands on Beems's naked shoulders, pushing him down until his head rested on top of the couch cushion. Forrest cocked his hips, drove forward with teeth clenched, penetrating deep into Beems's ass. He said, "Yeah. Sure."

"You mean that? This don't make me queer?"

"No," Forrest panted. "Never has. Never will. Don't mean nothin'. Not a damn thing. It's all right. You're a man's man. Let me concentrate."

Forrest had to concentrate. He hated this business, but it was part of the job. And, of course, unknown to Beems, he was putting the meat to Beems's wife. So, if he wanted to keep doing that, he had to stay in with the boss. And Mrs. Beems, of course, had no idea he was reaming her husband's dirty ditch, or that her husband had about as much interest in women as a pig does a silver tea service.

What a joke. He was fucking Beems's old lady, doing the dog work for Beems, for a good price, and was reaming Beems's asshole and assuring Beems he wasn't what he was, a fairy. And as an added benefit, he didn't have to fight the nigger tomorrow night. That was a big plus. That sonofabitch hit like a mule kicked. He hoped this McBride would tap him good. The nigger died, he'd make a point of shitting on his grave. Right at the head of it.

Well, maybe, Forrest decided, as he drove his hips forward hard enough to make Beems scream a little, he didn't hate this business after all. Not completely. He took so much crap from Beems, this was kinda nice, having the bastard bent over a couch, dicking him so hard his head slammed the wall. Goddamn, nutless queer, insulting him in public, trying to act tough.

Forrest took the bottle of baby oil off the end table and poured it onto Beems's ass. He put the bottle back and realized he was going soft. He tried to imagine he was plunging into Mrs. Beems, who had the smoothest ass and the brightest blond pubic hair he had ever seen. "I'm almost there," Forrest said.

"Stroke, Forrest! Stroke, man. Stroke!"

In the moment of orgasm, Beems imagined that the dick plunging into his hairy ass belonged to the big nigger, "Lil" Arthur. He thought about "Lil" Arthur all the time. Ever since he had seen him fight naked in a Battle Royale while wearing a Sambo mask for the enjoyment of the crowd.

And the way "Lil" Arthur had whipped Forrest. Oh, God. So thoroughly. So expertly. Forrest had been the man until then, and that made him want Forrest, but now, he wanted the nigger.

Oh God, Beems thought, to have him in me, wearing that mask, that would do it for all time. Just once. Or twice. Jesus, I want it so bad I got to be sure the nigger gets killed. I got to be sure I don't try to pay the nigger money to do this, because he lives after the fight with McBride, I know I'll break down and try. And I break down and he doesn't do it, and word gets around, or he does it, and word gets around, or I get caught . . . I couldn't bear that. This is bad enough. But a nigger . . . ?

Then there was McBride. He thought about him. He had touched McBride's balls and feigned disgust, but he hadn't washed that hand yet, just as McBride suggested.

McBride won the fight with the nigger, better yet, killed him, maybe McBride would do it with him. McBride was a gent that liked money, and he liked to hurt whoever he was fucking. Beems could tell that from the way the redhead was battered. That would be good. That would be all right. McBride was the type who'd fuck anyone or anything, Beems could tell.

He imagined it was McBride at work instead of Forrest. McBride, naked, except for the bowler.

Forrest, in his moment of orgasm, grunted, said, "Oh yeah," and almost called Mrs. Beems's name. He lifted his head as he finished, saw the hard glass eyes of the stuffed wild boar. The eyes were full of sunlight. Then the curtains fluttered and the eyes were full of darkness.

4:45 P.M.

The steamship *Pensacola*, outbound from Galveston, reached the Gulf, and a wind reached the *Pensacola*. Captain Slater felt his heart clinch. The sea came high and savage from the east, and the ship rose up and dived back down, and the waves, dark green and shadowed by the thick clouds overhead, reared up on either side of the steamship, hissed, plunged back down, and the *Pensacola* rode up.

Jake Bernard, the pilot commissioner, came onto the bridge looking green as the waves. He was Slater's guest on this voyage, and now he wished he were back home. He couldn't believe how ill he felt. Never, in all his years, had he encountered seas like this, and he had thought himself immune to seasickness.

"I don't know about you, Slater," Bernard said, "but I ain't had this much fun since a bulldog gutted my daddy."

Slater tried to smile, but couldn't make it. He saw that Bernard, in spite of his joshing, didn't look particularly jovial. Slater said, "Look at the glass."

Bernard checked the barometer. It was falling fast.

"Never seen it that low," Bernard said.

"Me either," Slater said. He ordered his crew then. Told them to take in the awning, to batten the hatches, and to prepare for water.

Bernard, who had not left the barometer, said, "God. Look at this, man!"

Slater looked. The barometer read 28.55.

Bernard said, "Way I heard it, ever gets that low, you're supposed to bend forward, kiss your root, and tell it good-bye."

6:30 P.M.

The Coopers, Bill and Angelique and their eighteen-month-old baby, Teddy, were on their way to dinner at a restaurant by buggy, when their horse, Bess, a beautiful chocolate-colored mare, made a run at the crashing sea.

It was the sea that frightened the horse, but in its moment of fear, it had tried to plunge headlong toward the source of its fright, assuring Bill that horses were, in fact, the most stupid animals in God's creation.

Bill jerked the reins and cussed the horse. Bess wheeled, lurched the buggy so hard Bill thought they might tip, but the buggy bounced on line, and he maneuvered Bess back on track.

Angelique, dark-haired and pretty, said, "I think I soiled my bloomers . . . I smell it . . . No, that's Teddy. Thank goodness."

Bill stopped the buggy outside the restaurant, which was situated on high posts near the beach, and Angelique changed the baby's diaper, put the soiled cloth in the back of the buggy.

When she was finished, they tied up the reins and went in for a steak dinner. They sat by a window where they could see the buggy. The horse bucked and reared and tugged so much, Bill feared she might break the reins and bolt. Above them, they could hear the rocks that covered the flat roof rolling and tumbling about like mice battling over morsels. Teddy sat in a high chair provided by the restaurant, whammed a spoon in a plate of applesauce.

"Had I known the weather was this bad," Angelique said, "we'd have stayed home. I'm sorry, Bill."

"We stay home too much," Bill said, realizing the crash of the surf was causing him to raise his voice. "Building that upper deck on the house isn't doing much for my nerves either. I'm beginning to realize I'm not much of a carpenter."

Angelique widened her dark brown eyes. "No? You, not a carpenter?"

Bill smiled at her.

"I could have told you that, just by listening to all the cussing you were doing. How many times did you hit your thumb, dear?"

"Too many to count."

Angelique grew serious. "Bill. Look."

Many of the restaurant's patrons had abandoned their meals and were standing at the large windows, watching the sea. The tide was high and it was washing up to the restaurant's pilings, splashing against them hard, throwing spray against the glass.

"Goodness," Bill said. "It wasn't this bad just minutes ago."

"Hurricane?" Angelique asked.

"Yeah. It's a hurricane all right. The flags are up. I saw them."

"Why so nervous? We've had hurricanes before."

"I don't know. This feels different, I guess . . . It's all right. I'm just jittery is all."

They ate quickly and drove the buggy home, Bess pulling briskly all the way. The sea crashed behind them and the clouds raced above them like apparitions.

8:00 P.M.

Captain Slater figured the wind was easily eighty knots. A hurricane. The *Pensacola* was jumping like a frog. Crockery was crashing below. A medicine chest so heavy two men couldn't move it leaped up and struck the window of the bridge, went through onto the deck, slid across it, hit the railing, bounced high, and dropped into the boiling sea.

Slater and Bernard bumped heads so hard they nearly knocked each other out. When Slater got off the floor, he got a thick rope out from under a shelf and tossed it around a support post, made a couple of wraps, then used the loose ends to tie bowlines around his and Bernard's waists. That way, he and Bernard could move about the bridge if they had to, but they wouldn't end up following the path of the medicine chest.

Slater tried to think of something to do, but all he knew to do he had done. He'd had the crew drop anchor in the open Gulf, down to a hundred fathoms, and he'd instructed them to find the best shelter possible close to their posts, and to pray.

The *Pensacola* swung to the anchor, struggled like a bull on a leash. Slater could hear the bolts and plates that held the ship together screaming in agony. Those bolts broke, the plates cracked, he didn't need Captain Ahab to tell him they'd go down to Davy Jones's locker so fast they wouldn't have time to take in a lungful of air.

Using the wall for support, Slater edged along to where the bridge glass had been broken by the flying chest. Sea spray slammed against him like needles shot from a cannon. He was concentrating on the foredeck, watching it dip, when he heard Bernard make a noise that was not quite a word, yet more expressive than a grunt.

Slater turned, saw Bernard clutching the latch on one of the bridge windows so tightly he thought he would surely twist it off. Then he saw what Bernard saw.

The sea had turned black as a Dutch oven, the sky the color of gangrene, and between sea and sky there appeared to be something rising out of the water, something huge and oddly shaped, and then Slater realized what it was. It was a great wall of water, many times taller than the ship, and it was moving directly toward and over them.

SATURDAY, SEPTEMBER 8, 3:30 A.M.

Bill Cooper opened his eyes. He had been overwhelmed by a feeling of dread. He rose carefully, so as not to wake Angelique, went into the bedroom across the hall and checked on Teddy. The boy slept soundly, his thumb in his mouth.

Bill smiled at the child, reached down, and gently touched him. The boy was sweaty, and Bill noted that the air in the room smelled foul. He opened a window, stuck his head out, and looked up. The sky had cleared and the moon was bright. Suddenly, he felt silly. Perhaps this storm business, the deck he was building on the upper floor of the house, had made him restless and worried. Certainly, it looked as if the storm had passed them by.

Then his feeling of satisfaction passed. For when he examined the yard, he saw it had turned to molten silver. And then he realized it was moonlight on water. The Gulf had crept all the way up to the house. A small rowboat, loose from its moorings, floated by.

8:06 A.M.

Issac Cline had driven his buggy down the beach, warning residents near the water to evacuate. Some had. Some had not. Most had weathered many storms and felt they could weather another.

Still, many residents and tourists made for the long wooden trestle bridge to mainland Texas. Already, the water was leaping to the bottom of the bridge, slapping at it, testing its strength.

Wagons, buggies, horses, pedestrians were as thick on the bridge as ants on gingerbread. The sky, which had been oddly clear and bright and full of moon early that morning, had now grown gray and it was raining. Of the three railway bridges that led to the mainland, one was already underwater.

3:45 P.M.

Henry Johnson, aided by "Lil" Arthur, climbed up on the wagon beside his wife. Tina held an umbrella over their heads. In the back of the wagon was the rest of the family, protected by upright posts planted in the corners, covered with the tarp that had formerly been on the roof of the house.

All day Henry had debated whether they should leave. But by 2:00, he realized this wasn't going to be just another storm. This was going to be a goddamn, wet-assed humdinger. He had organized his family, and now, by hook or crook, he was leaving. He glanced at his shack, the water pouring through the roof like the falls of Niagara. It wasn't much, but it was all he had. He doubted it could stand much of this storm, but he tried not to think about that. He had greater concerns. He said to "Lil" Arthur, "You come on with us."

"I got to fight," "Lil" Arthur said.

"You got to do nothin'. This storm'll wash your ass to sea."

"I got to, Papa."

Tina said, "Maybe yo papa's right, baby. You ought to come."

"You know I can't. Soon as the fight's over, I'll head on out. I promise. In fact, weather's so bad, I'll knock this McBride out early."

"You do that," Tina said.

"Lil" Arthur climbed on the wagon and hugged his mama and shook his father's hand. Henry spoke quickly without looking at "Lil" Arthur, said, "Good luck, son. Knock him out."

"Lil" Arthur nodded. "Thanks, Papa." He climbed down and went around to the back of the wagon and threw up the tarp and hugged his sisters one at a time and shook hands with his brother-in-law, Clement. He pulled Clement close to him, said, "You stay out of my sister, hear?"

"Yeah, Arthur. Sure. But I think maybe we done got a problem. She's already swole up."

"Ah, shit," "Lil" Arthur said.

4:03 P.M.

As Henry Johnson drove the horses onto the wooden bridge that connected Galveston to the mainland, he felt ill. The water was washing over the sides, against the wagon wheels. The horses were nervous, and the line of would-be escapees on the bridge was tremendous. It would take them a long time to cross, maybe hours, and from the look of things, the way the water was rising, wouldn't be long before the bridge was underwater.

He said a private prayer: "Lord, take care of my family. And especially that fool son of mine, 'Lil' Arthur.'"

It didn't occur to him to include himself in the prayer.

4:37 P.M.

Bill and Angelique Cooper moved everything of value they could carry to the second floor of the house. Already the water was sloshing in the doorway. Rain splattered against the windows violently enough to shake them, and shingles flapped boisterously on the roof.

Bill paused in his work and shuffled through ankle-deep water to a window and looked out. He said, "Angelique, I think we can stop carrying."

"But I haven't carried up the—"

"We're leaving."

"Leaving? It's that bad?"

"Not yet."

Bess was difficult to hook to the buggy. She was wild-eyed and skittish. The barn was leaking badly. Angelique held an umbrella over her head, waiting for the buggy to be fastened. She could feel water rising above her high button shoes.

Bill paused for a moment to calm the horse, glanced at Angelique, thought she looked oddly beautiful, the water running off the umbrella in streams. She held Teddy close to her. Teddy was asleep, totally unaware of what was going on around him. Any other time, the baby would be squalling, annoyed. The rain and the wind were actually helping him to sleep. At least, thought Bill, I am grateful for that.

By the time the buggy was hooked, they were standing in calf-deep water. Bill opened the barn door with great difficulty, saw that the yard was gone, and so was the street. He would have to guess at directions. Worse yet, it wasn't rainwater running through the street. It was definitely seawater; the water of the Gulf had risen up as if to swallow Galveston the way the ocean was said to have swallowed Atlantis.

Bill helped Angelique and Teddy into the buggy, took hold of the reins, clucked to Bess. Bess jerked and reared, and finally, by reins and voice, Bill calmed her. She began to plod forward through the dark, powerful water.

5:00 P.M.

McBride awoke. The wind was howling. The window glass was rattling violently, even though the windows were raised. The air was cool for a change, but damp. It was dark in the room.

The madam, wrapped in a blanket, sat in a chair pulled up against the far wall. She turned and looked at McBride. She said, "All hell's broken lose."

"Say it has?" McBride got up, walked naked to the windows. The wind was so furious it pushed him. "Damn," he said. "It's dark as midnight. This looks bad."

"Bad?" The madam laughed. "Worst hurricane I've ever seen, and I don't even think it's cranked up good yet."

"You don't think they'll call off the fight do you?"

"Can you fight in a boat?"

"Hell, honey, I can fight and fuck at the same time on a boat. Come to think of it, I can fight and fuck on a rolling log, I have to. I used to be a lumberjack up north."

"I was you, I'd find a log, and get to crackin'."

A bolt of lightning, white as eternity, split the sky, and when it did, the darkness outside subsided, and in that instant, McBride saw the street was covered in waist-deep water.

"Reckon I better start on over there," he said. "It may take me a while."

The madam thought: Well, honey, go right ahead, and I hope you drown.

5:20 P.M.

"Lil" Arthur was standing on the porch, trying to decide if he should brave the water, which was now up to the lip of the porch, when he saw a loose rowboat drift by.

Suddenly he was in the water, swimming, and the force of the water carried him after the boat, and soon he had hold of it. When he climbed inside, he found the boat was a third filled with water. He found a paddle and a pail half-filled with dirt. The dirt had turned to mud and was beginning to flow over the top of the bucket. A few dead worms swirled in the mess. The world was atumble with wind, water, and darkness.

"Lil" Arthur took the bucket and poured out the mud and the worms and started to bail. Now and then he put the bucket aside and used the boat paddle. Not that he needed it much. The water was carrying him where he wanted to go. Uptown.

5:46 P.M.

Uptown the water was not so deep, but it took McBride almost an hour to get to the Sporting Club. He waded through waist-deep water for a block, then knee-deep, and finally ankle-deep. His bowler hat had lost all its shape when he arrived, and his clothes were ruined. The water hadn't done his revolver or his razor any good either.

When he arrived at the building, he was surprised to find a crowd of men had gathered on the steps. Most stood under umbrellas, but many were bareheaded. There were a few women among them. Whores mostly. Decent women didn't go to prize-fights.

McBride went up the steps, and the crowd blocked him. He said, "Look here. I'm McBride. I'm to fight the nigger."

The crowd parted, and McBride, with words of encouragement and pats on the back, was allowed indoors. Inside, the wind could still be heard, but it sounded distant. The rain was just a hum.

Beems, Forrest, and the two oldsters were standing in the foyer, looking tense as fat hens at noontime. As soon as they saw McBride, their faces relaxed, and the elderly gentlemen went away. Beems said, "We were afraid you wouldn't make it."

"Worried about your investment?"

"I suppose."

"I'd have come if I had to swim."

"The nigger doesn't show, the title and the money's yours."

"I don't want it like that," McBride said. "I want to hit him. 'Course, he don't show, I'll take the money. You seen it this bad before?"

"No," Beems said.

"I didn't expect nobody to be here."

"Gamblers always show," Forrest said. "They gamble their money, they gamble their lives."

"Go find something to do, Forrest," Beems said. "I'll show Mr. McBride the dressing room."

Forrest looked at Beems, grinned a little, showed Beems he knew what he had in mind. Beems fumed. Forrest went away. Beems took hold of McBride's elbow and began to guide him.

"I ain't no dog got to be led," McBride said.

"Very well," Beems said, and McBride followed him through a side door and down into a locker room. The room had two inches of water in it.

"My God," Beems said. "We've sprung a leak somewhere."

"Water like this," McBride said. "The force . . . it's washing out the mortar in the bricks, seeping through the chinks in the wall . . . Hell, it's all right for what I got to do."

"There's shorts and boots in the locker there," Beems said. "You could go ahead and change."

McBride sloshed water, sat on a bench and pulled off his shoes and socks with his feet resting on the bench. Beems stood where he was, watching the water rise.

McBride took the razor out of the side of one of the shoes, held it up for Beems to see, said, "Mexican boxing glove."

Beems grinned. He watched as McBride removed his bowler, coat and shirt. He watched carefully as he removed his pants and shorts. McBride reached into the locker Beems had recommended, paused, turned, stared at Beems.

"You're liking what you're seein', ain't you, buddy?"

Beems didn't say anything. His heart was in his throat.

McBride grinned at him. "I knew first time I seen you, you was an Alice."

"No," Beems said. "Nothing like that. It's not like that at all."

McBride smiled. He looked very gentle in that moment. He said, "It's all right. Come here. I don't mind that."

"Well . . ."

"Naw. Really. It's just, you know, you got to be careful. Not let everyone know. Not everyone understands, see."

Beems, almost licking his lips, went over to McBride. When he was close, McBride's smile widened, and he unloaded a right uppercut into Beems's stomach. He hit him so hard Beems dropped to his knees in the water, nodded forward, and banged his head on the bench. His top hat came off, hit the water, sailed along the row of lockers, made a right turn near the wall, flowed out of sight behind a bench.

McBride picked Beems up by the hair and pulled his

head close to his dick, said, "Look at it a minute, 'cause that's all you're gonna do."

Then McBride pulled Beems to his feet by his pretty hair and went to work on him. Lefts and rights. Nothing too hard. But more than Beems had ever gotten. When he finished, he left Beems lying in the water next to the bench, coughing.

McBride said, "Next time you piss, you'll piss blood, Alice." McBride got a towel out of the locker and sat on the bench and put his feet up and dried them. He put on the box-ing shorts. There was a mirror on the inside of the locker, and McBride was upset to see his hair. It was a mess. He spent several minutes putting it in place. When he finished, he glanced down at Beems, who was pretending to be dead.

McBride said, "Get up, fairy-ass. Show me where I'm gonna fight."

"Don't tell anybody," Beems said. "I got a wife. A repu-tation. Don't tell anybody."

"I'll make you a promise," McBride said, closing the locker door. "That goddamn nigger beats me, I'll fuck you. Shit, I'll let you fuck me. But don't get your butthole all apucker. I ain't losin' nothin'. Tonight, way I feel, I could knock John L. Sullivan on his ass."

McBride started out of the locker room, carrying his socks and the boxing shoes with him. Beems lay in the water, giving him plenty of head start.

6:00 P.M.

Henry couldn't believe how slow the line was moving. Hundreds of people, crawling for hours. When the Johnsons were near the end of the bridge, almost to the mainland, the water rushed in a dark brown wave and washed the buggy in front of them off the bridge. The Johnsons' wagon felt the wave, too, but only slid to the railing. But the buggy hit the railing, bounced, went over, pulling the horse into the railing after it. For a moment the horse hung there, its back legs slipping through, pulling with its front legs, then the railing cracked and the whole kit and kaboodle went over.

"Oh Jesus," Tina said.

"Hang on," Henry said. He knew he had to hurry, before another wave washed in, because if it was bigger, or caught them near the gap the buggy had made, they, too, were gone.

Behind them the Johnsons could hear screams of people fleeing the storm. The water was rising rapidly over the bridge, and those to the middle and the rear realized they didn't get across quickly, they weren't going to make it. As they fought to move forward, the bridge cracked and moaned as if with a human voice.

The wind ripped at the tarp over the wagon and tore it away. "Shit," said Clement. "Ain't that something?"

A horse bearing a man and a woman, the woman wearing a great straw hat that drooped down on each side of her head, raced by the Johnsons. The bridge was too slick and the horse was moving too fast. Its legs splayed and it went down and started sliding. Slid right through the opening the buggy had made. Disappeared immediately beneath the water. When Henry ventured a look in that direction, he saw the woman's straw hat come up once, then blend with the water.

When Henry's wagon was even with the gap, a fresh brown wave came over the bridge, higher and harder this time. It hit his horses and the wagon broadside. The sound of it, the impact of it, reminded Henry of when he was in the Civil War and a wagon he was riding in was hit by Yankee cannon fire. The impact had knocked him spinning, and when he tried to get up, his leg had been ruined. He thought he would never be that frightened again. But now, he was even more afraid.

The wagon drifted sideways, hit the gap, but was too wide for it. It hung on the ragged railing, the sideboards cracking with the impact. Henry's family screamed and lay down flat in the wagon as the water came down on them like a heavy hand. The pressure of the water snapped the wagon's wheels off the axle, slammed the bottom of the wagon against the bridge, but the sideboards held together.

"Everybody out!" Henry said.

Henry, his weak leg failing to respond, tumbled out of the wagon onto the bridge, which was now under a foot of water. He got hold of a sideboard and pulled himself up, helped Tina down, reached up, and snatched his cane off the seat.

Clement and the others jumped down, started hustling toward the end of the bridge on foot. As they came even with Henry, he said, "Go on, hurry. Don't worry none about me."

Tina clutched his arm. "Go on, woman," he said. "You got young'uns to care about. I got to free these horses." He patted her hand. She moved on with the others.

Henry pulled out his pocketknife and set to cutting the horses free of the harness. As soon as they were loose, both fool animals bolted directly into the railing. One of them bounced off of it, pivoted, made for the end of the bridge at a splashing gallop, but the other horse hit with such impact it flipped over, turning its feet to the sky. It pierced the water and was gone.

Henry turned to look for his family. They were no longer visible. Surely, they had made the mainland by now.

Others had come along to fill their place; people in wagons, and buggies, on horseback and on foot. People who seemed to be scrambling on top of water, since the bridge was now completely below sea level.

Then Henry heard a roar. He turned to the east side of the bridge. There was a heavy sheet of water cocked high above him, and it was coming down, like a monstrous wet flyswatter. And when it struck Henry and the bridge, and all those on it, it smashed them flat and drove them into the churning belly of the sea.

6:14 P.M.

Bill and Angelique Cooper, their buggy half-submerged in water, saw the bridge through the driving rain, then suddenly they saw it no more. The bridge and the people were wadded together and washed down.

The bridge rose up on the waves a moment later, like a writhing spinal column. People still clung to it. It leaped forward into the water, the end of it lashing the air, then it was gone and the people with it.

"God have mercy on their souls," Angelique said.

Bill said, "That's it then."

He turned the buggy around in the water with difficulty, headed home. All around him, shingles and rocks from the roofs of structures flew like shrapnel.

7:39 P.M.

"Lil" Arthur, as he floated toward town, realized it was less deep here. It was just as well, the rain was pounding his boat and filling it with water. He couldn't bail and paddle as fast as it went in. He climbed over the side and let the current carry the boat away.

The water surprised him with its force. He was almost swept away, but it was shallow enough to get a foothold and push against the flow. He waded to the Sporting Club, went around back to the colored entrance. When he got there, an elderly black man known as Uncle Cooter let him in, said, "Man, I'd been you, I'd stayed home."

"What," "Lil" Arthur said. "And missed a boat ride?"

"A boat ride?"

"Lil" Arthur told him how he had gotten this far.

"Damnation," Uncle Cooter said. "God gonna put this island underwater 'cause it's so evil. Like that Sodom and Gomorrah place."

"What have you and me done to God?"

Uncle Cooter smiled. "Why, we is the only good children God's got. He gonna watch after us. Well, me anyway. You done gonna get in with this Mr. McBride, and he's some bad stuff, 'Lil' Arthur. God ain't gonna help you there. And this Mr. McBride, he ain't got no sense neither. He done beat up Mr. Beems, and Mr. Beems the one settin' this up, gonna pay him money."

"Why'd he beat him up?"

"Hell, you can't figure white people. They all fucked up. But Mr. Beems damn sure look like a raccoon now. Both his eyes all black, his lip pouched out."

"Where do I change?"

"Janitor's closet. They done put your shorts and shoes in there. And there's some gauze for your hands."

"Lil" Arthur found the shorts. They were old and faded. The boxing shoes weren't too good either. He found some soiled rags and used those to dry himself. He used the gauze to wrap his hands, then his dick. He figured, once you start a custom, you ought to stick with it.

7:45 P.M.

When Bill and Angelique and Teddy arrived at their house, they saw that the water had pushed against the front door so violently, it had come open. Water was flowing into the hall and onto the bottom step of the stairs. Bill looked up and saw a lamp burning upstairs. They had left so quickly, they had forgotten to extinguish it.

With a snort, Bess bolted. The buggy jerked forward, hit a curb, and the harness snapped so abruptly Bill and his family were not thrown from their seat, but merely whipped forward and back against the seat. The reins popped through Bill's hands so swiftly, the leather cut his palms.

Bess rushed across the yard and through the open doorway of the house, and slowly and carefully, began to climb the stairs.

Angelique said, "My lands."

Bill, a little stunned, climbed down, went around, and helped Angelique and the baby out of the buggy. The baby was wet and crying, and Angelique tried to cover him with the umbrella, but now the wind and rain seemed to come from all directions. The umbrella was little more than a wad of cloth.

They waded inside the house, tried to close the door, but the water was too much for them. They gave it up.

Bess had reached the top landing and disappeared. They followed her up. The bedroom door was open and the horse had gone in there. She stood near the table bearing the kerosene lamp. Shaking.

"Poor thing," Angelique said, gathering some towels from a chifforobe. "She's more terrified than we are."

Bill removed the harness that remained on Bess, stroked her, tried to soothe her. When he went to the window and looked out, the horse went with him. The world had not miraculously dried up. The water was obviously rising.

"Maybe we'll be all right here," Angelique said. She was drying Teddy, who was crying violently because he was cold and wet. "Water can't get this high, can it?"

Bill idly stroked Bess's mane, thought of the bridge. The way it had snapped like a wooden toy. He said, "Of course not."

8:15 P.M.

The fight had started late, right after two one-legged colored boys had gone a couple of rounds, hopping about, trying to club each other senseless with oversize boxing gloves.

The crowd was sparse but vocal. Loud enough that "Lil" Arthur forgot the raging storm outside. The crowd kept yelling, "Kill the nigger," and had struck up a chorus of "All coons look alike to me"—a catchy little number that "Lil" Arthur liked in spite of himself.

The yelling, the song, was meant to drop his spirits, but he found it fired him up. He liked being the underdog. He liked to make assholes eat their words. Besides, he was the Galveston Champion, not McBride, no matter what the crowd wanted. He was the one who would step through the ropes tonight the victor. And he had made a change. He would no longer allow himself to be introduced as "Lil" Arthur. When his name had been called, and he had been reluctantly named Galveston Sporting Club Champion by the announcer, the announcer had done as he had asked. He had called him by the name he preferred from here on. Not "Lil" Arthur Johnson. Not Arthur John Johnson, but the name he called him, the name he called himself. Jack Johnson.

So far, however, the fight wasn't going either way, and he had to hand it to McBride, the fella could hit. He had a way of throwing short, sharp punches to the ribs, punches that felt like knife stabs.

Before the fight, Jack, as McBride had surely done, had used his thumbs to rearrange as much of the cotton in his gloves as possible. Arrange it so that his knuckles would be against the leather and would make good contact with McBride's flesh. But so far McBride had avoided most of his blows. The man was a master of slipping and sliding the punches. Jack had never seen anything like that before. McBride could also pick off shots with a flick of his forearms. It was very professional and enlightening.

Even so, Jack found he was managing to take the punches pretty well, and he'd discovered something astonishing. The few times he'd hit McBride was when he got excited, leaned forward, went flat-footed, and threw the uppercut. This was not a thing he had trained for much, and when he had, he usually threw the uppercut by coming up on his toes, twisting his body, the prescribed way to throw it. But he found, against all logic, he could throw it flat-footed and leaning forward, and he could throw it hard.

He thought he had seen a bit of surprise on McBride's face when he'd hit him with it. He knew that he'd certainly surprised himself.

It went like that until the beginning of the fourth round, then when McBride came out, he said, "I've carried you enough, nigger. Now you got to fight."

Then Jack saw stuff he'd never seen before. The way this guy moved, it was something. Bounced around like a cat, like the way he'd heard Gentleman Jim fought, and the guy was fast with those hands. Tossed bullets, and the bullets stunned a whole lot worse than before. Jack realized McBride had been holding back, trying to make the fight interesting. And he realized something else. Something important about himself. He didn't know as much about boxing as he thought.

He tried hooking McBride, but McBride turned the hooks away with his arms, and Jack tried his surprise weapon, the uppercut, found he could catch McBride a little with that, in the stomach, but not enough to send McBride to the canvas. When the fifth round came up, Jack was scared. And hurt. And the referee—a skinny bastard with a handlebar moustache—wasn't helping. Anytime he tied McBride up, the referee separated them. McBride tied him up, thumbed him in the eye, butted him, the referee grinned like he was eating jelly.

Jack was thinking maybe of taking a dive. Just going down and lying there, getting himself out of this misery next time McBride threw one of those short ones that connected solid, but then the bell rang and he sat on his bench, and Uncle Cooter, who was the only man in his corner, sprayed water in his mouth and let him spit blood in a bucket.

Uncle Cooter said, "I was you, son, I'd play possum. Just hit that goddamn canvas and lay there like you axed. You don't, this shithead gonna cut you to pieces. This way, you get a little payday and you don't die. Paydays is all right. Dyin' ain't nothin' to rush."

"Jesus, he's good. How can I beat him?"

Uncle Cooter rubbed Jack's shoulders. "You can't. Play dead."

"There's got to be a way."

"Yeah," Uncle Cooter said. "He might die on you. That's the only way you gonna beat him. He got to just die."

"Thanks, Cooter. You're a lot of help."

"You welcome."

Jack feared the sound of the bell. He looked in McBride's corner, and McBride was sitting on his stool as if he were lounging, drinking from a bottle of beer, chatting with a man in the audience. He was asking the man to go get him a sandwich.

Forrest Thomas was in McBride's corner, holding a folded towel over his arm, in case McBride might need it, which, considering he needed to break a good sweat first, wasn't likely.

Forrest looked at Jack, pointed a finger, and lowered his thumb like it was the hammer of a revolver. Jack could see a word on Forrest's lips. The word was: POW!

The referee wandered over to McBride's corner, leaned on the ring post, had a laugh with McBride over something.

The bell rang. McBride gave the bottle of beer to Forrest and came out. Jack rose, saw Beems, eyes blacked, looking rough, sitting in the front row. Rough or not, Beems seemed happy. He looked at Jack and smiled like a gravedigger.

This time out, Jack took a severe pounding. He just couldn't stop those short little hooks of McBride's, and he couldn't seem to hit McBride any kind of blow but the upper-cut, and that not hard enough. McBride was getting better as he went along, getting warmed up. If he had another beer and a sandwich, hell, he might go ahead and knock Jack out so he could have coffee and pie.

Jack decided to quit trying to hit the head and the ribs, and just go in and pound McBride on the arms. That way, he could at least hit something. He did, and was amazed at the end of the round to find McBride lowering his guard.

Jack went back to his corner and Uncle Cooter said, "Keep hittin' him on the arms. That's gettin' to him. You wreckin' his tools."

"I figured that much. Thanks a lot."

"You welcome."

Jack examined the crowd in the Sporting Club bleachers. They were not watching the ring. They had turned their heads toward the east wall, and for good reason. It was vibrating. Water was seeping in, and it had filled the floor beneath the ring six inches deep. The people occupying the bottom row of bleachers, all around the ring, had been forced to lift their feet. Above him, Jack heard a noise that sounded like something big and mean peeling skin off an elephant's head.

By the time the bell rang and Jack shuffled out, he noticed that the water had gone up another two inches.

8:46 P.M.

Bill held the lantern in front of him at arm's length as he crouched at the top of the stairs. The water was halfway up the steps. The house was shaking like a fat man's ass on a bucking bronco. He could hear shingles ripping loose, blowing away.

He went back to the bedroom. The wind was screaming. The windows were vibrating; panes had blown out of a couple of them. The baby was crying. Angelique sat in the middle of the bed, trying to nurse the child, but Teddy wouldn't have any of that. Bess was facing a corner of the room, had her head pushed against the wall. The horse lashed her tail back and forth nervously, made nickering noises.

Bill went around and opened all the windows to help take away some of the force of the wind. Something he knew he should have done long ago, but he was trying to spare the baby the howl of the wind, the dampness.

The wind charged through the open windows and the rain charged with it. Bill could hardly stand before them, they were so powerful.

Fifteen minutes later, he heard the furniture below thumping on the ceiling, floating against the floor on which he stood.

9:00 P.M.

My God, thought Jack, how many rounds this thing gonna go? His head ached and his ribs ached worse and his insides felt as if he had swallowed hot tacks and was trying to regurgitate them. His legs, though strong, were beginning to feel the wear. He had thought this was a fifteen-round affair, but realized now it was twenty, and if he wasn't losing by then, he might get word it would go twenty-five.

Jack slammed a glove against McBride's left elbow, saw McBride grimace, drop the arm. Jack followed with the uppercut, and this time he not only hit McBride, he hit him solid. McBride took the shot so hard, he farted. The sandwich he'd eaten between rounds probably didn't seem like such a good idea now.

Next time Jack threw the combination, he connected with the uppercut again. McBride moved back, and Jack followed, hitting him on the arms, slipping in the uppercut now and then, even starting to make contact with hooks and straight rights.

Then every light in the building went out as the walls came apart and the bleachers soared up on a great surge of water and dumped the boxing patrons into the wet darkness. The ring itself began to move, to rise to the ceiling, but before it tilted out from under Jack, McBride hit him a blow so hard Jack thought he felt past lives cease to exist; ancestors fresh from the slime rocked from that blow, and the reverberations of it rippled back to the present and into the future, and back again. The ceiling went away on a torrent of wind, Jack reached out and got hold of something and clung for dear life.

"You stupid sonofabitch," Uncle Cooter said, "you got me by the goddamn head."

9:05 P.M.

Captain Slater thought they would be at the bottom of the Gulf by now, and was greatly surprised they were not. A great wave of water had hit them so hard the night before it had snapped the anchor chain. The ship was driven down, way down, and then all the water in the world washed over them and there was total darkness and horror, and then, what seemed like hours later but could only have been seconds, the water broke and the *Pensacola* flew high up as if shot from a cannon, came down again, leaned starboard so far it took water, then, miraculously, corrected itself. The sea had been choppy and wild ever since.

Slater shook shit and seawater out of his pants legs and followed the rope around his waist to the support post. He got hold of the post, felt for the rest of the rope. In the darkness, he cried out, "Bernard. You there?"

"I think so," came Bernard's voice from the darkness. And then they heard a couple of bolts pop free, fire off like rifle blasts. Then: "Oh, Jesus," Bernard said. "Feel that swell? Here it comes again."

Slater turned his head and looked out. There was nothing but a great wall of blackness moving toward them. It made the first wave seem like a mere rise; this one was bigger than the Great Wall of China.

Bill and Angelique lay on the bed with Teddy. The water was washing over the edges of the feather mattress, blowing wet, cold wind over them. They had started the Edison and a gospel record had been playing, but the wind and rain had finally gotten into the mechanism and killed it.

As it went dead, the far wall cracked and leaned in and a ripple of cracking lumber went across the floor and the ceiling sagged and so did the bed. Bess suddenly disappeared through a hole in the floor. One moment she was there, the next she was gone, beneath the water.

Bill grabbed Angelique by the arm, pulled her to her feet in the knee-deep water. She held Teddy close to her. He pulled them across the room as the floor shifted, pulled them through the door that led onto the unfinished deck, stumbled over a hammer that lay beneath the water, but managed to keep his feet.

Bill couldn't help but think of all the work he had put in on this deck. Now it would never be finished. He hated to leave anything unfinished. He hated worse that it was starting to lean.

There was one central post that seemed to stand well enough, and they took position behind that. The post was one of several that the house was built around; a support post to lift the house above the normal rise of water. It connected bedroom to deck.

Bill tried to look through the driving rain. All he could see was water. Galveston was covered by the sea. It had risen up and swallowed the city and the island.

The house began to shake violently. They heard lumber splintering, felt it shimmying. The deck swayed more dynamically.

"We're not going to make it, are we, Bill?" Angelique said.

"No, darling. We aren't."

"I love you."

"I love you."

He held her and kissed her. She said, "It doesn't matter, you and I. But Teddy. He doesn't know. He doesn't understand. God, why Teddy? He's only a baby ... How do I drown, darling?"

"One deep breath and it's over. Just one deep pull of the water, and don't fight it."

Angelique started to cry. Bill squatted, ran his hand under the water and over the deck. He found the hammer. It was lodged in its spot because it was caught in a gap in the unfinished deck. Bill brought the hammer out. There was a big nail sticking out of the main support post. He had driven it there the day before, to find it easily enough. It was his last big nail and it was his intent to save it.

He used the claw of the hammer to pull it out. He looked at Angelique. "We can give Teddy a chance."

Angelique couldn't see Bill well in the darkness, but she somehow felt what his face was saying. "Oh, Bill."

"It's a chance."

"But ..."

"We can't stand against this, but the support post—"

"Oh Lord, Bill," and Angelique sagged, holding Teddy close to her chest. Bill grabbed her shoulders, said, "Give me my son."

Angelique sobbed, then the house slouched far to the right—except for the support post. All the other supports were washing loose, but so far, this one hadn't budged.

Angelique gave Teddy to Bill. Bill kissed the child, lifted him as high on the post as he could, pushed the child's back against the wood, and lifted its arm. Angelique was suddenly there, supporting the baby. Bill kissed her. He took the hammer and the nail, and placing the nail squarely against Teddy's little wrist, drove it through the child's flesh with one swift blow.

Then the storm blew more furious and the deck turned to gelatin. Bill clutched Angelique, and Angelique almost managed to say, "Teddy," then all the powers of nature took them and the flimsy house away.

High above it all, water lapping around the post, Teddy, wet and cold, squalled with pain.

Bess surfaced among lumber and junk. She began to paddle her legs furiously, snorting water. A nail on a board cut across her muzzle, opening a deep gash. The horse nickered, thrashed its legs violently, lifted its head, trying to stay afloat.

SUNDAY, SEPTEMBER 9, 4:00 A.M.

The mechanism that revolved the Bolivar lighthouse beam had stopped working. The stairs that led up to the lighthouse had gradually filled with people fleeing the storm, and as the water rose, so did the people. One man with a young boy had come in last, and therefore was on the constantly rising bottom rung. He kept saying. "Move up. Move up, lessen' you want to see a man and his boy drown." And everyone would move up. And then the man would soon repeat his refrain as the water rose.

The lighthouse was becoming congested. The lighthouse tower had begun to sway. The lighthouse operator, Jim Marlin, and his wife, Elizabeth, lit the kerosene lamp and placed it in the center of the circular, magnifying lens, and tried to turn the beam by hand. They wanted someone to know there was shelter here, even though it was overcrowded, and might soon cease to exist. The best thing to do was to douse the light and hope they could save those who were already there, and save themselves. But Jim and Elizabeth couldn't do that. Elizabeth said, "Way I see it, Jim. It's all or nothing, and the good Lord would want it that way. I want it that way."

All night long they had heard screams and cries for help, and once, when the lighthouse beam was operating, they had seen a young man clinging to a timber. When the light swung back to where the young man had been, he had vanished.

Now, as they tried to turn the light by hand, they found it was too much of a chore. Finally, they let it shine in one direction, and there in the light they saw a couple of bodies being dragged by a large patch of canvas from which dangled ropes, like jellyfish tentacles. The ropes had grouped and twisted around the pair, and the canvas seemed to operate with design, folded and opened like a pair of great wings, as if it were an exotic sea creature bearing them off to a secret lair where they could be eaten in privacy.

Neither Jim nor Elizabeth Marlin knew the bloated men tangled in the ropes together; had no idea they were named Ronald Beems and Forrest Thomas.

5:00 A.M.

A crack of light. Dawn. Jim and Elizabeth had fallen asleep leaning against the base of the great light, and at the first ray of sunshine, they awoke, saw a ship's bow at the lighthouse window, and standing at the bow, looking in at them, was a bedraggled man in uniform, and he was crying savagely.

Jim went to the window. The ship had been lifted up on great piles of sand and lumber. Across the bow he could see the letters PENSACOLA. The man was leaning against the glass. He wore a captain's hat. He held out his hand, palm first. Jim put his hand to the glass, trying to match the span of the crying captain's hand.

Behind the captain a number of wet men appeared. When

they saw the lighthouse they fell to their knees and lifted their heads to the heavens in prayer, having forgotten that it was in fact the heavens that had devastated them.

6:00 A.M.

The day broke above the shining water, and the water began to go down, rapidly, and John McBride sat comfortably on the great hour hand of what was left of the City Hall clock. He sat there with his arms wrapped around debris that dangled from the clock. In the night, a huge spring mechanism had jumped from the face of the clock and hit him a glancing blow in the head, and for a moment, McBride had thought he was still battling the nigger. He wasn't sure which was worse to fight. The hurricane or the nigger. But through the night, he had become grateful for the spring to hold on to.

Below him he saw much of what was left of the Sporting Club, including the lockers where he had put his belongings. The whole damn place had washed up beneath the clock tower.

McBride used his teeth to work off the binds of his boxing gloves and slip his hands free. All through the night the gloves had been a burden. He feared his lack of grip would cause him to fall. It felt good to have his hands out of the tight, wet leather.

McBride ventured to take hold of the minute hand of the clock, swing on it a little, and cause it to lower him onto a pile of rubble. He climbed over lumber and junk and found a mass of bloated bodies, men, women, and children, most of them sporting shingles that had cut into their heads and bodies. He searched their pockets for money and found none, but one of the women—he could tell it was a woman by her hair and dress only, her features were lost in the fleshy swelling of her face—had a ring. He tried to pull it off her finger, but it wouldn't come off. The water had swollen her flesh all around it.

He sloshed his way to the pile of lockers. He searched through them until he found the one where he had put his clothes. They were so filthy with mud, he left them. But he got the razor and the revolver. The revolver was full of grit. He took out the shells and shook them and put them back. He stuck the gun in his soaked boxing trunks. He opened the razor and shook out the silt and went over to the woman and used the razor to cut off her finger. The blade cut easily through the flesh, and he whacked through the bone. He pushed the ring on his little finger, closed the razor, and slipped it into the waistband of his trunks, next to his revolver.

This was a hell of a thing to happen. He had hidden his money back at the whorehouse, and he figured it and the plump madam were probably far at sea, the madam possibly full of harpoon wounds.

And the shitasses who were to pay him were now all choked, including the main one, the queer Beems. And if they weren't, they were certainly no longer men of means.

This had been one shitty trip. No clothes. No money. No whipped nigger. And no more pussy. He'd come with more than he was leaving with.

What the hell else could go wrong?

He decided to wade toward the whorehouse, see if it was possibly standing, maybe find some bodies along the way to loot—something to make up for his losses.

As he started in that direction, he saw a dog on top of a doghouse float by. The dog was chained to the house and the chain had gotten tangled around some floating rubble and it had pulled the dog flat against the roof. It lifted its eyes and saw McBride, barked wearily for help. McBride determined it was well within pistol shot.

McBride lifted the revolver and pulled the trigger. It clicked, but nothing happened. He tried again, hoping against hope. It fired this time and the dog took a blast in the skull and rolled off the house, and hung by the chain, then sailed out of sight.

McBride said, "Poor thing."

7:03 A.M.

The water was falling away rapidly, returning to the sea, leaving in its wake thousands of bodies and the debris that had once been Galveston. The stench was awful. Jack and Cooter, who had spent the night in a child's tree house, awoke, amazed they were alive.

The huge oak tree they were in was stripped of leaves and limbs, but the tree house was unharmed. It was remarkable. They had washed right up to it, just climbed off the lumber to which they had been clinging, and went inside. It was dry in there, and they found three hard biscuits in a tin and three hot bottles of that good ole Waco, Texas, drink, Dr. Pepper. There was a phone on the wall, but it was a fake, made of lumber and tin cans. Jack had the urge to try it, as if it might be a line to God, for surely, it was God who had brought them here.

Cooter had helped Jack remove his gloves, then they ate the biscuits, drank a bottle of Dr. Pepper apiece, then split the last bottle and slept.

When it was good and light, they decided to climb down. The ladder, a series of boards nailed to the tree, had washed away, but they made it to the ground by sliding down like firemen on a pole.

When they reached the earth, they started walking, sloshing through the mud and water that had rolled back to ankle-deep. The world they had known was gone. Galveston was a wet mulch of bloated bodies—humans, dogs, mules, and horses—and mashed lumber. In the distance they saw a bedraggled family walking along like ducks in a row. Jack recognized them. He had seen them around town. They were

Issac Cline, his brother Joseph, Issac's wife and children. He wondered if they knew where they were going, or were they like him and Cooter, just out there? He decided on the latter.

Jack and Cooter decided to head for higher ground, back uptown. Soon they could see the tower of City Hall, in sad shape but still standing, the clock having sprung a great spring. It poked from the face of the mechanism like a twisted, metal tongue.

They hadn't gone too far toward the tower when they encountered a man coming toward them. He was wearing shorts and shoes like Jack and was riding a chocolate brown mare bareback. He had looped a piece of frayed rope around the horse's muzzle and was using that as a primitive bridle. His hair was combed to perfection. It was McBride.

"Shit," Cooter said. "Ain't this somethin'? Well, Jack, you take care, I gonna be seein' you."

"Asshole," Jack said.

Cooter put his hands in his pockets and turned right, headed over piles of junk and bodies on his way to who knew where.

McBride spotted Jack, yelled, "You somethin', nigger. A hurricane can't even drown you."

"You neither," Jack said. They were within twenty feet of one another now. Jack could see the revolver and the razor in McBride's waistband. The horse, a beautiful animal with a deep cut on its muzzle, suddenly buckled and lay down with its legs folded beneath it, dropped its head into the mud.

McBride stepped off the animal, said, "Can you believe that? Goddamn horse survived all this and it can't carry me no ways at all."

McBride pulled his pistol and shot the horse through the head. It rolled over gently, lay on its side without so much as one last heave of its belly. McBride turned back to Jack. The revolver lay loose in his hand. He said, "Had it misfired, I'd have had to beat that horse to death with a board. I don't believe in animals suffering. Gun's been underwater, and it's worked two out of three. Can you believe that?"

"That horse would have been all right," Jack said.

"Naw, it wouldn't," McBride said. "Why don't you shake it, see if it'll come around?" McBride pushed the revolver into the waistband of his shorts. "How's about you and me? Want to finish where we left off?"

"You got to be jokin'," Jack said.

"You hear me laughin'?"

"I don't know about you, peckerwood, but I feel like I been in a hurricane, then swam a few miles in boxing gloves, then slept all night in a tree house and had biscuits and Dr. Pepper for breakfast."

"I ain't even had no breakfast, nigger. Listen here. I can't go home not knowing I can whip you or not. Hell, I might never get home. I want to know I can take you. You want to know."

"Yeah. I do. But I don't want to fight no pistol and razor."

McBride removed the pistol and razor from his trunks, found a dry spot and put them there. He said, "Come on."

"Where?"

"Here's all we got."

Jack turned and looked. He could see a slight rise of dirt beyond the piles of wreckage. A house had stood there. One of its great support poles was still visible.

"Over there," Jack said.

They went over there and found a spot about the size of a boxing ring. Down below them on each side were heaps of bodies and heaps of gulls on the bodies, scrambling for soft flesh and eyeballs. McBride studied the bodies, what was left of Galveston, turned to Jack, said, "Fuck the rules."

They waded into each other, bare knuckle. It was obvious after only moments that they were exhausted. They were throwing hammers, not punches, and the sounds of their strikes mixed with the caws and cries of the gulls. McBride ducked his head beneath Jack's chin, drove it up. Jack locked his hands behind McBride's neck, kneed him in the groin.

They rolled on the ground and in the mud, then came apart. They regained their feet and went at it again. Then the sounds of their blows and the shrieks of the gulls were overwhelmed by a cry so unique and savage, they ceased punching.

"Time," Jack said.

"What in hell is that?" McBride said.

They walked toward the sound of the cry, leaned on the great support post. Once a fine house had stood here, and now, there was only this. McBride said, "I don't know about you, nigger, but I'm one tired sonofabitch."

The cry came again. Above him. He looked up. A baby was nailed near the top of the support. Its upraised, nailed arm was covered in caked blood. Gulls were flapping around its head, making a kind of halo.

"I'll be goddamned," Jack said. "Boost me, McBride."

"What?"

"Boost me."

"You got to be kidding."

Jack lifted his leg. McBride sighed, made a stirrup with his cupped hands, and Jack stood, got hold of the post and worked his way painfully up. At the bottom, McBride picked up garbage and hurled it at the gulls.

"You gonna hit the baby, you jackass," Jack said.

When he got up there, Jack found the nail was sticking out of the baby's wrist by an inch or so. He wrapped his legs tight around the post, held on with one arm while he took hold of the nail and tried to work it free with his fingers. It wouldn't budge.

"Can't get it loose," Jack yelled down. He was about to drop; his legs and arms had turned to butter.

"Hang on," McBride said, and went away.

It seemed like forever before he came back. He had the revolver with him. He looked up at Jack and the baby. He looked at them for a long moment. Jack watched him, didn't move. McBride said, "Listen up, nigger. Catch this, use it to work out the nail."

McBride emptied the remaining cartridges from the revolver and tossed it up. Jack caught it on the third try. He used the trigger guard to snag the nail, but mostly mashed the baby's wrist. The baby had stopped crying. It was making a kind of mewing sound, like a dying goat.

The nail came loose, and Jack nearly didn't grab the baby in time, and when he did, he got hold of its nailed arm and he felt and heard its shoulder snap out of place. He was weakening, and he knew he was about to fall.

"McBride," he said, "catch."

The baby dropped and so did the revolver. McBride reached out and grabbed the child. It screamed when he caught it, and McBride raised it over his head and laughed. He laid the baby on top of a pile of wide lumber and looked at it.

Jack was about halfway down the post when he fell, landing on his back, knocking the wind out of him. By the time he got it together enough to get up and find the revolver and wobble over to McBride, McBride had worked the child's shoulder back into place and was cooing to him.

Jack said, "He ain't gonna make it. He's lost lots of blood."

McBride stood up with the baby on his shoulder. He said, "Naw. He's tough as a warthog. Worse this little shit will have is a scar. Elastic as he is, there ain't no real damage. And he didn't bleed out bad neither. He gets some milk in him, fifteen, sixteen years from now, he'll be chasin' pussy. 'Course, best thing is, come around when he's about two and go on and kill him. He'll just grow up to be men like us."

McBride held the child out and away from him, looked him over. The baby's penis lifted and the child peed all over him. McBride laughed uproariously.

"Well, shit, nigger. I reckon today ain't my day, and it ain't the day you and me gonna find out who's the best. Here. I don't know no one here. Take 'em."

Jack took the child, gave McBride his revolver, said, "I don't know there's anyone I know anymore."

"I tell you, you're one lucky nigger," McBride said. "I'm gonna forgo you a beating, maybe a killing."

"That right?"

"Uh-huh. Someone's got to tote this kid to safety, and iff'n I kept him, I might get tired of him in an hour. Put his little head underwater."

"You would, wouldn't you?"

"I might. And you know, you're a fool to give me back my gun."

"Naw. I broke it gettin' that nail loose."

McBride grinned, tossed the gun in the mud, shaded his eyes, and looked at the sky. "Can you beat that? Looks like it's gonna be a nice day."

Jack nodded. The baby sucked on his shoulder. He decided McBride was right. This was one tough kid. It was snuggled against him as if nothing had happened, trying to get milk. Jack wondered about the child's family. Wondered about his own. Where were they? Were they alive?

McBride grinned, said, "Nigger, you got a hell of an uppercut." Then he turned and walked away.

Jack patted the baby's back, watched McBride find his razor, then walk on. Jack watched him until he disappeared behind a swell of lumber and bodies, and he never saw him again.

1910

1911

1912

1913

1914

1915

1916

1917

1918

1919

IF I SHOULD DIE BEFORE I WAKE

BY DAVID MORRELL

---

*The Lord doth build up Jerusalem; and gather
together the outcasts of Israel.*
*He healeth those that are broken in heart; and
giveth medicine to heal their sickness.*
*He telleth the number of the stars; and calleth
them all by their names.*

—The Book of Common Prayer

It wasn't the first case, but it was Dr. Jonas Bingaman's first case, although he would not realize that until two days later. The patient, a boy with freckles and red hair, lay listlessly beneath the covers of his bed. Bingaman, who had been leaving his office for the evening when the boy's anxious mother telephoned, paused at the entrance to the narrow bedroom and assessed immediately that the boy had a fever. It wasn't just that Joey Carter, whom Bingaman had brought into the world ten years earlier, was red in the face. After all, the summer of 1918 had been uncommonly hot, and even now, at the end of August, the doctor was treating cases of sunburn. No, what made him conclude so quickly that Joey had a fever was that, despite the lingering heat, Joey was shivering under a sheet and two blankets.

"He's been like this since he came home just before supper," Joey's mother, Rebecca, said. A slim plain woman of thirty-five, she entered Joey's room ahead of the doctor and gestured urgently for him to follow. "I found his wet bathing suit. He'd been swimming."

"At the creek. I've warned him about that creek," Joey's father, Edward, said. Elmdale's best carpenter, the gangly man still wore his coveralls and work boots and had traces of sawdust in his thick dark hair. "I've told him to stay away from it."

"The creek?" Bingaman turned toward Edward, who waited anxiously in the hallway.

"The water's no good. Makes you sick. I know 'cause Bill Kendrick's boy got sick swimming in it last summer. Breathed wrong. Swallowed some of the water. Threw up all night long. I warned Joey not to go near it, but he wouldn't listen."

"The creek through Larrabee's farm?"

"That's the one. The cattle mess in the water. The stuff flows downstream and into the swimming hole."

"Yes, I remember Bill Kendrick's boy getting sick from the water last summer," Bingaman said. "Has Joey been vomiting?"

"No." Rebecca's voice was strained.

"I'd better take a look."

As Bingaman went all the way into the room, he noted a baseball bat in a corner. A balsa-wood model of one of the Curtiss biplanes that the American Expeditionary Force was using against the Germans hung above the bed, attached by a cord to the ceiling.

"Not feeling well, Joey?"

It took an obvious effort for the boy to shake his head "no." His eyelids were barely open. He coughed.

"Been swimming in the creek?"

Joey had trouble nodding. "Shoulda listened to Dad," he murmured hoarsely.

"Next time you'll know the right thing to do. But for now, I want you to concentrate on getting better. I'm going to examine you, Joey. I'll try to be as gentle as I can."

Bingaman opened his black bag and leaned over Joey, feeling heat come off the boy. Joey's mother and father stepped closer, watching intently. Joey's cough deepened.

Ten minutes later, Bingaman put his stethoscope back into his bag and straightened.

"Is that what it is?" Edward asked quickly. "Bad water from Larrabee's farm?"

Bingaman hesitated. "Why don't we talk somewhere else and let Joey rest?"

Downstairs, the evening's uneaten dinner of potatoes, carrots, and pork chops cooled in pots and a frying pan on the stove.

"But what do you think it is?" Rebecca asked the moment they were seated at the kitchen table.

"How serious *is* this?" Edward demanded.

"His temperature is 102. His glands are swollen. He has congestion in his lungs."

"My God, you don't think he has diphtheria from the water." Rebecca's anxiety was nearing a quiet panic.

Edward stared at the floor and shook his head. "I was afraid of this."

"No, I don't think it's diphtheria," Bingaman said.

Joey's father peered up, hoping.

"Some of the symptoms are those of diphtheria. But diphtheria presents bluish white lesions that have the consistency of leather. The lesions are surrounded by inflammation and are visible near the tonsils and in the nostrils."

"But Joey—"

"Doesn't have the lesions," Bingaman said. "I think Joey may have bronchitis."

"Bronchitis?"

"I'll know more when I examine him again tomorrow. In the meantime, let's treat his symptoms. Give him one-half an adult dose of aspirin every six hours. Give him a sponge bath with rubbing alcohol. Both will help to keep down his fever. When his pajamas and bedding get sweaty, change them. Keep his window open. The fresh air will help chase the germs from his chest."

"And?" Joey's father asked.

Bingaman didn't understand.

"That's all? That's the most you can do?"

"That, and tell you to make certain he drinks plenty of water."

"If he can keep it down. It's water that got him into this trouble."

"Possibly. Did Joey tell you if any other boys went swimming with him?"

"Yes. Pete Williams. Ben Slocum."

Bingaman nodded. He not only knew them; he had delivered them, just as he had delivered Joey. "Take Joey's temperature every couple of hours. Telephone me if it gets higher or if other symptoms appear."

"Mrs. Williams, this is Dr. Bingaman calling. This might sound strange, but I was wondering—is your son, Pete, feeling all right? No fever? No swollen glands? No congestion?"

He made another call.

"Nothing like that at all, Mrs. Slocum? Your son's as fit as can be? Good. Thank you. Give my regards to your husband. Why did I telephone to ask? Just a random survey. You know how I like to make sure Elmdale's students are all in good health before they go back to school. Good night. Thanks again."

Bingaman set the long-stemmed earpiece onto the wooden wall phone in the front corridor of his home. Troubled, he shut off the overhead light and leaned against the wall, peering out his front-door window. Twilight was dimming. In the yard, fireflies began to twinkle. A Model T rattled past. On a porch across the street, illuminated by a glow of light from the living-room window over there, Harry Webster sat in his rocking chair, smoking his pipe.

"Jonas, what's wrong?"

Bingaman turned to his wife, Marion, whose broad-shouldered outline approached him in the shadows of the hallway. The daughter of a German immigrant, an ancestry that she had stopped mentioning given the war in Europe, Marion had been raised on a farm in upstate New York before she had received her nurse's training, and her robust appearance had been one of the reasons that Jonas Bingaman was initially attracted to her. Twenty-five years ago. Now, at the age of fifty-two, she was as robust as ever, and he loved her *more* than ever. True, the honey-colored hair that he enjoyed stroking had acquired streaks of silver. But then his own hair had not only turned silvery but had thinned until he was almost bald. Marion called it "distinguished."

"Wrong?" Bingaman echoed. "I'm not sure anything's wrong."

"You've been pensive since you came home for dinner after visiting Joey Carter."

"It's a problem I've been mulling over. Joey seems to have bronchitis. His father thinks he got it from swimming in infected water this afternoon. But bronchitis takes several days to develop, and none of the boys Joey went swimming with is sick."

"What are you thinking?"

"Whatever it is, Joey must have gotten it somewhere else. But usually I don't see just one case of bronchitis. It spreads around. So where did he catch it if no one else in town has it?"

Rebecca Carter fidgeted at the open screen door, impatient for Bingaman to climb the front steps and enter the house. "I was afraid I wouldn't be able to reach you."

"Actually, when you telephoned, I was just about to drive over. Joey was the first patient on my list this morning."

Feeling burdened by the weight he had put on recently, Bingaman started up the stairs to the second level, then paused, frowning when he heard labored coughing from the bedroom directly at the top. "Has Joey been coughing like that all night?"

"Not as bad." Rebecca's face was haggard from lack of sleep. "This started just before dawn. I've been giving him aspirin and sponge baths like you told me, but they don't seem to do any good."

The doctor hurried up the stairs, alarmed by what he saw when he entered the bedroom. Joey looked smaller under the covers. His face was much redder, but he also had a dark blue color around his lips. His chest heaved, as if he were coughing even when he wasn't.

Bingaman urgently went to work, removing instruments from his bag, noting that Joey's temperature had risen to 104, that his lungs sounded more congested, that the inside of his throat was inflamed, that his glands were more swollen, and that the boy didn't have the energy to respond to questions. The day before, Joey's pulse and respiration rate had been 85 and 20. Now they were 100 and 25.

"I'm sorry to tell you this, Mrs. Carter."

"What's *wrong* with him?"

"It might be pneumonia."

Rebecca Carter gasped.

"I know you'd prefer to keep him at home," Bingaman said, "but what's best for Joey right now is to admit him to the hospital."

Rebecca looked as if she doubted her sanity, as if she couldn't possibly be hearing what the doctor had just told her. "*No. I can take care of him.*"

"I'm sure you can, but Joey needs special treatment that isn't available here."

Rebecca looked more frightened. "Like what?"

"I'll explain after I telephone the hospital and make the arrangements." Hoping that he had distracted her, Bingaman hurried downstairs to the wall phone near the front door. What he didn't want to tell her was that the dark blue color around Joey's mouth was an indication of cyanosis; the congestion in the boy's lungs was preventing him from getting enough oxygen. If Joey wasn't hooked up to an oxygen tank at the hospital, he might asphyxiate from the fluid in his lungs.

"It certainly has the symptoms of pneumonia," the Elmdale hospital's chief of staff told Bingaman. His name was Brian Powell, and his wiry frame contrasted with Bingaman's portly girth. The two physicians had been friends for years, and Powell, who happened to be in the emergency ward when Jocy Carter was admitted, had invited Bingaman to his office for a cup of coffee afterward. Bingaman couldn't free his mind of Mrs. Carter's sobbing.

"But if it's pneumonia, how did he get it?" Bingaman ignored the steaming cup of coffee on the desk in front of him. "Do *you* have any patients who present these symptoms?"

Powell shook his head. "During the winter, the symptoms wouldn't be unusual. Colds and secondary infections leading to pneumonia. But in summer? I'd certainly remember."

"It just doesn't make any sense." Bingaman sweated under his suit coat. "Why is Joey the only one?"

"No." Rebecca Carter waited outside Joey's room in the hope that she would be allowed to enter. Her eyes were red from tears. "Nothing different. It was just an ordinary summer. We did what we always do."

"And what would that be?" Bingaman asked.

Rebecca dabbed a handkerchief against her eyes. "Picnics. Joey likes to play baseball. We go to the park, and Edward teaches him how to pitch. And the movies. Sometimes we go to the movies. Joey likes Charlie Chaplin."

"That's it? That's all?"

"Just an ordinary summer. I have my sewing club. We don't often get a chance to do things as a family because Edward works late on construction jobs, taking advantage of the good weather. Why do you ask? Didn't Joey get sick from the water in the creek?"

"Can you think of anything else that Joey did this summer? Anything even the slightest bit unusual?"

"No. I'm sorry. I—"

She was interrupted by her husband hurrying along the hospital corridor. "Rebecca." Edward Carter's leathery face glistened with sweat. "I decided to come home for lunch and check on Joey. Mrs. Wade next door said you and he had gone to . . . My God, Doctor, what's wrong with Joey?"

"We're still trying to find that out. It might be pneumonia."

"Pneumonia?"

The door to Joey's room opened. For a moment, the group had a brief glimpse of Joey covered by sheets in a metal bed, an oxygen mask over his face. Then a nurse came out and shut the door.

"How is he?" Joey's mother couldn't wait to ask.

"Light-headed," the petite nurse answered. "He keeps talking about feeling as if he's on a Ferris wheel."

"Ferris wheel?" Bingaman shook his head in confusion.

"He's probably remembering the midway," Joey's father said.

"Midway?"

"In Riverton. Last week, I had to drive over there to get some special lumber for a job I'm working on. Joey went with me. We spent an hour at the midway. He really loved the Ferris wheel."

"Yes, patients with fever, swollen glands, and congestion," Bingaman explained, using the telephone in Dr. Powell's office. "A possible diagnosis of pneumonia." He was speaking to the chief of staff at Riverton's hospital, fifty miles away. "Nothing? Not one case? Why am I . . . ? I'm trying to understand how one of my patients came down with these symptoms. He was in

Riverton last week. I thought perhaps the midway you had there . . . If you remember anything, would you please call me? Thank you."

Bingaman hooked the earpiece back onto the telephone and rubbed the back of his neck.

Throughout the conversation, Powell had remained seated behind his desk, studying him. "Take it easy. Pneumonia can be like pollen in the wind. You'll probably never learn where the boy caught the disease."

Bingaman stared out a window toward a robin in an elm tree. "Pollen in the wind?" He exhaled. "You know what I'm like. I'm compulsive. I think too much. I can't leave well enough alone. Except . . ."

"Yes?" Powell raised his eyebrows.

"Except in this case, my patient isn't doing well at all."

Marion watched him stare at his plate. "You don't like the pot roast?"

"What?" Bingaman looked up. "Oh. . . . I'm sorry. I guess I'm not much company tonight."

"You're still bothered?"

He raised some mashed potatoes on his fork. "I don't like feeling helpless."

"You're *not* helpless. This afternoon, you did a lot of good for the patients who came to your office."

Without tasting the potatoes, Bingaman set down the fork. "Because their problems were easy to correct. I can stitch shut a gash in an arm. I can prescribe bicarbonate of soda for an upset stomach. I can recommend a salve that reduces the itch of poison ivy and stops the rash from spreading. But aside from fighting the symptoms, there is absolutely nothing I can do to fight pneumonia. We try to reduce Joey's fever, keep him hydrated, and give him oxygen. After that, it's all a question of whether the boy is strong enough to fight the infection. It's out of my hands. It's in God's hands. And sometimes God can be cruel."

"The war certainly shows that," Marion said. She was American, stoutly loyal, but her German ancestry made her terribly aware that good men were dying on *both* sides of the Hindenberg line.

"All those needless deaths from infected wounds." Bingaman tapped his fork against his plate. "In a way, it's like Joey's infection. Lord, how I wish I were young again. In medical school again. I keep up with the journals, but I can't help feeling I'm using outmoded techniques. I wish I'd gone into research. Microbiology. I'd give anything to be able to attack an infection at its source. Maybe someday someone will invent a drug that tracks down infectious microbes and kills them."

"It would definitely make your job easier. But in the meantime . . ."

Bingaman nodded solemnly. "We do what we can."

"You've been putting in long hours. Why don't you do something for yourself? Go up to your study. Try out the wireless radio you bought."

"I'd almost forgotten about that."

"You certainly were determined when you spent that Sunday afternoon installing the antenna on the roof."

"And you were certainly determined to warn me I was going to fall off the roof and break my neck." Bingaman chuckled. "That radio seemed like an exciting thing when I bought it. A wonder of the twentieth century."

"It still is."

"The ability to talk to someone in another state. In another country. Without wires. To listen to a ship at sea. Or a report from a battlefield." Bingaman sobered. "Well, that part isn't wonderful. The rest of it, though . . . Yes, I believe I will do something for myself tonight."

But the telephone rang as he walked down the hallway to

go upstairs. Wearily, he unhooked the earpiece and leaned toward the microphone.

"Hello." He listened. "Oh." His voice dropped. "Oh." His tone became somber. "I'm on my way."

"An emergency?" Marion asked.

Bingaman felt pressure in his chest. "Joey Carter is dead."

Marion turned pale. "Dear Lord."

"With oxygen, I thought he had a chance to . . . How terrible." He felt paralyzed, and struggled to rouse himself. "I'd better go see the parents."

But after Bingaman put on his suit coat and reached for his black bag, the telephone rang again. He answered, listened, and when he replaced the earpiece, he felt older and more tired.

"What is it?" Marion touched his arm.

"That was the hospital again. Joey's father just collapsed with a fever: 102. He's coughing. His glands are swollen. The two boys Joey went swimming with now have Joey's symptoms, also. Their parents just brought them into the emergency ward."

"If it was only Joey's two friends, I'd say, yes, they might all have gotten sick from swimming in Larrabee's creek," Bingaman told Dr. Powell, who had returned to the hospital in response to Bingaman's urgent summons. It was midnight. They sat across from each other in Powell's office, a pale desk lamp making their faces look sallow. "The trouble is, Joey's father didn't go anywhere near that creek, and he's got the infection, too."

"You're still thinking of Riverton?"

"It's the only answer that makes sense. Joey probably got infected at the midway. Maybe a worker sneezed on him. Maybe it was a passenger on the Ferris wheel.

However it happened, he then passed the infection on to his father and his two friends. They showed symptoms a day after he did because they'd been infected later than Joey was."

"Infected *by* Joey. It's logical except for one thing."

"What's that?"

"Why hasn't Joey's mother—?"

Someone knocked on the door. Without waiting for an answer, a nurse rushed in. "I'm sorry to disturb you, but Mrs. Carter just collapsed with the same symptoms as her son and husband."

Both doctors stood.

"We'll have to implement quarantine precautions," Bingaman said, following the nurse from the room.

"Yes." Powell hurried next to him. "No visitors. Mandatory gauze masks for medical personnel, anybody who goes into those rooms. The emergency ward should be disinfected."

"Good," Bingaman said. "And the room where Joey died. The nurses who treated him had better scrub down and put on clean uniforms in case they've been contaminated."

"But we still don't know how to treat this, aside from what we've already tried."

"And that didn't work." Bingaman's chest felt hollow.

"If you're right about how the infection started, why haven't there been cases in Riverton?" Powell asked.

"I don't know. In fact, there's almost nothing I *do* know. When do we get the results from Joey Carter's autopsy?"

The stoop-shouldered man peeled off his rubber gloves, dropped them into a medical waste bin, then took off his gauze mask and leaned against a locker. His name was Peter Gingrich. A surgeon, he also functioned as Elmdale's medical examiner. He glanced from Bingaman to Powell, and said, "The lungs were completely filled with fluid. It would have been impossible for the boy to breathe."

"Could the fluid have accumulated subsequent to his death?" Bingaman asked.

"What are you suggesting?"

"Another cause of death. Did you examine the brain?"

"Of course."

"Was there any sign of—?"

"What exactly are you looking for?"

"Could the cause of death have been something as highly contagious as meningitis?"

"No. No sign of meningitis. What killed this boy attacked his lungs."

"Pneumonia," Powell said. "There's no reason to discount the initial diagnosis."

"Except that pneumonia doesn't normally spread this fast."

"Spread this fast?" Gingrich straightened. "You have other cases?"

"Four since the boy died."

"Good Lord."

"I know, this sounds like the start of an epidemic."

"But caused by what?" Bingaman asked.

"I'll try to find out," Gingrich said. "I have tissue samples ready to be cultured. I'll do my best to identify the microorganism responsible. What else can we—?"

Bingaman started toward the door. "I think it's time to make another telephone call to the Riverton hospital."

Blood drained from Bingaman's face as he listened to the doctor in charge of the emergency room at the Riverton hospital. "But I asked your chief of staff to get in touch with me if any cases were reported." *Damn him*, Bingaman thought. "Too busy? No time? Yes. And I'm very much afraid we're *all* going to get a lot busier."

As he turned from the telephone, he was struck by the apprehension on Powell's face.

"How many cases do they have?"

"Twelve," Bingaman answered.

"*Twelve?*"

"They were all admitted within the past few hours. Two of the patients have died."

Bingaman parked his Model T in his driveway and extinguished the headlights. The time was after 3 A.M., and he hoped that the chug-chug, rattle-rattle of the automobile would not waken his wife, but he saw a pale yellow glow appear in the window to the master bedroom and shook his head, discouraged, wishing he still owned a horse and buggy. The air had a foul odor from the car's exhaust fumes. Too many inventions. Too many complications. Even so, he thought, there is one invention you do wish for—a drug that eliminates infectious microbes.

Legs protesting, he got out of the car. Marion had the front door open, waiting for him, as he climbed the steps onto the porch.

"You look awful." She took his bag and put an arm around him, guiding him into the house.

"It's been that kind of night." Bingaman explained what was happening at the hospital, the new patients he had examined, and the treatment he had prescribed. "In addition to aspirin, we're using quinine to control the fever. We're rubbing camphor oil on the patients' chests and having them breathe through strips of cloth soaked in it, to try to keep their bronchial passages open."

"Is that working?"

"We don't know yet. I'm so tired I can hardly think straight."

"Let me put you to bed."

"Marion . . ."

"What?"

"I'm not sure how to say this."

"Just go ahead and say it."

"If this disease is as contagious as it appears to be . . ."

"Say it."

"I've been exposed to the infection. Maybe you ought to keep a distance from me. Maybe we shouldn't sleep in the same bed."

"After twenty-five years? I don't intend to stop sleeping with you now."

"I love you."

The patient, Robert Wilson, was a forty-two-year-old, blue-eyed carpenter who worked with Edward Carter. The man had swollen joints and congested lungs. He complained of a headache and soreness in his muscles. His temperature was 101.

"I'm afraid I'm going to have to send you to the hospital," Bingaman said.

"Hospital?" Wilson coughed.

Bingaman stepped back.

"But I can't afford the time off work," the heavyset carpenter said. "Can't you just give me a pill or something?"

Don't I wish, Bingaman thought, saying, "Not in this case."

Wilson raised a hand to his mouth and coughed again. His blue eyes were glassy. "But what have I got?"

"I'll need to do more tests on you at the hospital," Bingaman responded, his professional tone cloaking the truth: Whatever killed Joey Carter.

———

And killed Joey's father, Bingaman learned after he finished with his morning's patients and arrived at the hospital. Joey's mother and the boy's two friends weren't doing well, either, struggling to breathe despite the oxygen they were being given. And eight more cases had been admitted.

"We're still acting on the assumption that this is pneumonia," Powell said, as they put on gauze masks and prepared to enter the quarantined ward.

"Are the quinine and camphor oil having any effect?"

"Marginally. Some of the patients feel better for a time. Their temperatures go down briefly. For example, Rebecca Carter's dropped from 104 to 102. I thought we were making progress. But then her temperature shot up again. Some of these patients would have died without oxygen, but I don't know how long our supply will last. I've sent for more, but our medical distributor in Albany is having a shortage."

Conscious of the tightness of the mask on his face, Bingaman surveyed the quarantined ward, seeing understaffed, overworked nurses doing their best to make their patients comfortable, hearing the hiss of oxygen tanks and the rack of coughing. In a corner, a curtain had been pulled around a bed.

"Some of the patients are coughing up blood," Powell said.

"What did you just say?"

"Blood. They're—"

"Before that. Your medical distributor in Albany is having a shortage of oxygen?"

"Yes."

"Why?"

"Their telegram didn't say."

"Could it be too many other places need it?"

"What are you talking about?"

"The midway had to have come from somewhere to reach Riverton. After Riverton, it had to have *gone* somewhere."

"Jonas, you're not suggesting—"

"Do you suppose this whole section of the state is infected?"

"I'm sorry," the operator said. "I can't get through to the switchboard in Albany. All the lines are busy."

"*All* of them?"

"It's the state capital. So much business gets done there. If everybody's trying to call the operator at once . . ."

"Try Riverton. Try the hospital there."

"Just a moment . . . I'm sorry, sir. I can't get through to the operator there, either. The lines are busy."

Bingaman gave the operator the names of three other major towns in the area.

The operator couldn't reach her counterparts in those districts. All lines were in use.

"*They're* not the state capital," Bingaman said. "What's going on that so many calls are being made at the same time?"

"I really have no idea, sir."

"Well, can't you interrupt and listen in?"

"Only locally. As I explained, I don't have access to the other operators' switchboards. Besides, I'm not supposed to eavesdrop unless it's an emergency."

"That's what this is."

"An emergency?" The operator coughed. "What sort of emergency?"

Bingaman managed to stop himself from telling her. If I'm not careful, he thought, I'll cause a panic.

"I'll try again later."

He hung up the telephone's earpiece. His head was starting to ache.

"No luck?" Powell asked.

"This is so damned frustrating."

"But even if we do find out that this section of the state is affected, that still won't help us to fight what we've got here."

"It might if we knew what we were fighting." Bingaman rubbed his throbbing temples. "If we only had a way to get in touch with . . ." A tingle rushed through him. "I *do* have a way."

The wireless radio sat on a desk in Bingaman's study. It was black, two feet wide, a foot and a half tall and deep. There were several dials and knobs, a Morse-code key, and a microphone. From the day Marconi had transmitted the first transatlantic wireless message in 1901, Bingaman had been fascinated by the phenomenon. With each new dramatic development in radio communications, his interest had increased until finally, curious about whether he would be able to hear radio transmissions from the war in Europe, he had celebrated his fifty-second birthday in March by purchasing the unit before him. He had studied for and successfully passed the required government examination to become an amateur radio operator. Then, having achieved his goal, he had found that the demands of his practice, not to mention middle age, left him little energy to stay up late and talk to amateur radio operators around the country.

Now, however, he felt greater energy than he could remember having felt in several years. Marion, who had been astonished to see her husband come home in the middle of the afternoon and hurry upstairs with barely a "hello" to her, watched him remove his suit coat, sit before the radio, and turn it on. When she asked him why he had taken the afternoon off, he asked her to please be quiet. He said he had work to do.

Be quiet? She thought. *Work to do?* "Jonas. I know you've been under a lot of strain, but that's no excuse for . . ."

"Please."

Marion watched with even greater astonishment as Bingaman turned knobs and spoke forcefully into the microphone, identifying himself by name and the operator number that the government had given to him, repeatedly trying to find someone to answer him. Static crackled. Sometimes Marion heard an electronic whine. She stepped closer, feeling her husband's tension. In surprise, she heard a voice from the radio.

With relief, Bingaman responded. "Yes, Harrisburg, I read you." He had hoped to raise an operator in Albany or somewhere else in New York State, but the capital city of neighboring Pennsylvania was near enough, an acceptable substitute. He explained the reason he was calling, the situation in which Elmdale found itself, the information he needed, and he couldn't repress a groan when he received an unthinkable answer, far worse than anything he had been dreading. "Forty thousand? No. I can't be receiving you correctly, Harrisburg. Please repeat. Over."

But when the operator in Harrisburg repeated what he had said, Bingaman still couldn't believe it. *"Forty thousand?"*

Marion gasped when, for only the third time in their marriage, she heard him blaspheme.

"Dear sweet Jesus, help us."

"Spanish influenza." Bingaman's tone was bleak, the words a death sentence.

Powell looked startled.

Gingrich leaned tensely forward. "You're quite certain."

"I confirmed it from two other sources on the wireless."

The hastily assembled group, which also consisted of Elmdale's other physician, Douglas Kramer, and the hospital's six-member nursing staff, looked devastated. They were in the largest nonpublic room in the hospital, the nurses' rest area, which was barely adequate to accommodate everyone, the combined body heat causing a film of perspiration to appear on brows.

"Spanish influenza," Powell murmured, as if testing the ominous words, trying to convince himself that he had actually heard them.

"Spanish . . . I'd have to check my medical books," Kramer said, "but as I recall, the last outbreak of influenza was in . . ."

"Eighteen eighty-nine," Bingaman said. "I did some quick research before I came back to the hospital."

"Almost thirty years." Gingrich shook his head. "Long enough to have hoped that the disease wouldn't be coming back, that it had perished."

"The outbreak before that was in the winter of 1847–48," Bingaman said.

"In that case, *forty* years apart."

"Resilient."

"*Spanish* influenza?" a pale nurse asked. "Why are they calling it . . . ? Did this outbreak come from Spain?"

"They don't know *where* it came from," Bingaman said. "But they're comparing it to an outbreak in 1647 that *did* come from Spain."

"*Where it came from doesn't matter*," Powell said, standing. "The question is, what are we going to do about it? Forty thousand?" Bewildered, he turned toward Bingaman. "The wireless operator you spoke to confirmed that? Forty thousand patients with influenza in Pennsylvania?"

"No, that isn't correct. You misunderstood me."

Powell relaxed. "I hoped so. That figure is almost impossible to believe."

"It's much worse than that."

"Worse?"

"Not forty thousand *patients* with influenza. Forty thousand *deaths*."

Someone inhaled sharply. The room became very still.

"Deaths," a nurse whispered.

"That's only in Pennsylvania. The figures for New York City aren't complete, but it's estimated that they're getting two thousand new cases a day. Of those, a hundred patients are dying."

"Per *day*?"

"A conservative estimate. As many as fifteen thousand patients may have died there by now."

"In New York State."

"No, in New York *City*."

"But this is beyond imagination!" Gingrich said.

"And there's more." Bingaman felt the group staring at him. "The wireless operators I spoke to have been in touch with other parts of the country. Spanish influenza has also broken out in Philadelphia, Boston, Chicago, Denver, San Francisco, and . . ."

"A full-fledged epidemic," Kramer said.

"Why haven't we heard about it until now?" a nurse demanded.

"Exactly. Why weren't we warned?" Powell's cheeks were flushed. "Albany should have alerted us! They left us alone out here, without protection! If we'd been told, we could have taken precautions. We could have stockpiled medical supplies. We could have . . . could have . . ." His words seemed to choke him.

"You want to know why we haven't heard about it until now?" Bingaman said. "Because the telephone and the telegraph aren't efficient. How many people in Elmdale have telephones? A third of the population. How many of those make long-distance calls? Very few, because of the expense. And who would they call? Most of their relatives live right here in town. Our newspaper isn't linked to Associated Press, so the news we get is local. Until there's a national radio network and news can travel instantly across the country, each city is more isolated than we like to think. But as for why the authorities in Albany didn't warn communities like Elmdale about the epidemic, well, the wireless operators I spoke to have a theory that the authorities *didn't want* to warn anyone about the disease."

"Didn't . . . ?"

"To avoid panic. There weren't any public announcements. The newspapers printed almost nothing about the possibility of an influenza outbreak."

"But that's totally irresponsible."

"The idea seems to have been to stop everyone from losing control and fleeing into the countryside. Each day, the authorities evidently hoped that the number of new cases would dwindle, that the worst would be over. When things got back to normal, order would have been maintained."

"But things *haven't* gone back to normal, have they?" Gingrich said. "Not at all."

Gingrich's comment echoed ominously in Bingaman's mind as the meeting concluded and the doctors and nurses went out to the public part of the hospital. What the medical personnel faced as they resumed their various duties was the beginning of Elmdale's own chaos. During the half hour of the meeting, twenty new patients had shown up with what the staff now recognized as the symptoms of influenza—high fever, aching muscles, severe headache, sensitive vision, dizziness, difficulty in breathing. The litany of coughing made Bingaman terribly self-conscious about the air he breathed. He hurriedly reached for his gauze mask. He had a mental vision of germs, thousands and thousands of them, spewing across the emergency room. The mental image was so powerful that Bingaman feared he was hallucinating.

"Mrs. Brady," he told one of the untrained volunteer nurses who had been watching the emergency room while the meeting was in progress. "Your mask. You forgot to put on your mask. And all those new patients need masks, also. We can't have them coughing over each other."

And over us, Bingaman thought in alarm.

The end of normality, the chaos that had burst upon them, wasn't signaled only by the welter of unaccustomed activity or by the dramatic increase in new patients. What gave Bingaman the sense of the potential scope of the unfolding nightmare was that Elmdale's hospital, which was intended to serve the medical needs of the entire county, now had more patients than its thirty-bed capacity.

"What are we going to do?" Powell asked urgently. "We can put patients on mattresses and cots in the corridors, but at this rate, we'll soon use up those spaces. The same applies to my office and the nurses' rest area."

The head nurse, Virginia Keel, a strawberry blonde with a notoriously humorless personality, turned from administering to a patient. "This won't do. We need to establish an emergency facility, a place big enough to accommodate so many patients."

"The high-school gymnasium," Bingaman said.

The head nurse and the chief of staff looked at him as if he had lost his mind.

"With school about to start, you want to turn the gymnasium into a pest house?" Powell asked in amazement.

"Who said anything about school starting?"

Powell looked shocked, beginning to understand.

"A third of our patients are children," Bingaman said. "At the moment, I don't see any reason not to assume that we'll soon be receiving even more patients, and a great many of *them* will be children. It would be criminal to allow school to start. That would only spread infection faster. We need to ask the authorities to postpone school for several weeks until we realize the scope of what we're dealing with. Maybe the epidemic will abate."

"The look on your face tells me you don't think so," Powell said.

"Postpone the start of school?" Mayor Halloway, who was also the head of the county's board of education, blinked. "That's preposterous. School is scheduled to start four days from now. Can you imagine the response I'd have to suffer from angry parents? The ones who had telephones wouldn't stop calling me. The ones who didn't would form a mob outside my office. Those parents want their lives to get back to normal. They've had enough of their children lollygagging around town all summer. They want them back in front of a blackboard, learning something."

"A week from now, if this epidemic keeps growing at the present rate, those parents will be begging you to close the schools," Bingaman predicted.

"Then that'll be the time to close them," Halloway said, blinking again. "When the people who elected me tell me what they want."

"You're not listening to me." Bingaman put both hands on the mayor's desk. "People are dying. You have to take the initiative on this."

Halloway stopped blinking. "I'm not prepared to make a hasty decision."

"Well, make *some* kind of decision. Will you allow the high-school gymnasium to be turned into another hospital?"

"I'll have to consult with the other members of the school board."

"That's fine," Bingaman said angrily. "While you're consulting, I'll be setting up beds in the gym."

"This is really as serious as you say it is?"

"Serious enough that you're going to have to think about closing any places where people form crowds: the restaurants, the movie theater, the stores, the saloons, the—"

"Close the business district?" Halloway jerked his head back so sharply that his spectacles almost fell off his nose. "Close the . . . ? Maybe the saloons. I've been getting more and more complaints from church groups about what goes on in them. This prohibition movement is becoming awfully powerful. But the restaurants and the stores? All the uproar from the owners because of the business they would lose." Halloway guffawed. "You might as well ask me to close the churches."

"It might come to that."

The mayor suddenly wasn't laughing any longer.

He's worried about the epidemic's effect on business? Bingaman thought in dismay as he drove his Model T along Elmdale's deceptively sleepy streets toward the hospital. Well, there's one business whose prosperity the mayor won't have to worry about: the undertakers'.

His premonition was confirmed when Bingaman reached the hospital's gravel parking area, alarmed to find it crammed with vehicles and buggies, evidence of new patients. He was further alarmed by Powell's distraught look when they met at the entrance to the noisy, crowded emergency room.

"Eighteen more cases," Powell said. "Three more deaths, including Joey Carter's mother."

For a moment, Bingaman couldn't catch his breath. His headache, which had persisted from yesterday, had also worsened. The emergency room felt unbearably hot, sweat making his heavily starched shirt stick to him under his suit coat. He wanted to unbutton his strangling shirt collar but knew that his position of authority prohibited such public informality.

"Has anybody warned Ballard and Standish?" he managed to ask, referring to Elmdale's two morticians.

Powell nodded, guiding Bingaman into a corner, away
from the commotion in the emergency room. His manner
indicated that he didn't want to be overheard. "They didn't
need to be told," he whispered. "Each has been here several
times. I'm still adjusting to what Ballard said to me."

"What was that?"

Powell dropped his voice even lower. "He said, 'My God,
where am I going to get enough gravediggers? Where am I
going to find enough coffins?'"

"We're out of oxygen." Virginia Keel, the head nurse,
stopped next to them. "We're extremely low on aspirin, quinine, and camphor oil."

"We'll have to get everything we can from the pharma-
cists downtown," Powell said.

"Before the townsfolk panic and start hoarding,"
Bingaman warned.

"But without medical supplies . . ."

"Try to get fluids into them," Bingaman told the nurse.
"Do your best to keep them nourished. Soups. Custard.
Anything bland and easy to digest."

"But we don't have anyone to cook for our patients."

"The Women's League," Powell said. "We'll ask *them* to
do the cooking."

"And to help my nurses," Keel said. "Even with the volunteers who arrived this morning, I'm hopelessly understaffed."

"Who else can we ask to help us?" Bingaman tried desperately to think. "Has anyone spoken to the police department? What about the volunteer fire department? And the
ministers? They can spread the word among their congrega-
tions."

It was almost 2 A.M. before Bingaman managed to get home.
Again he extinguished the headlights of his Model T. Again

a pale yellow light appeared in the upstairs bedroom window. Despite his weariness, he managed to smile as Marion met him at the door.

"You can't keep pushing yourself like this," she said.

"No choice."

"Have you eaten?"

"A sandwich on the go. A cup of coffee here and there."

"Well, you're going to sit at the kitchen table. I'll heat up the chicken and dumplings I made for supper."

"Not hungry."

"You're not listening to what I said. You're going to sit at the kitchen table."

Bingaman laughed. "If you insist."

"And tomorrow I'm going with you. I should have done it today."

He suddenly became alert. "Marion, I'm not sure . . ."

"Well, *I* am. I'm a trained nurse, and I'm needed."

"But this is different from what you think it is. This is . . ."

"What?"

"One of our nurses collapsed today. She has all the symptoms."

"And the other nurses?"

"They're exhausted, but so far, they haven't gotten sick, thank God."

"Then the odds are in my favor."

"No. I don't want to lose you, Marion."

"I can't stay barricaded in this house. And what about you? Look at the risk you're taking. I don't want to lose you, either. But if *you* can take the risk, so can *I*."

Bingaman almost continued to argue with her, but he knew she was right. The townsfolk needed help, and neither of them would be able to bear the shame if they didn't fulfill their moral obligation. He had seen amazing things today, people whom he had counted on to volunteer telling him that he was crazy if he thought they would risk their lives to help patients with the disease, others who never went to church or participated in community functions showing up to help without needing to be asked. The idea had occurred to him that the epidemic was God's way of testing those who didn't die, of determining who was worthy to be redeemed.

The idea grew stronger after he ate the chicken and dumplings that Marion warmed up for him, his favorite meal, although he barely tasted it. He went upstairs, but instead of proceeding into the bedroom, he entered his study, sat wearily at his desk, and turned on the wireless radio.

"Jonas?"

"In a moment."

Hearing crackles and whines, he turned knobs and watched dials. Periodically, he spoke into the microphone, identifying himself.

Finally he contacted another operator, this one in Boston, but as the operator described what was happening there—the three thousand new cases per day in Boston, a death toll so fierce that the city's 291 hearses were kept constantly busy— Bingaman brooded again about God. According to the radio operator in Boston, there wasn't a community in the United States that hadn't been hit. From Minneapolis to New Orleans, from Seattle to Miami, from north to south and west to east and everywhere between, people were dying at a sanity-threatening rate. In Canada and Mexico, in Argentina and Brazil, England and France, Germany and Russia, China and Japan . . . Not an epidemic. A *pan*demic. It wasn't just in the United States. It was *everywhere*. Horrified, Bingaman thought about the bubonic plague, known as the Black Death, that had ravaged Europe in the Middle Ages, but what he was hearing about now was far more widespread than the Black Death had been, and if the mortality figures being given to him were accurate, the present scourge had the potential to be far more lethal. Lord, the cold weather hadn't arrived yet. What would happen when the worst of winter aggravated the symptoms of the disease? Bingaman had a nightmarish image of millions of frozen corpses strewn around the world with no one to bury them. Yes, the Spanish influenza was God's way of testing humanity, of judging how the survivors reacted, he thought. Then a further dismaying thought occurred to him, making him shiver. Or could it possibly be the end of the world?

"It appears to have started in Kansas," Bingaman told the medical team. They had agreed to meet every morning at eight in the nurses' rest area at the hospital: to relay information and squelch rumors. After the meeting, they would disperse to inform volunteers about what had been discussed.

"Kansas?" Powell furrowed his brow in confusion. "I assumed that it would have started somewhere more exotic."

"At Fort Riley," Bingaman continued. He had gotten only two hours' sleep the night before and was fighting to muster energy. His head throbbed. "That army facility is one of the main training areas for the Allied Expeditionary Force. In March, it had a dust storm of unusual power."

"Dust," Gingrich said. "I've been formulating a theory that dust is the principal means by which the disease is carried over distances." He turned to the nurses. "We have to take extra precautions. Close every window. Eliminate the slightest dust."

"In this heat?" Virginia Keel objected. As head nurse, she never failed to speak her mind, even to a doctor. "And with the patients' high temperatures? They won't be able to bear it."

Gingrich's eyes flashed with annoyance that he'd been contradicted.

Before angry words could be exchanged, Bingaman distracted them. "There might be another agent responsible for the initial transmission. I spoke to a wireless operator in

Kansas early this morning, and he told me the theory at the camp is that the dust storm, which turned the day into night for three hours, left not only several inches of dust over everything in the camp but also ashes from piles of burned manure."

Kramer's nostrils twitched. "Burned manure?"

Bingaman nodded. "I realize that it's an indelicate subject. My apologies to the ladies. But we can't stand on niceties during the present emergency. There's a considerable cavalry detachment at Fort Riley. Thousands of mules and horses. It's estimated that those animals deposit nine thousand tons of manure a month in the camp, an obvious hygiene problem that the fort's commander attempted to alleviate by ordering his men to burn the droppings. The smoke from the fires and then the ashes blown by the dust storm apparently spread infectious microbes throughout the entire camp. Subsequent to the storm, so many soldiers came down with influenza symptoms that the chief medical officer for the fort was afraid they would take up all three thousand beds in the fort's hospital. Fortunately, the outbreak abated after five weeks."

"And then?" Powell frowned. He seemed to have a premonition about what was coming.

"Two divisions were sent from the fort to join the rest of our expeditionary forces in Europe. Influenza broke out on the troop ships. When the soldiers arrived in France, they spread it to our units and the British and the French. Presumably also to the Germans. At last count, the Royal Navy alone has over ten thousand cases of influenza. Of course, the civilian population has been affected, too. After that, the disease spread from Europe throughout Asia and Africa and everywhere else, including, of course, back to America. An alternate theory about the pandemic's origin is that it started among farm animals in China and was introduced into France by Chinese coolies whom the allies used to dig trenches. Perhaps the *true* origin will never be known."

"But what about the death rate?" a nurse asked, obviously afraid of the answer.

"In three months, the flu has killed more people in Europe, soldiers and civilians, than have died in military operations on both sides during the entire four years of the war."

For several moments, the group was speechless.

"But you're talking about *millions* of deaths," Elizabeth Keel said.

"And many *more* millions who continue to suffer from the disease."

"Then . . ."

"Yes?" Bingaman turned to a visibly troubled nurse.

"There's no hope."

Bingaman shook his throbbing head. "If we believe that, then there truly won't be any. We *must* hope."

The nurse raised a hand to her mouth and coughed. Everyone else in the room tensed and leaned away from her.

"She's dead?"

Bingaman had just helped finish admitting twenty-five new patients to the gymnasium that had been converted into a hospital. As he and Dr. Kramer left the spacious building—which was rapidly being filled with occupied beds—they squinted from the brilliant September sunlight and noticed corpses being loaded onto horse-drawn wagons.

"How many died last night?"

"Fifteen."

"It keeps getting worse."

Bingaman faltered.

"What's the matter?" Kramer asked. "Aren't you feeling well?"

Bingaman didn't reply but instead took labored steps

toward one of the wagons. The corpse of a woman in a nurse's uniform was being lifted aboard.

"But I saw her only yesterday. How could this have happened so quickly?"

"I've been hearing reports that the symptoms are taking less time to develop," Kramer said behind him. "From the slightest hint of having been infected, a person might suddenly have a full-blown case within twenty-four hours. I heard a story this morning about a man, apparently healthy, who left his home to go to work. He wasn't coughing. None of his family noticed a fever. He died on the street a block from the factory where he worked. I heard another story."

"Yes?"

"Four women were playing bridge last night. The game ended at eleven. None of them was alive in the morning."

Bingaman's chest felt heavy. His shoulders ached. His eyes hurt—only from lack of sleep, he assured himself. He removed his gauze mask from his pocket, having taken it off when he left the hospital. "From now on, I think we're going to have to wear our masks all the time, even when we're not with patients. Day or night. At home or on duty. Everywhere."

"At home? Isn't that a little extreme?" Kramer asked.

"Is it?" Bingaman gave the dead nurse, in her twenties with long brown hair, a final look as the wagon clattered away. So young, so much to live for, he thought. "None of us is immune. The disease is all around us. There's no telling who might give it to us." He glanced at Kramer. "I keep remembering she was the nurse who coughed in the room with us yesterday."

"Don't touch me! Get away!"

The outburst made Bingaman look up from the patient he was examining. He was in the middle of a row of beds in the gymnasium, surrounded by determined activity as nurses and volunteers moved from patient to patient, giving them water, or soup if they were capable of eating, then rubbing their feverish brows with ice wrapped in towels. Another team of volunteers took care of the unsavory, hazardous problem of what to do with the bodily wastes from so many helpless people. A stench of excrement, sweat, and death filled the now hopelessly small area. Contrary to Dr. Gingrich's theories about dust and closed windows, Bingaman had ordered that all the windows in the gymnasium be opened. Nonetheless, the foul odor inside the building made him nauseous.

"I told you, damn it, get your filthy hands off me!"

The objectionable language attracted Bingaman's attention as much as the sense of outrage. The man responsible coughed hoarsely. There, Bingaman saw. To the right. Three rows over. Nurses, volunteers, and those few patients with a modicum of strength looked in that direction also.

"You bitch, if you touch me again—!" The man's raspy voice disintegrated into a paroxysm of coughing.

Such language could absolutely not be tolerated. Bingaman left the patient he had been examining, veered between beds, reached another row, and veered between other beds, approaching the commotion. Three men had evidently carried in a fourth, who was sprawled on a bed, resisting the attentions of a nurse. Bingaman's indignation intensified at the thought of a nurse being called such things, but what he heard next was even more appalling. His emotions made it difficult for him to breathe.

"You goddamn German!"

Marion. The nurse the patient shouted at was Bingaman's wife. The three men who had carried in the patient were pushing her away.

Outraged, Bingaman reached the commotion. "Don't you touch her! What's going on here?"

The patient's face reddened from the fury with which he coughed. Spittle flew. Bingaman stepped back reflexively, making sure that he stayed protectively in front of Marion.

"Put these masks on. No one comes in here without one. What's the matter with you?"

"*She's* what's the matter," one of the men said. His voice was slurred. He was tall, wore work clothes, and had obviously been drinking. "Lousy German."

"Watch what you're saying."

"Hun! Kraut!" a second man said, more beefy than the first. "Yer not foolin' anybody." He, too, was obviously drunk. "Yer the one who did it! Made my friend sick! Gave everybody the influenza!"

"What kind of nonsense . . . ?"

"Spanish nothing." The man on the bed coughed again. He was losing strength. Despite his feverish cheeks, he had alarming black circles around his eyes. "It's the *German* influenza."

The first man took a tottering step toward Marion. "How much did the Kaiser pay you, Kraut?"

"Pay her?" the second man said. "Didn't need to pay the bitch. She's a German, ain't she? Germans *love* killing Americans."

"I've heard *enough*." Bingaman shook with rage. "Get out of this hospital. Now. I swear I'll send for a policeman."

"And leave *her*?" The third man pointed drunkenly past Bingaman toward Marion, who gasped. "Leave *her* to kill more Americans? *She's* the one brought the influenza here. The *German* influenza. This is how the Kaiser thinks he's gonna win the war. Damned murderous Kraut."

"I won't tell you again! Leave this instant or I'll—"

Bingaman stepped toward the men, urging them toward the door. The first man braced himself, muttered, "The Huns killed my son in France, you goddamn Kraut-lover," and struck the doctor in the face.

Time seemed to stop. At once, it began again. Hearing exclamations around him, Bingaman lurched back, conscious of blood spewing from his lips beneath his mask. Something struck his nose, and he saw double. Blood spurted from his nostrils. He lost control of his legs. He felt as if he was floating. When he struck the floor, he heard faraway screaming.

Then everything was a blur. Hc had a vague sense of being lifted, carried. He heard distant, urgent voices. His mind reeled as he was set on something.

A cot. In a shadowy supply room at the rear of the gymnasium.

"Jonas, are you all right? Jonas?"

He recognized Marion's voice. Each anxious word sounded closer, as if she was leaning down.

"Jonas?"

"Yes. I think I'm all right."

"Let me get this face mask off so you can breathe."

"No. Can't risk contamination. Leave it on."

She was wiping blood from his face. "I'll give you a clean one."

"Jonas?" A man's voice. Worried. Powell.

"I'm only dazed," Bingaman answered slowly. "Caught me by surprise." His words seemed to echo. "I'll be all right in a moment." He tried to sit up, but he felt as if he had ball bearings in his skull and they all rolled backward, forcing his head down. "Those men. Are they . . . ?"

"Gone."

"A policeman. Did you send for a . . . ?"

"What would be the point? When they closed the schools, the restaurants, and the stores, they also emptied the jail. There isn't anyplace to put those men."

"Can't understand what got into them. Accusing Marion. Outrageous."

Bingaman managed to open his eyes and focus his aching

vision. He saw Marion's worried face. And Powell's, which had a reluctant expression.

"What is it? What aren't you telling me?" Bingaman asked.

"This isn't the first time."

"I don't understand."

"People are frightened," Powell said. "They can't accept that it's random and meaningless. They want easy explanations. Something specific."

"I still don't understand."

"Someone to blame. The Germans. Marion."

"But that's preposterous. How could they be so foolish as to think that Marion would . . . ?"

The discomfited look on Marion's face made Bingaman frown. "You've been aware of this?"

"Yes."

"How long has this been going on?"

"Several days."

"And yet you still volunteered to come down here and help? I'm amazed that . . ." But then Bingaman thought about it, and he wasn't amazed. Marion always did what was right, even when it was difficult.

"Don't get the wrong impression," Powell said. "It's not like everyone feels that way. Only a minority. A *small* minority. But they've certainly made their opinions known."

"I'm going to have to stay home," Marion said.

"No," Powell said. "You can't let them bully you."

"It isn't because of them. I have a more important job. Feel Jonas's forehead. Touch the glands in his throat. Put your hand on his chest. You don't need a stethoscope. You can *feel* the congestion. He has it."

The jolt of wheels into potholes and the noxious fumes of the Model T aggravated Bingaman's excruciating headache, making him nauseous as Marion drove him home. His injuries seemed to have broken the resolve with which he had subdued the symptoms that he had attributed only to fatigue. Now, as delirium took control of him, his last lucid thought was an echo of what he had said to Dr. Kramer after seeing the nurse's corpse: How could this have happened so quickly? By the time Marion brought him home, the pain in his swollen lips and nostrils was insignificant compared to the soul-deep aching of his joints and limbs. He was so light-headed that he felt disassociated from himself, seeming to hover, watching Marion struggle to get him out of the car and up the steps into the house.

He did his best to cough away from her, grateful that he had insisted she put a new mask on him. But the moment she eased him onto the bed, exhaling with effort, she loosened his shirt collar and took off the mask, which had become blood-soaked on the ride home.

"No," he murmured.

"Don't argue with me, Jonas. I have to get you cleaned up."

"Should have left me in the hospital."

"Not when you have a trained nurse to give you constant care at home."

She took off his shoes, his socks, his pants, his bloody suit coat and vest and shirt. She stripped off his underwear. Shivering, naked on the bed, clutching his arms across his chest, teeth chattering, he watched the ceiling ripple as Marion bathed him from head to toe. She used warm water and soap, dried him thoroughly, then made him sit up and slipped his nightshirt over his head, pulling it down to his knees. She tugged long woolen socks over his feet. She covered him with a sheet and three blankets. When that still wasn't enough and his shivering worsened, she brought him a hot-water bottle and put on the down-filled comforter.

Bingaman coughed and murmured about a face mask.

"It interferes with your breathing," Marion said.

"Might contaminate . . ."

"I don't think it does any good. Besides, I've already been exposed to it." Working, Marion breathed harder.

Minutes, perhaps hours later, she was spooning hot tea into him, and when the chills suddenly turned into alarming amounts of sweat oozing from him, she tore off the covers, stripped him again, bathed him with rubbing alcohol, ignored his coughing, and eased him out of bed onto the floor. He had lost control of his bowels and fouled the bed. She had to change the sheets, then clean him and change his nightshirt, then tug him up onto the bed and pull the blankets over him again because the chills had returned. She covered his brow with a steaming washcloth and spooned more hot tea into him, trying to make him swallow pieces of warm bread soaked in the tea.

He lost all external impressions and floated away into darkness. His mind was like a boat on an increasingly choppy sea. A night sea. Storm-tossed. Spinning.

He had no idea how long he was away, but gradually the spinning stopped, the weather calmed, and when he came back, slowly, dimly, he didn't think that his throat had ever felt so dry or that he had ever been so weak. His eyes hurt as if they had sunk into his skull. His skin was tight from dehydration, greasy from repeated sweating frenzies. At the same time, it seemed loose, as if he had lost weight.

These sensations came to him gradually. He lay passively, watching a beam of sunlight enter the bedroom window on his left. Then it went away, and eventually the sunbeam entered through the window on his right, and he realized that he had been in a semistupor while the sun passed from east to west. But he wasn't so stupefied that he failed to realize that nothing in the room had changed, that his nightshirt and covers were the same as in the morning, that no one had been in the room, that *Marion* hadn't been in the room.

He tried to call to her, but his lungs were too weak, his throat too dry, and nothing came out. He tried again and managed to produce only an animallike whimper.

Marion! He thought desperately. His fear was not for himself, not that he had been left alone, helpless. His terror was for Marion. If she wasn't taking care of him, that meant she wasn't *able* to, and that meant . . .

The effort to move made him cough. Congestion rattled in his chest. Breath wheezed past his swollen bronchial passages and up his raw throat. But despite his pain and lethargy, he had the sense that he was better, not as feverish. His headache didn't threaten to cause his skull to explode. His muscles ached, but not as if he were being stretched on a rack.

When he squirmed to the side of the bed and tried to stand, his legs wobbled. He slumped to the floor. *Marion!* he kept thinking. He crawled. The hand-over-hand movement reminded him of the fear and determination he had felt when learning to swim. A pitcher on a table attracted his attention, and he grasped a chair beside the table, struggling to raise himself, to tilt the pitcher toward his lips. Water trickled into his mouth, over his scabbed, cracked, parched lips, down his chin, onto his nightshirt. He clumsily set the pitcher back down, apprehensive about dropping it, the water too precious for him to risk wasting it. But as precious as it tasted, it was also tepid, stale, with a slight grit of dust. It had obviously been there a while, and with his premonition mounting, filling him with terror, he tried to call Marion's name, shuddered at the weak sound of his croaky voice, and crawled again.

He found her on the floor in the kitchen. His immediate panicked thought was that she was dead. But when he moaned, he thought he heard an echo, only to realize that the second moan had come from *her*, weak, faint, a moan nonetheless, and he fought to increase the effort with which he crawled to her. He touched her brow and felt the terrible heat coming off it. Yes! Alive! But the depth of her cough and the sluggishness of her response when he tried to rouse her filled him with dread, and he knew that his first priority was to get fluid into her. He gripped the top of a kitchen counter, pulled himself up, and sweated while he worked the pump handle in the sink, filling a bowl with water from the house's well. He almost spilled the bowl and barely remembered to bring a spoon, but at last he sat exhausted next to Marion on the kitchen floor, cradled her head, and spooned water between her dry, swollen lips. The heat coming off her was overwhelming. He struggled to the icebox, used an ice pick, and clumsily chipped off chunks from the half-melted block in the upper compartment. With the chunks of ice wrapped in a dish towel, he slumped yet again beside Marion and wiped the cool cloth over her beet-red face. He set the cloth on her forehead, spooned more water into her mouth, then gave in to his own thirst and drank from the bowl, only to have it slip from his grasp and topple onto the floor, soaking Marion and himself. He moaned, felt dizzy again, and lowered his head to the floor.

Time blurred. When he regained consciousness, he found himself on a chair in the parlor. Marion was on the couch across from him, a throw rug over her. Her chest rose and fell. She coughed. A plate of stale bread and a pitcher of water were on a side table. Someone found us, Bingaman thought, and coughed. Someone came in and helped. But during the next few effort-filled hours, he was forced to realize that he was mistaken, that no one had come, that somehow *he* had shifted Marion into the parlor, that *he* had brought the bread and the pitcher of water. The bread was so old and hard that he had to soak it in the water before he could gently insert it into Marion's mouth and encourage her to eat. He breathed a prayer of thanks when she swallowed. When she coughed, he feared that she would expel the food, but it stayed down with the unbelievably delicious water.

Again time blurred. It wasn't bread but strawberry jam and a spoon that he now found on the table beside the couch. He remembered having seen the jam in the icebox. Marion was coughing. He was rubbing her fiery brow with a towel that held the last of the ice from the box. He was spooning the jam into her mouth. He was raising a glass to her lips. He was drinking from another glass, feeling his parched mouth and throat seem to absorb the water.

Darkness. Light.

Darkness again. The cellar. Stumbling. Opening the door to the root cellar. Despite the coolness, sweating. Groping for two jars of Marion's preserves on a shelf. Coughing. Swaying. Stumbling up the cellar steps, reaching the kitchen, squinting from the painful brilliance of blazing sunset, discovering that the preserves he had expended so much effort to get were dill pickles.

Darkness. Light.

Darkness. Light.

Light again. Marion was no longer coughing. Bingaman later concluded that what saved her life was her robust constitution, although when she was alert enough she insisted that *he* had been the reason she stayed alive. His ministrations, she called them, and told him not to be so modest.

"Hush," he told her lovingly. "Don't waste your strength."

In the reverse, however, he had no doubt that Marion's own ministrations in the initial stage of *his* illness had been what saved *him*. The ruthless disease could be attacked only on the basis of its symptoms. After that, the patient would live or die strictly on the basis of his or her own resources, and now that Bingaman had endured the intimate experience of the influenza's devastating power, he marveled that *anyone* had the strength to resist it.

Perhaps strength was not the determining factor. Perhaps it was luck. Or fate. Or God's will. But if the latter was indeed the case, God certainly must have turned against a great many people. To a Presbyterian such as Bingaman, who believed in a contract that linked hard work and prosperity with salvation, the notion that the influenza might be God's display of worldwide disapproval was disquieting. Surely, even taking the war into account, the world couldn't be that bad a place. Or was the so-called *world* war, with its machine guns and tear gas, chlorine gas, phosgene gas, mustard gas, the mounting horrors, the millions of needless casualties, in fact the problem?

But in that case, did it make sense for God in turn to inflict millions of other casualties?

"Dr. Bingaman." The nurse stepped back in fright, her face suddenly drained of color, almost as white as her uniform. "It can't be!"

"What on earth?"

"I was told you were dead!"

"Dead?" Bingaman took another step toward the nurse in the hospital corridor.

She almost backed away. "After Dr. Powell died and Dr. Gingrich, I—".

"Wait a second. Dr. Powell is dead?"

"Yes, and Dr. Gingrich and—"

"Dead." Shock overwhelmed him. Dizzy, he feared that he was having a relapse and placed a hand against the wall to steady himself. He took a deep breath, repressed a cough, and studied her. "What made you think *I* was dead?"

"That's what I was told!"

"*Who* told you?"

"A lot of people. I don't know. I don't remember. It's been so terrible. So many people have gotten so sick. So many people have died. I can't remember who's alive and who isn't. I can't remember when I slept last or when . . ."

Bingaman's fatigue and his preoccupation when he entered the hospital had prevented him from realizing how exhausted the nurse herself looked. "Sit down," he said, realizing something else—the reason no one had come to his house to find out if he needed help. Why would anyone have bothered if everyone thought I was dead? And there must be a lot of people who have died.

"You need to go home," Bingaman said. "Get some food. Rest."

"I can't. So many patients. I can't keep the living straight from the dying. They keep going out, and others come in. There's so much to do. I . . ."

"It's all right. I'm giving you permission. Go home. I'll speak to Virginia." He referred to the head of the nursing staff. "I'm sure she'll agree."

"You can't."

"What?"

"Speak to her."

"I don't understand."

"Virginia's dead."

He found himself speechless, staring at her, horrified by the thought of being told that anyone else he referred to would also be dead. So much had happened so quickly. Stretcher bearers passed him, carrying the corpse of Mayor Halloway.

A further horrifying thought occurred to him. "How long?" he managed to ask.

The weary nurse shook her head in confusion.

"What I mean is . . ." His brow felt warm again. "What day is it?"

Confused, she answered, "Wednesday."

He rubbed his forehead. "What I'm trying to ask is—the date."

"October 9." The nurse frowned in bewilderment.

"October 9?" He felt as he had when he had been struck in the face. He lurched backward.

"Dr. Bingaman, do you feel all right?"

"A month."

"I don't understand."

"The last thing I recall it was early September."

"I still don't—"

"I've lost the rest of September and . . . A month. *I've lost a whole month.*" Frightened, he tried to explain, to give the nurse a sense of what it was like to spend so many weeks fighting to breathe through congested lungs, all the while enduring a storm-tossed black sea of delirium. He strained to describe the unbelievable thirst, the agony of aching limbs, the unbearable heaviness on his chest.

The disturbed way the nurse looked at him gave him the sense that he was babbling. He didn't care. Because all the time he struggled to account for how he had lost a month of his life, he realized that if it had happened to him, it must have happened to others. Dear God, he thought, how many others are trapped inside their houses, too weak to answer their phone if they have one, or to respond to someone knocking on their door? When he had left his house an hour earlier, he had knocked on the doors of his neighbors to his right and left. No one had answered. He had been troubled by how deserted his elm-lined street looked, a cool breeze blowing leaves that had turned from green to autumnal yellow with amazing rapidity in just a few days—except that he now realized it had been a month. And those neighbors hadn't gone away somewhere. He had a heart-pounding, dreadful certainty that they were *inside,* helpless or dead.

"Jonas, you look terrible. You've got to rest," Dr. Kramer said. "Go home. Take care of Marion."

"She's doing fine. Others are worse. She insisted I help take care of them."

"But—"

"You and I are the only physicians left in town! People are dying! I can't go home! I'm needed!"

Every church in town had been converted into a hospital. All of them were full.

The cemeteries no longer had room for all the corpses. Gravediggers could not keep up the labor of shoveling dirt from fresh pits. Corpses lay in rows in a pasture at the edge of town. Armed sentries were posted to stop animals from eating them, each man wearing a gauze mask and praying that he wouldn't catch the disease from the corpses. Funerals were limited to family members wearing masks, ministers rushing as fast as dignity would allow while they read the prayers for the dead.

"We have to keep searching!" Bingaman organized teams. "Who knows how many people need our help? Even if they're dead, we have to find them. There's too great a risk of cholera. Pestilence. The decomposing bodies will cause a secondary plague."

Leading his own group, Bingaman marched along streets and banged on doors. Sometimes, a trembling hand let them in, a bony, sunken-eyed face assuring Bingaman that everyone inside was over the worst, obviously not aware that Bingaman had reached them barely soon enough to try to save them. Other times, receiving no answer, Bingaman's team broke in. Weak coughing led them to a few survivors. Too often, the odor of sickness and decay made everyone gag. Whole families had been dead for quite some time.

> *I had a little bird.*
> *Its name was Enza.*
> *I opened the window.*
> *And in-flu-Enza.*

The rhyme, which Bingaman happened to hear a gaunt-cheeked little girl sing hypnotically, almost insanely, as her parents were carted dead from her house, festered in his mind. He couldn't get rid of it, couldn't still it, couldn't smother it. I opened the window and in-flu-Enza. The rhythm was insidious—like the disease. It repeated itself in his thoughts until it made him dizzy, and he feared that he would have another bout with Enza. Opened the window. Yes. The disease was everywhere. All around. In the sky, in the air. In every breath. Bingaman knew that after his ordeal he ought to follow Kramer's advice and rest, but no matter how dizzy he felt . . . in-flu-Enza . . . he persisted, as Marion urged him to do, struggling from home to home, performing the corporal works of mercy for the suffering and the dead. In-flu-Enza. He persisted because he had come to the firm conclusion that if this disease was God's punishment, it was also an opportunity that God was offering to make the world a better place, to eradicate evil and work for salvation.

Bingaman's team rammed the door open and searched through musty shadows, first floor, second floor, cellar, and attic. His apprehension had been needless. There was no one, alive or dead.

Grateful to return outside, scuffling their shoes through dead leaves, the team followed Bingaman along the wooden sidewalk.

"We haven't looked in *this* house."

"No need," Bingaman said.

"Why not?"

"It's mine."

"But what's that smell?"

"I don't know what you mean."

"It's coming from—"

"The house farther down," Bingaman said.

"No, *this* house. *Your* house."

"Nonsense. I don't smell anything."

"I think we'd better take a look."

"Stop."

"The door's locked."

"Stay away."

"The smell's worse here on the porch. Give us the key."

"Get off my property!"

"The drapes are closed. I can't see through the windows."

"I'm telling you to leave!"

"That smell is . . . Somebody help me break in the door."

Amid Bingaman's screaming protest, they crashed in, and the stench that made several men vomit came unmistakably from the parlor. Marion Bingaman had been dead for quite some time. Her gray-skinned, gas-bloated corpse was smeared with strawberry jam and camphor oil. Quinine and aspirin pills had been stuffed inside her mouth until her cheeks bulged and her teeth were parted. A dill pickle also protruded from her mouth. Her exposed back resembled a pin cushion, except that the pins were large hypodermics which the doctor had pressed between her ribs and inserted into her lungs, desperately trying to extract the fluid that had drowned her. Several pails contained foul-smelling yellowish liquid.

"Marion." Bingaman stroked her hair. "I'm sorry. I tried to keep them away. I know how much you like your naps. Why don't you try to go back to sleep?"

The pandemic's peak coincided with the armistice in Europe, the declaration of peace, November 11, 1918. Thereafter, as armies disbanded and exhausted soldiers began their long journey home, the flu did not return with them to reinforce the infectious microbes that were already in place. To the contrary, against all logic, the disease rapidly lost its strength, and by the end of the year, during the dead of winter, when the symptoms of the flu—exacerbated by cold weather—should have been at their worst, the pandemic slowed. A few remote areas—Pacific islands and jungle outposts—remained to suffer the onslaught. Otherwise, having scoured the entire world, making no distinction between Eskimo villages and European metropolises, the Spanish influenza approached its end.

Bingaman, whose face would never regain its former ruddy cheerfulness and whose thinning, silvery hair had fallen out, rested, as did his fellow survivors. Of Elmdale's population of twelve thousand, eight thousand had collapsed with the symptoms. Of those, twenty-five hundred had died. Many of the remaining four thousand had worked nonstop to care for the sick and to bury the dead. Some, of course, had refused to help under any circumstances, for fear of being infected. They would have to make their peace with God.

Humanity had been tested. During the major outbreaks of the Black Death in Europe during the Middle Ages, it was estimated that twenty-five million had died. The number of soldiers estimated to have been killed during the five years of World War I was eight and one-half million. The latter figure

Bingaman learned from his increasingly long nights communicating with radio operators in America and Europe. But the estimated number of those killed by the influenza was almost *forty* million. Even more astonishing, the total number of those presumed to have been infected by the influenza was one *billion*, more than half the world's population. If the disease had continued at its exponential, devastating rate, civilization as it was known would have been destroyed by the spring of 1919. Listening to his fellow radio operators around the country and around the globe, Bingaman shared their sense of helplessness and loss. But he also sympathized with a latent hope in some of their comments. Yes, the cream of American and European youth had been eradicated in the war. What the war had failed to accomplish, the flu had taken care of among other age groups. Society had been gutted.

But what if . . . and this idea was almost unthinkable, and yet a few had given it voice, based on their reading of Charles Darwin . . . what if the pandemic had been a means of natural selection and now that the strong had survived, humanity would be better for it, able to improve itself genetically? Such a materialistic way of thinking was repugnant to Bingaman. He had heard enough about Darwinism to know that it was based on a theory of random events, that at bottom it was atheistic and worshiped accident. For Bingaman, there was no such thing as randomness and accident. Everything was part of a cosmic plan and had an ultimate purpose, and any theory that did not include God was unacceptable. But another theory *was* acceptable, and it was this that gave him hope—that this plague, one of the horsemen of the Apocalypse, had been God's way of demanding humanity's attention, of warning the survivors about their sins, and of granting them an opportunity to learn from their transgressions, to make a fresh start.

"Like the war," Bingaman said to Marion, who had walked into his study three weeks after she had been buried.

He had looked up from his tears and smiled. He had been talking to her ever since.

"The flu was God's warning that there must never be another war like this one. Isn't that what they've been calling it? The War to End All Wars? I'm convinced that this is an opportunity to look ahead."

Marion didn't respond.

"Also, I've been reading about the movement to make prohibition an amendment to the Constitution," Bingaman said. "When the saloons were closed to help keep the flu from spreading, it was obvious how much better society was without them. People have seen the error of their ways. The saloons will stay closed."

Still, Marion didn't respond.

"And something else," Bingaman said. "You know I always try to be optimistic. I'm convinced that society will benefit in other ways from the flu's devastation. We came so close to dying, all of us, the world. So now we'll all learn to cherish life more, to respect it, to be better. This decade's ending. A new one's about to start. A fresh beginning. It's going to be fascinating to see how we recover from so much death."

Marion continued to remain silent.

"One thing troubles me, though," Bingaman said. "On the wireless last night, I heard about a medical researcher in New York City who discovered that influenza isn't caused by a bacterium but by a virus. In theory, that information ought to make it easier to develop a cure. Normally." He frowned. "All things being equal, we should be able to develop a vaccine. But not in this case. Because the researcher also discovered that the influenza virus is constantly mutating. Any vaccine would be effective only for a limited time. Meanwhile the ever-changing virus could come back in an even more deadly form. Or a different and worse plague could come along."

For the first time, Marion spoke. "God help us." She coughed. Blood-tinted saliva beaded her bluish black lips.

Bingaman shuddered, afraid that he was going to lose her for a second time, that the horror would be repeated, again and again. "Yes, that's what it comes down to. An act of faith. God help us. Remember how fervently we tried to have children, how deeply disappointed we were to find that we couldn't? We told ourselves that it wasn't meant to be, that God had given us a burden to test our faith. Well . . . Perhaps it was for the best." He sobbed as Marion's image began to fade. "I couldn't bear to lose anyone else."

Outside the study window, snow had begun to fall. A chill wind swept through the skeletal elms, burying the last of their fungus-wilted yellow leaves.

1920
1921
1922
1923
1924
1925
1926
1927
1928
1929

ARYANS AND ABSINTHE

BY F. PAUL WILSON

Germany is having a nervous breakdown.
There is nothing sane to report.

—Ben Hecht, 1923

Today it takes 40,000 marks to buy a single U.S. dollar.
Volkischer Beobachter, May 4, 1923

Ernst Drexler found the strangest things entertaining. That was how he always phrased it: *entertaining*. Even inflation could be entertaining, he said.

Karl Stehr remembered seeing Ernst around the Berlin art venues for months before he actually met him. He stood out in that perennially scruffy crowd with his neatly pressed suit and vest, starched collar and tie, soft hat either on his head or under his arm, and his distinctive silver-headed cane wrapped in black rhinoceros hide. His black hair swept back sleek as linoleum from his high forehead; the bright blue eyes that framed his aquiline nose were never still, always darting about under his dark eyebrows; thin lips, a strong chin, and tanned skin, even in winter, completed the picture. Karl guessed Ernst to be in his mid-thirties, but his mien was that of someone older.

For weeks at a time he would seem to be everywhere, and he was never at a loss for something to say. At the Paul Klee show, where Klee's latest, *The Twittering Machine*, had been on exhibit, Karl had overheard his sarcastic comment that Klee had joined the Bauhaus not a moment too soon. Ernst was always at the right places: at the opening of *Dr. Mabuse*,

der Spieler, at the cast party for that Czech play *R.U.R.*, and
at the secret screenings of Murnau's *Nosferatu,* to name just
a few.

And then he'd be nowhere. He'd disappear for weeks or
a month without a word to anyone. When he returned he
would pick up just where he'd left off, as if there'd been no
hiatus. And when he was in town he all but lived at the
Romanisches Cafe, where nightly he could be seen wandering among the tables, glass in hand, a meandering focus of
raillery and bavardage, dropping dry, witty, acerbic comments on art and literature like ripe fruit. No one seemed to
remember who first introduced him to the café. He more or
less insinuated himself into the regulars on his own. After a
while it seemed he had always been there. Everyone knew
Ernst, but no one knew him well. His persona was a strange
mixture of accessibility and aloofness that Karl found
intriguing.

They began their friendship on a cool Saturday evening
in the spring. Karl had closed his bookshop early and wandered down Budapesterstrasse to the Romanisches Cafe,
which occupied the corner at Tauentzien across from the
Gedachtniskirche: large for a café, with a roomy sidewalk
area and a spacious interior for use on inclement days and
during the colder seasons.

Karl had situated himself under the awning, his knick-
ered legs resting on the empty chair next to him as he sipped
an aperitif among the blossoming flower boxes and reread
Siddhartha. At the sound of clacking high heels he'd glance
up and watch the "new look" women as they trooped past in
pairs and trios, with their clinging dresses fluttering about
their knees and their smooth tight caps pulled down over
their bobbed hair, their red lips, mascaraed eyes, and coats
trimmed in fluffy fur snuggled around their necks.

Karl loved Berlin. He'd been infatuated with the city
since his first sight of it when his father had brought him here

before the war; two years ago, on his twentieth birthday, he'd dropped out of the university to carry on an extended affair with her. His lover was the center of the art world, of the new freedoms. You could be what you wanted here: a freethinker, a free lover, a communist, even a fascist; men could dress like women and women could dress like men. There were no limits. All the new movements in music, the arts, the cinema, and the theater had their roots here. Every time he turned around there was a new marvel.

Night was upon Karl's mistress when Ernst Drexler stopped by Karl's table and introduced himself.

"We've not formally met," he said, thrusting out his hand. "Your name is Stehr, I believe. Come join me at my table. There are a number of things I wish to discuss with you."

Karl wondered what things this man more than ten years his senior could wish to discuss with him, but since he had no other plans for the evening, he went along.

The usual crowd was in attendance at the Romanisches that night. Lately it had become the purlieu of Berlin bohemia—all the artists, writers, journalists, critics, composers, editors, directors, scripters, and anyone else who had anything to do with the avant-garde of German arts, plus the girlfriends, the boyfriends, the mere hangers-on. Some sat rooted in place, others roved ceaselessly from table to table. Smoke undulated in a muslin layer above a gallimaufry of scraggly beards, stringy manes, bobbed hair framing black-rimmed eyes, homburgs, berets, monocles, pince-nez, foot-long cigarette holders, baggy sweaters, dark stockings, period attire ranging from the Hellenic to the pre-Raphaelite.

"I saw you at *Siegfried* the other night," Ernst said, as they reached his table in a dim rear corner, out of the peristaltic flow. Ernst took the seat against the wall, where he could watch the room; he left the other for Karl. "What do you think of Lang's latest?"

"Very Germanic," Karl said as he took his seat and

reluctantly turned his back to the room. He was a people watcher.

Ernst laughed. "How diplomatic! But how true. Deceit, betrayal, and backstabbing—in both the figurative and literal sense. Germanic indeed. Hardly Neue Sachlichkeit, though."

"I think New Realism was the furthest thing from Lang's mind. Now, *Die Strasse*, on the other hand—"

"Neue Sachlichkeit will soon join Expressionism in the mausoleum of movements. And good riddance. It is shit."

"Kunst ist Scheisse?" Karl said, smiling. "Dada is the deadest of them all."

Ernst laughed again. "My, you are sharp, Karl. That's why I wanted to talk to you. You're very bright. You're one of the few people in this room who will be able to appreciate my new entertainment."

"Really? And what is that?"

"Inflation."

Before Karl could ask what he meant, Ernst flagged down a passing waiter.

"The usual for me, Freddy, and—?" He pointed to Karl, who ordered a schnapps.

"Inflation?" Karl said. "Never heard of it. A new card game?"

"No, no," Ernst said, smiling. "It's played with money."

"Of course. But how—"

"It's played with real money in the real world. It's quite entertaining. I've been playing it since the New Year."

Freddy soon delivered Karl's schnapps. For Ernst he brought an empty stemmed glass, a sweaty carafe of chilled water, and a small bowl of sugar cubes. Karl watched fascinated as Ernst pulled a silver flask from his breast pocket and unscrewed the top. He poured three fingers of clear green liquid into the glass, then returned the flask to his coat. Next he produced a slotted spoon, placed a sugar cube in its bowl, and held it over the glass. Then he dribbled water from the carafe, letting it flow over the cube and into the glass to mix with the green liquid . . . which began to turn a pale yellow.

"Absinthe!" Karl whispered.

"Quite," Ernst said. "I developed a taste for it before the war. Too bad it's illegal now—although it's still quite easily come by."

Now Karl knew why Ernst frequently reserved this out-of-the-way table. Instinctively he glanced around, but no one was watching.

Ernst sipped and smacked his lips. "Ever tried any?"

"No." Karl had never had the opportunity. And besides, he'd heard that it drove you mad.

Ernst pushed his glass across the table. "Take a sip."

Part of Karl urged him to say no, while another part pushed his hand forward and wound his fingers around the stem of the glass. He lifted it to his lips and took a tiny sip.

The bitterness rocked his head back and puckered his cheeks.

"That's the wormwood," Ernst said, retrieving his glass. "Takes some getting used to."

Karl shuddered as he swallowed. "How did that ever become a craze?"

"For half a century, all across the Continent, the cocktail hour was known as *l'heure verte* after this little concoction." He sipped again, closed his eyes, savoring. "At the proper time, in the proper place, it can be . . . revelatory."

After a moment, he opened his eyes and motioned Karl closer.

"Here. Move over this way and sit by me. I wish to show you something."

Karl slid his chair around to Ernst's side so they both sat facing the crowded main room of the Romanisches.

"Look at them, Karl," Ernst said, waving his arm at the room. "The cream of the city's artists attended by their cachinating claques and coteries of epigones and acolytes, mixing with the city's lowlifes and lunatics. Morphine addicts and vegetarians cheek by jowl with Bolsheviks and boulevardiers, arrivistes and anarchists, abortionists and antivivisectionists, directors and dilettantes, doyennes and demimondaines."

Karl wondered how much time Ernst spent here sipping his absinthe and observing the scene. And why. He sounded like an entomologist studying a particularly interesting anthill.

"Everyone wants to join the parade," he went on. "They operate under the self-induced delusion that they're in control: 'What happens in the Berlin arts today, the rest of the world copies next week.' True enough, perhaps. But this is the Masque of the Red Death, Karl. Huge forces are at play around them, and they are certain to get crushed as the game unfolds. Germany is falling apart around us—the impossible war reparations are suffocating us, the French and Belgians have been camped in the Ruhr Valley since January, the communists are trying to take over the north, the right-wingers and monarchists practically own Bavaria, and the Reichsbank's answer to the economic problems is to print more money."

"Is that bad?" Karl said.

"Of course. It's only paper. It's been sending prices through the roof." He withdrew his wallet from his breast pocket, pulled a bill from it, and passed it to Karl.

"An American dollar," Karl said.

Ernst nodded. "'Good as gold,' as they say. I bought it for ten thousand marks in January. Care to guess what the local bank was paying for it today?"

"I don't know," Karl began. "Perhaps . . ."

"Forty thousand. Forty thousand marks."

Karl was impressed. "You quadrupled your money in four months."

"No, Karl," Ernst said with a wry smile. "I've merely quadrupled the number of marks I control. My buying power is exactly what it was in January. But I'm one of the very few people in this storm-tossed land who can say so."

"Maybe I should try that," Karl said softly, admiring the elegant simplicity of the plan. "Take my savings and convert it to American dollars."

"By all means do," Ernst said. "Clean out your bank account, pull every mark you own out from under your mattress, and put them into dollars. But that's mere survival—hardly entertainment."

"Survival sounds good enough," Karl said.

"No, my friend. Survival is never enough. Animals limit their concerns to mere survival; humans seek entertainment. That is why we must find a way to make inflation entertaining. Inflation is here. There's nothing we can do about it. So let's have some fun with it."

"I don't know . . ."

"Do you own a house?"

"Yes," Karl said slowly, cautiously. He didn't know where this was leading. "And no."

"Really. You mean it's mortgaged to the hilt?"

"No. Actually it's my mother's. A small estate north of the city near Bernau. But I manage it for her."

Father had died a colonel in the Argonne, and he'd left it to her. But Mother had no head for money, and she hadn't been quite herself in the five years since Father's death. So Karl took care of the lands and the accounts, but spent most of his time in Berlin. He loved the city and loved the artistic renaissance it had spawned. His bookstore barely broke even, but he hadn't opened it for profit. He'd made it a place where local writers and artists were welcome to stop and browse and meet; he reserved a small area in the rear of the store where they could sit and talk and sip the coffee he kept hot for them. His dream was that someday one of the poor unknowns who partook of his hospitality would become famous and perhaps remember the place kindly. And perhaps someday he'd stop by to say hello with Thomas Mann or the reclusive Hermann Hesse in tow. Until

then Karl would be quite satisfied with providing coffee
and rolls to starving scribblers.

But even from the beginning, the shop had paid nonpe-
cuniary dividends. It was his entrée to the literati, and from
there to the entire artistic caravan that swirled through Berlin.

"Any danger of losing it?"

"No." The estate produced enough so that, along with
Father's army pension, his mother could live comfortably.

"Good. Then mortgage it. Borrow to the hilt on it, and
then borrow some more. Then turn all those marks into U.S.
dollars."

Karl was struck dumb by the idea. The family home had
never had a lien on it. Never. The idea was unthinkable.

"No. I—I couldn't."

Ernst put his arm around Karl's shoulder and leaned
closer. Karl could smell the absinthe on his breath.

"Do it, Karl. Trust me in this. It's an entertainment, but
you'll see some practical benefits as well. Mark my words,
six months from now you'll be able to pay off your entire
mortgage with a single U.S. dollar. A single coin."

"I don't know. . . ."

"You must. I need someone who'll play the game with
me. It's much more entertaining when you have someone to
share the fun with."

Ernst straightened up and lifted his glass.

"A toast!" he said, and clinked his glass against Karl's.
"By the way," he said, "do you know where glass clinking
originated? Back in the old days, when poisoning a rival was
a fad among the upper classes, it became the practice to allow
your companion to pour some of his drink into your cup, and
vice versa. That way, if one of the drinks were poisoned,
you'd both suffer."

"How charming," Karl said.

"Quite. Inevitably the pouring would be accompanied by
the clink of one container against another. Hence, the mod-

ern custom." Once again he clinked his absinthe against Karl's schnapps. "Trust me, Karl. Inflation can be very entertaining—and profitable as well. I expect the mark to lose fully half its value in the next six weeks. So don't delay."

He raised his glass. "To inflation!" he cried, and drained the absinthe.

Karl sipped his schnapps in silence.

Ernst rose from his seat. "I expect to see you dollar rich and mark poor when I return."

"Where are you going?"

"A little trip I take every so often. I like to swing up through Saxony and Thuringia to see what the local Bolsheviks are up to—I have a membership in the German Communist Party, you know. I subscribe to *Rote Fahne*, listen to speeches by the Zentrale, and go to rallies. It's very entertaining. But after I tire of that—Marxist rhetoric can be *so* boring—I head south to Munich to see what the other end of the political spectrum is doing. I'm also a member of the National Socialist German Workers' Party down there and subscribe to their *Volkischer Beobachter*."

"Never heard of them," Karl said. "How can they call themselves 'National' if they're not nationally known?"

"Just as they can call themselves socialists when they are stridently fascist. Although frankly I, for one, have difficulty discerning much difference between either end of the spectrum—they are distinguishable only by their paraphernalia and their rhetoric. The National Socialists—they call themselves Nazis—are a power in Munich and other parts of Bavaria, but no one pays too much attention to them up here. I must take you down there sometime to listen to one of their leaders. Herr Hitler is quite a personality. I'm sure our friend Freud would love to get him on the couch."

"Hitler? Never heard of him, either."

"You really should hear him speak sometime. Very entertaining."

Today it takes 51,000 marks to buy a single U.S. dollar.
Volkischer Beobachter, **May 21, 1923**

A few weeks later, when Karl returned from the bank with
the mortgage papers for his mother to sign, he spied something on the doorpost. He stopped and looked closer.

A mezuzah.

He took out his pocketknife and pried it off the wood,
then went inside.

"Mother, what is this?" he said, dropping the object on
the kitchen table.

She looked up at him with her large, brown, intelligent
eyes. Her brunette hair was streaked with gray. She'd lost considerable weight immediately after Father's death and had
never regained it. She used to be lively and happy, with an easy
smile that dimpled her high-colored cheeks. Now she was quiet
and pale. She seemed to have shrunken, in body and spirit.

"You know very well what it is, Karl."

"Yes, but haven't I warned you about putting it outside?"

"It belongs outside."

"Not in these times. Please, Mother. It's not healthy."

"You should be proud of being Jewish."

"I'm not Jewish," he said.

They'd had this discussion hundreds of times lately, it
seemed, but Mother just didn't want to understand. His
father, the colonel, had been Christian, his mother Jewish.
Karl had decided to be neither. He was an atheist, a skeptic,
a freethinker, an intellectual. He was German by language
and place of birth, but he preferred to think of himself as an
international man. Countries and national boundaries should
be abolished, and someday soon would be.

"If your mother is Jewish," she said, "*you* are Jewish. You
can't escape that. I'm not afraid to tell the world I'm Jewish.
I wasn't so observant when your father was alive, but now
that he's gone . . ."

Her eyes filled with tears.

Karl sat down next to her and took her hands in his.

"Mother, listen. There's a lot of anti-Jewish feeling out there these days. It will die down, I'm sure, but right now we live in an inordinately proud country that lost a war and wants to blame someone. Some of the most bitter people have chosen Jews as their scapegoats. So until the country gets back on an even keel, I think it's prudent to keep a low profile."

Her smile was wan. "You know best, dear."

"Good." He opened the folder he'd brought from the bank. "And now for some paperwork. These are the final mortgage papers, ready for signing."

Mother squeezed his hands. "Are you sure we're doing the right thing?"

"Absolutely sure."

Actually, now that the final papers were ready, he was having second thoughts.

Karl had arranged to borrow every last pfennig the bank would lend him against his mother's estate. He remembered how uneasy he'd been at the covetous gleam in the bank officers' eyes when he'd signed the papers. They sensed financial reverses, gambling debts, perhaps, a desperate need for cash that would inevitably lead to default and subsequent foreclosure on a prime piece of property. The bank president's eyes had twinkled over his reading glasses; he'd all but rubbed his hands in anticipation.

Doubt and fear gripped Karl now as his mother's pen hovered over the signature line. Was he being a fool? He was a bookseller, and these were men of finance. Who was he to presume to know more than men who spent every day dealing with money? He was acting on a whim, spurred on by a man he hardly knew.

But he steeled himself, remembering the research he'd done. He'd always been good at research. He knew how to ferret out information. He'd learned that Rudolf Haverstein, the Reichsbank's president, had increased his orders of currency paper and was running the printing presses at full speed on overtime. He watched in silence as his mother signed the mortgage papers.

He'd already taken out personal loans, using Mother's jewelry as collateral. Counting the mortgage, he'd now accumulated five hundred million marks. If he converted them immediately, he'd get ninety-eight hundred U.S. dollars at today's exchange rate. Ninety-eight hundred dollars for half a billion marks. It seemed absurd. He wondered who was madder—the Reichsbank or himself.

Today it takes 500,000,000 marks to buy a single U.S. dollar.
Volkischer Beobachter, September 1, 1923

"To runaway inflation," Ernst Drexler said, clinking his glass of cloudy yellow against Karl's clear glass of schnapps.

Karl sipped a little of his drink and said nothing. He and Ernst had retreated from the heat and glare of the late-summer sun on the Romanisches Cafe's sidewalk to the cooler, darker interior.

Noon on a Saturday and the Romanisches was nearly empty. But then, who could afford to eat out these days?

Only thieves and currency speculators.

Four months ago Karl hadn't believed it possible, but for a while they had indeed had fun with inflation.

Now it was getting scary.

For now, less than four months after borrowing half a billion marks, his ninety-eight hundred U.S. dollars were worth almost five trillion marks. Five *trillion*. The number was meaningless. He could barely imagine even a billion marks, and he controlled five thousand times that amount.

"I realized today," Karl said softly, "that I can pay off all of my half-billion-mark debt with a single dollar bill."

"Don't do it," Ernst said quickly.

"Why not? I'd like to be debt-free."

"You will be. Just wait."

"Until when?"

"It won't be long before the exchange rate will be billions of marks to the dollar. Won't it be so much more entertaining to pay off the bankers with a single American coin?"

Karl stared at his glass. This game was no longer "entertaining." People had lost all faith in the mark. And with good reason. Its value was plummeting. In a mere thirty days it had plunged from a million to the dollar to half a *billion* to the dollar. Numbers crowded the borders of the notes, everlengthening strings of ever more meaningless zeros. Despite running at twenty-four hours a day, the Reichsbank presses could not keep up with the demand. Million-mark notes were now being overstamped with TEN MILLION in large black letters. Workers had gone from getting paid twice a month to weekly, and now to daily. Some were demanding twice-daily pay so that they could run out on their lunch hour and spend their earnings before they lost their value.

"I'm frightened, Ernst."

"Don't worry. You've insulated yourself. You've got nothing to fear."

"I'm frightened for our friends and neighbors. For Germany."

"Oh, that."

Karl didn't understand how Ernst could be so cavalier about the misery steadily welling up around them like a rain-engorged river. It oppressed Karl. He felt guilty, almost ashamed of being safe and secure on his high ground of foreign currency.

Ernst drained his absinthe and rose, his eyes bright.

"Let's go for a walk, shall we? Let's see what your friends and neighbors are up to on this fine day."

Karl left his schnapps and followed him out into the

street. They strolled along Budapesterstrasse until they came upon a bakery.

"Look," Ernst said, pointing with his black cane. "A social gathering."

Karl bristled at the sarcasm. The long line of drawn faces with anxious, hollow eyes—male, female, young, old— trailing out the door and along the sidewalk was hardly a social gathering. Lines for bread, meat, milk, any of the staples of life, had become so commonplace that they were taken for granted. The customers stood there with their paper bags, cloth sacks, and wicker baskets full of marks, shifting from one foot to the other, edging forward, staying close behind the person in front of them lest someone tried to cut into the line, constantly turning the count of their marks in their minds, hoping there would be something left to buy when they reached the purchase counter, praying their money would not devalue too much before the price was rung up.

Karl had never stood in such a line. He didn't have to. He needed only to call or send a note to a butcher or baker listing what he required and saying that he would be paying with American currency. Within minutes the merchant would be at his door with the order. He found no pleasure, no feeling of superiority in his ability to summon the necessities to his door, only relief that his mother would not be subject to the hunger and anxiety of these poor souls.

As Karl watched, a boy approached the center of the line where a young woman had placed a wicker basket full of marks on the sidewalk. As he passed her he bent and grabbed a handle on the basket, upended it, dumping out the marks. Then he sprinted away with the basket. The woman cried out, but no one moved to stop him—no one wanted to lose his place in line.

Karl started to give chase but Ernst restrained him.

"Don't bother. You'll never catch him."

Karl watched the young woman gather her scattered marks into her apron and resume her long wait in line, weeping. His heart broke for her.

"This has to stop," he told Ernst. "Someone has to do something about this."

"Ah, yes," Ernst said, nodding sagely. "But who?"

They walked on. As they approached a corner, Ernst suddenly raised his cane and pressed its shaft against Karl's chest.

"Listen. What's that noise?"

Up ahead at the intersection, traffic had stopped. Instead of the roar of internal combustion engines, Karl heard something else. Other sounds, softer, less rhythmic, swelled in the air. A chaotic tapping and a shuffling cacophony of scrapes and dragging sounds, accompanied by a dystonic chorus of high-pitched squeaks and creaks.

And then they inched into view—the lame, the blind, the damaged, dismembered, demented, and disfigured tatterdemalions of two wars: the few remaining veterans of the Franco-Prussian War of 1870—stooped, wizened figures in their seventies and eighties, who had besieged Paris and proclaimed Wilhelm of Prussia as Emperor of Germany in the Hall of Mirrors at Versailles—were leading the far larger body of pathetic survivors from the disastrous Great War, the War To End All Wars, the valiant men whose defeated leaders five years ago had abjectly agreed to impossible reparations in that same Hall of Mirrors.

Karl watched aghast as a young man with one arm passed within a few meters of him, dragging a wheeled platform on which lay a limbless man, hardly more than a head with a torso. Neither was much older than he. The Grand Guignol parade was full of these fractions of men and their blind, deaf, limping, stumbling, hopping, staggering companions. Karl knew he might well be among them had he been born a year or two earlier.

Some carried signs begging, pleading, demanding higher pensions and disability allowances; they all looked worn and defeated, but mostly *hungry*. Here were the most pitiful victims of the runaway inflation.

Karl fell into line with them and pulled Ernst along.

"Really," Ernst said, "this is hardly my idea of an entertaining afternoon."

"We need to show them that they're not alone, that we haven't forgotten them. We need to show the government that we support them."

"It will do no good," Ernst said, grudgingly falling into step beside him. "It takes time for the government to authorize a pension increase. And even if it is approved, by the time it goes into effect, the increase will be meaningless."

"This can't go on!" Karl cried. "Someone has got to do something about this chaos!"

Ernst pointed ahead with his black cane. "There's a suggestion."

At the corner stood two brown-shirted men in paramilitary gear and caps. On their left upper arms were red bands emblazoned with a strange, black twisted cross inside a white circle. Between them they held a banner:

COME TO US, COMRADES!
ADOLF HITLER WILL HELP YOU!

"Hitler," Karl said slowly. "You mentioned him before, didn't you?"

"Yes. The Austrian Gefreiter. He'll be at that big fascist rally in Nuremberg tomorrow to commemorate something or other. I hope to get to hear him again. Marvelous speaker. Want to come along?"

Karl had heard about the rally—so had all the rest of Germany. Upwards of two hundred thousand veterans and members of every right-wing volkisch paramilitary group in the country were expected in the Bavarian town to celebrate the anniversary of the Battle of Sedan in the Franco-Prussian War.

"I don't think so. I don't like big crowds. Especially a big crowd of fascists."

"Some other time, then. I'll call you when he's going to address one of the beer-hall meetings in Munich. He does that a lot. That way you'll get the full impact of his speaking voice. Most entertaining."

Adolf Hitler, Karl thought as he passed the brown-shirted men with the strange armbands. Could he be the man to save Germany?

"Yes," he told Ernst. "Do call me. I wish to hear this man."

Today it takes 200 billion marks to buy a single U.S. dollar.
Volkischer Beobachter, **October 22, 1923**

"It's like entering another country," Karl murmured as he stood on the platform of the Munich train station.

"Not another country at all," said Ernst, who stood beside him as they waited for a porter to take his bags. "Merely an armed camp filled with people as German as the rest of us. Perhaps more so."

"People in love with uniforms."

"And what could be more German than that?"

Ernst had sent him a message last week, scrawled in his reverse-slanted script on the blank back of a hundred-million-mark note. Even with all its overworked presses running at full speed, the Reichsbank found itself limited to printing the new marks on only one side in order to keep up with the ever-increasing demand for currency. Ernst had found it amusing to use the blank sides of the smaller denominations as stationery. And this note had invited Karl south to hear Herr Hitler.

Karl now wished he'd ignored the invitation. A chill had come over him as the train crossed into Bavaria; it began in the pit of his stomach, then encircled his chest and crept up his spine to his neck, where it now insinuated icy fingers around his throat. Uniforms . . . military uniforms everywhere, lolling about the train station, marching in the streets, standing on the corners, and none of them sporting the comfortably familiar field gray of regular Reichswehr troops. Young men, middle-aged men, dressed in brown and black, blue, and green, all with watchful, suspicious eyes and tight, hostile faces.

Something sinister was growing here in the south, something unclean, something dangerous.

It's the times, he told himself. *Just another facet of the chaotic Zeitgeist.*

Of course Bavaria was like an armed camp. Less than three weeks ago its cabinet, aghast at what it saw as Berlin's cowardly submission to the continuing Franco-Belgian presence in the Ruhr Valley, had declared a state of emergency and suspended the Weimar Constitution within its borders. Gustav von Kahr had been declared Generalstaatskommissar of Bavaria with dictatorial powers. Berlin had blustered threats but so far had made no move against the belligerent southern state, preferring diplomatic avenues for the moment.

But how long would that last? The communists in the north were trying to ignite a revolution in Saxony, calling for a "German October," and the more radical Bavarians here in the south were calling for a march on Berlin because of the government's impotence in foreign and domestic affairs, especially in finance and currency.

Currency . . . when the mark had sunk to five billion to the dollar two weeks ago, Karl had paid off the mortgage on the estate plus the loans against his mother's jewelry with a U.S. ten-cent piece—what the Americans called a "dime."

Something had to happen. The charges were set, the fuse was lit. Where would the explosion occur? When?

"Think of them as human birds," Ernst said, pointing to their left at two groups in different uniforms. "You can tell who's who by their plumage. The gray are soldaten . . . regular Reichswehr soldiers, of course. The green are Bavarian State Police. And as we move through Munich you'll see the city's regular police force, dressed in blue."

"Gray, green, blue," Karl murmured.

"Right. Those are the official colors. The *unofficial* colors are brown and black. They belong in varying mixes to the Nazi S.A.—their so-called storm troopers—and the Reichskriegsflagge and Bund Oberland units."

"So confusing."

"It is. Bavaria has been a hotbed of fascism since the war, but mostly it was a fragmented thing—more feisty little paramilitary groups than you could count. But things are different these days. The groups have been coalescing, and now the three major factions have allied themselves into something called the Kampfbund."

"The 'Battle Group'?"

"Precisely. And they're quite ready for battle. There are more caches of rifles and machine guns and grenades buried and hidden in cellars in and around Munich than Berlin could imagine in its worst nightmares. Hitler's Nazis are the leading faction of the Kampfbund, and right now he and the Bavarian government are at odds. Hitler wants to march on Berlin, General Commissioner Kahr does not. At the moment, Kahr has the upper hand. He's got the Green Police, the Blue Police, and the Reichswehr regulars to keep the Kampfbund in line. The question is, how long can he hold their loyalty when the hearts of many of his troops are in the Nazi camp, and Hitler's speeches stir more and more to the Nazi cause?"

Karl felt the chill tighten around his throat. He wished

Ernst hadn't invited him to Munich. He wished he hadn't accepted.

"Maybe now is not a good time to be here."

"Nonsense!" Ernst cried. "It's the *best* time! Can't you feel the excitement in the air? Don't you sense the huge forces at work around us? Stop and listen, and you'll hear the teeth of cosmic gears grinding into motion. The clouds have gathered and are storing their charges. The lightning of history is about to strike, and we are near the ground point. I know it as surely as I know my name."

"Lightning can be deadly."

"Which makes it all the more entertaining."

"Why a beer hall?" Karl asked as they sat in the huge main room of the Burgerbraukeller.

"Because Munich is the heart of beer-drinking country," Ernst said. A buxom waitress set a fresh pair of liter steins of lager on the rough planked table before them. "If you want to reach these people, you speak to them where they drink their beer."

The Burgerbraukeller was huge, squatting on a sizable plot of land on the east side of the Isar River that cut the city in two. After the Zirkus Krone, it was the largest meeting place in Munich. Scattered inside its vast complex were numerous separate bars and dining halls, but the centerpiece was the main hall which seated three thousand. All those seats were filled tonight, with latecomers standing in the aisles and crowded at the rear.

Karl quaffed a few ounces of lager to wash down a mouthful of sausage. All around him were men in black and various shades of brown, all impatient for the arrival of their Führer. But he saw some in business suits, and even a few in traditional Bavarian lederhosen and Tyrolean hats. Karl and Ernst had made instant friends with their table neighbors by sharing the huge platter of cheese, bread, and sausage they had ordered from the bustling kitchen. Even though they were not in uniform, not aligned with any Kampfbund organization, and wore no armbands, the two Berlin newcomers were now considered komraden by the locals who shared their long table. They were even more welcome when Ernst mentioned that Karl was the son of Colonel Stehr, who'd fought and died at Argonne.

Far better to be welcomed here as comrades, Karl thought, than the opposite. He'd been listening to the table talk, the repeated references to Adolf Hitler in reverent tones as the man who would rescue Germany from all its enemies, both within and without, and lead the Fatherland back to the glory it deserved. Karl sensed that even the power of God might not be enough to save a man in this crowd who had something to say against Herr Hitler.

The hazy air was ripe with the effluvia of any beer hall: spilled hops and malt, tobacco smoke, the garlicky tang of steaming sausage, sharp cheese, sweaty bodies, and restless anticipation. Karl was finishing off his latest stein when he heard a stir run through the crowd. Someone with a scarred face had arrived at the rostrum on the bandstand. He spoke a few words into the increasing noise and ended by introducing Herr Adolf Hitler.

With a thunderous roar the crowd was on its feet and shouting, "Heil! Heil!" as a thin man, about five-nine or so, who could have been anywhere from mid-thirties to mid-forties in age, ascended the steps to the rostrum. He was dressed in a brown wool jacket, a white shirt with a stiff collar, a narrow tie, with brown knickers and stockings on his short, bandy legs. Straight brown hair parted on the right and combed across his upper forehead; sallow complexion, almost yellow; thin lips under a narrow brush of a moustache. He walked stooped slightly forward with his head canted to the left, and his hands stuffed into his jacket pockets.

This is the man they call Führer? He looks like a shop-keeper, or a government clerk, Karl thought. This is the man they think is going to save Germany? Are they all mad or drunk . . . or both?

Hitler reached the rostrum and gazed out over the cheer-ing audience, and it was then that Karl had his first glimpse of the man's unforgettable eyes. They shone like beacons from their sockets, piercing the room, staggering Karl with their startling pale blue fire. Flashing, hypnotic, gleaming with fanaticism, they ranged the room, quieting it, challenging another voice to interrupt his.

And then he began to speak, his surprisingly rich baritone rising and falling like a Wagnerian opus, hurling sudden gut-turals through the air for emphasis like fist-sized cobble-stones.

For the first ten minutes he spoke evenly and stood stiffly, with his hands trapped in his jacket pockets. But as his voice rose, and his passion grew, his hands broke free, fine, grace-ful, long-fingered hands that fluttered like pigeons and swooped like hawks, then knotted into fists to pound the top of the rostrum with sledgehammer blows.

The minutes flew, gathering into one hour, then two. At first Karl had managed to remain aloof, picking apart Hitler's words, separating the carefully selected truths from the half-truths and the outright fictions. Then, in spite of himself, he began to fall under the man's spell. This Adolf Hitler was such a passionate speaker, so caught up in his own words, that one had to go along with him; whatever the untruths and specious logic in his oratory, there could be no doubt that this man believed unequivocally every word that he spoke, and somehow transferred that fervent conviction to his audience, so that they, too, became unalterably convinced of the truth of what he was saying.

He was never more powerful than when he called on all loyal Germans to come to the aid of a sick and failing

Germany, one not merely financially and economically ill, but a Germany on its intellectual and moral deathbed. No question that Germany was sick, struck down by a disease that poultices and salves and cathartics could not cure. Germany needed radical surgery: The sick and gangrenous parts that were poisoning the rest of the system had to be cut away and burned before the healing could begin. Karl listened and became entranced, transfixed, unmindful of the time, a prisoner of that voice, those eyes.

And then this man, this Adolf Hitler, was standing in front of the rostrum, bathed in sweat, his hair hanging over his forehead, waving his arms, calling for all loyal Germans who truly cared for their Fatherland to rally around the Nazi Party and call for a march on Berlin where they would extract a promise from the feeble Weimar Republicans to banish the Jews and the communists from all positions of power and drive the French and Belgian troops from the Ruhr Valley and once again make the Fatherland's borders inviolate, or by God, there would be a new government in power in Berlin, one that would bring Germany to the greatness that was her destiny. German misery must be broken by German iron. Our day is here! Our time is *now*!

The main hall went mad as Hitler stepped back and let the frenzied cheering of more than three thousand voices rattle the walls and rafters around him. Even Karl was on his feet, ready to shake his fist in the air and shout at the top of his lungs. Suddenly he caught himself.

What am I doing?

"Well, what did you think of the Gefreiter?" Ernst said. "Our strutting lance corporal?"

They were out on Rosenheimerstrasse, making their way back to the hotel, and Karl's ears had finally stopped ringing. Ahead of them in the darkness, mist rising from the Isar

River sparkled in the glow of the lights lining the Ludwig Bridge.

"I think he's the most magnetic, powerful, mesmerizing speaker I've ever heard. Frighteningly so."

"Well, he's obviously mad—a complete loon. A master of hyperbolic sophistry, but hardly frightening."

"He's so . . . so . . . so anti-Semitic."

Ernst shrugged. "They all are. It's just rhetoric. Doesn't mean anything."

"Easy for you to say."

Ernst stopped and stood staring at Karl. "Wait. You don't mean to tell me you're . . . ?"

Karl turned and nodded silently in the darkness.

"But Colonel Stehr wasn't—"

"His wife was."

"Good heavens, man! I had no idea!"

"Well, what's so unusual? What's wrong with a German officer marrying a woman who happens to be Jewish?"

"Nothing, of course. It's just that one becomes so used to these military types and their—"

"Do you know that General von Seeckt, commander of the entire German army, has a Jewish wife? So does Chancellor Stresemann."

"Of course. The Nazis point that out at every opportunity."

"Right! We're everywhere!" Karl calmed himself with an effort. "Sorry, Ernst. I don't know why I got so excited. I don't even consider myself a Jew. I'm a human being. Period."

"Perhaps, but by Jewish law, if the mother is Jewish, then so are the children."

Karl stared at him. "How do you know that?"

"Everybody knows that. But that doesn't matter. The locals we've met know you as Colonel Stehr's son. That's what will count here in the next week or so."

"Next week or so? Aren't we returning to Berlin?"

Ernst gripped his arm. "No, Karl. We're staying. Things

are coming to a head. The next few days promise to be *most* entertaining."

"I shouldn't—"

"Come back to the hotel. I'll fix you an absinthe. You look like you could use one."

Karl remembered the bitter taste, then realized he could probably do with a bit of oblivion tonight.

"All right," he said. "But just one."

"Excellent! Absinthe tonight, and we'll plan our next steps in the morning."

Today it takes 4 trillion marks to buy a single U.S. dollar.
***Volkischer Beobachter*, November 8, 1923**

"Herr Hitler's speaking in Freising tonight," Ernst said as they strolled through the bright, crisp morning air, past onion-cupolaed churches and pastel housefronts that would have looked more at home along the Tiber than the Isar.

"How far is that?"

"About twenty miles north. But I have a better idea. Gustav von Kahr, Bavaria's honorable dictator, is speaking at the Burgerbraukeller tonight."

"I'd rather hear Hitler."

It was already more than a week into November, and Karl was still in Munich. He'd expected to be home long ago but had found himself too captivated by Adolf Hitler to leave. It was a strange attraction, equal parts fascination and revulsion. Here was a man who might pull together Germany's warring factions and make them one, but then might wreak havoc upon the freedoms of the Weimar Constitution. But where would the constitution be by year's end with old mark notes now being overprinted with EINE BILLION?

Karl felt like a starving sparrow contemplating a viper's offer to guard her nest while she hunts for food. Surely her nest would be well protected from other birds in her absence, but could she count on finding any eggs left when she returned?

He'd spoken to a number of Jews in Munich, shopkeepers mostly, engaging them in casual conversation about the Kampfbund groups, and Herr Hitler in particular. The seismic upheavals in the economy had made them frazzled and desperate, certain that their country would be in ruins by the end of the year unless somebody did something. Most of them said they'd support anyone who could bring the economic chaos and runaway inflation under control. Hitler and his Nazis promised definitive solutions. So what if the country had to live under a dictatorship for a while? Nothing— *nothing*—could be worse than this. After all, hadn't the Kaiser been a dictator? And they'd certainly done better under him than with this Weimar Republic, with its constitution that guaranteed so many freedoms. What good were freedom of the press and speech and assembly if you were starving? As for the anti-Semitism, most of the Munich Jews echoed Ernst's dismissal: mere rhetoric. Nothing more than tough talk to excite the beer drinkers.

Still uneasy, Karl found himself drawn back again and again to hear Hitler speak—in the Zirkus Krone, and in the Burgerbraukeller and other beer halls around the city—hoping each time the man would say something to allay his fears and allow him to embrace the hope the Nazis offered.

Absinthe only added to the compulsion. Karl had taken to drinking a glass with Ernst before attending each new Hitler speech, and, as a result, he had acquired a taste for the bitter stuff.

Because Herr Hitler seemed to be speaking all the time.

Especially since the failed communist putsch in Hamburg. It failed because the German workers refused to rally to the red flag and Reichswehr troops easily put down the revolution in its second day. There would be no German October. But the attempt had incited the Kampfbund groups to near hysteria. Karl saw more uniforms in Munich's streets than he'd seen in Berlin during the war. And Herr Hitler was there in the thick of it, fanning the sparks of patriotic fervor into a bonfire wherever he found an audience.

Karl attended his second Hitler speech while under the influence of absinthe, and there he experienced his first hallucination. It happened while Hitler was reaching his final crescendo: the hall wavered before Karl, the light dimmed, all the color drained from his sight, leaving only black and white and shades of gray; he had the impression of being in a crowded room, just like the beer hall, and then it passed. It hadn't lasted long enough for Karl to capture any details, but it had left him shivering and afraid.

The following night it happened again—the same flash of black and white, the same aftershock of dread.

It was the absinthe, he was sure. He'd heard that it caused delirium and hallucinations and even madness in those who overused it. But Karl did not feel he was going mad. No, this was something else. Not madness, but a different level of perception. He had a sense of a hidden truth, just beyond the grasp of his senses, beckoning to him, reaching for him. He felt he'd just grazed the surface of that awful truth, that if he kept reaching, he'd soon seize it.

And he knew how to extend his reach: more absinthe.

Ernst was only too glad to have another enthusiast for his favorite libation.

"Forget Herr Hitler tonight," Ernst said. "This will be better. Bavaria's triumvirate will be there in person—Kahr, General Lossow, and Colonel von Seisser. Rumor has it that Kahr is going to make a dramatic announcement. Some say he's going to declare Bavaria's independence. Others say he's going to return Crown Prince Rupprecht to the throne and restore the Bavarian monarchy. You don't want to miss this, Karl."

"What about Hitler and the rest of the Kampfbund?"

"They're frothing at the mouth. They've been invited to attend but not to participate. It's clear, I think, that Kahr is making a move to upstage the Kampfbund and solidify his leadership position. By tomorrow morning, Hitler and his cronies may find themselves awash in a hysterical torrent of Bavarian nationalism. This will be worse than any political defeat—they'll be . . . irrelevant. Think of their outrage, think of their frustration." Ernst rubbed his palms with glee. "Oh, this will be *most* entertaining!"

Reluctantly, Karl agreed. He felt he was getting closer and closer to that elusive vision, but even if Generalstaatskommissar Kahr tried to pull the rug out from under the Kampfbund, Karl was sure he would have plenty of future opportunities to listen to Herr Hitler.

Karl and Ernst arrived early at the Burgerbraukeller, and a good thing, too. The city's Blue Police had to close the doors at seven-fifteen, when the hall filled to overflowing. This was a much higher-class audience than Hitler attracted. Well-dressed businessmen in tall hats and women in long dresses mingled with military officers and members of the Bavarian provincial cabinet; the local newspapers were represented by their editors rather than mere reporters. Everyone in Munich wanted to hear what Generalstaatskommissar Kahr had to say, and those left in the cold drizzle outside protested angrily.

They were the lucky ones, Karl decided soon after Gustav von Kahr began to speak. The squat, balding royalist had no earthshaking announcement to make. Instead, he stood hunched over the rostrum, with Lossow and Seisser, the other two-thirds of the ruling triumvirate, seated on the bandstand behind him, and read a dull, endless anti-Marxist treatise in a listless monotone.

"Let's leave," Karl said after fifteen minutes of droning.

Ernst shook his head and glanced to their right. "Look who just arrived."

Karl turned and recognized the figure in the light tan trench coat standing behind a pillar near the rear of the hall, chewing on a fingernail.

"Hitler! I thought he was supposed to be speaking in Freising."

"That's what the flyers said. Apparently he changed his mind. Or perhaps he simply wanted everyone to think he'd be in Freising." Ernst's voice faded as he turned in his seat and scanned the audience. "I wonder . . ."

"Wonder what?"

He leaned close and whispered in Karl's ear. "I wonder if Herr Hitler might not be planning something here tonight."

Karl's intestines constricted into a knot. "A putsch?"

"Keep your voice down. Yes. Why not? Bavaria's ruling triumvirate and most of its cabinet are here. If I were planning a takeover, this would be the time and place."

"But all those police outside."

Ernst shrugged. "Perhaps he'll just take over the stage and launch into one of his speeches. Either way, history could be made here tonight."

Karl glanced back at Hitler and wondered if this was what the nearly grasped vision was about. He nudged Ernst.

"Did you bring the absinthe?"

"Of course. But we won't be able to fix it properly here." He paused. "I have an idea, though."

He signaled the waitress and ordered two snifters of cognac. She looked at him strangely, but returned in a few minutes and placed the glasses on the table next to their beer steins. Ernst pulled his silver flask from his pocket and poured a more than generous amount of absinthe into the cognac.

"It's not turning yellow," Karl said.

"It only does that in water." Ernst lifted his snifter and

swirled the greenish contents. "This was Toulouse-Lautrec's favorite way of diluting his absinthe. He called it his 'earth-quake.'" Ernst smiled as he clinked his glass against Karl's. "To earthshaking events."

Karl took a sip and coughed. The bitterness of the worm-wood was enhanced rather than cut by the burn of the cognac. He washed it down with a gulp of ale. He would have poured the rest of his "earthquake" into Ernst's glass if he hadn't felt he needed every drop of the absinthe to reach the elusive vision. So he finished the entire snifter, chasing each sip with more ale. He wondered if he'd be able to walk out of here unassisted at the night's end.

He was just setting down the empty glass when he heard shouting outside. The doors at the rear of the hall burst open with a shattering bang as helmeted figures charged in, brandishing sabers, pistols, and rifles with fixed bayonets. From their brown shirts and the swastikas on their red armbands Karl knew they weren't the police.

"Nazi storm troopers!" Ernst said.

Pandemonium erupted. Some men cried out in shock and outrage, while others shouted, "Heil!" Some were crawling under the tables, while others were climbing atop them for a better view. Women screamed and fainted at the sight of a machine gun being set up at the door. Karl looked around for Hitler and found him charging down the center aisle holding a pistol aloft. As he reached the bandstand he fired a shot into the ceiling.

Sudden silence.

Hitler climbed up next to General Commissioner von Kahr and turned toward the crowd. Karl blinked at the sight of him. He had shed the trench coat and was wearing a poorly cut morning coat with an Iron Cross pinned over the left breast. He looked . . . ridiculous, more like the maître d' in a seedy restaurant than the savior of Germany.

But then the pale blue eyes cast their spell, and the familiar baritone rang through the hall announcing that a national revolution had broken out in Germany. The Bavarian cities of Augsburg, Nuremberg, Regensburg, and Wurzburg were now in his control; the Reichswehr and State Police were marching from their barracks under Nazi flags; the Weimar government was no more. A new national German Reich was being formed. Hitler was in charge.

Ernst snickered. "The Gefreiter looks like a waiter who's led a putsch against the restaurant staff."

Karl barely heard him. The vision . . . it was coming . . . close now . . . the absinthe, fueled by the cognac and ale, was drawing it nearer than ever before . . . the room was flickering about him, the colors draining away . . .

And then the main hall of the Burgerbraukeller was gone, and he was in blackness . . . silent, formless blackness . . . but not alone. He detected movement around him in the palpable darkness . . .

And then he saw them.

Human forms, thin, pale, bedraggled, sunken-cheeked, and hollow-eyed, dressed in rags or dressed not at all, and thin, so painfully thin, like parchment-covered skeletons through which each rib and each bump and nodule on the pelvis and hips could be touched and numbered, all stumbling, sliding, staggering, shambling, groping toward him out of the dark. At first he thought it a dream, a nightmare reprise of the march of the starving disabled veterans he'd witnessed in Berlin, but these . . . people . . . were different. No tattered uniforms here. The ones who had clothing were dressed in striped prison pajamas, and there were so many of them. With their ranks spanning to the right and left as far as Karl could see, and stretching and fading off into the distance to where the horizon might have been, their number was beyond counting . . . thousands, hundreds of thousands, millions . . .

And they were all coming his way.

They began to pick up speed as they neared him, breaking

into a staggering run like a herd of frightened cattle. Closer, now . . . their gaunt faces became masks of fear, pale lips drawn back over toothless mouths, giving no sign that they saw him . . . he could see no glint of light in the dark hollows of their eye sockets . . . but he gasped as other details became visible.

They had been mutilated—branded, actually. A six-pointed star had been carved into the flesh of each. On the forehead, between the breasts, on the belly—a bleeding Star of David. The only color not black, white, or gray was the red of the blood that oozed from each of those six-pointed brands.

But why were they running? What was spurring the stampede?

And then he heard a voice, shouting, faint and far off at first, and then louder: *"Alle Juden raus!"* Over and over: *"Alle Juden raus! Alle Juden raus!"* Louder and louder as they approached until Karl had to clasp his hands over his ears to protect them.

"ALLE JUDEN RAUS! ALLE JUDEN RAUS!"

And then they were upon him, mobbing him, knocking him to his knees and then flat on his face in their panicked flight through the darkness, oblivious to him as they stepped on him and tripped over him in their blind rush to nowhere. He could not regain his feet; he did not try. He had no fear of being crushed because they weighed almost nothing, but he could not rise against their numbers. So he remained face-down in the darkness, with his hands over his head, and listened to that voice.

"ALLE JUDEN RAUS! ALLE JUDEN RAUS!"

After what seemed an eternity, they were past. Karl lifted his head. He was alone in the darkness. No . . . not alone. Someone else . . . a lone figure approaching. A naked woman, old, short, thin, with long gray hair, limping his way on arthritic knees. Something familiar about her—

"Mother!"

He stood paralyzed, rooted, unable to turn from her nakedness. She looked so thin, and so much older, as if she'd aged twenty years. And into each floppy breast had been carved a Star of David.

He sobbed as he held his arms out to her.

"Dear God, Mother! What have they done to you?"

But she took no notice of him, limping past as if he did not exist.

"Moth—!"

He turned, reaching to grab her arm as she passed, but froze in mute shock when he saw the mountain behind him.

All the gaunt living dead who had rushed past him were piled in a mound that dwarfed the Alps themselves, carelessly tossed like discarded dolls into a charnel heap that stretched miles into the darkness above him.

Only now they had eyes. Dead eyes, staring sightlessly his way, each with a silent plea . . . *help us . . . save us . . . please don't let this happen . . .*

His mother—she was in there. He had to find her, get her out of there. He ran toward the tower of wasted human flesh, but before he reached it the blacks and whites began to shimmer and melt, bleeding color as that damned voice grew louder and louder . . . *"ALLE JUDEN RAUS! ALLE JUDEN RAUS!"*

And Karl knew that voice. God help him, he knew that voice.

Adolf Hitler's voice.

Suddenly he found himself back in the Burgerbraukeller, on his feet, staring at Adolf Hitler who still stood at the rostrum. Only seconds had passed. It had seemed so much longer.

As Hitler finished his proclamation, the triumvirate of Kahr, Lossow, and Seisser were marched off the stage at gunpoint. And Hitler stood there with his feet spread and his arms folded across his chest, staring in triumphant defiance at the shocked crowd mingling and murmuring before him.

Karl now understood what he had seen. Hitler's hate wasn't mere rhetoric. This madman meant what he said. Every word of it. He intended the destruction of German Jewry, of Jews everywhere. And now, here in this beer hall, he was making a grab for the power to do just that. And he was succeeding!

He has to be stopped!

As Hitler turned to follow the captured triumvirate, Karl staggered forward, his arm raised, his finger pointing, ready to accuse, to shout out a denunciation. But no sound came from his throat. His lips were working, his lungs were pumping, but his vocal cords were locked. Hoarse, breathy hisses were the only sounds he could make.

But those sounds were enough to draw the attention of the Nazi storm troopers. The nearest turned and pointed their rifles at him. Ernst leaped to his side and restrained him, pulling his arm down.

"He's not well," Ernst said. "He's been sick, and tonight's excitement has been too much for him."

Karl tried to shake free of Ernst. He didn't care about the storm troopers or their weapons. These people had to hear, had to know what Hitler and his National Socialists planned. But then Hitler was leaving, following the captured triumvirate from the bandstand.

In the frightened and excited confusion that followed his exit, Ernst steered Karl toward one of the side doors. But their way was blocked by a baby-faced storm trooper.

"No one leaves until the Führer says so."

"This man is sick!" Ernst shouted. "Do you know who his father was? Colonel Stehr himself! This is the son of a hero of the Argonne! Let him into the fresh air immediately!"

The young trooper, certainly no more than eighteen or nineteen, was taken aback by Ernst's outburst. It was highly unlikely that he'd ever heard of a Colonel Stehr, but he stepped aside to let them pass.

The drizzle had turned to snow, and the cold air began to clear Karl's head, but still he had no voice. Pulling away from Ernst's supporting arm, he half ran, half stumbled across the grounds of the Burgerbraukeller, crowded now with exuberant members of the Kampfbund. He headed toward the street, wanting to scream, to cry out his fear and warn the city, the country, that a murderous lunatic was taking over.

When he reached the far side of Rosenheimerstrasse, he found an alley, leaned into it, and vomited. After his stomach was empty, he wiped his mouth on his sleeve and returned to where Ernst awaited him on the sidewalk.

"Good heavens, man," Ernst said. "What got into you back there?"

Karl leaned against a lamppost and told him about the vision, about the millions of dead Jews, and Hitler's voice and what it was shouting.

Ernst was a long time replying. His eyes had a faraway look, almost glazed, as if he were trying to see the future Karl had described.

"That was the absinthe," he said finally. "Lautrec's earthquake. You've been indulging a bit much lately, and you're not used to it. Lautrec was institutionalized because of it. Van Gogh cut off one of his ears under the influence."

"No," Karl said, grabbing the front of Ernst's overcoat. "The absinthe is responsible, I'll grant that, but it only opened the door for me. This was more than a hallucination. This was a vision of the future, a warning. He's got to be stopped, Ernst!"

"How? You heard him. There's a national revolution going on, and he's leading it."

A steely resolve, cold as the snow falling around them, was taking shape within Karl.

"I've been entrusted with a warning," he told Ernst softly. "I'm not going to ignore it."

"What are you going to do? Flee the country?"

"No," he said. "I'm going to stop Adolf Hitler."

"How?"

"By any means necessary."

We do not have the right or authority to execute—yet.
Hermann Goering, November 8, 1923

The rest of the night was a fearful phantasm, filled with shouts, shots, and conflicting rumors—yes, there was a national revolution; no, there were no uprisings in Nuremberg or the other cities.

One thing was clear to Karl: a revolution was indeed in progress in Munich. All through the night, as he and Ernst wandered the city, they crossed paths again and again with detachments of brown-shirted men marching under the swastika banner. And lining the sidewalks were men and women of all ages, cheering them on.

Karl wanted to grab and shake each one of them and scream into their faces, *You don't know what you're doing! You don't know what they're planning!*

No one was moving to stop the putsch. The Blue Police, the Green Police, the Reichswehr troops were nowhere in sight. Ernst led Karl across the river to the Reichswehr headquarters, where they watched members of the Reichskriegsflagge segment of the Kampfbund strutting in and out of the entrance.

"It's true!" Karl said. "The Reichswehr troops are with them!"

Karl tried to call Berlin to see what was happening there but could not get a phone connection. They went to the offices of the *Munchener Post*, a newspaper critical of Hitler in the past, but found its offices ransacked, every typewriter gone, every piece of printing equipment destroyed.

"The putsch is not even a day old and they've started already!" Karl said, standing on the glass-littered sidewalk in the wan dawn light and surveying the damage. "Crush anyone who disagrees with you."

"Yes!" a voice cried behind them. "Crush them! Grind them under your heel!"

They turned to see a bearded middle-aged man waving a bottle of champagne as he joined them before the *Post* offices. He wore a swastika armband over a tattered army coat.

"It's our time now!" the man said. He guzzled some of the champagne and held it aloft. "A toast! Germany for the Germans, and damn the Jews to hell!" He thrust the bottle at Karl. "Here! Donated by a Jew down the street."

Icy spikes scored the inner walls of Karl's chest.

"Really?" he said, taking the half-full bottle. "Donated?"

"Requisitioned, actually." He barked a laugh. "Along with his watch and his wife's jewelry . . . after they were arrested!"

Uncontrollable fury, fueled by the growing unease of the past two weeks and the horror of his vision in the beer hall, exploded in Karl. He reversed his grip on the bottle and smashed it against the side of the man's head.

"My God, Karl!" Ernst cried.

The man stiffened and fell flat on his back in the slush, coat open, arms and legs akimbo.

Karl stared down at him, shocked by what he'd done. He'd never struck another man in his life. He knelt over him.

"He's still breathing."

Then he saw the pistol in the man's belt. He gripped the handle and pulled it free. He straightened and cradled the weapon in his trembling hands as he turned toward Ernst.

"You asked me before how I was going to stop Hitler. Here is the answer."

"Have you gone mad?" Ernst said.

"You don't have to come along. Safer for you if you return to the hotel while I search out Herr Hitler."

"Don't insult me. I'll be beside you all the way."

Karl stared at Ernst, surprised and warmed by the reply. "Thank you, Ernst."

Ernst grinned, his eyes bright with excitement. "I wouldn't miss this for the world!"

Throughout the morning, conflicting rumors traveled up and down the Munich streets on both sides of the river with the regularity of the city trolleys: the triumvirate has thrown in with Hitler . . . the triumvirate is free and planning counter-moves against the putsch . . . the Reichswehr has revolted and is ready to march on Berlin behind Hitler . . . the Reichswehr is marching on Munich to crush this putsch just as it crushed the communist attempt in Hamburg last month . . . Hitler is in complete control of Munich and its armed forces . . . support for the putsch is eroding among some police units and the young army officers . . .

Karl chased each rumor, trying to learn the truth, but truth seemed to be an elusive commodity in Munich. He shuttled back and forth across the Isar River, between the putsch headquarters in the Burgerbraukeller on the east bank and the government offices around Marianplatz on the west, his right hand thrust into his coat pocket, clutching the pistol, searching for Hitler. He and Ernst had separated, figuring that two searchers could cover more ground apart than together.

By noon Karl began to get the feeling that Hitler might not have as much control as he wished people to think. True, the putschists seemed to have an iron grip on the city east of the river, and a swastika flag still flew from a balcony of the New City Hall on the west side, but Karl had noticed the green uni-forms of the Bavarian State Police gathering at the west ends of the bridges across the Isar. They weren't blocking traffic, but they seemed to be on guard. And Reichswehr troops from the Seventh Division were moving through the city. Reichswehr headquarters on the west bank was still held by the Reichskriegsflagge units of the Kampfbund, but the headquarters itself was now surrounded by two Reichswehr infantry battalions and a number of artillery units.

The tide is turning, Karl thought with grim satisfaction.

Maybe he wouldn't have to use the pistol after all.

He was standing on the west side of the Ludwig Bridge, keeping his back to the wind, when he saw Ernst hurrying toward him from the far side.

"They're coming this way!" Ernst shouted, his cheeks red with the excitement and the cold.

"Who?"

"Everyone! All the putschists—thousands of them. They've begun a march through the city. And Hitler's leading them."

No sooner had Ernst spoken than Karl spied the front ranks of the march—brown-shirted Nazis carrying their red-and-white flags that whipped and snapped in the wind. Behind them came the rest, walking twelve abreast, headed directly toward the Ludwig Bridge. He spotted Hitler in the front ranks, wearing his tan trench coat and a felt hat. Beside him was General Ludendorf, one of the most respected war heroes in the nation.

A crowd of putsch supporters and the merely curious gathered as the Green Police hurried across to the east side of the bridge to stop the marchers. Before they could set up, squads of storm troopers swarmed from the flanks of the march, surrounding and disarming them.

The march surged across the bridge unimpeded.

Karl tightened his grip on the pistol. He would end this here, now, personal consequences be damned. But he couldn't get a clear view of Hitler through the throng surrounding him. To his dismay, many bystanders from the crowd joined the march as it passed, further swelling its ranks.

The march streamed into the already-crowded Marianplatz, in front of City Hall, where it was met with cheers and cries of adulation by the thousands mobbed there. A delirious rendition of "Deutschland Über Alles" rattled the windows all around the plaza and ended with countless cries of "Heil Hitler!"

At no time could Karl get within a hundred yards of his target.

And now, its ranks doubled, the march was off again, this time northward up Wienstrasse.

"They're heading for Reichswehr headquarters," Ernst said.

"It's surrounded," Karl said. "They'll never get near it."

"Who's going to stop them?" Ernst said. "Who's going to fire on them with General Ludendorf at Hitler's side and all those civilians with them?"

Karl felt his jaw muscles bunch as the memory of the vision surged through his brain, dragging with it the image of his elderly, withered, unclothed, bleeding mother.

"I am."

He took off at a run along a course parallel to the march, easily outdistancing the slow-moving crowd. He calculated that the marchers would have to come up Residenzstrasse in order to reach the Reichswehr building. He ducked into a doorway of the Feldherrnhalle, near the top of the street, and crouched there, panting from the unaccustomed exertion. Seconds later, Ernst joined him, barely breathing hard.

"You didn't have to come," Karl told him.

"Of course I did. We're witnessing the making of history."

Karl pulled the pistol from his coat pocket. "But after today someone other than Adolf Hitler will be making it."

At the top of Residenzstrasse, where it opened into a plaza, Karl saw units of the Green Police setting up a barricade.

Good. The march would have to slow as it approached the barricade, and that would be his moment.

"Here they come," Ernst said.

Karl's palms began to sweat as he searched the front ranks for his target. The pistol grip was slippery in his hand by the time he identified Hitler. This was it. This was his moment in history, to turn it from the horrors the vision had shown him.

Doubt gripped the base of his throat in a stranglehold. What if the vision was wrong? What if it had been the absinthe and nothing more? What if he was about to murder a man because of a drunken hallucination?

He tore free of the questions. *No. No doubts. No hesitation. Hitler has to die. Here. Now. By my hand.*

As he'd predicted, the march slowed as it neared the barricade, and the storm troopers approached the Green Police shouting, "Don't shoot! We are your comrades! We have General Ludendorf with us!"

Karl raised the pistol, waiting for his chance.

And then a passage opened between him and Hitler's trench-coated form.

Now! It has to be now!

He took aim, cautiously, carefully. He wasn't experienced with pistols. His father had taken him hunting with a rifle or a shotgun as a young man, but he'd never found much pleasure in it. He found no pleasure in this, only duty. But he knew how to aim, and he had the heart of this strutting little monster in his sights. He remembered his father's words . . . "Squeeze, don't pull . . . *squeeze* . . . be surprised by the shot . . ."

And while Karl waited for his surprise, he imagined the tapered lead cylinder blasting from the muzzle, hurtling toward Hitler, plunging into his chest, tearing through lung and heart, ripping the life from him before he could destroy the lives of the hapless, helpless, innocent millions he so hated. He saw Hitler twist and fall, saw a brief, violent spasm of rage and confusion as the milling putschists

fired wildly in all directions, rioting until the Green Police
and the regular army units closed in to divide their ranks,
arrest their leaders, and disperse the rest. Perhaps another
Jew hater would rise, but he would not have this man's
unique combination of personal magnetism and oratory
power. The future Karl had seen would never happen. His
bullet would sever the link from this time and place to that
future.

And so he let his sweat-slick forefinger caress the curve
of the trigger . . . *squeezing* . . .

But just as the weapon fired, something brushed against
his arm. The bullet coughed into the chill air, high, missing
Hitler.

Time stopped. The marchers stood frozen, some in mid-
stride. All except for Hitler. His head was turned Karl's way,
his pale blue eyes searching the doorways, the windows.
And then those eyes fixed on Karl's. The two men stared at
each other for an instant, an eternity . . . then . . . Hitler
smiled.

And with that smile time resumed its course as Karl's
single shot precipitated a barrage of gunfire from the Green
Police and the Kampfbund troops. Suddenly there was chaos
on Residenzstrasse. Karl watched in horror as people ran in
all directions, screaming, bleeding, falling, and dying. The
pavement became red and slick with blood. He saw Hitler go
down and stay down. He prayed that someone else's bullet
had found him.

Finally the shooting stopped. The guns were silent, but the
air remained filled with the cries of the wounded. To Karl's
shock he saw Hitler struggle to his feet and flee along the sidewalk, holding his arm. Before Karl could gather his wits and
take aim again with his pistol, Hitler had jumped into a yellow
Opel sedan, which sped him away.

Karl added his own shouts to those of the wounded. He
turned to Ernst.

"It was you! Why did you hit my arm? I had him in my sights, and you . . . you made me miss!"

"Terribly sorry," Ernst said, avidly scanning the carnage on the street before them. "It was an accident. I was leaning over for a look and lost my balance. Not to worry. I think you accomplished your goal: This putsch is over."

The Munich putsch definitely eliminates
Hitler and his National Socialist followers.
New York Times, **November 9, 1923**

Karl was overjoyed when Adolf Hitler was captured by the Green Police two days later, charged with high treason, and thrown into jail. His National Socialist Party was disbanded and declared illegal. Adolf Hitler had lost his political firmament, his freedom, and, because he was an Austrian, there even was a good possibility he would be deported after his trial.

While waiting for the trial, Karl reopened his bookstore and tried to get back into a normal routine in Berlin. But the vision and the specter of Adolf Hitler haunted him. Hitler was still alive, might still wreak the horrors Karl had seen. He hungered for the trial, to see Hitler humiliated, sentenced to a minimum of twenty years, or deported, or best yet: shot as a traitor.

He saw less and less of Ernst during the months leading to the trial. Ernst seemed bored with Berlin. New, gold-backed marks had brought inflation under control, the new government seemed stable, there were no new putsches in the works . . . life was far less "entertaining."

They met up again in Munich on the day of Hitler's sentencing. Like the trial, the sentencing was being held in the main lecture hall of the old Infantry School because the city's regular courtrooms could not accommodate the huge crowds. Karl had been unable to arrange a seat inside; nor, apparently, had Ernst. Both had to be content to stand outside under the bright midday sky and wait for the news along with the rest of their fellow citizens.

"I can't say I'm surprised to see you here," Ernst said, as they shook hands.

"Nor I you. I suppose you find all this amusing."

"Quite." He pointed with his cane. "My, my. Look at all the people."

Karl had already studied them, and they upset him. Thousands of Germans from all over the country swarmed around the large brick building, trying in vain to get into the courtroom. Two battalions of Green Police were stationed behind barbed-wire barriers to keep the crowds at bay. During the twenty-five days of the trial, Karl had moved among them and had been horrified at how many spoke of Hitler in the hushed tones of adoration reserved for royalty, or a god.

Today the women had brought bouquets of flowers for Hitler, and almost everyone in the huge throng was wearing ribbons of red, white, and black—the Nazi colors.

"He's a national figure now," Ernst said. "Before the putsch no one had ever heard of him. Now his name is known all over the world."

"And that name will soon be in jail," Karl said vehemently.

"Undoubtedly. But he's made excellent use of the trial as a national soapbox."

Karl shook his head. He could not understand why the judges had allowed Hitler to speak at such length from the witness box. For days—*weeks*—he went on, receiving standing ovations in the courtroom, while reporters transcribed his words and published them for the whole country to read.

"But today it comes to an end. Even as we speak, his sentence is being pronounced. Today Adolf Hitler goes to prison for a long, long time. Even better: Today he is deported to Austria."

"Jail, yes," Ernst said. "But I wouldn't count on deportation. He is, after all, a decorated veteran of the German Army, and I do believe the judges are more than a little cowed by the show of support he has received here and in the rest of the country."

Suddenly there were shouts from those of the huge crowd nearest the building, followed by wild cheering as word of the sentencing was passed down: five years in Landau Prison . . . but eligible for parole in six months.

"Six months!" Karl shouted. "No, this can't be! He's guilty of treason! He tried to overthrow the government!"

"Hush, Karl," Ernst said. "You're attracting attention."

"I will *not* be silenced!" Karl shouted. "The people have to know!"

"Not these people, Karl."

Karl raised his arms to the circle of grim faces that had closed about him. "Listen to me! Adolf Hitler is a monster! They should lock him up in the deepest darkest hole and throw away the key! He—"

Sudden agony convulsed through his back as someone behind him rammed a fist into his right kidney. As Karl staggered forward another man with wild, furious eyes and bared teeth punched him in the face. He slumped to the ground with cries of "Communist!" and "Jew!" filling his ears. The circle closed about him, and the sky was shut out by enraged, merciless faces as heavy boots began to kick at his back and belly and head.

Karl was losing his last grip on consciousness when the blows suddenly stopped and there was blue sky above him again.

Through blurry eyes he saw Ernst leaning over him, shaking his head in dismay.

"Good God, man! Do you have a death wish? You'd be

a bloody pulp now if I hadn't brought the police to your aid!"

Painfully, Karl raised himself on one elbow and spit blood. Scenes from the dark vision began flashing before his eyes.

"It's going to happen!" he sobbed.

He felt utterly alone, thoroughly defeated. Hitler had a national following now. He'd be back on the streets and in the beer halls in six months, spreading his hatred. This trial wasn't the end of him—it was only the beginning. It had catapulted him into the national spotlight. He was on his way. He was going to take over.

And the vision would become reality.

"Damn you, Ernst! Why did you have to knock off my aim?"

"I told you, Karl. It was an accident."

"Really?" During the months since that cold fall day, Karl's thoughts had returned often to the perfectly timed nudge that had made him miss. "I wonder about that 'accident,' Ernst. I can't escape the feeling that you did it on purpose."

Ernst's face tightened as he rose and stood towering over Karl.

"Believe what you will, Karl. But I can't say I'm sorry. I, for one, am convinced that the next decade or two will be far more entertaining *with* Herr Hitler than without him." His smile was cold, but his eyes were bright with anticipation. "I am rather looking forward to the years to come. Aren't you?"

Karl tried to answer, but the words would not come. If only Ernst knew . . .

Then he saw the gleam in Ernst's eyes and the possibility struck Karl like a hobnailed boot: Perhaps Ernst *does* know.

Ernst touched the brim of his hat with the silver head of

his cane. "If you will excuse me now, Karl, I really must be off. I'm meeting a friend—a new friend—for a drink."

He turned and walked away, blending with the ever-growing crowd of red and white, black and brown.

1930

1931

1932

1933

1934

1935

1936

1937

1938

1939

TRIADS

BY POPPY Z. BRITE
AND CHRISTA FAUST

—*For Su Wei*

What a riot of brilliant purple and tender crimson,
Among the ruined wells and crumbling walls.

—Tsao Hsueh-Chin,
"A Dream of Red Mansions"

Backstage at the Lucky Dragon Theater, the air was thick with the smell of greasepaint and incense and the sweat of young boys. Small warriors in richly embroidered red-and-gold jackets crowded before fragments of mirror, painting lips and smooth-lidded eyes with long brushes. Pairs took turns stretching each other's muscles in the complex and painful positions that prepared their bodies for the rigors of Peking Opera. Thighs made fluid 360-degree rotations in hip sockets; spines bent backward like grasses in a wind. An older boy, fourteen or so, hooked a long white beard over his ears and struck an arthritic pose, his pleated sleeves quivering.

Against the far wall, a boy in an iridescent green-and-silver tunic squatted with his arms crossed. He was tall for his age and broad-shouldered, with bony wrists and wide, expressive hands. The angles of his painted face were strong and lean, and might have been considered harsh if not for a pair of comically large ears that stuck out like the handles on a jug.

He tipped his head back against the splintery wall and drew in a slow breath. His body felt as tight as a finely tuned string waiting to be plucked. The wet ribbon tied across his forehead was beginning to dry beneath his peaked cap, tightening the skin above his eyes until it was impossible to blink. After an hour or two, it dried out his eyeballs to the point of agony.

But the burning of his eyes and the hot itch of his skin beneath the makeup were familiar torments. After eight years, these were no more noticeable than the ache in his empty belly or the endless pain inflicted by his daily routine of punishing exercise.

"Ji Fung."

The soft voice pulled him from the well of mindless contemplation. He looked up into the wide painted eyes of his best friend, Lin Bai, in the white-and-silver robes of the seductive White Snake.

In full dress, Lin Bai was transformed from an unusually pretty boy to a vision of beauty that disturbed Ji Fung every time he saw it. Seeing his friend's familiar face eclipsed by fantasy made Ji Fung's belly boil with a stew of contradictory emotions. He would recall the long hungry nights when he and Lin Bai had huddled close under their thin blankets, whispering small dreams and secrets in the cavernous silence of the dormitory hall.

Master Lau was old-fashioned and still believed that real women were bad luck onstage. He had given Lin Bai his name, which meant *hidden lotus*, more like a girl's name. And Lin Bai was brilliant in the roles of pretend women. He played female warriors like Mu Lan and tragic heroines like Chu Ying-tai with equal finesse. Ji Fung's own broad chest and natural acrobatic dexterity conspired with his mediocre singing voice to keep him in the grueling roles of soldiers and other sword fodder.

Lin Bai was born to play the leads. He possessed the grace of a swallow, the flagrant lushness of a full-blown orchid, the cool beauty of white jade. His voice was plangent and full of color. He had already struck sparks of competition in stars ten years his senior. His fellow students despised him as a cosseted lapdog, the Master's favorite, who had a mouthful of hot rice even when everyone else went hungry. Ji Fung was his only friend.

"Help me with my banners." Lin Bai's cherry mouth turned up slightly at one corner.

Ji Fung took the padded harness with its four white banners, motioning for Lin Bai to turn around. Lin Bai obeyed silently, head down; he knew how to take an order. Ji Fung pulled the straps across his friend's narrow chest and knotted them tight, tugging lightly to make certain they would hold. Lin Bai shook his upper body, testing. The silver embroidery flashed as the four banners fluttered like wings.

Lin Bai smiled, and Ji Fung felt suddenly hot and cold at once. He turned away.

Dusty purple curtains at the far end of the dressing room parted, and Master Lau strode into the midst of the bright chaos. The boys' musical chatter died.

"Enough playing around!" The Master's heavy eyebrows dipped low over his eyes, then shot up alarmingly. He was a tall man, well muscled, with a sensuous mouth that seemed misplaced beneath his blade of a nose and sharp, stony eyes. Displeasure in those eyes was every boy's nightmare, for the Master's punishments were dispensed often and without warning. Ji Fung had known them all: forced to dance and somersault until his ligaments screamed in agony; made to bend over and count off the strokes as his tender bottom was caned raw; ordered to balance on his hands so long that he could not unbend his wrists for hours afterward.

The Master was their teacher, their father, and their god. They longed for his rare praise and lived in terror of his disapproval. Many could not imagine their lives without him.

"The performance is beginning," said the Master. "No mistakes."

The boys lined up for inspection. Master Lau walked down the row, critical eyes burning through his young charges. Here, a crooked pompon on a headdress earned a cruel ear twist; there, an imperfectly painted face brought a stinging slap to the back of a neck. The Master passed over Ji Fung and the other bit players with little more than a nod, but he stood before Lin Bai for nearly a full minute, glaring at him as if he could see through cloth and flesh and into the ruby depths of the boy's beating heart. Lin Bai would not meet his Master's gaze. His female garb and the demure cast of his eyes made him seem coy. Only Ji Fung knew him well enough to read the hatred in his stiff spine and taut jaw.

Lin Bai loathed Master Lau with a vehemence Ji Fung had never fully fathomed. Ji Fung knew what it was to curse the Master in his heart while he bit back tears under the sting of the rattan cane, or during the long hours spent motionless in a single excruciating position. But Lin Bai's hate was different, deeper, a thing he hid inside himself like a sharp-edged crystal treasure, a dark pupa whose final shape could not be guessed. There was a peculiar intensity in the air between the Master and his star pupil that made Ji Fung feel weak and sick, yet fiercely protective of his friend.

"Good," Master Lau said suddenly, and then the music began to wail, and it was time to slip into that other world.

The audience was nearly empty. Nothing but small clusters of gray heads and fidgeting children. As Ji Fung stood in the wings, he found himself wishing he were one of those children. A small boy whose mother and father sat on either side of him in the stuffy red-and-gold theater. A boy who would go home to sweets and a soft bed, not a small bowl of rice and a crowded dormitory.

He had been a boy like that, in another life. Somewhere in him was a barely remembered dream of a fine house and a smiling *amah*. Of silver toys that wound up and a little black dog with the softest fur. Of family, uncles and aunts and cousins; rich noisy banquets full of laughter and strange tales.

But Ji Fung was too old to long for the mindless comforts of childhood. And if he let his mind wander too far down those old paths, he knew he would end up at the terrible crossroads of the night he had been taken from his home forever.

Back then he had just been called Ji, or son. He had another name that was much longer and finer, but at home it was Ji; sometimes Siu Ji, or little son. But on that night everything had been taken from him, even his true name.

His mother's desperate hands had dragged him up from uneasy sleep. She had put him to bed a few hours earlier with no supper, ignoring his cries for his *amah* and the steamed lotus buns he loved. Now she was shaking him awake and buttoning him into a plain cotton jacket. She wore a dull blue tunic and loose trousers, her shining hair coiled at the nape of her neck, her pale face scrubbed clean of makeup. She looked like a servant, not the first wife of a rich and powerful man.

Ji had known, in the way children know without understanding, that something was terribly wrong. He felt sick to the bone and sure the world was ending. His mother had not spoken more than a handful of words to him in his seven years of life. Now she was calling him *good boy* and *little man* while she stared past him into nothing. Her eyes shone in the darkness like moonlight on treacherous water.

When he was able to speak, he cried softly for his father. Father always had time for him, brought him presents from Macao and Shanghai, would make important business associates wait while thoughtfully considering a scraped knee or a broken toy. Yes, Father spoiled his only son, but never to the point of helplessness, for sons must grow strong and brilliant. Ji would sit behind that desk one day, would understand the mysterious transactions his father engineered, would engineer them himself.

Already Father had presented him with his own name

chop, a carved seal of jade Ji kept with him always. It was in his sweating hand now, snatched from under his pillow as he woke, its cool angles and tiny characters as familiar and soothing as his father's voice. If he could only see his father now, the night would lose this skewed sense of menace.

But when he called out, his mother turned away. Her spine was stiff and strange.

"Never speak of your father again," she said.

The hatred in her voice paralyzed him like spider's venom. Ji knew then that the world had already ended.

She led him through the still house, moving wraithlike through the long, silent hallways. Their cloth slippers made no sound on the heavy rugs and polished marble floors. He asked where they were going, but she did not answer. He asked for Second Mother and his little half sisters. For Third Mother with her big round belly and placid eyes. For his *amah*. For the houseboy with the broad chest and strong arms. For anyone who might be able to stop Siu Ji from sliding out of control down a slick incline, toward some unfathomable future. But his mother would not answer any of his cries. She only twisted his arm and made him walk faster.

Moving through the dark kitchen, he saw the forms of his *amah* and the cook curled on the floor by the stove. His *amah*'s head was haloed with shiny black fluid on the clean while tile. The air was stale with old food and smelled faintly of vomit.

"*Amah*," he called, straining toward the crumpled body.

His mother shushed him. "*Amah* is sleeping. She is very tired." She looked away. "Everyone is very tired. We must be quiet, and not wake them."

Ji tried to look back as she dragged him through the servants' entrance, but it was too dark, and the door swung closed too quickly behind them.

They walked all night, taking a twisted, nonsensical route through the streets, down dark alleys reeking of fish guts and urine. They slipped unnoticed through staggering battalions of foreign sailors with ruddy faces and foul drunken breath. When they passed an open noodle shop, bright and crowded behind glass windows opaque with steam, Ji tried to pull his mother toward the good doughy smell. He was faint with hunger now, but she would not turn aside.

The Hong Kong night was a collage of images, horrific and fantastic. He saw hollow-eyed prostitutes flaunting shrunken breasts, and beggar children licking the blood of slaughtered chickens from the filthy pavement outside a charnel house. He saw lurid neon reflected in the glossy black skins of long automobiles carrying millionaire tai-pans and their exotic red-haired women. Glamour and squalor lay belly to back, intimate as lovers.

For Ji, seven years old and exhausted, it was brutal sensory overload. He clutched his jade chop until its edges dug into his palm, resolving not to cry, not to *see*, to blindly put one foot in front of the other until this incomprehensible journey was over. Perhaps he was still dreaming in his own bed, and his *amah* would soon wake him with a bowl of hot rice porridge.

Foul toothless mouths muttered close to him, but he would not look up to see their owners. Glittering light danced temptingly in the corners of his eyes, but he would not turn to see its sources. He saw only his own feet, clad in rough-stitched peasant shoes. Black cloth shoes, worn around the edges, shuffling over greasy cobblestones. One step after the other and his mother's hand like a mouthful of sharp teeth around his own, never letting him slow down. His room, his bed seemed impossibly far away. Perhaps there had never been anything but this endless walking. Perhaps his whole life had been a dream, the invention of a wandering mind while his body plodded on.

He began to gray out, his consciousness coming slowly untethered, and he might have gone forever if his toe had not struck something stiff but yielding. His vision snapped back to razor clarity.

There was a dead girl in the alley before him, half-hidden behind stinking bins of garbage. She was almost pretty, her little hands curled like seashells. Her long graceful neck parted in a wet red smile. Her bloodstained Western-style dress was rucked up over her hips. To Ji's childish eyes, the pink folds of her exposed and battered labia looked like some dreadful mutilation, a wound far worse than the one in her throat, a deep cut that could never heal. He hitched in a great shuddering sob.

If his mother had slapped him or ordered him to be quiet, he might have been able to keep loving her. But she only stared at him without seeing, lost in some private hell where the terror and sorrow of her only child was no more important than the buzzing of the flies in the garbage bins. The blankness in her face was so terrible, so unforgivable that Ji's tears died inside him, leaving a coldness so deep that it would never quite thaw again.

They arrived at the Hong Kong Opera School as dawn was bleeding into the deep blue sky. At the gate, his mother paused and laid her hands on his trembling shoulders. Since she had pulled him up from sleep, Ji had been wishing for her to look at him, to acknowledge him in some way. But now that she fixed her burning eyes on his, he was more afraid than he had ever been.

"Your new name is Wang Ji Fung," she said. Her voice was devoid of emotion. "Your father was Wang Sau. He pulled a rickshaw, but he died. Say it."

He repeated the lie, not understanding but terrified of making a mistake. *Fung* was *phoenix*. His new name meant *phoenix son*.

"If you ever tell anyone your real name, bad men will come and cut out your tongue. Do you understand, Wang Ji Fung?"

He pictured hard-faced men in dark suits coming after

him with oily black guns and knives as sharp and cruel as their eyes. He nodded. His terror was huge and pure.

The sun broke red over the horizon. With it came an eerie lilting keen, high and strong, echoing off the mossy stone walls of the main school building. It was a sound that would define his life for the next eight years: the sound of young boys singing their morning exercises. It gave him a sick precognitive chill that brought cold sweat to his shivering skin.

In a shadowy office, he stood still and silent beside his mother as Master Lau read the contract aloud. Ji came to understand that he would belong to this man for the next ten years, a raw bit of property the Master would endeavor to polish and make valuable. He would receive food, shelter, and training, and if he disobeyed, he could be beaten to death.

The newly born Wang Ji Fung felt nothing but coldness as his mother pressed her thumb into the sticky black ink and set her mark on the bottom of the page. She knew how to write the characters of her own name perfectly well, but he supposed she was pretending to be the illiterate widow of a poor rickshaw puller.

She bowed her head and turned to her son. Ji Fung felt those bleak, hot eyes settle on him again.

"Never forget what you have been told," she said.

He watched her as she walked away, her shoulders set beneath the cheap blue tunic. He tried to memorize the wisps of ebony hair against her pale neck, her delicate wrists, the proud set of her spine. He thought of running after her, of hurling himself onto her back and smashing her fragile skull against the cold stone floor. Instead, he looked away. That was the last time he ever saw her.

"Dreaming of your dinner?"

Lin Bai tweaked Ji Fung's earlobe. "Pay attention. If you miss your cue, Master will take it out of you later."

Ji Fung was about to answer, but Lin Bai heard his own cue, bowed quickly to the opera gods, and swirled away, small feminine steps carrying him onstage. Ji Fung and the other boys in White Snake's army of sea creatures poured out behind him in tight formation, and the battle began.

Ji Fung tried to lose himself in the dullness of routine. He knew the moments and motions of this story so well. Forward and back, tassel shake and spear flash, flip in the air and land on his feet, mirroring his three partners. But in his mind he saw himself truly fighting for the honor of his love, Lin Bai in White Snake's garb. He imagined slitting open the bellies of the rival soldiers, slashing off the head of White Snake's unworthy husband, who rejected her love and conspired to destroy her. He imagined bringing the severed head to White Snake and being rewarded with a deep, warm kiss.

This thought coiled around his spine, hot and distracting. As his opponent struck a wide, dramatic death blow, Ji Fung's balance wavered, skewing his backward somersault, making him land hard and slightly off center. Pain shot through his left arm, but he recovered flawlessly, following through with a series of flips that carried him offstage.

Leaning against the splintery wall, Ji Fung rubbed his sore shoulder and watched Lin Bai battle the others. Spears flew and twirled like so many straws. The deep tragedy in the curve of Lin Bai's shoulders and graceful hands always broke Ji Fung's heart a little. Anyone could see that White Snake didn't want to fight, that she still loved her husband in spite of his betrayal, and that this futile love only increased her pain.

Ji Fung felt that strange protectiveness welling up in him again, as if it were not an ancient female character but Lin Bai himself who had been so betrayed. He tried to push it down inside himself, as always. But each time it was a little harder to push down.

Later, Ji Fung knelt before a basin of greasy water, rinsing the paint from his stinging skin. Around him, naked boys gathered up armfuls of discarded costumes and carefully folded them into trunks of scented wood. Weapons were gathered and wrapped in soft cotton, pots of paint stacked in lacquer boxes. When everyone was scrubbed and dressed in plain gray uniforms, they lined up and waited for their Master.

It was an hour before he finally arrived, his jaw tight, his eyes squeezed down to thin slits. He stood for a long time staring at the line of boys. Then he turned away.

"Tonight's performance was our last here at the Lucky Dragon." Master Lau spoke to the wall, his body still as stone. "Mr. Sung tells me he will have no more Peking Opera." His chin trembled, barely perceptible. "From now on, jazz music only."

The students were silent, eyes down. Ji Fung felt as if he had taken a hard blow to the sternum, the kind you sometimes got when you landed badly and hit a piece of scenery or another boy's knee. He wondered what would become of him now. His ten years were nearly up, and the Opera was all he knew. He had always assumed he would join a troupe and spend the rest of his life performing. What other choice did he have, and if this was no longer a choice, had his body and soul been sold to a dying art?

But this thought was too vast and slippery to hold. It was much easier to walk the familiar streets that led back to the school, Lin Bai in step before him and another boy behind, all helping to carry their prop trunks like ants with a heavy load. Ji Fung calmed himself by staring at the back of Lin Bai's neck, at the silky blue-black stubble hugging the vulnerable curve of his skull. He tried to make his mind as blank as the pale gray sky.

Back in the darkened dormitory, the two lay on their narrow cots, close but barely touching. All around them, boys were rustling, sighing, settling into sleep. Lin Bai's and Ji Fung's cots were pushed together in one corner of the big common room, up against the stones of the wall. This spot was cold and dank, but afforded them a small measure of privacy.

"No more performances at the Lucky Dragon," Ji Fung whispered. He still could not get used to the idea; the musty smell of the old theater and its dank backstage area were as familiar to him as the sagging frame of his own cot. "Hard to believe. Maybe that dragon's not so lucky after all."

Lin Bai nodded. "People would rather go to the cinema." His voice grew soft and dreamy. "See films made in America. In Hollywood."

The name meant nothing to Ji Fung. It was simply a foreign-sounding word.

Lin Bai reached under the thin pad of his mattress and pulled out a tattered magazine. His delicate fingers were reverent on the slick sweat-stained cover. Ji Fung could barely make out the image of a pale-haired woman in a tight dress that pushed her breasts up under her chin and nipped her waist down to the size of a spider's. He wondered how she could breathe. The words on the cover were loopy and incomprehensible.

"One day I'll go there," Lin Bai said. "To Hollywood. I'm tired of boring old Chinese operas. The same stories over and over. I'll go to America and become a famous film star."

He slid down in the bed and pulled Ji Fung after him, yanking the covers up over their heads. Ji Fung was acutely conscious of Lin Bai's body warmth mingling with his own, of Lin Bai's bony shoulder and hip touching his.

"We'll go together," Lin Bai whispered. "We'll be action heroes. Partners. We'll fight cowboys and gangsters and ride in automobiles and drink fine champagne."

"Sham-peh-yin? What's that?"

"I'm not sure," Lin Bai admitted, "but all the film stars drink it. It must be very sweet."

"Yes, yes," Ji Fung said, warming to the fantasy. "We'll wear leather shoes and grow our hair long. We'll lie in bed all morning, and a servant will bring us champagne and cakes."

"People will cry when they see us perform." Lin Bai giggled. "We'll hide in the theater and watch our faces ten feet high on the silver screen. We'll watch the people watching us and see how their intestines are tied into a hundred knots by our brilliance."

"And Master Lau will be sorry to have lost such fine actors."

There was a short, loaded silence. When Lin Bai spoke, his voice was full of a dark poison, a hatred as lethal as ground glass.

"Master Lau will be dead."

The silence grew, hot with unspoken truths and the boys' breath beneath the covers.

"The Master has not called you tonight." Ji Fung's voice was soft, on the verge of breaking. He was terrified to speak of this. Never before had he mentioned Lin Bai's nightly lessons alone in the Master's room. It was the source of much speculation and cruel innuendo among the other boys: since Lin Bai was so good at playing a woman onstage, perhaps he also played one in the Master's bed.

More silence, like an organic, malignant blackness between them. Ji Fung expected Lin Bai to turn away angrily, lost in his secret hurt. He wished for a way to call back his thoughtless words, to offer Lin Bai some meager comfort, some shelter from his internal storms.

Then, out of the dark, came the softest sound. A sound that obliterated the gulf between them, made the scant space separating their bodies crawl with strange heat. It was the low, broken whisper of tears.

Ji Fung hardly dared to breathe. His wrist lay against the curve of Lin Bai's shoulder, and he was excruciatingly aware of this tiny contact. He felt Lin Bai's body shudder with stifled sobs, and thought of White Snake weeping for the death of her heartless husband. Ji Fung realized that what he really wanted was to take Lin Bai in his arms and kiss the tears from his face, to protect him from the Master and all the world, but most of all from the fierce pain devouring him from the inside out. This realization brought hot blood rushing to Ji Fung's cheeks and his stiffening penis.

He pulled his wrist away, rolled his body away. His heart hammered wildly. He wanted to jump up and run outside, bathe his body in the cool wet nighttime air, anything to escape this hot cave of blankets and shame and the intoxicating scent of Lin Bai's body. He felt as if he might drown in the heady hormonal stew raging inside.

He almost broke loose, almost got up. Then Lin Bai's bony little hand curled itself around his, and Lin Bai whispered, "Don't go."

And then he brought Ji Fung's fingers to his lips, those cynical, vulnerable pink lips still stained cherry red at the corners. Ji Fung let himself be drawn down into an awkward embrace that felt like falling off a mountain, like stepping into a languorous dream. Like coming home.

Lin Bai's skin beneath the coarse cloth of his pajamas was so fine and soft that Ji Fung felt sure he must be bruising it with his rough clutching hands, but he could not stop himself. He was no longer aware of the other boys in the room around them, no longer cared whether anyone was watching. He wanted to press harder into that silken smoothness, to feel the warm, half-painful friction of Lin Bai's nakedness against his own. He wanted to crush Lin Bai's ivory bones, to tear into the vulnerable flesh of his mouth with savage starved teeth. The vicious intensity of his desire frightened and ignited him.

Lin Bai's hands were slender, callused, cool-skinned, so very gentle. They traced the muscles of Ji Fung's chest, spidered down his belly, cupped his aching penis. Ji Fung bit his own tongue to stifle a cry and began spiraling into pure pleasure.

Then the cocoon of blankets was ripped away like the fragile layer of skin covering a newly healed wound. Ji Fung felt hard fingers dig into the back of his neck. Before he knew what was happening he had been hauled out of bed and thrown against the wall. His skull hit hard, and the inside of his head shimmered with stars: red, blue, silver, like New Year's fireworks.

He barely had time to slide to the floor before he was yanked up again. As his vision cleared, Master Lau's face appeared inches from his own, disfigured with fury. Behind the Master were the rows of cots, the other boys pulling their covers over their heads, pretending not to see. Ji Fung's desire curdled in his belly, giving way to sick guilt and sharp-edged fear.

Master slammed Ji Fung against the wall again, sending tremors of agony up and down his spine. Then the unthinkable happened: Master's fist came looping down into Ji Fung's upturned face. His head filled with more glitter, and a sound like a glass bowl of fruit being smashed with a padded club.

He knew then that he was going to die. The Master had beaten Ji Fung and every other boy more times and more ways than they could count. But never did he hit a student in the face. *Your face must be as clean and pure as blank paper waiting for the ink.* This was one of the Master's countless rules, the ones he would make them recite as he burned the tender skin at the insides of their elbows with a hot iron or whipped their naked asses bloody with a bundle of twigs. Master Lau was a man of unshakable rules and routines. This was what made him a brilliant teacher. This was what terrified Ji Fung now: if the Master broke one rule, he could break any of them.

As Master Lau's grip tightened, Ji Fung's throat began to fill with thick, choking blood. His fists clenched, aching to break the hold and fight back. But an immovable block inside him forbade any resistance to the Master. His mother had handed him over to this man. He was Master Lau's property, to keep or kill.

He remembered standing behind his mother in the Master's office that chilly morning, listening to the Master's dry voice tick off the points of the contract. *If he disobeys, he will be beaten to death.*

Ji Fung felt his consciousness receding into grayness as the Master dragged him across the room and shoved him into a closet full of dirty laundry. He lay curled on his side vomiting sticky gouts of blood and rice, clutching fistfuls of rough sweat-stenched cloth. The door slammed, the lock clicked home, and Ji Fung's darkness was complete.

Lin Bai crouched against the wall, feeling the heat of a hundred eyes peering out from under blankets, crawling over him like shiny black insects, judging him with gutter words. He spread his hands over his face, knowing how weak this gesture would make him appear, but unable to bear the scourge of so many eyes. He wanted to unleash all his rage upon them, to destroy them.

But he had no power, no flammable source of anger. He had nothing but his agility and his beauty, nothing but his grace and his wiles. These were the things that had made Ji Fung love him.

His hands smelled of Ji Fung's body. Silently Lin Bai sentenced himself to a thousand torments for pulling his friend down into his own private nightmare. Master Lau's nightly ministrations were a burden he had always borne alone, a secret tattooed on the meat of his soul. Anyone who ate of that tainted meat would suffer, just as he had suffered. Just as his parents had suffered, burned to death in their tiny tea shop for the crime of bearing him. Just as the small son of his auntie had suffered, choking to death on a bit of sweet beef jerky four days after Lin Bai had come to live with them.

The day his auntie brought him to the opera school, she had called him a bad-luck child, cursed to bring pain and death upon anyone close to him. He had never wanted that to happen to Ji Fung, so he had kept his friend at arm's length, all the while aching to pull him close and never let go. Tonight his need had overwhelmed him. Now both he and Ji Fung would pay the price.

Master Lau tore Lin Bai's hands from his face, gripped the boy's jaw hard enough to abrade the skin.

"Whore," he whispered through clenched teeth.

Lin Bai's whole body trembled in anger and shame. The air around them was gravid with silent listening. Dreams of death and murder unspooled behind his eyelids, but he offered no resistance when Master dragged him away into the privacy of his studio. From these rooms the other boys might catch an odd whimper or shriek, but they would not really know what was going on behind the heavy door.

Lin Bai's thoughts beat against each other like trapped birds in the razor-wire cage of his skull. His body remained passive as always, as it had been trained to do since he was barely old enough to walk: feet together, head bowed, alone and motionless in the void of the studio, facing the man he had hated and serviced for years. His body remained passive as Master Lau bound his wrists above his head with a red silk cord, passive as Master tore away his threadbare pajamas and laid into his bare flesh with a length of soaked rattan. The pain was as familiar as breathing.

"How dare you give yourself to another man?" Master demanded. His breath was hot and harsh against the downy hairs on Lin Bai's neck, right at the juncture of his skull. He imagined Master Lau sinking his teeth into that spot and barely managed to suppress a shudder.

"Worthless gutterslut. Stinking little whore."

These insults were familiar, too, though not as comforting as the sting of the cane. On other nights, in this same scene, Lin Bai had played his role just as he played all the other roles he knew so well. *Forgive me, Master. I am not worthy of your hands' wisdom, of your cock's power.* Like a song to stretch his voice, an exercise, sounds with no meaning.

But tonight his anger burned hotter than his terror, hotter even than his shame at his reluctant desires. In his blackest moments he had to admit to himself that, sometime in the last two years, he had begun to like the way the Master touched him. Not tonight, though, not after feeling Ji Fung's heavenly hands on his hipbones, not after seeing Ji Fung's face beaten bloody. Lin Bai bit back his anger as the Master's fingers skittered over his rattan-striped flesh, into the cleft of his lacerated ass. He gnawed on his fury as the Master thrust a long blood-greased finger up into his anus.

"Did you let him inside you?" the Master hissed, his voice crawling with contempt. "Did you accept his puny little noodle? I doubt you could even feel it after mine."

Acid boiled up over Lin Bai's tongue.

"I'm not your wife," he said.

The finger slid out of his asshole too fast, a sickly scraping sensation. This weak pain was eclipsed by the sharp one of a slap to the face. He could smell himself on the Master's hand.

"I own you," the Master spat, Lin Bai's face squeezed between thumb and ass-pungent forefinger. "I created you. I carved the womanhood out of the scrawny peasant boy your aunt sold me nine years ago. You are more than my wife. You are my *possession.*"

Master Lau spun him around and wrapped a crushing forearm around his ribs, lifting his bare feet off the ground and stealing his breath. Lin Bai was struck with a wave of nauseous vulnerability as he felt the Master's fingers working to loosen his trousers. He heard the Master hawk deep in his throat, spit into a rough palm. Then, though he had known the sensation many times, he shrieked as the thick length of the Master's erection slid up inside him.

It felt like a fist punching at his intestines, like a tree trying to grow in his gut. Lost in a vortex of swirling pain and sick, guilty pleasure, Lin Bai groped for some solid emotion, something to keep him from drowning in shame and fear. He thought at once of Ji Fung, the taste of his skin, the silken-muscle feel of his hard cock pulsing between Lin Bai's palms, the sound of his skin splitting under the Master's blows.

He was certain that, afire with sex, the Master would go back to the closet and kill Ji Fung. A dark part of Lin Bai's mind even wanted to embrace this brutal logic. He was evil luck, poison, and anyone foolish enough to get close to him would die.

But bubbling up out of the chaos was a fierce new emotion, one that swallowed the desire for passive acquiescence. Born of his bottomless bitter fury, the fury he could no longer chew like a cud, this new emotion was raw and complex. And it brought with it a need to fight: against apathy, against the prison of sadistic routine. But not with random anger. Not with pointless resistance that would only earn him harsher pain, but with a single controlled act that would free him and his lover.

An icy wash of clarity drained away the last of his confusion, and Lin Bai knew what he had to do.

He arched his spine, melted his insides around the

Master's thrusting penis, and moaned as if he had found himself back in Ji Fung's arms. He threw himself into the performance with every bit of strength he had. Somewhere along the way, as always, he lost himself in the role. The pleasure he pretended became real, and he let his body work with the Master's as he would with a fellow actor. Speaking with words and without, he told the Master everything he needed to hear. Soon the Master's orgasm erupted inside him, and Lin Bai felt himself coming, too. It felt like a premonition of victory.

When the red cord that bound his wrists was undone, Lin Bai crumpled to the floor, seeming to swoon. His senses were clearer than they had ever been, and he was very aware of where they had tumbled in their passion. The Master was half-drunk on the nectar of Lin Bai's submission, and noticed nothing. But a few feet away, with the other props, was a rack of battle spears. These were richly ornamented with silk and inlay, designed as stage props, not weapons. Still, they had some heft, and the tips were sharp enough to puncture skin. Lin Bai had seen boys pricked with them more than once during practice.

As always, he kept his face averted until Master had wiped off and stuffed himself back into his trousers. Soon Master's voice came, gruff but no longer as angry as before. "Get up, woman."

Lin Bai could not see the Master, but sensed him standing close. If his judgment was even the tiniest bit off, he would die before Ji Fung tonight.

"Master," he whispered, "I am too weak to stand."

His hand crept ever so slowly toward the lowest spear, red and gold, adorned with silk pompons and a horse's tail tied on with a black ribbon.

"Help me, my husband." The word was sour bile in his mouth. He turned what he hoped were helpless, flirtatious eyes up to the Master.

The Master made a hoarse sound in his throat, the closest

he ever came to smiling. He took a step closer and bent to help his star pupil, his woman.

Lin Bai heaved out a long breath. He was filled with the ecstatic terror he always felt before trying a difficult trick onstage for the first time. This time there had been no rehearsal, and error meant his life. He knew he could carry out the necessary motion. But this was the man who had taught it to him.

The Master grabbed his wrist and yanked. Lin Bai came up fast, using the other man's motion to propel his own. His arm shot out—he had the spear—it was slicing forward, forward, toward Master Lau's shocked face. He saw the Master's hand coming up to stop it, fast as a stroke of lightning but not fast enough, reflexes dulled by sex and sadism. The tip of the spear was at Master Lau's throat, punching into the *V* of his collarbone and through the wattled skin there.

Lin Bai twisted the spear, then pulled up. The blade caught on something hard in Master's throat and snapped off. Master's hands clawed at it, pulled it out with a dreadful sucking sound, and sent it clattering away. The wound came open like a fruit or flower, edges parting cleanly, bloodless for an instant. Then there was blood everywhere, streaming down the front of Master's body, raining on Lin Bai's face. He tasted it on his lips, salty as the man's sperm.

Master Lau staggered backward, trying to hold the two halves of his neck together, failing. A wet choking sound forced its way out of his crushed larynx. The look of surprise on his face was exquisite.

Lin Bai sprang to his feet as the Master fell. He caught sight of himself in the small looking glass the Master kept over his basin. In the blue moonlight, blood glittered black on his pale face, symmetrical as makeup around his wide eyes. He struck a delicate pose, with the spear held close.

"The sun rules all heavenly beings," he sang, "but the moon can deceive it by patience and reflection."

He tossed the spear high, spinning, and twisted his bare body to catch it. The blade glittered, and the horsetail swished wildly. Lin Bai laid the spear on the floor at his feet and bowed before the corpse of his Master.

Ji Fung lay curled into himself, entombed in blackness and roaring pain. A voice twisted through his head, through his gut, whispering the same words over and over.

It's happening again.

The mindless routine of his life had been blown wide open. Beneath its sundered skin was his childhood demon of raging chaos, of huge horrible events he could not control or even understand, events that swept him along in their wake.

When the closet door swung open, he almost screamed. Hands clutched at him, tried to drag him out. He flailed at them, certain Master Lau had returned to beat him to death.

"Ji Fung!"

A spitting whisper close to his face, and a rich coppery scent. Ji Fung opened his eyes and saw Lin Bai, with dark blood splashed across his high cheekbones, streaking his pale forehead, dripping off his pointed chin. There was a sheen of madness in Lin Bai's gore-rimmed eyes that froze Ji Fung's heart. It was as if his mother's lunatic passion had returned to haunt the familiar face of his only friend, his almost-lover. He was paralyzed before this madness; it threatened to pluck him from this life and send him spinning into the past.

"We need to get out of here! *Now!*"

Ji Fung squeezed his eyes shut and shook his head. He felt his arm being yanked, but he could not move. "I want to see my father," he heard himself saying in a child's voice.

"Ji Fung . . ." Lin Bai's voice was suddenly softer, saner. He cupped his friend's face between bloody hands. "I can't leave you behind. I would die without you. If you stay here, I will stay, too, and die with you instead."

Ji Fung opened his eyes. He saw tears making crystal tracks through the congealing blood on Lin Bai's face. His body went limp and unresisting as Lin Bai slid warm arms around him and whispered the words he needed to hear more than any others.

"I love you," Lin Bai said.

The ancient armor around Ji Fung's heart shattered. He was still half-sick with terror, but he could do this. He could escape the prison of the opera school with Lin Bai at his side, could look for a new life where he had thought there was none.

He hugged back fiercely for a long moment, incapable of anything else. Then he remembered. "Wait," he said, pulling away.

Under the curious eyes of the other students, who had watched the entire scene without moving to interfere, Ji Fung raced across the dormitory to his cot. The blankets still held traces of warmth from their bodies. He touched the loose weave of the cloth for a moment, regretting the interruption.

But that interruption, and whatever hell Lin Bai lived through in the Master's studio, had given them their chance at freedom. There would be time for warm blankets and warmer caresses later, if they were lucky. Ji Fung reached beneath the thin cotton mattress and closed his fist around the jade chop. He pocketed it and ran back to Lin Bai, who was staring at his hands and smiling strangely.

"Come on. You said we had to hurry."

Lin Bai looked up, and his eyes cleared. "Yes. Let's go."

Hand in hand, urging one another through the dark passages and haunted halls, they fled the school that had been their world for more than half their lives.

The streets were alive with people. Westerners with bulbous noses and fearful pale eyes. Merchants proclaiming in song the perfection of their pears or crabs or shoes. Tough-looking boys lounging in doorways, their pockmarked faces lit orange by the glow of foreign cigarettes. Hard-eyed women offering, for a few pennies, to do things the boys had never even heard of. They ran and ran, dodging bicycles and pedicabs, becoming drunk on the night wind and freedom.

Lin Bai stopped briefly to wash the blood from his face in a marble fountain filled with carp, the big orange-gold fish that would someday grow into dragons. Ji Fung wondered whether the blood of their murdered Master would nourish these creatures or poison them.

Soon they found themselves down by the waterfront. The harbor was full of glitter, swarming with life. The junks with their strabismic eyes and the flat-bottomed sampans ranged far out into the pea green bay. The people who lived on the boats comprised their own lanternlit, floating village. They cooked sizzling fish on small stoves of charcoal, hung tattered laundry out to dry as best it could in the humid air. A girl sat on the prow of a much-repaired sampan, combing long hair that fluttered in the sea breeze. Her little brother pissed into the water, laughing.

"Where can we go?" asked Ji Fung, looking out across the water to the distant lights of Kowloon. "We know no one. We have no money."

Lin Bai smiled, struck a wide-armed pose, and sang out. His strong, clear voice carried far out over the harbor.

"It's sooooo cold!"

"Shhh," Ji Fung hushed, waving his hands. A perfect sequence from *Twice a Bride* might have gained Master Lau's approval, back in that other life, but it would do them no good here.

"The icy wind cuts like a dagger," Lin Bai chanted, eyes wide. "With stomach empty, I'm forced to be a beggar."

"Have you gone crazy?" Ji Fung glanced wildly around. "Stop singing! Someone will take you back to the school!"

"For a poor scholar, little the future holds in store. I am starved and cold. How can I endure any more?"

The boys had gained a small audience of curious faces. Ji Fung grabbed Lin Bai's hand and bowed his head.

"Sorry to be disturbing you. Suddenly my brother thinks he is an opera star!" Ji Fung tried to force a laugh, but Master Lau had squeezed his throat raw. His laughter sounded sickly, more like a choke. Their little crowd vanished, and they were alone with the sound of water lapping at the wooden flanks of a hundred boats.

"Why did you do that?" Lin Bai hissed. "They were going to give me some money."

"Stupid! They don't have any money."

"Food, then."

Ji Fung smelled the cooking odors from the sampans: sliced ginger, bubbling oil, fish so fresh and tender it would melt in the mouth. His stomach rumbled, and he wondered whether he should have let Lin Bai sing after all.

"That was very pretty," said a new voice, raspy and sneering, directly behind them.

They turned to face a boy two or three years their senior. He was thin as a dog, with cold slitted eyes, long filthy hair, and a smile like a saber cut.

"Tell me," said the boy, taking a step closer. "What other tricks can you do?"

The back of Ji Fung's neck prickled. He moved in front of Lin Bai and tried to stare the boy down, hoping he looked tougher than he felt. "Piss off," he said. "You don't want any trouble with us."

"Ai, don't scare me so." The boy's narrow smile grew wider. From the darkness behind him materialized four others, even thinner and more ragged than their leader. "Did you hear this bald-headed faggot try to threaten me?" he asked them.

Ji Fung and Lin Bai found themselves flanked on either

side by grinning boys with broken teeth and missing fingers, closing in. Ji Fung's blood was screaming, ready to fight. When two of the boys made a grab for him, he lashed out madly, loving the sensation of skin splitting beneath his knuckles. He flipped out of their reach and came back with both legs extended, catching a boy in the abdomen, feeling ribs crack as his feet connected.

For a few moments he thought he could beat them all. Then an arm slid round his neck, and the icy bite of a blade under his chin froze him, with his heart galloping in his chest.

He heard the leader's raspy voice again. "Get the pretty one."

Lin Bai clawed the eyes of one scrawny boy, landed a flying kick in another's testicles. But there were too many, and he was dragged before the leader, whose face he spat in. The leader trailed a filthy finger through the spit, licked away a stray drop near the corner of his mouth. He smiled, and in that instant Ji Fung believed this boy would kill them both.

Then suddenly there came a series of sharp pops like a string of New Year's firecrackers going off. Ji Fung felt something buzz past his shoulder, barely grazing his collarbone. The boy holding him dropped the knife and ran. A second later the others scattered, too, quick as a nest of insects frightened by footfalls. The leader threw one last evil glance over his shoulder at them as he disappeared into an alleyway.

Ji Fung swayed on his feet, nauseous and dizzy. He had been struck again in the face, and on top of the beating Master Lau had given him, his skull felt full of metal shavings. Lin Bai was beside him, and Ji Fung leaned into his friend's bony shoulder, trembling like an old man.

But Lin Bai was nudging him, gesturing at something. As Ji Fung managed to raise his head, a new voice called out. "Get in if you want to live!"

A long, sleek, dove gray sedan had pulled up in the lane

ten feet away. A shadow-shrouded figure sat in the back, beckoning to them with one hand, holding a gun as small and shiny as a toy in the other.

Lin Bai and Ji Fung didn't even have to look at each other. Sick and exhausted and utterly out of options, they headed for the long gray automobile.

The marksman wore a white Western-style suit and shiny black shoes. *Leather* shoes, Ji Fung noted. He was alarmingly pale, though his long black hair was glossy and neatly styled. His clothes, his skin, the inside of his sedan smelled at once sweet and stinging. But the strangest thing about him was his eyes. They were Chinese in shape, with lashes as long and black as Lin Bai's, but their color was a milky jade like the eyes of some predatory animal.

After ordering his chauffeur to drive on, he tucked the gun away and offered them a slim silver flask from some inner pocket. "Here, have a nip."

The boys stared at him, uncomprehending.

The young man sighed. "You *do* speak Cantonese? You didn't just tumble off a passing boat, by any chance?"

Ji Fung found his voice. "Yes, we speak Cantonese." *More clearly than you,* he thought, but did not say it. Their savior's accent was mainland, maybe Shanghaiese. And it was tinged with something even stranger, something Ji Fung could not begin to guess at.

He felt those milk-jade eyes on him and bowed his head. "In ten thousand lifetimes we could never repay you for saving our worthless lives. For this, we are forever indebted to you."

The man smirked. "A small thing, not even worth mentioning. It's a pleasure to practice my marksmanship on those urchins. And I would not have wanted the world to lose such a lovely and talented singer."

A flush crept into Lin Bai's smooth cheeks. Ji Fung was unsure whether to smile or feel jealous.

"But," the man continued, "since you *are* forever indebted to me, you might at least grant me the favor of trying my refreshment."

Again he offered the flask. Ji Fung was afraid to sully the gleaming silver surface with his grimy, bloody fingers. But Lin Bai reached out and grabbed it. He drank deep, then smiled, licked his lips, and passed the flask to Ji Fung. Emboldened by the flavor of Lin Bai's mouth on the metal, Ji Fung took a swig.

The taste went blazing down his throat, seared his stomach like a branding iron, filled his skull with translucent amber fire. He choked, coughed out a spray of saliva and stinging liquor, clapped his hands to his face in consternation, and dropped the flask. Lin Bai caught it neatly in midair.

Their savior was laughing. "Not your poison, eh?"

"Poison?" Ji Fung's stomach clenched in horror, and even Lin Bai looked alarmed.

"No, no, don't be so stupid. It's only a saying, a ridiculous American saying. That's Jack Daniel's whiskey you just drank."

Lin Bai was unable to hide the excitement in his voice. "Are you American? From Hollywood?"

"God, no." The man rolled his eyes. "Americans make good whiskey and good music, but they don't know how to live. *Especially* not in Hollywood. I am French."

Manners did not allow any show of curiosity about the obvious tinge of Chinese blood in the veins of this exotic being. The boys remained silent. Lin Bai's disappointment was almost tangible.

At last Ji Fung asked, "What can we call you?"

"My name is Pierre Jean-Luc LeBon. My friends call me Perique." His pause was laden with erotic tension. "If you want to be my friends, then call me Perique."

Lin Bai frowned. "Pei-week?"

Perique's laughter was low and, Ji Fung thought, ever so slightly cruel. "If you intend to go to Hollywood," he said, "you're going to have to work on that accent."

Perique took them to a hotel that was more like a fantasy, the corridors all blue and silver, brightly lit, ultramodern. He smuggled them through a back entrance, down hallways with carpet so lush the boys could barely keep their footing, and into a suite bigger than the Lucky Dragon's auditorium. The baroque furniture was draped with clothing of the latest cuts and fabrics, soft trousers and thin shirts and silk neckties in deep, brilliant jewel tones.

Ji Fung tried to remain aloof, suspicious of all this wealth and casual generosity. But Perique had saved their lives, and there was no way to leave without shaming him and themselves.

Besides, Lin Bai was utterly seduced. The glamour had sucked him in deep, the soft bright clothes everywhere, the novels with gilt-edged pages, the box of French chocolates Perique offered. Ji Fung could not swallow the jealousy in his throat each time Lin Bai's face lit up over some new luxury.

Perique ordered food for them, Western delicacies that were both disgusting and fantastic. Everything seemed too sweet, too soft. Ji Fung found himself longing for some noodles fried in hot oil, a meal Master Lau had always given them as a New Year's treat. Thinking of the Master reminded him of Lin Bai's crime, such a monstrous thing. Killing one's Master was as bad as murdering one's father. Ji Fung felt suddenly hunted, terrified, unable to forget. For an instant, the chocolate smeared across Lin Bai's mouth looked like blood.

But it was so difficult to remember that they were fugitives, murderers. So difficult, when Perique was constantly offering a taste of this, a sip of that, and encouraging him to feel this jacket's lining, the finest silk, and wouldn't he like to try it on? They drank champagne, which was not sweet after all, but a sharp bubbling drink that stung the roof of Ji Fung's mouth and slowed time to a languid crawl.

Soon Perique was pushing the furniture against the walls and begging the boys to perform. Ji Fung was reluctant at first, but Lin Bai needed no convincing. The sound of that clear, rich voice banished the ache in Ji Fung's throat, and he plunged in. They sang to each other, battled with curtain rods, died in each other's arms. Perique's rapt smile urged them on, and the champagne wet their throats until it seemed they could continue for hours.

As they grew more and more tipsy, the boys began to forget the words that had once seemed branded on their tongues. Perique suggested making up new words, a concept so shocking that it had them first giggling self-consciously, then trying to outdo each other in vulgarity and silliness. "Your balls are succulent as ripe kumquats—let me suck their juice," Lin Bai sang in flawless operatic tones, and Ji Fung collapsed laughing even as he realized the offer was heartfelt.

Perique played the part of a Hollywood director, making them kiss like long-separated lovers, pretending they hadn't gotten it right, making them do it again and again. Then they were naked together on Perique's bed, a cloudlike fantasy of white linens and goose-down pillows, their limbs tangled and their mouths joined, just as if they knew how to make love.

Perique was still murmuring directions, but Ji Fung scarcely heard him, scarcely heard anything but Lin Bai's breath and heartbeat. Under those watchful eyes that were somehow at once Chinese and foreign, in this place that was like nothing they had ever imagined, Ji Fung and Lin Bai finally discovered each other.

———

Ji Fung awoke to shrouded sunlight. His first thought was *It's late, the Master will kill us for sleeping so long . . .*

Then his head began to pound and a slick nausea twisted in his guts, and he remembered everything. His muscles ached; his cock felt hot and raw. Lin Bai curled asleep beside him, one familiar thing in this terrifying new world. Perique was gone, leaving behind the sweetish miasma of his various grooming products. Ji Fung slid his arm around Lin Bai's waist, hid his face in the silken curve of Lin Bai's shoulder.

Lin Bai stirred, groaned low in his throat, then shot bolt upright and stared wildly around the darkened room. His eyes met Ji Fung's, and Ji Fung saw memory seeping back in.

"Ai-yaa," said Lin Bai at last. "My head feels ready to burst."

"My *bladder* feels ready to burst. I wonder what the toilet looks like here."

"Probably carved out of jade."

"With gold fittings."

"And squares of fine silk to clean yourself."

Laughing blearily through their pain, the boys stumbled around the room, opening door after door. They found several enormous closets crammed full of Perique's clothes and shoes—Ji Fung had assumed their host's entire wardrobe was strewn around the room, but that was hardly a fraction of all he had to wear. Everything was scented with sandalwood and sharp cologne. One door swung open to reveal a claw-footed tub; behind another was a gleaming porcelain toilet.

"Almost a shame to piss in there," Ji Fung said. But the boys stood hip to hip and did so anyway, streams of urine crossing before they splashed into the clear water.

Perique returned in a rush of sugar smells and fresh sea air. He tossed his jacket across the bed and pulled the boys to him.

"It seems you've been very naughty," he said.

Ji Fung stiffened in Perique's perfumed embrace. "What do you mean?"

Perique retrieved a much-folded sheet of newspaper from his jacket and smoothed it out on the bedspread. "Look."

Ji frowned at the paper. He could feel the blood rushing to his cheeks. "Bad eyesight," he said. "You read it."

Perique looked up, realization dawning in his eyes. "You can't read, can you?"

"Of course I can." Ji Fung waved a dismissive hand. "Too much drinking last night gave me a headache. That's all."

Perique smiled and shrugged to show that he knew Ji Fung was lying, but that he was not entirely without manners.

"It says that Lau Tung Ho, Master of the Hong Kong Opera School, was murdered last night. Stabbed to death. Two pupils are missing, wanted in the murder. Their names are Lin Bai and Wang Ji Fung."

Perique turned the page and laid the paper out flat. Lin Bai sat up and leaned over Ji Fung's shoulder to look.

"Here is their picture."

It was a portrait of their class, taken a year ago by the owner of the Lucky Dragon Theater. The fugitives' heads were circled. Ji Fung stood in the back row with the tallest boys, his face a nondescript pale blur. But Master Lau had posed his star pupil at the front, and Lin Bai's fine features were instantly recognizable.

Ji Fung felt a helpless surge of anger. Lin Bai had destroyed his safe, complacent world and dragged him into this incomprehensible whirlwind of a new one. He had killed their guardian, and now they were at the mercy of this new one, Perique, who was fascinating but surely insane.

At once he realized the pettiness of his feelings. *He* was not the one who had endured nightly humiliation and rape at the hands of Master Lau. *He* was not the one who had faced the torment of all the other boys for doing something he hated. Those dubious honors belonged to Lin Bai alone.

Lin Bai had had to kill Master Lau, had done it to save Ji Fung's life as well as his own. And Lin Bai had had to run. Ji Fung had chosen to run with him, and now they were bound to each other for all time. If rotting in prison was part of their destiny, then they would rot together.

He looked up at Perique. "Are you going to turn us in?"

Perique burst out laughing. Ji Fung thought again that their new friend's laughter was not entirely kind, but now it came as a relief. "And miss more of your command performances? Don't be stupid!" He swept the newspaper away and gripped the boys' hands tightly. "I have my own habits that are, how shall we say, outside the law. They seldom extend to murder, but I'm forced to be tolerant of those who enjoy that sort of thing."

"I didn't enjoy it!" Lin Bai shouted, then clapped his free hand over his mouth.

Perique raised one perfectly shaped black brow. "It was you, Little Gift?" He was making a pun on Lin Bai's name. *Siu Lai* was *little gift*. Ji Fung had become *Jung*, or *seed*.

Lin Bai nodded, defiance and shame warring in his face.

Perique stroked Lin Bai's smooth cheek, ran a gentle hand over the stubbly growth on his head. The Master had shaved them once a week, and they had nearly seven days' growth now. "Good for you. I guessed it was Jung, but the petals of the lotus may conceal a wasp with a sharp sting, no?"

Lin Bai shrugged. His eyes were brimming, about to spill over. Ji Fung wanted to embrace him, but if Lin Bai felt sorrow for his murdered Master, he must face it alone. It should not be diluted by meaningless comfort.

"He must have been very cruel to you," Perique said. "I only want to help."

Ji couldn't restrain himself. "You don't know us—you like our looks, true, but we're nobody in your world. Why be so generous to us? Why risk trouble for yourself by helping two criminals?"

"I enjoy trouble."

"Well, but . . ." Ji Fung struggled for a way to say what he meant without robbing Perique of face. "Perhaps you are of noble birth, or an important international businessman. We are only poor actors unused to such a life. It is not right that you should endanger yourself for our sake."

"In other words," smiled Perique, "you're not going to trust me until I've told you something about myself."

Ji Fung and Lin Bai stared. Surely Perique was not, could not be Chinese. No Chinese would dream of slicing so neatly through a veil of polite obfuscation.

"I don't mind. I speak five languages, and I like talking about myself in all of them. Let's have a pot of coffee, shall we?" Perique ordered it, then pulled up a gilt armchair next to the bed. "Where to begin? I was born twenty years ago in Shanghai. My father was an artist from Paris, an adventuring madman whose talent greatly exceeded his wealth. My mother was the daughter of a rich coastal trader who owned a fleet of opium junks. I have five brothers and sisters, three living in France, two in London. I often spend summer overseas, so you're lucky to find me here now!"

The coffee arrived, rich black brew that smelled delicious but tasted bitter and strange.

"My parents are dead now. My Chinese mother left me a fortune; my French father, a dream. I was like him, he said. If the world ever ceased to amuse me, I would perish. And I believed him. So I travel the world filling my brain with the newest ideas, my stomach with the finest delicacies, and my bed with the loveliest creatures I can find."

Ji Fung looked at Lin Bai, then back at Perique. "Why both of us?"

A tinge of crimson flushed Perique's pale cheeks, but he was smiling. "I like to watch," he said.

Perique ushered the boys from the silver sedan into an alley that smelled of joss sticks and oyster shells. A woman with powder-white skin and wanton red lips stood by an unpainted metal door. Perique spoke rapidly to her in an unfamiliar language. Hearing the word *jazz*, Ji Fung guessed it was English. The woman pushed the door open and ushered them in.

The interior was dimly lit, thick with the smoke of tobacco and opium. Onstage, an exotic beauty in a white satin dress sang strange quick notes. Her voice was nimble and light, sparkling like champagne. Her skin was dark as strong tea, her brown eyes heavy-lidded, her mouth impossibly full and lush. Perique winked at her, and she smiled.

Perique led them backstage, into a tiny dressing room filled with cut flowers. The sweet, humid scent was at once refreshing and overwhelming. When the song was over, the singer came sailing in, followed by waves of applause and shouts for an encore. She kissed Perique lightly on the mouth and began speaking in that same unfamiliar language, slurred and slow.

Perique gestured at the boys as he replied. The singer nodded thoughtfully.

Perique turned back to the boys. "Lai, Jung, this is Clarise. She is going to help you prepare for the most important roles of your acting career—the roles that will save your lives."

With a slow smile, Clarise unfastened her dress and let it fall. The soft points of her breasts fell with it, for they were sewn into the bra cups of the dress. Beneath it her chest was flat, small brown nipples showing above a tightly laced corset.

"You see?" she said in Cantonese, her accent thick and lisping. "I am a boy like you."

She caressed the bulge in her silk panties.

"But it is my own secret. And now it will be your secret, too."

Ji Fung shook his head, horrified at the sight of the cruel corset, the manhood swathed in lace and silk, the idea that he could ever look like this creature. "Lin Bai plays the woman," he said. "Not me."

Perique grinned at his distress. "If the police catch you, you will be executed. Lai, too."

"But who will believe that I am a woman? It's impossible." Ji Fung grabbed his ears, tugged them out like jug handles. "Look at these! I would be the homeliest woman in China."

Perique shrugged. "Do you have a better idea?"

Ji Fung turned to Lin Bai. "Tell him! You know it isn't possible!"

Lin Bai turned his head, smiling behind his fingers.

Ji Fung jumped up. The scent of blossoms nearly sent him reeling. "You're all against me!"

"Stop fighting it," Clarise scolded softly. "You fight it, you see, no one will believe in you."

He felt Lin Bai's hand on his arm. "Don't be so upset, Ji Fung. I'd love to see you as a girl." Ji Fung let his head drop and his shoulders sag. He knew when he was defeated.

"Undress," Clarise told them. "Before you can be a woman, you must let go of the man." She held up a gleaming straight razor.

Ji Fung was halfway through the door before Perique stopped laughing long enough to gasp, "Shaving, Jung. Only shaving."

Clarise brought a basin of water, soaped the boys' legs and armpits, and scraped away the lather with her shiny blade. Afterward, they could not stop stroking their own skin, marveling at the newly silky texture.

Perique's eyebrows lifted as Clarise opened her makeup kit. "They're both so pretty. Surely they don't need that."

Clarise snorted. "Shows how much you know about being pretty." Perique looked hurt until Clarise leaned over and gave him another kiss on the mouth, not so light or quick this time.

"We can do our own makeup," Lin Bai volunteered. "We know how."

They dived into the kit, outlining their eyes with kohl, accenting their eyebrows and the hollows of their cheekbones, painting their lips, and powdering their skin. Even Clarise's stage makeup felt light and dry compared to the sludgy greasepaint they knew from school. Still, the act of decorating their features was a small comfort, something familiar in this sea of strangeness.

Lin Bai appeared to enjoy being laced into a complex corset of elastic and whalebone, but Ji Fung refused the frightening contraption. Clarise clucked her disapproval and said he would have a flapper's figure. Ji Fung didn't know what a flapper was, but he insisted on being able to breathe.

Next came brassieres with cotton padding sewn in, just a hint of swelling for Ji Fung, fuller cups for Lin Bai. The heavy false breasts looked incongruous on his slight frame, but Perique pronounced them sexy. Then slippery stockings held up by elastic bands, and Western-style dresses of bright silk, summer sky and shimmering jade. And leather shoes, high-heeled pumps that hurt to walk on, but felt wonderful when sitting still.

Finally, the crowning touch: their wigs. Clarise fussed over the possibilities, holding up one glossy shell of hair, tucking it back in its box and pulling out another, cupping the boys' chins and turning their faces this way and that. Lin Bai's face lit up when she brought out a blond bob, but Perique called it implausible. Lin Bai sulked until Perique chose him another wig in the same style, this one dark brown with brilliant reddish highlights.

For Ji Fung, the selection was harder. Clarise finally settled on a tumble of shiny black waves that fell past his shoulders and easily covered his offending ears.

When Clarise led them before a full-length mirror, Ji Fung could not believe he was looking at himself. Lin Bai was stunning, of course, as flawlessly feminine as any of his roles. But Ji Fung could not stop staring at the woman he himself had become. She was not half as beautiful as Lin Bai, but she was undoubtedly female. A little on the plain side, taller and broader in the shoulders than she ought to be. A girl who would have to settle for marriage to an older man—a widower, maybe—but a girl nonetheless. It was frightening. He felt as if part of himself, the wholly masculine part, had died back at the school with Master Lau. For the second time in his life, his identity had been erased and recreated. It made him feel lost and dizzy. He reached for Lin Bai's hand.

"Brand-new girls must have brand-new names," Perique told them. "American names, suitable for American movie stars."

He cupped Lin Bai's chin. "You will be Betty Lee."

"Betty," Lin Bai repeated as if hypnotized.

With his other hand, Perique stroked Ji Fung's powdered cheekbone. "And you will be Jenny Lee. Betty's sister."

If you ever tell anyone your real name, bad men will come and cut out your tongue. Do you understand?

"Jenny Lee," said Ji Fung, feeling the slow fear of a dream. He would not forget. He would never tell.

Two months passed. Ji Fung felt himself learning to move like a woman, like Lin Bai. They were used to spending hours each week practicing and performing together. In lieu of that, their bodies exchanged information in every other way, all the time—side by side on a crowded street, hips swaying in tandem; in the marvelous bathtub all slippery with soap and sweat; making love under Perique's hungry gaze.

One night Perique took them to The French Quarter, a posh nightclub decorated with curling vines and ornate ironwork. Perique said it was modeled after New Orleans, a beautiful city in America. He promised to take them there one day as he bought them tall crimson drinks called Hurricanes. "A hurricane is like a typhoon," Perique explained as the boys sipped the fruity concoction, "but in America they give them girls' names."

"What? Storms?"

"Yes. Perhaps this year Hurricane Betty will wipe out New Orleans!" Perique teased a lock of Lin Bai's wig round his manicured finger. Lin Bai was ravishing in a black dress that left his back exposed, plunging to the tailbone and hinting at the sweet cleft of his ass. It was all Ji Fung could do to keep from stroking that tempting length of spine, sliding a finger into that silken cleft.

Perique showed no such restraint. He scarcely touched the boys in private, but made a great show of pawing them in public. Like his style of gesture and dress, like his ostentatious displays of wealth, it was as if he were saying to the world, *Look what I have. Look what I can get away with.*

Ji Fung sipped at his Hurricane. It was sweet enough to set his teeth on edge. He found himself wishing for a champagne chaser to cut through the cloying flavors of fruit and rum. He had become used to the small vice of champagne, just as he had become used to the word itself. Perique was teaching them English, drilling them on their pronunciation until they could say, "I'm very pleased to meet you" just like proper ladies. They spent hours in the cinema and hours afterward imitating their favorite stars, struggling to pronounce names such as *Greta Garbo* and *Marlene Dietrich.*

Perique was proud of his students, who drank information

like thirsty sponges. When they wanted something, he would make them ask in English. He had even taught them to read and write it a little; Ji Fung found that he had an aptitude for the magic of words on paper. Perique was like an angel compared with the harsh master they had known before, but still there were times when Ji Fung wondered if their savior was a bit too fond of his superiority.

There were also times when he wished he had never learned English. He had been standing at the bar of a Western jazz club one night, getting a drink for Lin Bai while Perique danced with him, when a slick-haired American sneered at them and asked his stylish (but homely) companion, "Who brought the little Chinks?"

The woman's grin seemed to split her sharp face like a hatchet cut. "Perique LeBon, I'm sure."

"That boy likes to pass himself off as white, but the yellow is starting to show through."

"At least they're *girls*. You should have seen the creature he dragged in here last month . . ."

Ji Fung never mentioned this to Perique, but it stayed in the back of his mind, twisting.

Setting the empty Hurricane glass back on the table, he took a compact from the silver mesh bag in his lap and examined his face, rubbing at an imaginary smudge of eyeliner, applying an unnecessary dash of lipstick. He still could not believe the face he saw in the mirror was really his. Lin Bai saw Ji Fung gazing at himself, smirked, and poked him in the ribs with a long, red-painted nail.

As he tucked the compact away, he felt something square and smooth in the bottom of the purse. His jade name chop. He'd kept it with him since the night of their escape, but had scarcely thought of it in recent days. Now he pulled it out and turned it over and over in his hand. His head was swimming with alcohol fumes and clubland glitter, and he suddenly felt as if this small relic was the only thing linking him to his previous two lives, a seed from which he might someday regrow his true identity.

Ji Fung pressed the cool jade to his lips. Glancing around the club, he noticed the silent bartender, an impossibly tall European with long black hair, serving a pair of Chinese men in suits and black fedoras. They exuded a predatory nonchalance, and Ji Fung wondered if anyone would dare to call them Chinks.

Perique planted a liquor-scented kiss near the corner of his mouth and mumbled something about going to spend a penny, but Ji Fung could not take his eyes off the pair by the bar.

Lin Bai noticed the focus of Ji Fung's attention. "Who are they?"

"I don't know," Ji Fung said. Part of him wanted to forget about them, leave this club, take Lin Bai home and spend the night devouring his smooth, skinny body. But he could not look away. There was something familiar about these men, about the curious stiff way they held their fingers as they raised cigarettes to their lips.

One of the men spoke to the bartender, a few short explosive syllables. The bartender nodded, brought out a thick envelope from beneath the bar, and handed it over. Slipping it into an inner pocket, the man turned his head and caught Ji Fung's gaze.

Ji Fung turned away, heart rocketing, but it was too late. The man was coming over, was at their table.

"Good evening, ladies." His smile showed off a mouthful of perfect teeth, but never touched his eyes. It vanished altogether when he saw the jade chop in Ji Fung's hand.

Ji Fung tried to slip the chop back into his purse, but it was too late. The man grabbed his wrist and yanked him to his feet.

"Where did you get this?"

Blank terror flooded Ji Fung's vision. He knew now who

these men must be. They were the gangsters his mother had warned him about, the ones who would cut out his tongue if he ever told. His mind was spinning out of control, dizzy with panic. He knew he was going to lose his tongue. He could not remember what he must never tell. His name— what was that? Wang Ji Fung? Jenny Lee? Or something else entirely?

The man twisted his hand, caught the chop as it fell. "Answer me, bitch!"

But Ji Fung could not. When he felt the cold kiss of a gun against his ribs, he closed his eyes and waited to die. Instead, the two men gripped his elbows and hustled him toward the door. Dimly he heard Lin Bai shrieking syllables that might have been his name.

In a fetid alley behind the club, the man with the perfect teeth examined Ji Fung's jade chop in the meager light. His friend held Ji Fung against a slimy wooden gate, murmuring vile endearments that were more like threats of torture.

"Thief," said the first man softly, as if speaking to a lover. "Tell us how it is you came to have a precious item belonging to Gong Wa Toi."

His father's name. Ji Fung had not heard it spoken in years. All at once he remembered his mother's mad eyes on that long-ago dawn, her hot breath as she ordered him, "Never speak of your father again."

The other man loosened his grip on Ji Fung's throat. The pearl choker Perique had bought just this afternoon broke, scattering the pale spheres across the stinking mud of the alley. Ji Fung could not speak, only shake his head.

The man made a spitting sound, twined his fingers in Ji Fung's hair, and yanked. When the long black tresses came off in his hand, the expression on his face was almost comical. He tore the front of Ji Fung's dress open and cursed at the sight of the naked, boyish chest.

Of course they beat him then. Ji Fung offered no resistance, giving in to the blows just as he had once given in to Master Lau's rattan cane. When consciousness receded, he welcomed the blackness and prayed that he would never wake up.

The gods did not answer his prayer. Awareness descended bit by painful bit: a wrenching pain in his elbow, a throbbing in his kidneys, a dull ache in his right eye. He awoke to find his sore cheek pressed against the weave of a fine rug, its rich red-and-gold pattern writhing in the blurred vortex of his vision. He felt cool air on his back and thighs and realized that he was nearly naked, the expensive dress reduced to rags.

Ji Fung closed his eyes, seeking the comfort of oblivion. But suddenly rough hands were touching him, shaking him. He looked up into the face of his attacker.

The man was white as a ghost, his eyes bright with panic. He showed his perfect teeth in a desperate smile that was more like a rictus. "Drink this," he said, holding out a translucent blue cup. "It will make you feel better."

Ji Fung sat up, wincing and baffled. He took the cup, since the man's hands were shaking so badly that the liquid inside threatened to slop onto the rug. It was tea, strong and honey-smooth. He drained it in three swallows. The man was there at once to refill the cup. "I am Chi Gwai, your servant. I have brewed you a pot of Cloud Mist, which grows only on the highest mountain peaks, where men cannot climb. Monkeys have been trained to pluck the tea and bring it down in baskets. A very special infusion. Please tell me at once if there is anything else you require."

Ji Fung's mind was all jagged edges, unable to grasp the puzzle of his attacker's behavior. He sipped the tea and inventoried his body. Nothing broken, but his flesh felt bruised and torn, low aches punctuated by clusters of pins and needles. His lower lip was split, though not badly, and several teeth wiggled in their sockets when he poked them with his tongue. His head rattled with half-formed questions.

"I humbly offer you these clothes," said Chi Gwai, bowing his head. "Poor quality, but the best I own."

He held up a Western-style three-piece suit, charcoal gray with thin white stripes, and a black silk shirt. The clothes were exquisitely made. Ji Fung took them, feeling as if the world had completely ceased to make sense.

"Please accept these shoes also." Chi Gwai handed him a box. The shoes were black-and-white leather, shiny as glass. They fit his feet perfectly.

Chi Gwai brought him hot water to wash the crust of blood and lipstick from his face, and a comb to slick back his growing mop of hair. Dressing himself in the suit, he found his jade name chop tucked discreetly into a vest pocket.

At last he looked into the mirror—and saw yet another brand-new person. He was stylish, almost handsome. The bruises and split lip lent him a sinister air. He looked like the gangsters of whom his mother had warned him.

Chi Gwai led him along a hallway and into a great room half-filled with a carved table and rows of inlaid chairs. A niche in the wall held a statue of Kwan Ti, the fierce general-god of loyalty and brotherhood, with three sticks of incense burning before him. On the far wall hung an enormous painting of a village in winter, full of tiny people performing a thousand busy tasks. Ji Fung recognized the painting an instant before he saw the man sitting at the head of the table.

"Hello, Siu Ji."

The name of his childhood. The first name he had ever known, the one he had almost forgotten.

Ji Fung remembered eating meals at this table, staring at the painting and wishing for a way to step into that perfect miniature world. He and his parents had always been welcome at this man's table. His uncle's face was heavier now, his hair beginning to thin. But his eyes had not changed.

They were like Father's, high-lidded and clear brown—but he remembered his father's eyes as kinder than this man's. A thin American cigarette was pinched tightly between his nicotined fingers, smoldering. Ji Fung remembered the constant smell of tobacco smoke that had pervaded all their meals.

"Uncle," Ji Fung murmured, bowing his head to cover his confusion.

Gong Sut Fo stood and took his nephew by the shoulders. "At first I did not believe my eyes. The ghost of my brother's son, come back from the grave as a woman."

Ji Fung's face burned with shame, but he did not understand. Had his mother told his family he was dead?

Gong Sut Fo eyed him like an antique dealer appraising rare jade.

"I curse myself for failing to recognize your picture in the paper, but it was blurred, and I could not bring myself to believe that your mother was capable of such wickedness. Now that I see you with my own eyes, there can be no doubt."

Ji Fung's heart began to swell with cautious joy. His mother had done a terrible thing by taking him away from his family, but now he had found them, and it was she who would be sent away.

"Where is Gong Wa Toi?" he asked. "Why is my father not here to greet me?"

His uncle's face went blank as still water. Silence spun out for an endless moment, and Ji Fung thought his heartbeat must surely be the loudest thing in the room. Then Gong Sut Fo took a cautious slurp of tea.

"You must be hungry." He stared for a moment into the depths of the painting, then clapped his hands. In a few seconds a servant girl appeared.

"Bring my nephew some soup and steamed dumplings." He held up his cup. "And some more tea."

"No, please," said Ji Fung, struggling with long-rusted manners. "It is too much trouble."

In truth he was not very hungry; his belly was full of acid from anxiety and the Hurricane he had drunk. But he knew better than to refuse outright.

"It is no trouble," Gong Sut Fo said, his face creased with a peculiar sunless smile. "Only leftovers."

When the food arrived, it was twice what he'd expected, each dish fresh and hot: a spicy pork filling in the dumplings, succulent bits of shark's fin in the soup, little sweet cakes and pickled vegetables and a big bowl of steaming, sticky white rice. Ji Fung's appetite came back in a nostalgic rush. He had forgotten how sick he was of Western food, with its stodgy lumps of meat and thick bland sauces. The fragrant Cantonese dishes before him brought back memories of huge banquets at this table, of him and his two small sisters running back and forth like little playful dogs, snatching a morsel of fish, a sticky rice cake, a slice of candied lotus root.

He ate hugely under his uncle's watchful gaze and waited for the answer to his question. But it was not until Ji Fung had finished every dish that Gong Sut Fo spoke again.

"Your mother was from Soochow, a middle-class girl whose family made musical instruments. She was known for her sweet voice and beautiful face, and her father was ambitious, refusing offers from respectable men. He was holding out for a wealthy man from Hong Kong, a man with power. A man mentioned to him by a local fortune-teller."

Ji Fung refilled his cup and drank, listening intently.

"I met your mother, Miao-Ying, in Shanghai." Gong Sut Fo paused. "We fell in love."

Ji Fung frowned, but his uncle's eyes looked right past him.

"Foolish," he said. "We had not been introduced. But it was true. I adored her odd little ways, the faraway look in her eyes. How bad we were—she allowed me to hold her hand,

and even to kiss her fingers! But she was a strange girl. She said she didn't want to depend on men all her life, and everyone knows a woman must depend on men.

"Miao-Ying went home and told her father that she had met the husband of her dreams. She told him I was from a powerful Hong Kong family, just as the fortune-teller promised, and she begged him to let us marry. Her father was pleased, but being ambitious, he investigated my family and found out that my older brother was also unmarried. He thought, *Why give my daughter to the second son of the Gong family when she could be the first wife of the first son?* And he offered Miao-Ying to Wa Toi instead of to me.

"At the time I thought I would die, seeing her every day, knowing she slept with my brother every night. Now I realize that losing her may be the only reason I am still alive. Her odd ways—that faraway look—I believe they were signs of her madness."

Ji Fung's hands twisted together in his lap. The delicious meal lay uneasy in his belly.

"After the wedding, Miao-Ying became like a ghost in the house, never speaking to me or my brother, and to the servants only when she had no choice. In my youthful arrogance, I imagined she was pining for me. She was ill all through her pregnancy. When you were born, she didn't seem to recognize you as her son. When you cried for her, she would hand you to a nurse, but then she would disappear, and the servants would find her staring at you while you slept.

"Wa Toi tried to love her, I think. And he worshiped you. But when she returned none of his affections, he took a second wife, the mother of your sisters, and later a third, who was carrying a child that spring. Miao-Ying withdrew further, as if she thought nothing more was required of her.

"Even though by that time I had wives and children of my own, I was still tormented by thoughts of Miao-Ying. I imagined us running away together, foolish dreams that haunted me endlessly. I imagined that I would save her. I wish we had run away—I could not have saved her from herself, but I might have saved my brother.

"It was early that spring, during the season of the vernal equinox, when she took you away. I had been out drinking all night and well into the morning, and I came to the decision that I could not live without her. I went to my brother's house and banged on the door, demanding that he divorce Miao-Ying without further delay. When there was no answer, I pushed the door open and walked inside. What I found in there I will never forget.

"First, the smell. Awful, like a sick person who has not washed in months, like an overflowing toilet. I came upon servants lying where they had fallen, their clothes streaked with shit and vomit—black vomit, the sign of a certain poison much employed for murdering. I ran upstairs to look for my brother, only to find him tangled in stinking, bloody bedclothes, stiff and dead, with his second wife beside him.

"As I continued my search, I found nothing but death. I have seen many terrible things in my life, but few rival the sight of my brother's third and youngest wife lying with your two small sisters in her arms, her legs spread wide to reveal the wrinkled blue head of the baby emerging as if it had tried at the last moment to escape its mother's fate, but hadn't had quite the strength.

"I was enraged in my drunkenness, swearing vengeance upon the man-headed demon that had poisoned my brother's family. I had left Miao-Ying's chambers for last, dreading the sight of her poor body wracked with poison, but needing to know. I stood at the door with tears on my face, and as I took a deep breath to ready myself, I detected a new odor. Kerosene. I pressed my ear to the door and was able to make out the faintest of sounds, like muffled weeping.

"Enthralled by the idea that Miao-Ying might still be alive, I pushed open the door and saw her kneeling in the center of the room. Her pale arms encircled a small child swathed in a blanket. I could not see his face—I assumed it was you. The stink of kerosene was overwhelming; I could see that her hair and clothes were soaked with it, as was the blanket wrapped around the child. I realized it was he who was crying, his sobs muffled in the thick cotton that covered his head.

"When Miao-Ying turned to look at me, I knew it was she who had poisoned my brother. Her face was as composed and lovely as always, but her eyes were hot like a mad dog's, full of sickness and loathing. I watched in horror as she struck the match and gave herself to the flames.

"The child screamed and struggled in her arms, trying to cast off the burning blanket, then writhing as the fire took his flesh. Miao-Ying held him tight, her face beneath the flames at once serene and ecstatic. I could only stand and watch the fire eat away the face that had haunted me for so many years.

"To this day I am ashamed to admit I made no move to save her, or the child I thought was you."

Gong Sut Fo turned his gaze to Ji Fung, though he did not seem to see his nephew.

"Now that I have told you a story, you must tell me one. The story of how you came to be here in my house eight years after your mother murdered you."

At first, no words would come. Ji Fung could only think of questions. What depths of emotion had curdled in his mother to make her capable of such an act? Her heart must have been like a thousand-year egg, preserved in ash and lime, buried until it was black as a millennium of midnights. What had finally driven her to do it—could he ever comprehend her reasons? If he could, did that make him a possible murderer? Did that prove he was his mother's son?

And what child had died in his place? Too easily he could imagine her leaving him at the opera school, then luring some half-starved waif back to the house of corpses, promising him food, giving him death. He imagined the boy's dirty face blackening and shriveling in the flames. It seemed more real than the face of his uncle before him, more real than the memory of his mother's face.

Ji Fung was sick to the bone, sure that he would never speak again. But eventually he did. Once he had begun the process of unburdening after so many years, the story took on momentum beyond his control, pouring forth like blood from a wound he had thought healed.

His uncle listened intently, always pulling at his cigarette, pockmarked face empty of emotion. When Ji Fung had trailed off into helpless silence, Gong Sut Fo clapped for more tea.

"I have already taken care of this trouble with the police," he said, refilling Ji Fung's cup. "They are no longer interested in you as a suspect."

"Uncle, you are too generous." *But what about Lin Bai?*

Gong Sut Fo's mouth turned up in the chilly grimace that passed as his smile. "It is the least I can do for the only son of my only brother."

Ji Fung knew he could not ask reprieve for his friend. If he knew what sort of friends they were, his uncle would probably have them both killed. Could Lin Bai remain a woman forever? Ji Fung felt as if the favor were a weight settling onto his heart. He could not imagine what he would be asked to pay in return.

For an hour they spoke of ordinary things, like any nephew and uncle visiting after a long absence. Gong Sut Fo showed photographic portraits of his five daughters, all well married or promised to good families, and Ji Fung remarked on what lovely young women they had become. They spoke of a granduncle who had died, a cousin Ji Fung barely remembered. Of mah-jongg and the weather and a trip Gong Sut Fo had recently made to Peking. Ji Fung was beginning to feel he had truly returned home.

Gong Sut Fo pushed his chair back. "Well, and it is late, nearly morning."

"Yes, it is," Ji Fung answered. He was exhausted, as if the evening's chaos had drained every drop of vitality from his bones.

"There is only one small thing I must ask of you before we retire."

Ji Fung's breath caught. This was it. He nodded, wary.

"Only a small favor, but one that would be much appreciated."

"Anything, Uncle."

"It is like this." Gong Sut Fo put a match to the latest of what seemed a hundred cigarettes. "I have a very important new business associate in Shanghai. An American. He is considering doing business with us, but would first like a sample of our product."

"What product is that?"

His uncle beckoned to the serving girl, who brought an intricately carved jade box to the table. Gong Sut Fo opened the lid, took out a bundle tied in red cloth, unfolded the cloth to reveal a sticky black pellet as long and thick as a man's finger. A rich, sweet odor emanated from it, strong enough to make Ji Fung's head swim.

"Opium?" he whispered.

"Does this shock you?"

Ji Fung could not speak. He stared down at his shiny new shoes. The gangsters, the murdering men his murdering mother had warned him of—they were his own family. But surely his father had not been an evil man . . . ?

Ji Fung realized he knew nothing about his father save that the man had given him sweets and spoken kindly to him. Outside of his role as father, Gong Wa Toi could have been any sort of man at all. Was it even barely possible that something—a life of festering corruption, perhaps—might have justified Miao-Ying's murdering him and stealing his son?

It was not possible. And even if it were, nothing could justify the wanton murder of the other wives, the faithful servants, the children. And the boy who had died for him, who had suffered the ultimate loss of face for him, his features burned beyond recognition.

Seeming to read the confusion in his nephew's face, Gong Sut Fo spoke. "We are not criminals. We are revolutionaries, acquiring capital by any means necessary. Capital gives us power to fight the imperialist cowards who would drive China into the ground to satisfy their own greed. The Triad brotherhood is like a family, and a family must bind together in times of strife and sorrow." His voice grew tense with emotion. "It is a family you were born into, and from whose arms your mother tore you. Your rightful place is here with us. I thank the gods that you are with us again. You are the first son of my father's first son. I have no sons of my own, only daughters. It would be an honor to consider you my son."

All the long cold nights at the opera school came rushing back, all the times Ji Fung had dreamed of running away to find his lost family. The memories filled him with hope and gratitude, so much so that tears stung his eyes. He blinked them away and waited, knowing his uncle was not finished.

"But first there is one thing," said Gong Sut Fo, his eyes grim. "I must know beyond a doubt that you are the son of my brother, not of Miao-Ying. If Gong blood runs in your veins, then you will not disappoint me. Do this favor for your uncle as a demonstration of loyalty to your father's memory."

Ji Fung bowed his head.

"Tell me what to do, Uncle, and I will do it gladly."

"In three days it will be Yue Lan, the Festival of Hungry Ghosts. At that time, take the ferry to Kowloon and walk up Tung Tau Tsuen Road to the Walled City. Enter the City by way of Fui Sing Street, where the illicit dentists practice their trade. A hundred steps in you will see a butcher's shop, and

beyond it an alleyway where an old man sells shoes. Ask to
see some woven grass sandals. When he tells you he has only
one left, you say, *I only need one for the journey I must make.*
Hand him the money like this."

Gong Sut Fo held a folded note in his left hand between
the first and second fingers, the other fingers tucked into the
palm, the thumb holding them down. Ji Fung took the money
and mimicked his uncle's motion. Gong Sut Fo nodded, slipping the note back into his pocket.

"The old man will give you a box. Take this box to
Shanghai by train. On the Bund, the main street that runs
along the Whangpoo River, you will find an establishment
called the Shanghai Club, where our new friend sups each
day with his French associates. You will meet him there and
give him the box. He already has the key. The man's name is
Herbert Hinchcliffe."

Ji Fung repeated the difficult name twice, softly.

"Your English pronunciation is excellent," Gong Sut Fo
said. "Did they teach you that in the opera school?"

Ji Fung smiled, just a little, and his uncle returned it with
more genuine feeling than he had yet shown.

"You are a good boy." He stood and patted Ji Fung's
shoulder. "I have one more thing for you."

Gong Sut Fo motioned to the girl, who vanished. Seconds
later, the two men from the alley sidled in.

"Nephew, you have already met Chi Gwai. This is Lam
Bao, his associate." The two men bowed. Both looked pale and
nervous. "They have come to apologize for causing you injury."

Ji Fung stood stiff and uncomfortable through the excruciatingly formal apologies. He could see that both men were
terrified of his uncle. When the second man stumbled to a
halt at the end of his ill-prepared speech, Gong Sut Fo
reached into a drawer and took out a small silver-plated
revolver. He handed the gun to Ji Fung, who took it with
great reluctance.

"Do you forgive them?" Gong Sut Fo asked.

Ji Fung balanced the gun's cool weight in his right hand. The two men before him were silent and wild-eyed, their faces slick with sweat. Ji Fung realized there was a part of him that wanted to shoot them both, to make them feel the fear and pain he had felt when they dragged him away from Lin Bai.

Thinking of Lin Bai brought its own pain. Where was he right now? Was he mourning Ji Fung for dead, just as Gong Sut Fo had done for so many years?

Ji Fung bit down on the inside of his lip. He had to concentrate. This was not a question of revenge. It was a test. He closed his eyes for a long moment, then looked his uncle full in the face.

"I do forgive them," said Ji Fung. "They were only protecting the memory of my father. And I would not have found my family without them."

Gong Sut Fo nodded. He clearly approved of this answer. "My nephew's generous nature has spared your lives," he told the men. "But in my eyes, the road to forgiveness is long and painful."

He took the gun from Ji Fung and fired two shots. Blood exploded across the floor. Vivid red flowers blossomed on Ji Fung's black-and-white shoes. The two men fell screaming, each clutching a shattered leg.

Gong Sut Fo replaced the gun in its drawer and laid his hand on Ji Fung's shoulder again. This time Ji Fung struggled not to flinch.

"By the time their wounds have healed, you will have returned from Shanghai. From that day on, they will be your personal bodyguards. They will protect you with their lives and perform any other services you require."

Ji Fung forced himself to look away from the blood pooling on the beautiful rug. His eyes fell on the statue of Kwan Ti brandishing his sword, and he remembered that this was also a Triad god, one of three generals known as The Three

Brothers because of their great loyalty to one another. He noticed that Kwan Ti's left hand was curled in the same way that his uncle had shown him to hand over the money.

It was all too much. Like a tired child, Ji Fung let his uncle lead him around the writhing men and out into the long hallway.

"It has been a long night for you," said Gong Sut Fo. "Today you will sleep undisturbed. You begin your journey at the next nightfall."

Lin Bai lay naked on his belly, head spinning, mouth dry as sand. His cheeks were scaly with tears that had flowed and dried, flowed and dried. Perique had gone out hours ago, desperately optimistic, certain that with money and what he called his connections, he would be able to find Ji Fung.

Lin Bai had no such hope. He understood what was happening here. Everyone who tried to love him died, so Ji Fung was dead. Lin Bai had not thwarted his ill luck by murdering Master Lau; he had only sent it astray for a bit. Now it had found him, and Ji Fung was surely devoured in its jaws.

He knew he should leave this hotel before his poison luck spilled over onto Perique, who was rather weak and silly but sweet, who had saved his unlucky life and Ji Fung's. But perhaps the poison had already touched Perique. Inevitably, it would touch anyone he cared for. He could go far away, deep into the mountains, become a hermit. But he knew he would not survive two moons. He had an actor's heart. He would wither and die without an audience. Perhaps he should.

Hot helpless tears began again, and Lin Bai rolled onto his side to let them drip slowly into the sweaty silk sheets. He reached for the bottle of American whiskey beside him only to find the coverlet sodden with its reeking contents. He hurled the empty bottle against the wall. It did not shatter as he had hoped, but landed dully on the carpet.

Lin Bai closed his eyes. Thick pain pulsed in his head, his stomach cramped with misery, and he realized that more than anything, he wanted to die. Death would put an end to his pain—but more importantly, it would put an end to the pain of everyone around him.

How to do it? The window was not high enough. Perique had taken his gun with him. There were razors, but the blood would remind him of Master Lau. He did not want to die as Master Lau had died.

He looked desperately around the room, seeking the instrument of his own demise. His eye fell upon the bedside table, where Perique had set half a plate of little baked cakes full of red bean paste and sweet opium. Yesterday Perique had warned him and Ji Fung not to eat more than one at a time, for they were very strong.

Lin Bai began to eat the cakes with quick delicate bites, their brash flavor clenching the dry tissues of his mouth. When he had finished four, the plate fell away from his hands. He lay back and waited for the void to claim him.

Ji Fung paused for a moment before the door to Perique's suite, suddenly apprehensive. He straightened his new tie and ran his palms over his slicked-back hair, nervous and unsure of himself. He had come so far, changed so much in the course of one night. He was no longer an orphan on the run. He was a man with a powerful family, the long-lost first son welcomed back home. Was it even possible to return to this nightside world, this sex-scented opium dream of a life?

He shook his head. He had no choice. He owed Perique for saving his life, and that life would be meaningless if he could not share it with Lin Bai.

He had to fit together these two halves. There must be some way. He could introduce Lin Bai to his family as Betty Lee—or better yet, Betty LeBon, Perique's cousin. His uncle would never believe Perique was from a good family, but perhaps a rich one would do. What had he said about the strange brotherhood, the shadowy gangster/revolutionaries whose true purpose Ji Fung had not even begun to fathom? "We gain capital any way we can."

Perhaps Perique would even know where to buy him children. Then he could have sons, and replenish the family his mother had devastated. He imagined street urchins saved from lives of wretched hunger, from miserable deaths like that of the boy who had taken his place. Perhaps he could atone for that boy's agony, placate his burning ghost.

He was smiling and full of the future as he opened the door and strode through the suite to the bedroom. Lin Bai's naked body lay limp and accusatory on the bed, surrounded by the sticky remains of half-eaten opium cakes.

Ji Fung ran to the bed, yanked Lin Bai up by the shoulders, slapped his pale face lightly, then harder. Lin Bai's head lolled on his neck as if it were barely attached. His skin was cold and clammy, his eyes slitted silver-white.

"Lin Bai, wake up! Don't be dead now! I beg you, my brother, my lover!"

Lin Bai made a soft noise like a sleeper disturbed. A faint pulse jumped in his neck. Ji Fung hauled him to his feet, struggling to support his slight but inert bulk.

"Walk with me," Ji Fung commanded. "Dance with me! Come on, graceful feet, stand up."

Perique burst through the door, cursing in French.

"Jung, you're alive!" He rushed to help support Lin Bai. "What's happened to Lai?"

Ji Fung gestured with his chin at the half-eaten cakes.

"*Mon Dieu!* I should never have left him alone. But he's not too far gone yet. I've seen worse." Perique rushed into the bathroom and began to fill the tub. "Bring him in, quickly."

They laid Lin Bai in the cool water and splashed his face, rubbed his hands and his feet.

"Lin Bai," Ji Fung called. "My love, can you hear me?"

He began to sing. *"Since ancient times, how few lovers have remained constant to the end?"*

Lin Bai's eyelids fluttered. He rolled his head back and forth, groaned softly. Perique pursed his lips in approval.

"That's right, sing with me. *But those who were true have come together at last. Even though thousands of miles apart. Even though torn from each other by death."*

Lin Bai's lips were moving, his voice a soft whisper, barely audible.

"How does the rest go?" Ji Fung asked. "You know I always forget the words. Help me remember."

Lin Bai's mouth turned up at the corners, faintest ghost of a smile. His voice was high and wandering, but now there was a hint of strength behind it. *"And all those who curse their unhappy fate are simply those lacking in love."*

There were tears on Ji Fung's cheeks, and his voice cracked as he and Lin Bai sang together.

"True love moves heaven and earth. Metal and stone shine like the sun and light the pages of old histories."

Lin Bai rested his head against the shoulder of Ji Fung's new suit, now damp with bathwater. "You never remember the words," he scolded. "Daydreaming instead of practicing. How will you become a star in Hollywood?"

Ji Fung pressed his lips to the crown of Lin Bai's head, remembering the feel of stubble where silky hair now grew. "I need you there to remind me," he said.

Lin Bai opened his eyes and looked at Ji Fung, fully aware now. "You're alive."

Ji Fung nodded.

"And so am I."

"Yes, you are."

"I didn't bring you bad luck."

Ji Fung smiled. "Definitely not."

With Lin Bai dried off and swaddled in a white terry-cloth robe, the boys lay embracing on the bed. Perique sprawled in his armchair, chin propped on his fist, regarding them owlishly. Ji Fung stroked his lover's damp hair while he unfolded the story of last night.

When he told them of the favor his uncle had requested, Perique's pale eyes lit up. "Shanghai," he exclaimed. "The only civilized city in this wretched hemisphere. How wonderful!"

He leaned over and stroked Lin Bai's cool cheek.

"We're going on a trip, beautiful Betty. We're going to Shanghai!"

None of them had ever been inside Kowloon Walled City, but they had all heard frightful tales. The place was a teeming nest of villains, where decay and dissolution throve. A man who entered at night was unlikely to see morning, and a woman would be foolish to enter at all, particularly if she were beautiful. Perique told them of squalid rooms where women were kept, drugged and shackled, forced to perform any abomination a customer's mind could dream up. For the right price, Perique said, one could even mutilate or kill a girl.

Even so, Lin Bai insisted on coming along. He could not spend another night waiting at the hotel; he said he would go mad. Remembering the image of his lover's limp body sprawled on the bed, Ji Fung gave in. He reasoned that anyone attempting to interfere with Betty Lee would get more than they bargained for; no one would expect such a demure young lady to be capable of turning a somersault in midair or delivering a double-footed flying kick strong enough to shatter a skull.

The Walled City met none of their expectations. Its

claustrophobic mass of masonry and wood was nearly deserted. Once this place had been the Manchu stronghold against the British, fortified with walls fifteen feet thick, ruled by the iron hand of the *yamen*. After the British takeover the place had become a no-man's-land, governed only by the law of a razor across the throat.

In Hong Kong, and in other parts of Kowloon, the Festival of Hungry Ghosts was in full swing. Ji Fung and Lin Bai knew this celebration well, since it included special performances of operas to entertain the dead. Small bonfires dotted every lane and alleyway, every pavement and courtyard. The smoke from spiraling coils of incense mingled with that from the fires. The damp air smelled sweet, faintly singed. Paper replicas of necessities and luxuries—furniture, automobiles, clothes—were burned on this night to protect one's dead ancestors from want. Ji Fung thought again of the boy who had died in his place, fed to the flames so that his father would not lack a son in the afterlife.

Inside these walls, though, the festival itself was like a ghost—and an exceedingly hungry one at that. Most of the ramshackle structures were dark and empty. Some sagged and swayed, ruins ready to fall but held upright by buildings on either side, like a corpse supported by two cripples. Here and there, tiny fires were fueled by chips of bone and dried human shit, tended by crouching souls who occasionally fed them spirit-gifts fashioned out of cheap newsprint. The streets were so narrow that the boys had to edge past these miserable celebrations in single file to avoid scorching their feet. The inhabitants of the City paid them no mind. Most did not even look up when they passed, and those who did looked quickly away again.

"It's almost as if they're scared of us," Lin Bai whispered, as a muscle-roped young man peered at them from the doorway of a filthy shop, then ducked inside.

"They think we're Triad," said Perique.

Ji Fung glanced at him. "We are."

"*You* are. I'm on vacation. Ha." Perique neatly avoided a puddle of foul, oily mud. "Shanghai is going to look damned good after this."

They came to the butcher's shop Gong Sut Fo had mentioned. Roast pigs' heads were displayed in the window, eyes popped in their sockets, skin brittle and translucent, lower jaws split down the middle and splayed to reveal two rows of razor-sharp teeth. Above them hung a phalanx of badly preserved ducks, moldy and flyblown. A single taper burned in the shop, and by its light a small boy was skinning a dog. The colorful mass of its guts lay on the floor beside him. His naked body was greased with blood, his long black hair stiff with it.

They hurried past the shop and turned into the narrow alley just beyond it. The old shoeseller's stall and household were set up in a slight recess in the wall of the butcher's building. His territory was marked by a heap of cloth slippers and rough hide sandals. Beyond that were his cookpot and sleeping mat.

He put aside his bowl of noodles as Ji Fung entered the alley. His dark face was as desiccated as the hide of his sandals, but his eyes were sharp and bright.

"Shoes for the young gentleman?" he asked.

"I would like to buy some of your grass sandals," said Ji Fung, feeling as if he were onstage again.

The old man smiled, revealing a single tooth.

"Ah," he said. "I am ashamed to admit that I have only one left."

He reached into the pile of shoes and pulled out a single old-fashioned woven sandal, like those worn by monks.

"Best quality, though. Hand-woven from fine reeds."

Ji Fung looked over his shoulder at Perique and Lin Bai hovering at the mouth of the alley. Perique shrugged. But Lin Bai gave him a slight nod and frown, as he had always done when Ji Fung needed prompting.

He took a deep breath and delivered his line. "I need only one for the journey I must make." Then he fished out the note he had carefully folded on the ferry, tucked it between his left thumb and forefinger, and handed it over as he had been instructed.

The old man nodded, his gnarled brown fingers snatching the money and spiriting it away more quickly than Ji Fung's eyes could follow. He lifted his cooking pot to reveal a deep hollow, removed a red lacquer box, brushed away some dirt and ashes, and placed it in Ji Fung's hands.

It was larger than he had expected. Big enough to require two hands to hold, with an ornate brass lock. This he must carry safely to Shanghai. Weighing it in his grasp, he could barely conceive of the value this simple box represented. Not only the cash value, but the amount of trust his uncle had placed in him. Ji Fung silently promised his father's spirit that the brotherhood would not be disappointed.

The train had stopped again. This was the seventh time, and they had not even reached Soochow.

Perique rolled his eyes and shook his head, but the boys ignored him, hanging out the window surrounded by hordes of itinerant vendors. These people had become so used to seeing trains stopped on the tracks that they loitered about with their wares, waiting for it to happen. When it did, they rushed up with trays of snacks and clay cups of tea, curious baubles and playthings. It disgusted Perique to see the way these yokels swarmed, like flies or some other sort of minor but annoying vermin. He wished his boys would not encourage them.

When Ji Fung and Lin Bai finally sat back down, their arms were full of junk. Brown pears and rice balls steamed in lotus leaves. Paper cones full of noodles fried in rapeseed oil. A little mirror with a red-and-gold dragon on the back. A bamboo crab with waving eyestalks and moving legs. A painted tin monkey on a stick.

They began sharing out the food, unwrapping the limp gray-green leaves amid clouds of steam, dipping into the paper cones with fancy chopsticks. Perique wrinkled his nose. "How can you eat that?"

"It's good!" Lin Bai said. His lipstick was almost entirely gone. Only the corners of his mouth were still bright red.

"Here." Ji Fung offered him a pear, but Perique shook his head violently.

"Don't you know anything? These country people use human shit to fertilize their crops. Their food is filled with all sorts of disease. Cholera. Dysentery."

Lin Bai laughed. "No diseases can live with these." He held up a wrinkled red chili between his silver chopsticks, then popped it into his mouth.

"Besides," added Ji Fung, "that food in the dining car is terrible. Tastes like pale meat boiled in baby's vomit."

Perique hissed in exasperation. His hopes of turning these wild animals into civilized young men receded further each day.

A devious look passed between the boys, and Ji Fung reached over to pull the curtains on their compartment.

"Now, just a minute," Perique began, but then they were all over each other, kissing and sucking and moaning and letting him see everything, and he remembered why he loved his little animals so much.

Later, over supper, the dining car was abuzz with talk of war. Shots had been exchanged by Chinese and Japanese troops on the Marco Polo Bridge near Peking. A Japanese lieutenant and his driver went missing, and were later found near the Hungjao aerodrome.

"Sexually mutilated, what?" a red-faced Brit elaborated

with no little relish. "Cut off their willies don't you know. Appalling what these Chinee get up to."

His companion, a pale young wisp of a woman with ashy blond hair and faded blue eyes, spoke up. "D'you suppose there's any sort of danger?"

The Brit's enormous white moustache quivered. "Don't be so bloody thick, Enid! These things go on all the time in China. It isn't going to affect any civilized people."

At sundown, the train still hadn't moved. Perique sat in the stifling compartment with a tumbler full of whiskey and ice, Lin Bai's head pillowed on his lap. The boy was so beautiful, with his long bangs falling over his pale forehead, with those nymphet eyes and that lush pink mouth. His hair had grown into a short bob, so he could dispense with the wig, a blessing in these summer months. And his features were so fine and well trained that he scarcely needed makeup to look like a girl.

Across from them, Ji Fung sat looking stylish and perhaps even a little dangerous in his new gray suit and shiny two-tone shoes. He was the yang to Lin Bai's yin, just as beautiful, but in a hard-edged, masculine fashion. His square chin, broad shoulders, and lean waist were a perfect complement to Lin Bai's graceful reediness. They looked ever so good together.

Ji Fung noticed Perique's attention and smiled, cocking his head in a way that displayed the fine muscles of his throat. "Tell us more about Shanghai," he said.

Lin Bai chimed in without opening his eyes. "Yes, tell us."

"Well . . . I remember the library at the Shanghai Club." He laughed softly. "The club is famous for its bar, which is the longest in the world—150 yards, and I will buy you both a drink there, I promise—but when I was a boy, I cared nothing for bars. I remember the old men playing chess in the library, the scent of their pipe smoke. I remember the books, shelves and shelves of them rising up as far as the eye could see, with long ladders you climbed to reach the high ones. I would spend long summer days reading there, breathing the dust of leather and paper, the effluvia of imagination. I had few friends, so I comforted myself with those I found in books."

"Surely you must have had some friends," Ji Fung said.

"Who? I didn't know any other half-breeds my age. The Chinese children thought I was a snob, and the white children called me—"

"What?" Lin Bai propped himself up on one elbow. "What did they call you?"

Perique stared out the window at the motionless landscape. "A Chink and a bastard," he said finally.

Ji Fung leaned over and patted Perique's knee. "Then they were stupid, and you didn't need to know them."

Perique nodded, but even to this day he remembered how lonely he had felt for the company of other boys, so lonely that he would gladly have siphoned out either his Chinese or his white blood if he had been able to do so. To be pure white in Shanghai's French Concession would have been heavenly. All the city's pleasures and opportunities would have been open to him. But even to be pure Chinese—to fully belong *anywhere*—just to have some friends—

Ji Fung's voice jolted him out of his reverie. "What about your brothers and sisters?"

Christ. "Oh yes," he said lamely, "I often played with them."

He remembered once commanding the children of some servants to play with him. The two boys had done so with cold politeness, waiting patiently for this new duty to be finished so they could go back to plucking ducks in the kitchen. Agonized and enraged, Perique had dragged them to a vine-swathed pagoda at the back of the family compound and made them pleasure each other with their mouths while he watched. They exhibited signs of excitement, but after it was over, they had

looked at Perique with such hatred that he never dared speak
to them again.

He reached across the compartment and pulled Ji
Fung over to his side, slipped his arm around the boy's
narrow waist, ran his other hand through Lin Bai's thick
soft hair. "But now I have you, my boys. And when we
get to Shanghai, I will show you the Paris of the Orient,
or the Whore of the Orient if you like. Only a few years
ago a visiting Christian missionary claimed the city was
so decadent as to call for an apology by God to Sodom
and Gomorrah."

Both boys frowned in confusion.

"Never mind. I'll take you walking on the Bund, by the
river, where the Shanghai Club and all the other grand buildings are. We'll go shopping at Sincere's and Wing On, where
you can buy absolutely anything your pretty hearts desire.
We will go to the Great World Theatre and see the Shanghai
Ballet, or the Russian Opera. Would you like that?"

He received a chorus of emphatic yeses. Just then the
train lurched to a start, and cheers resounded along the length
of the car.

It was the middle of the night when they finally pulled
into the Shanghai railway station. In spite of the late hour, the
station was packed with people. There were elegant blond
mothers surrounded by matching suitcases, gossiping to each
other about the "Oriental troubles" while Chinese nurses
tried to soothe whining blond children kept up far too late.
There were old European dandies and their handsome young
companions of both sexes. There were Shanghai natives,
well-dressed couples and businessmen and wealthy women
with painted eyebrows and severe, rice-powdered faces.

All were fighting to get on a train and get out of
Shanghai. The tension was beginning to wear thin the mask
of civilized manners; Ji Fung was shocked to see a pretty
young mother push an old woman aside to get her children

on the departing train. The old woman tottered and almost fell onto the tracks.

"Why is everyone in such a hurry?" Ji Fung asked, hefting three of their seven suitcases.

"How should I know?" Perique muttered, looking around for a porter. The last leg of the journey had wilted him, and he was annoyed at the prospect of carrying his own luggage.

"Is it because of the fighting?" Lin Bai asked, toeing a small case with the tip of his high-heeled pump.

"*Fuck* the fighting!" Perique barked. He raised an imperious hand. "Porter!" But the few uniformed porters they could spot were already laden down with far too many bags.

"Listen," Perique said. "This isn't a bunch of ignorant country people squabbling over worthless bits of land. This is the civilized world. If we ran away every time these people started shooting at their enemies, there would be no Shanghai."

"These people?" Ji Fung dropped the bags he was holding. "You mean Chinese people?"

Perique rolled his eyes. "I'm talking about uncivilized people."

Lin Bai tried to push between them. "Here. I'll take two suitcases and Pei take two and Ji Fung take the rest. If we wait for a porter, we'll be here all night." They ignored him.

Ji Fung spat on the floor beside Perique's shoes. "If it weren't for all those uncivilized people, who would clean your fancy porcelain toilets and do your laundry and cook your food and spoon-feed it to you like the baby you are?"

"How dare you speak to me in that way?" Perique's face was flushed, his green eyes blazing. "Without me, your precious *people* would have cut your throat and left you dead on the Hong Kong waterfront."

"Yes, and you can turn a philosopher into a biting dog if you starve him long enough!"

"Why, you ungrateful little—"

"What?" Ji Fung screamed into Perique's face. *"What were you going to call me?"*

Perique had no answer. Ji Fung turned to Lin Bai, who was watching them in horror. "Will you stay and be his pet Chink, or are you coming with me?"

"Where?" Lin Bai's hands worked in unconscious operatic gestures of distress, shaping the stale smoky air of the train station. "Where would we go? We need a friend." He turned to Perique. "You are Chinese. You are as entitled as anyone to criticize your own countrymen. Only try to be more compassionate. The lives of most Chinese people are not as fortunate as yours."

"I'm not Chinese," said Perique in a strangled voice. "I'm not anything. My name isn't even LeBon, it's Lee."

"What?" said the boys in unison.

The crowd kept pushing and flowing around them. Their own silence spooled out. At last Perique said, "It doesn't matter. I suppose you'll want to leave, seeing as I'm not only a racist but a liar, too."

Lin Bai tilted his head. "What do you mean, Pei?"

"I told you I was born in Shanghai twenty years ago. That much is true. Everything else was a lie. I have no brothers or sisters. My father was Chinese, a trader of things legal and not. Mostly not, and he was extremely wealthy.

"My mother was a dance-hall hostess from Paris, working in Shanghai. Not a whore, just a free spirit . . . but in my father's eyes it amounted to the same thing. He spent money on her, dazzled her, made her think he loved her. Soon enough he got what he wanted from her, and soon enough he tired of it and dropped her. She had other admirers, and wasn't one to chase a man. My father didn't hear from her until three months later, when she contacted him and told him she was going to have his child.

"At first he didn't believe that she knew he was the father, but she convinced him somehow. After that he took her in and treated her as his wife. She received the richest food, the softest bed, and the best herbal medicine. My father treated her exquisitely until the day I was born."

"Then what?" Lin Bai urged when Perique stopped. "Did he throw her out?"

"No. He had her killed."

The boys' eyes grew large.

"He sent two underlings into her room that very night. One held a hand over my mouth so I wouldn't cry and wake her. The other pushed a long hatpin through her nostril and into her brain. My father had her body dumped off an opium junk in the middle of the South China Sea."

"But why?"

Perique shrugged. "He wanted a son. He didn't want to be burdened with a wife, much less a Parisian slut, as he called her. I was suckled and raised by an *amah*. I don't think he was really very interested in women. If I'd been born a girl, he would have killed me, too."

"How do you know all this?" Ji Fung asked.

"My father told me the story himself when I was ten years old. He wanted me to know what sort of man he was, and what sort of woman my mother had been. Like your uncle, Jung—he was worried that I would turn out to be my mother's son. I suppose I did. Five years later he called me a soft French faggot and ordered me out of his house."

"Then how . . ."

"How do I live so comfortably? It's easy. Chinese family ties can never really be broken. Until he died, my father paid me thousands of pounds a year to use a name other than his own. He promised that if I would live this way until his death, I would inherit his fortune, and I did. Publicly he wanted nothing to do with me. But whenever I was in Shanghai to collect a payment, he always seemed to know what I'd been up to."

Perique stood silently for a moment, his arms hanging

limp at his sides. He looked tired and defeated. Ji Fung's heart went out to him in spite of the snobbery and petty racism. These things seemed pathetic now, like a man lashing out uselessly at a system that has ultimate power over him.

Ji Fung felt a new kinship with Perique: they both knew the pain of losing a beloved parent to a mad one. For Perique obviously loved his mother's ghost, though he had spent only a single day with her while she lived. Ji Fung imagined Perique as a child, a sheltered prisoner in his father's world, just as he and Lin Bai had been prisoners of the opera school. But while they had had each other, Perique had had no one.

He reached out and gave Perique's hand a quick squeeze. Perique looked surprised, then relieved. "So you don't want to go?" he asked.

Ji Fung allowed himself a slight smile. "Not unless you want us to."

"Don't tease me," said Perique as he stooped to pick up his share of the luggage. "You two are the first real friends I've ever had."

"Then let's find somewhere to store these damned bags, and you can start showing us the Whore of the Orient."

The Shanghai Club was as fabulous as Perique had described it. High ornate ceilings, cool shady rooms, long windows overlooking the river and the rococo skyline. The world's longest bar was staffed by a hundred expert bartenders and stocked with every potable poison in the world. Perique bought them Brandy Alexanders, frothy, creamy drinks whose sweetness cloaked a sharp alcoholic bite.

They wandered tipsily through the library, trying to read the Roman characters stamped in gilt on the leather spines of the books, driving themselves into fits of giggles with their slurred pronunciations. They almost missed their six o'clock appointment with the Westerner. When Perique saw the clock and reminded them, they lost another five minutes saying "Herbert Hinchcliffe" to each other and laughing at the sound of it.

Taking a moment to sober up in the washroom, Ji Fung stood before the mirror breathing deeply, as he had often done just before going onstage. He tapped one manicured fingernail against the brass lock on the red lacquer box, searching for a confidence he didn't feel. When he could delay no longer, he squared his shoulders and went out to speak to the maître d'hôtel.

The maître d' was an officious little Fukienese fellow with threads of gray in his neatly trimmed moustache. He eyed Ji Fung and his associates with polite suspicion.

"I am looking for the American, Herbert Hinch—kwiff." Ji Fung struggled to keep his voice low and authoritative, though he knew he had botched the man's name.

"Who is it who is looking?" the man asked. His tone was supercilious, not quite rude.

"I am the nephew of Gong Sut Fo. I bring a package from my uncle to give to our client, Mr. Herbert."

"Hinchcliffe," Perique hissed. "The surname is Hinchcliffe."

But the little man did not seem to notice Ji Fung's mistake. As soon as he heard the name Gong Sut Fo, the man had gone from haughty and dismissive to desperately servile.

"Mr. Gong, I am happy to receive you and your friends in our humble establishment. Please allow me to offer you our finest meal free of charge."

"You are very kind," Ji Fung said. "But first, can you tell me where to find our American friend?"

The man's face fell as if he were suddenly the bearer of terrible news. "So sorry, Mr. Gong, but Mr. Hinchcliffe has not come in for three days." He scribbled quickly on a scrap of paper. "Here is his address where you might find him. If there is anything else I can do to assist you . . ."

Ji Fung pocketed the scrap. "Thank you," he said, his chin high. "That will be all."

"Well spoken," Perique murmured as the maître d' led them to a table by the window. "I believe there's hope for you yet."

Herbert Hinchcliffe's house was in the French Concession, on Route Lafayette across from the Parc Français. The little park was overrun with squatters, and the moist evening air was full of cooking smoke and the sibilant sound of Shanghaiese.

Ji Fung pushed open the heavy iron gates of the pristine white house. A brick path, green with moss, wound through a lush garden to the veranda. Shanghai had been built on top of a river swamp, which meant the city was slowly sinking into its soft underpinnings. But the vegetation that sprang from this mud was riotous and verdant. The scent of night jasmine filled the garden and followed them up onto the porch.

The tall double doors were adorned with brass knockers shaped like lions' heads. Ji Fung was used to the Chinese lion, a smiling creature usually seen playing with a colorful hollow ball. Herbert Hinchcliffe's lions were cold-eyed, their mouths frozen in eternal snarls. He forced himself to grasp one of the heavy brass rings and knock three times. Then he stepped back, listening for sounds of life inside.

It was a full five minutes before the door was hauled open by an old woman in a black cloth jacket. Her hair was thinning, her back twisted in a dowager's hump that reduced her height to less than four feet.

"We're here to see Mr. Hinchcliffe," said Ji Fung. At last he had gotten the name right. He held the red lacquer box before him like a peace offering.

The old woman shook her head. "Too late." Her Mandarin was clipped with a strong Shanghai accent.

"What do you mean, too late?" Perique asked.

"Gone." She made flapping wings out of her wrinkled hands. "Back to America. Afraid of war, he says. Chinese-Japanese fighting all the time now. I am afraid, too, but I am old grandmother." She laughed. Almost any sentiment could be expressed by Chinese laughter; this was the laugh that meant *I am empty of hope*. "All my life I work for Hinchcliffe family. Tell me, where would I go?"

The old woman, whose name was Mrs. Yuan, gave them tea while they decided what to do about the box. It sat on the table between them, still locked, while the man with the key was thousands of miles away. Ji Fung found his fingers tracing the edges of the box while they debated their options. Should they leave it with Mrs. Yuan? Take it back to Gong Sut Fo? Ji Fung's heart was heavy in his chest. He was sure that, whatever action they chose, he had failed his uncle.

At last they decided to send a telegram to Gong Sut Fo asking for further instructions. They thanked Mrs. Yuan for the tea and left her alone in the empty house.

The sedan Perique had hired was still waiting outside. As they piled in, Perique took a long pull from his silver pocket flask and ordered the driver to turn on Route Pierre Robert.

Lin Bai accepted a dainty sip from the flask. "Where are we going?"

"I want to show you something." There was an odd light in Perique's strange eyes. He leaned forward and told the driver to go very slowly along Route de Zikawei. When they drew up alongside a set of tall iron gates much like Herbert Hinchcliffe's, Perique drained the flask and dragged the boys out of the automobile.

"This is the house where I was born and raised. It is where my mother was murdered, and where my father died in his sleep of old age."

Ji Fung and Lin Bai exchanged wary glances, unsure what Perique wanted of them.

"I don't know who lives here now, but I'm sure they won't mind us having a wander through the garden. There used to be roses, every color you can imagine . . ."

"Pei, no." Lin Bai dug his nails into Perique's shoulder. "It's dark. These people won't want us sneaking through their garden. What if they think we're Japanese soldiers?"

But Perique was already pushing open the gates and striding in. The boys followed, intending to seize him. Instead they nearly ran into him, for he had stopped at the head of the overgrown path and was staring at the moonlit remains of the house.

The paint was gray and leprous, falling away in scabby clumps. The graceful windows were smashed, only a few jagged points of glass embedded in the rotten frames. The roses were still there, leggy and wild, their pale whorls edged with brown. The delicate skeletons of what might have once been fruit trees lay on their sides, tangled roots ripped out of the swampy ground. The front door hung open, revealing an unhealthy darkness inside.

Perique stood as motionless as the moss-covered, vine-draped statues that inhabited the garden. His back was to Ji Fung, but the sag of his shoulders bespoke bitter disappointment. Ji Fung wondered what Perique had hoped to find there.

"Pei," he said, laying a hand on his friend's shoulder. "Let's go."

There was a low rustle from inside the house. Perique's chin snapped up. His whole body seemed to focus with a predatory intensity on the darkness inside the open door. Ji Fung looked, too, just in time to see a young girl step out onto the veranda.

Painfully thin beneath her gray scrap of a dress, she was hauling the frame of a wooden chair with no seat. She saw them and froze.

Ji Fung could hardly believe what happened next, even

though he saw it with his own eyes. Perique reached into his jacket and whipped out his tiny gun as easily as a cowboy in an American movie. Before Ji Fung could react, a fire-cracker pop sounded in the still evening air, and the girl's dirty cheek exploded in a hot red spray. She crumpled like paper. The chair lost a leg as it hit the moldering tiles of the veranda.

The boys stood stunned, as Perique ran up the steps and kicked the fallen girl. "Thief!" he shouted. "I'll teach you to steal from my father's house!"

He kicked the body again and again until it tumbled off the veranda and into the weeds. Falling to his knees, he care-fully set the chair up on its three remaining legs.

"My father had eight of these chairs, and a table to match." Tears sparkled on his pale face in the moonlight. "At the banquets he gave for his business associates, I was always seated on his right side. It was the only time I ever thought he was proud of me."

Perique's sobs grew heavier, shaking his body.

"Everything is gone," he whispered. His voice was nearly lost beneath the song of crickets in the dying garden.

That night, Ji Fung could have sworn Perique dragged them to every bar and nightclub in Shanghai. Each place was packed with people who seemed desperate for a good time. Jazz lubricated the sultry night air. Glasses were filled and emptied and filled again. The impromptu carnival swelled and spilled out onto the streets, and the boys let it carry them like a warm alcoholic tide.

Ji Fung tried to hold himself aloof from the revelry. Under every gay drunken smile seemed to lurk a rictus of despera-tion. There were soldiers here and there in the crowd, many of them pitifully young, all drinking as if it were their last day on earth. Prostitutes swarmed like rats. Even the oldest and the most diseased were doing a brisk business. Everyone seemed to be trying to grab the last handful of a good time.

The night soured early for Ji Fung, but it took hours to drag Perique back to the Cathay Hotel.

Standing alone by the window, Ji Fung stared out over the predawn harbor. He could make out several Japanese boats, including a huge flagship flying the Rising Sun. Unease gnawed at his belly, and when Lin Bai slid warm arms around his waist, Ji Fung flinched.

"Things are going bad here," Lin Bai whispered, pressing his lips to the back of Ji Fung's neck. "Can you feel it?"

Ji Fung nodded. "I think there will be war soon in Shanghai."

"No, not just Shanghai." Lin Bai rested his chin on Ji Fung's shoulder and stared out over the harbor. "I mean all of China. You weren't paying attention tonight, but everyone is talking about war. About revolution. Crazy talk. There is fighting all over."

Lin Bai gripped Ji Fung's waist, just above the swell of his buttocks. "I think we should leave."

Ji Fung turned his head to look into Lin Bai's face. "Go back to Hong Kong?"

"No." Lin Bai kept staring out the window. "To America."

"Don't be silly. Where would we get the money?"

"Pei has money."

Ji Fung turned to look at Perique, who slept restlessly in tangled covers.

"Leave the old world behind," said Lin Bai. His naked skin was warm and silken against Ji Fung's back. "Leave bad luck behind. Start a new life in Hollywood, like our dreams."

Ji Fung turned and took Lin Bai in his arms. The angles of his lover's body felt so precious, so fragile. "I can't leave my family," he said.

Lin Bai pushed away, his eyes dark and narrow. "I am your family. Pei would be, too, if you let him."

Ji Fung was silent. His uncle had given him back his lost identity. He gave Ji Fung a lineage, a history, made him feel connected not only to his lost blood family, but to the greater brotherhood of the Triads. And, after finding his long-lost nephew, Ji Fung didn't think Gong Sut Fo would be happy to lose him again. In fact, if he did anything to make his uncle believe he was his mother's son, he suspected he would not be allowed to live.

"Bai," he said. His voice felt ragged, torn. "Please don't make me choose."

All next day they shopped. Perique was more manic than ever, throwing away money on whatever trinket caught his fancy, accepting first price on everything. He loaded Lin Bai's arms with jade bracelets and bought Ji Fung a shamefully expensive diamond tiepin. For himself, he chose a new gold watch with his initials inside in fine, spidery script.

As the day wore on, Ji Fung found himself walking a few steps behind Lin Bai and Perique. As the wet afternoon heat beat down on their skulls and glued their clothes to their bodies, their petty squabbling intensified. Ji Fung usually found it amusing; he would address them as "you girls" and refer to them as "the girls" until they both turned on him. But now their sharp voices scraped his nerves raw. His head throbbed in time with his uneasy heart. Something was going to happen.

In a candy shop, "the girls" argued over whether to buy chocolates or salted plums. Ji Fung leaned against the doorway, nauseated by the smell of burnt sugar. He had gone earlier to the telegraph office to wire his uncle, but the tiny storefront was packed beyond capacity, the anxious crowd spilling out onto the streets. He tried the telephone, but all lines had been co-opted for military use. Now he felt lost and adrift, disconnected from both of his families.

The only useful article Perique had bought him today was a roomy black valise, perfect for holding the red lacquer box. Stepping out of the path of a fat European lady with a snarling dog under each huge white arm, Ji Fung squatted and unbuckled the valise, just to check. Just to run his fingers over the cool surface of the precious box, reassuring himself that it was still there. He had been afraid to leave it behind in the hotel room. He was almost certain that he had failed his uncle and the Triad brotherhood . . . almost. The box was his one link to that life. As long as he had it, there was a chance he still belonged there.

At last Perique and Lin Bai came out of the candy shop with a box of chocolates, a bag of salted plums, and a handful of the fragrant, near-bitter black ropes Ji Fung had developed a taste for back in Hong Kong. Ji Fung chewed slowly as they walked, still uneasy, but beginning to be lulled by the drowsy heat. A light rain began to fall, slicking the sidewalks, turning the sky a watery gray, blunting the harsh edges of the afternoon. Perique's fragmented memories took them on a nonsensical route through the city, and Ji Fung let himself be led.

"Sincere's," Perique sighed as they reached the intersection of Nanking Road. "I must take you to Sincere's and buy you anything your hearts desire. I promised you I would." His jade eyes were overbright in his flushed face.

Ji Fung tried to protest. "Pei, you've bought us enough. Why not go back—"

Lin Bai cut him off. "Let him keep buying. It makes him happy; he loves to show off for us. And how do you know we won't need these things?"

"Jade and diamonds—"

"Can be traded for other things," Lin Bai said with an air of finality.

Sincere's turned out to be a vast department store with palm trees flanking its doors like sentinels at the entrance to some ancient temple. Inside it was dark and cool, redolent of fine cloth and subtle oils. Everywhere he looked, Ji Fung saw something he had never seen before. Candied ducks' tongues and torturous devices for curling ladies' hair. Jade carvings the size of small children. Shiny modern appliances and conveniences side by side with celadon goddesses and lucky red banners for long life and good fortune. Standing in the midst of all this wealth, Ji Fung could almost believe the promises made by the flowing golden characters.

There was a small commotion outside. At first Ji Fung ignored it, but it grew louder and louder. He drifted toward the doors, leaving Perique and Lin Bai with their heads bent over the glass jewelry cases.

"What's happening?" he asked a running boy in an American baseball hat.

The boy looked at him quizzically, poised to flee. Ji Fung clasped his shoulder and repeated the question in English.

"Chinese planes are bombing the *Idzumo*!" the boy said, squirming out of Ji Fung's grasp.

"The what?"

"The Japanese warship," the boy called over his shoulder. "Get down to the harbor, or you'll miss it!"

Ji Fung stepped into the street and looked up into the pale gray sky. The rain had tapered off, but he couldn't see any planes. He heard distant thunder and the growling of engines in the east. All around him people were huddled together, staring into the empty sky.

A wry-faced old man with a cage of geese on the end of a pole was reporting to everyone around him. He had been on the bank of the Whangpoo when the attack began.

"Pah!" he spat. "Not one bomb hit that ship. Just falling into the water, impotent. I am ashamed for the sons of China. How can we hope to save our country from the Japanese devils when our planes are worst quality and our pilots are untrained?"

"Look!" A pregnant woman with a baby on her back stabbed a finger at the sky. The whine of engines grew louder, and a brace of four Chinese planes cast their crucifix shadows on the cobblestones of Nanking Road.

"See how they retreat in shame," said the old man, shaking his white head and making his wispy beard fly. "No hope for China."

"Grandfather." A young girl with ribboned braids tugged at the old man's sleeve. "What are those black spots in the sky?"

The old man's rheumy eyes grew huge, and nearly as round as a foreigner's. "It cannot be," he whispered. But the wobbling black specks grew and grew, their cylindrical shapes and finned back ends becoming clearer as they fell.

A dreadful lazy paralysis gripped Ji Fung's bones as he watched the bombs falling toward him. Their descent seemed almost leisurely, like the gait of a man strolling to meet a lover he had known for years. He might have stood there staring until his eyes were blinded in their sockets by the blast if an image of Lin Bai's face had not risen before him like a foreshadowing of explosion.

His sick complacency shattered. He turned and ran back into Sincere's. After staring into the sky for so long, the store's dim interior seemed completely black.

And then the bombs fell to earth.

There was only a split second of terror, a split second of Lin Bai's name hot in his throat. Then the muscular push of the shock wave filled his head with thunder, picked him up, and threw him like the hand of an angry god. There was pain and vertigo and a huge soft impact that blotted out the world.

Ji Fung resurfaced with a feeling of great weight, of suffocation. He thrashed against the yielding mass that surrounded him until he reached light and air. He was battered but not seriously hurt, and he saw that he had been buried under bolts of fine silk. Their vibrant colors were dimmed with soot and plaster dust, stained with dark blood. He dug frantically in the pile, his heart screaming in his chest. He had to find his valise. Where was the red box? Ji Fung knew he had lost it, had failed his uncle, his father, their myriad brotherhood.

When his fingers touched the buttery leather of the valise, tears of relief filled his stinging eyes. He sank down into the pile of silk, clutching the valise to his chest for what seemed an eternity, his mind washed clean of thought.

Again the thought of Lin Bai penetrated his haze, a blinding aftershock that pulled him back from catatonia. Ji Fung heaved himself up, still clutching the valise, and began to look for his friends. The few landmarks he had noticed in the store were jumbled and broken, leaving Ji Fung disoriented, unable to locate the jewelry case where he had left them admiring a large ruby set into a heavy gold ring.

The store was in a shambles, all the beautiful things smashed and ruined. The cable that lifted the glass elevator to the upper floor had snapped. The elevator's twisted carcass lay at the bottom of the shaft, seeping oil and blood. The remains of its passengers were a mangled stew. The whole thing looked somehow organic, a monster of flesh and metal, freshly dead.

Toward the back of the store, the ornate ceiling had collapsed, crushing shoppers beneath tons of stone and plaster. The dead and dying were everywhere. Hands clutched at Ji Fung, voices begged for help or a quick blow to the head, but he refused to heed them. He picked his way through the wreckage like a blind man, the image of Lin Bai's face his only guide.

He found Perique first.

He was dead. That much was obvious from ten feet away. His body lay twisted, head skewed at an angle that defied anatomy. When Ji Fung got closer, he could see the metal skeleton of the display case. A million shards of glass had exploded out of that frame, and Perique had been standing directly in front of it. Ji Fung knelt beside his friend to make sure of what he already knew.

Perique's handsome face was almost unrecognizable. Precious stones glittered in the flayed meat of his cheeks, diamonds and emeralds embedded there by the force of the blast. His eyes were filled with slivers of fine crystal. His white linen suit was scarlet with blood.

In the soft flesh under Perique's chin, Ji Fung saw the ruby ring Lin Bai had admired. It was reluctant to part with the open muscle into which it had sunk, but Ji Fung was determined. Eventually it came free with an unwholesome sound, and he tucked it into his vest pocket. A single thought filled his mind, blotting out the shrieks and sobs around him. Lin Bai had liked this ring. Ji Fung would give it to him. He had found the ring; therefore, he would find Lin Bai.

But in the end, Lin Bai found him.

"Is he dead?" asked the familiar resonant voice. Ji Fung turned to see Lin Bai standing almost gracefully in the death and rubble. His silk stockings were laddered, his fancy red shoes spattered with darker blood. His face and arms were laced with cuts.

Ji Fung stood, longing to sweep Lin Bai into his arms, but unable. "He was a good man," he heard himself reciting. "Generous and brave." Why was he being so formal? He wanted to laugh, scream, anything that would break the grip of this strange coldness.

Lin Bai dropped to his knees beside Perique and touched the shattered, jewel-encrusted curve of his jaw. Then he opened the white linen jacket and removed Perique's money clip. He hesitated for a moment, then took the new gold watch and the gun in Perique's waistband as well.

Ji Fung frowned. "Stealing from the dead?"

Lin Bai's chin was set, determined. "He will not need these things in heaven."

A woman began screaming a few yards away. They could not see her, but her shrill sounds of agony pierced their brains.

"Come." Lin Bai took Ji Fung's hand. "It will be better outside."

It was worse. Shanghai was no longer an oasis of elegance and decadence, untouched by the inconvenient machinations of revolution. The gilded carapace that protected the soft-bodied foreigners from the reality of China was shattered forever. War had arrived at their doorstep, and when they failed to hear it knocking, had come smashing in.

Death was the great equalizer. Chinese and Europeans lay side by side, washed in each other's blood, some bodies driven into each other by the force of the blast. Limbs and unidentifiable chunks of flesh lay bleeding on the rain-damp cobblestones. Drivers slumped over the wheels of expensive cars, their rich passengers cooked in the backseats like smoked ducks in a restaurant window.

The old man who had feared for the future of China sat naked in the street, clothes ripped from his body by the concussion. His wispy white beard was reduced to char on his scorched cheeks. In their bamboo cage, his geese had been churned into a pink stew of innards and feathers. The old man held a mass of carbonized flesh to his scrawny chest. Ji Fung could barely make out the clutching shape of a tiny hand, the bright scrap of a colored ribbon in a smoking black tangle of hair.

"No hope!" the old man cried. "No hope for China!"

Lin Bai pulled Ji Fung to a clear area in the middle of the street, away from walls that might crumble at any second. "Listen to me. We have to get out of the country. You would not believe me before—believe me now. The old man is right. There is no hope in China, only death. We have no choice. We must open your uncle's box."

Ji Fung clutched the valise. "You are talking crazy. I cannot open it. And what would we do with the contents if I could?"

"The opium in that box is worth a fortune. We could sell it cheaply and still have more than enough for two tickets to America."

Ji Fung turned his face away. "I told you. I cannot betray my family."

"Tell me one thing," said Lin Bai. His fine black brows drew down over his eyes, which were spitting dark fire. "Where is *my* place in your new family? Will you leave me behind to marry some suitable girl of your uncle's choosing?"

"Of course not. I planned to introduce you as Pei's cousin—"

"Pei is dead. And your uncle lives today because he was not allowed to marry the woman of his choosing, your mother. What makes you think he would allow you to choose your wife?"

"I would not abandon you," Ji Fung murmured. But Lin Bai raged on.

"Even if he did, I am not a woman! Even if you have forgotten this, I have not. Do you expect me to play this role until the day I die? You have found your own identity, but you care nothing for mine. Who killed Master Lau so that you could live? Who has been like a brother and a lover to you? Was it your precious family?"

Lin Bai's well-trained voice sliced through the shrieks, moans, and crashes that made up the aftermath of the explosion. Ji Fung's cheeks burned with shame, and he looked around to see if anyone could hear. The few people still able to stand and walk paid them no mind, but he cringed at the thought of this conversation falling on the ears of a dying person. "We mustn't talk here."

"Will you not listen?" Lin Bai lowered his voice. "We can sell or trade the opium and be on our way to America by tomorrow. Your uncle will assume you were killed in the bombing. He is rich. You know that he would not trust you with more than he could afford to lose."

"I cannot steal from my own family."

Lin Bai's face was dark with fury. "You dare to speak to me about stealing. You are stealing my future to please a man you barely knew."

"My father . . ." Ji Fung felt as if he were being pulled inside out, as if his heart were being fought over by dogs.

"I had no father. I have no uncle, no rich influential family. If I cannot escape from China, I will die. I do not want to be a ghost in your family's house."

He reached out to Ji Fung, still achingly beautiful under the plaster dust and sticky blood that streaked his face.

"Give me the box."

Ji Fung gripped the valise tighter. "I cannot."

Tears clung to Lin Bai's dark lashes, then spilled over, tracing crystal lines on his lacerated cheeks. "Then you leave me no choice," he said. He reached into his red leather handbag and took out Perique's gun. As if in a dream, he pointed it at Ji Fung's face. "Give me the box."

For a long moment, Ji Fung was too shocked to speak. His mind raced with irrelevant memories. He recalled a time when Lin Bai had played the female warrior Mu Lan, and Ji Fung had been one of the evil henchmen. It was the only time they had had to fight each other, and throughout the scene they had to struggle to keep from laughing. But now there was no humor in Lin Bai's eyes, only a shiny glaze of desperation.

"You would shoot me?"

"I have no choice," Lin Bai said. His agony was evident in his trembling voice, but the gun's barrel did not waver.

Ji Fung's chest was tight and icy. "Don't do this. Come home with me."

"Put the box on the ground." Now Lin Bai's voice was barely audible above the sounds of the wounded and dying.

Moving as if trapped in the thick syrup of nightmare, Ji Fung laid the valise on the pavement between them. He watched from what felt like a great distance as Lin Bai snatched it and pulled out the red box. Searching in the rubble, Lin Bai found a fist-sized stone and began smashing the brass lock. The gun was no longer aimed at Ji Fung, but he did not think of rushing Lin Bai. He knew the quickness of his lover's reflexes.

It took five strikes. The final blow smashed the red lacquer lid and sent lock and contents spilling across the bloody cobblestones.

It was sand. Fine white sand.

Lin Bai dropped the gun. He grabbed a double handful of the stuff, sifting it through his fingers, whipping his head back and forth in wordless denial. Ji Fung saw a scrap of paper in the splintered remains of the box and bent to retrieve it.

"Mister Hinchcliffe," it read in English. "If my nephew delivers this box to you unopened, please give him five hundred American dollars, which you will be soon repaid. I am very grateful for your assistance."

Below this was his uncle's chop. Ji Fung let the note fall from his numb fingers.

Lin Bai's hands were still buried in sand, but now he turned his face to the sky. "Ji Fung. Listen . . ."

Again the drone of engines from above, coming fast and low. Ji Fung tried to speak, but the words that might have healed all that lay shattered between them were swallowed in a second volley of explosions that sent him sprawling flat on the ground, face pressed into the bloody sand.

When he was able to open his eyes, he saw Lin Bai's face

washed with fresh blood from a deep gouge on his temple. He could not tell whether his lover still lived. As he gathered Lin Bai into his arms, Ji Fung began sobbing at last. It felt as if the sobs were being wrenched up from the depths of his trained lungs, from the pit of his belly, from the root of his genitals. He wanted to close his eyes and never open them again. But even as he realized this, he felt the faintest thread of a pulse in Lin Bai's throat, and he knew he could not die while Lin Bai lived.

The hospital was a fresh kind of hell. Doctors and nurses moved like sleepwalkers through an ocean of trauma, treating only those who seemed to stand a chance of survival, injecting the rest with morphine and leaving them in the hallways to die. It was full dark before Ji Fung could get someone to examine Lin Bai. The doctor was English, scarcely older than Perique. His blue eyes were ringed with purple fatigue, his arms gloved in blood past the elbows.

"Your wife has a concussion and, I suspect, a hairline fracture of the skull. You must try to keep the wound clean, since infection of the brain could result in death."

The doctor took out a handkerchief and wiped his sweating brow.

"I would give you medicine, but there is none left. I would give you extra gauze to dress the wound, but we have none to spare. There is nothing more I can do for her."

Outside, the night was hot and foul. The living had done their best to clear the dead from the streets, but the task was overwhelming and the heat unforgiving. The stench of burned, rotting flesh had already begun to pervade the humid summer breeze. They walked along the Bund, where the river freshened the air a little, looking for their hotel. They could not find it. The Japanese ships were still anchored in the dark water, impassive, perhaps gloating over the city's self-destruction.

Ji Fung held Lin Bai while he vomited blood and chocolate against the Hong Kong and Shanghai Bank Building. The smell of bile was almost welcome, for at least it smelled of life.

"Ji Fung," Lin Bai gasped as if reading his lover's thoughts. "I'm dying."

"Hush," Ji Fung whispered. "Stop that bad luck talk."

"Bad luck is all we have," Lin Bai wailed. "The world is dying. No escape."

"Don't worry." Ji Fung smoothed back the sweaty, bloody hair straggling into Lin Bai's face. "We're going home to Hong Kong. We'll be safe there."

"No escape," Lin Bai repeated. "Oh, I'm *so dizzy* . . ." He crawled away from Ji Fung and began to vomit again.

A crowd had formed across the street, shouting and jostling. Taking a few steps closer, Ji Fung saw that the commotion was centered around an open military vehicle. The crowd seized its occupants and dragged them into the street, attacking them with stones, long jagged splinters of wood, whatever deadly thing came to hand.

As Ji Fung watched, a young Japanese soldier tore free from the mob and stumbled across the street toward him. The man's face was a bloody sponge, nose smashed, lips and ears split open. His uniform was in tatters. Beneath his close-cropped hair, Ji Fung could see deep gashes in his scalp. The skull gleamed dully through in several spots. One hellish porridge of a wound exposed the man's brain.

The soldier grabbed Ji Fung's lapels and shouted something in rhyming staccato syllables. Then he was falling. Before he fully knew what he was doing, Ji Fung caught him and lowered him gently to the ground. The soldier's hands found his own, and Ji Fung gripped them tightly. The Japanese might be invading, torturing devils. But the Japanese were an abstract. This young man was like him, a pawn in an implacable system, set upon by forces beyond his understanding.

Ji Fung cradled the dying soldier, staring into his eyes. One of his pupils was blown, filling the iris with bottomless blackness. As Ji Fung gazed into that eye, it seemed that images from the man's damaged brain imprinted themselves on his own. People he had never seen, landscapes he had never known. A silent room where a master meditated, his still body a vessel brimming with the fluid motions of combat. A girl in an embroidered kimono, cherry blossoms woven through her long black hair.

A bubble of thick blood swelled and burst at the man's lips. His body stiffened in Ji Fung's arms, and a long wet rattle came from deep in his chest. As life left the soldier, the images in Ji Fung's head seemed to foretell the future. He saw the man's body decomposing where it lay, bursting open in the wet heat, flyblown and ripe with the juices of decay. He saw an old man and woman reading a letter, their faces sagging with grief. He saw what looked like a line of ghost-children in a shadowed hallway, translucent and insubstantial, stretching into infinity. The children this man would have had, perhaps, and their children, and their children's children. Their little hands were curled against their chests as if they knew they would never be born.

The soldier's fingers closed on his sleeve, a reflex of death. And suddenly Ji Fung thought he was in a strange city, the city where this man and all his family had lived. Something had fallen from the sky—a bomb, but more terrible than any bomb Shanghai had seen. He was running from a fearsome heat that baked his skin and made his eyes feel as if they were frying in their sockets. His organs were cooking inside him. He could go no farther.

He fell, rolled over on his blistering back, and stared at a sight utterly beyond his comprehension. A swelling crown of fire rose into a striated sky. Beneath it was a great column of smoke in which he could make out blackened shapes twisting, swirling. It must be a million *li* high. How could anyone live in a world where such a thing was possible? He was not sure whether he had closed his eyes or been blinded, but either one was preferable to the sight of that devil's cloud.

Ji Fung blinked. He was crouching on the steps of the Hong Kong and Shanghai Bank Building cradling a dead man in his arms. Behind him, he could hear Lin Bai still gagging and spitting; it seemed only a few seconds had passed. He stared into the soldier's ruined face. "What have you shown me?" he whispered. "Would you have lived to see that? If so, then be thankful you are dead tonight."

He laid the soldier's body aside and went to help his lover.

On the crowded deck of an old junk called the *Devil Fox*, Ji Fung sat with his back against a pile of rotting hemp rope, cradling Lin Bai's head in his lap. It was a good spot, occasionally shaded by the ragged brown sails that made him think of enormous curved insect wings. Ji Fung had traded his diamond tiepin, Perique's gold watch, and all but one of Lin Bai's jade bracelets for passage to Hong Kong, silently thanking Perique for that last frantic shopping spree.

Now their faces were burned by wind and sun, their lips dry with salt spray. Ji Fung had eaten nothing since sharing the last of the candy with Lin Bai two days ago. Letting the thick chocolate melt over his tongue, it had been difficult to believe he had ever stood in the doorway of the candy shop on Nanking Road listening to "the girls" squabbling. There was still fresh water on the junk, but with so many people on board, it wouldn't last more than another day or two.

Lin Bai stirred in his lap and whimpered softly, a hopeless painful sound. Ji Fung did his best to soothe him, checking the crusted bandage that covered the wound in his temple. It was foul and stinking, but Ji Fung had used the last strip of cloth from his shirt, and he was reluctant to start tearing up his jacket, the only sunshade they had.

"Hing," whispered Lin Bai. *Older Brother*, a nickname he had not called Ji Fung for many years. "I'm thirsty."

"You'll have some water soon. They'll come round with the bucket." Ji Fung stroked Lin Bai's cheek. Neither of them needed to shave yet, but there was the faintest shadow of fine black hair on the line of Lin Bai's jaw. Ji Fung wondered how much longer his lover would be able to pass for a woman, and what would happen if they were found out. Would the crowd of refugees gang up on them, throw them overboard to save a few mouthfuls of water? Did the hatred run that deep? Or did the less important taboos fall by the wayside in desperate times such as these?

Luckily, the people closest to them were unlikely to notice anything amiss: an ancient half blind man with three exquisitely carved cricket cages on a string; a pair of exhausted women with a brood of hollow-eyed children who demanded all their attention.

That night, the weather turned bad. They had come into the wake of a typhoon, and could not tell whether they were sailing around its edges or straight into its heart. Ji Fung covered Lin Bai with his jacket and huddled in the rain with nothing but his thin silk vest and bloodstained pants. The sea flexed angrily beneath them. Lin Bai's face was icy pale, his lips bruise blue. He lapsed into occasional delirium, babbling to Ji Fung or Perique or Master Lau, then sobbing as if his heart would break. Ji Fung sang every song he knew, trying to soothe him, but Lin Bai would not join in, not even when Ji Fung forgot the words.

The old man with the cricket cages gave them sips of plum wine from a small bottle he had hidden inside a cloth shoe, saying he would do anything to help young lovers. He told them a story about two lovers who had turned themselves into crickets to escape disapproving parents. Ji

Fung was glad for the endless rain because it masked his tears.

In the morning the old man was dead, his toothless mouth filled with rain. The crew dumped him overboard and took the lovely cricket cages. Ji Fung managed to salvage the bottle of plum wine, nearly empty now. He watched the swirling water toss the old man's thin frame until cruising sharks pulled it under. He shuddered and held Lin Bai closer. They were still three days from Hong Kong.

The rain did not let up. Instead the sea became more violent. Looking into the sky was like watching a silvery veil slowly descending in a huge spiral pattern. Ji Fung's bones ached from cold and wet and from fighting the wind. Waves towered higher than the boat, walls of slate-green death that could swallow them in an easy second if the gale turned. Sometimes water sheeted across the deck, washing away seasick-vomit and untethered bundles. People lost the few precious items they had been able to salvage from the wreck of Shanghai. The waves around them were peppered with silk wedding dresses and gilded teapots, portraits of stern ancestors and lacquer chests much like the one Lin Bai had smashed open in Nanking Road. So many treasures, now all as worthless as a few handfuls of sand.

The water began to claim children and old people who could not hang on. Passengers were tying themselves to the masts and rigging, grimly aware that they were almost sure to drown if the junk capsized, but willing to risk it rather than be swept overboard. Ji Fung used a piece of wet hemp rope to lash himself and Lin Bai to a heavy iron hook embedded in the deck. His mind was empty of any thought but survival.

By the time they made it into Hong Kong harbor, more than half the passengers were gone.

The typhoon pulling the junk in its wake had already reached the island city. It was as if the destruction of Shanghai had followed them home, using water and wind instead of fire to attack the familiar landscape. The junks and sampans in the harbor were battened down tight, but the swells still tossed them cruelly. At the top of a long pole on the pier, a warning flag fluttered. Two triangles, one stacked on top of the other, apex to apex. Ji Fung thought the symbol looked like an hourglass with its time running out.

It took almost all night to find a hotel. Thousands of travelers, refugees, and Kowloonese who had missed the last ferry were holed up waiting for the storm to pass. Finally he was able to trade Lin Bai's last jade bracelet for a tiny room in one of the rough hotels that catered mostly to foreign sailors.

He laid Lin Bai on the stained mattress, peeled off the torn stockings and wet rag of a dress, covered him with a thin gray blanket. It was not necessary; Lin Bai's naked flesh radiated the heat of sickness like a well-stoked furnace.

"Hing . . . Tell the Master I am too sick to go to him. I cannot bear it tonight."

He groped the air, and Ji Fung seized his hand. It felt like a fleshless claw, almost too hot to hold. "The Master is dead," Ji Fung said. "He will never touch you again."

"Chen Bau will have to play White Snake." Lin Bai's yellowed eyes roamed from side to side, unseeing. "Tell him to use the quail-feather headdress."

Ji Fung saw a crystal drop splash into the hollow of Lin Bai's collarbone. Was the wretched roof leaking? He touched a fingertip to it, then tasted it. Warm and salty. A tear, his own.

"Ji Fung?" Lin Bai's voice was thick and low, clotted with infection. "One day we'll leave this place, won't we? We'll go to Hollywood. No more boring Chinese operas for us. We'll be cowboys and gangsters."

"That's right," Ji Fung said. He undressed and slid under the blanket, enfolding Lin Bai's hot, skeletal body in his arms. "When you get better, I promise you we'll leave this place. But first you must promise me you will get better. Do you promise?"

But Lin Bai was silent, his breathing ragged and tortured. Ji Fung spent the rest of the night holding him, trying to think of everything he had ever wanted to say, murmuring it all into the sweat-damp hair at the back of Lin Bai's neck. Sometimes he sang snatches of opera, pretending to grope for the words, trying to make Lin Bai join in.

"But those who were true have come together at last." He remembered Lin Bai lying limp in his arms after the near-fatal overdose. *"Even though thousands of miles apart . . ."*

But he could not bring himself to sing the next line, though his mind spoke it soft and clear.

Even though torn from each other by death . . .

Ji Fung looked down into Lin Bai's white face and knew that he was dying. As bloody light seeped into the sky, he lay listening to his lover's final breath, long and slow, the sound of his soul slipping out from between his parched lips.

Ji Fung kissed those lips. They were dry, faintly sweet, as slack as death itself.

He lay holding Lin Bai's body for a long time, listening to the storm screaming outside. He was not afraid; he knew Lin Bai would never hurt him, had known it even when the gun was pointed at his face. But when he felt a chill stealing over the corpse in his arms, he shuddered and sat up to put on his vest.

As he fastened the little carved buttons, he felt a lump in the left pocket. Unbuttoning it, he discovered the forgotten ring from Sincere's and the jade chop that had once been the receptacle of all his hopes and dreams. The blood-dark jewel was as dazzling as it had been when Lin Bai pointed it out to Perique in the glass display case, a thousand years ago.

He imagined how Lin Bai's face would have looked when Ji Fung slid the ring onto his slender finger. But it was too late for that. The world was dead. Lin Bai was dead.

There was nothing left. The family that had meant so much
to him seemed worthless without Lin Bai there to share it. As
worthless as two handfuls of sand. He curled up on the bed
and sobbed into his lover's cooling shoulder, wishing he
were dead, too.

But as the day wore on, he found his wish unfulfilled. His
body was stiff, filled with aches and covered with bruises, a
far cry from the numb comfort of death. Unless he wanted to
kill himself, he would have to live. He turned the ring and the
chop over and over in his hands. As the daylight died away,
so did the typhoon. A limpid, eerie hush fell over the city.
The eye of the storm had arrived, and Ji Fung felt the stir-
rings of a plan.

Selling this ring would give him enough money for the
two things he needed.

First, a ticket to America. Second, a bottle of kerosene.

He thought Lin Bai would approve of both purchases.

Gong Sut Fo was taking his pleasure with an American singer,
a red-haired, long-legged beauty with wide amber eyes and
coral pink nipples. Her temperament was as fiery as her color-
ing, and this tryst had cost him a great deal in both money and
peace of mind. When a pallid, trembling servant interrupted
with four taps on the door, he was furious.

"You dare to disturb me?" Gong Sut Fo yanked on a robe
of black-and-red silk. "What is it that cannot wait until a man
is finished with—is—is finished?"

"A ghost, Gwan." Ghost, indeed. Gwan was a fawning
term of respect, ghost meant a matter that couldn't be discussed in front of the singer, and the servant looked as
though someone had just murdered his only son.

The singer understood some Cantonese. She pulled the
blanket up over her pendulous breasts and frowned. "A
ghost! What's he talking about?"

Annoyed by this turn of events, his cock wilting like an old turnip, Gong Sut Fo found that her flat American voice grated on his nerves. He kissed her manicured fingers. "Mimi, my sweet . . ." He took a deep breath, remembered the cushiony feel of her body. "I swear I will return to you without delay."

As he rushed down the stairs, he could hear shouting in the alley behind the kitchen. He pushed the cowering servant out of the way and strode past the crowd of cooks and scrubbers, out through the servants' entrance, into the alley. The smell hit him at once, the unforgettable smell that had branded itself on his memory eight years ago in an upstairs hallway of his brother's house. It was an odor of tallow, of dripping fat, of frying hair and meat, foul yet somehow savory.

There was a burning corpse in his alley.

"Fools!" he spat, shoving servants toward the kitchen door. "Do you want the whole neighborhood to go up in flames? Go! Get water!" The gawking servants quickly formed a brigade of water pots and buckets. Even so, it was several minutes before they extinguished the flames.

Gong Sut Fo knelt to examine the body. Its limbs were shrunken, drawn up into the fetal position. Its face was a nightmare rictus of charred flesh and scorched bone. But the feet were hardly burned at all, and he easily recognized the shiny black-and-white shoes he had ordered Chi Gwai to give his nephew. Gong Sut Fo felt a sinking sensation in his chest as he saw that the corpse was clutching something in its hand.

It was difficult to pry open the tight black fists, and he was able to do so only by snapping some of the fingers. They crumbled like burned noodles. In the end, he found what he was looking for.

The jade was cracked from the heat, but the carved characters still spelled out his nephew's name.

The servant who had disturbed Gong Sut Fo's pleasure now knelt before him, trembling even more violently than before. There was a folded piece of paper in his hand.

"This was found in the kitchen door," he said, and scuttled away as soon as Gong Sut Fo took the paper.

The English words were written in a scrawling, childish hand. The note read simply, "I am my mother's son."

When their master went back inside, the servants threw an old blanket over the smoking remains of the corpse and shooed a small crowd of onlookers out of the alley. In the shuffle to retreat, no one noticed the tall homely girl with a gray kerchief pulled down over her large ears. No one asked why she was smiling even though there were tears on her face.

1940

1941

1942

1943

1944

1945

1946

1947

1948

1949

RIDING THE BLACK

BY CHARLES GRANT

The buck stops here.

—Harry S. Truman

When the sun rose, it was summer white, and the shadows it cast weren't shadows at all, but simply places in the air where things went to hide until the moon returned. In a small stable too weathered to be quaint, a pair of horses shifted uneasily; in a small two-room cabin too worn to be real comfort, boards creaked and a kettle whistled faintly and a curtain stirred when a breeze slipped past the cracked window and died on the bare floor.

When the kettle stopped, there was no sound at all.

In the front yard, mostly bleached dirt and sagging grass and a handful of cacti barely the height of a child, a blue-tail lizard darted from stone to rock, freezing, darting, slipping under the low porch where the sun couldn't reach and the heat was less a furnace than a sullen, crouching thing.

What horizon there was in what directions there were might have been cut from impressive mountains had the mountains had color, had the haze not smeared the slopes and softened the peaks.

A man sat on the porch, holding a tin cup of coffee between his palms. There was no chill to dispel, but he felt one just the same, and sipped the thick liquid as if winter had somehow found its way to his marrow.

When he finished, he placed the cup beside his chair and watched the black road that passed by what passed for his home these days.

The land rolled unevenly, and out there in the high desert

were sage and piñon, cactus and scrub, freestanding boulders shaped by the wind, and in the distance straight ahead a line of full-crowned pale trees that marked the bend of a narrow river that teased but never came near.

Nothing moved.

An hour later he took a slow breath and pushed himself to his feet. He stretched, rubbed an eye with a knuckle, and stretched again. He was a man without height until he was angered, without much in his face until anger tightened the sun-baked creases and narrowed the midnight eyes, without much on his bones no matter how he felt.

His shirt was plaid, cuffs rolled back once, buttons open two down, collar worn and separated from what had once been a white yoke. Jeans. Scuffed boots. A leather belt scratched thin. A Stetson with front brim dipped low.

He watched the road.

Nothing moved.

He nodded once, slowly, and slowly he turned, stepping off the porch to make his way to the relative cool of the stable. There he fed and watered the skittish black, fed and saddled the placid roan, let the black make its way into the partly grassy, spring-fed corral, where it headed immediately for the false promise of shade beneath a cottonwood too old to care. The horse wasn't quite skin and bones, but to look at him would tell anyone a good run would kill him.

When it reached the tree, it turned its head.

The man nodded, a promise, and turned away, stroking the old roan's neck, whispering to her, flattering her, telling her he had a feeling they wouldn't be alone for long.

Once in the saddle, hat settled low, he let her find her own way out to the road, to the shoulder between the macadam and the wide ditch beside it. They moved easily, the man and the long-tail horse, seldom if ever in a hurry. He was late this morning. Usually, when he left, he left just after dawn, before the day had a chance to ignite the white fire. There had been a dream, though, and the shimmering faces of absent companions long awaited and long missed; they were alone as well, and, like him, they were searching.

He rode east toward a town the land's easy rise-and-fall tucked out of sight, not bothering to try to beat the sun. There was no sense moving faster; the day and the distance would have done them in. Not even when he glanced over his left shoulder and saw the dust cloud moving toward him. He didn't stop. He rode on. An engine rode the air.

Nothing moved.

Not even the roan.

Eventually, no time at all, horse and car were abreast, ignoring one another until the car sped up and drew onto the shoulder a hundred yards ahead. The roan was forced onto the road, snorting, one ear laid back.

The driver leaned out his window, shook his head, and stared at the rider through narrow sunglasses that mirrored nothing but the sky.

"You," the driver said, smiling, "are one son of a bitch to get hold of, you know that?" A round face, little tan. Shark's teeth.

The rider looked down patiently, saying nothing.

"I swear to Christ, Rob, when the hell you gonna get a telephone?" Matt Dumont rubbed his brow, and propped his arm on the opened window. "Damn, I hate coming out here. It's like driving in a goddamn furnace."

Rob Garland moved his lips, maybe a grin, maybe not. "So don't come." A voice much deeper than the engine, or the desert night.

"How the hell else am I going to get in touch?" A voice so average, most people barely heard it. "Jesus." He patted the door gently. "Like it? Roadmaster. Picked it up for a song last month, when old Davidson packed up for Los Angeles. He bought into the Frazer people, claimed he didn't want to be disloyal." He brayed. "A banker. Can you believe it? A disloyal banker?" He brayed again.

"I'm busy, Matt. What do you want?"

"You."

Rob grunted.

"I swear, Rob, that's all. I just want to talk. Is that so bad? A cuppa at Dinah's, what do you say?"

In shifting his other arm, Dumont's elbow accidentally hit the horn rim.

The swift blare was smothered under the weight of the heat.

The roan didn't move.

"You don't need me, Matt. Hell, you don't even like me."

Dumont cocked his head and grinned, a gap between his two front teeth. "So?"

"So there ain't nothing you can say I ain't already heard a hundred times before. I didn't like what I heard then, and I sure won't like it at Dinah's." He touched fingers to hat brim. "Drive slow, Matt. You hit something out here, ain't nobody gonna find you."

"You live out here, you'll find me."

Rob touched the roan's neck to get it moving. "No," he said. "I don't think so."

"Goddamnit, Garland," Dumont shouted at his back, exasperation high. "The war's over, you idiot! When are you gonna learn times change?"

A moment later the car sped past, horn shrieking, tires stirring dust into a bloated dervish as it swept over a rise and vanished.

Rob and the roan rode on, slow as the heat that rode with them.

He was annoyed that Dumont had shown up, annoyed that his peace had been disturbed by that long-front vehicle. He had nothing against cars, but they were virtually useless out here, and idiots like Dumont drove as if the Devil himself were perched on the roof. He hoped the man wouldn't be in town when he got there. He had no desire to talk. He had done his talking, and his fighting, and his running, and his bleeding.

That was then; this was now.

And now they passed a building that had once been a spur depot when the nearby mines were still working; but the mines had been hollow since FDR died, and the tracks were long gone, forged into tanks; the roof had caved in; the doors were splintered, the windows without glass; coyote tracks in the dust; tumbleweed nesting where the conductor once stood and wiped his face with a handkerchief half as long as his arm.

They passed an old buckboard collapsed in the ditch, wheels a memory, bolts rusted, the bed filled with pebbles and weeds and the bones of a hawk's meal. Planks missing; he had taken a couple himself when winter demanded a fire.

They passed a work crew planting telephone poles, stringing wires, wondering aloud who the hell in his right mind would order all this done all the way out here in the middle of nowhere, and nowhere to go.

They ignored him.

That was fine.

A hawk on the wing drifted as the sun rose.

Shadows sank into the ground.

Eventually, no time at all, he took the roan through the high open doors of the town's only remaining stable, dismounted, and told Solomon Winks to take it easy on the old gal, she was feeling the heat worse these days.

"Shouldn't ride her so hard in weather like this, Mr. Garland," the stable hand chided, shaking his head sorrowfully at the horse, clucking to it, easing off the saddle, reaching for a damp cloth to cool the beast down.

"We walked."

The black man sighed. "She walked. You rode."

Rob laughed quietly and fed the horse a sugar cube, let her nuzzle his chest.

Solomon, wearing nothing more than coveralls and a sleeveless undershirt, hosed water into a trough. "You mind me asking why you come in, Mr. Garland? I didn't think I'd see you for another couple weeks."

"Just looking around, son, just looking around."

The white-haired man squinted at him, scars across his forehead as if he'd been chewed in his sleep. "You never just look around."

Rob shrugged. "You get the urge, you got to move, that's all." He swatted the roan's rump a good-bye for now. Then he pointed at the stable hand. "Make nothing of it, Solomon, you hear me? Believe it or not, sometimes a man gets damn bored out there all alone."

Solomon nodded.

Rob knew it was a lie.

After scooping a palmful of water from the trough, wiping it over his face, he walked on through the long high building, smelling hay and sweat and cool and warm, until he reached the door that led into the back of the feed store. He walked through to the street without greeting the clerk and paused under the motionless fringed awning.

Cars at the curb, cars at the new traffic light; pedestrians in suits and jeans and dresses and work clothes handed out when the owners were discharged and came home from the ocean to the desert. He used to know them all; now he hardly knew a dozen. They moved on, the young did, to the cities on the coast across the mountains, and the cities across the plains.

The old stayed.

The young died.

The old didn't.

And the place itself had hardly changed: the long main

street shimmered darkly, heat lifting ghost arms in the distance, hiding the mountains, twisting the poles that took the place of trees, wires for branches, crossbars for twigs. The buildings mostly clapboard, some stone, a few brick. The houses, the churches, the school, all on streets behind the two-story offices and shops.

A small town lying in the desert, waiting for a city to find it.

Two blocks later he slipped through the door of the area's first restaurant, now its smallest, least-used, red-check oil-cloth and standing fans and a counter along the left-hand wall, booths along the right, a handful of tables down the center and in back. A translucent shade drawn halfway down the front window to keep the glare out. Three men in the first booth, hats on wall pegs; nobody at the tables.

Nobody at the counter until he took a stool nearest the register, dropped his hat on the stool beside him, and plucked a menu from between the sugar and the catsup. As he glanced down the list, not really reading since he could recite it by rote, he heard sniggering behind him, quick whispering, an outright laugh.

His eyes closed briefly.

In the old days, he thought wistfully; in the old days.

In that moment of blessed dark he heard the faint squeak of the swinging door in the back wall and the footsteps of a woman.

"Hey," one of the men said. "Hey, cowboy."

When his eyes opened, he saw her standing in front of him, arms folded under her breasts, one thick eyebrow cocked. Her fair hair was bobbed. Her uniform equal measures of pale stains and pale color too long gone to have a name.

"Hey, you, cowboy."

Her face was high angles and soft hollows, lips dark and thick, eyes dark and seldom wide. In his youth he would have done the dance, said the words, made the promises, anything at all to see what lay beneath the buttons that strained down her front. But the century turned, and in his age he only watched, and smiled, and waited for the question.

"Sixty-two?" she asked, tip of her tongue at the corner of her mouth.

"Nope."

"Damn."

"Hey! Cowboy!"

His eyes closed again, opened, and he watched her face for one sign or another.

Your call, her expression answered; it's too damn hot to think.

He knew how she felt, and let the stool turn him gradually to face the booth, and the men, and their stupid grins as they saw the years on his face, and on the backs of his hands resting lightly on his thighs.

"Sorry, old man," one of them said. "We thought you were someone else."

The other two snickered.

"Maybe you'd be right, then," he answered calmly.

Waiting.

Nothing moved.

The whir and roar of the fans in the back corners.

The whicker of a horse somewhere outside, its hooves hard on the hard road.

The youngest and tallest of the three slid easily out of the booth, his tie slightly off-center, broad lapels shrinking an ordinary chest, baggy trousers giving him a giant's legs. He moved cautiously, peering at Rob through the dust hanging starlike in the air. When one of his friends hissed at him, he shook his head violently, once, and slipped his thumbs into his high waistband.

"Do you have any idea who I am?" he asked. The gap between nose and lip was filled with a moustache, Douglas Fairbanks, and his hair was slicked back, Tyrone Power.

Rob shrugged.

"Clark," the waitress said wearily, "go someplace else, okay? I don't need this."

Clark Mitchell winked at her over Rob's shoulder. "Dinah, no trouble. Just asking a question, that's all."

His companions grinned.

Rob watched.

Clark perched on the edge of a table, one foot swinging. "So. Do you have any idea who I am?"

Stagecoach rumbling down the street behind six lathered horses, a woman and child in matching bonnets, four cavalry riders, their horses prancing. A man peering through the window, a large silver star pinned to his rawhide vest. Rob glanced at him; he moved on.

"Hey," Clark said softly. Not kindly.

Rob put his back to him, tapped the menu, and cocked an eyebrow at Dinah. "Coffee, eggs, toast, bacon, ham, butter if you got it."

"Rationing's over," she said with a quick smile. "You know, you really ought to get into town more often."

He laughed without sound, but didn't miss the question in her expression.

Or the apprehension.

It had nothing to do with the three men behind him.

"Hey, cowboy, I'm talking to you."

She plucked the menu from the counter and slid it back into its place. "Do me a favor," she said, heading for the kitchen. "Don't make a mess. I'm alone today."

A hand reached under his thigh to the stool and spun it around.

Clark smiled; there was nothing there.

"You're not very polite, old man, you know that? I ask you a question, and you ignore me. How do you expect to be a star if you ignore me?"

Rob frowned.

"See?" Clark said to the others. "I told you he doesn't know me."

Without apparent motion Rob stood, grabbed the suit's lapels, and lifted, effortlessly carried the young man to the booth, and dropped him on the seat. He leaned over, one hand now at the knot of the young man's tie, the other hand on the tongue, pulling it, making a noose.

"I don't much care who you are," he said quietly, "and I definitely don't care why you're here. You touch me again, and I'll skin you. Alive."

Clark's face mottled, his eyes bulged.

His friends gaped.

The noose tightened.

"You're a television man," Rob said, leaning closer, speaking softer. "I'm not impressed."

He released the tie with a twist and snap of his wrists, and the young man gasped, sputtered, slumped forward, as his friends finally decided to come to his rescue.

Rob stared them down.

"You were right, by the way," he told them, heading back to the counter.

"Impossible," one of them sneered. "You're too damn old."

Rob sat, smiled. "Son, you don't know what old is."

Turned his back.

Waited until he heard the batwing doors stop their creaked swinging, waited until the footsteps stomped away on the wood-slat boardwalk, waited until the jingle of spurs was overlaid by the sputtering grumble of a bus, waited until the faint odor of an oiled gun was replaced by the aroma of his meal.

The three men had gone.

Dinah leaned a hip against the counter and watched him eat, saying nothing, saying it all, while he watched her watching him, and guessed her to be settling around her mid-forties about now. She had no husband—he had run off to fight in the

Pacific and hadn't returned, maybe dead, maybe not; she had no children, and no family to speak of. She had the restaurant, that was all.

And a couple of times a month, she had him, on the stool at the counter, watching her watching him.

"Rob?" she said, a young woman's voice, uncertain and a little frightened.

He ate.

"Solomon just came to the back while I was cooking."

He grunted. "The man talks too much."

"He says—"

Rob looked at her, nothing more, and she turned away to pick up a clean cloth to wipe down a counter touched with nothing but Rob's plate, and a light coat of dust.

The Horseshoe Tavern, across the street from Dinah's and one block up, had been at its corner location, it seemed, since the world had formed, a gold mine for the owners who took the gold from miners fresh from their claims, took the silver from travelers on their way to California, took the dollars from soldiers who still hadn't found time to change out of their dress uniforms and find themselves work.

It was not, and never had been, a peaceful place.

Piano players and girl singers had eventually given way to flashy jukeboxes, and now, in the back under a gallery, a half dozen men stood around a dusty Panoram, shaking their heads in amazement, but not putting in another dime. They didn't stay long. The rectangular movie screen on top of the jukebox-sized cabinet was faded, and Rita Rio and her All-Female Orchestra sounded tinny and too fast, their images scratched and fluttery. It was better to sit in the Deluxe and watch the same performers on the big screen, more for the money and easier to take.

Clay Poplar had put the soundie in five years ago. When the company stopped making them because the war needed the iron and glass and copper, he hadn't the heart to take the thing out. Not even when he had to splice the short music films together himself.

"Gonna burn that son of a bitch one day," he muttered, handing a shot glass to Rob. A grizzly in a white shirt and apron, he filled the room even when it was empty.

"Times change," Rob said. Drank. Felt the fire. Tapped the glass with a finger.

Poplar looked at him sideways. "You sure? Damn early."

Rob tapped the glass again.

The bartender poured and stood back, fussed with some glasses and a towel. "I like the movie place, you know? The Deluxe?"

Rob nodded.

"They had a picture of the Bomb on the newsreel the other night."

Rob drank.

"Hell of a thing, Rob, hell of a thing." He fussed with the bottles stacked before the etched mirror. "Truman says the Russians, they ain't our friends anymore, they got that bomb stuff, I don't know what it's called." He fussed with his apron, his voice low now, much younger. "If they got it, Rob, they'll blow up the world. That NATO thing ain't gonna be worth spit."

"You don't say," he answered, letting the last drop settle on his tongue.

Poplar had the sense to sound embarrassed when he faked a laugh. "There's a guy out there these days, a preacher man. He's got Mildred talking about the goddamn end of the world. You know, the Apocalypse and all."

"You don't say."

"Not me. I got enough to handle with drunks and whores. I leave that church stuff to her and her old lady."

Rob felt as if he'd been sitting on stools all his life. He slid off this one and dropped a dollar on the bar. Hitched at his gun belt and walked out into the sun.

A small man stood on the corner beneath the full branches of one of the few trees left on Main Street. A hand-lettered poster was tacked to the bole, tent meeting tomorrow tonight, on the east end of town, the Reverend Carl Thomas. The man wore a black suit, the trousers too short, the jacket sleeves exposing bony wrists and frayed cuffs. His left hand was held at his shoulder, gripping an open Bible, whose pages were edged with gold; his right hand beseeched passersby, long fingers in constant fluid motion, languid in the tide of heat.

Rob leaned against the tavern wall and watched as the man spoke well and earnestly to a half dozen women, all of them nodding, and a half dozen men, most of them bemused.

"There is no coincidence that both the Beast and the Bomb begin with the same letter." He clutched the open Bible to his chest, lovingly, near rapture. "There is no coincidence that the color of the Enemy is as red as the color of your young babies' blood."

Rob listened as the dozen became two dozen, and a passing policeman reminded them all, officially tolerant, that the tent was someplace else, the meeting another time, it was time to move along. The preacher smiled and told him he was merely passing the Word to those who might find themselves at the theater instead, or in some unfortunate's living room where the television had taken root.

The crowd drifted away, unspoken promises of attendance the following night.

The policeman shook his head and walked away.

The preacher looked at Rob. "Will you be there, Brother?"

Rob pushed away from the wall, touched the brim of his hat, and walked away.

"He who lives by the sword, Brother!" the preacher called.

Rob turned, walking backwards, and smiled as he tipped his hat.

The preacher blinked once in astonishment, then staggered against the tree, gripping it with one hand while the other slapped the Bible again to his heart.

"Used to be," Rob said to the little girl on the swing, "there were buffalo, and you couldn't see the ground because there were so many. Millions, I expect. Millions. And when they moved, darlin' . . . oh Lord, when they moved."

Rage and thunder trapped beneath the surface, setting horses to rearing and cattle to running and walls to shaking dust from their joints; sudden geysers of earth miles away from the running herd, trees quivering and some falling; the feeling in a man's bones, as if he were listening to God, or the Devil, screaming inside.

He leaned against the schoolyard's stockade fence, one hand in a pocket, the other tucked in his waistband. His hat was low, one leg crossed over the other at the ankle. A dozen or more boys stood around him, grinning at his stories, demanding more and begging their teacher not to send him away yet, recess was still going, and this was more fun than playing catch in the sun.

The girl, her name was Jean, wanted to know if Dale Evans was really a cowgirl.

"Oh, I think so," he said, not minding the lie. The child had little else in the desert but the look to get away. "But I think you're prettier."

She blushed.

The boys hooted.

The teacher clasped her hands and shook her head. "Mr. Garland, you're incorrigible."

He grinned at her. "Best thing I've been called all day, Miss Amy."

The boys hooted again, and started shoving each other. They were being ignored; they didn't want the old man talking to a stupid girl, or their teacher. Besides, he was old enough to be her grandfather, for gosh sake, and she shouldn't be looking at him the way she was.

"Hey," one of them said. Rob knew him as Pete. "Did you see the atomic bomb, Mr. Garland?"

The children fell silent.

Jean stopped swinging.

Pete looked around, suddenly fearful he'd said something dreadfully wrong.

Amy Russell said, "I don't think Mr. Garland is really—"

"No," Rob said gently. "I didn't see it."

"I saw it on my uncle's television. It was big."

He nodded. "I'll bet it was."

"It won the war, you know."

He nodded again. "I know."

"It looked really bad."

"I've seen worse."

Amy seemed flustered, and Rob tilted his head until he could see her, sun aura behind her auburn hair, almost but not quite penetrating her dress. When she looked away and down briefly, he couldn't help but smile, although it didn't move his lips.

"The buffalo," Jean said, close to pouting. "I want to hear about the buffalo and the Indians."

He could feel the heat, the weight of the sky.

"Too late," he said. "It's too late."

A bell rang in the schoolhouse, and there was a sudden whirlwind of children running, calling, waving good-bye, laughing at Jean, who hadn't known the old man had known that recess had ended.

Amy moved closer, edging away at the same time. "Rob, I've missed you."

He wanted to reach out, to touch her arm, but a stout woman stood in the distant doorway. "I'll be back again." He grinned, and this time his lips did the work. "You know I will. Those kids can't get enough."

She didn't move. "They're scared, Rob. It's all they talk about—the Bomb. Most of their fathers were in the Pacific." She looked around the empty yard helplessly. "I don't know what to tell them."

"Nothing," he said.

Another bell rang.

"What are you doing here, Rob? What's—"

He touched his hat brim to silence her and walked through the gate and down the street. He knew she watched; he knew others watched, too, from front lawns and behind curtained windows, and he wished little Jean hadn't asked him what it had been like, out there, before it changed.

Worse; he wished he couldn't remember.

But he couldn't help it.

Campfire to electricity, Pony Express to the telephone, railroads to trucks and cars, trenches to jet fighters; it was like riding the black when the black was young. Too fast to see anything, and when they got where they were going, it wasn't the way it had been when they started. Which is why he rode and walked slow now, taking his time, taking all the time, making sure he knew what he saw before what he saw wasn't there anymore, before it was behind him and falling behind.

He had been to Los Angeles, to San Diego, had taken the train from Denver to St. Louis. He was not, as Dumont complained bitterly to anyone who listened, a man who lived in the Past, hating the Present and sabotaging the Future. He enjoyed going to the movies, the telephone fascinated him as much as it unnerved him, and he had more than once blessed the air-conditioning in Clay Poplar's bar. Not, he amended, that it always worked, especially in the high days of late July.

But times changed.

Sooner or later, he would have to tell them.

Sooner or later, his friends would arrive.

Dumont caught him coming out of the hardware store, a small bag of nails in one hand, hammer in the other. There was a round body to go with the round face, short legs and pudgy hands, and the suit he wore was too expensive and tailored to have been purchased around here.

"Talk to me," he demanded.

"I'm going home."

"I'll dog you."

Rob laughed. "You will, that's for sure."

In the distance, the lonely cry of a locomotive, its plume rising above the rooftops because there was no wind to take it.

A mongrel rooted at the base of a hitching post, snuffling loudly.

A coolie quick-walked around the corner, saw them, and bowed himself out of sight.

"Quit it," Dumont said.

Rob walked on. The man would follow or not, he didn't much give a damn.

"Listen, Rob," the man said, keeping his voice low, leaning close without touching, "there's a guy here in town, his name is Clark Mitchell. He works for the National Broadcasting Company—NBC, like on the radio—they want to expand their television network. You know what that is, a network? People in New York can watch the same programs at the same time as the people in Los Angeles? All the places in between? They're setting up relay points and local stations. Rob, you *have* seen a television set, right? Jesus, do you have any idea what I'm talking about?"

Rob walked on; the man would keep on, or he wouldn't.

"At least tell me you've heard of Ed Sullivan and Milton Berle."

Reluctantly Rob nodded.

Dumont glanced skyward. "Thank you, God, for small favors. Anyhow, this Mitchell guy, he's like a reporter. He goes on the television at night and tells the news. Pretty big man this side of the Mississippi."

"I already have a radio," Rob said, glancing in a shop window, thinking it was about time he bought himself a couple of new shirts. He had four—one had been patched too many times to be worn in polite company, and two had stained holes. The fourth he only wore once in a while.

Later, he decided; maybe tomorrow.

"We're talking the future here, Rob," Dumont insisted, grabbing his arm, letting it go as if he'd been scorched. "All I want is ten acres, man. Ten lousy acres. Christ, you've got what, five, six thousand? What the hell would ten acres of goddamn sand lose you?"

Rob looked down at him. "Ten acres of goddamn sand."

"Very funny." Dumont mopped his face with an already sweat-stained handkerchief. "We are talking rich, Rob. You sell to me, I sell to them, and we split it."

At the corner, Rob waited for a stage to rumble by, shotgun rider saluting him with a touch to his hat. Inside, a woman in a feathery hat smiled coyly.

"I could sell it to him myself," Rob said, crossing the street.

"No, you wouldn't. But you'd sell to me, right?"

They passed the feed store, and Rob paused at the building's edge. "No."

"Why, damn it?" Dumont demanded to his back.

Rob didn't answer.

"Jesus Christ, if they drop the goddamn Bomb, all you'll have left is five, six thousand acres that won't grow a goddamn weed."

Solomon was gone.

Rob saddled the roan and walked her into the open.

Dumont shied away from the animal, mopping his face again. "Rob, please, you've got to listen to me. Mitchell isn't going to be here forever. He'll move on if we don't act now, pick someplace else." He clutched at the stirrup. "Jesus, Rob, you've got to help me get out of here, man. You're the only hope I've got left."

The stirrup twitched; the hand fell away.

"God *damn* you, Garland! You come riding in like this, on that goddamn horse, you've got half the town scared to death."

Rob leaned over and tapped the man's shoulder. "Good," he said. "They have reason."

As he rode out to the road's shoulder, a trio of young boys sped by in a convertible.

They laughed and blew the horn.

The roan didn't move.

He sat on the porch and watched the mountains turn to blood, thick and dark as the sun crept behind them. And dark motion in the sagebrush as the desert returned to life and the sky filled with birds with dark arrow wings that held them against the night wind until they dropped. Like a bomb. Until the small creatures died without making a sound.

He drank from the tin cup, but it wasn't coffee this time. A bottle rested on the porch beside his chair, and as he sipped he remembered it once tasting so fine, and wondered with a shudder why it tasted now like paint.

322 —

CHARLES GRANT

He finished the cup and filled it again without spilling a drop, drawing his denim jacket snug across his chest as the heat finally ended and the desert chill settled. Sounds around the cabin, scuttling and scurrying, rustling, a pebble rolling. A sweet smell on the air. A soft feel to the twilight slipping swiftly to dusk.

He drank, and saw a street, not here, down near Denver, where he had ridden in one morning and had been stopped by a kid who had a large gun in his waistband. There were pox scars on the kid's cheeks, and one ear had been mangled, but he had been determined to try, and had been insulting and snide, and Rob had killed him with one shot without ever leaving the saddle.

He paid for the funeral.

He rode on, south this time, and found work on a ranch near the hills of Santa Fe. A year later the word arrived, and someone tried, and he moved on.

He spent a winter in a cave, and a summer in a prison that finally failed to hold him; he rode a barge on the Great River, hauling wood for the steamboats and cotton for the ships and women for the men who worked the docks and levees. A year later the word arrived, and someone tried, and he moved on.

He drank again and saw more clearly, and closed his eyes and saw it all.

Something screamed in the desert just before it died.

Headlights dragged a guttering roar from east to west, never slowing.

At the back of his head an ache took root; he scowled and willed it away. This wasn't the time.

There were stars, then, and a dreamlike howling that made him smile, raise his head, return the favor. He suspected they laughed at him, the coyotes and wolves, but it always made him feel better.

Amy drove out and sat on the steps at his feet, her pleated skirt hugged around her shins. They talked about the children, the ones who were her favorites and the ones who drove her crazy and the ones who burst out crying because their daddies woke at night, hearing gunfire and fighter planes, deck cannon and grenades.

Four years after, and the dying hadn't stopped.

"And now this," she said angrily.

He lit a lantern and hung it on its hook in the porch roof. The light wasn't much, but at least he wasn't listening to a ghost.

"Which this?" he said, sitting again, crossing one leg over one knee, sipping from the cup refilled again.

"You know what I mean." She reached out and touched his boot, gripped it and tugged until he scooted the chair close, and she laid her cheek against his knee. His free hand hovered above her head, feeling it without touching it, fire in the lantern mirroring the fire in the hair. "I mean, you've seen so much, Rob. Cars and planes and more wars than I think you want to admit. You're a walking history book, and you don't even know it." She shifted a little, a finger brushed her hair and snapped away. "I've been to school, and I don't know anything, and I'm supposed to tell those kids not to be afraid."

He couldn't help it; he touched the hair, molding it to her skull, following its fall to her spine.

She sighed, and hugged his leg.

The coyotes sang.

A stagecoach thundered past, horses snorting, whip cracking.

Out of the dark.

Into the dark.

"I hate you," she said dreamily.

He grunted.

She shifted, snuggled closer. "Why are they afraid of you?"

He didn't know how to answer, and so kept his silence, hoping that this time, with this woman, there would be no time but the time they had.

So young, so soon old.

"I was thinking about driving out to that tent meeting tomorrow."

"Oh?"

She laughed, just a little. "I feel sorry for that preacher, that's all. He's so little. I don't know if anyone will take him seriously."

They would; he knew they would.

They always do.

And they're always wrong.

She drew away and turned to lean back against the post, lantern light giving her face soft shadow and softer age. "I know who you are, you know."

He said nothing.

She grinned, the age vanished. "I'm a teacher, remember? I can look things up, read, write, magical things like that."

He said nothing.

"You're an outlaw."

He inhaled deeply, let it out slowly.

She shook her head in amazement. "It's practically the middle of the century, and we've got a living, breathing outlaw living right outside town." Lantern light in her eyes. "I thought they were all dead."

The coyotes sang.

"They are," he whispered.

A gust of wind, the lantern creaked and swung, her face slipping in and out of shadow.

"Is that why they're so afraid of you? Because they think you'll—"

A long-nosed automobile pulled up behind Amy's wood-sided station wagon. Headlights cut the night and died. The engine raced. A door slammed. She adjusted her skirt, scowling at the intrusion, looking to him for a clue what to do, what to say, but he only shook his head, just enough for her to notice, and sagged just a little, abruptly adding heavy decades to his frame.

She blinked, then smiled, and turned as a man crunched across the yard.

"Mr. Garland, good evening."

Rob nodded. "Mr. Mitchell."

"Ah, you know me at last. I'll take it as a compliment." Mitchell stopped at the reach of the light, put a foot on the porch, and leaned forward, resting on an arm. Tipped his hat back, touched his chin. "And you're the schoolteacher, am I right? Miss . . . ?"

"Russell," she said primly.

He nodded. "Of course." A smile at Rob, not a shark, just a wolf. "It seems to me, Miss Russell, that we have a celebrity here in our midst."

"Is that so?"

"Well, sure. Mr. Garland here is what we in the television business call a personality."

His gaze didn't move.

"Is he really?"

"Oh, come now, Miss Russell. Are you telling me you didn't know?" Wolf's teeth. "Robert Garland, birth date unknown, death date not applicable, no fancy names like Billy the Kid or Six-gun Morgan, has served time in several jails and prisons across the West. For murder. Unfortunately it seems there isn't a jail around that can hold him."

"Is that so?"

Mitchell stopped smiling. "He's a killer, Miss Russell. I'm willing to bet there are a dozen outstanding warrants for his arrest in every state east of the Rockies and west of the Mississippi. Would you say that's right, Mr. Garland?"

"Be a hell of a coup," Rob said hoarsely. "Call the Law

and tell them to arrest a tired old man who can barely sit on his old horse. Hell of a coup."

"I don't want you arrested, Mr. Garland. I just want your land."

The lantern still swinging, still creaking.

Mitchell's face, in and out of shadow.

"Do you know," he said, ignoring Amy now, "that there are over a million television sets in the country already? Do you have any idea how many people see my face every week? Do you have any idea how many people would see *your* face every night if I give the word?" He ducked his head, looked up again. "There isn't a cop in this country who wouldn't know your name."

He straightened, smoothing his tie with the flat of his palm.

Amy said, "Why?" She gestured at the night. "There are a dozen towns you could go to. Scores of them. And every one of them is bigger than ours. What the hell do you want us for? Why are you picking on Rob?"

He tipped his hat and walked away, looked over his shoulder, and said, "Because I can."

She kissed him good night.

The coyotes sang.

He lay on his bed, moonlight across his chest.

He didn't think he was a stupid man; he had seen too much not to know that worlds change and worlds collide, that people like him and Solomon, Dinah and Clay, either stood aside on their own or were moved—shoved or nudged, it didn't make much difference. It was the way of it. A young wolf sooner or later took the fight out of an old one; a young buffalo sooner or later took care of a slow bull.

He reached over the side and picked up the tin cup, realized it was empty, closed one eye in thought, then tossed the cup aside. He picked up the bottle.

He drank.

He had met them all, and loved a few, and had ridden on when he could no longer watch them die, when he could no longer bear the looks in their eyes or the feeble kisses they gave him or the quivering touch of their fingers soft on his skin, when they began to wonder and began to ask questions and began, at the last, to hate the sound and sight of him, riding on.

When he saw the way of it.

The sky held stars and a moon and shadows that flew from one slope to another.

The way of it.

Until one night held a sun.

It didn't last, but it was there, and so was the wind that battered the slopes and scoured the earth, and nothing that walked there ever walked again, and nothing that flew there ever drew another breath.

He drank.

He had ridden there that night, on the night of the sun, and had felt the wind and had seen the black the sun left behind. It neither frightened nor thrilled him.

But it saddened him, just a little.

He had grown used to it, just a little: the places, the faces, the killing and the saving; the whiskey, the mead, the wine, and the water; the huts, the towers, the long roads and mountain passes.

The riding.

He drank.

Yet there had never been a time like the time he had had today, never a time when he could finally see the road's end. Dirt or macadam, concrete or cobblestone, they always took a bend, crossed a river, wound around a mountain, slipped into a valley he hadn't noticed as he traveled.

It saddened him.

Just a little.

Not for the road's end, but for them and their not knowing.

He was old.

He was slow.

He supposed, as moonlight faded, it really was getting to be time.

But it saddened him.

Just a little.

He drank the bottle dry.

He slept.

He didn't dream.

He woke near the end of the sun's slide, rolled to sit up, held his head in his hands, and stared at the floor.

because I can

He walked to the door and held on to the jamb, squinting in the dying daylight, watching the trucks and the stages, shaking his head with a soft simple smile at the slipping back and forth, then and now. When a long gray bus passed without pausing, he turned away and wondered how it was that Dumont and Amy were the only ones who saw. He hadn't thought them all that special, a con man and a teacher, but he hadn't thought that night sun had been all that special either.

It still wasn't.

Not the way they thought.

He turned back and stood on the porch, testing the air, listening, and knew that his friends wouldn't be arriving tonight. It puzzled him for a moment; he was almost sure they'd be here, until a truck guttered by with several crates in its bed. Stenciling on the side. Television sets. One of them, he was sure, would be for Clay Poplar and his wife.

No bombs in there.

The end, just the same.

"Well," he said softly. A decision finally made.

He moved around the large room, picking up things he thought he'd like to save, and putting them back when he realized what he was doing. And as he moved, raising dust, he breathed deeply and hummed tunelessly, touching, always touching, until the day had gone. Then he reached under the bed and pulled out an old steamer, leather straps brittle and brass fittings tarnished. The leather snapped when he touched it, the lid crumpled when he lifted it, and from the black inside he used both hands to lift the black onto the mattress.

"Well," he said to the clothing he hadn't worn in so long. "Well."

He stripped.

He dressed.

He picked up his hat, wide-brimmed and black, and stepped onto the porch.

The coyotes sang.

He answered.

A shower of meteors flashed and burned, flashed and died, traces of light hopeless in their wake.

He walked around the cabin to the stable, still not truly sure he had to ride tonight until he moved inside and saw that the roan was on her side in her stall.

"Oh, Lord," he whispered, as much for himself as for the horse. He knelt beside her and stroked her warm flank, suggesting with a whisper that it would be all right, old girl, you don't want to be here, not now, not this time.

When he stood, joints popping, back stiff, a soft whicker in the next stall made him turn, raise an eyebrow, say nothing as he walked the sleek black into the yard and saddled him. And as he did, he watched the sky, watched the road, thinking there were a few things he could still do before he had to do what he had to.

A step, smooth and easy, set him on the horse's back.

A cluck, a touch, and they were on the road, riding down the center, nothing behind them and nothing above.

The coyotes stopped singing.

And in no time at all he stopped at the stable doors, seeing a light inside.

The black crossed the open space loudly, nearly prancing, and Solomon came out, scowling, until he saw Rob.

"Oh, Jesus," the old man said. He looked around frantically, every jerk and gasp telling Rob he was thinking to run, wanting to hide, terrified to do anything but stand there. Then he put a hand over his face until he stopped trembling. "I was going to go to the tent meeting, but all this work . . . Damn, I should have gone." He leaned over to look behind the black, frowned again, and scanned the yard. "You alone?"

"For a while," Rob said. "You don't have to worry."

Solomon nearly sagged, so great was his relief. "You mind me asking how long?"

Rob laughed. "You're a pest, Solomon. You want to know too much."

"I got a right."

Rob considered, and smiled. "Not very long, as these things go. But too long for you. All right?"

"Hell, no. I'm living forever."

The man on the black leaned over and shook the black man's hand, long and hard, and wheeled his horse around to head for Main Street.

Riding down the center.

Streetlights and houselights and the lights in the shops dimming as he rode past, and not brightening again.

He stopped a second time when he reached the Horseshoe Tavern. He dismounted and pushed through the door, not caring about the silence that cut the piano player off in mid-note, or the looks he received from the men at the tables back near the jukebox. He went straight to the bar and took a stool beside Dumont. The bartender was a young man, who just managed not to gape when he saw Rob sit, the surprise quickly replaced by a sneer and a word to the two women who sat at the bar's end. They looked up and giggled.

"What the hell do you want?" Dumont demanded.

Rob reached into his shirt pocket and pulled out a roll of bills bound in a string. He took the man's hand and placed the money in the palm, closed the fingers around it.

"Get out, Matt," he said, lowering his voice. "Get in that fancy Roadmaster of yours and get the hell out."

Dumont stared at the bills, blinked once, and stood. "Which way?" he said, starting for the door.

"It doesn't matter," Rob told him as he tossed a bill on the bar for Dumont's drink, stood, and followed.

Outside, easy and swift, he sat on the black and watched Dumont hurry away, stop as if he'd remembered something vital, and hurry back, reaching for but not grabbing the stirrup.

"Why me?" he asked.

Rob grinned at him. "Clay's at the meeting."

"You son of a bitch."

"Maybe. Maybe not."

Dumont nodded and left, not looking back, swinging around the corner where the tree that held the poster stood alone amid the scattered litter of its leaves.

The black tossed its head and snorted.

They rode on.

Lights dimming, fading, one or two popping out in brief sparks.

Hooves, metal hooves, echoing off stone and wood long after the town was left behind.

He saw the light in the distance, a bright white made brighter because the night was so dark.

They rode on.

Turned through a gap in a makeshift rope fence, beyond which several score automobiles and a handful of wagons were parked around the bulge of a large circus tent. Torches on poles burned around the entrance just high enough for a tall man. Bunting wrapped around the guy wires. Pennants drooped around the top.

He could hear a voice inside, but he couldn't hear the words. Not that it mattered. He knew what they said: sin and corruption and salvation and damnation and ascension and descent into a black chasm ringed with fire.

He rode inside, holding the black in check when the hundred or more on hard folding chairs realized he was there.

In front, on a high stage, the little preacher in his black suit held up his Bible, stuck in the middle of a verse, mouth open, eyes wide, a finger pointing to the canvas roof.

"You!" the preacher cried. "You . . . *dare!*"

Rob ignored him.

He eased the black forward, down the center aisle, looking at the faces for the one face he needed.

"You! Dare! In the House of the Lord!"

Amy sat on the aisle.

He saw her, he smiled, he rode on.

"Begone, Satan!" the preacher commanded.

When the black reached the stage, it snorted, laid back its ears, stamped once, and wheeled.

No one spoke, no one cried, no one prayed, no one moved.

Rob rode back up the aisle, slowly, without a sound, until he saw Amy again.

She had half risen from her seat, dropped back when he reached her, and leaned over, and said, "Tell Jean and Pete the buffalo are coming."

He straightened before she could speak, scanned the faces until he saw him, smug and dapper in a new pin-striped suit, hat in his lap, looking for all the world as if all the world knew his face.

"Satan!" the preacher cried, the first sound in a while.

The second was the wind that began to billow and ripple the tent's walls, and the pennants and bunting snapped, gunshots and thunder.

Rob drew his gun and aimed it at Clark Mitchell.

"With me," he said simply.

Mitchell laughed and shrugged.

The hammer was cocked.

"With me."

Mitchell smoothed his tie, unsure and wondering.

A woman whimpered, a man muttered, the wind bulged the walls and began roaring in the desert.

"I won't say it again," Rob told him.

Mitchell defied him for a single second before rising and making his way apologetically to the aisle. "I'm sorry, Reverend," he called as he put on his hat. "You won't get away with this," he said to Rob.

The black advanced.

Mitchell backed away.

"Satan, begone from these people!" the preacher cried.

Rob looked over his shoulder, lifted his head, and the preacher froze.

You know, Rob thought, as if the preacher could hear, you know, but you won't tell them.

Mitchell broke then, yelling for help as he sprinted out of the tent.

Rob followed without haste, paused once outside to let the wind tell him where the man had gone. To the road, it seemed, and the black began to trot, puffs of dust turned to sparks, steam from its nostrils, steam from its hide.

The pennants cracked; the bunting writhed; a guy wire snapped, and the roof began to sag.

Once on the road, Rob swung the black east and let the animal run. He couldn't see Mitchell, but that was all right. The man had no imagination; he would seek cover in the night, then try to double back when he was sure Rob had passed him by.

The black ran.

Fire and smoke.

And slowed when Mitchell faded in directly ahead, hat gone, jacket flapping, looking over his shoulder and trying to run faster when he saw Rob coming toward him.

The chase didn't last long.

Rob drew even, reached down, and swatted the man's shoulder. Mitchell sprawled onto the macadam and skidded, rolled over, and scrambled to his knees, hands clasped and begging, blood between his fingers, as Rob turned and waited.

The gun was still drawn.

Blood masked the right side of Mitchell's face, oozing and sliding, bits of pebble and grit embedded in his cheek and brow, a patch of his hair pulled free, the scalp raw.

"You can't do this," Mitchell said, quaking so hard he nearly toppled. "You don't know who I am."

Rob said nothing.

"They'll have your face on every newspaper, on every screen. You can't do this!"

The black lowered its head and shook it.

"They'll know who you are, you stupid son of a bitch!" He sobbed and covered his face.

Winter wind and tumbleweeds.

"No," Rob said. "They won't."

Mitchell lowered his hands, blood smeared even to his lips and teeth. He didn't understand; an outstretched hand pleaded, *What the hell did I do to you?*

The man on the black looked back toward the tent, toward the flames just beginning to crawl up the sides, erasing some of the stars, tiny figures running away from the fire.

"You showed them the Bomb," he said, slowly turning his head back. Midnight eyes.

Mitchell swallowed, gagged, and spit. "So what?"

The man on the black jerked his head toward the tent. "The preacher tells them that means Armageddon."

"Jesus Christ, so the hell what?"

"He's wrong."

Mitchell tried to stand, fell back to his hands and knees, and whimpered. "Crazy," he whispered. "Jesus God, he's crazy."

"You are," the man told him.

He pulled the trigger.

Mitchell stiffened upright, back rigid, until the wind knocked him over.

Rob waited until another gust rolled the body into the ditch, waited until he was sure Amy had escaped the burning.

Waited until the black grew tired of standing.

And then he rode on.

A short road, this time.

And it saddened him.

Just a little.

1950
1951
1952
1953
1954
1955
1956
1957
1958
1959

THE OPEN DOORS

BY WHITLEY STRIEBER

As for the nights, I warn you the nights are dangerous
The wind changes at night and the dreams come
It is very cold
     there are strange stars near Arcturus
Voices are crying an unknown name in the sky.

          —Archibald MacLeish,
          Epistle To Be Left in the Earth

The meteor cut a trench of light in the sky, was followed by silent howling, left a sense of strange life. The doctor, a doctor of the sky, turned away as if from something plagued. He dragged in a breath of the flushed suburban air, felt it stretch his chest, felt also the slight pulling beneath his chest that was the pulling of death.

Of death, as alien as the meteor, coming from an unknown place, going to an unknown place.

Of death, and the things seen. What could he say of them?

What could he say?

"There are quanta of meaning, determinations, the inflexibility of sin, the inoperable condition of the soul. My soul."

Princeton's lights shone intermittently along the hills, beads of memory that recalled the strong, foolish days when he had taught there. He took another breath, grabbing for it in a way that struck him as rather horrible.

"How you cling, von Neumann," he said to the air. "Von *Noo*man," he said again, pronouncing it like an American. "How can *you* be the one?"

The physicist, the Commissioner, the Hungarian Jew in the three-piece suit, the Smartest Man in the World. The Catholic.

He wondered if the neoplasm was pale or translucent, or the same color as the liver where it lived. He could feel a pushing bulge, could feel the pressure, as of a child's gentle hand upon the interior of his belly, or a pregnancy. He touched his temple. "Typically, this neoplasm will metastasize to the brain, often lodging in the seat of consciousness." Rubbing, he made breathy sounds, feeling his hair rolling under his fingers. In a child, the sounds would have been screams, and the hair would have been torn from the roots.

He sighed with the next gust of breeze. How he despised the night. Sleep was horrible; they watched him sleep, watched from the *inside*, their eyes on him, their long lips grinning with lascivious eagerness.

The most awful part, though, was not that. The most awful part was waking up. First, the good, slow return to consciousness, then the sudden weight of memory coming back, then with a gasp and a tightening of every muscle in his body: They're real.

Three of them ran across the sidewalk—scuttled. Three of them tonight. Their odor drifted on the garden air: smoldering paper.

"The possibility exists that our initial interpretation was not correct, not even directionally. The possibility exists that—"

They said: His mind grows weak. They said: It's a symptom. But they did not know what he'd seen.

His colleagues condescended gently about his return to the Church. He could not explain himself to them, because to do that, he would have to reveal the secret, and if he revealed it, his finger would pop out of the dike.

That finger was the safety of the world: the gate was kept closed by ignorance.

They would ride into reality on a tide of knowledge— and this was the reason he was dying. Nature had detected his knowledge and was rejecting the disorder it implied by filling him with cancer.

Unfinished letter to President Eisenhower, 1956, Top

Secret Ultra: "Something about the different way they view reality means that, in our world, they literally *are not real* and must use our belief in them as a bridge. For this reason, official denial must be absolute and aggressive. The public must not know that they are here."

If the people knew what was there at the bottom of the garden . . . if they knew what now awaited at the moment of death, what doomed passengers would see dancing in the aisles of crashing planes, what enters the cabin with them

" . . . traffic emergency . . ."

before they fall like broken butterflies. Then what, then what? emergency . . .

"Your liver is not operational, Dr. von Neumann. We may get it started again, but you cannot expect a cure."

You will not see 1957, 1958, 1959, 1960 sixty-one sixty-two sixtythree sixtyfourfivesix—

He gazed up at the sky. "God, take me. Christ, take me. Virgin, take this man who has killed millions."

"John, your work is no sin. Your work is on behalf of the greater good of the commonweal. In that sense it is an extension of the body of Christ."

"I burned fifteen thousand children to death, Father, and maimed thirty-six thousand more."

"You must trust the Lord's power. You must trust his forgiveness. Christ wants your sins. Take them to him."

"Nobody wants my sins! Or no—*they* want my sins."

"They want you to feel too guilty to open your soul to grace. This is where they feed."

"They feed on us all."

A face stares into his own from a foot away, and he sees in its black universal eyes the destruction of man. If the evil are evil enough, then all the souls will be delivered up, even the souls of the elect and of the good.

"I don't believe that."

"Father, it is true!"

"God cannot let go of the good. The saved are saved."

"Even them! Heaven itself is invaded. God is losing, don't you see? His own creation is destroying him, and that—*that*—is the secret of the ages."

"Pray with me, John. Pray simply. Hail Mary, full of grace, the Lord is with thee—"

"She's nothing, a mere woman—a little lost Jewess from the distant past."

"The cocreator of being. Star of the Sea. Queen of the May. She lays her feet upon the brow of the serpent."

"Words! Silly words!"

"Words are the foundation of the world. He made it all with words."

"The original formation of matter reached critical mass and exploded."

"The *Word* was with God and the *Word* was God. We speak of the same thing, you see."

"What happens to you when you die, Father?"

"Whatever God wishes."

"If he gives your soul—" He stopped himself, then turned away, trying to conceal his distress from the brilliant, baby-faced old priest. But the *word* came after him, for the *word* was not God, not anymore.

Then he sees in the eyes, his own father's face—and the eyes fade. "Forgive me, O my God, forgive me my foolish sins."

The priest also fades, the talk of three months ago fades, and his fingers run along the pages of the Bible. Too dark to read now, not with these deceiving eyes. "God, let me keep my finger in the dike that my mind has broken. Let the flood not drown me. God, the tumor is so terribly, terribly hard."

He is sick again. His meal has been too rich. So it is bile, then, bile becomes a poison that enforces his death dreams . . . dreams also of Magyar days, childhood songs, father's cigars and whiskers, the joy of running with leaves in autumn. Bile brings him poetry, bile sentences him to his memories.

After his diagnosis—late that night—he had awakened and vomited it pure and bitter. He had lain down on the tiles in the bathroom, lain on his side in his gray pajamas and listened to the toilet finish its roaring, and then to the puttering of moths against the glaring ceiling light.

The Smartest Man in the World had in that moment become only another body—

which had seen their strange blue clothing, the uniforms that shimmer and slip between reality and nightmare

which had felt the tearing prick of their claws and the softness of their deer skin.

Buried in a cellar at that airfield, buried beneath the runway, beneath the gasoline storage area, beneath the refrigerator units, beneath the weapons-storage platforms, where the pipes were crusted and white roaches played, they lay in blue-breath cold and compressor-humming silence, their dead lips surrounding what appeared to be a sort of rapture.

Had they come because of the fire of the bomb, somehow attracted by its fury—or was it that an atomic explosion is so violent that it poisons also the world of the soul?

For a time after the diagnosis, he had worked furiously. For a few weeks. Then he had been told to stop smoking, and that had made him feel naked somehow, and he had begun to see more directly what he wished he could not see.

He spent time with Father Dubois, following his tight, rhythmic smoking, listening to his explanations, his cajolery, marveling at the ponderous, poetic and soulful tales that comprised the Church.

He had approached the ones who were supposed to be dead, led by that polished bright soldier Arthur . . . what? The brain again, what was the man's name? Arthur . . . a lieutenant colonel in the new Air Force uniform . . . Exner? And the young man had said, "They are decomposing, Dr. von Neumann, but they do not seem dead."

How could another world be so strange? How could its

entire reference to reality be so completely different, yet so consistent? They saw nothing as we did, and yet everything they did still made sense.

Dead, out of his body, he would not be safe from them.

Dr. von Neumann, you are dying. Sky doctor, doctor of the tiny world, thief of God's secrets, Promethean fool: you are dying. And look, there's another one out there in the shadows, just under that tree, as still and squat as some gray fungus.

Hollow-earth theory. Perry as he approached the end of the north: "I see a fantastic sight, I am at the edge of another world, a great, gaping fissure where the pole should be . . ."

Doctor?

"I had the feeling that it was here collecting souls," the little man had said. Little man who had come to the Air Force, little bit of nothing from somewhere near Roswell, New Mexico, with that terrible secret in his mind. Veins bulging on his head. His big, screwed hands had twisted, sweat stains under his arms, clutching a hand-rolled cigarette he called a pill, and Dr. von Neumann had said, "You must never repeat this." And had thought: A member of the public knows the truth. And had thought: He must die if he talks. But he did not talk.

His son talked. The boy talked and talked in the Navy, in civilian life, spilled wild stories of demons in the desert. Disappeared, he did; just another boy. Died looking straight into the face of the gun, died as if he was examining its blue metal skin for faults.

They left his car at a roadside.

"Now, Doctor, we are here to collect thy soul. Thine, excuse us. Thine soul. Archaic possessive sounds more final, doncha think?"

It is possible to calculate the rate at which the tumor adds to itself, and thus identify the speed at which it squeezes and closes and impedes. As bile backs up, blood becomes sewage, eyes tinge yellow, skin gleams orange. And the blood is brown, as brown as the frozen offal hanging from the tail of his plane in Anchorage, when they had gone to see . . . what to call it? The source of all whispers, the *thing* from the ice. He remembered the sense of celebration on the plane, fancy War Department—no, that's changed, Defense Department—food, all the luxuries in that wonderful Super Connie in USAF livery. They had thought they were going to crack the secret of the ages.

Then seeing the stiff brown stalactite jutting out the rear of the plane—their sewage had frozen solid as it left the toilet. Haw haw haw, Colonel This and Colonel That had laughed, and General Walter—spit, what's his name, your memory is going—had laughed, too. Then they'd crossed the tarmac to the cars, more cigars, more drink, and you think, here you are the Commissioner of it all, Commissioner von Neumann in a fine suit, because you can send the calculations soaring in your mind . . .

Can measure the breadth of time, the white-hot whoop of the atom's death, the probability that Saint Augustine actually *did* understand the nature of the world.

You, the master, did not know that to see the *thing* was to enter its body, as Jonah had, and to lie in its pulsating gullet for the rest of your days, knowing that *it* had you and would have you forever.

Had they brought *it* there and buried *it* in the ice because *it* was too terrible even for them to bear, too powerful for demons to control? Was there actually an evil beyond Satan—more corrosive, more invasive?

The priest had once said a curious thing: "God complies with the darkness. It is God's love that makes Satan's fire."

City of God, Garden of God: not a physical place, really, but one outside the nature of time. The earth, he saw now, was not a globe at all: the energy of time was what rounded it and set it on its perfect traverse of the sky. In reality the world was an immense tapestry, its leading edge being woven by the busy worms of life. Yes, a tapestry in the palace of God's mind: that was what was meant by "complies with the darkness." The Smartest Man in the World knew, now, that the dark and light were one another's foundation. God and Satan were married.

And they look at the part of the tapestry *you* have made, and they are not satisfied. *You* have introduced the ugly brown thread of your arrogance and your wet, gobbling, tempted orifice. *You* have said, yes, let me publish this, let me calculate that, let me decode the secret of the dark and light, that you are one, that you always have been one, let me then manage and mastermind the revelation.

So I stole also, as Prometheus, as Eve. I stole your real secret, that behind the goodness of God and the evil of the shadow, you are.

The colonels saw it, too, in the sleek body of the *thing* from the northern ice. And they fell silent because of what *it* reflected back at them—not their handsome faces but their grotesque old souls. They all saw that they were somehow part of the *thing*, that they had added to *it* and made *it* grow until *it* had fashioned machineries out of the damned, and was flying them in the common air of the world. So much for those colonels and their cars and cigars. Instead of being killed, they had been locked in a windowless madhouse, tended by deaf nurses. A compromise between the President and the Smartest Man in the World.

"Shoot them down, General," he had said when they began slipping through the skies; said it in acid irony. But the poor stupid creature had replied, "Damn right!"

So here come the planes . . . so high, so terribly dramatic, crossing the sky of 1951 . . . flown by young men with shiny cheeks, reading paperback novels and chewing gum . . . young men who think about the Brooklyn Dodgers and the St. Louis Browns . . . who carry, in their craft's metal bellies, the end of the world . . .

We applaud. Clatter, clatter, clip clap clatter. "Blue Moon" had been playing on the radio in the ready room: "Blue Moon," was it Dorothy O'Shea? The Manhattan Colleen.

Dear, the delicious food of Manhattan, Manhatta, the Indian word . . . all gone. All the celebrations of his various ships (professorship, commissionership, sinking ship)—the rolling out of planes, the rolling out of bombs, the unveiling of reactors—were a single blur now of uniforms and the pervasive whiff of Brasso that emanates from collections of officers.

He dropped into an iron garden chair, wet with evening dew. His next long breath brought the soft scent of leaves . . . Manhattan Project, where we sorted the leaves of death, decoding, decoding, calculating, finding the balances of atomic justice . . . while *they* watched from the soaring sky . . . hungering, hoping that we would succeed.

He wanted to light a cigar so badly that he went through the motions of slapping his sides to find cutter and lighter, then reaching into his breast pocket for the sweet Cuban that ought to be nestled there.

Tightly packed in his tumor, on this clear summer night, must be the whole history of the planet. In every tumor. And those meteors—were they just stone and iron from the land of far away, or were they really flying cancers, seeking across the cosmos for a victim to infest?

Had not one come down, hovered in the back garden, slipped sizzling along the grass?

No, surely not.

Had it not floated quietly in through the window?

No.

And come along the hall, spitting where it touched the walls?

No.

Leaving a smoke that stank of sizzling human skin?

No.

Had it not come into the bedroom?

No.

Had it not come to the bed?

No!

Closer and closer

NO.

To the little, trembling edge of the skin . . .

NO!

And then . . . in. Insertion of the syringe: There now, John, it isn't painful, it is uncomfortable . . . she in her white linen that crackled through the warm afternoon, in the deep marble well of the toilet, kneeling, his naked buttocks exposed to her wide peasant attentions . . . Magda smelled like that, smelled like the deep sharp sweet of all flesh.

Out of death and the memories of home, Magda, a Jewess . . . suffocated. Who had nursed and tended, bathed and brushed, who had held him in her enormous room of a lap and given him to understand that every woman, Jewess or not, bears within her the sparkling presence of the Virgin. "God and Goddess," Magda had said. "She is His mother and His wife." Magda: a Jewish Catholic Pagan. His father had chuckled and said he should learn his catechism from a priest.

Magda in the rain, her big hands of comfort grabbing the edge of the door, sucking air scented by apple blossom as they clattered slowly up the spine of Europe . . .

How difficult it is to find one's sins in this life. Magda was not my responsibility; she was a hired servant, they all were.

God, we got out: first the Communisti, then the Iron Guard trampling down the lace blue empire of childhood, the Austro-Hungarian contraption.

God, we left our servants behind.

God, I think that I loved this Magda who nursed me,

raised me up, carried me on her hip, slept on a bed of picked rags at the side of my crib. I remember—or the cancer remembers—the exact taste of her milk.

Can you believe it, Hungary is part of Stalin's empire now? He was clever to get the Magyars, finally to steal them from themselves. O that daddy-moustached, pipe-stuffing monstrosity—

With his own planes. You, Josef. Harry called him Uncle Joe. Ike does not, Ike has no illusions about him. "Those Russian soldiers were like animals." No illusions: "Jesus Christ, John, can't you people make me a bigger bomb? And faster, for God's sake, make 'em faster! Build the facilities, who cares if they leak? Are you a patriot or not? Build, for the love of God!"

Build these imperfect chambers, sir, wherein we alchemize poisons for the ages, sir?

"I authorize long gray buildings filled with fans and vents and ducts, and the hell with the children in that park!"

Plutonium is so complex that it amounts to a living species, with needs and rights and desires, even morals and ethics—and a conscience served, as ours is, only by its own survival.

Rocky Flats, O God it is so imperfect. Oak Ridge—ironic, bucolic name—also imperfect. Vents opening into the wide blue afternoon, tin shrieking, fans going *suck suck suck* and a thousandth of a gram sailing across out into the picture pretty world full of long blue cars and pale houses, echoing with the song of Princess Summerfallwinterspring and Howdy's howdy howdy do, and the spitting of sprinklers and the gleam of the sun upon Dixie Peach pomaded flattops . . . in Oak Ridge, where the late night brought the stealthy rhythm of fornication, and the baby-packed women rolled caged baskets through the Piggly Wiggly, filling them with Uneedas and red beefsteaks and cartons of Fatimas and Corn Flakes and Hydrox Cookies, and upon them all the mark of the beast, rising and falling in the flush of the cheek, appearing in the liquid glance of a happy, happy eye.

Land of the proud and free.

Ike: "We are here to protect those children, Doctor. Give me bigger bombs! Do it now! Yesterday!"

And how lovely they are, the new hydrogen bombs with their slim fuselages and silver fins, sailing down through the blue Pacific silence, winking like silver leaves in the breezy tropic sky. And lovely also are the boys aiming with those clear American eyes, their gum cracking, baseball scores floating in their heads like God's perfect numbers.

It is about the dying of the light. Lights going out all over Europe . . . I remember them now, the lights in the ballrooms of Pest, of Wein, of Berlin, the churning cabarets and the spider-slow arts of us Jews. Juden. Judenratt. Osweicim. That longing my servants and my friends must have gotten, for the open snow. Jew to Catholic to von. *Von* Neumann. Our Father who art . . . Christ, okay, we give up, he's the Messiah.

"Father, forgive me."

"God forgives."

And further back, in the First War, how we suffered for the lack of coffee and the sweet, cold wines of the Rhine country, for the champagne of France and the tall noble pastries of our own Empire . . . and then the fatal gossip of the guns.

Buda in 1918: a city made old in three brass-band years, suddenly foggy from the burning of raw coal, of bits of wood, even the snow arriving gray and sad. And in the sadness, a thin sort of *noblesse*; and high, high above, moving silently and impossibly beneath the vast dome of the overcast, I saw the ghostly silver airplanes of the future . . . which has arrived with its own swiftness.

And now, America: "I consider myself the luckiest man in the world . . ." Lou Amyotrophic Lateral Gehrig, voice inaugurating the future, echoing as if in a cathedral of empty parks, nerves humming the fatal sclerosing dance of a whole nation.

For the sclerosis was released, escaping with me, coming—with me—on a mystical journey into the deepest nature of the country, coming as I came in a silver airplane from the future, bringing (with me) the cruelties of Europe to the Hollywood Hills with their cantilevered houses and swishing blue dresses and long, long cars, and softly, swiftly coating it all with ageless sadness.

He thought often of Lou Gehrig, who had died the most perfectly terrible of all deaths. The most athletic man in the world had been reduced micron by micron to absolute, dead paralysis until he lay frozen and silent, his eyes sunken closed on dreams of the highest, farthest, most amazing of all home runs. He died like you will die, my adopted land. Smiling, I open my hands. In them, I see the searching glow of plutonium. "I have your medicine."

Of course the Smartest Man in the World was also the most dangerous. He sat with his feet in the grass, gazing at the daffodils that tumbled away down the garden, sweet silent shadows in the dark. He sat, also, in that silver airplane of his first approach and thought: O Adolf of the Guerlain cologne and the clandestine cigars and your own golden spectacles like Harry's but more secret, you escorted our children into the crusted cellars of your chambers, and we Jews combined, just so, this and that little ingredient, and replied with the bomb.

In the tremendous sense, we work for God. We work for God, we who are too elegant of mind to bear God—we work for a girl of twelve with corn gold hair and lips like Sharon's roses, who in the middle years of your life, darling Adolf, stood naked, her corn gold hair crawling with three stages of the lives of the louse, and listened in the dark to the tinkling fall of the crystals and then to the wide shrieks

of eight hundred other children with corn gold hair and lips
of Sharon, and tasted of the gas, and thought in her terror
and last humiliating confusion that the silver Gott Mit Uns
belt buckle of the gentle man who had ushered her in was a
talisman of deliverance. And so she held her hands up to the
peephole that one thousand six hundred other hands were
scrabbling at and thought she saw gleaming from its polished Hakenkreuz another light—

the light that was then in my mind
light of steel
light of Europe's sins and America's young journey
blue, glowing light of Sharon's vale.
"John, you will get cold."
Voice? Real? No.
"You can have a little cognac now."
"Yes."
Dutiful, aware that the lighted living room will cast
accents upon his Halloween skin, aware that they will all give
him those awful cow looks, the women whose hands will
wash his dead body soon, he moves obediently toward the
door. And also continues his other journey, bringing the shadows of old Europe into America's swiftly contracting sun.

O America, I did not know you then, but now I sit above
you, transported by thy (thine) silver-winged youth on my
death mission, the cancer-packed, thickly accented old "guy"
with his slightly rounded figure and his sweetly tailored
suits, who can converse with Ike like you do with Charlie
from Charlotte—O America.

Strange creature coughed up by the death of Europe, I
have come to devour you with atomic poison.

Ike sucks a cigarette, this fierce, intense man, smilin'
Ike. "How about giving me two bombs a month? That can't
be so hard. Two a month." He twirls his high leather chair
around, stares out across nodding roses to the White House
lawn. "Goddammit, I think she's drunk," he says with a

priest's muttered conviction. A square, small woman moves along the grass as if searching for a lost earring.

"Mr. President, we do not have the capacity to double production in a year."

Whoosh the chair comes hard around. The eyes, now wet, regard him with the fearless sadness of a cornered panther. "Stalin is going to come here and he is going to have bombs by the thousands."

"Sir, that is—"

"Don't you tell me it's impossible, Johnny! Don't you even breathe it! I tell *you* what's possible!"

"We will have sixty bombs by mid '54. Sixty."

"Guaranteed? Certain?"

"I am the administrator of bombs."

Me, the administrator. Commissioner of the Atomic Energy Commission. Why? I dreamed too well, so well that they put me, a foreigner, in charge of all the other dreamers.

"Dr. von *Noo*man, I am asking if the Atomic Energy Commission guarantees the president sixty atomic bombs in operational status by January 1, 1954. What is your answer?"

"Just driftin' and dreamin' down Moonlight Bay . . ."

The cancer says, "Hey, dreamer."

The cancer says, "How about a musical about me?"

The cancer says, "You can call it . . . hmm . . . lessee . . . you can call it—maybe—*Mister Slow*."

"Come in for your cognac, John."

Down Moonlight Bay.

Nobody knows anything about the sexuality of death, which is one of the most awful things about dying slowly. Falling off a mountain, waking up in a firestorm, being crushed beneath a dropping safe: these are the deaths of the blessed.

The slow deaths belong to us accursed, who will be able to see the strange, childish demons that I see, drawing closer, closer yet . . . see them, and see off there a million miles above, the ordinary people sailing in a rainbow I cannot touch.

The fruit of the tree of knowledge: I got fat on it and so saw *them* and saw the *thing* that is worse than Satan and better than God and so lost my place completely. "All I could do, Father, was jam my finger in the dike—the very finger that had broken the hole in the first place!"

"I don't quite follow."

No, certainly not, because if you did, I would have you killed for your own safety and the safety of the world. The more you know, America, the deeper you go.

"Father, what if one has a sin that cannot be confessed?"

"To receive absolution, all sins must be uttered in the confessional. We cannot say simply, 'I have a sin, absolve me.' It must be *uttered*."

"What if the uttering of it is itself a sin?"

The priest, at last, had been silenced. He was without an answer, and John von Neumann knew then that he was himself lost. He, of all men who had ever been, had committed an unpardonable sin.

In the slow death, there is passion, there is release, there is a horrible sexuality. Why do you think that public executions are worked by whores? Why did the dying body spring to rapture as the noose tightened or the gas hissed? Why did *they* appear to be in rapture, they who had given their lives?

Being cut off from living breath—suffocated, poisoned, mashed—touches the body also with pleasure . . . yes, and so the cancerous old man becomes revoltingly sensual. After he is done with his wife, she creeps off into the depths of the house. Soon he hears muffled choking and knows that she is vomiting from the sensation of him.

He loves her anyway.

"Come in, we're going to have a fire."

"I am coming."

Then, on the beetle-rustling silence, from the black

window of the house next door, a voice . . . the English, English . . . it seems suddenly important to understand . . . what is Gillgillyosenfeffercastenellenbogen by the sea? Ah, a song. A song from the radio. *If I ever needed you, I need you now . . . If I ever needed love, I need it now . . .*

He moves slowly closer to the house in his black suit and waistcoat, gold fatherly chain tinkling darkly. *If I ever needed you . . .* Is it a waltz, meine Liebchen? *If I ever needed love, I need it now . . .* I feel so all alone, I don't know what to do.

Prometheus, you devil, passed down the ages from scientist to scientist, like a virus of the mind . . . the Promethean sorrow . . . fire-thieves . . . *take me in your arms and never let me go* . . . O God are you out there . . . everybody's sleeping so it's quite all right . . .

He finds another bench, this one touched by the scent of nameless flowers. Night-blooming jacaranda—or no, that cannot be, the jacaranda is a Californian. No jacaranda in Princeton.

"What is blooming?"

"Speak up, John. Are you saying you are ill?"

"What flower is blooming?"

"No flower now. Come in, come in."

Formally, as the pope might, he extended his arms toward the soft voices of the radio. America, save me, ba ba ba boom. America, you swept me off my feet. Now's the time, America, make love to my sarcoma.

You smell with cancer of the liver, yes, and in the cancer ward there is an odor combined of rotted esters, chemical breakdown, and the stink of bilious skin.

What do they do, since they can't stop the tumors? They shunt. Build little temporary openings for the bile to flow through. Here a shunt, there a shunt. They shunt you up.

Again he hears sounds down by the gate. He hurries, going to another weak point, going to close it off.

"Oh, he's going back down the path!"

He has assigned himself the task to walk back and forth in this little European garden in the middle of America, to walk here, guarding against them in the night.

"John, I must demand that you come in."

"There are children here."

"Come in."

"Only a moment more."

They do oppress this Jew who followed after the long boats of migration in a silver ship, came upon the grandeur of the sky, bearing the fire into the hands of these happy, these better . . . *bum bum bum Mr. Sandman, bring me your dreams* . . . Amerikaner with their gum and their paperbacks who will not line up men just to test the bomb . . .

As Josef did . . . thirty-six thousand dead in an instant. What did he expect, putting them in idiotic uniforms and sending them out on "atomic maneuvers"?

But we, the bearers of Prometheus . . . We did not need maneuvers, we had whole cities to test our bombs. Stripped earth, burned harder than it was ever meant to burn.

The souls of Hiroshima and Nagasaki: In his worst dreams, even the souls are gone.

"Hi, Dr. von Neumann."

"Good evening."

She is swinging on the gate, her pale lips of Sharon glowing with night glow. "They had you on the radio." Says, raadio . . . aahdio.

"Ah."

"You're the smartest man in the world."

"Ah, hah! They have not talked to Herr Doktor Einstein, then, I don't think."

She extends her hand, crooks her finger, bidding him near. And he goes with—I know a dark secluded place— trepidation yes because of the horrible weakness of the body and the terrible embrace he is in of temptress death and feels

instantly the electric burning fire in his gut that is the urgency
of the body to leave its seed behind, the closest thing there is
on earth to the love of God—rich, wet, smelly, sensual, licking, sucking, rubbing, screaming love of the dear old God at
the bulging dark imploded center of everything—

olay.

"Why doncha ever wear just a shirt?"

"I am a gentleman."

"Oh."

He knows that she's wondering about his body, and how
she would react if she saw it. Of course, it would bring out
her Magda, not her Lorelei. She would come smiling, her
smooth arms powdered by the twilight, her eyes darkened by
the infinite, and say, "Ya wanna piece a gum?"

O Magda momma, I am so afraid. Were you in the gas,
afraid? Were you when the lights went out with a bitter electric thump, and were you when the Zyklon-B crystals came
rattling down like hard, hard rain? Were you when you
smelled their chloric stink and the stink of urine and feces
releasing in the howled storm of the women around you, fingers working locks, fingers trembling in the pouring vents,
and the hard gulping screams of all the Magdas of Europe—

"What is your name? Are you the daughter of my neighbor, Mr. Chilton, I think?"

"Nope."

"Then—" He stopped. Sweat burst out all over his body.
Steel fingers closed his throat.

"Who am I, Jancsi?"

There can be no answer. But how have they done it?
How have they come here in this terrible form, the form of a
little girl who walked down the long ramp to darkness?

Again the smile. The lips rise from the teeth like terrible
wings, the teeth themselves are long and wet, the tongue
within bears a crystal eye.

It.

They found *it* in the desert near some dreary, unutterable little town. *It* appeared in the form of a splayed-open machine that had vomited maggots onto the pure earthen land. Maggots from space, maggots from the beyond, maggots from right out of the center of his liver—

"You wanna sit down? With me?"

Cannot, dare not, say no. "I—of course—"

So they sit on the last bench he installed here with his own hands in '49 . . . was it the summer? The Guardian Bench at the edge of the garden, borderland of the world. "Jancsi, be calm. Sit, sit."

"Yes, I will sit with you."

She leads him, she sits, he sits, he expects and she does draw him down so that he lies on the bench with his head in her lap, looking up as at Magda in boyhood, Sylvia Maria in youth, at the long necks and pride of the women, up along the lines of the gentle godly faces, touched more than any man's by the shadow of the soul.

"My mom and dad say you sure are sick."

"It is so, child."

She lays fingers as light as flies upon his cheek. Another hand lies upon his folded hands. His eyes are closed then by other fingers and other fingers touch his neck . . . he is not used to intimate fingers touching him, that is not in his background . . . he is naked now, an unsure babe in the lap of the goddess the enormous, with her hair in the cosmos of stars, her eyes breathing an infinity of houses and hearths, her teeth grinding with hunger for soul meat.

And there comes from him a scream. A scream. A scream, and—

"Jancsi?"

There was a story about him that made the rounds at Princeton, land of the sucking minds, that he was not human but a demigod who had made a detailed study of the humans and could imitate them perfectly.

Ironic, now that he is in the hands of a real demigod, a chortling demon in the form of a girl-child whose corn blond hair carries with it a faint numbing whiff of Zyklon-B.

Upper-middle-class Budapest families such as his had generally put great emphasis on the development of social skills; a courteous and charming manner was nurtured as an essential tool for advance *advance*, the tanks flying over the smoking earth, *advance* glorious tank armies! Here come the guns . . . here come the planes . . .

The men in the B-36, listening to WEAF on their radio while they arm their bomb. "The Fat Man is up. Three. Two. One. Armed. Prepare for delivery. Open doors . . . the open doors . . ."

The high blue afternoon, the doors opening upon the face of the land, the land smiling up at the sky, the sky smiling down and this droning demon beetle full of men from Jackson and Chicago Cubs and false Cleveland of the eradicated Indians—"Hey, guys, the Cubbies're gonna make it all the way."

"Nah, no way, 'sgonna be the Reds."

"You got a go? That 'Shima?"

"Yeah. You got it. We—Countdown to release."

"No flak, flak's good."

"Okay, releasing baby."

"I have it."

"Cubbies."

"Reds."

"Release. Clean."

O *Enola Gay* did you see what I see, we tore 'em right up, wow them Nipponeses ifyapleezes—lookit—

Cubbies.

Reds.

Fuckin' Yanks, you guys, what?

Hey, I wonder if a bomb could burn up a soul.

You a Nip lover, Jernigan?

Not me. It's just, it's awful quiet in my heart right now. *I had the feeling that it was here collecting souls.*

"Please, please don't make me relive that."

"It is your achievement."

"No! My—my sorrow."

She probes deep into his mind, carrying with her sheets of burned Japanese skin that she hangs on the line of his memory, in the beloved morning sun of his childhood, to dry and get clean in its freshness.

The most awful thing about being punished by demons is that they enjoy it so much. It doesn't wear them out like human torturers. The SS had to be given counseling. Herr Doktor Schleicher with his briefcase full of Schutz Staffel foolscap would come and give you Zigaretten, and say, "So many Jews for the Fatherland, eh?" And you would, in the privacy of that room, allow yourself to weep, eh?

"But that is not my sin. My sin is—"

"Is?"

"Is—to—be." And there is his whole self, and he weeps in the seeing of his whole self, in the tremendous agony of knowing and seeing that all sin belongs to all sinners, and so for his perishing soul, he does weep.

Demons do not weep. In fact, the more you suffer, the stronger they get. Your agony draws them into a state of climax. It becomes permanent, like the balance of the sun, your agony, their pleasure: the alpha and the omega, locked in perfect harmony.

She says, "I want to come over and see you every day."

"Oh, child, you needn't do that."

Of course he is not lying with his head in the lap of a girl—no such, ach—but seated beside her in proper attire and demeanor, inhaling nevertheless a freshness of skin and hair and hearing the purity of voice that gets to why the mystical heart of Judaism migrated to America and made of it a redoubt protected by bombs.

Ben Bernie's voice drifts out from the television: "Ya wanna buy a duck?"

Milton, Uncle Miltie, Texaco, you can trust your car to the man who wears the—

Stars in the heavens like dust hanging in der Morgenlicht.

Morning light, so soon? "Where am I, O Father in Heaven, where am I?"

You are in your mind, John. You have reached singularity. You are a superposition, neither here nor there.

The mind sees the B-36 46 56 66 76 86 96 what will it be like in 2006, when mankind judges mankind, takes the clean skin at last from the lines of the mind, O God preserve me. . . .

John, I am going to place your soul into another flesh, into the body of this very girl, who will in the year 1962 bear you forth in her flesh, yes, this girl who swings now eleven on your garden gate will after Orion passes thrice the moon, be your mother.

You touch the hand of the child, the hand of your mother, who will lift you back into the world, bringing your foolish diamond of a soul back into the fatal light. "What is your name, child?"

"I'm Sally. You met me, you know."

"You are not Sally. You are not a child."

"Are you scared?"

"Yes, Sally, I am."

"Come with me, then."

"No."

"You must come with me."

"No!"

Something leaps upon his back, he cries out, staggers under the weight, hears a rough whisper: "You will come with us! I'll ride you there, you fat old nag!" Plump, hard boy hands grab his ears and yank until comets blaze in the corners of his eyes, and he lurches out the garden gate, into the common alley with its rutted track and its garbage bins, turvy fences, and overhanging willow boughs. She flits in among the brushy shrubs, passing easily toward some childhood bower, a secret place, he supposes, where there are—

dozens

—the children of the damned world, the inheritors of quantum indeterminacy and the fallout from *Enola Gay*: a world condemned to suffer what has saved it.

"Hey, she's brought the Jew. The Jew! He's here!"

"Hey, mister, you gonna get nekkid? Let's see yer Jew dick all uncovered, like wow, they burned 'em off 'em in Poland. My dad got it at Monte Casino, Mr. Jew, how did you figure in that, hmm?"

"Well, God gave Hitler Himmler and Zyklon-B, but He gave us Jews Albert Einstein and me."

"My *dad* got it!"

"I bend my grateful knee at the grave of thy father, O America. I bring you in return for your blood, the key to the future of the world."

Principle:

Once the mind adopts experience as quanta, it ceases to believe in itself as a controlling factor, and the world begins then to unfold in a more true, more real, and—paradoxically—less determined manner. It is only from within the context of minds in this condition that genuinely new and useful thought can now occur.

Exposition of principle:

"Commissioner of Atomic Energy Dr. John von Neumann, considered by many to be the smartest man in the world, stated at the International Symposium on the Future of Science held at Dumbarton Oaks that mankind must 'begin the process of developing intelligences greater than human, if we are to continue to progress toward a single functional theory that explains all physical operations.' Dr.

von Neumann also said that 'Human intelligence, it will be found, will not be sufficient to achieve the unified theory that we now seek. To do this, we must, in effect, create a new God, one that will converse with us.' The Reverend Dr. Herb Trickler of the United Churches of God lodged a formal protest at the conference, describing Dr. von Neumann as a 'misguided heretic of the Jewish persuasion and a godless communist.'"

Memories are made of this . . . shoop shoop . . . are made of this . . .

So many conferences and so many executed, boiled, desiccated and served chickens later, Dr. von Neumann has become the victim of a gamma ray or a high-speed neutron emitted past the lead at Los Alamos or Oak Ridge or some other blighted reactor, and now his liver has a cancer in it like a living chunk of anthracite and the Reverend Trickler has become Congressman Trickler, who wears his trousers high and his collars tight and twangs about communism, and says, "This National Foundation of Science will never receive a penny of public funds"—a pronouncement that Ike thankfully ignores.

"I could bathe you like I bathe my dollies."

"Excuse me?"

"You keep scratching. If I bathed you all over with castile soap, would you feel better?"

"I would feel better, O and in the cool water . . ."

Magda: little love, little dove, I am singing to you. I am singing, little love, little dove. O know, know it is so, that the Magyar once touched Heaven with their voices, when the Magyar were free.

And as a man dieth, he leaves layer after layer of himself dead before, until there is only nakedness and the grave, and that is the path that John von Neumann is traversing in his stumpy, plump, slow way, with his yellow eyes and a billiard ball dragging at his gut.

"Doctor, I am sorry to tell you that science has not advanced enough to offer you something that would be curative."

"Is there a surgical option, Doctor?"

"I'm afraid not, Doctor. There are chemicals, but that sort of treatment is in its infancy. We probably wouldn't do anything but make you even sicker."

"Doctor, you understand that I am in a very sensitive position, with regard to my employment? Which is why I feel that I must ask you: Are there heroic measures?"

"Theory is that an organ could be transplanted. But it's only theory."

"Why not just resect the liver?"

"We can't. There's no way to control the bleeding."

Sixty-six, 76, last train, 86, all aboard, 96, Belsen, Belsen, train to Belsen, Therienstadt, Auschwitz, and Biarritz . . .

"So, Doctor, you are telling me that I must die?"

"I am afraid so, Doctor."

He just stood there feelin' like he got a bum steer, him bein' only fifty-three and such, and they thought O bitter that it was the damn gamma rays got released at Oak Ridge or Los Alamos, because some kid's attention wandered . . .

An American kid, an American attention, Cubbies, Yanks, Philly A's, dying Commish von Neumann. "But Doctor, I can't die, I'm a *resource*. The country needs me. The whole Western World does. I am a bastion against the isms."

"I'm sorry, Doctor. Truly sorry."

"Doctor, it would serve the country best if you could give me as much productive time as possible."

"Of course, Doctor."

Regimen: thin diet, aspirin, novacristin, then the attempt to resect fails. He wakes up, knows just from their faces that—"Prognosis?"

"Radiotherapy to the abdominal cavity may bring on

other complications due to the fact that we cannot target the tumor perfectly and the liver is so damn sensitive."

"Is this going to occur soon?"

"Not soon. First, Dr. von Neumann, you'll be eaten. Slowly. Because you have committed an incredibly subtle and terrible sin, and God wants to give you a good bit of time to contemplate it, in hope that you can gain forgiveness before you run out of time. Otherwise, one of the very best souls ever created is going to have to be destroyed."

Children in the moonlight, angels maybe or maybe demons, standing hand in hand, sang to an old man in his fear and in his dying:

Did you not hear my lady
Go down the garden singing?
Blackbird and thrush were silent
To hear the alleys ringing

Old, dear Handel, he had not heard it since a boy! A boy, a kissing, dreaming boy. The purity of their voices seemed to contain the whole of wisdom.

O saw you not my lady
Out in the garden there
Shaming the rose and lily
For she is twice as fair

"John, what is this? I have brought you your shawl."
"My soul?"
"Shawl! Is your hearing gone, too, my love?"

Tho I am nothing to her
Tho she must rarely look at me
Tho I could never woo her
I love her till I die

His wife paused, looked toward the children. "How beautiful. Songs on a sweet evening."

"The saddest voices I have ever heard."

"Especially for a man who saved a whole world. You children, sing him a happy tune!"

"Don't! Don't talk to them!" He heaves his thick arms about. "No, don't listen to her. Please, dear heart, return to the house."

A vast weight out of the black of the sky swarms down upon him and again he is in the poison of death, the brown of blood and the growing granite fist in his gut. He touches his side, stretches, can feel hard inner pulling. There is a terrible itch connected with this miserable thing, and he wishes he had the lotion to spread over his puckered skin. And he wishes again to smoke, pats his pockets, searching for a fat Cuban. It is a ritual of the dying that they are deprived of tobacco.

He sees then that time has passed, magically swept and slept away. He is no longer standing in the garden watching the sky, he is somewhere dark and warm—dead?

No, in his bed. And there is in his hand another that is soft and cool and damp, and it squeezes as he awakens, and he sinks for a spare, sweet moment into the deep of his marriage. But the hand seems more like a worm or a snake that wraps his wrist the moment he notices. He tries to pull away, hears a soft, warbling voice, looks—

into vast black oceans

where swim the histories of the fallen worlds

and he sees his place in the histories

and knows that they are waiting to eat the part of him that would otherwise have been immortal

as he would eat a leg of lamb.

Instantly the sun comes up, the doves begin to hoo, the scent of coffee and bacon comes in from the kitchen, the radio croons, *because it's yooooooo.*

There will be a graduate student come to take dictation today. They are hanging on the words of the demigod. *Classified*: "It is probable that a quantum barrier would exist between entities, due to the absolute lack of perceptual referents. This would mean that the first difficulty would involve actually seeing one another, for we would of necessity see what our expectations allowed us to see and no more. I refer here to a neuronal and informational difficulty. We literally could not see what we could not anticipate. I suspect, incidentally, that a milder form of this problem affected the Mesoamerican peoples when they confronted the Spaniards. This is why the Spaniards reported such a curious passivity in their armies, and why just a relatively few Spaniards could work the defeat of thousands.

"However, it is my belief that the perceptual barrier will be of a double nature, that is to say, that neither side will be able to 'get it right' until the other does.

"What will we see, in the absence of reality? I can only refer here to 'the sleep of reason begets monsters,' for that, thus far, is all we have encountered."

Jim Forrestal in the dark deep of night, behind the guards in the Bethesda hospital, on a high floor, came face-to-face with the complicated, buzzing awfulness itself, so old and wearing all its sins on its vile face. Jim leaped out the window and into the black air rather than face that . . . sleep with it . . . let it lick him, whatever it had wanted.

How can we have courage, when at eight in the morning, we concoct such fantasies?

"What is it like, Father, to die? When does control cease, and what does it feel like, this peculiar winding-down of the mind?"

"I feel so vulnerable, you see, like the philosophers and the geniuses in the gas, I suppose, standing there stripped naked, knowing that the little bedraggled cadre of children

they had seen hanging about in the vulture halls would soon
be tearing out the gold of their mouths . . . chosen because
there were no tools for it, and their fingers were small."

"Doctor, I cannot understand. You are speaking
Hungarian. When you speak Hungarian, I cannot understand."

"Magyar . . . It is a close tongue, you know, close to the
root tongue of all the Aryans."

"I don't doubt it, Doctor. What is your question today?
Your concern?"

"If I took my sin directly to God, and uttered it only to
Him—"

"No, to my ears. God will hear you only then. That is the
binding of the Church, and it cannot be loosed. Just say your
sin and be done with it. You have little time."

Father Dubois, at last, grows impatient with his elaborate intellectual.

I who am that dying man, fat and bloated and yellow and
itching in my sheath of cream, here on this reeking chair in
the home I soon must leave

—my children and the children of the children

—those generations, yes, who will walk to the edge

—fifty years, no more, and they will be able to predict
the end of their days.

"Magda?"

"Magda is dead, John."

"Of course. I slipped. I thought I was back in the old
house."

But no, I am naked, here in her sunny boudoir. The priest
is gone, long gone, and she takes up the lotion, spreads it
across my naked skin, she who has tended me all these long
years, who has been awed by me and enjoyed the slender
pumping thread of my sex, who has laughed in the rain of my
kisses and received my adoration and passion, who has
looked upon me and pronounced sentence that time when I

was shaving: "Is that the light, John, or do you look a little yellow?"

"Oh, yellow. It's the damned Chinese; they're giving us trouble in Korea."

"No, I think you have the jaundice. Do you feel well?"

And then he felt for the first time that gravity had a bit more of a hold on him, and there was in his temples a sort of sluggish pounding, and he was not at all well.

He had gone off, still, to the work of that last immortal day, where they speculated about monsters in elegant phrases, where they used the language of physics to babble about the impossible that had become real.

He had told them a story, beginning it with the line: "They have always been hiding in the nature of the world . . ."

He had once entered a cave in the Thüringer Wald—this was what, forty years ago?—a strange cave that had been an iron mine, a place where they had taken iron even during the Aryan Dawn—and before, perhaps, when the first of us dragged the first metal through the first smelting . . . it could easily have been the first of all mines.

Down inside the drips rushed and the way was steep, the walls blue in the glow of their hard carbide headlamps, and he and that Thuringian . . . dead in the First War, of course . . . a wonderful, civilized fellow with a delightfully careless mind . . . they had loved each other a little, kissed but only the cheek, between fellows, yes, you know, it's nothing, and they had come upon such an odd, old place, a strange chamber deep within that cave, with a tall ceiling and then . . . beyond . . . a sort of trick in the earth . . . and had there not been blue, glowing shapes . . . kobolds, the people of the mines, yes, interesting, perhaps some form of life? Quite real, of course, although denied by the life scientists. But who are they to visit deep mines in Thuringia, in the year 1914?

Dear old world, so handsome in your sunset, never was

there such elegance or tolerance or purity of human hope—
all signed away in articles of war. It was possible for a Jewish
boy from Hungary to pass naturally across half a dozen borders by train and never a word, no, nor even so much as a disquieting glance from a fellow traveler. A Jew? Who cares, we
are all Europeans together, are we not?

There was that cabalist from Poznan who said, "We did
remarkable things, Dr. von Neumann, created astonishing
conjurings, spread good and prosperity among all the Polish
Jews, we shtetler magi. But we did not see the shadow . . .
until suddenly, there they were in their black tanks and their
screaming planes, and we saw that, by ignoring the dark,
we had released it."

Yes, yes, he had said with an amused chuckle. "And
what did you conjure—chickens for the pots of the Jews?"

Now he knows: They had conjured the demon kobold.
Cobalt. Cobalt bomb. Radioenergetic cobalt, the most terrible of poisons. Behind the lead shield, behind the foot-thick
quartz window lighted as if with Lucifer's very lamp, horribly blue and horribly bright, lay the flesh of the demon,
which he had seen in living form in Thuringia, in the underground.

He told all of that as a story, and they had listened, their
eyes narrow with awe, knowing that they were hearing something from beyond the limits of the human mind. And it was
such stories that gave rise to the tales of the demigod, the
impostor among men.

Am I? Is this little Jancsi an impostor, deceiving even
himself? Perhaps so, perhaps that is why I cannot find the
final turning in this maze, the forgiveness of my life.

When he had first seen cobalt that had been rendered
radioactive, he had stepped back, startled by how much it
looked like the skin of the kobolds he had glimpsed in that
mine. He had thought that it must be the very flesh of Hell.

"It will poison the world, Mr. President."

It is also that dark glowing blue. The way it buzzes, as if it was made of many flies . . .

Jim Forrestal dashing toward the window, Jim opening the window, Jim falling like a comet in fluttering sheets to the concrete below, Jim's blood leaking through his shroud.

I had the feeling that it was here collecting souls.

There was a fearful thing, there was a fearful, fearful thing: and what of that film, a black egg racing through the sky, chasing that pulsing, burning shape? What was that? What did it mean?

Captured souls. Captured species. Captured world.

The first meeting had been held two days after Roswell. John von Neumann remembered every word.

HST: We have the bomb.

JVN: We have a great problem, I fear.

HST: Well, solve the damn problem.

JVN: I cannot, Mr. President.

HST: You're supposed to be the smartest man in the world.

How helpless he had felt then. Even more so today.

"Today, I think it is time for good-byes."

"Do you feel so terrible, John?"

"Oh, certainly terrible. I need morphia, I fear."

Then will come the young men with their gum to protect him from babbling his secrets. The plan was that, at the very last, he would be left alone in a soundproof room, so that nobody could be infected with his knowledge. No, he would die with it, go with it to the demons and pull the door to Hell closed behind him.

America, then, would be paralyzed not all at once by sudden knowledge, but by a process of infinitely patient revelation that, hopefully, would not be complete before a defense was found. If his knowledge somehow escaped that room—well, then the world would end.

You unearthed them with your atomic nonsense. To save civilization you enslaved it. Ah, the cunning of it. We did the same as the shtetler cabalists. By fighting the demons who had entered the body of man, by defeating Hitler and Tojo, by containing Uncle Joe and Chairman Mao, we gentle, musical people of the West have caused them to come looming out of the night even larger than before, to jump straight in from Hell, their talons poised to hook our souls. Those who are going to embrace the good must therefore find a way to appease evil. Anything else is arrogance. Mozart, arrogance. Dear Handel, arrogance. Electric light, blue cars, freckled boys, girls with corn blond hair, women in summer dresses, arrogance, arrogance.

"Father, the Church is arrogant."

"No."

"Arrogant to imagine that it can simply forgive sin. What of Hitler?"

"If his faith had taken the measure of his sins, they would have been washed away."

"But they were not washed away."

"God alone knows that."

What will they say in a thousand years, of our age? It was a time of music and science, the chief products of this civilization. Prior to the West, man had only a little music, the curious myxolydian twanging of the Greeks, the long mourning Roman horns, the elaborations of China. But then there came the bursting flower of five centuries of song and thought, the discovery of the natural world curiously linked to the invention of instrument after instrument, the lost chord to the unified field, the chance missed by music also missed by science, and thus no fusion between science and religion, no service to the divine.

God in his chariot going on to the next place, the next chancy planet covered with howling desperate apes . . . and the next decision: evolve or extinguish?

"Has God abandoned us, Father?"

"No."

"Can you be certain?"

"John, to believe something is to know its truth intellectually. Faith is that same truth flowing in the blood. My blood makes me certain."

"But what if you die and Christ is not there? No Virgin, no Heaven, nothing as you expected?"

In His anger and His love, He left us to the kobolds, that boy-god who, in his search for companionship, has fashioned an entire cosmos . . .

O Dionysus my love, sweet immortal animal in the flesh of a child . . . understood partly by Petronius Arbiter and partly by William Blake and fully by Dr. John von Neumann, of whom let it be said, "He understood all that was put before him."

And walked the past and the future, and hid himself away from the gum-cracking horde with their baseball and their silver bombers on the towers of air, with their stupid paperback novels and their electronic magic—the television, such a miracle—given over to the *Texaco Star Theater*, See the USA in your Chevrolet, America's the greatest land of death, and Beulah, black Magda in the back room where the happy Negro is compelled to smile and to dance.

Dance. Yes, Magda wrote: "They have made us dance today. We were out on the yard, something went wrong, I did not hear, and then of a sudden, we are beginning to dance. We are dancing. The countess does not know our dancing, and must waltz about—and she so thin—in the cold that stings your skin every place it touches—she had all that silken lace—and then at four, I think, they unloaded a dump of potatoes and the children ate even the worms—O my Jancsi, I am writing this only because I am the Therienstadt special Jewess, She With Paper, a showcase Jewess, carried out to smile at the Red Cross but at least I can give this paper for America, I say you is my son, you see—only we send to relatives, none other—and I want to say that this Nazi cleaning of Jews it is not too good. I am here with all Deutsche and French Jews because you are noble name and they know you are famous in America they do not want me to hurt too much."

What would it have been, when they left, to simply take her along? But no, she was left to manage the house, and there must have been some fine days in there for Magda and Pyotr with all the champagne and sturgeon and cognac left behind, some of it from before the First War, yes they could fill their faces, they could manage with a little coal for the kitchen . . . until the soldiers came, he had seen film of it, O God how dreadful, and to have these letters these photogs he was so much in agony, she had in her effort bequeathed him a terrible punishment—

which he deserved always as a boy, when he dissected that accursed chicken and got the blood in her sewing, she upended him in her huge servant's way and he knew how it was that the peasants punished their issue, and ah how his father had laughed to hear the tearful story . . . O Mag, you gave him a proper Magyar hiding, good, good! Ha ha. What a surprise that had been, to hear him laugh that this peasant had raised welts on the buttocks of a von. He'd thought they'd have her head, had thought even to denounce her to the Emperor. Ha ha, if he crosses you, lay on another! Good! Good!

How proper he had been with her then, no longer her pretty von master, but just another upendable bitter peasant boy, always cracking nuts and sweating. No more jokes on her. O but there had been such good love in that house.

He had seen films of Jewesses herded naked in the streets, sophisticated, educated women clutching their poor jellied udders—God—and the men with their circumcised penises exposed and pointed at by the sallow, jeering crowds.

Where were the children of Schiller, where were they going, how was it that they had never escaped the dark woods of Vercingetorix after all, what awful curse was upon them?

He had wished, yes and heartily wished, that Berlin had lasted longer than Toyko, because Harry would certainly have dropped one of their little Semitic eggs on old Adolf's accursed head. Yes, the stupid Semites with their idiotic science. Hitler had said, "I'm inclined to believe that the world is surrounded by ice . . ." He had dismissed his own heavy water project, hadn't understood, not with his indistinct and cruel peasant's mind. He was not like Roosevelt or Harry or Ike, who worshiped what they did not understand.

Oh, you fine man. What did you do with that heavy water they made for you, you wretched south German boob, drink it? Take it in a fine enema? You devil, killer of my poor plump old Mag . . .

Half the world dies in terror, the other half in amazement. Death has a secret sensuality. He'd seen it long ago, a boy coming upon a casual execution—some rough brigand—in the Romanian fastness, a little town . . . they'd hauled him up and he'd gone hard as a stick as he twitched and turned black . . . dick and tongue both sticking out . . . hideous memory to enter the skull of a dying man . . . what am I to do if my daughters surround me and I come to some sort of paroxysm? But no, I am too filled with secrets, I forget that I will die alone, with only the gum boys and their baseball, the thrice-shaved joes and mikes cleared to the top, what nonsense—what are they doing with all these secrets in a republic?—I will die alone, with only a secured military orderly to witness my terror and my abnegation . . . and then, at the last, even he will leave me.

Ike, who has that smile, do they not see the violence in it? Do they not see how hard a man he is? No.

Amazing. He goes out and golfs. Who could golf, how do they endure the extreme dullness? Golfs, eats hamburgers, reads those strange books about the cowboys. How far Stalin is ahead of Ike, intellectually. But mad, thank God . . .

O what does it matter? Only the deeper secrets matter, the ones so terrible that I keep forgetting. You awaken to such brightness and such birdsong and such sweet air, and then you feel your aching, nauseous weight and remember your brown blood and the secrets and the granite plug at the base of your liver and the gamma rays that put it there, when you were viewing the cobalt flesh of the demon, the cobalt that killed you, in the end, because you saw it in its living form in a mine . . .

That's something that not even Einstein could understand. It would overturn his world entirely. But he only pretends to wisdom, he only pretends.

I am not wise, I am too intelligent for that. I know too much to be anything but absolutely terrified.

O Mag, please be there for me on the other side. Mag, please take me in your big lap, take me and sing, yes, the old, old songs—titles words names elude me—but the ones from the days of your milk, O mother Mag.

"I am thinking again of thee, my Magda."

"John, you do so much remembering now. It's good. You had no time to remember before—"

"Before I was dying."

She nods, but her eyes do not rise to meet his. She twists her hands together. She has whispered, "Mother of Mercy, Mother on High, preserve him and cleanse him of this terrible disease." They have discussed Lourdes. Yes, and here one of the greatest of minds, physicist and mathematician and theorist, one of the ones surely free of the rosaries and the mumbo—put a tumor in his belly and off he goes to Lourdes, you see?

Bless me, Father, for I have sinned, I abandoned a good woman to be horribly murdered by the Germans and I did it needlessly, out of selfish concern for a useless old house that

I lost in any case. Bless me, Father, for I have eaten of the
fruit also of the tree of knowledge—the high fruit, excuse
me, that Eve missed. Yes I have, and I have discovered there
the maggots beneath the surface, the spirit maggots who wait
for heavy souls, for souls like mine to become tired of tread-
ing the surface, to sink down and become entangled in the
machineries of immortal agony. Yes I have, and now they
have been unleashed on the surface, been sent raging into the
houses of the innocent, because I tore down with my bombs
thy holy wall, O my God.

Father Dubois: "Excuse me, John, you're talking
Hungarian again. You say you have made a bomb? What sort
of a bomb?"

"Father, I am desperate for absolution, desperate
because I have seen, I have seen what they, I have seen what
they do, what they—I have walked down in the halls of Hell,
Father—"

"Yes, go on."

"I have committed the greatest of all sins, stolen the fire
behind the fire, the fire that even Prometheus missed. I have
stolen God's very soul and made it into a bomb, Father. I have
stolen it and made it into a bomb and spread terror in the
world, Father."

"Anything else?"

"In what sense, Father?"

"Any other sins? Ate meat on Friday, perhaps, while you
were fooling with your bomb?" (Lowers voice.) "Touched
yourself, perhaps?"

"Meat . . . yes . . . of course . . . thousands of times. I've
been an agnostic, you see."

"Oh, no agnostics. There are only Catholics and hea-
thens. Those fine distinctions are just nonsense. Well, now
we have some real sins, here. Sins that God can forgive. Ate
meat on Friday, did you? Well, we know that the Holy Father
forbids this. It's a mortal sin."

"Father?"

"Yes?"

"I think that I have destroyed mankind."

"Ah. So be it, God's will. But give the good Lord three Hail Marys for that meat . . . *ego te absolvo* . . . go and sin no more . . ."

He wrote to Bishop Pearsall: "Is it possible that there is a priest who is security cleared?" And then the Secretary of Defense—the new Secretary, Jim Forrestal was long dead—the same. But there was no priest for the classified.

"My wife, I wish to kneel at thy feet."

"John?"

"I wish it, to beg forgiveness for my sins."

"The priest—"

"Has nothing to do with it. You are closer to God. Being with you is like being with God. The coital moment is the most sacred and prayerful moment."

In her lush white nightgown, blushing, she sits upon the straight chair before her table and receives his supplication, a sick naked old man at her feet, and when he lays his head upon her knees, she somehow manages, by the way she touches his bald scalp, to preserve his dignity. "We have had such a sweet life," she says. Then, in Magyar: "The flowers still are smiling."

He feels the comfort of her song-lifted voice, feels her quiet hands upon his head, and knows by the gentleness and the nobility of her presence that this god he has invented for himself is compassionate indeed—

and then he knows that she is not herself

and then also knows that these are not the knees of his good wife

and he hears the buzzing, eager song of the beast

and he knows that the Lord of the Flies is his wife, and he is but a naked supplicant at the feet of Hell.

He could not leap up, he had not the strength anymore,

but instead reared back and glimpsed briefly the whizzing blue mandibles and his own sallow, shocked reflection in the lenses of the ancient compound eyes of *it*. And then she was there, coming down over *it* like molten wax, the body and face of his wife covering *it* until he reached out with trembling fingers and touched her neck, feeling the neat patter of her pulse . . . but knew—of course—*it*.

"You can confess yourself, John," she said in the softest of tones. She spread her arms. "Come, husband, you can, yes."

He was so appalled that he could not move, there on his knees, knowing that all along he had been married to, had conceived children with, had taken the pleasure of something . . . dreadful.

She reached out to him. "Don't shrink away, John." A girl's smile. "I'm nobody to fear." In the tone, the rising of the humanity, so entirely soft, so entirely of love that he was disarmed and settled again and muttered to her:

"There is something here, a terrible thing, that has threatened that if we tell of *it*, if we reveal to the rest of mankind that *it* is here, then *it* will annihilate us all."

"This is the disease."

"Certainly, the disease of the universe. God's universe, abandoned and horribly diseased, an unimaginable multitude of rotting suns, a horrible mistake, a desert of murdered worlds." He buried his face in her lace. "And we—I did it. I murdered the world."

"Oh, John, this is no sort of sin. What have you done, gone with the girls? Or boys, John, I understand that. I know how it goes, it's a little accident, nothing more. John, you must not fear to tell these sins before you die. No, I will be your priest, I will absolve you in the name of the Virgin Mother, I will grant you forgiveness." Her hand pressed against his cheek; he smelled the sweetness of her nightgown. "Already, even before I know."

"I have wanted . . . Dionysus."

"A young man?"

"No, no, a god. A god, you see. Fell in love—a child with the body of a man and the wisdom of the ages—"

"The Christ Child?"

"Wild child. Child of the forests and the rushing stream, child of the sacred woods and the leaping hind. That—I loved—once—in Thuringia . . . in a mine . . . O God, in a mine—"

"I can't understand."

Suddenly he went up from her lap. He knelt facing her, clasped his hands. "I have eaten meat on Friday, please my beloved, forgive me."

She smiled softly. "I can only forgive the sins of the heart. I can't even understand a thing like that. Is that a sin in the American Church?"

His mind wanted to laugh at how idiotic he must appear, a fat yellow man balancing on knob knees, his enormous old schlong dangling practically to his ankles. He could not confess his secrets because nobody could comprehend them. The gulf between what he knew and how they imagined their world worked was simply too great. They could not understand the nature of indeterminacy, and therefore could not comprehend the harm he had done by causing the lost, amorphous reality of the demon to suddenly become fixed and absolutely real.

"Come." She stood, drew him to his feet, and together they went to the bed. She held her head in a proud way, she treated him with such grace, with such gravity, and he pretended that he had not seen her quiver of revulsion when he kissed her sweet skin.

She laid her hand upon him and lowered her eyes and a blush came into her cheeks. They were never so forward with each other, never so blunt as this, and he was ashamed, it was the light of day, she should not see this. But she did see, she looked full upon his naked, erect species, his hanged man. "John," she said, and drew her fingers along the shaft until she touched the most naked place, where the flesh lifted out of the root of his body.

He stirred, he thrust from his mind the fact that *it* was present, for *it* was present at the edge of everybody, *it* sought to enter the world through two billion doors. For that was what mankind really was, a vast engine of doorways, ready to open, ready to let the dark flood into the sweet lighted house of God.

Demigods know such things; unlike men, demigods are condemned to the consequences even of actions they do not understand. In this sense, Oedipus was a demigod because he had to suffer the consequences of a nature he could not control. And so also John von Neumann, who had to suffer because he fulfilled the tragic destiny of his own mind.

She drew him to her, then lay him back upon his conjugal bed. She dropped away her gown and let his eyes fall upon her, upon her softly smiling lips and the eyes of God's own gentle side, upon the line of her breasts and the perfect earthly curve that they bore, upon her sweet-scented imperfect skin, tightened by her suffering of babies, and the mound of Venus also and the secret within.

But he knew, and could not escape the knowledge, that straining to free itself from behind her grace and dignity was the whole buzzing fury of Hell.

"Oh, it looks fine," she said, and in that narrow, tiny moment was happy, was happy with him

and with her magic they were young again

and death was far away

the sky was empty but for stars

Enola Gay was still iron in the Thuringian depths, and the nation of the happy had not yet filled the world with its planes and its bombs

and Adolf Hitler was a quaffing peasant and Albert Einstein was a Swiss clerk and O then, O then she shone like a star, and shook her head with the pleasure of it, and he saw the moonlight in her hair.

Now, the sunlight. She hung over him, a dear old crow of a woman, bouncing on him and throwing her head about and laughing. He was done quickly, he had no strength, and then his heart was crashing like a trout in a creel and his temples were grinding and his stomach was heaving, but all he could do was turn his head to one side and retch white bitter froth.

Thus did the grace of the flesh leave him forever. She came off him, tossed her head like a proud exciting filly, and set about cleaning him up, which she did with a cool cloth and two pink towels. "Now, there you are love, none the wiser." She went into the bathroom and he saw her sit upon the toilet and weep, expelling what was undoubtedly the last of her husband.

He lay as still as possible, wishing that his heart would burst right at this perfect ending. But no, it ground tiredly on. He fought to quell his stomach, breathing deep, his attention moving from nausea to sickening headache and back again. From nausea to headache to memory:

He had known instantly, the horrible moment that the call came in. "Doctor, this is General Roger Remy, and I would like to be the first to inform you that the Eighth Air Force has a disk and the remains of three alien fliers."

How stupid they were. Alien fliers. These bodies without internal organs, with only vestigial windpipes, could not be what they seemed. The Air Force and all the others thinking—imagining, poor fools—that the things were anything other than a cruel and cunning trick. He had always sensed that *it* would come, the demon would come . . . but how clever this was.

The coming of the flying saucer was the beginning of the end of man. He saw it as a rupture of reason, a breach of the dike, the rising of a chaos that history and love and hope had folded away in the dark.

At first, there had been excitement, even elation—plans to go out to New Mexico and meet the "aliens," even the President, with their flags, their dreams. The fools had formed committees and study groups and Jim Forrestal and Harry Truman had invented high secrecies to control the flow of knowledge, and O the days were full of gold and promise.

For them, for the fools. He'd gone straight to Father Peter Dubois and had made entrance into the Church, had returned, yes, had gone back to mass, had abandoned his old agnostic ways, had knelt and prayed, dear Jesu and Maria, protect this thy child from that which he in his ignorance has unbound. Dear Jesu and Maria, show me the way to forgiveness.

Then *they* had in some cunning manner located Secretary Forrestal in the midnight and removed him from his body like drawing the pulp from a fruit, and he saw them as they really are, and in a day was completely mad. He had written diaries, and Truman had asked, "Should I read them?"

"Burn them, Mr. President, with your own hands, right there in that fireplace. Never open them again. Burn them." He knew what would be in them, of course: the alchemy that would dissolve the walls of the world. "Burn them and kill everybody who knows about this. Me. Yourself."

How Truman had laughed, with his little spectacles gleaming and his cheeks going pink. Truman, who smelled of bath powder. Little man with precise, nervous hands. Truman, who had been granted the right to make the two greatest human decisions: to drop the bombs that let them through; to then conceal their presence.

A day passed, one of those timeless days that occur in the lives of the very sick, when the body seems to be gliding in an endless, unchanging haze that is not quite death, not quite yet.

Then it had been two days he had remained in the bed,

never rising from that moment of coitus. Never rising. She sponged him and gave him the bedpan. He was helpless now, entirely so. He could not rise, not even if he tried.

That night he had dreamed an odd dream, of pure children, blond and pale and cruel, who had made a place for him in the barn offal. He had not understood why a gentleman and a doctor would be billeted in a barn, until he saw his own tracks and realized that he was a pig, a fat pig, and saw that he had died and become this filthy beast to whom table leavings and even his own shit smelled sweet. He became aware that the dancing children were fattening him and that he could not resist the crusts of bacon and the boiled carrots that they tossed to him, even though he saw the cool interest in their eyes.

His pig body was so richly alive that he felt like a demigod on tiny hooves. When he cried out, there was song in it—high song—and an ancient, mysterious sense of incantation. He was powerful in his pigdom, the glorious, the king, the recipient of fine foods. He loved their long arms and their pudgy hands, but not their dark, deep eyes—no, the eyes opened into the unknown—but they served him in their shorts and boots, the girls in their starched aprons.

Where their hands grasped him, he felt a dread electricity, as if they were made of shivering fire. He sang his song, he raised his eyes, but his servants had become his masters, and suddenly there was white heat in his throat and the pouring blood, and then their own cries of pleasure, and he heard the melody and was dead.

When he awoke from this death, he was in a white room, and there were men around his bed.

Saying their gentle good-byes.

He had worked until the end, they said.

He had been noble, they said.

He said: But I'm a pig.

They said: This young man will stay with you.

There was a boy in the uniform of the Air Force, a

bright-cheeked youth who smelled, inevitably, of fruit gum and cigarettes.

"Good morning, sir," he said. "I'll be here for the duration."

The duration! Wo ist meine Frau? My wife?

She'll be waiting outside. And my children? Outside.

The secret, John. Remember the stakes.

Oh, God—if we tell them, then it is the end: mankind devoured. But what does it matter? Even if we don't tell, they're going to be devoured in secret.

"Devoured, devoured, what is the etymology of that word in English, gentlemen? Isn't it from the Latin, from *devorare*—a stressed stem, related to devout?" (Look at their faces, they understand nothing.) "*Devorare, devotate*—a matter of the ending, you see?"

They do not see. They think in terms of weapons, of fighting, but you cannot fight this, you cannot fight a beast who can enter the world by two billion doors—and more, O my God, as time passes. More and more doors. They think that they are dealing with something essentially ordinary, but this is not essentially ordinary.

"At the least, *it* can maintain the grace of the quantum world in the macrocosm, do you see that?"

Blank faces, heads that turned, that shook with some misbegotten sadness.

"I cannot die, gentlemen, if nobody but me understands this!"

The youth smiled. He laid his hand upon von Neumann's forehead. "Fever," he said.

"How old are you?"

"Nineteen, sir."

"A lieutenant, so young . . ."

"I'm from the Academy." Chosen for his ignorance, no doubt, and told never to tell a soul what he had heard, under penalty of death.

He struggled in his sheets, glared about, finally finding the Secretary. "What is this? Where is Colonel Ford?"

"Do you recall, 'the marginal man is always relatively the more civilized human being'?"

"Ah, Veblen. I suppose I share the concept." It was, of course, the reason that the Colonel had been replaced by the boy. He looked from face to face. Secretary of Defense. Secretaries of the Army, Navy, and Air Force, the Chiefs of Staff like a platoon of dog soldiers at the back of the room. "Where is Ike?"

"Ike is in the desert."

He waved his hand, not wanting the boy to hear more. "Nobody understood what I said—about the ending? No, I see not. Then send Wiener, send Pauli. They may understand."

There was silence. His young nurse-boy laid a cloth upon his forehead. In the sparkle of his fresh eyes, John von Neumann could see the peculiar truth of Veblen's concept: The boy's ignorance was indeed a peace, indeed civilized, and they had been right to bring him.

"Send someone. Anyone. At least try to understand."

Slowly, like old women leaving a cathedral, the gentlemen of power withdrew.

"Don't fight," he called after them, half-rising from the bed, then being lifted by the boy, lifted to a sitting position. "Don't you dare fight!" A hand raised, waved . . . as if waving him away. "You stupid Americans, listen!"

He struggled frantically, but they did not stop.

Then all the strength left him. He sank in the boy's arms.

"The tar baby. The tar baby."

"Sir?" The boy laid him back on the bed.

"The tar baby."

"Yes, sir."

The boy didn't understand; none of them did or could understand. The only mind that could prevent this was dying.

He struggled through the day, felt vaguely disquieted when the boy bathed him and relieved him. "You are a nurse, also?"

"I'm in premed. I'm going into high-altitude medicine."

"And you know—you are on a need-to-know basis?"

"Yeah."

"How do you feel, boy? What about your girl? You have a girl?"

"No, sir."

"No. Children . . . Will you raise children, continue your line?"

"Sir, I think I'll pass on that."

"Yes, of course you will. They would all pass on it, if they knew."

"I meant, pass on the question. Until I have a girl."

"Don't have children! Don't do it!"

The boy's smile flickered. "No?"

Von Neumann reached for him. "I'm a pig, I'm being slaughtered!"

"Yes, sir."

"Leave here! Leave the room!"

Instead, the boy came closer, and in that moment John von Neumann understood the one last thing that he had not understood. It caught his breath, snapped his heart, to realize that the boy knew, that they all knew just as he did, had known it always just as he had known, these ancient souls who were the creators of the gods and the bombs and the dreams.

As von Neumann's breath swooned upward and outward, he felt the warm arms of the boy embracing him more and more tightly, saw in his blazing eyes the eyes from beyond, felt in the power of his arms both the serpent and the angel. In the boy's fearsome smile, the dying man saw at last who it is that waits for us all, beyond the open doors.

1960
1961
1962
1963

FIXTURES OF MATCHSTICK MEN AND JOO

BY ELIZABETH MASSIE

1964

—For Amy, Kurt, and Ananda

1965

───────────────────────────

1966
1967
1968
1969

When I look up to the sky
I see your eyes a funny kind of yellow
I rush home to bed I soak my head
I see your face underneath my pillow
I wake next morning tossing, yawning
See your face come peeking through my window
Pictures of matchstick men and you
Mirages of matchstick men and you
All I ever see is them and you—

—The Status Quo, "Pictures of Matchstick Men"

He scrambled around the wounded guy and dropped behind a rusted trash barrel on the street corner. The blood on his hands belonged to the wounded guy, to a woman, and to himself; he had tried to help the wounded guy, to pull him out of the way of the projectiles and the billowing clouds of gas, but the guy had been knocked unconscious, and was too heavy to pull. And as he stood to look for help, to raise his arms amid the madness to wave for someone, something to come to their aid, a screaming goon lashed out with his club and split the skin of his palms and broke the tips of two fingers.

"I got to get out," he said, panting, his body crouched down behind the barrel, his chin tucked to avoid flying glass. His words came through jaws that chattered with the speed of a wind-up toy. "This ain't right. This ain't fucking right."

A cry came from his left, just beside the barrel. "Ayeeeeeeee!" He squinted and looked up. A man in a torn jacket, his face a banshee's grin, waved a North Vietnamese flag and tap-danced. The man nearly stepped on the wounded guy, but didn't seem to notice that he was there. Then something flew over the man's head and shattered on the wall behind him. The man let loose a war cry and dashed back out into the chaos on the street.

Behind the barrel, he wondered how long it would go on before someone with more power than he could drag it to a halt. It had gone on day after day now. Insanity and hurt. Hate and blood. Not what he'd pictured, not what he'd signed up for.

No sir.

This isn't some distant land of rice paddies and water buffalo and mine fields. This isn't Southeast Asia. This is fucking Chicago, for God's sake. Shit like this doesn't happen here.

A hand came down on his shoulder, and he flinched, raising one bloody hand before his face as a shield.

Don't hit me, man, I'm already hurt, I ain't going out there no more, leave me alone!

But the voice that came down from above was soft and gentle, barely audible over the battle in the streets.

"You need this, son," the voice said.

He squinted around the web of his broken fingers to see a smile, and a piece of paper being handed to him.

"Need what?" he asked. His throat hurt.

"This," said the voice. "Read it. Don't lose it."

He lifted his good hand and pulled the paper free. He looked from the smile to the pamphlet, which was already smudged in red.

What was it, a fucking advertisement? Come eat at Sam's after the battle, we serve patriots and communists alike . . . ?

But there was a line drawing of trees and a sun. Beneath it were the words SUNRISE. WE WELCOME YOU.

He crammed the paper into his shirt pocket. Maybe he'd take a closer look later. But now he was hurt, and there was a wounded guy around the barrel who wouldn't last much longer if he stayed out there in the madness.

"Hey, man," he began. "There's a guy out there if you could . . ."

But looking back up, he saw the smile was gone. Sunshine pamphlet guy had vanished. He peered around the barrel. The hordes were still swarming, some in one direction, some in another.

It would be a while before he could get out.

"Fuck it," he said. He held his shattered fingers to his chest and tried to think of the lyrics to "A Little Help from My Friends," but he couldn't because there were no friends here. Whatever friends he'd found earlier were out there somewhere, and he'd never find them again. Most weren't friends at all.

No friends.

No help.

The Beatles were lucky, they had both.

SEPTEMBER 1968

Lord, this can't be happening.

Sharon dropped to her knees in a stall inside the first-floor girls' bathroom.

Her heart pounded.

God, you have to hear me, she prayed silently. *I was supposed to start today. I have to start, it's been almost four months since I started! Please, don't let this happen!*

Outside the stalls, other girls sat on sinks and drew on their cigarettes. "At St. Mary's, you have to kneel, and if your skirt doesn't touch the floor, they send you home." It was Susan talking. "They try to do that here, I'll tell 'em fine, I'll go home! Getting kicked out would be groovy, don't you think?"

"Yeah." It was Mary Jane. She rolled her skirts up higher than anyone else in school. She loved the low drink fountains, where she had to bend way over.

Sharon drove her fists together, trying to squeeze out the sound of the girls' voices in case the Lord answered. *Lord, hear me!*

Susan and Mary Jane giggled and coughed.

Lord!

There was a banging on the door to the hall. Someone rushed in to the sinks, and said, "Teacher's coming! Lose the butts!"

Stall doors slammed open. Smokes hit the toilet water with a hiss; pots were flushed.

Sharon doubled over and drove her fist into her stomach. Again. Again. Again.

How do you like this? Huh? I said listen! Forgive me now!

She could hear the girls fleeing the bathroom. After a moment, there were teacher footsteps on the tile floor. "Someone smoking in here?"

Forgive my sin, God!

"Anyone in here at all?"

Listen to me! Answer me!

The teacher went into the stall next to Sharon's, sat down, and cut a long, sputtering fart.

It was all the answer Sharon was going to get.

Gary didn't think his knee would need stitches, but it still hurt like blazes. The gash ran across the kneecap, not deep but bloody as hell. His overalls were torn, and he didn't have anything to sew them up with. He cursed under his breath, touched the gash one more time just to see how much he could make it hurt, then looked out at the road and the pass-ing cars.

He'd never jumped from a moving vehicle before. Trippy thing to do, he knew, but the old man who had given him a ride had grabbed at his privates, and there was no other recourse. Gary had hitchhiked all the way from Chicago to Virginia, a good thousand miles he'd guessed, or at least a couple hundred, and up until now, all the rides had worked out fine. One girl had been blitzed and Gary wasn't sure they were going to stay on the road, but even that had turned out okay. He'd only gone with her fifteen miles before he told her thanks, this is as far as I'm going, my grandma lives just up that little driveway, see you later.

Things had been tolerable over the past week. His broken fingers, the tips bound together with some masking tape he'd pulled off an auction-sale sign on a country road back in Illinois, felt like they were beginning to heal.

But this old hayseed he'd hitched with last was enough to make Gary debate the merits of maybe walking the last thirty miles. The man had looked harmless enough, about seventy, with a John Deere cap and a stack of Farm Bureau flyers on the front seat. But a couple miles along, halfway up the mountain toward the Blue Ridge Parkway, the man had started talking about bulls.

"You a farm boy, son?"

"Nope. I'm from Worth originally."

"What's that?"

"Near Chicago."

The man nodded as if he heard but didn't really care. He whirled his arm out the window of his Ford Falcon, indicating the person in the car behind him to go on and pass and quit tailgating.

"Been living on the road the past few days," Gary said. "Ain't been easy, but I've made it so far."

"You ever spend much time with cows?"

Gary had glanced at the man without turning his head. He didn't know where this was leading. Maybe the old guy had some wisdom he wanted to share and nobody to share it with. Gary decided to go along. He had decided a week ago that he would try to be fair in all things. Open to all things, all people. To embrace peace and understanding. Judge not, and all that good shit. A vow he'd made to himself to counter all the bad he'd seen recently. All the bad he'd done. Lead me blindly. Let me trust.

"No," Gary answered. "Don't know much about cows."

"Thought you might, wearing them overalls."

Gary was wearing overalls. He'd been a little embarrassed over them at first but had forced himself to get over it. When he left the city, he didn't go back home first. It was easier just to take off with what he already had with him, a duffel bag containing sunglasses, a rolled-up cardboard sign, a flashlight, a pack of cigarettes and couple of joints, a black plastic comb, and two hundred dollars from his job last spring as a street-construction flagman. After two days on the road he'd met with a thunderstorm that drenched his only clothes, a pair of bell-bottoms and a T-shirt. So he'd stolen the overalls and a second shirt, a blue one with long sleeves he proceeded to tear off, from a clothesline behind a little brick house along the way. He left a few dollars clothespinned to the line.

And so every other day, Gary had changed back and forth between the two sets of clothes. Today was an overalls day.

"No," Gary said, working his elbow onto the armrest of the Falcon. He liked to hold his broken fingers up when he could. "I just wear 'em 'cause they're comfortable."

The old man coughed, spit out his window, and sucked on a molar. Then he said, "You like comfortable things?"

"Well," said Gary. He paused, then said, "Sure."

The man laughed at that, although Gary wasn't following his bemused train of thought.

"Ain't that the truth for everybody?" said the man. "We all like comfortable stuff. Stuff that feels good."

Gary felt something tighten in the back of his mouth with a click. "We're just about up the mountain now, looks like. You can let me off here, okay? Don't want to take you out of your way any."

"Nah," said the old man. "I'm going all the way. You can, too." The man licked his lower lip and his old, furry white eyebrows began to twitch.

Gary slipped his elbow through the strap of the duffel bag and put both hands on the armrest. The muscles in his legs tensed.

"You kind of pretty, there, you know, with that long hair," said the man. "You like somebody running their fingers in that hair, boy?"

"Let me out," said Gary. His vow to fairness added, "Please."

"You got that nice hair on your face and chin, just like a real man. Bet you got nice hair 'tween your legs, too, don't you? Bet it feels good!"

And the man shoved one hand into Gary's crotch with a squeal of delight, and Gary popped the door and jumped out.

As he rolled clear of the car onto the shoulder of the road, he saw with relief that the old man didn't slow down. The opened car door slammed shut with the angle of the climb and the speed of the car as it continued up the mountainside.

Then Gary sat up and saw the gash in his leg.

"Goddamn pervert!" Gary shouted at the vanishing Falcon. The leg stung, and Gary picked at the cut for a while. But the bleeding eased up and he stood, appraised the ruined overalls, and slung his duffel bag over his shoulder.

He had thirty-some miles to cover, and he wasn't feeling like giving another car a try at the moment.

Vow of peace and understanding or not.

From the dining room her mother called, "Did you walk home from school today?"

In the foyer, Sharon called back, "Yeah. Rachael wanted to go shopping before the football game. I didn't want to go."

Dishes were clinking, being put into place. Her mother was always on time, always proper, always a good wife to Dr. Louis Richards, Jr. Dinner was taken in the dining room, never the breakfast nook. Napkins were always cloth, plates always the china.

"My goodness, Sharon. You and Rachael aren't on the outs, are you?"

"No."

Sharon wrapped her arms around her book bag and took the steps two at a time, pausing at the top when a cramp caught her stomach.

Yes, God, please let this be it. The beginning of the end.

But the cramps stopped as quickly as they had come, leaving nothing but a mild burn. She walked down the hall-way to her bedroom and shut the door behind her.

Her books were dropped onto her desktop. She sat on her bed, keeping care not to rumple the covers much so she wouldn't have to remake it before dinner. All around her were tasteful furnishings, chosen by her mother. White chairs, white window coverings, white canopy. Pure and white, like their daughter. On a framed corkboard were pictures of Davy Jones and Walter Koenig, torn from issues of *16 Magazine*. There were no posters, though. Posters were "tacky."

Someone knocked on the bedroom door, and from the hallway her little brother, Lou, said, "I get the TV tonight. There's a Banana Splits special at seven-thirty."

"Fine," Sharon said. "Now get lost."

She lay back on her bed and reached out to pull open the drawer in her nightstand. From inside, she took out a small scrapbook. She opened it, held it over her head, and stared up at the news clippings she'd been saving since April.

Current events had always been a dirty word, until this past spring. Anything beyond her town of Neison had nothing to do with her, with them. Who had time to care for more than family, friends, and the pep squad? But then Sharon had fallen in love. She saw him on the after-dinner news, and it was the face, the eyes, that caught her heart. He was beautiful.

Sharon's father hated him, of course. The man was a radical, the man was anti-American. The man wanted equal rights for Negroes. The man wanted to end the war. The man was a liberal. The government needed to watch out for slick men like that.

Sharon's friends didn't even know who the man was. Well, perhaps they'd heard his name around and about and certainly knew about his dead brother, but they never read the news, never watched the television except for *Wild Wild West* and *Gomer Pyle*.

Bobby.

Sharon had written his name on the insides of all her spiral notebooks. She'd taken her old Girl Scout scrapbook, torn out all the camp mementos, and begun a Bobby book.

And then they killed him. Shot his brains out in a hotel kitchen on June 5. Died June 6. Her friends had shrugged their shoulders. Her father had said, "Things fall into place if you let them. I'll bet our good government had something to do with it. They're smarter than some want to think."

On June 7, Sharon had invited Darrell Harner over to her house while her parents were out. In the backyard, behind the gazebo, she had fucked the football star to relieve her grief.

It hadn't helped. She spent the rest of the summer avoiding Darrell's persistent phone calls.

And now.

Sharon gently put the scrapbook back into the drawer. Then she pounded her stomach with her fist again, gritting her teeth, praying this time to the Devil, since God seemed so disinterested.

It was early evening. Many cars had passed him on his hike along the road heading up the mountainside, but he'd stepped way off the shoulder and ignored them. One Volkswagen van, full of what seemed to be college students, even slowed and honked. A girl in the front asked him if he'd like to squeeze in with them, they were heading to Virginia Beach, but Gary had waved them on. Bruises had welled up on all sorts of odd places of his body, and he felt the burn of new scrapes with every other step. If physical torment were cleansing, then he was as clean as rainwater. In spite of what he actually looked like.

When he reached the road sign announcing that it was only a mile and a half to the crest of the mountain, Gary found a soft, mossy spot beneath a tree. He dropped into the undergrowth, leaned his head against the bark, and dozed.

His dreams were of wars and blood, and it was not without relief when he woke up to the spattering of rain on his overalls.

Dinner discussion centered around her father, of course. As Sharon's mother passed bowls around the table, smiling and nodding in rhythm with her husband's monologue, Louis Richards, Jr., M.D., discussed a warehouse he had just purchased.

"It's going to be a moneymaker of the near future," he said. "I divide the place up into many small compartments, each with its own door and key. The rooms can be rented on a monthly basis."

"Mmmm," said Sharon's mother.

The family sat in the dining room. Sharon, her parents, and little brother Lou. Lou the third. Lou was itchy, hoping dinner would be over before the Splits came on.

"Make it convenient, available twenty-four hours a day. Hire one security man to wander. I could get upward to one hundred compartments out of that place I figure." Dad took a bite of meat loaf. It was nasty meat loaf; Mom was a good decorator, a pitiful cook. But Dr. Richards had too much on his mind to notice.

"The funny thing is that the little old man who owned the warehouse had no idea of the gold mine he was sitting on. I paid a pittance for it. Ignorance is hardly bliss, is it?"

"No, I wouldn't think so," said Sharon's mother.

Sharon said, "I'm sick. I want to go upstairs."

"Do you need some Pepto-Bismol?" Her mother finally looked at her. "You can't be sick, honey, we have a luncheon at your grandparents' tomorrow."

Dr. Richards said, "I'll triple the investment in less than two years, I've got it figured. There are a few other warehouses on the south of town I want to snatch up before anyone else figures what I've got going."

"May I be excused? Please?" Sharon's fists balled reflexively. She put them in her lap, so her parents wouldn't see. Nothing they hated more than slipping emotional control.

"Honey?" said her mother, who then looked at her husband for the cue. He tapped his teeth together, then flicked his hand in the air—a mildly irritated dismissal.

Sharon went upstairs to the bathroom. She sat on the toilet and watched between her legs for the sign that either the miracle she'd prayed for or the pummeling she'd given herself was working.

She strained, and watched.

There was nothing but pee.

She went into her room, heart hammering, and sat for a minute on the edge of her bed. Then she grabbed her purse, climbed out her window, onto the sunroom roof, and dropped to the ground.

She thought for a moment of going to Darrell's house, but that would be useless. It would cost him nothing. It was costing her everything.

"A pretty bad investment, Daddy," she said. "You won't be bragging about this one at the next family reunion."

She went down the driveway toward the road, and began walking east, toward the foot of the mountain. Before she got a block, she was already shivering in the early-evening air.

He reached the top of the mountain, sweating and aching. The dried blood on his knee itched. But the view at the crest took some of the discomfort away. At an empty overlook, Gary stood against a stone wall and took it in. They were stunning, these vast blue mountains. Miles after miles of rolling, tree-softened ridges. Roads hidden by nature; houses, if there were any, swallowed up. Clouds hanging above, seeming ready to come down and embrace the world.

"Yes," Gary said. He took a deep breath. "Yes."

This was nearly the place. He could feel it. The stress from the past week drained from him like air from an old balloon. Lifting his arms, he tipped back his head and smiled at the sky. Below him, from mountainside trees, a rush of wings caught the air, and, in an instant, a flock of birds was around him, beside him, above him. Gary said, "Oh, yes!" The birds scattered then, and were gone.

Gary left the overlook for the road again.

Close by, he found a tiny spot of civilization—a gas station and a Howard Johnson's restaurant. Gary, watchless, guessed the time to be about eight o'clock, so most of the supper business had gone on. Only a few vehicles sat in the lot. The orange on the roof needed paint.

Gary tried the door to the gas-station bathroom, but it was locked. He found a water spigot around the side of the building and ran water into his cupped hands and splashed it on his face. In the station's plate-glass side window, he appraised himself, more curious with what he saw than disgusted. His hair was now past his shoulders, straight and brown. He'd washed it in a roadside creek yesterday, but it was still flat and oily. His beard was bushy. His eyes were rimmed with circles from the little sleep he'd been getting on leaf piles he kicked together at night and covered with the duffel bag.

And his stomach was angry at the lack of concern it had received since Chicago. There'd been one long parade of burgers and baked beans at dives in small, tar-bubbly towns. Sometimes there'd been no admittance to the dives at all because the managers didn't care for his looks and wouldn't let him inside, so his meals had been assorted leftovers from the Dumpsters out back.

Tonight, though, he wanted something he could taste, something that he could close his eyes to and let sing an easy song to his taste buds.

Clams, he thought. Clams, fresh bread, and a salad. He wiped his hands on his overalls, raked his fingers through his hair, and sniffed his pits.

Not great, but the inside of the restaurant was probably air-conditioned, and it wouldn't be as noticeable.

As he walked toward the restaurant, the Howard Johnson sign hummed and sputtered into life. Flying bugs were immediately drawn to its monotonous tune. Gary stopped in the parking lot, lit a cigarette, and took a few drags. A couple came out of the restaurant, arm in arm, and paused to kiss on the front step. Gary allowed himself a small smile; here was love. It did still exist in little pockets of the world, even in these blue mountains of Virginia.

The boy broke from the girl, looked at Gary, and said, "What the hell is your problem, you filthy hippie?"

But even in Virginia, love wasn't blind.

The restaurant was a Howard Johnson's. Sharon had been to this place many times before when her family took weekend drives along the Parkway to Raven's Roost. But she had never climbed the mountain before, never hiked the four miles from Neison to the crest, and the restaurant was a wonderful shrine to a weary pilgrim.

Sharon sat for a moment on the bumper of a station wagon in the parking lot, her stinging feet out of her tennis shoes.

Although her body was worn, her mind was fresh and haughty. *But now what are you going to do?* it persisted. Sharon brushed the question off. She wouldn't think about anything now except getting something to eat and drink. Her throat was raw from breathing through her teeth on the steep slopes.

After the meal, she'd look again at her situation and the two choices. A leap from the overlook down the road or life with her parents and a baby and the stigma and the self-hate and shame.

Eeny-meeny-miney-mo.

She stepped back into her shoes and went inside. The hostess gave her a booth. Sharon slid onto the vinyl seat and rubbed her eyes. She knew there were tears behind them, but they didn't want to come out. That was okay. That was good. Losing it would do no one any good. As she waited for the waitress to bring her some water and a menu, she noticed the customer seated in the booth next to hers.

He was a small man, dark hair to his shoulders, with a black, ragged beard. He surely wasn't from around here. He looked like he'd been sleeping in a barn. His eyes were focused out the restaurant window at some distant, unmoving point. Sharon gave him a quick perusal, then rummaged in the bottom of her purse to total up enough change for at least a Coke and bowl of chowder.

Great planning, Sharon. Lou has a damn piggy bank full you could have taken.

It was the man's sigh that brought her gaze back to him,

and the furrow between his brows that kept her looking long enough for him to realize she was there. The man glanced from the spot outside the window to her. His eyes were as dark as his hair, and the intensity of emotion—fear, anger, sorrow, she wasn't sure—pinned her to the back of her seat and took her breath away.

And then she nodded slightly, a polite, benign gesture taught her well by her mother ("Be nice to strangers, not too nice, but never rude, Sharon"), and returned her attention to her handful of change.

"Help you?" It was a gum-chewing waitress, no older than Sharon.

"I didn't get a menu," Sharon said. "How much is the clam chowder?"

"Cup is forty-nine cents," said the waitress. "Bowl is sixty nine."

"And the chili?"

The gum snapped. "Same. You want a menu?"

"How about soup? You do have soup here."

The waitress put a hand on her hip. "We got soup."

"How much for minestrone?"

The eyes rolled, the gum flashed at the front of the waitress's mouth. "I'll get you a menu." She strode off. Sharon looked at the change in her hands.

She had one dollar and sixteen cents, not counting whatever stray pennies still hid in the folds of the cloth-purse bottom. A cup of soup and a glass of water would have to be it for now. Her stomach, having turned up its nose at the meat loaf back home, growled.

Sharon got up and went to the ladies' room. She didn't want to be there when the smart-ass waitress brought the damn menu. For a minute, she ran the water in the sink and let her fingers play in it. The heat felt good, the steam rising to her chin and making the stray hairs in her braid curl up like birthday ribbons.

"Lord have mercy," she whispered.

She exited the ladies' room for her booth. The waitress was just putting the menu down, so Sharon lingered at the pie display until she had left. Then she walked over and sat.

Next to the menu, the corner poking up from under the salt shaker, was a five-dollar bill.

It hadn't been there before.

Sharon touched the bill, then glanced around. Behind her, a family with three children crammed in the booth argued over one child who was refusing to eat her cheeseburger. Across the restaurant, on stools at the counter, lone diners chewed their meals and stared at their plates. At the booth in front of her, the bearded man watched something out the window.

The bill was crumpled, clearly from someone's pocket. Sharon's father always kept bills neatly folded in his wallet. This one seemed to have been hastily crammed in a pocket and drawn out again. Sharon pulled it out from under the salt shaker.

The waitress was back. The gum popped.

"Looked at the menu?" she asked.

Sharon felt the skin of her face tighten. "You looked at the mirror? You look like a slob with that gum. It's disgusting."

The waitress's eyes narrowed. She hesitated, fighting for something to say. Then she pulled on a snippy smile and said, "What have you decided you can afford for under a dollar? Ma'am?"

Sharon stood up, stuck the five-dollar bill into her skirt pocket, and said, "I can afford to walk away from this place. And you're stuck here. Enjoy yourself."

Outside, it was dark. Sharon walked to the far side of the parking lot and stood, her arms crossed, her elbows caught in her hands. Tears tried to fall, but Sharon bit the inside of her cheek to stop them. The HoJo light above her head droned like a hornet caught in a bag.

"You need this?"

Sharon looked around, her fingers still clutching her arms, and saw the man who had been in the booth next to her. He was indeed short, no more than five-five, and his clothes were horrendous. A sleeveless blue cotton shirt and overalls that looked as if they'd been run over by a truck. He was holding out a handful of napkins.

"No. Thank you."

"Sure?"

She nodded.

The man was early twenties at most. He looked like some of the hippies Sharon had seen in the newspaper. Scraggly. Ragged. He had a duffel bag which looked almost empty. She wondered if he was a radical, a communist. She wished he would leave.

He just stood there.

She said, "What do you want?"

"Is there anything I can do to help?" His voice was soft and unassuming. "You didn't get anything to eat back there. I have some crackers, left over from my clams."

"No," she said. "Thanks. But I guess I'll take the napkins after all."

He gave them to her. She rubbed her face.

"Anything else?"

"No."

The man nodded. He walked away a few yards, then sat down on a large rock at the side of the parking lot. He stared out at the road in the same way he had stared out the restaurant window.

Sharon crammed the napkins into her purse. There was an overlook not far down the road. Bobby had found his end violently. Hers would be similar. She wondered if her head would split open like the brain of someone shot in the skull. She wondered if she deserved the same kind of death Bobby had suffered. Didn't Saint Peter have himself crucified upside down because he felt unworthy to be executed the same way as Jesus?

She walked out to the roadside.

On impulse, she called back to the man, "Have a good life."

It was that comment, she realized later, that kicked all her plans in the big fat butt.

It was her last comment before she headed off down the road that made Gary follow her. Good life?

His cheek twitched with anxiety. He kept back a ways, watching her moving in the cloud-mottled moonlight, not wanting her to think he was a dangerous man creeping after her, but wanting her to know he was back there just in case.

In case what? "Fuck it, I don't know," he hissed to himself. The girl was young, perhaps seventeen or eighteen, he guessed. She was tall, with red hair in a single braid that hung halfway down her back. Her clothes were a green miniskirt and white, sleeveless shell. Gary bet she was chilly, with the mountain breeze and all. She had nothing but a purse. She must be a local girl out for a stroll.

He thought, for some reason, that she was going to continue down the long mountain road into the little town at the bottom, but, instead, she turned off onto the overlook. Gary stopped beside a scabby sycamore tree at the edge of the overlook's entry drive and watched. The girl went to the stone wall that separated the lookers from the sheer drop down the mountainside. She stood and looked over at the distant valley, at the dots of lights that indicated human presence, human dominance over the dark.

She's pretty, he thought.

And then she stepped up onto the stone wall and swung her arms back, and Gary thought, *Does she think she can fly?*

She swung her arms back, pistons prepared for the thrust. Good people died all the time. Old people, young people. Famous people, those without a name.

There was freedom in dying. There was innocence in death. No one would need to know the truth.

"Lord, see me. I repent."

She leaned forward, the sudden upcurrent of air from the fragrant valley holding her suspended for the barest of moments.

"I repent. I—" She jumped back off the wall. Her knee hit a stone and scraped a long chunk of skin away.

"Goddamn it," she said. "I can't." Her lungs drew in, crushing her hopes and her vision. "Goddamn it all."

And suddenly someone was running at her and grabbing her and throwing her to the toothed gravel of the overlook's parking lot.

Her head bounced, once, on the ground. She fought to right herself. Her hands batted the air. The bearded man was there, staring at her.

"What the hell are you doing?" Sharon shouted. The man sat back on his heels and said nothing. "Get away from me!"

The man's breathing was irregular, heavy, as if he was as scared as she was. He rubbed his face. Then he eased down on his butt and scratched his beard.

"I said get away from me!" she shouted.

"I thought . . ." he began.

"What?" Sharon demanded. She reached over and slapped him on the shoulder. "What did you think?"

"I thought you were going to jump off."

Sharon hesitated. "So what if I was? What business is it of yours? Who are you to screw with what I want to do?"

Sharon thought she saw his shoulders rise and fall in a shrug.

Sharon pointed at the specks of blood on her skinned knees. "You made me hurt myself," she said.

"I'm sorry."

Sharon scooted back to lean against the stone wall. *What the hell is this, Lord? You adding insult to injury?*

Like the bearded man, God said nothing.

After a minute, Sharon said, "Who are you, anyway?"

The man didn't look at her. He said, "Gary."

"Yeah, well, Gary, you shouldn't be so anxious to get into someone else's business."

They were silent. Then Sharon said, "You can go on now."

Gary looked up at the stars, then back at Sharon. "I've got time."

"Time for what?"

"Time to not go on yet."

Sharon shut her eyes. Even though only three months pregnant, she thought she could feel the movement of the fetus deep inside her, like a little goldfish checking the boundaries of its bowl. If only it were that simple, to take a net and dig it out and flip it onto the blacktop where it would just take a few gulps and die. If only she had the money to go to London like the rich ladies did. Daddy had the money. Sharon had nothing but righteous anger and a scraped knee.

She shivered violently.

Gary looked over. In the pale light of the nighttime, Sharon saw the same intense emotion she'd seen in his eyes at the restaurant. She caught her breath. It was at once frightening and curious.

"Are you cold?" Gary asked.

She was. "No."

"You shivered. I have another shirt in my duffel bag. You want it?"

"Does it stink like you do?"

Gary shrugged. "I don't know. Maybe it does. But that doesn't make it less warm."

"No thanks."

"I'm heading south of here, just a little ways," Gary said.

"About another twenty-five miles down the Parkway. Looking for a place called Sunrise. You from around here?"

"Yeah."

"You heard of Sunrise?"

"No."

Gary nodded. "It's a wonderful place, although I've never been. I found out about it a little over a week ago. I've dreamed about it ever since. A place on the mountaintop. It's the answer to everything I've wanted. Peace. Freedom." Gary reached into the front pocket of his overalls. He pulled out a folded brochure. He handed it to Sharon. It was printed in purple mimeograph ink, like the worksheets at school.

"It's hard to read in the dark," said Sharon.

Gary opened his duffel bag and took out a flashlight. He clicked it on and gave it to Sharon.

She read the notice.

"Sunrise. We welcome you. You won't find what you are looking for anywhere else. We love you even though we don't know you yet. Come, find us."

"What is this?" said Sharon.

"What it says it is. I'm looking for a place to live. Far away from the shit I've dealt with the last year."

At the top of the brochure was a drawing of trees and a smiling sun. At the bottom were directions.

"I've traveled from Chicago to find it."

"Chicago? You look like a farmer," said Sharon. She gave the brochure back.

Gary stuck it into his pocket. "You want to come with me?" he asked.

"Why do you think I'd do that? I live in Neison, down at the bottom of the mountain. I have a good family, my dad's a doctor." She took a deep breath. It hurt. "I'm not a transient. I don't even know you. You could kill me in a second."

Will you kill me, Gary? Make it quick. Shoot me in the skull.

"Guess it seemed like you had nowhere to go," he said.

A strand of hair caught in Sharon's mouth. She brushed it away, angrily. He wasn't going to kill her after all.

"So are you going?" Gary asked. "Back to Neison?" Sharon opened her mouth to speak, to tell him to get lost, to tell him to just kill her, please, to tell him she was pregnant and she couldn't believe they had murdered Bobby, he was beautiful, oh, so beautiful, but this man's eyes were beautiful like Bobby's, this ugly man in stinking, torn overalls had eyes full of concern and care. And so all that came out was a rush of tears and racking sobs. The first tears shed since June 6. Her father would have applauded her stoicism if he'd known.

Gary scooted beside her and put his arm around her. She put her face against his shoulder. Her nose was stopped up with the crying, so the smell wasn't so bad.

And he was warm.

He hurt dreadfully in the morning. The girl had slept against his shoulder for a very long time, and so he had sat still, accommodating her. His arm was asleep and full of needles. Add to that his cut knee and broken fingertips, and he was on a roll. And now, with the sky orange and newly awake, Gary had to piss.

"Hey," he said, shaking her.

The girl groaned.

"Hey, I have to get up." The girl's eyes fluttered, then opened. She stared at Gary, her eyebrows drawing up in disbelief.

"I have to get up. Move over."

The girl blinked, then flinched. "What happened?"

"You slept. I sat. Now I have to get up."

"I slept here?" she asked.

"Yeah." Gary stood up. There were trees at the edge of

the overlook. A quick trot over there and a few seconds would do it.

"I slept here with you?"

"Yeah. And I have to pee." He felt stupid, as if he were asking her permission. He said, "I'll be right back."

Gary went to the trees and stepped behind a thick-trunked oak. As he unbuckled his overalls and relieved himself, he wondered if she would leave while he was preoccupied. She was a strange one, but she was in need of something. He didn't even know her name.

He came back out from the trees and walked across the gravel toward the stone wall. The girl was up, rummaging through her purse for something. She looked rumpled, but still pretty.

The girl turned when she heard him. She was frowning. "I have to go," said the girl.

"I thought you didn't want to go home. Last night you seemed so sad, so scared."

The girl rolled her lips in between her teeth. She stared down at her feet. "My shoes look terrible."

"Better than mine."

"I look terrible, too."

Gary said nothing.

"Don't I?"

"You look fine. Looks aren't everything."

The girl shook her head. "You're wrong. Looks tell people things. Looks are important, they say what kind of person you are. My mother won't even let me go shopping in a pantsuit. I have to wear dresses. Dresses tell people I take time for myself. That I have class."

Gary said, "What do my looks say?"

"I can't tell with you."

Gary shoved his hands into his overalls pockets. "Well," he said, "I've got to find Sunrise. It was nice meeting you."

"Sharon," she said.

"Sharon."

He lifted his duffel bag and slung it over his arm. He gave the girl a smile, the only thing he could offer. Then he turned and crossed the overpass to the road. Twenty-five miles would do it. Due south on the Parkway.

"Maybe I should come with you," she called after him. "That is, if you don't mind company."

Gary turned back to her. "No," he replied. "I don't mind."

She shouldered her purse and trotted across the gravel, her braid swinging. "Let's pick up some breakfast from HoJo's first. I've got a five."

Gary nodded. They set off.

A third choice had come along. Not an overlook dive, not returning to her parents. But tagging along with a bruised and scraggly man in overalls to a place on the mountain she'd never heard of.

They walked a good fifteen miles before it began to grow dark. Sharon was tired, but she gritted her teeth and didn't let it show. Each time a car passed, and she suggested they flag it down, he said no.

They talked, first about the wildlife they saw at the road-side, then about family, then about current events. Sharon asked Gary what he thought of Bobby Kennedy being shot. He told her it was a damn sin.

Sharon thought she was going to like this man, in spite of his overalls.

Another mile, and Sharon had told Gary that she was pregnant.

At six-thirty, Sharon stopped dead in her tracks and waited for Gary to notice she wasn't keeping up. He stopped ten yards ahead and looked back.

"What's up?"

Sharon sighed. "I wish you would reconsider hitching a ride. What do we have, another ten miles tomorrow?"

"What if the ride is dangerous?"

"What if it isn't? Most people are nice, aren't they?"

"I don't know."

"Hey, if they slit our throats you can blame me. Okay?"

"We'll rest tonight and start tomorrow."

"Wait, someone's coming." Sharon's head tilted, listening to the vehicle approaching from behind the curve.

"I don't—"

Sharon began to wave. "It's an old man. He looks okay!"

"Great," said Gary. The truck shuddered on the road and pulled over. Sharon went to the window and spoke softly for a moment. Then she waved to Gary. "He's going in our direction! Come on."

Gary picked up his duffel bag and walked over. He said, "If the guy starts talking about cows, I'm out before you can blink."

"What do you mean?"

"Nothing."

The driver's name was Mitchell. He had nothing to say about cows or overalls. Sharon sat between the two men.

"Only ten or fifteen miles to Conner Falls, and your brochure says the place is near there," she said.

Gary nodded but didn't say anything.

That was okay, she thought. If he didn't appreciate it, at least his feet would.

The car stopped at a small country store just off the Parkway. Thick fog was beginning to roll in from the higher ridges all around.

"Got to make a phone call," he told Gary and Sharon. "Let my wife know I'm going to be another hour. When it gets like this, it takes a damn long time to make it to the farm. She worries."

While Mitchell wandered to the phone booth beside the gas pumps, Gary and Sharon went into the store. It had been a long time since they'd eaten Gary's packs of crushed crackers and the doughnuts from Howard Johnson's, and Sharon was more than hungry.

The interior of the store smelled of pine jewelry boxes and plastic mountainy souvenirs. Every mountain vacation Sharon had ever taken with her family had smelled like this. Behind the counter was an old woman with red lipstick and blue-rimmed glasses. She smacked her lips in distrust, and said, "What is it you two want? I'm closed in ten minutes."

Sharon felt the backs of her hands flush with instant anger. "I beg your pardon, but we're customers."

"I do wonder at that," the woman said.

"You don't care for customers in your store?"

The woman's eyes narrowed. "Customers look like customers. I see 'em all the time. You ain't them."

Gary said softly, "Sharon, it's cool, let it go."

"You two look like them freaks that live up the road," the woman continued. "I don't trust 'em far as I could throw 'em. And I'd throw 'em down the side of the mountain if I could."

Sharon strode toward the counter, jaws clenched. "How dare you speak of looks? Didn't your mother teach you common courtesy? Who do you think you are?"

"Sharon," said Gary. Sharon heard him approach. He touched her arm. She jerked away.

"I suppose manners don't reach this far up the mountain, do they?" Sharon hoped the woman would get into it with her. A fight would feel so good now. No philosophy, just an old-fashioned screaming session. Like she had with her mother over dress colors or skirt lengths.

And I'm pregnant, Mom, how do you like that?

But the woman was so angry she couldn't speak or move. The corners of her eyes trembled with rage. Her hands were palsied on the countertop.

There was silence for a long moment. Then Gary said, "I guess it would be worthless now to ask you directions to the Sunrise Camp."

It was.

They walked for a while without speaking. The fog caressed Gary's face, and he felt the cleansing of its cold, moist hands. *Take me into this blindly,* he thought. *I want to trust.* He was so excited, he could hardly swallow. And Sharon, he knew already that he loved her.

She was exhausted, he could tell. Not much farther now, he kept telling her. And she didn't complain.

Mitchell, who was hanging up the phone when Sharon and Gary came out of the store, had given them directions.

"See Route 947, right next to the store? Heads east? Take it about a quarter mile or so. Then there's a graveled road with no number at all. I think that's the road to Sunrise. Why you want to go there, anyway? Nothing but hippies. You ask me, our feds ought to kick them all out on their asses and let them sink or swim somewheres else."

Gary had only said, "Thanks for the directions."

The road to Sunrise had been at least a half mile down Route 947. The gravel surface was easy to follow but impossible to predict. They could see six feet ahead of them but no farther. Gary's flashlight burned out a few minutes after they turned onto the road. Curves seemed to take them spiraling upward until there surely could be no more ground left. It was like walking into Heaven. Trees visible on the sides of the road were ghostly. Every few minutes, a hint of moonlight shot a spear through the fog, but then it would vanish, and the two would be wandering on faith again.

"How on Earth are we going to know when we're there?" Sharon asked.

"I think we'll just know."

I'll know. Almost there, yes, almost there!

They walked.

Sharon said, "Want to sing? I know all the Monkees' songs."

"I don't."

"How about 'Yellow Submarine'?"

Gary shook his head. This was a serious moment; he couldn't sing about a party under the ocean.

"I like to sing. We used to sing at Girl Scout camp, when we were out in the woods like we are now."

"That's nice," said Gary.

Sharon took a breath. She began to sing. "When I look up to the sky I see your eyes, a funny kind of yellow."

Gary couldn't help but grin. "Pictures of Matchstick Men." A great one.

"I rush home to bed, I soak my head, I see your face underneath my pillow," sang Sharon.

And together, "I wake next morning tossing, yawning, see your face come peeking through my window. Pictures of matchstick men and you, mirages of matchstick men and you, all I ever see is them and you."

Sharon broke off, laughing. "What does that mean, Gary? I don't get a lot of the psychedelic songs."

"Guess it's different for different people."

"That's a cop-out!"

Gary conceded. "Maybe it is."

A skunk waddled across the gravel in front of them, and they froze. It blinked at them and disappeared into the trees.

And then Gary held up his hand to stop Sharon.

"What?" she asked.

"I think we found it."

A cedar at roadside was decorated like a Christmas tree. It was covered with little tin ornaments, cut, it seemed, from old vegetable and fruit cans. Paper chains, most of them discolored and torn from past rains or winds, looped about the tree branches. Little people, made from wooden sticks, dangled among the chains.

"Look what the children did," Sharon said.

Gary said, "Here's a gate."

There was a pipe gate, unlatched, across the road. Gary pushed it open, and the two of them walked onto the shrouded grounds of Sunrise.

It was another three minutes before they could distinguish anything other than more trees and more gravel road. There were softened circles of light ahead, off the path to the right.

"A house?"

Sharon nodded. "I think so."

They walked toward the lights. As they neared, the square sides of a small shack became visible. There was a screened porch on the front and a swing hanging from the porch roof on the left. The lights were the lanterns that were nailed to either side of the shack's door.

"You want me to knock?" Gary asked.

"I will if you don't want to," she said. Gary felt a rush of affection for her determination, and he reached out to pat her face gently.

She didn't move away, and she didn't scowl. He knew, then, with certainty, that he loved her. Gary walked up and across the screened porch and tapped on the door. Waiting for an answer from behind the wood, Gary wondered for a moment if there might be some insane mountain man waiting inside, shotgun in hand.

Take me into this blindly. What is there is there.

There were footsteps, then the door was yanked open.

A smiling woman in a white nightgown said, "You're looking for Sunrise?"

Gary nodded. He looked back at Sharon. She had come to the porch. She, too, nodded.

They went inside, leaving the foggy night behind.

———

Sunrise rose with the sun; men and women came from their assorted shacks and gathered on the ridge-top pasture and watched as the red spot ascended from behind a distant ridge and began its climb in the sky. They were silent in this morning ritual. All stood and gazed heavenward.

Gary and Sharon, who had slept on mats in the shack they'd found in the fog, came out to the porch to watch the community's early-morning assembly. The woman who had greeted them last night had left before Sharon and Gary awoke. But she had told them last night that her name was Gem.

"It's a bigger place than I thought," Gary whispered to Sharon, but she shushed him, afraid that if they spoke before it was proper, they would be banished back down the gravel road.

There were perhaps one hundred Sunrise citizens, most of them men and women in their twenties and early thirties. A few of the women tended children, none of whom was older than three. The clothes worn were strange combinations, all certainly practical for the weather of an early fall, but ugly and clashing and without any sense of style. Not a fashionable Nehru pantsuit or shift dress in the bunch. Sharon felt a sting of superiority, then felt ashamed for it. Gary's clothes were as bizarre as those of these people. And Gary was truly a good person.

The other shacks stood near the one in which Gary and Sharon had slept—some of them in the open, some beneath the trees. Sharon bet this place had been a church or 4-H camp at some time.

After ten minutes of gazing, the people broke and moved around, speaking freely. Gary left the porch and walked toward a couple who sat beneath a nearby tree, holding hands. Sharon followed.

"Hello," Gary said.

The two looked up. They blinked and smiled. The man had dirty blond hair to his waist. The woman, of Asian descent, wore her hair in many braids intertwined with dead honeysuckle vines.

"Well, hello there," said the man.

"We got here last night," Gary said. "We slept in that cabin, with a woman named Gem. We're new."

"Right on, man," said the man. He seemed to have a speech impediment, his words dragging on his tongue a little. He blinked a lot; the whites of his eyes not quite white. He tossed back his hair and extended his hand to Gary and Sharon. "You must come meet Abraham."

"Who?" asked Sharon.

The woman giggled. It seemed strange, a woman of thirty giggling like a girl. But it was such a happy sound that Sharon couldn't help but smile. "Abraham to Wind. Jonah to me. He's the one who founded Sunrise, the one who welcomed us here." Her voice, too, was a bit slurred. Sharon wondered if the altitude of the place played tricks with sounds.

The blond man stood and took the woman by the arm. "Come with us. He is not asleep, although he didn't come out for the sunrise. He is busy, rarely seen, planning for us, doing for us."

"Doing what?" asked Sharon.

The man giggled then, and the woman joined him. The sound of the laughter was sharp and open and free. Gary looked from the couple to Sharon, and when Sharon laughed, he did, too. The couple led Sharon and Gary across the pasture to a distant row of trees, where one shack, a bit larger than the rest, sat alone. They passed a woman sitting on the grass, watching two little children. One child, a girl, had a head much too tiny for her body. The other child, a boy of not quite two, was missing both arms.

Sharon felt her lungs contract, and she made herself look ahead and not at the children.

At the shack, Wind stepped onto the stoop and tapped on the door.

"He is busy but never too much for newcomers," Wind said. He tapped again. There was a call from inside, a deep, hearty sound that seemed a blend of Santa Claus and Charlton Heston.

"Do come in!"

As Sharon and Gary stepped forward, Wind put out his hand and held Sharon back.

"Oh, only one at a time," Wind said. "He must meet us one at a time, to know us, to understand us."

Sharon looked at the woman. The woman played with one of her braids and smiled.

"Okay," Sharon said.

She sat on the bottom step of the shack's stoop as Wind and the woman wandered away.

Gary went inside.

The shack was much like the one in which they'd spent the night. There clearly was no electricity. Kerosene lanterns sat on a rough wooden table beside a fireplace. A few chairs were lined against the walls beneath the windows. A door to a second, rear room was closed. There were posters tacked onto the bare spots on the wall. WAR IS NOT HEALTHY FOR CHILDREN OR OTHER LIVING THINGS. WE SHALL OVERCOME. And the Desiderata, GO PLACIDLY AMID THE NOISE AND HASTE . . .

The man was standing beside the table, lighting a pipe. He was tall, thin, with a beard that lay on his chest like a bird's nest. His head, though, was bald.

"My friend!" he said. "You found us. No one deterred you, did they?"

"Deterred us?"

The man's eyes winked. "Those who hate us. Those who think we should believe what they believe. The police, the F.B.I., the military. The government, damn them. You were given a flyer?"

"Yes."

"And where did you get it?"

"Democratic National Convention. Chicago. A little over a week ago."

"Ah, yes, a bad scene, my friend. We welcome all who want no more bad scenes, no more bad trips."

"Yes," said Gary.

"So tell me, my friend." The man stepped up to Gary and leaned his head down. "Whisper to me. Why are you here?"

Gary looked at the man. He felt stupid, suddenly. Who was this guy? Was this what he had come so long to find?

Trust, help me trust, help me go into this blindly and freely.

"I came to get away from the harm of the world," Gary managed.

"Yes," said the man. "You have hurt others, have you not?"

"Yes."

"Tell me."

"I've done what I shouldn't have. I haven't done what I should have. On the streets at the convention, I threw bottles. Glass bottles. I hit a woman. I may have killed her, I don't know."

"Go on."

"I have friends who went to war. I didn't. They were killed. I miss them. I wish I could have saved them."

"You want to get away from violence."

"I have made a vow of peace. I want to find that, and life. And love."

"You will have it here," said the man. He stood straight and smiled at Gary. It was a good smile.

This is going to be okay.

"Name me what you will," said the man. "I want to be what you need."

Gary paused. What to call this man. Then he said, "I'll call you Friend."

"Whisper to me. Why are you here?"

Sharon said, "I want innocence again."

"You are innocent now."

"No, I'm not. I'm pregnant."

The man smiled. Sharon wanted to reach out and touch him. He understood. What hint of concern she had seen in Gary was outblazed by the fire of sympathy in this man. What luck she had followed Gary here, she thought.

"Innocence," said the man, "is in us all. If we open ourselves to all experiences, we are innocent. It is when we hesitate that we are lost."

"I didn't love the boy I was with."

"Love is innocent. So is sex. So is pain, joy, sorrow. What we are created to experience is innocent. We should experience it all."

Sharon nodded.

"Name me what you will," said the man. "I want to be what you need."

"Anything?" asked Sharon.

The man nodded.

"May I call you Bobby?"

OCTOBER 1968

They shared the shack with the woman named Gem and her three husbands. The shack, having only two rooms, left one for Gem's family and one, the front room, for Sharon and Gary. Gem was sweet and her husbands (in God's eyes, she told them) were quiet and unassuming, one as much like the other two as brown-haired triplets. They spent their days drawing pictures, hoeing the pumpkin and squash patches, singing, and sleeping.

It was all Gary could do to lie beside Sharon at night and not draw her to him and make love to her. He loved her. He ached with love. She didn't braid her hair anymore; she let it go free, and the sight of it in the wind made him hard. At the communal meals, held on the pasture when the weather was good or in the large dining hall when the rain came, he could barely eat sometimes, watching her graceful movements and her open, honest smile.

This place had done wonders for her.

Why hadn't it done wonders for him? He felt lost and alone. *It would only take time,* he told himself. Not everyone could let go of distrust easily. He prayed at night to the power of the universe to let him be taken with the freedom, but as yet, he still fought.

One thing that kept him edgy was the fact that Sharon seemed infatuated with the leader, whom she called Bobby. His appearances, once in the morning at breakfast, once at night at supper, played in her conversation the whole day through. Gary didn't think he liked the man much for this, and calling him Friend was difficult.

Fucking Sharon would help ease the bad feelings, although now that thought only made him feel more guilty.

At first, Sharon could have sworn that everyone at Sunrise had speech impediments, but after the first few weeks, it didn't seem so anymore. Either that, or Sharon and Gary had grown used to the sounds.

Or they, themselves, had acquired the slur. Sharon found she didn't care one way or the other.

As the October days grew longer, Sharon helped fix the

meals for the community and, at times, helped watch the children.

There were seven children in all. When she was first approached by Gem for help with a children's game, Sharon had balked. They all had defects. Two were missing limbs. One had scaled skin. Another had been born with no mouth, and Bobby had done emergency surgery on the girl, opening a hole through which the child now ate.

But Bobby had talked with Sharon after hearing of her hesitation.

Innocent, they all were. Even more the innocent for their imperfections, and therefore more capable and needy of love. Where but here could they receive that love? Certainly not in the outside world, where wars were fought and money reigned supreme.

Sharon threw herself into the children's care with enthusiasm. She helped bathe them and feed them. They played games with rocks and flowers. They made silly little men out of used matchsticks from the kitchen and fixed them to the cedar tree at the entrance to Sunrise. Sharon couldn't wait for her own child's arrival in March. At night, sometimes, in the silence of the front room, she apologized to the baby for the hate she'd had for it at first. Then she would go to sleep, safely by Gary's side.

And dream of Bobby.

Gary hated the food. It all tasted as if it was on the verge of spoilage, and seemed more so as time went on. The women of Sunrise might be able to paint a picture or weave a robe, but they couldn't cook worth crap. Friend was in charge of the food preparations. He was the one who ordered the supplies, and he was the one who monitored what went on in the kitchen, but clearly the man knew nothing about palatability. Gary wondered more and more what the hell the man did with his spare time. It wasn't spent researching cook-books.

After eating, Gary never felt quite well. His tongue seemed thick and stupid. His speech slurred like that of the other Sunrise citizens. He moved more slowly. Sometimes, he only pretended to eat, then would sneak down off the Sunrise property to the old woman's country store on Route 947 and buy snacks from the outdoor vending machine with the little cash he had left in his duffel bag.

Somehow, he knew if Friend found out, the man wouldn't be happy at all.

But somehow, Gary couldn't care. He was biding his time until he felt the life force he'd sought. Until he was engulfed with the peace and love the others all around him seemed to have captured.

I need it now, bring it now, let me trust enough to have it!

The only life force he was aware of was the burning he felt when he was close to Sharon. She would hug him and smile at him, but nothing more. He knew she was in love with Friend. Most of the women at Sunrise seemed to be. Some of the men, too. So where did that leave him?

Gary threw himself into his gardening and into the repair of Sunrise's many buildings. He traded mild jokes with the others who worked beside him, hoes or hammers in hand.

And he waited for his salvation, daydreaming of Sharon.

NOVEMBER 1968

Sharon sat in the grass on the edge of the pasture, feet dangling down the slope. Her hands were wrapped around the growing bulge in her stomach. The sun was going down, and the evening gathering had dispersed. Beyond the slope, buzzards circled. On a grass blade near her a katydid poised, probing the air with its antennae. Gary was off with some of the others, bringing in the last of the late-season pumpkins. There was a breeze blowing up the slope and across the pasture. The air smelled like copper and cinnamon.

Bobby came and sat next to Sharon. He picked up her hand and patted it. Sharon wanted to move into him, but didn't dare. He was too important for that. That he would come out in the day just to see her was all the glory she needed.

"Thank you for everything," Sharon said shyly.

"Thank yourself. You are a lovely, innocent woman." They sat in silence. Sharon was suddenly afraid that if she said no more, Bobby would leave. So she asked, "I wonder who won the election today?"

"Election?"

"The president?"

"I don't know what you're talking about," said Bobby, and Sharon knew he was right in his oblivion. She needed to forget as well as he had. How wise he was. How good. How innocent.

God, thank you, she thought.

Bobby sat a bit longer, then got up and walked to his shack to do the work he did. Whatever that was. He knew, and that was all that was important.

DECEMBER 1968

There was snow. Gary stood on the screened porch and looked out at the white.

Damn, but it's going to be a long winter.

The door opened behind him, and Sharon stood there, wrapped in a blanket she had made herself of old cloth scraps.

"Look at that!" she said. "I love snow."

And I love you, Sharon. Can't you see that? But he said, "I had my share in Chicago. Just looking at it wears me out."

"Gem has snowshoes she made last year. She'll show us how to make some if we would like."

"Sure."

Sharon came over and threaded her arm through Gary's. "Isn't this so wonderful? I don't think I've ever been so happy. Bobby knows how to care for us, doesn't he?"

Gary said, "You think it's all wonderful."

"Yes."

"Nothing seems strange to you?"

"Strange? Of course. My life was nothing but prom dresses and luncheons and the Monkees. This would have to be strange, wouldn't it? Gloriously strange."

"I wonder what today is?"

"Hmmm," said Sharon. "Does it matter? I'm just happy."

"Maybe it's Christmas already. If it was, I'd give you a gift, Sharon. Do you know if it's Christmas?"

"I don't care if it's Christmas or Easter or Groundhog Day. It doesn't matter, Gary."

"And if it was Christmas, would we have a Christmas dinner? And what would it taste like? Like the shit we have every day? The shit that makes me sick? Don't tell me you don't feel it, Sharon."

"Feel what?" Her voice began to rise defensively. God, he wished she loved him and trusted him. Sharon stepped away, her eyes and her blanket drawing up in one motion. "What do you mean?"

"This place isn't what I'd hoped."

"You aren't giving it a chance, Gary."

"I've given it lots of chances. There's something not right here."

"Please don't say that."

"Why not?"

"They'll hear you."

Gary grabbed her arm. One side of the blanket slid free, exposing her naked body to the winter air. She didn't move to pick it up. Her gaze was locked on him.

"Who will? Who would care? This is a place for freedom,

right? Sharon, listen to yourself. You may not agree with me, but I have the right to my own words. I can't believe you, of all people, have gone for this place, hook, line, and sinker!"

"You brought me here. You believe in it, too!"

"Sharon, just think for a minute. No one even looks healthy. Their eyes are dimmed, Sharon."

"Shut up! Please, just shut up, Gary!"

Gary stared at her. Her red hair, brushing her breast. Her eyes, wide and frightened, and yes, innocent if not somewhat dimmed themselves. At least she'd found what she wanted. She had her innocence.

"Okay," he said finally. "I'll shut up. I'm sorry, Sharon. Forget what I said."

Sharon said nothing.

"Okay?" Gary said.

Sharon pulled the blanket up over her shoulder. "Okay," she said. She took a deep breath. A small smile pulled at her lips. "Want to make snowshoes?"

There was a hand over his mouth, and Gary woke with a start, unable to cry out. He blinked in the darkness of the cabin, trying to see who straddled him and held him down.

The voice told him.

"Gary, Gary," said Friend. "Are you doubting our sincerity here?"

Gary could smell the pipe tobacco on the man's breath. One of Friend's knees was pressed into Gary's chest. It hurt like hell.

"Gary, we love you. How do you doubt that? We are not part of the world. We must stay strong and believe in ourselves. Do you believe in yourself, Gary?"

Gary didn't know what to do except to nod. Sharon had told on him. A child at school, ratting on the bad boy.

"That's good. Doubting is so very sad. Remember, I am

here for you. If you have doubts, come talk with me directly. Don't frighten our sisters with silly talk."

The hand came away from Gary's mouth. Gary coughed, then said, "Whatever you say."

There was a pause, and then Friend bent over and gave Gary a passionate kiss. "I am what you need," he said, pulling away. "Don't even think of leaving. Not even in your dreams, my friend."

Gary nodded.

The man got up and quietly left the cabin. Gary lay shuddering.

I wasn't going to hate I wasn't going to hate I wasn't going to hate.

He whispered, "I hate you, you bastard."

FEBRUARY 1969

The pains began just before dawn. Sharon sat up on her mat and wrapped her arms about herself until the pains were so strong she didn't think she could keep quiet.

Women do this all the time, she told herself. *Since the dawn of whenever. Bobby said so. Pain is part of it.*

"Gary?" she whispered.

Sweat ran down her chest and buried itself in the fold above her belly. Her lips caught between her teeth as a contraction clawed her belly. *Should I awaken Gary? I don't know anything about this. How long should it take? What if something is wrong?*

Pain is part of it.

"Gary?"

Pain is innocent.

Another contraction came, stealing her breath and her mind for a moment. The muscles in her neck drew her head back until she was staring at the cobwebbed ceiling.

"Gary! Gem! Help me!"

Gary was up then, leaning over her, taking her head and cradling it in his arms.

"Gem!" he cried.

Gem was at their sides a moment later. She held Sharon's hand, chanting and smiling.

Ten hours and many heat-tortured delusions later, the baby was born. It was twisted, with fins for legs, but it was beautiful. And innocent.

Bobby was ecstatic. He came to see Sharon, who had been brought out onto the shack's porch to rest in spite of the cold winter wind. He kissed her forehead, then held the baby up to examine it. Sharon watched the gentle, loving man as he held the little girl to his cheek, then turned to present her to the congregation outside on the snow.

"A precious little one!" he said. "An innocent babe in the world, given to us. Free from the terrible laws of the world. Free to be what she is supposed to be."

There were murmurings in the crowd, most of them sounds of pleasure and awe.

Bobby turned back to Sharon. His eyes were rimmed and wet. "I've named the child Jewel," he said. "A jewel of our love. A jewel to sparkle in our hearts. She will be part of us forever."

Kiss me, Sharon thought.

Bobby leaned over and kissed Sharon's cheek. Her soul soared. Bobby gave the baby back, and Sharon cuddled its tiny body against her neck. He tramped down the porch steps and spelled the baby's name by stomping letters in the snow. Big letters, for all to see.

"Jool."

Bobby turned, winked, and then walked back to his cabin. Through her own tears, Sharon could see Gary, shifting from one foot to the other, standing in the crowd. She wanted to call out to him, to tell him to smile, the baby was fine and she was fine and their little part of the world was fine, but her throat was raw with the birthing screams, and so she shut her eyes and let Gem and Willow pat her and tend her and then take her inside when her body had cooled down.

He's making fun of us.

Gary stared at the name in the snow, the name the others so carefully and reverently stepped around so not to mess it up.

He's a smart man. He is literate. He can spell. He's making fun of us, and we're worshiping him for it.

JULY 1969

Gary stood beside the dining hall, holding a rake. He had skipped dinner, and was watching the community members stroll out into the afternoon mist, arms around each other, singing, laughing. Happy.

Fools.

"We're going to take the babies down to the blueberry patch," said Sharon, as she and some of the other mothers passed by. The slurred speech made Gary's skin crawl. He couldn't bear to look at the baby. "Would you like to come?"

"No, thanks," said Gary. "I have to get rid of some of this clipped grass and then weed in the beans."

Sharon smiled, shrugged, and shifted the baby Jewel on her hip. The child wore a small white dress that Gem had made, embroidered with the child's nickname, "Joo."

"Bobby's coming down, too," Sharon said. "He told us he can be with us for a whole hour if we'd like!"

"That's nice, Sharon," Gary said. He smiled. She didn't know the difference anymore between a real smile and a forced one. How different from the desperate, haughty girl he'd met in September. She was desperate now, but out of love for her Bobby. She would run naked through thorns for him if he asked. She would bear more children if he wanted, more deformed creatures if he only snapped his fingers or looked at her with a grin. She would jump off an overlook wall for the man.

Gary's heart kicked painfully at beauty gone mad. But it wasn't just Sharon who was mad. The whole damn community was gone.

It had been a long time since Gary had eaten food prepared by the Sunrise ladies. Out of money since October, he had stolen from unopened boxes of bread and fruits in the kitchen and drunk water he collected in a nearby stream. Certainly, he was eating no worse than he had on his trip from Chicago to Virginia. And this, itself, had been the most amazing trip of all.

This trip had kept him rational and had brought one truth to light.

Friend was drugging them.

Why, Gary couldn't fathom. What Friend wanted with a slow-moving, speech-slurred community was beyond him. They weren't bringing him riches. They weren't his sexual slaves.

It made no sense.

So Gary had made a second vow to himself in the past months, a vow as important to him as that of peace. He would stop the bastard when the chance presented itself. How, he had no idea. What it would involve, he couldn't imagine. Sometimes he felt as bumbling and stupid as the most mind-fried of the Sunrise citizenry. But when the time came, he would do it. This for the love for Sharon.

"I love you, Sharon," he whispered to Sharon's back as she took the baby away. And the second vow, once again, set his teeth on edge, and made his muscles twitch under his skin.

When the dining hall was empty and Gary was certain all were off doing their afternoon rituals, he began raking. Along the front of the dining hall, around the side, then moving in a straight but slow line into the trees toward Friend's shack. Gary's mind grabbed onto the tattered fabric of logic he'd been picking at and began to explore the cloth again.

Who the hell was Friend? He certainly was no religious messiah. Gary had never heard the man talk on the coming end of the world or the righteous rising up against the outside devils; he never preached salvation or everlasting life.

A professor, Gary guessed. A man fired from his university job, a chemistry professor, experimenting with a little flock of sheep. Fun to watch, especially with the variety of birth defects that popped out of the cookers.

The man went to a hell of a lot of trouble for his jollies. Flyers distributed as far west as Chicago. Money for the constant influx of food and supplies.

Gary gripped the rake so hard it felt as if his knuckles popped. He worked the teeth in the grass and leaves, getting ever closer to Friend's porch. Sharon said the man was going to spend an hour with them, picking blueberries. He raked around for a few minutes and listened.

The shack was empty.

Gary took the rake with him. He stepped onto the stoop, looked behind him, then slipped inside.

Nothing will do short of evidence, he thought. *Lead me blindly, show me something that will convince Sharon to leave with me.*

The front room was the same as it had been when he and Sharon had first met Friend. Chairs unmoved. Lanterns in the same place. Clearly the man spent little time in this room. The back room was his business.

And what do we find there? A chemistry set?

With the trust Friend seemed to have in those around him, Gary was surprised to find the door to the back locked.

He took out a bobby pin he'd stolen from Sharon and worked it into the keyhole. His childhood in Chicago paid off. The door swung open.

It took a moment for his eyes to adjust to the lack of light. There was a single window in this room, and it was covered with newspaper.

And then he could see, but what was there only made Gary cross his arms and shake his head.

There was a small electric generator. It was hooked to a television and two-way radio. In front of the television was a recliner, well used.

"Damn," said Gary. "This is the man's big secret? He watches *Laugh-In?*" Gary almost smiled, but then his jaw clenched tightly. His fists drew up. "Hardly," he said softly.

There was a small bed, a lantern, a rag rug, probably made for Friend by one of his ardent communal admirers.

No boxes, no powders.

Just the stinking radio and television. A stack of newspapers and magazines on the floor. Not exactly hard evidence.

He must have a stash somewhere else.

Gary heard footsteps on the stoop outside. He gasped, and pulled the back-room door shut, then felt his way to the bed. It had been a low-sitting cot. He lay down and squeezed beneath it.

Friend's voice came from the front room.

"What were you thinking, Gillian?"

Gillian, Gary thought. A young woman he'd seen but never really noticed. Twenty-something. Plain.

"What, Gillian?" Friend repeated.

Gillian's voice was faint. "I don't know."

"Honey, we've talked about this before, haven't we? You are here because you are one of the special people who wants freedom from what's out there. Don't you remember that?"

Gillian said, "Yes."

"But twice now, you've been found wandering away from Sunrise. Almost as if you didn't want to stay here anymore."

Gillian said nothing.

"Is that true? Do you really want to leave?"

Gillian said nothing.

Something that felt like a spider crawled up the side of Gary's face. He brushed it away.

"Gillian, we can't have people leaving. I told you that the first time it happened. It's not for the best. Now sit. I have to make sure this doesn't happen again."

Gary tipped his head, straining toward the closed door. "No," whispered Gillian.

"Sit."

There was silence. A long pause. Then Gillian said, "No, please."

"There is joy in all experiences," said Friend. "Remember that? Love, sex, work, pain."

"No, please!"

And there was a scream, and then sobbing, and Friend saying, "I'll bandage those. No one need know the circumstances, Gillian. We can make them bright bandages, don't you think? Pretty ones, for the summertime?"

Gillian fell into muffled sobs. There was movement around the room, and after what seemed like an endless time, the front door was opened.

"I'll help you to the blueberry patch where you can watch the babies. You can enjoy the sun and be grateful for all you have here. Lean on me, Gillian."

The door closed. Gary scrambled out from under the bed and opened the door. Carefully, he walked to the front window and peered out.

Gillian and Friend walked down to the pasture, arm in arm like lovers. Gillian leaned heavily on him.

She had been hamstrung.

Sharon could barely contain her happiness. As Joo suckled on her breast and Gem lay beside her in the grass, counting leaves on an overhead branch, she played over in her mind what Bobby had told her as they had collected blueberries.

"We have a very special treat tonight at dinner," he'd said.

"What is it?" she asked. God, the man was beautiful, even more beautiful than the first Bobby. She couldn't even remember the first Bobby's last name, or why she'd loved him.

"Now, it wouldn't be so special if I told you," he said, putting his arm around Sharon and touching her chin playfully. "But it has to do with our friend Gary. Don't tell him. I'll need your help. You will help me tonight, won't you?"

"Oh," Sharon had said. "Of course!" Joo coughed, and Sharon put the baby over her lap and patted her back gently.

Gem said, "I've got over three hundred!"

Of course I'll help! Sharon thought.

He played the game for the rest of the day. He was a happy, drugged citizen of Sunrise. He finished his raking, pulled weeds from among the beans, and joined in lunch on the pasture. He even held Sharon's baby, taking care not to look directly at the legs. He hoped the cold sweat on his arms passed as mere hardworking sweat. When Gillian hobbled to join the lunch crowd and everyone mumbled that the poor thing must have hurt herself—but aren't those paisley bandages cheerful?—Gary fought to keep a rush of bile down.

Fucking mad professor.

No, worse than that. A fucking mad emperor, king of all he surveyed, isolated on the mountain, safely away from the terrible world he so often babbled about.

Sharon, dear God, what are we in for here?

Gary could not let this madness go on. But he hadn't been able to figure out how to stop it.

Other than kill Friend, and he'd made a vow never to do violence again.

In the afternoon, mending the railing on a shack, he scrambled for ideas. Nothing seemed possible. There would be no convincing the community of what was happening. They loved this place. They loved their Bobby, their Abraham, their Jonah. His Friend.

Perhaps, then, he should simply take Sharon and run. Leave the others to their euphoria.

Yes, he decided as the dinner bell was struck, and the other gardeners grinned and shouldered their tools. After dinner, he would take Sharon and get the fuck out of this place.

Even if he had to gag her. Even if he had to gag and tie her and throw her over his shoulder.

Sharon sat between Gem and Gary, holding her baby. They were in the dining hall again because rain had returned, and it pattered on the metal roof and through the open windows. Sharon's foot bounced up and down with the rhythm of the rain. She couldn't stop it and didn't want to. Tonight, Bobby was going to let her do something special.

The serving bowls moved around the tables, everyone scooping out dollops of mashed potatoes and creamed corn. Bobby sat at his usual place at the front table, his hands folded, smiling. It was so sweet that he never served himself when the others ate. He said he always wanted to make sure there was enough for them, first. Gary sat silently, stirring potatoes on his plate.

"Cheer up," she said to him, giving him a nudge. He smiled at her.

"That's better," she said.

And then Bobby stood up and held his hand aloft for the attention of all who were present.

"Gary," said Friend. "Come up here."

Gary dropped his spoon. It clattered across the tabletop. All talking ceased, and everyone looked at him.

"What?"

"Come up here, my friend. And Sharon, you, too." Sharon was up in a flash, handing Joo to Gem, then moving between the tables to stand beside Friend. She whirled her hand in the air, urging Gary to come on, come on!

Gary stood. He walked to the front of the dining hall. *What the fuck?* His heart twisted, uncertain, terrified. He stopped between Sharon and Friend, between the innocent and the guilty, and looked out at the smiling crowd. The drugged, insipid, giddy smiles trained not on him, but on the man beside him. Friend.

"Gary," said Friend. "I've been noticing you as a special member of our community. You are a true seeker, are you not?"

"Well," said Gary. "Yeah."

"Sometimes it is fitting to reward seekers. Seeking is not always its own reward. We don't always find what we are looking for. At least, not right away."

What the fucking hell?

Sharon nodded, pretending to understand what the mad professor was saying.

"You and Sharon came here together. Her way was easy. You've struggled. I want to honor your struggle." He lifted a mug from the table before him. He held it up to the community members. "I offer a toast to Gary in all his persistence! We shall drink to him, and he to himself. Sharon, as his first friend, see that he drinks every drop so that he doesn't diminish this honor out of humility."

All the people raised their glasses. Sharon, grinning, held the mug to Gary's lips.

Oh, God.

He could try to run. The crowd was drugged.

But Friend was not.

Maybe he truly wants to honor me. Maybe it is nothing more than a reward for remaining and not causing trouble since the night visit.

"Drink it, silly!" giggled Sharon.

Maybe.

"Gary, come on!"

Probably not.

He had no choice. He took the cup in his hands. *Lead me blindly. Let me trust.*

And he drank.

The television was on, droning softly, its blue, pulsing light washing the floor of the room. Friend was sprawled out on his recliner, drinking a bottle of beer. It sounded like a news event was on. There were intense men's voices and no music. Gary glanced at the set over Friend's shoulder, but could make no sense of what he was seeing. Black-and-white. Indeterminable movement. It increased his dizziness. He dropped his gaze back to the floor.

Oh, God, his head hurt. His stomach drew up, and he leaned over the side of the cot and spit.

"We don't always find what we are looking for, do we, Gary?" said Friend, not turning around. "At least, not right away."

Goddamn. "What . . . ?" he began.

Friend sighed. "What the hell was it you were looking for when you came here to Sunrise? I forgot exactly what you said, but I'm sure it wasn't much different from what the other dregs were after. Life? Something like that. And what were you looking for in my cabin this morning? Drugs?"

Gary pulled himself to a sitting position, eased his feet over the edge of the cot and placed his feet beneath him. Vision flickered.

"Just look at this," said Friend. He raised the hand with the beer bottle and motioned toward the television set. Gary squinted at it once more. Black-and-white. Fuzzy movement. A movie, it looked like. A rocket of some sort, sitting on a dusty landscape. Gary shook his head, trying to clear away the buzzing. The televised voices, excited and garbled, congratulated someone in the craft. Then the voices spoke to television viewers, to each other, teetering on the verge of great emotion.

"They've landed on the moon," said Friend.

Gary tilted his head and stared. "The moon?"

"So it seems," said Friend. He took a swig and sighed. Then he looked back at Gary and made a little tsking sound. "Almost four years in this job, and I've never had anyone break into my private living space. Guess I should have expected it eventually, but I got used to the easy life."

On the television, a hatch was opened. There were men in strange suits. *Landed on the moon? Impossible.*

"Easy life," Gary repeated.

"Very easy," said Friend. "Government jobs are the cushiest, Gary. Good pay, benefits. Well, if you can call this pisshole cabin a benefit. But it's better than Indochina; no hazards here. I keep in touch with my superiors constantly; they know what's going on and couldn't be happier with my work. Everyone here in line, everyone believing in their own special search. Just June bugs exploring the inside of a Clorox bottle is all."

"You knew I was in here," Gary said.

"Well, hell, Uncle Sam may be cushy, but he doesn't hire morons. You left a rake in my front room this morning. You were the only one with a rake after breakfast. I notice things. And where else could you have been but in the back room?"

"I . . . I wasn't—"

"Now, Gary." Friend turned the recliner around and gestured with the beer bottle. "Let's not play stupid with each other anymore. You're the seeker. I'm the truth. I'll give you something interesting. Then—" he nodded toward the stack of newspapers. A syringe lay on top of the pile. "Then you'll have to join the ranks of the permanently happy."

"Why all the trouble?"

"Trouble?" asked Friend. "You idealistic shits are the trouble. We have communes like this all over the country. We give flyers out at all the rallies, all the protest meetings. Draws 'em in like flies. A place to escape the sins of America, right? We bring 'em in, keep 'em buzzed and peaceful, and they are out of the way."

Gary stood up. For a barest second he thought he'd fall over, but he fought to hold his stance, to hold his mind. He needed his mind, his body.

"And what are a few deformed babies?" asked Friend. "They won't grow up to challenge us, I don't think."

Vow against violence, Gary. Vow of peace.

"To Uncle Sam and his wisdom," said Friend. He took a drink. He smiled.

Vow of peace!

On the television, a space-suited man's head appeared through the hatch. The moonscape was like night.

"Ready for the prick?" asked Friend. He stood, planting his feet and facing Gary like a gunslinger. "A prick for a prick?"

And Gary dived forward. He fell into Friend, who skipped backward over the arm of the recliner and struck his head against the floor.

"Nonviolence!" Friend screeched. "Remember, peace and love and . . . !"

Gary grabbed the television with both hands. Rage coursed his arms, bringing the bulky set up and over his head. On the television, a sputtering voice said, "That's one small step for a man."

"Gary, wait, we can . . . !"

Fuck peace!

Gary brought the set down on Friend's head. There was a satisfying crack. The picture on the screen bobbed like a ball dropped into a lake, then cleared again. Gary scooted back along the floor, staring. Blood oozed from beneath the set, running out to catch in Friend's outstretched fingers.

"One giant leap for mankind."

He didn't wait for Sunrise to find him. There would be no explaining. They would curse him in slurred voices, and Sharon would have the burden of two losses: her friend and her god.

Sharon.

Gary stood at the wall of an overlook off the Parkway. He'd walked for hours in the darkness, and was soaked in sweat. He wondered if anyone had yet been curious enough to see if Friend was in his cabin.

Of course not. They respected his isolation. Disturbing the man was not something they would fathom. It could go for days. No one would notice.

Gary watched the world to the west, waiting patiently for the sun to come up behind him and curse him.

When he felt the first heat of the morning and saw the first red-pink strokes around him, he climbed onto the wall. These blue mountains were indeed beautiful. Roads and houses hidden by lush and persistent growth. Above, the clouds turned from pink to gold to white. A breeze blew up from the sheer rocks below.

Sharon.

Gary lifted his arms to the heavens.

"One small step for a man," he said.

From the thick trees beyond and beneath the wall, a rush of wings caught the air. In an instant, a flock of helicopters rose, swirling around Gary and beside him. They passed above him, cutting and wounding the sky, moving in the direction of Sunrise.

Someone had noticed.

Looking down, Gary wondered if his head would split open like that of someone shot in the skull.

"One giant leap," he said.

1970

WHATEVER

BY RICHARD CHRISTIAN
MATHESON

1971

1972

1973

1974

1975
_____

1976   *You're gonna come around*
        To the sad sad truth
        The dirty lowdown.

1977

                    —Boz Scaggs, "Lowdown"

1978

1979

Rolling Stone
Inter-Office MEMO

To: Michael Blaine, Senior Editor.
From: Lisa Frankel, Executive Editor.

M:
Bad news. Looked over Matheson's pages. Frankly puzzled. They're indeed a fascination. Yet somehow elusive. Despite the horror of what actually happened, they amount to nothing more than a scrapbook. Evocative. But transient. Not surprised *Esquire* and *The New Yorker* decided to pass. My best suggestion, we do the same.

I know this writer is a friend of yours. But I feel strongly if we get into this, we make a real mistake. Bottom line: the band once mattered, but in my mind is not legend; simply forgotten. And the manuscript, while accomplished, is unpublishable. Wish I had better news.

Awaiting your thoughts.
L.

cc: M. Blaine/L. Frankel/J. Wenner

FORTRESS OF THE DEAD CITY. AIX-EN-PROVENCE, FRANCE. AUGUST 27, 1969.

Flies.

Striking skin; bullets with eyes of dried blood. Clinging to smooth stone, fortress walls, sleeping in chunks of shade that creep; shadow icebergs.

Tourists. Heat.

Salty half-moons under armpits. Sandals scuffing ancient rock. Turkish cigarettes. Lovers hold humid hands.

A deserted city. Long dead. Before Christ was born. Hated. Pounded onto wood with nails; left to bleed, a slaughtered calf. Cries unanswered. Reasons unprovided.

A couple.

Young. Nineteen. Seventeen. Him. Her.

A relationship. Two months. Moods beyond control. Passion and fear.

Suffering.

Her Nikon slicing moments off time; a gently clicking scalpel. Memories for a book. An album. A cocktail table mausoleum.

Always fighting. Driving from Paris to Monte Carlo. Stopping for iced espresso in a town. A charming village. Staring in silence; a joint burial.

He opens his guitar case. Metal strings hot under sun; branding fingers. Plays a new ballad. Sings softly. Children gather. He smiles, a barefoot saint. It's about her. She tries not to hear. Feels her life washed away. He isn't hers anymore. This trip was an epitaph.

She begins to cry.

He's going back to America. To that bastard Tutt. To record; to find fame.

To Whatever.

FROM A TAPED CONVERSATION. MONTSERRAT.
NEW YEAR'S DAY, 1972.

"I'm fuckin' exhausted. Bad influenza."

Jagger; straw to gimlet. Horse teeth shoving out lips; gaudy fenders. "Is that a pun? Christ . . ."

When he talks it looks like oral sex. He's tanning. A lewd little boy in Spandex; the Groin Gatsby, afloat on a 150-foot bauble. Right now, he has the sniffles and a hundred temperature. His features are a water-retentive Halloween mask; not a face that should host a head cold.

The other Stones are down there somewhere, in wet slow-mo, with rented air, scoping out the coral and triggers. Scaring the specimens with horned, goateed jewelry. Scarred arms. Albino eels worth too many million to pester the math.

"Sunken cheeks amid sunken treasure," Mick suggests. "So . . . what is it? You want my opinion?" He likes the idea, disaffected glee trickling. He lights an antique pipe, tokes. Answers, tucking air in lungs, sounding inside a heavy sack.

". . . okay. They're us. If we were good enough to be them."

I jot it down. He dimples Learjet cool. Licks the edge of his perfect little glass, a pink rag sponging. Then, as suddenly, looks off into a place he wants out of, fast. A place of torrential wrongness.

"But that shit they write is intense. These guys are tormented." He shrugs. "It's not Woodstock anymore. Besides, like Keith says, that was just mud and bad acid."

He blows Barnum air, yawns like the world's richest kitty.

"But same time . . . I wouldn't want to be them. The light they use inside those heads . . . too fuckin' bright. You can see everything. You heard 'Error of the Opposite' from the first album? The songs are fuckin' brilliant but . . . where you get a light like that?"

Sunglasses reflect yachts, refrigerator magnet–sized boats sliding across his lenses. He says nothing. Sneezes. Coughs S-M Caruso guck from a throat insured by Lloyds. Groans, unhappily.

"I'd hate to see everything. That's why they invented . . . what did they invent, again, mate?"

"Shadows?"

He shakes his head. No, that's not it.

"Limits?"

He's losing interest. You can tell when that happens to rock stars. They dive into perfect sea and soak you.

BAM *MAGAZINE.*
DECEMBER 9, 1969.

BLOOD SPATTERINGS AND FLORAL ARRANGEMENTS

Petals, a soft rock group that specialized in emotion-drenched lyrics, has broken up, and its members have left to form other groups. Founder Rikki Tutt is rumored to be working in an L.A. studio with ex–Seance member Greg Magurk, known for his acerbic lyrics and dark wordplay in such well-known songs as 1967's top ten hit "Miss Take." Magurk recently returned from a honeymoon in France, during which his much-publicized marriage to Bibi Rousse, a former colonic hygienist, was abruptly canceled.

Drummer Stomp McGoo, late of Louisiana funk band Pressure, is manning the sticks. Phil Zapata of folk duo Zapata and Lake is rumored to be jumping ship from the latest Z+L European tour to join. Lake has reportedly filed a lawsuit against his partner. Their *Take A Guess* album has been top ten for over five weeks.

Sounds like something plenty interesting getting rolled and lighted here, kids. Keep you posted.

LYRICS FROM "HERE PUSSY" FROM SECOND SEANCE ALBUM. WRITTEN BY GREGORY MAGURK. COURTESY VOICE RECORDS. 1968.

When I met you,
I wasn't good for much.
A six-pack of nowhere.
Wasn't safe to touch.

You cooked me eggplant,
Ironed my flaws and clothes.
Now I'm just a house cat.
Don't suffer all those lows.

ROLLING STONE.
RANDOM NOTES. FEBRUARY 1970.

Newly formed group Whatever is currently recording, working with L.A. studio producing whiz Purdee Boots. Rumor is various Beatles and Hollies are sitting in and that the tracks, so far, are monsters. The as-yet-untitled album is due out within the year on VOICE Records.

FROM MY NOTES.
FILLMORE WEST. SAN FRANCISCO.
BILL GRAHAM'S OFFICE.
JUNE 5, 1970.

Portion of taped interview with Whatever manager Lenny Lupo.

Q. How would you describe the band's sound?
A. It's the death knell of nitwit rock. Got melody. Got ideas. You know Zappa's a fan? Wants to sit in on the next album. If it was the seventeenth century, these guys would be writing operas. Tell you, if I was Bob Dylan, I'd shoot my rhyming dictionary in the head and open a dry cleaners.
Q. You represented folk acts and surf bands in the sixties. How did you decide to manage the group?
A. I listened. I liked. Instinct.
Q. The debut album *Know Means Know* is rumored to be amazing.
A. Tell you something. Whatever is the American Beatles. I defy anyone to listen to their music and not be profoundly blown away.
Q. Surf is dead. The British invasion is dead. Where are the seventies going?
A. Ask me in ten years.

NEW YORK TIMES. MUSIC REVIEW.
"WHATEVER," BOTTOM LINE.
FEBRUARY 4, 1972.

Whatever, a band said to have an I.Q. too big for its own good, escaped imperious repute last night and shook the earth.

Their first album, the exquisitely produced *Know Means Know*, has been enjoying the view from the top of nearly every critic's list this year. Its exacting mosaics of song and voice, via producer Purdee Boots, is a radiant marvel. But live, the Los Angeles–based quintet is even better.

Their compositions, the work of moody, ponytailed guitarist Greg Magurk and angel-faced bass player/ lead vocalist Rikki Tutt, are like small novels set to highly original scores.

However, not content with mere literate Beatle-esquery, the wordplay, observation, and heartache of Messrs. Magurk and Tutt are only part of the hat trick. Their vocals and tunesmithing are also fed by primal rhythms—a voodoo body blow. Make no mistake, this is not a vinyl meringue abloom with tender nothings. It is rock and roll that keeps its mouth open while it chews.

And it is music nearly impossible to resist.

Last night, playing to a stunned crowd which packed the Bottom Line, Whatever was a dizzying Houdini. Mr. Tutt's vocals were choirboy-sweet and soared without effort. Mr. Magurk's baleful arias were darker, oozing sly carnality. Wicked lyrics overflowed with estimable ironies, yet never felt like self-indulged puzzles.

While the rest of rock and roll (with few exceptions, like John Lennon and Paul McCartney, Joni Mitchell or Bob Dylan; perhaps a stray, poignant phrasing from Neil Young, Paul Simon, or Lou Reed) revel in stick drawings, Whatever is doing full figure studies.

Mouth-dropping chops from drummer Stomp McGoo gouged a groove so deep it's amazing no one fell in and got hurt.

Keyboardist Phil Zapata, a former child prodigy, is all grown-up now; a honky-tonk Chopin who smokes

Camels while sledging keyboard, and wears shades so dark he takes on the appearance of some Steinway thug.

Rhythm guitarist G.G. Wall, draped in trademark fringe jacket and skintight jeans, chugged the songs into a trance state, power-plucking a Fender neck that must've needed a cigarette afterward.

Apart from the astonishing songs of Messrs. Tutt and Magurk, this band could be hugely successful on its own. Working with Messrs. Tutt and Magurk, a supergroup seems probable.

Like some fugitive smoke, Whatever has risen quickly from the horizon of poseurs and record-company puppets that stultify top 40 rock and roll. They are not kings yet. But there is royal talent here.

With its pristine vocals and lyrical savagery, Whatever has ascended to meaning and wonder. Something rare touches these young men.

CRAWDADDY *MAGAZINE.*
AUGUST 1976.

"It's Hubris.

"Stanley Hubris. One of our finest filmmakers," says Greg Magurk, Rikki Tutt's partner and cofounder of Whatever, grinning. He's currently at pool's edge, under a hundred pounds of zinc oxide—a 5'11" can of Crisco.

"We're forever accused of trying to make the journalists trip up, you know? Like we trade in some quicksand prattle and dare initiates to step closer." Tutt is fed up.

It's an ultramarine, vaporizer day in Honolulu. Tutt, Magurk and the rest of Whatever are taking a few days off from L.A., swatting bugs from freshly written songs for the new album, *Philip's Head*, a tribute to band member Phil Zapata, who died last month in Greenwich Village. Tutt, a private pilot, flew the band to the funeral in Sag Harbor in a retired Avianca 707 the band bought and refurbished—a floating retreat, gutted and filled with warm, fuzzy hedonisms.

The jet, which Whatever members call *SPOT*, brought them to the islands and rockets the entourage to all shows. Random guests on the passenger list have included a prime minister's wife who ran away to join Tutt and Magurk's free-associative sock hop, and a Catholic bishop who lost his faith after discovering sex that didn't involve himself exclusively, shed his red hat and ended up living with one of the members of Sister Sledge.

In passing, I ask if it's true about the hole in Zapata's head.

Tutt nods, dripping pineapple on the decking of this rented house on Diamond Head. "Trepanation. Did it to himself. Decided on the drill-bit size and . . . in he went."

Magurk plays with a telescope, squints through precision optics, trawling for undesirables.

"He always wanted a higher state of mind. Way Phil figured it, babies are born with skull unsealed . . . and it's not until we become adults that the . . ." He searches for an image.

" . . . ossified helmet," Tutt suggests.

" . . . right. Anyway, that it's formed, which encloses membranes that moat the brain and block pulsations from the heart. Idea is the brain gets too compressed and starved for sun in there and would love a little fresh air. So, Phil gets it into his head . . ."

" . . . temporarily, anyway," adds Tutt.

" . . . that he was losing touch with dreams, aberrant ideation and so forth. Then, he figures his mental balance is tending toward egoism and eventual psychosis, which Phil argued was man's inheritance, collectively and individually. That's when he decided to drill a hole in his head."

Tutt is humming and wrestling a coconut that keeps escaping his lap and knife, rolling away.

"Anyway he did it by hand with this weird tool he bought at a surgical store. Called a trepan. Corkscrew thing you work by hand. Sort of a metal spike surrounded by a ring of saw teeth," explains Magurk.

Tutt takes over. "Spike was meant to be driven into the skull. Then you hold the trepan steady until the revolving saw makes a groove, after which it can be retracted. If all goes well, the saw band removes a disc of bone and exposes the brain."

"Assuming one's in there," says Magurk. He lowers his voice, sadly. "It was a total mess. He bagged it, halfway."

"Cops said it looked like he had a big flower on his forehead."

Magurk focuses his telescope. "You can't force imminent well-being. Who said that?"

"That guy on *McHale's Navy*?"

They nod somberly.

While Tutt and Magurk have been criticized for trading in flippant and cruel conversation, after an afternoon with them, it's clear this sort of talk is only their private walkie-talkie humor, which delights in esoteric couplings. Indeed, they plan to give a sizable percentage of the *Philip's Head* profits to Zapata's widow, Joyce, who is left with two young sons, Lon and Will. Tutt and Magurk are the godfathers of the boys and call them often from the road. Meanwhile, they've brought various studio legends in to take over Zapata's keyboard chores on the album.

And what about the new songs themselves?

"We like them. Phil would've liked them. But before we record, we just want to try the new stuff out in smaller clubs. It's perfect here. Very low-key. Everybody's happy in Hawaii."

"Even the lepers are upbeat."

"Anyway, we've come to avoid the evil ink-ees."

He means the critics. It's not that the band gets bad reviews. It's that Tutt and Magurk can't help but be appointed *the* voice of their time. They never angled for that pulpit.

"They treat us like we're a cortex on a marquee. I mean, c'mon guys, who nominated us the skewering conscience of the posthippie stupor? We're just song-writers."

"Look," says Magurk, "we don't deny what's going on. When you've got the last few years filled with venal kings in the palace, with their duplicitous munchkins bugging the competitor's HQ, and the country in that ghastly war, burning children alive, how can you just write about love?"

They fall silent. We watch waves break. Clouds inch.

Magurk scribbles in a notebook, rewriting lyrics for a new song the band has already laid down tracks for in L.A.'s Music Plant. It's called "Flesh Diction."

"It was easy ten years ago," says Tutt. "You just dressed better than John Sebastian and quoted from *Siddhartha* to get laid." He glances at the spearing sun with a misanthrope's half-interest. ". . . Marmalade skies, y'know?"

Magurk isn't even listening. "Hawaii is a complex

braid of man and nature," he says to no one in particular, eyeing a buxom palomino rising from the surf.

BILLBOARD *MAGAZINE.*
SEPTEMBER 1971.

Nominations were announced today in all Grammy categories. To no one's surprise, Rikki Tutt and Greg Magurk's Whatever is being considered in the Best New Rock Group and Best Album categories. The group's debut album, *Know Means Know*, has been a huge seller and critical favorite and ranks at Number 2 in this week's *Billboard* top 100 albums.

FROM TAPED CONVERSATION.
PARIS, FRANCE. EIFFEL TOWER.
DECEMBER 20, 1974.

G.G. Wall swears it's true.

"I guess it was like some metaphor. You know, outwardly represented. It was strange."

He claims the child would simply bleed. Instead of tears, blood would run down her eight-year-old face, and stain her dress red. Otherwise, she remained expressionless, hands folded calmly in her lap, flies sipping on her cheeks.

"I don't see how they could've faked it. But people came from all over, just fascinated. They felt sorrow and remorse. But they also seemed to feel an odd sense of relief."

He thinks that maybe it helped them work through their own pain and quiet tortures. The girl never left the chair, for the several hours she was on view. Never spoke.

"It gets fucking hot in Italy that time of year, too . . . it was summer, you know? And her parents just forced her to sit there in that white dress while folks lined up and walked by."

He begins to dislike the memory.

"We were on tour, all through Europe. Played Italy for a couple weeks. I went to see her every day."

Silence.

"After a few days, I started to feel ashamed. Watching her like that. I don't know what it meant or why it picked her, but it was wrong what we all did . . ." He looks out from the Eiffel, studying nothing, lost in Paris as huge painting.

It's been two years since Whatever played Italy. Wall says word is, the girl continues to bleed.

KING BISCUIT FLOWER HOUR.
NATIONAL RADIO BROADCAST.
MARCH 19, 1972.

"And now the song that's skinning the charts alive . . . Whatever's 'Yeah, Right,' a tantrum-anthem which seems to have taken the fevered temperature of an entire generation. Pete Townshend: take notes."

> *This deal is crap,*
> *I want my mommy.*
> *My mantra died.*
> *Page my swami.*
>
> *Is this a joke?*
> *Who's in charge?*
> *They brought me small,*
> *I asked for large.*
>
> *I'm having no fun,*
> *I've lost my zip.*
> *Where's the laughs?*
> *Life's a gyp.*

> *It's not like it was.*
> *The beer is flat.*
> *The sun is cold.*
> *I smell a rat.*
>
> *Leave me for dead,*
> *I'll be fine.*
> *There's nothing left.*
> *But it's all mine.*
>
> *Cut my throat,*
> *Watch me gush.*
> *Don't cry, baby.*
> *Enjoy the rush.*

FROM MY NOTES.
DURANGO.
FEBRUARY 1973.

Tutt's getting married.

Inga from Germany. They say she never smiles. Just stares through your pupils, making you feel like cheap, toy binoculars. She makes normal men nervous. Rockers happy. Knows all their doors and windows, how to pick locks, break in. Knows how to chat and laugh. Wears clothes so tight some say you can hear the ambition leaking through the fibers.

They also say her mother was Hitler's private masochist, her exquisite skin his personal ashtray, the moody Führer polka-dotting her with petulant tobacco scorches whenever the Reich hit a snag.

Inga is beautiful. She couldn't have married anyone other than a star. And when she smiles at Tutt, his sky fills with puffy clouds, tweeting birds.

They all wanted Tutt. He wasn't just an SRO pheromone. He was the one with the pretty face, sweet worry. The child without a mother who took your hand, smiled tentatively at any kindness. He was the poem only you could rhyme. The yearning vocal that stilled a stadium.

Made it weep.

Joke was he bled internally when he sang. But nobody could get over him. Even his ex-collaborator, Truce Wood.

"Know what he wanted to call our band, Petals? *Cry*. He always liked that name. Fit him, y'know? He's a morose fuck. Real mood disorder."

But what about the music? I ask Wood. He keeps throwing his knife into a tree. This succulent-laden ranchette is what he bought with what he had left, a cacti-nippled nowhere.

"It's sorta like this. Everybody else is writing songs. Tutt and Magurk hear God. Set it to music. Bleed for our sins."

And we all get a chance to listen to the downpour. It's a nice image. Or is it just that Truce is born again? He won't answer, prefers not to talk about it.

Knife pulled from tree. A lost glance. After Petals broke up, Truce released some solo work. Band called Fat Couch. First album in '70, *Happy Nap*, just sat in a dull puddle and died. Nothing clicked. Label cut them before a second album even made the climb into headphones.

Now he runs a bar, TRUCE, in Durango. He admits when everything in his world bent sideways, he lost his voice and dropped acid like it was vitamin C. Soon became so despondent and paranoid, he hired a private detective to track his voice down.

The guy charged him $250.00 a day, plus expenses. Told Truce he tracked the voice to a diner in Wichita Falls and cornered it but that it got away. He finally claimed to have found it and sent it by registered mail in a padded box to Truce. Truce still keeps the unopened box on his fireplace mantel.

"That's what drugs'll do to you." He smiles. "I keep it there as a lesson to myself. I lost everything, man. I'm lucky I'm fucking alive." He wipes the blade on his Levi's. "Things change. And you gotta live with the ghosts."

And now Rikki Tutt is marrying a hundred pounds of Mercedes austerity, and Truce is worrying about just the right wedding gift.

"Tell you this, females on seven continents are in mourning."

He's right. Rikki is more than the one who got away. He's the only one who ever managed to find the way in.

"Maybe I'll get him his own box for the mantel." Truce is nodding, dead serious. "Fame swallows you when you ain't looking."

MUSIC CITY NEWS.
NASHVILLE.
APRIL 1971.

Twenty-two-year-old G.G. Wall, lead guitarist for Whatever, was named guitarist of the year by *Playboy* magazine in its annual music poll. He beat out Clapton, Segovia, Beck, Hendrix, Wes Montgomery, Joe Pass, Kenny Burrell, and George Harrison. His composition "Tight Squeeze" was also voted best instrumental of the year.

Wall, who quit school at fourteen, has suffered with emotional problems since childhood and spoke about it on a recent *Dick Cavett Show*. When asked about the place intellect plays in the music of Whatever, Wall replied to Cavett that his mind "doesn't stop by much, anymore. Guess it had other plans."

And about the psychotherapy he's been in for over ten years: "I believe in it. Psychology is like restoring paintings. Bringing back the original colors."

Much of Wall's teen years were spent in and out of

juvenile facilities for burglary. He always broke into places of worship and is known to have stolen religious artifacts from literally hundreds of churches.

"Why should the churches keep it, man?"

And what has he done with all those artifacts?

"Well . . ." he manages, mischief clowning on his face. "Just say I couldn't recall and replied with an opaque stare."

THE DAVID FROST SHOW.
LONDON. RITZ HOTEL.
SEPTEMBER 1972.

"Mr. President, let's talk a bit about your private life with the First Lady. I understand you and Pat very much like to watch sports on TV."

"The Soviet gymnast Olga Korbut is a remarkable athlete. I'm no fan of their government, but excellence can occur in surprising places."

"I also have spies who tell me you have a passion for the music of Stan Kenton. Do you dance in the White House? The two of you? Alone?"

Nixon laughs. Takes a sip of water offered by Frost.

"I don't think I'd better answer that without getting the go-ahead from Pat. She's very private about romantic things."

"Favorite movies this year?"

"We screen movies at the White House, as you know. Have some friends over. We very much liked *The Poseidon Adventure. Jeremiah Johnson. What's Up Doc?* I liked *Deliverance*, but Pat was uncomfortable with the violence."

"And rock 'n' roll?"

"Pat is a Helen Reddy fan. Roberta Flack's 'First Time Ever I Saw Your Face' is quite lovely."

"I'm talking about real rock 'n' roll."

He chuckles.

"Ask me another question."

"Certainly you're well aware of the Rolling Stones, the Beatles . . ."

"Of course. Very talented young men."

"And Whatever?"

Nixon blinks. Sees it coming.

"Are you aware of how critical they've been of your foreign policy?"

"I haven't heard that, no."

"I can assure you, Mr. President, they seem to speak for their generation and mirror a huge dissatisfaction among the young people of America."

"The people of Southeast Asia need our help."

"Then what of other issues? One of the band's number one songs, 'World of Hurt,' indicts what band members have been quoted as saying they perceive to be Washington's apathy in regards to the dumping of toxic materials. Surely you've been told."

Nixon grins darkly, jowls gathering; judgmental tuck and roll.

"Is that a question or a pointed object?"

"Why were members of the band beaten by police and arrested last month during a peace rally at the Washington Monument? You know about the arrests?"

"Are we discussing politics or rock music?"

"We're discussing your waning popularity with the youth of the United States, sir."

Nixon wipes upper lip.

"They believe that your office is running an undeclared and immoral campaign of military violence in Southeast Asia—and that you wish to mitigate voices who are raised in opposition. That you are leading the young men of your country to slaughter."

"You don't burn the American flag. You do not. This band . . . they did that on stage."

"And what of their outrage and despair . . . indeed, that of young people throughout your country?"

"You do not burn the flag."

PORTION OF UNPUBLISHED ESQUIRE *ARTICLE.*
JUNE 5, 1973.

When Tutt first saw her, he says he saw the end.

It flashed like a precognitive REM warning, a half frame. A keyhole glimpse of a murdered form, slumped somewhere in his thoughts. A sense nothing good could come from being with her.

Tutt remembers her saying little. A smile that revealed something. Nothing. Everything he needed to believe. It was her gift; he realized it too late.

She was dark. Hair. Eyes. Jewelry. Her eyebrows were perfect on her beautiful face. She seemed strong; certain. Yet tears probably fell somewhere in her. Tutt felt it in a blink. A moment.

She smiled too easily, he remembers thinking. Wishes he'd paid more attention to the fleeting impression that soon blurred, raced away. He'd pay later for the oversight.

He was feeling at home in her eyes. Liked the heat of her skin, though he hadn't touched it. But he sensed it was warm, like a solar beam that slips silently through shutters.

He could smell her perfume and thought for a moment it had always been his favorite scent, though he couldn't place it. He could place nothing about her. But he knew her . . . at least, he says, he felt he must.

The astrologer he'd met at the recording studio during the first album mix had predicted the meeting with Inga. Told him he'd meet the woman he'd stay with forever. His soul mate. The companion who'd been imprinted in his flesh like the tiny colored threads which suffuse paper money.

Yet he knew nothing right could ever come from their life together. Even the day he married her, he was scared. Something was wrong. On that day, in that beautiful church above the glimmering sea, filled with friends and family, he felt sick. As they kissed, Rikki felt he was dying.

FROM MY NOTES.
MALIBU, CALIFORNIA.
JULY 1972.

"Look closely enough, everybody wants it."

She's nineteen. A lapsed Botticelli angel. Her own band, Crazy Tea Cup, tried it on Elektra but didn't fly. Girls with guitars. Forget it. Gets on people's nerves, like polka.

She watches guys; Kama Sutra no-nos fill her mind. There's none of the cloying penance of her mother's generation—shame over sexual abandon. The moral imprisonment of past generations of female sexuality is going up in flames, burned with all those bras outside the White House, a sky gone cotton and auburn outside Nixon's front lawn.

And for Jamie, rock 'n' roll cock is the best Ohio Blue Tip around.

"My mother's generation were nice women with a lot of fucked-up frustrations."

That pleasing curvature seeps from sheer blouse, tight bell-bottoms. Her skin is pearly, hands delicate.

"I'm just making up for lost time." She rolls some Hawaiian and pouts for effect—a cannabis Lolita.

By her estimate, she's meaningfully convened with over a thousand rock luminaries. Just doing it for Mom. But for Jamie, Whatever takes the sweaty cake. She's had them all and travels with the band whenever it hits the road. In fact, her territorial beekeeping of their privates' lives and lives private consumes her at all times, and she often acts as nursemaid and confessional. She seems to feel her tonic closeness will ease their journey through life. Deepen their music. Make her part of it all.

"Magurk always says I'm quite up for the safari. 'Warm clothes, a trenchant undertow to my casual asides. It's all in the suitcase.' He talks like that," says this Radcliffe dropout who has traveled with Zep, Supertramp, Dr. Hook, and even Cat Stevens before, as she says: " . . . he boarded the 'Preach Train.' "

She tried to move on from life on the road with Whatever, but the trackmarks of being that close to world level touring kept her on a backstage leash.

She tried it different. Even dated a cop, a bruised genie, who lived in a Smirnoff bottle after hours.

"Lasted a week. It was my mother's idea. She thinks I'm attracted to guys like my father because he's unavailable. Like if he were available, I'd fucking care."

She drinks some ouzo. Licks those lips that take famous temperature in a special way. Would rather talk about Tutt and Magurk.

"They're geniuses. Not the usual peacock clods."

She giggles. "Definitely not pea cocks."

LETTER TO ME FROM MAGURK.
LAUSANNE, SWITZERLAND.
JULY 1974.

Dear Yourself,

A jotting from the disjointed and convex.

Thanks for the letter. We're actually okay to do the interview with you in Miami. Only possible snag is we're doing *Midnight Special* remote feed from the Cameo Theater. We're in town to do a Bobby Seale rally, or raise money to get Joan Baez some tits or some damn thing.

Crosby, Stills + Nash (the fucking tumbleweed sleeping pills) are support. We need an afternoon to sound-check. How about we do the interview the next day so we can rest? Otherwise we're distant signals.

We'll be at the Bel Aire. We like it because, as narcissistic plunderers, we can push them around and demand a full-time nanny to attend to our impossible demands. Particularly of a sordid, crotchy sort.

Tutt wants to buy an overcoat in Miami. His was grilled to a sickly mound by his latest coin-operated woman while tramping around Lennon's estate. Something about someone starting a fire and needing wood. She thought they said wool.

Do you suppose John actually mows the place himself? Probably forces Ringo to do it in exchange for being allowed into Apple offices to drain his snout.

We don't know Miami well and are easily manipulated into believing anything, the dream tourists. We're really quite happy to be led about like odd species on loan from a West Coast zoo and would love to check out whatever is fascinating, utterly debasing or easy to dance to.

Wrote four new songs last night with Tutt. He

must've swallowed a piano. No matter where you touch him, you get music.

See you in Miami.

MAGURK

FROM MY NOTES.
AIRBORNE. THE IRISH COAST.
JANUARY 1975.

"I hated the war. Hated the weapons. You know what napalm does? You know how long it takes to burn right through to the fucking bone? Cooks the marrow. I know about U.S. guys who ate the cooked marrow of Vietnamese children like it was Colonel Sanders. Guys in . . . Thin Lizzy or Ginger Baker's Air Force had pictures. I forget which one."

Stomp paradiddles Lucchese cowboy boots, leather pants scabbed with stains of unknown origin; scuffed rock-gladiator wear. The helicopter angles over the stage on the Scottish island where twenty-five superstar rock acts will perform this weekend and raise money for handicapped orphans of the war.

"'Calley's kids,' we call them. Think he'd mind? Get pissed, put us in a trench?"

He manages to get a hit of hash. Cannons it out.

"We bought a cathouse in Saigon. Sent all the girls to another one in Gia Dinh. We turned it into a hospital. Give these kids a place. They got no arms. No legs. Pizza where they had eyes. It's horrible. Really."

He solos fingers on leather, legs crossed, staring down at the mossy island, sprouted from the sea—a giant shamrock. Tutt and Magurk are coming in from London, later. They were up all night at Abbey Road studios doing a mix.

G.G. Wall is finishing a two-day vacation in Moscow with latest girlfriend, Vera, a Russian spy type. There is talk he's also dating Goldie Hawn, one of Donovan's ex-girlfriends, and a nun. Stomp grins, disavows nothing. Wants to get back to his version of politics.

"Fucking Kissinger. Fucking military industrial complex. Fucking John Wayne." It's a comprehensive dismissal from the quiet one of the group. Perhaps naive; a jumble of anger and buzzwords. Perhaps something more personal.

His own brother, Steven, flew in Vietnam, pouring Orange Julius from death choppers, killing trees, stunting limbs.

"John Wayne . . . another asshole. Take his legs and arms. What does he need 'em for? Turn him into an organ bank. Help the kids. Just shoot him in close-up. He'll still work."

He smiles, but means every word, a hopeless fluid in this particular syringe. "These guys are killing America. When you're old and mean and can't get it up, war is the best fuck around. You can bet they're looking for the next one, right now."

The helicopter gets smacked in the head by Atlantic wind. Stomp bites a snack-sized bit of lip. Closes his eyes.

"God, I hate flying."

UNPUBLISHED ARTICLE.
SEAHORSE PARTY. HOLLYWOOD HILLS.
JANUARY 1979.

Blowtorch moon.

The crazies are out; waxed Kraut cars valet park before a Frank Lloyd Wright mansion. Rock gushes from inside, kicking hard from deco arches.

Inside, the place is crawling with rock 'n' roll lemmings, golden arms. Thrashed glitter faces laugh and vacuum psyches over white lines. Perfect, naked bodies slip into churning tubs. Loud music peels us alive as L.A. twinkles and speedballs, far below. Somewhere out there, Sid Vicious killed his girlfriend, and pimply goons line up to see *Grease*.

The freak who leased the place for the month snorts with the group's soundman, Feeder. They talk about the tour, cranked. Seahorse cleaned plate through Europe. The new album, *High Horse*, shipped gold.

"They're leaving bands like Whatever in the dust," says Snuffy Hawkins, music editor of *Whirl*, the fastest-growing music magazine since *Rolling Stone*. Even though the backup singers and occasional musicians who've played on Whatever albums have enjoyed malarial perks of that association, such days are over.

Other Seahorse members pass, glazey, berserko. The fifteen-country tour burned them into their boots; they need this blowout. Four of them: drummer, two guitars, lead singer. Zep rip-off. Heavy, waste-the-pussies hostility. Bad-boy snits under plague eyes. Guttural secrets passed with knowing smirks, word-codes.

Girls everywhere. Willing, eyes wide. They watch in needful silence, a harem of casualties, taking a number, hoping to win a member of the band.

Seahorse is laughing, drinking around the gelato-bright pool with their friend from Whatever, G.G. Wall. They all just finished an interview with me for *Rolling Stone* and trashed everybody. The band's lead roadie, Dino, tells them they fucked up. Nobody gives Jann Wenner shit, not even cut-edge crotch royalty like Seahorse.

Seahorse bass player, Lick Clean, spreads something new around. Heroin. Brown. Chinese. Calls it Rocky Road. Stuff plays with chemical matrices like they were soup recipes.

G.G. takes the bad dessert into his arm. Wanders into the cavernous party palace, starting to ride what Feeder promises is Elvis, blow jobs, and mercy spit from one needle. He immediately starts to convulse.

Twenty minutes later, he's pale and cold.

The morgue wagon got lost, trying to find the place.

"He had leukemia. I'm sure that was it," says Whatever manager Lenny Lupo. "Living with a death sentence was too hard for him. Stuff coulda flared anytime. He was a take-charge guy. He took charge."

"Bullshit," says Seahorse lead singer Vinnie Perito. "I saw him that night. He looked good. He was digging it. Maybe he got out before Etcetera or Noteven or Whatever-The-Fuck became the fucking Monkees, okay? No disrespect intended. I liked to party with the guy. And I used to dig them, when they mattered. But then again, am I lying? Message shit is yesterday. I say he knew it."

Perito is currently in rehabilitation at Synanon after surviving a second O.D. Rikki Tutt, reached in Aspen on a skiing trip, said Wall was a brilliant musician and ". . . an old soul."

FROM MY NOTES.
SÃO PAULO, BRAZIL.
BEJEJOS WOMEN'S PRISON.
DECEMBER 1977.

"I got caught." No expression. "Life."

Inga is in the visitor's area. She's smoking. Smirking. Can't believe she's here, especially with Christmas coming.

"Look, I can't say anything about the case, all right?"

Word is she was framed. Bringing a few kilos into Rio for the big Whatever concert on Copacabana.

She'd managed to get off with community service for the dope buy in L.A. But this was different. South America is a bad place to smuggle or score. They cut off hands; cut off lives.

Word coming from the Whatever camp is that Magurk and his legal team are trying to meet with Rio police officials again. Work some kind of appeal. Maybe buy a deal. But it doesn't look good.

"If you see him, tell him I love him. They won't let me get mail or send it."

I'm told visiting time is over by a tough-looking, dark-skinned matron. Inga shows no fear, upset.

"I'll get out of here. Just watch. Magurk isn't gonna let me die in here."

I promise to tell Magurk she loves him.

CASHBOX MAGAZINE.
SEPTEMBER 1974.

For the new Whatever album on VOICE Records, *Just Forget It*, music retailers around the globe are going to highly unusual lengths to associate with the super-group. Several major music chains have announced plans to give all their display space to *Just Forget It*, and embossed T-shirts and sweatshirts will be given to buyers.

Wallach's Music City in L.A. will also have Whatever displays taking up the entire side of the store facing Sunset Boulevard. On the roof, the album cover, a two-story brain with a red diagonal line through it, will be flanked by 20-foot reproductions of the recently reissued Whatever debut album.

On the night of the release, VOICE Records will hold an invitation-only party at L.A.'s elite Kaleidoscope Club featuring members of the band. Among events on the East Coast will be a caravan of

VOICE party trolleys transporting customers from Central Park to Manhattan record stores until the wee hours.

Other "Midnight Madness" parties scheduled internationally will include laser shows, giant listening sessions, and a live concert screened in movie theaters via satellite.

Asked about the promotional blitz, Rikki Tutt and Greg Magurk of Whatever shrug. "Images in search of meaning."

ARTICLE PORTION.
ALBUQUERQUE, NEW MEXICO.
JULY 1977.

Stomp is acting.

Dressed like Jesse James and sweating under that prop hat. The 25-year-old director, Mitch Meyer, is right out of UCLA film school and cattle-prodding an exhausted crew through this five-and-dime Peckinpah spur opera. It's called *Blood of Earth* and the plot has something to do with: (A) a whorehouse that's hiding the gold from a train robbery (and Buffy Sainte-Marie is the madam . . . hey, you got to love this country), (B) a schizophrenic outlaw who shaves badly and consorts with grinning sadists, and (C) a sheriff who sings.

Are you happy yet?

Where exactly the blood or earth part fits in, or where the earth might be bleeding, is not clear. I guess if you're deep enough, it adds up.

Meanwhile, you could say things haven't been going so well on the set.

The production is running so far over budget they may have to just draw the rest of it with crayons. Two producers have quit, the unit production manager lost an important finger in a local bar fight (word is the finger started it), numerous crew members have gotten dysentery from traveling to Mexico for a night of fun and admitting sombrero bugs into their colons. And while the film is being touted as a Jungian tale of cowardice and primal truths, rumor is, from those who've seen dailies, it looks like bad dinner theater *Oklahoma*.

It's currently so hot in New Mexico, flies roll onto their sides, begging for a Corona. Location trailer tires are going Wrigley. Gaffers are hosing down the horses so they don't faint, and everything around this set has a tortured, dehydrated look. It had to have been cooler when they shot *Lawrence of Arabia*.

Even *Our Mr. Sun*.

To complicate the less than thrifty morass, the studio, back in L.A., hates the rushes. The look, the lighting, the performances. They like Stomp. Think he has a moody, erogenous ease. A natural.

Lenny Lupo, manager for Whatever, agreed to let Stomp take this part after costar Lenda Bruxton saw the band in concert and thought Stomp had just the right look. Half-ugly, a little sexy, engagingly hairy.

The director wrote the script and demanded he direct or he wasn't selling. Beatty wanted to do it. Newman. Burt Reynolds fought to get it, couldn't, and is now trying to get into a project called *The Man Who Loved Cat Dancing*. Do people really want to see cats dance with Burt?

The director is losing a pound a day to heat, lack of appetite, and terror; the guy looks like a roller-coaster car is loose in his digestive tract. He knows his neck has a very expensive dotted line across it right now, and the short subject he won first place for in Cannes doesn't mean Dick York.

He's dining on peeled cuticles as he huddles with the cameraman and the director of photography, trying to get a shot that seems impossible; make points with the hundred-dollar haircuts in L.A. who are threatening to gas the shoot. One of the crew said growing gospel is, Mitch is lost in the frosting, and "there ain't no cake."

The studio has already brought a new writer aboard; a hundred-grand-a-week gunslinger who's in a trailer right now, restructuring and doctoring, neck-deep in fresher verbs. But this is no punch-up. It's a quadruple bypass.

Stomp has had his own off-camera problems.

He left his girlfriend, Jane, for one of the extras in the film, a Hawaiian beauty-contest winner with breasts so impressive she's actually named them after American presidents. But set rumor is that Jane found them naked in Stomp's hotel room and heaved 110 pounds of stacked aloha out the second-story window. The breasts survived, Jane split, and Stomp refocused on his work.

Right now, he's in his folding director's chair, writing lyrics for a song called "Floozy Woozy." A book of William Blake's poems and Daniel Berrigan's speeches ride sidesaddle in his script pouch. He's anxious to finish production, get back to L.A. and work on Whatever's new double album, *Skin and Bones*. And he's anxious to be taken seriously as a songwriter.

More and more, he feels Tutt and Magurk have that monopoly, and it's his time to put up hotels on Park Place. He's gotten a new personal manager, Karen Dellinger, who has guided Illinois Speed Press, Peaches and Herb, Livingston Taylor, and Eric Carmen. Thus far, he's written a jingle for a toothpaste company and an album of children's songs that's ready to be recorded called *The Big Stinky Ape*. And he thinks there's more nifty manna where that came from. He's also engaged to Dellinger, a former bookkeeper, who says Stomp is every bit the talent Magurk and Tutt are. While he plans to continue as the drummer for Whatever, he's also taking guitar lessons.

Stomp fingers his Martin, customized with his name in pearl. Wants to share.

"Just messing with it . . . you know. Wanna hear some?" He erases a word, blows red rubber shavings away—bouncy confetti.

"Very rough. Something like . . . 'Sitting in the cheap seats . . . sleeping on the torn sheets . . . listening to her thoughts . . . my attention drifts and rots.'" He tries to decide if he likes it. Wrestling with what he's scribbled.

"Anyway . . . it goes on: 'She's there for me . . . she's there for you . . . she's a bleak reminder . . . that some things never grew/ She makes me feel off-center . . . not a buyer . . . just a renter.'" He grins, Likes that part. Takes a sip of iced coffee, under the beating sun. Chomps a cube. Reads on.

"Floozy Woozy . . . I'm sick of her face. Floozy Woozy . . . she's a mind without a trace." He rubs his unshaven jaw—part of the role's look, a widowed sheriff, hollowed by grief; nightmare shakes. And evidently left unable to shave. Did I mention he sings, too? Maybe in the rewrite he'll tap like Sammy.

"Rest is . . . bit vague. Playing with: 'She thinks I like her . . . she thinks she's intriguing . . . to me she's proof of inbreeding.'" He wipes sweat. It could be flop sweat if we were anywhere but this kiln that's firing us like cowboy raku.

The stunt coordinator, a polite Stockholmer with a name too hard to spell, is passing by, and Stomp reads the lyrics again. Wants to know how the stunt Swede likes them. The S.S. smiles, politely.

"Maybe Magurk and Tutt can fix it," he says under his breath, clogging away.

NEWSWEEK.
SEPTEMBER 11, 1974.

What are Ronni Tutt and Greg Magurk of Whatever thinking? The darkness of their second and newest album, *Just Forget It*, released last week, is a harrowing ride that borders on diatribe.

While the band's first album, the intoxicating *Know Means Know* was a Lewis Carroll surrealism, filled with post-psychedelia braininess, addictive pulses and lyrical whimsy, this second outing is harder to place. There is none of the delighted feeling of the band caught under a bit of Magritte drizzle, from earlier efforts; no more nose-snubbing invention for its own pleasure.

The band is changing. Philip Zapata, now fully Moog synthesized, and G.G. Wall, his axe haunted by Jimi and experience, cannot rescue their faithless leaders. Listening to Whatever's new music is almost like watching an eloquent friend fall into a suffocating depression.

Could it be that Watergate antics and the body counts of Vietnam have left Tutt, Magurk, and company in a cheerless funk that won't let go? While *Just Forget It* is a brilliant set of songs, lyrically stunning, there is no mistaking the lightless bondage of its mood. The assassination of pop culture fills its every note and word, graff and bullies of sour headlines their prime targets. Our government tops the list.

"Addicts" is a toxic pin-the-tail-on-the-heartless mockery about the Watergate break-in that swarms with bitter imprecations. None gets out alive, including G. Gordon Liddy, John Dean, John Ehrlichman, and former President Richard M. Nixon.

The fountain of youth is red, not clear.
The secret of love is playing on fear.
You shouldn't resist, there's no point.
It's life's dirty trick, the rules of the joint.

Their gifts and tricks never abate, but the songwriters seem to have forgotten the joy of it all. This is an album of myriad gifts, however massively troubled. Whatever needs to lift its head from the bleakness of U.S. war policy and the bleating rancor of protesters before Tutt and Magurk have nothing good left to say about anything.

HIGHLY RECOMMENDED

FROM MY NOTES.
KITTRIDGE ARMY HOSPITAL. MISSOURI.
NOVEMBER 4, 1974.

"He can't hear me."

The room is stuffy. View of cornfields. Smokestacks. A train filled with frightened livestock rattles by.

A small town; farming, some industry. They don't see guys like Stomp McGoo coming through too often from atop their tractors and fundamentalism. All that hair and velvet. Bracelets jangling; a scrawny faggot. Makes their necks redden just thinking about it.

He's holding his brother Steven's hand. Steven landed his chopper on a mine in Vietnam, and when he came to there was less of him. Two arms gone. A leg. Most of his face. He's blind now. Being fed through a tube.

"You shoulda seen how he threw, man. Fuckin' Steven was the whole varsity team. Could pass into a thimble from half a mile."

Steven moans. Stomp strokes his hair.

The nurse says visiting time is almost up. Stomp nods, leans down to whisper to Steven, hold him. I can't hear what he says. Stomp holds him more tightly. Turns to look at me for a moment. He's crying.

On the drive away from the hospital, Stomp never said a word. As the jet took off, he looked out the window at the town left behind. Closed eyes. Said something about how Steven could never cry again. There was nothing left of his face that would allow it. Tear ducts had been destroyed.

The next night, Stomp did the longest and most amazing drum solo anyone could remember.

L.A. WEEKLY *ARTICLE. FROM MY NOTES.*
LOS ANGELES, CALIFORNIA.
DOWNTOWN L.A. ALAMEDA RAILROAD TRACKS.
JANUARY 3, 1975. 2:37 A.M.

Bad streets, bad people. Bars that hose death off their sidewalks every morning. A loft building rises, crapped-out—cheap. Inside, a guy who had an emotional blowout at a million miles an hour and kept going is waking.

His name is Oz Peterson, and he used to be a Chi-town blue. Until he and his partner got grabbed by Peruvian smack monkeys, and Oz watched the guy he rode with get unlaced slow style, tortured for DEA leads.

His partner, Nicky, never told. But it took three days to finally kill him. And Oz still has nightmare flashes of Nick, hung like beef, inch-long knife cuts venting his body, bled to death.

Oz rubs puffy features awake, fixes coffee, as a smoggy sun comes up in his loft space. It's filled with towering canvases painted with self-exorcising images. Oz disappeared after the death and flaked, drank, got lost, hoped he'd never get found.

Ended up in L.A. painting, doing dipshit P.I. work when he needed the gig. Divorce surveillance, riding a telephoto, getting fat. He'd go home at night, talk to a few shots of Huerredura and paint until the images scared him. Faces. Screaming children. Blades slitting skin. Red trickles that dripped onto his loft floor and made him sit cross-legged and think about just yanking his fucking cord.

But a knock at the door stopped him.

She stood there, and he'd seen her before. But he looked down, not wanting to make the connection, not wanting to chance even liking anybody. And so they rode in the loft building elevator a thousand times and he buried his face under a dead mask and she never asked. He always read her as a hooker. Pale, flashy. Edgar Winter hair, a teased abstraction. Pretty face, smart eyes. Eyes that probably knew he was cocooned and wasn't going to ask.

But then she said she needed to score. Was he holding? It was for a friend. A hungry arm that needed some yummy.

He said nothing. And she knew.

She talked him into bed and did some magic tricks on him that fried the hangover. And they held each other and he watched her, guilt pooling. What was someone like her doing down here?

"People here just get left on the curb to be collected." He likes her. Being next to her.

He battles a decision. Finally pulls cuffs from the bedside table, anchors her thin wrist to bedpost.

She writhes, yells bad words.

He calls the cops.

And as Inga gets taken away, he sketches her face. She's shrieking at him, in the back of the squad car. He stands on the filthy sidewalk, finishes the charcoal. Goes back to his room. Hangs up the sketch and gets drunk.

This year's Oval Office mouseketeer, "Gerry," was starting to clamp down on drugs, big-time. Nickel-and-dimers were gulping years without parole. Maybe Magurk wouldn't be able to buy Inga out of this one.

Even though he'd sent her.

TIME.
APRIL 10, 1978.

It's been a long wait. And the result is a troubling masterpiece.

The first cut from the new Whatever double album, *Skin and Bones*, is "Mainline," and, like the rest of the album, it's a full-frontal indictment.

> *Disease and glitter,*
> *Just take my hand.*
> *I'll never hurt you.*
> *I'm your biggest fan.*

And so it goes throughout this lethal stroll through the neon Styx of media imagery and false dreams. In the eyes of Tutt, Magurk, Wall, and McGoo, L.A. is one big ghastly appetite, rendered in inhuman, industrial grays and gunshot reds. They cut a deep incision and pull back flesh to dismiss show business as chic destitution, a party that dips its young in lies before eating them.

In Whatever's bloodied testimony, the city of glitz-gloom swallows lives, and the streets are littered with sick flesh, tar-pit stares. Hookers strut, peddling death, and everywhere the poison landscape ingests hope and spreads while no one is looking; city cancer. From "Hurting Inside" comes this merry shudder:

My schedule is murder.
I'm hurting inside.
Another new friend
Washes up in the tide.

I feast on misfortune.
I make a questionable friend.
I'm good on the full moon.
I'm a hip seventies trend.

I eat men for breakfast,
Drink women for lunch.
I soak in their essence.
It's my favorite punch.

It can't be stopped.
Can't be found.
To me, you're all barking dogs,
Put to sleep in my pound.

(chorus)

I'm hurting inside.

No one understands.
I'm a priceless addition,
Just lending a hand.

There's too many people,
Not enough love.
The world is a cliff.
I'm just a shove.

(end chorus)

I make a killing,
Transporting lost souls.
Some question the method,
But life's about goals.

My schedule is murder.
It's just my way.
Another lost dream.
Another fine day.

Not content to shoot at neon falsity, they plunge into deeper trauma with their pro-environmentalist "Black Sky," set to a fierce piano and raging vocal by Tutt.

The birds are hiding,
Bleeding in dead trees.
Clouds infected.
Bringing sick men to their knees.

Bad things are coming.
I can hear them on the stairs.
Coming down the hallway.
Death is in the air.

(chorus)

Black sky.
The clock has stopped for good.
Black sky.
Flames have reached the wood.

Black sky.
Bad man's coming with a smile.
He's hungry and he's empty
Be staying for a while.

But all is not nihilism. In the dulcet "Shade of a Blue Affair," the band changes emotional octaves, and Magurk sings a pleading ballad, backed only by Wall's melancholic guitar. On side three, the band's opening track is the sultry "Spanish Lies," a lulling Castillian sway.

The twenty songs, despite frequently scathing lyrics, never oppress melodic invention nor become brittle allegations. In past albums, Tutt and Magurk have deadened their own heartbeats with polemics and bile. In *Skin and Bones*, they don't pull any punches, but nor are they self-pitying and lost. What felt like thinly camouflaged star-malaise in past work is nowhere to be found on this album. Only perception and sleek production. And the usual tunesmithing that soars.

Maybe Bob D. was right, and the times truly are changing. This is not an album that could have been appreciated or forgiven a few years ago. But the way things are going, this is an album which fills an ominous vacancy.

FIVE STARS.

JOYCE HABER'S COLUMN.
LOS ANGELES TIMES.
FEBRUARY 4, 1978.

ROCKER's GAL PAL FOUND DEAD. Inga Johanneson, former wife of Whatever cofounder Rikki Tutt, was found hanged in her São Paolo, Brazil, prison cell. Prison officials say Johanneson committed suicide, using a belt. Tutt was unavailable for comment, but it is known he had tried to secure her release for several months. Whatever manager Leonard Lupo said the entire band was in shock and that Tutt is in seclusion, under doctor's supervision. Those close to Tutt have declined comment on the troubling coincidence that Johanneson's death occurred on his birthday.

FROM MY NOTES.
MINNEAPOLIS MEMORIAL STADIUM.
NOVEMBER 1979.

Rikki Tutt is bare-chested, staring at himself in the mirror. His band, Whatever, is in Minneapolis, opening for Latin rock group Malo, about to perform for a half-filled stadium. The days of SRO and number one albums have faded; this juxtaposed billing of differing musical styles places things in telling relief.

In recent years Whatever has suffered poor record sales and concert attendance. The group seems a casualty, at least partially, of disco music. In recent months, they were booed offstage when opening in Sarasota for KC and the Sunshine Band. Equally, they have had more than their share of genuine tragedy.

Their brilliant guitarist, G.G. Wall, died of a heroin overdose at a party in the Hollywood Hills, hosted by megagroup Seahorse. In further misfortune, drummer Stomp McGoo was jailed for sexual assault with a minor, though the girl later admitted she'd lied. Stomp rejoined the group for its ill-fated, disastrously unpopular double album *Skin and Bones*.

Wall was replaced for one tour by Snap Brown, who had played with Billy Preston, Blood, Sweat and Tears, the Eric Burdon Band, Howlin' Wolf, and was a session player in London and New York.

Brown left the group after eight months to form SHAKE, an enormous international concert draw which features upbeat dance music and colorful calypso costumes. The first album from SHAKE, *Boogie Bay*, is number one in America and Britain, and all compositions are Brown's.

Although Magurk and Tutt are openly critical of Brown's music, and aghast at Brown's status as a superstar, Brown never responds in the press. His solo album, *French Eyes,* has been ridiculed by Tutt and Magurk, who termed it *French Fries* and compared its musical instincts to fast food.

Meanwhile, Whatever remains on the road to pay spiraling legal expenses arising from their ongoing lawsuit with former manager Lenny Lupo, who they claim misappropriated royalties from their four albums. Lupo counterclaims it's fiction and that he was fired while still having a stake in all the band's past albums and future projects—if any.

"Invented sewage," says Tutt.

The group has also been sued by the parents of the fifteen-year-old girl who was beaten to death at their Athens concert in 1978. Greek police say private security hired by Whatever did nothing to help when the girl was attacked by an unruly crowd, unhappy that Whatever had to shorten their concert to only one hour when G.G. Wall collapsed on stage. It's hard to say whether the group has recovered from his overdose and death.

"I miss him," admits Tutt. "I don't know . . . maybe he was smart to get out. The world is falling asleep. No one cares. It's global torpor. I mean, a fucking actor is running for president."

"Pedestrian one at that," adds Magurk.

"Oh, is he walking now?" Tutt chews celery.

Magurk almost smiles.

"Something went wrong somewhere," he says. "I mean, Donna fucking Summer is number one. I went to visit my mother in Sarasota, and she has a Pet Rock."

Tutt sips a tequila shooter. "Maybe it's just your father. He's awfully quiet." He points. "Tell ya, people used to think we had something to say."

"Did we?" Magurk asks.

Tutt says nothing. Finishes the shooter.

"Ask the Bee Gees."

REUTERS NEWS SERVICE BULLETIN.
JANUARY 1, 1980. 1:15 A.M.

The rock band Whatever, a group which many fans and critics felt defined thinking man's rock and the intellectual cutting edge of early-seventies music, died in a fatal air crash last night outside Montreux, Switzerland.

The group had been returning to the United States after a New Year's Eve performance. All three members were killed when their private aircraft collided with snow-covered mountains.

The group's manager and original producer, Purdee Boots, reached in his Los Angeles offices, said, ". . . we're all in shock."

Swiss police investigators at the scene of the disaster said the interior of the crashed jet had been filled with the remains of religious objects.

"They must've been holding mass up there, or something," said Detective Claude Thoin. "Some kind of gloomy thing going on."

OPEN MIKE NIGHT. THE COMEDY STORE.
HOLLYWOOD, CALIFORNIA.
JANUARY 7, 1980. 11:50 P.M.

"So, here's my question . . .
    "Whatever?
    "I mean, talk about a band hitting its peak . . ."

FROM MY NOTES.
NEW YORK CITY.
JANUARY 15, 1980.

I'm writing this at three o'clock in the morning.

I was unable to complete this article as I'd hoped. I'd wanted to get into the childhood of each member, the matrices of their lives prior to forming Whatever. But they ran out of time.

I hope that what I've gathered, while fragmentary, compared to the red-blood dimension of real lives, and while tending toward mosaic, captures some of their lives and extraordinary gifts. Maybe it doesn't work. Maybe I won't either. Life. Just like Inga said.

When I arrived at the site of the fatal collision, my eye was caught by Swiss police plastic-bagging bits of religious objects found around the crash site. It was quite cold on the mountain and as the bodies were taken away by helicopter and I watched them lift off, I remembered the night I'd flown with the group, after a show they'd done at the Forum, in Los Angeles, five years ago.

We were on our way to Dallas, and I'd been around the

band long enough to earn their trust. That night they shared something enormously private with me: a ritual. They allowed me to witness it, though I was asked to take an oath that I'd never talk about what I'd seen.

Because of their untimely deaths, I feel I can now talk about it. I hope that instinct is right. This is what I remember:

The night we left LAX, ten minutes off the ground, Rikki Tutt put the band's 707 on autopilot. Then, he came into the back with the rest of the band. The cabin of the jet had no seats, only big throw pillows. It was almost 2 A.M.

Rikki put on a haunting album of a beautiful choir as it sang at Robert F. Kennedy's funeral service. The voices were filled with pain, and it had a strangely opiate effect on us.

Greg Magurk dimmed the small spotlights throughout the fuselage and the others lighted exactly one hundred candles of different sizes. I don't know what the number signified. But it was observed; somehow essential. They used candleholders from the innumerable churches Wall had robbed.

The five joined hands, closed eyes. Then, one by one, each asked for truth always to be there. Wax bled onto countless candleholders, marring the tarnished divinity like Christ's blood.

In my mind, I can still see Tutt and Magurk, cross-legged on pillows. More serious than I'd ever seen them, faces shadowed by candlelight, eyes seeming to await some onrushing fact of being.

G.G. Wall, Philip Zapata, and Stomp McGoo sat next to one another and joined hands with Greg and Rikki. All were exhausted from the show and in the flame-flicker, they glistened; Indian braves readying to meet the Great Spirit.

Truth.

It became their church. Their fortress in a city which had died.

In the end, maybe it was the seventies that did it. Who the

fuck knows. Magurk once told me that the " . . . meretricious bacteria of the American dream" offended him. "The sordid dealings and thieveries." He meant the music business. Washington. Democrats. Republicans. Bad music. Bad leaders.

A gravity without planet.

In music, Whatever felt the no-talents with vacuous product had ruined things. The money machine that co-opted art and used it like cheap gas ran the show.

Whatever came into mythic immensity and were enthroned in a world filled with barrels of oil worth $19.00, sold for $46.00. With peace accords that had ghostly half-lives. With meanings devoid.

I wonder if they knew the mountain was there. That they had seen enough; that the distance between what they valued and what the world had become took them before they even collided, buried in steel and snow.

It's a thought. But it doesn't change the fact that I miss them. That they should never have stopped mattering. That they were forgotten and replaced, entombed by the manic decay of a vain decade.

This is the last note I received from Greg and Rikki. They were in Amsterdam just before Christmas, working on the sound track for a low-budget film called *Void of Course*, about an American president who suffers a nervous break-down and no one notices. They were proud of their compositions. The note read:

Hola Fine Man,

We've thought about your suggestion of doing a book about the band. We're going to pass. Not even sure we want to do the long piece you envision in *Rolling Stone*. Bands shouldn't be novels. Or manifestos. Anyway we're over. Just an oldies-but-goodies tape.

Stomp says the seventies were just the sixties with worse hair. We say the seventies never even existed. We ought to know.

You thought we were about ideas, a certain Escher perception set to music. But it's just rock 'n' roll. Comes. Goes. Fades in the rearview.

Hey, man . . . we've been at this party long enough.

How about you?

DISMANTLING FORTRESS ARCHITECTURE
56   28 1 34   7

1980

BY DAVID J. SCHOW
AND CRAIG SPECTOR

1981

1982

1983

1984

He has played a trick on us. This Hitler, I think he'll remain with us until the end of our lives.

1985

—Heinz Krüger,
The Shattered House: A Youth in Germany

1986

1987

1988

1989

A child of six, he lives and breathes for the dead—family, friends and strangers, all rendered equal by machines that grind. Whispers suggest the sifted dust is used to form mortar (to build their prisons) or bake bread (to fool their bellies); such grand jokes are beyond his comprehension. To ghettos and ovens and mass graves he has borne witness. At his sooty face and blackened hands, his guards always laugh.

He amuses his masters with his pluck and skill. It is sufficient to earn him a new job, a new name, and to keep him alive. At least until he turns seven.

Hirohiko Ozawa's backbar mirror was a piece of Art Deco trash with layered glass that fractured his visage into many overlapping duplicates. The floor-to-ceiling windows of his tenth-floor executive suite commanded a splendid view across the Tiergarten. Outside, below, the Berlin Wall was coming down a chunk at a time. Adrift in a world of transparency, false images, and unexpected change, Hiro, a consummate lover of puns, could permit himself the luxury of reflection.

When it came to success and survival in the arena of corporate cutthroats, chameleonism was a vital knack, and Hiro had strategized his career according to the injunctions of constant change: make decisions of stone, on paper, then turn those edicts to water when the time was right. Turn one face as stocks rose; show another when they plummeted, and never let them see you sweat. Become famous, then feared, then infamous . . . then invisible. Work change as one man, and subterfuge as someone else. A great many people returned Hiro's stare from the mirror.

The Koramitsu Corporation had founded much of its success on one of Hiro's favorite conceits—the concept of the airtight alibi. In this world, when you said Koramitsu, you were talking software, and when Koramitsu desired bold strides in product design, they called upon the man they knew as Hirohiko Ozawa. Hence, the office, the perks, the view from on high. The mirror had been selected by Hiro, along with the aqua-colored clamshell monstrosity that was the wet bar. Hiro enjoyed vulgarities. He was a connoisseur of the garish, especially when it was bought and paid for by below-the-line nonentities.

Alone, arrogantly, he toasted himself. Not at all the humble, shielded, self-deprecating Japanese. Fuck all *that* noise.

Hiro was about to shape-shift again. From European werewolf to Asian weretiger, he fancied. A fortnight from today he would be in Hong Kong, assuming a brand-new post under the name of Seko Kobayashi . . . whose berth had been secured by the smuggling of certain top-secret microprocessor designs out of Koramitsu's German manufacturers, the Mohler Partners, GbH. The designs had been a mere bargaining chip—pardon the pun—in the predestined merger between Koramitsu and Mohler. But when the theft was discovered, the guy picking up the guilt tab and taking the big fall would be—wait for it!—"Hirohiko Ozawa."

Thanks to an à la carte subsidiary sale, Hiro had ensured that leverage against him via the pilfered tech would be impossible in six months. By then, the new boys in Hong Kong would *need* Seko Kobayashi to save their butts . . . and Seko had big plans for Hong Kong, prior to the end of the party there in 1997.

Beyond the glass, soundlessly, youngsters with nothing better to do were having a bash at the Wall. They teemed and swarmed, anxious to get their countenances recorded by news cameras during this fleeting moment of pocket history.

The Wall had been standing for most of Hiro's life, first as a barbed-wire barricade erected by the East German police in 1961. Berlin had always been a city of walls, dating back to 1735, when King Frederick William I threw a wall around the growing city to facilitate the collection of taxes. Historically, walls had unified Berliners, until this most infamous one, which was specifically intended to divide them into *ossis* and *wessis*.

Hiro knew of the scheme to greet the incoming ossis with "welcome funds" of 100 DM each, and did not plan on hanging around for the almost-guaranteed economic chaos that would ensue once the Western sector was flooded with Easterners who were, by Hiro's standards, fiscally subviable. East German currency was not convertible. The going black market exchange rate of 1 DM (West) per ten marks (East) would soon nose-dive to near–Weimar Republic levels, leaving many of the current celebrants of reunification poor and surly.

Either way, there would be long lines in front of the banks here, soon.

After forty years of economic miracle, the West had grown plumply complacent: a crowded market, highly specialized, hierarchical, dominated by silver-haired dinosaurs who were all about to get their rumps rudely shocked. The air was cold and depressing, tainted with what the locals called the "typical Communist smog" of burning coal and carbon monoxide, wafting westward. What was that line about knowing which way the wind blew?

Opportunism is a great productive force, claimed the editorials in *Der Spiegel*. It sure was, thought Hiro, who knew that in the USSR such "opportunism" had turned the entire bureaucracy inside out. If the Berlin Wall could be torn down, then all bets were off; a divided Deutschland had formerly been a notion as immutable as the monolithic stability of the Soviet Union.

At least *some* things never changed.

The 1980s had commenced with Polish tanks comminuting citizens like bugs, Soviet troops swarming into Afghanistan, and the insane American president, Ronald Reagan, lavishing $2.4 *trillion* on a militaristic spending spree. Now the decade was in twilight, and dominoes were falling all over Eastern Europe. This was what happened when a country committed its national identity to a war . . . and the enemy resigned. Time to split.

Hiro would slip away amid the pop of champagne corks and the gritty crunch of sledgehammers kissing the Wall. Soon bulldozers would crush the painted concrete into smaller and smaller particles, like that Western saying about making little ones out of big ones. Eventually, the Berlin Wall would become nothing more than souvenir fodder for tourists, and, inevitably, the smarter stone-breakers might realize that *any* fragment of convincingly spray-painted rock might cadge a few bucks from dupes on the Venice Beach boardwalk, a world away in California.

At the *peep* of a card swiping through the coded slot that accessed his office door, Hiro turned, still holding his drink. Guilt was not in his makeup, but surprise still was, and his gaze leapt to the Halliburton case on his desk, neatly packed with stolen barter.

The unannounced visitor was a short man, almost equal to Hiro's own height, though older—Hiro guessed his age at fifty-plus. A man whose neat gabardine suit and choice of neckties proclaimed efficiency and bespoke anonymity. A man like Hiro. He wore steel-rimmed spectacles, and his right hand was completely encased in a strange sleeve of matte black about the size of three videocassettes stacked together.

That was all Hiro could record before a small-caliber subsonic round pierced his aorta. He dropped his glass, gobbled blood, and weaved dumbly until all sensation drained from his legs. He piled up on the carpet.

The intruder looked toward the Halliburton case, then back to Hiro. Another silent bullet smashed in exactly where the man's eyes told it to go.

The next round, fired directly into Hiro's temple, had been chosen for its lack of residual velocity; it penetrated, expanded, and did not exit. It ricocheted madly around inside Hiro's skull, pureeing the secrets there, even though Hiro was already nerve-dead.

If Hiro's still-open eyes could have seen, they would have registered the reflections in the backbar mirror, now that the Halliburton case no longer blocked the view, of the distant Wall coming down at last, spectators and rabble-rousers capering over the ruins like army ants.

Kommandant smiles when he sees the boy leading the fire tenders in their horned leather headgear. It is a good morning for burning.

Troopers march the meat out in columns five deep and shoot them in full view of the pyres that will consume their remains. The boy watches the soot swirl skyward, as black as coal tar, flecked with ashen gray. No time, not anymore, for ovens or deceptive relocation schemes; if processing is not sped up, the Reich will drown in a stinking sea of Jewry.

A visiting SS officer from IV-B4 assesses the boy with limpid eyes, mistaking him at first for a mere sex toy. He asks about the nickname Kommandant has bestowed upon this small charge.

Kommandant's eyes offer the SS man an answer. Just

watch, they seem to say with a glimmer of pride. One like this comes along only once per war. Watch what my Aschmaus does.

The man known to the hotel staff as Herr Erich Barstow shuffled from one sofa to another in his suite, checking his Rolex too many times. Almost lunchtime. Almost time to fill that little hole in your life, he thought, by becoming a man of action.

He felt like a movie extra, thrust into the coveted star spotlight only to find that with such light comes unbearable heat. If your audience saw you sweat, you lost. If his guests, today, got the slightest whiff that Herr Erich Barstow was as fake as his rich man's wristwatch . . . well, the dead don't sweat, do they?

Gelft stood sentry near the foyer door. Soon there would come a knock, and Gelft would admit three men—all the genuine item, real as poison. And Erich Barstow would be onstage.

Gelft himself was a piece of work. Strapping, blond, possibly the most Aryan-looking Israeli Erich had yet seen in his new calling as ersatz spy. The Institute had set up this ambush, and seeded the costly suite (eight hundred American dollars a night, Erich marveled) with mini-microphones. They had also insisted on a bodyguard for Erich, a professional whose cool made Erich ache to scream *Cut!* from the nearest windowsill . . . though he was boundlessly thankful, as the time drew closer, that his big ally was right at hand.

Erich's Armani was a loaner whose tailored fit was a happy coincidence. Happy, he thought ruefully, wishing he could slip into character as easily as he had donned the jacket.

Today's lunchtime guest list was comprised of Koepp, the politician; Hessler, prime mover of the Phoenix

Foundation; and Jaeckel, the sole Nazi of vintage in this new Holy Trinity of National Socialism.

One drizzly morning in the spring of '43, Jaeckel's SS Einsatzgruppen hung two hundred butchered, headless Jews on meat hooks, with signs labeling them *Carne Kosher*, in mockery of Talmudic law. The execution of over 130,000 undesirables in Poland and Latvia had also been overseen by Jaeckel . . . and the heirs to the adjudicators of Nuremburg had spent the past four decades scratching and sniffing for him.

Herr Erich Barstow had found him. Finding men like Jaeckel was simple if one had the right connections, such as the Phoenix Foundation, based in America and headed by a man whose name had been legally changed to Karl Hessler.

Hessler's club was the sort that *always* welcomed sympathetic contributors with apparently bottomless bank accounts, if for no more modest purpose than reminding the world at large that the so-called Holocaust was a lie, the Final Solution a myth, and the scoop on crematoria and Zyklon-B just plain nonsense perpetrated by ZOG, the Zionist Occupation Government.

In bald fact, Jaeckel was an impotent relic, and Hessler, a clown with a bullhorn. Ernst Koepp was the prize. A man of dramatic presence, pull, and influence in the new Germany, Koepp had an almost-divine knack for glad-handing the grass roots—the Volk. He could make a logical speech about law and order sound like an equally logical return to the old-fashioned virtues of National Socialism . . . then make private jokes at the fund-raising smokers afterward about being able to smell a Jew from four blocks away. Koepp's brand of tunnel vision appealed to a worldwide audience hungry for swift, settling solutions; his platform translated easily, continents distant, into Molotoved churches in Orange County, and hate crimes from Brooklyn to Johannesburg to Bialystock.

Enter Erich Barstow, collaborator.

With the help of his nom de guerre and a PO box, Erich's racial credentials were provably impeccable. His identity as a Washington, D.C., lobbyist was considered invaluable by Hessler, who claimed a sixth sense about such things (as he confided to Erich in several of his egregious communiqués). Just in time, too—cash flow was urgently needed for safe houses, for arms, for publications, for Koepp's political war chest.

Enter, next, the polar opposite of the Phoenix Foundation: A group which called itself—this year, at least— the Institute. What *they* urgently needed was a "face" for a sting against Hessler and his cronies; not a hero, just someone to help deliver a small piece of the world from evil. The Institute knew how to exploit weak patches in human resolve. They knew how to make normal men say *yes* to playing spy.

Perhaps it was destiny that this man be Herr Erich Barstow today. Or perhaps it was one more grab at capturing a piece of his soul he'd always felt had wandered away while he wasn't paying attention.

Erich tried to harden his resolve. Fourteen floors below the windows of the hotel suite, twenty-eight miles of concrete and steel spanning twenty-eight oppressive years lay like the excavated spine of some extinct saurian monster. Eastern border guards schooled to shoot on sight now traded unaccustomed grins with their Western counterparts, all of them wondering what might happen next. History was built on moments like these, and the autumn air was charged. Something was coming . . . but what? What if the great beast down there suddenly awoke and decided to eat a few of the Lilliputians dancing on its sundered vertebrae?

Erich suffered a moment of flash panic. He wished he could be down there, among the celebrants. If he walked out now . . .

If only the dummkopfs at the Vienna Academy had given

that little schmuck painter a shot, way back when. No, it was more important that the world not suffer one more piss-poor artist, and thus require Erich to be here, now.

On the third knock, Gelft opened the door to the suite. Erich was still around a blind corner, by the window. He straightened all seams and prepared to do good.

Gelft was gone.

The door was being closed—quietly—by a smallish man in a neutral-colored gabardine suit. He smiled blankly at Erich. Glare from the overhead lights formed two equally blank white rectangles in the lenses of his glasses. As he smiled, he shot Erich twice in the solar plexus with some sort of soundless, baffled gun. Traumatic shock hit with textbook speed. Erich's knees unhinged, and he hit the floor.

He saw blood. From his own lungs. He could not speak. Or inhale.

The assassin's shooting hand was smothered in some boxy, black device. Still smiling, the man produced a tatter of ancient cloth and laid it gently over the pumping wounds in Erich's chest.

In the quarter second that made up the rest of his life, Erich recognized the shape, remembered it from an old photograph. Two overlapping triangles forming a six-pointed star. Then another dot of fire spat from the business end of the black box, taking him right between the eyebrows.

Exit Erich Barstow.

Kommandant's favorite anecdote wins the humor of his officers and makes him more human, a man from whom it is not so bad to take harsh orders. As he tells the tale, there is usually a toast or two as punctuation. And how his men marvel.

I saw a twitching nerve the size of a child, Kommandant usually begins. Nothing in its eyes but hunger and the will to survive.

That nails them.

You know what a nuisance they are to herd. Shepherds can only goad them so much. Row upon row of Jews, wailing and shrieking, waiting to see children get shot. But one zigzags out. The whore to whom it belonged starts making noise. It is running straight for me! The Schupos put her down with a rifle butt and prepare to pick off the little vermin before it can soil my coat or bite me on the ankle. No shot comes. My staff and I are in the line of fire. And just as it reaches me, it stops, clicks its heels together, and salutes. "Heil, Hitler!"

Never once does it look back at its mother. What can I say to this?

I let him watch. That morning we burned three thousand. The bone fragments alone would fill several trucks—trucks we did not have. A diesel mixer was requisitioned to grind the bone material to powder. To facilitate this, there were large steel balls inside the drum. They were crude, inefficient. The boy proves this to me by climbing into the drum and fetching out a skull. He combed warm embers and found gold that our cleanup crews had missed. When he removes the detritus, the powder is better, finer.

Some people tend pet rats. I had my nerve the size of a small Aschmaus. And as for the Judenflour, you all know what happened to that.

According to the crap in her bag, the bitch's name was Heike Strab. German name, but American documentation and passport. She was some sort of lawyer, but more importantly, she was obviously a race traitor. Stanz and Wolfie took turns raping her on the stone floor of the pump station. No one would hear them, thanks to the secret sanctity of their latest squat, and the din of the revelry scant meters from where they did the dirty.

Stanz and Wolfie had found all this make-happy about the Wall vomitus, and went on the prowl, spoiling to break a few skulls. Potential victims milled everywhere like narcotized zombies, mindlessly celebratory. It was like a riot, but without the fun. At least the alcohol was flowing, and mostly free for the snatch, so Stanz and Wolfie sniffed the throng for pussy and ultraviolence, not necessarily in that order.

They had found Heike, and her camera. Snapshot of a pair of skull-shaven Aryan punks: One mark. The cheapest memento on the open market. Right this way.

This lamb from abroad had no way of knowing that Stanz and Wolfie were not punks, or even post-punks. From their red-laced combat boots to their tribal tattoos, they were as rigidly uniformed as young men of their aspirations could ever hope to be. Both of them had actually read *Mein Kampf* board-to board (the same hardcover copy); it was the closest either of them would ever come to reading for pleasure. Wolfie packed an SS dagger in his boot (bragging that it was genuine, nicks and pits and all); he even slept wearing it. Apart from Wolfie being six months Stanz's junior and possessing unfortunately brown eyes (Stanz's were blue, just like the Führer's), the pair were fundamentally indistinguishable from each other, inseparable, two vital young skinheads programmed with a solo track of cryptofascist dogma. Mostly for them it was an excuse to cripple strangers and thieve food, but lately they had begun to feel the warm rumblings of some oncoming millennium, the way you can feel air acquire the heat of an oncoming sunrise before the light. Perhaps they *had* been doing something right, intuitively, all along.

In Heike Strab's faraway world of black and white and right and wrong, heroic policemen would helicopter in any moment to save her. A rescue would be effected, charges would be filed, and the boys would receive due punishment. In her world, the grade-school psych evaluations of this pair would become admissible evidence. If anyone cared to decipher the poor carbon on yellow flimsy, they would see innocuous, normal names for these two—names long-discarded—and labels for their disposition like *contumacious* and *depressed*. One might read that their weight was *subnormal*, their speech patterns *frenetic* and *circumstantial*, and their sleeping and eating patterns, *aberrant*. Conclusions? *Schizothymia*, *overanxiety*, and something no one could ever figure out, yet was named "Mixed Specific Development Disorder." The solution to the problem of young Stanz and Wolfie had a name, too: Ritalin SR, in twenty-milligram dosages that the boys ultimately sold to schoolkinder even younger than they were. In Heike Strab's world, such socially disaffiliated ingredients formed a recipe for an individual who might frequently toy with suicidal thoughts. Misfits, in Heike Strab's deluded worldview, nearly always self-destructed.

Suicide, however, would never be an option for Stanz or Wolfie unless they got drunk enough to kill each other accidentally. The world had spit them out, and they took every opportunity to spit right back. It was not their fault Heike Strab had made the mistake of eye contact. Heike's dynamic new learning experience was reinforced each time one cock or the other penetrated her anus.

How simple and pleasant, to take advantage of the town's mood tonight. Never mind how we *look*; we're all allies now, ja? Target acquisition was a snap in such a carnival atmosphere, and once they'd taped the gym sock into her face, this target was not too much hassle. A tightish fuck, for a Jewbitch.

Though weak and simpering, she had been so much more diverting than their original target, a sawed-off guy with mean little steel glasses, nakedly out of place in the melee as he tried to hustle from some hotel with a bag in each hand—an attaché case and one of those silver Halliburton jobs favored by drug dealers in the cinema. What had been in the cases? Money? Secrets? Tempting. But by the time the boys had dogged him, Wolfie had spotted the fair Heike and her camera, and while he and his partner Stanz enjoyed and even invited mayhem, they weren't *fags*.

Their current squat was unique. It permitted them both the privacy to turn Heike Strab's life to garbage and the wall-flower invisibility of being situated right in the heart of the partiers making merry at the Wall.

Built prior to the fall of Berlin, the flat, blockhouse-style structure had originally been intended as a pump station fed by the Landwehrkanal. Forty percent of the bricks used in its construction had arrived in Berlin by rail from the Rademacher Brickworks, which utilized crude ash supplied by the Mendhausen labor camp during the war.

One statistic that had always impressed Stanz and Wolfie was that some 367,000 Jews had contributed substantially to Mendhausen's output of ash.

Repeated and relentless night bombings had miraculously spared the edifice but left the city's water system damaged and unsanitary. So maddeningly constant was the rain of fire at the close of 1944 that the new station never got a chance to serve its people. Once the Iron Curtain demarcated East from West, the Wall had been built right through the existing structure. All petcocks had been sealed; all accesses, formidably bricked up.

With common bricks, this time.

One generation later, Stanz and Wolfie had broken and entered, and discovered a secret.

The rear of the station paralleled the riot of graffiti that was the Western face of the Wall. There was a gap of about two meters between the exterior of the station and the Wall itself. Someone had tried to tunnel through. An excavation in the back room wound down about ten feet, then eastward. Aboveground, past the width of the Wall, lay a two-hundred-yard no-man's-land of guards, dogs, barbed wire, nail-mesh mats, and batteries of self-firing weapons. The tunnelers had given up after about forty yards. The back room of the station was choked with debris—fill dirt, shattered rock, stones, and clumps of concrete. Obviously, some underground through-way for escapees had been planned, then abandoned. Similar mole-holes had worked, such as one that snaked up into an abandoned bakery and permitted fifty-seven people to escape in 1964 . . . until sentries began firing into the tunnel on the Eastern end. How old this forsaken operation might be, Stanz and Wolfie had no way of knowing, nor the intellectual equipment for guessing, or caring.

Wolfie glided back with an easy Bier score, and the boys calmed their lupine thirst while Heike drifted in and out of consciousness. They toasted her, toasted their choice of victim, toasted each other, and at last got pretty toasted themselves.

Sometime past the toll of midnight, a maul or hammer thudded heavily against the exterior of the abandoned and forgotten station. Stanz and Wolfie jolted awake, and shook their heads at each other sadly. This squat was destined to fall to dust, thanks to the Wall, and a new one would have to be hunted.

Before they went back to sleep, angry at their forthcoming eviction, they dragged what was left of Heike Strab into the back room by her heels. Stanz mashed her face into the dirt pile left by the tunnelers, then sat on the back of her head until she stopped breathing and went to meet her ancestors.

Then Wolfie opened her up with his fake SS dagger, and they began to tag the flaking stone walls with her blood.

A good burn is three hundred or so, stacked young to old and fat to thin, to make the fires run hot enough to forge steel.

Wiggling the jawbone of one of yesterday's skulls, Aschmaus mimes speech for the amusement of Kommandant.

He finds many glass eyes and starts a collection. More browns, here, than anything else.

Aschmaus will mock them all if it means he is allowed to breathe and eat until one more sunrise. He can force Mama's face to fade from his memory. He blocks out the sounds of strangers en route to Heaven. He erases their expressions, building walls inside his head, just like another hobby, a secret one . . . the only private thing he has.

Sometimes, after Kommandant's boots are off and the Gramophone plays, Aschmaus is permitted a quarter-moon of sausage or an apple core from the table of his master. He sits at the feet of Kommandant and sometimes dozes. The light sleep allows him to imagine being spirited away by the music, to float high above the guards like a forgotten bit of ash, out of sight of the towers, and beyond the pyres forever.

Aschmaus builds his walls, and collects his eyes, and floats when he can. Sunrise always comes.

Nearly a century earlier, in 1888, Jack the Ripper had also murdered two in one day. His murders of East End prostitutes Catherine "Kate" Eddowes and Elizabeth "Long Liz" Stride had become notorious as his "Double Event."

Clouder reflected upon his own busy morning, and wondered if, a hundred years from today, the scrutiny of history and hindsight would yield up motives, connections, irrefutable theories . . . all the disposable tripe that made for many a nonfiction best-seller, and lent armchair Sherlockians a reason to keep using air. Serial killer books were big right now.

The "connection" part was a near-given. While Clouder had employed two different handguns to assassinate his two outwardly unrelated targets, the chilly, deliberative style he brought to all his work might become worthy of the sort of editorial comment that would flag the jobs as contract hits or execution-style murders. Which was all the evidence anyone would ever have to chew over. Which was precisely why Clouder had chosen this methodology. He never left accidental clues, always left purposeful voids—something on which second-rate intellects could nibble, eagerly, endlessly. Uselessly.

He hung up his topcoat in the foyer and blotted his face lightly with the tip of his scarf—a natty affectation he had never bothered to ponder. Perhaps it was a luck gesture.

"Hirohiko Ozawa" had not seemed surprised to be killed, and because of this, Clouder felt a fleeting kinship with the man. It was business, a risk Herr Ozawa had ventured with the potential consequences in clear sight. The hit had been a snack for Clouder.

"Erich Barstow," on the other hand, had behaved as though Clouder's visit was the biggest surprise of his truncated life. For Clouder, this second hit had left a spoiled taste on his intellectual palate all afternoon. As he fed the contents of the file jacket on Herr Ozawa to the shredder, and thence to his fireplace, Clouder brewed strong tea in the Russian fashion and left a long spoon in the glass as a heat sink, to cool it. When it came to the disposal of the file on Herr Barstow, Clouder uncharacteristically flipped through it one last time. It was thicker than the file summing up Ozawa's history and habits.

Amateurs should never play the only international game that matters. What had inspired the creation of the man Clouder had killed as Erich Barstow?

The folder was fattened by a pamphlet-style book titled *Holocaust Hoax!* It had been published—typos, fingerprinty layout, and all—by the Phoenix Foundation in 1983, three years before an abused copy had been purchased on a whim by a Georgetown University history teacher named Eric Greene.

Holocaust Hoax! was a transparently primal, foamingly

anti-intellectual rant. Its proud author, Karl Hessler, was prominently pictured with an extensive though modest bio of his accomplishments. Clouder had only to look at the photo of Hessler to infer the man's sheer baseness and fanaticism: He was sloppy and flabby, with a fetish for uniforms; low cunning smoldered from his eyes. Exactly the cartoon real Nazis would never condone . . . except where financial contributions were concerned. Clouder dropped the booklet next to the remainder of the file.

Eric Greene's backstory was as depressingly thin and predictable as Hessler's motives. His mother had been a Gentile who died when Greene was six. His father had been flattened by a thromboembolism the size of a kosher salami. Finding himself the de facto patriarch of the bloodline, Eric began to seek "meaning" in his life.

Clouder rolled his eyes. Never content, are the drab ones, to teach history and remain good consumers. On the other hand, Greene had been reminded of his own mortality and acted to change the course of his existence. Perhaps there had been a mote of depth to the man.

The collision between Greene and *Holocaust Hoax!* appeared random. It was the sole accidental confluence of the chain of events Clouder had recently terminated with gunfire. Greene's passions had been ignited by Hessler's diatribe, so perhaps the booklet had achieved some good.

Using a fake name and a mail drop, Greene had cast a line into the turbid waters of intrigue and reeled Hessler closer—not surprisingly, given Hessler's obvious hunger. Through expedient lies and judicious use of the blind spots provided by long-distance contact, Greene was able to present himself as "Erich Barstow" . . . Washington lobbyist, closet Nazi, sympathetic ear, and Karl Hessler's newest benefactor and best friend.

Clouder sipped his tea and paged forward. Once Greene had Hessler's ear, he attracted the notice of the Institute. The

Institute had come forward and filled in a few gaps regarding the family bloodline.

Greene's father, it turned out, had survived Auschwitz and come to America as a displaced person in 1948. Clouder shook his head. The background pull on Greene's family was shallow, trivial. But the Institute people had a hole card—a photograph, which they produced for Greene's scrutiny at precisely the right moment.

Mother and child, anonymous Krakow street; little boy waving as Mama holds him up. Stitched on the sleeves of both, a crude, six-pointed star of cloth.

Clouder only had a blurry facsimile of the photo. He read the mother as careworn but hopeful. She and the child were smiling, though the circumstances seemed bleak. In an instant he felt a twinge, a trace memory, something like the recognition Greene must have felt when the Institute had ambushed him with this picture.

Eric Greene had seen his father's face in the boy. His father had made it out of a death camp. His grandmother, the young, proud woman in the photo, had not . . . but here she was, waving hello to the grandson she would never hold or know.

Clouder fed the facsimile of the photo into the shredder.

The timing was more critical than Eric Greene ever could have suspected. Hessler phoned, brimming over with some exciting project for which the new Reich would be honored to request the participation of "Erich Barstow." Almost simultaneously, the Institute let Greene know they needed a neo-Nazi "face" for their latest sting operation. Past and future, history and reality had all rammed together for Eric Greene in that moment, and he had agreed, perhaps impulsively, to play hero.

The rest of the jacket was insignificant. Greene had a brown-eyed Hausfrau back in Georgetown named Ellen Rachel. No children. His tenure was up for review at the school. No pets.

Clouder cleaned up the hearth with a small whisk broom once he had consigned the rest of the "Erich Barstow" jacket to the fire. He felt mild annoyance. Greene had sought to plug a gap in his spiritual life; silly to blame him for anything, since the man had never known how exposed he had been all along. Reconsidering Greene's history, now, had opened a similar chasm in Clouder's calm. Never a good idea, he reflected, to feel involved with the targets.

Greene was banal and hopeless. He was the *late* Herr Greene.

Clouder passed from his living room to his billiards room. Both were identical in configuration, separated by an archway that had been a nonsupporting wall. Clouder's residence had once been the east wing of a middle-income apartment warren erected on postwar rubble as a filing cabinet for human beings—mirror-image rooms ranked with military monotony. After a flurry of rezoning, Clouder moved in along with upscale refurbishments, occupying two apartments now fused into one.

Only bills were mailed here, addressed to a name other than Clouder's. Technically, Clouder had not possessed a traceable name for decades, only a pack of identities shuffled and discarded at will. Soon, there would no longer be a distinction between East and West; Clouder might have to change the way he return-addressed his bills. They were calling it Reunification. Now it could all be "Germany" again. Past the jubilation of the crumbling Wall waited all manner of nasty ghosts from the past. Once reunified, how else might the reborn Germany become like the old?

The realization hit Clouder like tea leaves on the tongue; mentally brackish. Had Eric Greene been conned into sacrificing his life by the dolts at the Institute?

The Institute people had found a well-intentioned but ignorant Jew. They had leveraged his distaste for Nazis with exactly the right pep talk. They had strategically advantaged his family's past, and, when the time came, shoveled him onto the firing line.

The Institute was after something else, and Eric Greene had been a pawn to play.

Clouder made more tea. He always chose a new glass for each refill. He was fastidious in small rituals. It was a fairly quick puzzle exercise to dope out what had happened backstage, before his second assignment of the morning.

Clouder's data pull on Greene/Barstow had come from Die Schwarze Spinne, a puppet-master conference of new Nazis who specialized in stringing along outmoded warhorses like Hessler's Phoenix Foundation, in the hope that the Ultimate Destiny of that gang of political mummies would include growing up and getting real. The go-between had been a double agent from Die Schwarze Spinne, code-named "Gelft."

That would be the man to whom Clouder had given a curt nod, as the man opened the door and stepped out . . . so Clouder could step in, and close the door, and kill Eric Greene and Erich Barstow with the same shots. Gelft had probably read the same deep background on Greene that Clouder was now destroying.

Gelft was an interesting game piece. Clouder enjoyed deduction.

The fair-haired Gelft had invested enough time ducking bullets and catching the desert sun in the Sinai to pass as a card-carrying member of the Mossad Aliyah Beth, and thus penetrate the American Embassy in Berlin . . . that is, West Berlin. He could just as easily pass as German; his accent, as Dutch. By exploiting contacts made at the embassy, Gelft could alert the Institute to a Nazi powwow, which had caused the Institute summarily to send "Erich Barstow" to slaughter. The Institute would interpret Greene's instantaneous exposure not as a leak, but as a slap in the face. A warning. The Institute had been in bed with the Arabs ever since the manufactured petrol crises of the early 1970s, and, to Clouder's recollection, the Arabs had never been overly fond of the Mossad. The Greene sting had been necessarily flimsy because assisting Israel could never bear too obviously high a price tag.

As a wild card in this international deck, Gelft (or however he was called in the real world) was fraught with inscrutability and freighted with ghost details—ephemeral facts that cumulated to fog. Given the major premise that Eric Greene was a Jew masquerading as a Nazi, and the minor premise that Gelft could just as well be working for either side, a syllogist would conclude that if Greene had been targeted for any motive other than a neatening of the international deck (like whacking the cards to make their edges true up) . . . then something was missing. An ingredient Clouder could not yet perceive; some concealed advantage that might come into play late in the game.

It might be stimulating to interfere on purpose, given what Clouder already knew or could deduce. He could affect the outcome of short-term future events. Otherwise, the Double Event that used up most of his morning would hold no satisfaction for him at all. Killing was not enough, anymore.

Not a sacrifice, Clouder concluded. More typically of Institute ops, Eric Greene had become a victim of budget.

Satisfied that his morning's work was now not such a mystery, Clouder phoned a secure night line in Zurich to confirm that two deposits had been posted to his private accounts as of closing time, this date. Thanks to a device called a Solander Box, Clouder had one of the "hardest" telephone lines in Europe. Any attempt at a trace or tap would be routed to random numbers all over the city; a multiplicity of unknown names behind which Clouder could remain safe. Too bad Eric Greene had lacked such a parachute, such a spare persona.

The special silencer Clouder had employed this morning

had been custom-built to swaddle a broad assortment of revolvers or autos. Its wing-nut port was designed to lock any barrel into thick exit baffles. As Clouder was fond of thinking, *the bang jumps from the chamber, not the muzzle.* All it took was a microsecond, but it was the *loudest* microsecond of the whole process of discharging a firearm. He told this to the gunsmith who fabricated the silencer. Barrel silencers, both men knew, were a conceit of popular cinema. Clouder's silencer, similar to a camera blimp, was the real deal. Along with both job guns and the attaché case that had contained them, it had been mashed into a characterless cube of scrap by the big junk compactors near the Berlin Wall, where a lot of demolition would be taking place for a good long while. Clouder regretted the loss of the silencer, because it was the work of an artisan, an exemplar of a craftsmanship the New Germany had lost sight of.

But since Clouder was a methodical man, he had already ordered two more just like it.

Clouder's home was riddled with hidey-holes for such things as weapons and silencers and all manner of currency and ID. Some were simple safes, or sliding-panel compartments sophisticated enough to outfox any snoop wearing a uniform. Others were capable of withstanding multiband scanning or nuclear attack . . . not that flying missiles were much of a downside possibility, given the cheerful, chaotic tone prevalent in the newspapers and on TV.

After stashing the Halliburton case from the Hirohiko Ozawa job in the boot of a planted Mercedes, Clouder had come home empty-handed. Lacking a new contract, and not wanting the phantom of Eric Greene spoiling the rest of the day, he thought about die Berliner Mauer. He had walked through some of the crowd assembled for its deconstruction. He had felt no sense of community.

Berlin, "sister city" to Los Angeles as Cannes was to Beverly Hills, was once again girding to act as the capital for a unified Germany. American military—250,000 strong during the height of deployment in 1987—would be packing their bags, and the historic "Berlin Brigade," commanded by Colonel Alfred W. Baker, would be the first to leave during this massive drawdown. The Brigade would vacate offices formerly used by the Luftwaffe, in an East German building erected for Field Marshall Hermann Goering—until recently, the sole U.S. base behind enemy lines.

Clouder's admiration for Colonel Baker was twofold; first, there was boundless respect for the man's ability to re-create himself from the ground up. In 1969, Baker had been blown apart by a satchel full of Viet Cong explosives. His bones sundered as the blast hurled him twenty feet into the air; he landed with half his face ripped away and his back broken in two places. Medics abandoned him in a triage section. When a priest began giving him last rites, Baker spat out bits of teeth and shredded gums to say, "Get the fuck away. I'm not Catholic, and I'm not going to die."

The second reason was something Baker had said as a young lieutenant assigned to patrol East Berlin in the early 1960s, words that Clouder had memorized because they not only spoke to a capacity deep inside him, a space in his soul long dormant and almost forgotten, but also summed up the bisected, bleeding place the city had become then: "It was like looking into day on one side and night on the other, like living in sunshine while looking into a storm. As I drove around, people would sometimes signal, *'Don't forget us.'*"

Something had been forgotten. Something was missing. That was why Eric Greene's face kept nagging Clouder. An American Jew with a hole in his past had become a pretend Nazi with a hole in his brain. Some vital truth had been mis-placed. Not overlooked; Clouder was too painstaking to be sloppy. It was like the name of a popular song just near the tip of the tongue—teasing, seductive, elusive.

Clouder meditated in an abrasively hot needle shower,

and lay down naked, to nap. Counting prep for the morning's work, he had been awake for eighteen hours. Before he closed his eyes he turned on his stereo. Now it was Mahler time.

The tuneless song mumbled by the Ash and Death Brigades holds hope neither for victim nor tormentor:

> Hey, SOB, hey, SOB,
> Why did you give birth to me?
> Such a life, such a life;
> Better if you had a miscarriage.

Days become weeks, become months, metered out in sweat and hunger, stench and dread. The superstitious wisdom of dead Mama's God means nothing to a boy born into a world of pogroms and ghettos. He knows no justice or meaning, family or tribe. There is no "God" here.

The new eye he finds for his collection is perfect blue, like the Führer's, blue like the sky. It will watch over him, as the others sense his power and avert their gaze. They are already corpses, all of them, rough fuel for flames. But he is Aschmaus, king of the liars, and he will always find a way to survive.

Henri startled awake, in a nightmare sweat, the strains of dreamed music fading, to be replaced by a headache. So real, the dreams, so narcotic, but no match for the ringing phone. He tried to locate his glasses, his robe, his composure, in time to hear the bad news. Calls were infrequent, and calls like this one, potent enough to slap the mist from his brain, if not the crust from his eyes.

Though his phone was connected to an answering machine (a genuflection to encroaching technology), Henri did not believe in intermediaries. He nodded to himself and hummed monosyllables to indicate he was paying attention.

The Black Spider was spinning dark webs again. An Institute-sponsored grab had been sabotaged; an American friendly, killed. Henri's mouth drew taut, a reflex too familiar and never comfortable. One less for our side.

Then, the rest: A convocation had been called. Henri was to note the address. Tonight, at 33 Gelderstrasse, players would rally to savor some new proof that the old Reich was not all dust and ashes.

Henri rang off and worked on ways to deflect his oncoming headache. He felt destabilized and hung over.

He was a small man of common cut, with hair that was vibrantly white and a posture unbent by time, the sort of person who amortized his regrets by aiming high at his aspirations. His hands were deft and capable; his eyes, unclouded. Henri saw things clearly. He had watched the Wall come down, mostly on television, and his opinion of the coming Reunification was guarded.

Holes were being kicked in the Brandenburg Gate. Stasi guards and Berliner Polizei were seen drinking in public, as a jolly mob danced on the dividing line between Then and Now.

Whenever Henri heard talk of the past, the scar on the inside of his left forearm would pulse, as though it was trying to communicate something arcane and revelatory. It was a puckered groove about three inches long, barely whiter than the unviolated flesh surrounding it. Henri preferred this bent serpent of scar tissue to the number that had once been tattooed there. He had performed his own anesthesia and carved the meat himself, using a sterilized straight razor. It had hurt very much. Henri had been blessed with a high tolerance for pain, ever since childhood.

He was alive. According to the phone call, a foreigner named Eric Greene was dead. Henri wondered about Herr

Greene's tolerance for pain. He had no doubt that Eric Greene had been young, and brave . . . but he had never worn a cloth star, nor borne a number, and probably had never had to make cannibalistic choices to survive.

The code name for Henri's phone source was "Doppelgänger." Thanks to modern electronics, not even timbre of voice could be trusted, and it was of technology Doppelgänger had also spoken.

The meeting at 33 Gelderstrasse was coalescing around some stolen bit of hi-tech which had cost yet another life. To a man, those who were to gather there would count anyone with Henri's convictions as their most hated enemy.

Henri knew the address—a sprawl of granite situated midway between Checkpoint Charlie and the Topographie des Terrors, where the crimes of the Fatherland were enshrined in the husk of the former headquarters of the Gestapo. Hosting tonight's affair would be the fairest-haired of New Germany's politicos, Ernst Koepp, who had inherited the formidable house from his father, and so could hold court with an equidistant vantage of the world past and the world to come.

Such a chance, to straddle the past and the future, was one Henri did not want to miss.

In the East German state of Saxony, a dissident pastor-turned–Interior Minister named Heinz Eggert was getting tough. Eggert had formulated the idea of an elite police unit to deal especially with neo-Nazis and right-wing violence; soon his Soko REX, or "special commission for right-wing extremism," would be cleaning up Saxony's crime stats in a fashion designed to impress the entire planet. Other states, such as Brandenburg, were said to be considering the deployment of similar units.

Meanwhile, the Kremlin and the Americans and the Mossad shot for the big, splashy scores: the Mengeles, the Barbies, the Eichmanns, the fish capable of garnering the hottest international press, and the fattest appropriations.

While Eggert waited for all Germans to evolve, and while the higher-profile hunters of Nazi big game drew all the best reviews, between them existed Henri, right now, doing something about all this injustice, today, but unobtrusively. Ostentation and public accolades were both phobic to him.

Henri usually kept his television set turned on, sound down. It was an outmoded tube model, and reception was chancy with no cable hookup. Visual noise, not resolution, was the object. Occasionally he paid attention to the news. Just now he could see the excitement outside, trapped and boxed into his snowy screen—rapture reduced to spectacle.

The parade of color and motion on the silent television provided nondemanding companionship, and helped wall away the crippling toxins that lived in his mind. He could shave the number from his forearm, but never from the inside of his head. Crossing the room to a bookshelf, he drew out a cloth edition of *Mein Kampf*—illegal to sell, he knew, but not to own. The dust on the shelf reassured him nothing had been disturbed since the last time he had used the book. Nestled within the thickness of its gutted pages was a keypad. Henri entered his number: 56281347.

The chamber hidden behind the sliding bookcase was the width of two opposing desks, with room for a chair between them—a *small* chair—and headroom low enough to brush against Henri's hair when he sat down. It was fully cluttered with Henri's burden of proof—his sociopolitical research and bulging files. Tucked away in his computer database were many of the names who would show up at Koepp's house tonight. Like a detective plotting a drug bust, Henri knew how bad these men were. So did they. He had proof. They had protection. The trick, which never changed, was to catch them hot: right place, right time.

From a drawer he lifted a pistol he had never fired. It was a relic of the old war and a reminder of his hijacked youth. Henri utilized the gun, on occasion, to pry cooperation from men who were evil. The weapon was for sweeping up, not scoring kills; to settle old debts, not inspire new ones. That was why the Institute would forever call on Henri— their think-tankers already knew that business didn't matter, nor did politics. For Henri, it was all personal, and there were not many like Henri left. Whenever the Institute signaled, Henri would unleash himself as a bloodhound. It was cleaner, left a clear trail of blame, and made for less paperwork.

The part Henri's exploiters would never realize (and, in fact, did not give un verdammt about) was that Henri, to his own mind, could never bring down enough of the enemy to balance any set of scales. If he could burn the guilty ones, a hundred per day, the fire would last a century beyond the end of his life.

Bitterly, he wondered how many glass eyes he might reap from those cinders.

The monocular TV screen showed him his fellow citizens all coming gloriously unglued. The world had changed in a matter of days.

The hegira of East Berliners to Hungary and Czechoslovakia had resulted in demonstrations in Leipzig and Dresden. It all came to a head in the Alexanderplatz: three-quarters of a million people causing the Politburo stalwarts to blush and sweat like weight lifters, as they promised change and tried to buy time.

Two days ago the Reissepass law had been announced. For the first time in forty years, exit visas would permit the *ossis* to visit the Western sector, starting the following morning. Simple. Profound.

Except that Party publicist Gunter Shabowsky had only lent the new law a cursory skim, while en route by limousine to a TV press conference. When asked *when* the law would go into effect, Shabowsky riffled his paperwork and, finding no answer, told the journalists and live cameras what sounded best:

As far as he knew, *immediately*.

At every gate from the Reichstag down to Checkpoint Charlie, they massed by the tens of thousands, demanding the right to pass . . . fourteen hours early. The Tinterpisser Burokrats were completely blindsided, while the border guards at the Borhomler Street crossing wondered if they should start shooting everyone.

Finally, it was a lean, alcelaphine Stasi captain named Helmut Stossi who was the first to open his gates, and begin the flood tide that would eventually topple the Iron Curtain . . . without a shot fired, a world-shaking result of what was essentially a clerical error.

Captain Stossi wondered, aloud and touchingly, just why he had been standing at that gate for the last twenty years. Henri had seen him, on television, the one man who had made a difference through action.

Henri despised predictability.

He decided to take the gun with him to the party.

The computer chip that had cost Hirohiko Ozawa his multi-form life resembled a silicon centipede with jutting, tine-like legs of copper. The slim box that contained it in a nest of antistatic foam was in Hoff's breast pocket; the way Hoff paranoiacally patted himself down between bites and after each sip of wine confirmed for Ernst Koepp that the man was a twitch, unstable, too furtive even for a mad scientist.

But Hoff was undeniably a maestro in the orchestration of data, in the careful coaxing of machines; in the alien (to Koepp) subworld of optical drives and gigabytes and superprocessors, Hoff could make music. Hoff knew how to interpret the songs of a billion lifetimes, all distilled to incomprehensible chains of zeros and ones, all stored in one one-hundredth the area of the head of a pin.

Hoff had his job and was happy in his work. Koepp's job, this night, was to wed Hoff's technological sorcery to the half-century-old ideal of a Thousand Year Reich . . . and make the marriage work.

At the foot of the table, Karl Hessler was busy being seen and sucking up. Hessler had always reminded Koepp of a blowfish, and he had wanted to shoot the fat man himself after that abortive, Institute-sponsored show-and-tell. Getting nailed in the down-market company of the Phoenix Foundation and crusty old sieg-heilers like Jaeckel inside a soft-target hotel could only wreak detrimental effects on Koepp's image-building.

Tonight, he had mandated the meeting place: The Gelderstrasse manse boasted crenellated battlements; a gated stone wall bespoke its aristocratic heritage. It was one of the few private residences not leveled by Allied bombs, and it was rumored that Prince Albert of Prussia had once kept a mistress there. Such history pleased Koepp, whether it was true or not. The residence had been handed down to him by his father, a much-valued Party member who had liberated it from the previous tenant, a well-to-do glassmaker named Schulman. The only thing Koepp knew about Herr Schulman was that he had gone flying up a smokestack at Treblinka . . . that, and Herr Schulman's Big Secret.

In the heady days prior to the Kristellnacht, Herr Schulman (clever Hebrew that he was) had dug out a sec- ondary cellar and provisioned it as a hiding place spacious enough to sustain his family—he had fathered six children— for several weeks. A sliding door, veneered to appear as a fea- tureless wall of plaster, accessed the room, which was laid out like a rail flat at six by sixteen meters, and incorporated cook- ing and sanitation facilities—the vents for which had been the fatal giveaway. Koepp knew well the rule about being careful when it came to what billowed from one's flue, and had eradicated all exterior evidence of the chamber's existence years ago, beyond all decent memory. He had fed in modern wiring and track lighting and air filtration. Up until this historic night, Koepp had used the space primarily as a gallery for his oil canvases—Impressionists, a few pre-Raphaelites, and several Klees—another legacy from Papa Koepp, the deserving Party man.

Security was handled by Koepp's handpicked staff, spearheaded by two pewter-eyed pups named Rudi and Klaus, both wired as tight as a Gestapo smile. Inside this house, Koepp could allow fools like Hessler and antiques like Jaeckel the courtesy of dismissive indulgence, and let his hair down among the men who were the true hope for a restored Reich.

Up table were Heidrick and Drexler, aggressive, third-generation National Socialists from the United States. At Koepp's right hand was Volmer Saphire, in from Stuttgart. Saphire was Koepp's first choice for vice chancellor, when the time came. To Koepp's left was Biermann, who, despite his comical name, was the best-case argument for a modern-day Göering Koepp could summon; not so much a man as a big, solid *thing*, cold and unyielding, a wall of rock. Then Hoff, all frizzy hair and frazzled thoughts and fractured composure, fretting through the dessert course and afire with the nearly sexual thoughts concerning what he could make his beloved computer chip do. Past him, Stohler, newly returned from Argentina just two days prior to his sixty-ninth birthday. Then there was Conrad Bleuel, a master prestidigitator of identity who had been wooed by the Palestinians the moment the Middle East replaced Vietnam as the hot spot of the seventies. Past him sat Esslin and Zille, both present by dint of untainted postwar identities supplied courtesy of the American CIA, in a heartwarming display of morality-free barter. Then came the briefcase brigade: Adenauer, Gelft, and

Broger, respectively representing the Order, Die Schwarze Spinne, and the Aryan Nation. Directly across from Koepp sat his boyhood friend (and current lover) Werner Uedey.

This, reflected Koepp, was what Reinhard Heydrich must have felt like, presiding over Wannsee—a conference of dedicated men, some more reliable than others, some better at their jobs than the men next to them, some simply better men, but all of them aimed at a common accord, sipping good cognac, changing the world.

Adenauer called for a toast in remembrance of the Phantom Nazi, and Koepp listened while the legend was recited, for those who had not yet caught up.

According to the story, the Phantom Nazi was a key player in the waking hours of the Kampfbund, a man so over-looked by scholarly history that he now bore all the seductive mystique of a subordinate Kennedy assassin. Shortly follow-ing the Beer Hall Putsch, the Phantom Nazi had staged a phony attempt on the Gefreiter's life in Munich—meticu-lously planned, and timed to raise public consciousness. All it had taken was a single gunshot, fired from a hidden van-tage in the Feldherrnhalle. A riot between Nazis and police ensued, and the rest was history they all knew. The man who had been instrumental in Hitler's rise to dominance had never claimed credit, nor enjoyed status in the Third Reich. Having humbly worked a miracle for the good of Germany, he had chosen to remain invisible for all time. Admirable. Glasses clinked.

At the opposite end of the table, Hessler noisily pro-posed some counter-toast Koepp felt comfortable ignoring. Instead, he monitored the varying degrees of enthusiasm around the table, and gauged the plaudits given the Phantom Nazi to bode well for the presentation he had planned, which would begin as soon as the requisite form of stinking cigars and antiseptic brandy could be dispensed with.

When it was time to make the pitch, Koepp tapped his

table knife against a water glass. Hessler, as usual, was the last to fall silent.

While they sat, feasting, observed Koepp, a new Germany was taking shape outside. Agreements were murmured all around.

It was a revolution. Not just in Germany, but all over the world. The not-so-superpowers were doomed. Communism would implode from its own top-heaviness. Gangsters would hold sway, Ivan in pinstripe, as America the long-distance runner wheezed and wobbled and finally toppled. From the void would issue chaos, inflation, black-market rule. The resultant feeding frenzy would leave the rest of the globe on the slave auction block. As the Zionists hatched futile plots, the Mideast would sunder, and China would rouse from its Maoist coma. The world would cry out for order at any price, and welcome the first iron hand that could guide it. They would be ready.

Hearty assent, from the group, as Koepp now spoke of the *new* blitzkriegs. He invoked the technological gris-gris of computers, of internets, of information superhighways, of fiber-optic filaments through which any security, anywhere, could be penetrated. Of how the new assaults would be fast, fluid, mutable, like viruses overwhelming nations before a single shot could be fired, or missile retargeted. Resistance? Topple it from within. Make bank accounts evaporate with a phone call. Make the enemy disappear by turning them into non-persons with a salvo of keystrokes simpler than playing "Chopsticks" on the piano.

Hoff bobbed his skull in approval, particularly when Koepp used the chrome-plated, mathematically romantic buzzwords. There were no walkouts.

Outside the battlements of 33 Gelderstrasse, Berliners were drunkenly partying on behalf of German rebirth. This, too, fit and seemed apt.

Koepp put on his very best Party face and rose to lead his

fellow Soldaten downstairs, where a better future awaited them all.

The front bell rang just late enough to turn Rudi's edginess to hostility. His partner Klaus was already deep into full-blown pique. Neither enjoyed Herr Koepp's proper, political shindigs, because Germany had always been the most caste-conscious of countries, and the coven of Nazis who had just spent two hours guzzling and gorging and farting in the dining room reminded these two young aspirants that they were not yet Party members, did not rate Party privileges. Not yet.

Tonight, they walked through their roles as Koepp's most trusted adjutants, sneaking swift gulps of schnapps and bitching with minty breath about the ways they could become point men in the new Fourth Reich, if only Koepp would grant them a window.

The bell sounded just as Koepp was leading his guests to the wine cellar for the evening's members-only divertissements. Instead of relaxing a notch, Rudi and Klaus probably had to deal now with some inebriated Scheisskopf from the revel outside. They could pitch the interloper back to the mob, or—Klaus caught the chilly sparkle in Rudi's eye—perhaps they could escort him to where the cars were parked and pummel the grease out of him, wholesale.

Either way, the entertainment prospects for the evening were looking up.

Gelft drew a deep and careful breath, showing no outward sign of reaction or shock. The visitor standing on Koepp's threshold was of small stature and bookish mien, like an accountant, a man of no abrasive surface detail. He seemed to know where he was; he had come here on purpose. He exuded friendliness and solicited cooperation. Peter Kurten, the Dusseldorf Vampire, had been a man such as this—smartly dressed, tranquil, polite, even deferential . . .

. . . rapist, arsonist, a murderer who loved bestiality and killed men, women, children, animals, *anything*, using hammer, knife, scissors, and garrote, not that he favored those tools specifically. He killed with whatever came to hand and did the job. Kurten had committed the first of his ghastly crimes and shocked all of Germany the same year as Hitler's Beer Hall Putsch.

The man in the doorway smiled, inquired, acted formal. Rudi backstopped Klaus; neither of them was smiling.

Just yesterday, Gelft and this guest had passed each other, Gelft exiting, the other man entering to blow Eric Greene, aka Nazi manqué Erich Barstow, clean out of his patent leather shoes. Gelft had admired the polish of the hit, after the fact. Now, he calmed; no struggle, since he, too, was a pro.

The killer at the front door returned Gelft's glance with absolutely no recognition. *This gentleman is good*, thought Gelft. *This gentleman is a cube of ice.*

As the other guests trooped down to Koepp's cellar or bomb shelter or whatever it was, Gelft had excused himself to use the bathroom and swipe sixty extra seconds for tactical considerations. Now a solution to his worry had just knocked on the front door. Gelft had the power to order Rudi and Klaus to back off, so he did; Rudi and Klaus didn't like it, and Gelft didn't care. The stranger entered, doffing hat and umbrella and directing a curt smile of acknowledgment—no more—to Gelft. Still, deep in those killer's eyes, no hint or giveaway clue.

Good.

Gelft escorted the newcomer downstairs. The look of disappointment on the faces of Rudi and Klaus was as palpable as fresh-molded clay. Gelft switched his briefcase to his free hand in order to clap his comrade on the shoulder as they descended, the better discreetly to inquire as to what alias he would prefer to be called when he was introduced to the guests.

The answer held no significance for Gelft.

Below, Koepp had run out of armbands. Gelft saw the others sporting them—classic black swastikas in white circles on fields of crimson—and preening fatuously like hormone-drunk Hitler Youth at their first circle jerk. If Koepp had a prevalent talent, it was for making everyone belong. He would remind them all that aboveground, in a world where modern Berliners danced atop the tombstone of Stalinism, it was illegal to wear such insignia. It was a crime to sell a copy of Germany's most influential autobiography. It was against the law even to give the Nazi salute.

Koepp fancied himself the father of change, a man who would favor his chosen and give them back their pride, and, tonight, confer on them all the honor of being in the vanguard. Yes, even Hessler.

The interstices of wall space between Koepp's collection of stolen paintings were absorbed by pegged oaken shelves displaying a fastidiously kept library—books on one side of the corridor-shaped chamber, videocassettes and discs on the other. Gelft could smell processed air, and suspected dehumidifiers.

A large projection monitor spanned the far end of the underground room; in earlier decades, this space could have been a stage. The beaded screen was enormous, taller than Gelft. On standby, it glowed a bright, expectant blue.

Gelft watched his guest squint at the shelves, examining the sleek treasure trove of Nazi lore, filed with care and tended with something like love. Every book imaginable. Every frame of archival footage ever exposed to light: Der Führer in uniform, in civvies, making speeches, shaking hands, leading troops, doing a jig, dancing with his dogs, disporting with Eva. Here were Goebbels's home movies. It was all in evidence—the largest and certainly one of the most comprehensive databases on the little painter Gelft could imagine. He suspected it even went the distance of including psychiatric profiles, past and present, and reports by modern authorities on the likely makeup of the very chemicals in Hitler's brain.

Koepp nodded to Hoff, the electronics man, and finished distributing snifters. With a *Phantom of the Opera* flourish, Hoff seated himself at a terminal that looked complex enough to administer a Swiss bank on autopilot. He removed the stolen Koramitsu chip from its case and plugged it into a cylindrical socket that withdrew into the main terminal once a few commands had been tapped into the keyboard. A tiny port irised shut, and the chip was gone, swallowed.

Hoff's explanation that the chip converted digital samples into virtual reality analogues sailed clear over the intellects of most of the men present. There was more. Koepp motioned for him to get on with it. Hoff persisted long enough to emphasize that this hybrid computer could not only assimilate information, but also produce resultant artificial intelligence that was capable of free association.

Ja, right. Hessler, near the rear of the group, picked his nose and wheezed in awe at a fully accoutred SS uniform preserved in a stand-up glass case near the door. While Hessler was a tourist in this idiom, Jaeckel was nostalgic, openly coveting the outfit's ceremonial dagger.

Hoff pecked in a few more directives. His brow furrowed. He stroked his upper lip longwise with his index finger, as though awaiting telepathic approval from the device. Deep within sandwiched circuitry, discs whirled into a simulacrum of life.

Koepp glanced at his watch and made sure that Hoff saw him do it. Gelft almost stepped forward to introduce his guest, but that would have been a mood breaker. When the big monitor glitched—a digital hiccup—Gelft sighed and put his attaché case down, shrugging to the visitor (who had become his special charge until the presentation was finished). It looked like they were going to have to play audience for a while.

Pixel by pixel, a face began to resolve onto the big screen, like a monochromatic sketch in ice, slowly surfacing through murky water. Hoff nodded affirmatively at Koepp.

At first, it was just a blurry video composite, the features jumping about in crude planes and curves, the idiographic shock of dark hair and toothbrush moustache little better than a bad cartoon caricature; Disney does Dachau. Its eyes were closed. Its expression, if you could call it that, was one of perfect, regal peace.

Shadows overlaid themselves as the machine extrapolated and exponentially built on what it knew. The image acquired depth and perspective. Topography melted into physiognomy. For Gelft, it was akin to watching really good polarized 3-D, without the glasses. He swore he could make out *pores* on the face. The very tips of the moustache hairs were white. The nostrils flared as the image gave the appearance of breathing.

Those watching were trapped between breaths. When the giant face onscreen at last opened its eyes—blue eyes— and seemed to look right at them, they were transfixed.

Koepp made his move. Gelft could see the speckles of feverish perspiration on his forehead. The politician strode forward and proclaimed *Alle Juden Raus*!

It was not the reaction of the guests, but the expression on the face of the onscreen image that drew Gelft's startled attention: It *altered* at the sound of Koepp's voice; it was both imperious and innocent, half-child, half-god. It *looked* from Koepp to the rest. The way it seemed to be seeing them all, individually, somehow knowing what it was doing, was the thing that captured Gelft's astonishment. It had to be wired into pinhole cameras. Maybe they were all being monitored from a dozen vantages right now, and fed into Hoff's monster on a nanosecond-to-nanosecond basis. The machine would be digesting what it took in, and reacting to it.

Beaming, Koepp waited while the image answered.

What it said was: *H-h-hi-hhei-Heil-hh.*

The face wrestled with its first spoken word, its voice careening from basso profundo to adenoidal squeak. As the image continued to refine, softening and becoming more organic, Hoff's expression grew unreal as he mumbled apologies and excuses to Koepp and abused the keyboard, seeking rectification with pursed, white lips and the cheesy skin tone of a cadaver.

H-h-hhe-Heil . . . HIT-hiii . . . HEIL hit-hit-hit . . .

It blasted them all from hidden speakers like a retarded child doing do-re-mi in surround sound and fast motion. Half the men had put down their brandy glasses in discomfort. Adenauer glanced at Gelft and shrugged. Most of the rest, being very German, waited with neutral expressions and vaunting disdain for what might happen next.

Hoff banged out another flurry of keystrokes. The face de-rezzed and reconfigured in a quarter second, as though someone had slapped it in the back of the head.

Heil Hi-Hi-HITT-lrr!

Koepp snapped to, saluting and repeating the invocation correctly. It worked on about half of the guests, like Jaeckel, who thrust out his chicken-bone chest as though galvanically prodded. Some of the younger men, like Drexler and Broger, were anxious to err on the side of inclusion, if for no bigger reason than not to be ambushed by some tricky pop quiz on loyalty.

The face looked back to Koepp. *At* him, thought Gelft; if it was a trick, it was a fancy one. The face seemed to consider anger, then think better of it. To Koepp, it said, *"Heil, Hitler!"* . . . this time, without the electronic stutter. Damned near perfect.

Koepp lit up. The program recognized him, and was

actually communicating! Now almost everyone joined him in returning the salute.

Almost everyone.

When Gelft saw the expression on the face of the little man, his "guest," he literally could not summon a definition for it. There was no time for speculation. At the back of the chamber, someone was laughing.

Karl Hessler, founder and embodiment of the Phoenix Foundation, dropped his brandy glass. His face was bright red. The bulbs spotlighting Koepp's display uniform picked out the fat man, too clearly, as his chuckle broke free, into a guffaw. He brayed. He was on the verge of a rupture. Heidrick and Saphire actually stepped *back* from him, as though he was contagious; probably more afraid that they might start laughing themselves.

Gelft watched the others as Hessler pawed air, trying to justify himself, to explain, if only by pantomime, that . . .

That he was thinking helplessly of playing Pong. Of trying to place a simple long-distance phone call in Europe. Of an Interactive Adolf to order them all around, leading to a portable version, the Ronco Pocket Führer . . .

That this was the silliest fucking thing he'd ever seen in his life.

The American at last had to lean against the glass cabinet that contained the SS gear. He was gasping now. Struggling to draw air, thought Gelft, so he could laugh some more. It might serve as a distraction.

Gelft saw the rage in Koepp hit the flash point. Before he could retaliate, and attempt to save face, a decision was reached from the other side of the room. Someone else had chosen what to do, and without messy emotional noise.

The face on the screen spoke Koepp's name—perfectly—then added something new, also without flaw: *"Ausrotten."*

At first Gelft misunderstood; he thought he had heard *all*

is rotten. Koepp understood. So did Hessler, who stopped laughing as though switched off. It was a word he had creatively misused throughout his amateur career to rationalize booklets like *Holocaust Hoax!* The gauntlet of faces, like a jury in the semi-dark, parted as Koepp came for the fat man.

Hessler backed away, his mind positively lusting for an explanation. Gelft saw his opportunity, and knew in his soul that the time had come for extirpation, for extermination. For ausrotten.

The perpetrator of the Phoenix Foundation managed three backward steps before the nape of his neck stopped against Gelft's ten-millimeter Glock. The single, unsilenced shot hit hard in the tomblike acoustics of the subterranean room. Everyone flinched. Hessler's overactive vocal gear sprayed to fleck the monitor from which the projected image observed his demise, not with hatred, or fulfillment, but with total concentration. Hoff, unaccustomed to tasting dots of honest-to-god dead guy on his face, almost bolted. Gelft aimed the gun at him next. In less time than it took Hessler's corpse to fall, Hoff sat back down to mind his own business, tend his keyboard, and sit in his own urine as the inseam of his trousers darkened.

Onscreen, their Führer smiled.

Gelft saw the light: Every scrap of information on Hitler had been synthesized here, and the product knew history, politics, strategy, economics, and human nature better than any ten of them. It would learn more by the millisecond and never forget anything it knew. It could see where errors had occurred before, dissect mistakes from a million angles, and forge unheard-of strengths from former weaknesses. The longer it thought, the better it would get, and it *never* stopped thinking. It could transcend the frailties of the flesh as a being of pure will, and this time, that will could triumph . . . if they all listened to what it would have to say.

It reminded them all, zum Beispiel, that in 1945 the Red

Army's ukase to de-Nazify Poland and Germany led to the deaths of over seventy-five thousand Germans—men, women, and children, all noncombatant civilians—in more than twelve hundred "incarceration camps," where they subsisted on starvation rations if they did not die of typhus or overcrowding. Russia's Office of State Security deliberately recruited survivors of the so-called Holocaust to round up Germans and subject them to this vengeful punishment . . .

. . . and these hypocrites dared to wail Never Again?

Gelft saw the eyes of his companions in the dark, glittering now, transfixed by the conjured image, but more so by the reinvigorated dream. They were all reflected in their leader's cool phosphor gaze in an endlessly expressed duality. All of them, save the eyes of his guest, the belated observer with the unplugged calm of a professional killer . . . or a man who could read the evil in this place, who had perhaps even tasted it.

The little man was trembling. He tore a Luger from his coat and shouted a single word. It was supposed to be dramatic, a showstopper. Instead, Gelft saw that the man was on the verge of weeping, the impact of his gesture sabotaged by the quaver in his voice.

The word was genug, and all it meant was *enough.*

Koepp's glare was alive with bloodlust. The resolve of his lieutenants had been consecrated by the sacrifice of Hessler; their minds, pleasured by the seductions of their church. Now a new victim had just presented himself—a stranger, a coward who had drawn down on a roomful of men while their backs were turned.

Gelft felt the glandular kick of his own need to act. To terminate Koepp would amount to a symbolic decapitation of the Hydra. Killing any of the others would be a futile grab at bettering already-suicidal odds.

His guest fired at the face on the screen.

There came no satisfying explosion of sparks and shrapnel. The screen was a rear-projection apparatus of bounce Mylar. All the bullet did was punch a neat, round hole in the center of the oversize image's forehead, a flaw the face itself could not see.

The face smiled again, the mouth twitching upward halfway to express the crooked sort of pleasure one takes in squashing an insect. Hoff made a noise from the console. He had not typed a command for whole minutes.

There was only the time for one surprise move, one round fired, and Gelft acted before anyone else could. He trapped the shooter in an elevated full nelson while Adenauer unhesitatingly plucked the Luger from his grasp—probably to keep it as a trophy, Gelft thought. Eager to score points now that the danger was past, Biermann buried a pile-driver fist into the stranger's stomach that folded him and arched his feet off the floor. The stranger woofed air and sagged into Gelft's arms.

Gelft was instantly targeted by Koepp; this disruptive troublemaker was Gelft's fault. A good answer at this moment could mean the difference between a promotion . . . and another execution.

Gelft opted for clarity. This, he explained, was not an enemy of the Reich, but a man whose contributions, much like those of Adenauer's Phantom Nazi, had helped them behind the scenes, to obtain the chip, to neutralize vendetta-mongers like Eric Greene. Perhaps, Gelft suggested, his guest had drunk too freely, or was overwrought on some other front. Perhaps he was subsumed with passion for the miracle he had just witnessed.

Koepp demanded to know a name. Gelft slapped down the only card he had left to play: *Aschmaus.*

The name woke Joseph Jaeckel like a set of cardiac paddles. It seemed to renew the ultraviolet fire buried deep in his eyes, jump-start him like Frankenstein's lightning. With surprising vitality he grabbed and twisted the arm of the man held immobile by Herr Gelft of Die Schwarze Spinne. The shirtsleeve bunched back, and there Jaeckel saw the crooked forearm scar, peeking free of the cuff like a serpent from a burrow.

His smile was an incision in his face. He asked this "Aschmaus" where he had lost his number.

Today, Jaeckel was aware that most of the others viewed him as a fossil. In 1944, however, he had been SS Sturmbahnführer Jaeckel. He was old now, yes, and tired . . . but he would have to have been a potted plant not to recall the nickname bestowed upon the six-year-old he had once watched frolic among the ashes of his own people.

Just watch, Kommandant's eyes seem to say, with a glimmer of pride. One like this comes along only once per war. Watch what my Aschmaus does.

Here, there was no retreat into mounds of pestled bone and the raw, pulverized residue of lives sacrificed. Jaeckel swore he could see something *behind* this man's eyes, suddenly tearing apart, a barrier vaporizing without warning. Despite the ridiculous position in which he was being restrained by Gelft, this *Juden* managed to knock his heels together and deliver a *sieg heil* for the cincture of accusatory eyes engirding him, his palm snapping flat as his trapped arm jutted the wrong way.

Jaeckel watched the gesture *hold* all present, as it had mesmerized Kommandant. But only for an instant.

The men sizing up their would-be spoiler laughed, breaking the tension, elbowing each other. Koepp was back in charge, still seeking an explanation for the intruder, who was Gelft's responsibility.

Jaeckel said nothing. He wanted to see how these latter-day masters played it.

The man Gelft was excellent. He quickly proposed to

escort this Aschmaus, this secret agent, away, to deal with him elsewhere, precisely because it was his responsibility. The late Karl Hessler would have to be cleaned out of Koepp's carpeting. There was no need for more wet melodrama inside of Koepp's house. Gelft wanted to acknowledge chain of command and demonstrate respect.

Jaeckel's opinion was confirmed when he saw the thing with the bullet hole in its televisual head nod in silent agreement.

Henri ascended at gunpoint toward guaranteed death. He had failed to exterminate even one of the monsters at the bottom of these stairs. He was not a religious man, and so could seek no comfort in last rites or prayers.

What had he accomplished?

He had walked right into their lair, a Jew in the thick of Nazi connivance, a transgression punishable by a bullet to the brain. He had been unafraid. Had, in fact, felt an inexplicable sense of safety and closure, of good being done, ever since he had been admitted to Koepp's home unchallenged, with the help of the man who now intended to murder him.

Why?

Gelft, the man prodding Henri ever-upward with his gun, answered all his unspoken questions by whispering a single word.

Doppelgänger.

Space spiraled in Henri's vision; he tasted a blurt of dizzy nausea. Gelft was Doppelgänger? Until now, that code name had been nothing more than a voice on the phone, ageless, sexless. Gelft was Institute, double-agenting within the webwork of Die Schwarze Spinne, then performing another half twist, like a gymnast of intrigue, to land feet-first, with a perfect score, right inside Koepp's inner circle.

Gelft stayed completely in character and urged Henri

toward the foyer upstairs. Freedom at gunpoint. Henri's heart surged. Perhaps there was genuine good in this world after all. With the front door scant meters away, Gelft asked if Henri could remember his history.

Before Henri could respond or ask what that meant, the world became one bright light.

The explosion seemed to hoist the entire building, then drop it in a huff. Koepp's castellated home met the ground crookedly, with enough motive force to rearrange the teeth of passersby. All that stood, fell over; all breakables broke. The stones of the foundation were microscopically bullied into new alignment, after centuries in the same position.

Most of the living beings inside the house ended life as flaming litter. The fortified stairway channeled the fireball that plumed up from the basement, like a pipe bomb the size of a U-Bahn tunnel. It would burn hellishly and reduce 33 Gelderstrasse to rock and ashes, leaving nearby Berliners with something to prattle about the next morning besides the fall of the Wall.

Hoff, the techno-wizard, became one with his control panel as blast heat fused his skeleton to puddled circuitry. Solder boiled. The projection screen crisped faster than celluloid held to a lit match.

There was no God down below, amid the flames. There was also no longer a Führer.

Two thoughts marked the end of the newborn silicon consciousness: It remembered what happens when officers leave meetings early, and it was stung with the irony of burning in a bunker, twice in the same century.

Upstairs, Gelft was hurled bodily into Henri as the concussion vented. The front door before them bowed, tindered, ignited, and burst outward. Debris fell, collided, and made more debris as plaster dust billowed poisonously. This was what it must have been like inside the gas chambers, inside the heart of the pyres.

The man called Henri as a child, then Aschmaus, then Henri again, was smashed floorward by Gelft's heavier form. Then he was gone, perhaps forever.

Clouder came to amid smoke and fire and panic, flames licking at the sweat and blood on his face, a hot rivet of pain incapacitating his left shoulder. His legs were pinned beneath a fallen body.

He remembered everything.

Now that he could see, he had no time to admire. His educated nose told him that the still-falling rubble in which he sprawled stank of C4—too much, just to erase a roomful of sitting ducks. Perhaps the plastique artist was attempting to compensate for the house's thick stone masonry.

Everyone below them had to be dead. Up here, there were still spasms of life. Clouder saw one of the watchdogs—the kid named Rudi—grayed to ghost hue and bleeding from both ears, pushing his way lopsidedly through strewn junk, headed for where the cellar doorway had been. He seemed mildly crazy, yet full up with glory. Here was an opportune chance to prove his worth to Koepp.

Gelft groaned, rolled off Clouder, and shot Rudi in the cheek. His head came apart in a whip crack of bloodstained hair, and he went down.

Freed, Clouder tried to stagger upright against a bowed lintel. He had doped out Gelft in the instant it took Rudi to die—Gelft had more switchbacks in his cover than a snake had vertebrae. He had shoved Eric Greene out into the traffic of intrigue just to validate his own RSVP to Ernst Koepp's get-together. Greene's life had paid the admission for Gelft's attaché case.

Remember your history?

When this trick had first been tried, Hitler had been

saved by a section of conference table which shielded him
from the blast. Some tricks improved with time.

Klaus, who had seen the part where Rudi ate the floor,
attempted to tackle Gelft from behind a tipped-over sideboard.
Clouder saw the charge coming. Despite his injured shoulder,
he managed to step forward and intercept.

The boy was taller. But what Gelft witnessed was worthy of awe.

Clouder seemed to take to the air on toe tip, arresting
Klaus's head in the crook of his arm and using the momentum of descent to separate the boy's neck with a pop that
went unheard in the general chaos. It was all a single, balletic
move on Clouder's part. Klaus's eyes rolled to white. When
he was released, he slid lifelessly down, lacking only funeral
arrangements.

Gelft had never seen Henri before in his life. But Gelft
had seen Clouder, that morning, in the hotel.

It all swam together elegantly. But there was still no time
to savor the unique kinship Clouder felt with this man, a kind
of psychic doubling that brought a thousand questions to the
fore. No time, now, for any of them. Sirens and uniforms
were seeking the house, wending closer to the incident that
had just lit up the night.

Gelft was trying to hold half his scalp on, wobbling to
stand, still able to wave Clouder away, to try and make him
leave the scene immediately. Their single electric moment of
eye contact told Clouder more than any interview.

His instincts told him to make for the Wall. Get lost in
the crowds there. Find water to clean himself up, improvise
bandages.

Clouder stumbled away from the remains of Koepp's
house, working his way up Wilhelmstrasse, leaving the mystery man known as Gelft behind. Doppelgänger stood sil-
houetted in the entryway, framed by fire, poised to continue
with his life of deceit.

The coverage by West Berlin television and radio is nonstop. Reporters shove microphones toward jubilant citizens, asking their impressions. Almost everyone responds that it is crazy, really insane.

Clouder fits right in.

The lath and grit speckling his clothing are attributed to the wounds visible all over the Wall—gouges where keepsake pieces have been extracted. It is thirsty, dusty work, swinging pickaxes and mauls. No one gets hurt. For now, there is exuberance. Scant days later, there will be displeasure and hostility at the traffic jams, the long queues, the overcrowding.

A young woman who breathlessly introduces herself as Gisela produces a first-aid kit, as if by magic, and proceeds to attend Clouder's cuts. As she works, Clouder is absurdly reminded of a combat medic. Someone hands him a half-empty bottle of cheap champagne; Clouder gulps two mouthfuls to cut the aridity in his throat. When Gisela finishes and tells him he'll be okay, she kisses him and blends into the crowd, never to be seen again.

Clouder slumps against the Wall, half in relief, half in rebound. The tidal swell of the mob moves him around, yet holds him up as individuals are shoved fore and aft like plankton.

No one will come here, looking for him. His arm still throbs venomously; he will have to seek proper medical attention. But just for this moment, he stands as one more face in the crowd, a blur that no historian will ever single out or find cause to remember. The moment of surcease is to be savored.

Brandishing a can of spray paint, a modern primitive shoves through. People clear the way as he sloganizes the Wall in letters three feet high, right next to where Clouder is standing. *DIE MAUER IST TOT*. Wild cheers. With exaggerated gestures, like a mime showing off, he laughs, swapping the spray-paint can for the champagne bottle in Clouder's grasp. He drains the last of the bubbly with a grin as the crowd watches the lettering on the Wall drip.

Clouder has accidentally brushed against the graffito. When he looks at his free hand, it is wet with paint, bright red.

He exhibits his hand to the graffiti artist, apologetically, almost sheepishly. Before he can speak, he is taken by force, and no one sees it happen.

It is crazy out here tonight, really insane.

Two in one, two in one, two in one . . .

Wolfie was capering about like a monkey or a Chink (which, come to think of it, were the same verdammt thing, ja?), brimming over with piss and rowdiness. They'd just rifled a cash-rich billfold, and the steal meant fat times for both of them, because Wolfie and Stanz had had themselves a two-in-one kind of day.

Stanz put in a steel-toed boot and heard a rib strut crack. Blood was running out of the old fucker's nostrils; more blood delineated his yellow teeth. Not that they'd had to *try* to hurt this guy; he'd been dusty and scuffed when they found him, like a secondhand carpetbag.

Wolfie had recognized the guy first.

Their second catch of the day vindicated every reactionary rule by which they lived. Chance never favored them. Yet here came the exception, the logic crack through which their entire lives might slip, the aberrant cosmic loophole that permits mutants to be. Their admittedly limited horizons had been reached, then surpassed.

The point was, they were enjoying this victory just too damned hugely.

Stanz had played wacky artist with the spray paint, while Wolfie took care of coshing the guy. Wolfie had been photopositive: Here was the same mark they'd passed up earlier in the workday for the pleasures of the late Heike Strab. Same compact little business type; simply adjust for lack of eyeglasses and briefcase, but still a grab of worth, sighted while Wolfie and Stanz were larking about within the masses more obsessed with petricide—the killing of stone—than the killing of anything else.

Once all eyes were staring at Stanz's graffito, it was easy to chaperon their dazed victim to their pump-station hideaway, for turning out. *Pardon my Papa; he's had too much to drink.* Amen.

Fireworks were popping in the night sky, and there had been one major loud-ass bang that turned everyone's head just a few moments before Stanz and Wolfie made their lucky score. The whole damned city was losing its collective wits, and that suited the boys just fine. It made for better cover.

As they peeled the old man, Stanz caught sight of the telltale scar on his left arm, and less than soberly helped Wolfie conclude that their latest victim was, in fact, Juden. They commenced casually kicking the shit out of him, giving his limp form another well-deserved blow whenever he threatened to regain consciousness. They amused themselves by watching the patterns his blood made in the dirt.

Tomorrow morning, Berlin would awaken with a worldclass hangover. The citizenry would be less forgiving. Time for Wall rats, in particular, to blitz out. When the industrial cranes hoisted entire sections of the Wall free, each gap would become a new ingress for the ossis. The pump station would inevitably be leveled.

Now they had the means to move on to their next destination in a brutal and possibly foreshortened life. That fun would follow a few more judicious, last-minute taunts and punches and kicks. Alibis? Why? They would not be caught tonight. There was no wedding band to hock, or other evidence that some Schätzchen would be pining for this old Schwanz. There would be no questions to be asked of the boys.

By the time their pump station had been either circumvented or demolished, Stanz and Wolfie would be inside new clothes, hanging hard with a warm place to crash and money in their pockets. They would toast—many times—the anonymous old fart whose life they had stolen, that they might fill their own glasses to the top.

Their benefactor was still breathing raggedly when the boys draped him over Heike Strab's corpse in a mannequin parody of sexual intercourse. As his staved-in head thudded to her non-respiring breast, he groaned and mumbled names.

None of them meant anything.

The last time Aschmaus sees his mother's face, it is masked in blood. She has long since stopped screaming. She has stopped moving. She is dumped into the pyre and falls in cruciform, as if waiting to receive a lover in the flames.

Henri, he thinks, though no one is asking. My name is Henri.

But there is no one to call him that here, not anymore. His name sails away, a gray fleck on a black cloud, until Aschmaus is all that is left behind.

He does not see Mama as she smolders and curls, crisping ligaments pulling her fetal, as if still warding off blows. Part of him wishes he could tell her he's sorry, but that part is better left consigned to the flames. There is no place for sorrow, or pity, or remorse. Aschmaus stands at attention before the crackling fire, then gets on with the business of staying alive.

Still boggled by the explosion at Koepp's house, seduced by a transient caesura at the Wall, he never saw the champagne bottle arcing toward the back of his head. He does not now feel the wedges of broken glass embedded amid hair matted with fresh blood, his own. After a lifetime's worth, he is inured to simple pain.

He never felt the scampering hands probing his pockets, exposing his identities, stripping him clean. He is malfunctional and disoriented. All he knows is that if he blacks out again, there may be no waking.

His guard had been dulled, just for that one moment. Normally, two like his tormentors would have been short, effortless work. He could have taken them even with his injured arm; it is the damage that concerns him, not the pain. He decides that when he opens his eyes, he will kill them both.

But hours have passed. Hours, since they have gone for good.

The woman is inert, half-entombed beneath gray dust under inadequate light. She seems featureless; her upturned face is a wash of dried blood and ashen dirt. She is cool to the touch and does not seem to mind his weight. It is easy for him to make the substitution. Mama died like this. A tragedy, a bad thing. But at least he has survived, to . . .

To do what? Accomplish what?

He remains quiet. So tired. Outside, large machines treadmill, muffled by the bricks of this, his newest prison.

He has been sundered, to hunt and kill and survive, then slammed back together, to suffer more as his very soul tries to divide and conquer, as his body tries to force him to survive anew. His eyes have been opened to his own elaborate inner machinations . . . but all they can see are crude proclamations in dull maroon on the walls surrounding him.

ACHTUNG JUDEN. ALLE JUDEN RAUS!

No one will come to move him. No one will shift him

closer to the block walls for more efficient obliteration. He cannot reach the incomplete escape tunnel in this tiny room; if he could, he'd be going the wrong way, toward a dead end.

No one will recycle his ashes, to forge bricks to build places like this. He has achieved the invisibility that for all his life has been his shadow-dancing partner.

Outside, another piece of the Wall is cleaved free. It strikes the ground with a vibration like thunder. Germans and tourists swarm over it, bloodying their hands in a mad rush to obtain souvenirs and fragments for sale. There will always be takers, and there will never be enough pieces. Soon, even the watchtowers and guard dogs will be available, for the right price.

Loose soot trickles groundward in the forgotten back room of the pump station, adding another coat of dust to the still-open eyes of the woman who could be his mother, returned to him. He clings to her and shivers. Now the child can finally put its head down safely, to rest.

As he sleeps, Aschmaus realizes that the terrible sound he hears outside, in the night, is not the awakening of some long-dormant evil. It is the stertorous death rattle of something else, something that has been far too long in dying.

1990

1991

1992

1993

1994

1995

———————————————————

1996

1997

1998

1999

THE WORD

BY RAMSEY CAMPBELL

—For S.T. Joshi

Truly this was the Son of God.

—John Wayne in *The Greatest Story Ever Told*

Nobody tries to speak to me while I'm waiting for the lift, thank Sod. Whenever you want to go upstairs at a science-fiction convention the lift is always on the top floor, and by the time it arrives it'll have attracted people like a dog turd attracts flies. There'll be a woman whose middle is twice as wide as the rest of her, and someone wearing no sleeves or deodorant, and at least one writer gasping to be noticed, and now there's a vacuumhead using a walkie-talkie to send messages to another weekend deputy who's within shouting distance. Here comes a clump wearing convention badges with names made up out of their own little heads, N. Trails and Elfan and Si Fye, and I amuse myself trying to decide which of them I'd least like to hear from. Here's the lift at last, and I shut the doors before some bald woman with dragons tattooed on her scalp can get in as well, but a thin boy in a suit and tie manages to sidle through the gap. He sees my *Retard* T-shirt, then he reads my badge. "Hi there," he says. "I'm—"

"Jess Kray," I tell him, since he seems to think I can't read, "and you sent me the worst story I ever read in my life."

He sucks in his lips as if I've punched him in the mouth. "Which one was that?"

"How many have you written that are that bad?"

"None that I know of."

Everyone's pretending not to watch his face doing its best not to wince. "You sent me the one about Frankenstein and the dead goat and the two nuns," I say for everyone to hear.

"I've written lots since."

"Just don't send any to *Retard*."

My fanzine isn't called that now, but I'm not telling him. I leave him to ride to the top with our audience while I lock myself in my room. I was going to write about the Sex, Sects, and Subtexts in Women's Horror Fiction panel, which showed me why I've never been able to read a book by the half of the participants I'd heard of, but now I've too much of a headache. I lie on the bed for as long as I can stand being by myself, then I look for someone I can bear to dine with.

We're at Contraception in Edinburgh, but it could be anywhere a mob of fans calling themselves fen take over a hotel for the weekend. As I step into the lobby I nearly bump into Hugh, a writer who used to have tons of books in the shops, maybe because nobody was buying them. Soon books will all be games you play on screens, but I'll bet nobody will play with his. "How are you this year, Jeremy?" he booms.

"Dying, like everyone else."

He emits a sound as if he's trying not to react to being poked in the ribs, and the rest of his party comes out of the bar. One of them is Jess Kray, who says "Join us, Jeremy, if you're free for dinner."

He's behaving like the most important person there, grinning with teeth that say we're real and a mouth that says you can check if you like and eyes with a message just for me. I'd turn him down to see how that makes him look, except Hugh Zit says "Do by all means," so his party knows he means the opposite, and it's too much fun to refuse.

Hugh Know's idea of where to eat is a place called Godfathers. I sit next to his Pakistani wife and her friend who isn't even a convention member, and ignore them, so they stop talking English. I've already heard Hugh Ever say on panels all the garbage he's recycling, about how it's a writer's duty to offer a new view of the world, as if he ever did, and how the most important part of writing is research. He still talks like the fan he used to be, like all the fen I know talk, either lecturing straight in your face or staring over your shoulder as though there's a mirror behind you. Only Kray couldn't look more impressed. Hugh Cares finishes his pizza at last, and says "I feel better for that."

I say "You must have felt bloody awful before."

Kray actually laughs at that while grimacing sympathet-ically at Hugh, and I can't wait to go back to my room and write a piece about the games he's playing. I write until I can't see for my headache, and after I've managed to sleep I write about the rest of the clowns at Contraception, until I've almost filled up the first issue of *Parade of the Maladjusted and Malformed*, which is what conventions are. On the last day I see Kray buying a publisher's editor a drink, which no doubt means he'll sell at least a trilogy. That's what I write once I'm home. Then it's back to wearing a suit at the bank in Fulham and having people line up for me on the far side of a window, which at least keeps them at a distance while I turn them and their lives into numbers on a screen. But there's the smell of the people on my side of the glass, and sometimes the feel of them if I don't move fast enough. Playing the game of never saying what I think just about sees me through the day, and the one after that, and the one after that. I print my fanzine in my room and mail it and wait for the clowns I've written about to threaten to sue me or beat me up. The year isn't over when among the review copies and the rest of the unnecessaries publishers send to fanzines I get a sheet about Jess Kray, the most exciting new young writer of the decade, whose first three novels are going to give a new meaning to fantasy.

Sod knows I thought I was joking. I ask for copies to see how bad they are, and they're worse. They're about an alter-nate world where everyone becomes their sexual opposite, so a gay boy turns into a barbarian hero and a dyke becomes his lover, and some of the characters remember when they return to the real world and most of them try to remind the rest, except one thinks it's meant to be forgotten, and piles of similar crap. I just skim a few chapters of the first book to get a laugh at the idea of people buying a book called *A Touch of Other* under the impression that it's a different kind of junk. Apparently the books go on to be about some wimp who teaches himself magic in the other world and gets to be leader of this one. It's nine months since I saw Kray talking to the editor, so either he writes even more glibly than he comes on to people or he'd already written them. One cover shows a woman's face turning into a man's, and the second has a white turning black, and the third's got a tinfoil mirror where a face should be. That's the one I throw hardest across the room. Later I put them in the pile to sell to Everybody's Fantasy, the skiffy and comics shop near the docks, and then I hear Kray will be there signing books.

How does a writer nobody's heard of put that over on even a shop run by fen? I'm beginning to think it's time someone exposed him. That Saturday I take the books with me, leaving the compliments slips in so he'll see I haven't bought them. Maybe I'll let him see me selling them as soon as he's signed them. But the moment I spot him at the table with his three piles on it he jumps up. "Jeremy, how are you! This is Jeremy Bates, everyone. He was my first critic."

Sod knows who he's trying to impress. The only customers are comics readers, that contradiction in terms, who look as if they're out without their mothers to buy them their funnies. And the proprietor, who I call Kath on account of his caftan and long hair, doesn't seem to think much of Kray trying to hitch a ride on my reputation, not that he ever seems to think of much except where the next joint's coming from. I give Kray the books with the slips sticking up, but he carries on grinning. "My publishers haven't sent me your review yet, Jeremy."

I should tell him that's because I won't be writing one, but I'm mumbling like a fan, for Sod's sake. "Write something in them for me."

In the first book he writes "For Jeremy who knew me before I was good," and "To our future" in the second, and "For life" in what I hope's the last. When he hands them back like treasure, I stuff them in my armpit and leaf through some tatty fanzines so I can see how many people he attracts.

Zero. Mr Nobody and all his family. A big round hole without a rim. Some boys on mountain bikes point at him through the window until Kath chases them, and once a woman goes to Kray, but only to ask him where the *Star Trek* section is. Kath's wife brings Kray a glass of herbal tea, which isn't even steaming and with the bag drowning in it, and it's fun to watch him having to drink that. We all hang around for the second half of the hour, then Kath says in the drone that always sounds as if he's talking in his sleep "Maybe you can sign some stock for us."

I can hear he doesn't mean all the books on the table, but that doesn't stop our author. When Kray's defaced every one he says "How about that lunch?"

Kath and Mrs Kath glance at each other, and Jess Kidding gives them an instant grin each. "I understand. Don't even think of it. You can buy lunch next time, after I've made you a bundle. Let me buy this one."

They shake their heads, and I see them thinking there'll never be a next time, but Jess Perfect flashes them an even more-embracing grin before he turns to me. "If you want to interview me, Jeremy, I'll stand lunch. You can be the one who tells the world."

"About what?"

"That'd be telling."

I want the next *PotMaM* to spill a lot more blood, and

besides, nobody's ever bought me lunch. I take him round the corner to Le Marin Qui Rit, which some French chef with too much money built in an old warehouse by the Thames. "This is charming," Kray says when he sees the nets full of crabs hanging from the beams and the waiters in their sailor suits, though I bet he doesn't think so when he sees the prices on the menu. As soon as we've ordered he hurries through the door that says Matelots, maybe to be sick over the prices, and I rip through his books until he comes back with his grin, and says "Ask me anything." But I've barely opened my mouth when he says "Aren't you recording?"

"Didn't know I'd need to. Don't worry, I remember everything. My ex could tell you."

He digs a pocket tape recorder out of his trench coat. "Just in case you need to check. I always carry one for my thoughts."

He heard an ex-success say that at Contraception. A sailor brings us a bottle of sheep juice, Mutton Cadet, and I switch on. "What's a name like Kray supposed to mean to the world?"

"It's my father's name," he says, then proves I was right to be suspicious, because it turns out his father was a Jewish Pole who was put in a camp and left the rest of his surname behind when he emigrated with the remains of his family after the war.

"Speaking of prejudice, what's with the black guy calling himself Nigger when he gets to be the hero?"

"A nigger is someone who minds being called one. Either you take hold of words or they take hold of you."

"Which do you think your books do?"

"A bit of both. I'm learning. I want to be an adventurer on behalf of the imagination."

I can hardly wait to write about him, except here's my poached salmon. He waits until I've taken a mouthful, and says "What did you like about the books?"

I'm shocked to realise how much of them has stuck in my mind—lines like "AIDS is such a hell you'll go straight to heaven." I want to say "Nothing," but his grin has got to me. "Where you say that being born male is the new original sin."

"Well, that's what one of my characters says."

What does he mean by that? His words keep slipping away from me, and I've no idea where they're going. By the time we finish I'm near to nodding in my pudding, his refusing to be offended by anything I say has taken so much out of me. The best I can come up with as a final question is "Where do you think you're going?"

"To Florida for the summer with my family. That's where the ideas are."

"Here's hoping you get some."

He doesn't switch off the recorder until we've had our coffee, then he gives me the tape. "Thanks for helping," he says, and insists on shaking hands with me. It feels like some kind of Masonic trick, trying to find out if I know a secret—either that or he's working out the best way to shake hands.

He pays the bill without letting his face down and says he's heading for the station, which is on my way home, but I don't tell him. I turn my back on him and take the long way through the streets I always like, with no gardens and no gaps between the houses and less sunlight than anywhere else in town. While I'm there I don't need to think, and I feel as if nothing can happen in me or outside me. Only I have to go home to deal with the tape, which is itching in my hip pocket like a tapeworm.

I'm hoping he'll have left some thoughts on it by mistake, but there's just our drivelling. So either he brought the machine to make sure I could record him or more likely wanted to keep a copy of what we said. Even if he didn't trust me, it's a struggle to write about him in the way I want to. It takes me days and some of my worst headaches. I feel as if he's stolen my energy and turned it into a force that only works on his behalf.

When I seem to have written enough for an issue of *PotMaM* I print out the pages. I have to pick my way around them or tread on them whenever I get up in the night to be sick. I send out the issue to my five subscribers and anyone who sent me their fanzine, though not many do after what I write about their dreck. I take copies to Constipation and Convulsion and sell a few to people who haven't been to a convention before and don't like to say no. When I start screaming at the fanzine in the night and kicking the piles over I pay for a table in the dealers' room at Contamination. But on the Saturday night the dealers' room is broken into, and in the morning every single copy's gone.

It isn't one of my better years. My father dies and my mother tells me my ex-wife went to the funeral. The branch of the bank closes down because of the recession, and it looks as if I'll be out of a job, only luckily one of the other clerks gets his back broken in a hit-and-run. They move me to Chelsea, where half the lunchtime crowd looks like plainclothes something and all the litter bins are sealed up so nobody can leave bombs in them. At least the police won't let marchers into the district, though you can hear them shouting for employment or life sentences for pornography or Islamic blasphemy laws or a curfew for all males as soon as they reach puberty or all tobacco and alcohol profits to go to drug rehabilitation or churchgoing to be made compulsory by law . . . Some writers stop their publishers from sending me review copies, so at least I've bothered them. I give up going to conventions for almost a year, until I forget how boring they are, so that staying in my room seems even worse. And at Easter I set out to find myself a ride to Consternation in Manchester.

I wait most of an hour at the start of the motorway and see

a car pick up two girls who haven't waited half as long, so I'm in no mood for any crap from the driver who finally pulls over. He asks what I'm doing for Easter, and I think he's some kind of religious creep, but when I tell him about Consternation he starts assuring me how he used to enjoy H.G. Wells and Jules Verne, as if I gave a fart. Then he says "What would you call this new johnny who wrote *The Word*? Is he sci-fi or fantasy or what?"

"I don't know about any word."

"I thought he might be one of you chaps. Went to a publisher and told him his ideas for the book and came away with a contract for more than I expect to make in a lifetime."

"How come you know so much about it?"

"Well, I am a bookseller. Those on high want us to know in advance this isn't your average first novel. Let me cudgel the old brains, and I'll give you his name."

I'm about to tell him not to bother when he grins. "Don't know how I could forget a name like that, except it puts you in mind of the Kray brothers, if you're not too young to remember their reign of terror. The last thing he sounds like is a criminal. Jess Kray, that's the phenomenon."

I'd say I knew him if I could be sure of convincing this caricature that he isn't worth knowing. I bite my tongue until it feels as if my teeth are meeting, then I realise the driver has noticed the tears that have got away from me, and I could scream. He says no more until he stops to let me out of the car. "You ought to tell your people about this Kray. Sounds as if he has some ideas that bear thinking about."

The last thing I'll do is tell anyone about Kray, particularly when I remember him saying I should. I wait in my hotel room for my headache to let me see, then I go down to the dealers' room. Instead of books, a lot of the tables are selling virtual-reality viewers or pocket CD-ROM players. I can't find anything by Kray, and some of the dealers watch me as if I'm planning to steal from them, which makes me feel like throwing their tables over. Then the fat one who always wears a sombrero says "Can I do something for you?"

"Not by the look of it." That doesn't make him go away, and all I can think of is to confuse him. "You haven't got *The Word*."

"No, but Jess sent us each a copy of the cover," he says, and props up a piece of cardboard with letters in the middle of its right-hand side:

JESS KRAY
THE WORD

I can't tell if they're white on a black background or black on white, because as soon as I move an inch they turn into the opposite. I shut my eyes once I've seen it's going to be published by the dump that stopped sending me review copies. "What do you mean, he sent you it? He's just a writer."

"And he designed the cover, and he wants everyone to know what's coming, so he got the publisher to print enough cover proofs for us all in the business."

I'm not asking what Kray said about his book. When Fat in the Hat says "You can't keep your eyes shut forever" I want to shut his, especially when as soon as I open mine he says "Shall we put you down for a copy when it's published?"

"They'll send me one."

"I doubt it," he says, and he'll never know how close he came to losing the bone in his nose, except I have to take my head back to my room.

Maybe he wasn't just getting at me. Once I'm home I ring Kray's new publisher for a review copy. I call myself Jay Battis, the first name that comes into my head, and say I'm the editor of *Psychofant* and no friend of that total cynic Jeremy Bates. But the publicity girl says Kray's book isn't genre fiction, it's literature, and they aren't sending it to fanzines.

So why should I care? Except I won't have her treating me as though I'm not good enough for Kray after I gave him more publicity than he deserved when he needed it most. And I remember him thanking me for helping—did he mean with this book? I ask the publicity bitch for his address, but she expects me to believe they don't know it. I could ask her who his agent is, but I've realised how I'd most like to get my free copy of his world-shaking masterpiece.

I don't go to Kath's shop, because I'd be noticed. On the day the book is supposed to come out I go to the biggest bookshop in Chelsea. There's a police car in front, and the police are making them move out of the window a placard that's a big version of the cover of *The Word*—I hear the police say it has been distracting drivers. I walk to a table with a pile of *The Word* on it and straight out with one in my hand, because the staff are busy with the police. Only I feel as if Kray's forgiving me for liberating his book, and it takes all my strength not to throw it away.

Even when I've locked my apartment door I feel watched. I hide the book under the bed while I fry some spaghetti and open a tin of salmon for dinner. Then I sit at the window and watch the police cars hunting and listen to the shouts and screams until it's dark. When I begin to feel as if the headlights are searching for me I close the curtains, but then I can't think of anything to do except read the book.

Only the first few pages. Just the prospect of more than a thousand of them puts me off. I can't stand books where the dialogue isn't in quotes and paragraphs keep beginning with "And." And I'm getting the impression that the words are slipping into my head before I can grasp them. Reading the book makes me feel I'm hiding in my room, shutting myself off from the world. I stuff *The Word* down the side of the bed, where I can't see the cover playing its tricks, and switch on the radio.

Kray's still in my head. I'm hoping that since it's publi-
cation day, I'll hear someone tearing him to bits. There isn'
a programme about books any longer on the radio, just one
about what they call the arts. They're reviewing an Eskimo
rock band and an exhibition of sculptures made out of used
condoms and a production of *Jesus Christ Superstar* where
all the performers are women in wheelchairs, and I'm sneering at myself for imagining they would think Kray was worth
their time and at the world for being generally idiotic, when
the presenter says "And now a young writer whose first novel
has been described as a new kind of book. Jess Kray, what's
the purpose behind *The Word*?"

"Well, I think it's in it rather than behind it if you look
And I'd say it may be the oldest kind of book, the one that's
been forgotten."

At first I don't believe it's him, because he has no accent
at all. I make my head throb trying to remember what accent
he used to have, and when I give up the presenter is saying
"Is the narrator meant to be God?"

"I think the narrator has to be different for everyone, like
God."

"You seem to want to be mysterious."

"Don't you think mystery has always been the point? That
isn't the same as trying to hide. We've all read books where the
writer tries to hide behind the writing, though of course it can'
be done, because hiding reveals what you thought you were
hiding . . ."

"Can you quote an example?"

"I'd rather say that every book you've ever read has been
a refuge, and I don't want mine to be."

"Every book? Even the Bible? The Koran?"

"They're attempts to say everything regardless of how
much they contradict themselves, and I think they make a fun-
damental error. Maybe Shakespeare saw the problem, but he
couldn't quite solve it. Now it's my turn."

I'm willing the presenter to lose her temper, and she says "So to sum up, you're trying to top Shakespeare and the Bible and the rest of the great books."

"My book is using up a lot of paper. I think that if you can't put more into the world than you take out of it, you shouldn't be here at all."

"As you say somewhere in *The Word*. Jess Kray, thank you." Then she starts talking to a cretic—which is a cretin who thinks they're a critic, such as everyone who attacks my fanzines—about Kray and his book. When the cretic says she thinks the narrator might be Christ because of a scene where he sees the light beyond the mountain through the holes in his hands I start shouting at the radio for quite a time before I turn it off. I crawl into bed and can't stop feeling there's a light beside me to be seen if I open my eyes. I keep them closed all night and wake up with the impression that some of Kray's book is buried deep in my head.

For the first time since I can remember I'm looking forward to a day at the bank. I may even be able to stand the people on my side of the glass without grinding my teeth. But that afternoon Mag, one of the middle-aged girls, waddles in with an evening paper and nearly slaps me in the face with it as though it's my fault. "Will you look at this. Where will it stop. I don't know what the world is coming to."

CALL FOR BAN ON "BLASPHEMOUS" BOOK

I don't want to read any more, yet I grab the paper. It says that on the radio programme I heard, Kray said his book was better than the Bible and people should read it instead. A bishop is calling for the police to prosecute, and some mob named Christ Will Rise is telling Christians to destroy *The Word* wherever they find it. So I can't help walking past the

shop my copy came from, even though it isn't on my wa
home. And on the third day half a dozen Earnests with plac
ards saying CHRIST NOT KRAY are picketing the shop.

The police apparently don't think they're worth mor
than cruising past, and I hope they'll get discouraged
because they're giving Kray publicity. But the next day ther
are eight of them, and twelve the day after, and at the week
end several Kray fans start reading *The Word* to the pickets t
show them how they're wrong. And I feel as though I've ha
no time to breathe before there's hardly a shop in the coun
try without clowns outside it reading *The Word* and the Bibl
or the Koran at one another. And then Kray starts touring a
the shops and talking to the pickets.

I keep switching on the news to check if he's bee
scoffed into oblivion, but no such luck. All the time in m
room I'm aware of his book in there with me. I'd throw
away except someone might end up reading it—I'd tear it u
and burn it except then I'd be like the Christ Will Risers. Th
day everyone at the bank is talking about Kray being in tow
during my lunch hour I scrape my brains for something els
to do, anything rather than be one of the mob. Only suppos
this is the one that stops him? That's a spectacle I'd enjo
watching, so off I limp.

There must be at least a hundred people outside the book
shop. Someone's given Kray a chair to stand on, but So
knows who's arranged for a beam of sunlight to shine on him
He's answering a question, saying "If you heard the repeats c
my interview, you'll know I didn't say my book was bette
than the Bible. I'm not sure what better means in that contex
I hope my book contains all the great books."

And he grins, and I wait for someone to attack him, bu
nobody does, not even verbally. I feel my voice forcing it
way out of my mouth, and all I can think of is the questio
vacuumheads ask writers at conventions. "Where did you ge
your ideas?"

So many people stare at me I think I've asked the question he didn't want asked. I feel as if he's using more eyes than a spider to watch me, more than a whole nest of spiders—more than there are people holding copies of his drivel. Kray himself is only looking in my general direction, trying to make me think he hasn't recognised me or I'm not worth recognising. "They're in my book."

I want to ask why he's pretending not to know me, except I can't be sure it'll sound like an accusation, and the alternative makes me cringe with loathing. But I'm not having any of his glib answers, and I shout "Who are?"

The nearest Kray fan stops filming him with a Steadicam video and turns on me. "His ideas, he means. You're supposed to be talking about his ideas."

I won't be told what I'm supposed to be saying, especially not by a never-was who can't comb her hair or keep her lips still, and I wonder if she's trying to stop me asking the question I hadn't realised I was stumbling on. "Who did you meet in Florida?" I shout.

Kray looks straight at me, and it's as if his grin is carving up my head. "Some old people with some old ideas that were about to be lost. They're in my book. Everyone is in any book that matters."

Maybe he sees me sucking in my breath to ask about the three books he wants us to forget he wrote, because he goes on. "As I was about to say, all I'm asking is that we should respect one another. Do me the honour of not criticising *The Word* until you've read it. If anyone feels harmed by it, I want to know."

I might have vanished or never been there at all. When he pauses for a response I feel as if his grin has got stuck in my mouth. The mob murmurs, but nobody seems to want to speak up. Any protest is being swallowed by vagueness. Then two minders appear from the crowd and escort Kray to a limo that's crept up behind me. I want to reach out to him

and—I don't know what I want, and one of the minders
pushes me out of the way. I see Kray's back, then the limo is
speeding away, and all the mob are talking to one another
and I have to take the afternoon off because I can't see the
money at the bank.

Whenever the ache falters my head fills up with thoughts
of Kray and his book. When I sense his book by me in the
dark I can't help wishing on it—wishing him and it to a hell
as everlasting as my headache feels. It's the first time I've
wanted to believe in hell. Not that I'm so far gone I believe
wishes work, but I feel better when the radio says his plan's
gone wrong. Some Muslim leaders are accusing him of
seducing their herd away from Islam.

I keep looking in the papers and listening in the night in
case an ayatollah has put a price on his head. Some book
shops in cities that are overrun with Muslims are either hiding their copies of *The Word* or sending them back, and I
wish on it that the panic will spread. But the next headline
says he'll meet the Muslim leaders in public and discuss *The
Word* with them.

A late-night so-called arts programme is to broadcast the
discussion live. I don't watch it, because I don't know anyone who would let me watch their television, but when it's on
I switch out my light and sit at my window. More and more
of the windows out there start to flicker, as if the city is riddled with people watching to see what will happen to Kray. I
open my window and listen for shouting Muslims and maybe
Kray screaming, but I've never heard so much quiet. When it
starts letting my head fill up with thoughts I don't want to
have, I go to bed and dream of Kray on a cross. But in the
morning everyone at the bank is talking about how the
Muslims ended up on Kray's side and how one of them from
a university is going to translate *The Word* into whatever language Muslims use.

And everyone, even Mag who didn't know what the

world was coming to with Kray, is saying how they admire him or how they've fallen in love with him and the way he handled himself, and wish they'd gone to see him when he was in town. When I say I've got *The Word* and can't read it, they all look as though they pity me. Three of them ask to borrow it, and I tell them to buy their own because I never paid for mine, which at least means nobody speaks to me much after that. I can still hear them talking about Kray and feel them thinking about him, and in the lunch hour two of them buy *The Word*, and the rest, even the manager, want a read. I'm surrounded by Kray, choked by a mass of him. I'm beginning to wonder if anyone in the world besides me knows what he's really like. The bank shuts at last, and when I leave the building two Christ Will Risers are waiting for me.

Both of them wear suits like civil servants and look as though they spend half their lives scrubbing their faces and polishing the crosses at their throats. They both step forward as the sunlight grabs me, and the girl says "You knew him."

"Me, no, who? Knew who?"

Her boyfriend or whatever touches my arm like a secret sign. "We saw you making him confess who he'd met."

"Let's sit down and talk," says the girl.

Every time they move, their crosses flash, until my eyes feel like a whole graveyard of burned crosses. At least the couple haven't swallowed *The Word*, and talking to them may be better than staying in my room. We find a bench that isn't full of unemployed and clear the McDonald's cartons off it, and the Risers sit on either side of me even though I've sat almost at the end of the bench. "Was he a friend of yours?" the girl asks.

"Seems like he wants to be everyone's friend," I say.

"Not God's."

It doesn't matter which of them said that; it could have come from either. "So how much do you know about what happened in Florida?"

"As much as he said when I asked him."

"You must be honest with us. We can't do anything about him if we don't put our faith in the truth."

"Why not?"

That throws them, because they're obviously not used to thinking. Then they say "We need to know everything we can find out about him."

"Who's we?"

"We think you could be one of us. You're of like mind, we can tell."

That's one thing I'll never be with anyone. I nearly jump up and lean on their shining shampooed heads so they won't follow me, but I want to know what they know about Kray that I don't. "Then that must be why I asked him about Florida. All I know is that last time I met him he was going there and he wrote *The Word* when he came back. So what happened?"

They look at each other across me, then swivel their eyes to me. "There are people who came down a mountain almost a hundred years ago. We know he met them or someone connected with them. That has to be the source of his power. Nothing else could have let him win over Islam."

I wouldn't have believed anyone could talk less sense than Kray. "He was like that when he was just a fantasy fan. He's got a genius for charming everyone he meets and promoting himself."

"That must be how he learned the secret that came down the mountain. What else can you tell us?"

I don't mind making them more suspicious of Kray, but I won't have them thinking I tried to help them. "Nothing," I say, and get up.

They both reach inside their jackets for pamphlets. "Please take these. Our address is on the back whenever you want to get in touch."

I could tell them that's never and stuff their pamphlets in

their faces, but at least while I've the pamphlets in my fist nobody can take me for a Jess Kray fan. At home I glance at them to see they're as stupid as I knew they would be, full of drone out of the Bible about the Apocalypse and the Antichrist and the Antifreeze and Sod knows what else. I shove them down the side of the bed and try to believe that I've helped the Risers get Kray. And I keep hoping until I see *Time* magazine with him on the cover.

By then half the bank has read *The Word*. I've seen them laughing or crying or going very still when they read it in their breaks, and when they finish it they look as if they have a secret they wish they could tell everyone else. I won't ask, I nearly chew my tongue off. Anyone who asks them about the book gets told "Read it" or "You have to find out for yourself," and I wonder if the book tells you to make as many people read it as you can, like they used to tell you on posters not to give away the end of films. I won't touch my copy of *The Word*, but one day I sneak into a bookshop to read the last page. Obviously it makes no sense, only I feel that if I read the page before it I'll begin to understand, because maybe it can be read backward as well as forward. I throw the book on the table and run out of the shop.

At least they've taken *The Word* out of the window to make room for another pound of fat in a jacket, but I keep seeing people reading it in the streets. Whenever I see anything flash in a crowd I'm afraid it's another copy drawing attention to itself. At home I feel it beginning to surround me in the night out there, and I tell myself I've one copy nobody is reading. But I have to take train rides into the country for walks to get away from it—they're the only way I can be certain I'm nowhere near anyone who's read it. And coming back from one of those rides, I see him watching me from the station bookstall.

He looks like a recruiting poster for himself that doesn't need to point a finger. While I'm pretending to flip through the magazine I knock all the copies of *Time* onto the floor of the booking hall, except for the one I shove down the front of my trousers. All the way home I feel my peter wiping itself on his mouth, and in my room I have a good laugh at my stain on his face before I turn to the pages about him.

The headline says WHAT IS *THE WORD*? in the same typeface as the cover of his book. Maybe the article will tell me what I need to put him out of my mind for good. But it says how he bought his parents a place in Florida with part of his advances, and how *The Word* is already being translated into thirteen languages, and I'm starting to puke. Then the hack tries to explain what makes *The Word* such a publishing phenomenon, as she calls it. And by the time I've finished nearly going blind with reading what she wrote I think it's another of Kray's tricks.

It says too much and nothing at all. She doesn't know if the word is the book or the narrator or the words that keep looking as if they've been put in by mistake. Kray told her that if a book wasn't language, it was nothing. "So perhaps we should take him at his, you should forgive it, word." He said he just put the words on paper, and it's for each reader to decide what they add up to. So she collected a gaggle of cretics and fakes who profess and that old joke "leading writers" and got them to discuss *The Word*.

If I'd been there I'd have mashed all their faces together. It was the funniest book someone had ever read, and the most moving someone else had, and everyone agreed with both of them. One woman thought it was like *The Canterbury Tales*, and then there's a discussion about whether it's told by one character or several or whether all the characters might be the same one in some sort of mental state or it's showing a new kind of relationship between them all. A professor points out that the Bible was written by a crowd of people, but when you read it in translation you can't tell, whereas she thinks you can identify to the word where Kray's voices change, "as many voices as there are people who understand the book." That starts them talking about the idea in *The Word* that people in Biblical times lived longer because they were closer in time to the source, as if that explains why some people are living longer now and the rest of what's happening to us, the universe drifting closer to the state it was in before it formed. And there's crap about people sinning more so their sins will reach back to the Crucifixion because otherwise Christ won't come back, or maybe the book says people have to know when to stop before they have the opposite effect and throw everything off-balance, only by now I'm having to run my finger under the words and read them out loud, though my voice makes my head worse. There are still columns to go, the experts saying how if you read *The Word* aloud it's poetry, and how you'll find passages almost turning into music, and how there are developments of ideas from Sufism and the Upanishads and Buddhism and Baha'i and the Cabala and Gnosticism, and Greek and Roman and older myths, and I scrape my fingernail over all this until I reach the end, someone saying "I think the core of this book may be the necessary myth for our time." And everyone agrees, and I tear up the magazine and try to sleep.

I can still hear them all jabbering, as if Kray is using their voices to make people read his book to discover what they were raving about. I hear them in the morning on my way to the bank, and I wonder how many of them his publisher will quote on the paperback, and that's when I realise I'm dreading the paperback because so many more people will be able to afford it. I'm dreading being surrounded by people with Kray in their heads, because then the world will feel even more like somewhere I've wandered into by mistake. It almost makes me laugh to find I didn't want to be shown that people are as stupid as I've always thought they were.

When posters for the paperback start appearing on bus shelters and hoardings I have to walk about with my eyes half-shut. The posters don't use the trick the cover did, but that must mean the publishers think that just the title and his name will sell the book. At the bank I keep being asked if I don't feel well, until I say I'm not getting my Sunday dinner any more since my mother had a heart attack and died in hospital, not that it's anyone's business, but as well as that I can hardly eat for waiting for the paperback.

The day I catch sight of one there's a march of lunatics demanding that the hospitals they've been thrown out of get reopened, and in the middle of all this a woman's sitting on a bench reading *The Word* as though she can't see or hear what's going on around her for the book. And then the man she's waiting for sits down by her and squashes his wet mouth on her cheek, and leans over to see what she's reading, and I see him start to read as if it doesn't matter where you open the book, you'll be drawn in. And when I run to the bank one of the girls asks me if I know when the paperback is coming out, and saying I don't know makes me feel I'm trying to stop something that can't be stopped.

Or am I the only one who can? I spend the day trying to remember where I put the interview with him. Despite whoever stole all the copies of *PotMaM* at Contamination, I should still have the tape. I look under my clothes and the plates and the tins and in the tins as well, and under the pages of the magazine I tore up, and under the towels on the floor in the corner, and among the bits of glasses I've smashed in the sink.

It isn't anywhere. My mother must have thrown it out one of the days she came to clean my room. I start screaming at her until I lose my voice, by which time I've thrown just about everything movable out of the window. They're demolishing the houses opposite, so some more rubbish in the street won't make any difference, and my fellow rats in the building must be too scared to ask what I'm doing, unless they're too busy reading *The Word*.

By the end of the week, two of the slaves at the bank have the paperback and will lend it to anyone who asks. And I don't know when they start surrounding me with Kray's words. Most of the time—Sod, all the time—I know they're saying things they've heard someone else say, but after a while I notice they've begun speaking in a way that's meant to show they're quoting. Like the girl at the window by mine would start talking about a murder mystery on television and the one next to her would say "The mystery is around you and in you," and they'd laugh as if they were sharing a secret. Or one would ask the time and her partner in the comedy team would say "Time is as soon as you make it." And all sorts of other crap: "Look behind the world" or "You're the shadow of the infinite," which the manager says once as if he's topping everyone else's quotes. And before I know it at least half the slaves don't say "Good morning" any more, they say "What's the word?"

That makes the world feel like a headache. People say it in the street, too, and when they come up to my window, until I wonder if I was wrong to blame my mother for losing the tape, if someone else might have got into my room. By the time the next catchphrase takes root in the dirt in people's heads I can't control myself—when I hear one of the girls respond to another "As Kray would say."

"Is there anything he doesn't have something to say about?"

I think I'm speaking normally enough, but they cover their ears before they shake their heads and look sad for me and chorus "No."

"Sod, listening to you is like listening to him."

"Maybe you should."

"Maybe he will."

"Maybe everyone will."

"Maybe is the future."

"As Kray would say."

"Do you know you're the only one who hasn't read him, Jeremy?"

"Thank Sod if it keeps me different."

"Unless we find ourselves in everybody else . . ."

"As fucking Kray would say."

A woman writing a cheque gasps, and another customer clicks his tongue like a parrot, and I'm sure they're objecting to me daring to utter a bad word about their idol. None of the slaves speaks to me all day, which would be more of a relief if I couldn't feel them thinking Kray's words even when they don't speak them. I assume the manager didn't hear me, since he was in his office telling someone the bank is going to repossess their house. But on Monday morning he calls me in and says "You'll have been aware that there's been talk of further rationalisation."

He was talking before that, only I was trying to see where he's hidden *The Word*. At least he doesn't sound like Kray. "Excuse me, Mr Bates, but are there any difficulties you feel I should know about?"

"With what?"

"I'd like to give you a chance to explain your behaviour. You're aware that the bank expects its staff to be smart and generally presentable."

I hug myself in case that hides whatever he's complaining about and hear my armpits squelch, and me saying "I thought you were supposed to see yourself in me."

"That was never meant to be used as an excuse. Have you really nothing more to say?"

I can't believe I tried to defend myself by quoting Kray. I chew my tongue until it hurts so much I have to stick it out. "I should advise you to seek some advice, Mr Bates," says the manager. "I had hoped to break this to you more gently, but I must say I can see no reason to. Due to the economic climate I've been asked to propose further cuts in staff, and you will appreciate that your attitude has aided my decision."

"Doesn't Kray have anything to say about fixing the economy?"

"I believe he does in world terms, but I fail to see how that helps our immediate situation."

The manager's beginning to look reluctantly sympathetic—he must think I've turned out to be one of them after all, and I won't have him thinking that. "If he tried, I'd shove his book back where it came from."

The manager looks as if I've insulted him personally. "I can see no profit in prolonging this conversation. If you wish to work your notice, I must ask you to take more care with your appearance and, forgive my bluntness, to treat yourself to a bath."

"How often does he say I've got to have one?" I mean that as a sneer, but suppose it sounds like a serious question? "Not that I give a shit," I say, which isn't nearly enough. "And when I do I can use his book to wipe my arse on. And that goes for your notice as well, because I don't want to see any of you again or anyone else who's got room in their head for that, that . . ." I can't think of a word bad enough for Kray, but it doesn't matter, because by now I'm backing out of the office. "Just so everyone knows I know I'm being fired because of what I say about him," I add, raising my voice so they'll hear me through their hands over their ears. Then I manage to find my way home, and the locks to stick the keys in, and my bed.

There's almost nothing else in my room except me and *The Word*. So I still have a job, to stay here to make sure it's the copy nobody reads. I do that until the bank sends me a cheque for the money they must wish they didn't owe me, and I remember all my money I forgot to take with me when I escaped from the bank.

I'm waiting when they open. At first I think the slaves are pretending not to know me, then I wonder if they're too busy thinking Kray's thoughts. A slave takes my cheque and my withdrawal slip and goes away for longer than I can believe it would take even her to think about it, then I see the manager poke his head out of his office to spy on me while I'm tearing up a glossy brochure about how customers can help the bank to help the Third World. I see him tell the clerk to give me what I want, then he pulls in his head like a tortoise that's been kicked, and it almost blinds me to realise he's afraid of what I am. Only what am I?

The slave stuffs all my money in an envelope and drops it in the trough under the window, the trough that always made me wonder which side the pigs were on. I shove the envelope into my armpit and leave behind years of my life. I'm walking home as fast as I can, through the streets where every shop either has a sale on or is closing down or both, when I see Kray's face.

It's a drawing on the cover of just about the only magazine which is still about books. I have to find out what he's up to, but with the money like a cancer under my arm I can't be sure of liberating the magazine without people noticing. I go into the bookshop and grab it off the rack, and people backing away make me feel stronger.

I've only read how *The Word* is shaping up to outsell the Bible worldwide, and how some campus cult is saying there's a different personal message in it for everybody, and anyone who can't read it should have it read to them, when a bouncer trying to look like a policeman tells me to buy the rag or leave. I've read all I need to, and I have all I need. The money is to give me time to do what I have to.

Only I'm not sure what that is. The longer I stay in my room, the more I'm tempted to look in *The Word* for a clue. It's trying to trick me into believing there's no help outside its pages, but I've something else to read. I find the Christ Will Rise pamphlets that *The Word* has done its best to tear up and shove out of my reach, and when I've dragged them and my face out of the dust under the bed I manage to smooth out the address.

It's down where most of the fires in the streets are and the police drive round in armoured cars when they go there at all, and no cameras are keeping watch, and hardly any helicopters. By now it's dark. People are doing things to each other standing up in doorways if they aren't prowling the streets in dozens searching for less than themselves. I'm afraid they may set fire to me, because I see dogs pulling apart something charred that looks as if it used to be someone, but nobody seems to think I'm worth bothering with, which is their loss.

The Risers' sanctuary is in the middle of a block of hundred-year-old houses, some of which have roofs. Children are running into one house holding a cat by all its legs, but I can't see anyone else. I feel the front steps tilt and crunch together as I climb to the Risers' door, and I hold on to the knocker to steady myself, though it makes my fingers feel as if they're crumbling. I'm about to slam the knocker against the rusty plate when a fire in a ruin across the street lights up the room inside the window next to me.

It's full of chairs around a table with pamphlets on it. Then the fire jerks higher, and I see they aren't piles of pamphlets, they're two copies of *The Word*. The books start to wobble like two blocks of gelatin across the table toward me, and I nearly wrench the knocker off the door with trying to let go of it. I fall down the steps and don't stop running until I'm locked in my room.

I watch all night in case I've been followed. Even after the last television goes out I can't sleep. And when the dawn brings the wagons to clean up the blood and vomit and empty cartridges, I don't want to sleep, because I've remembered that the Risers aren't the only other people who know what Kray was.

I go out when the streets won't be crawling—when the taken care of have gone to work, and the beggars are counting their pennies. When I reach Everybody's Fantasy it looks as if the books in the window and the Everything Half Price sign have been there for months. The rainy dirt on the window stops me reading the spines on the shelf where Kray would be. I'm across the road in a burned-out house, waiting for a woman with three Dobermans to pass so I can smash my way into the shop with a brick, when Kath arrives in a car with bits of it scraping the road. He doesn't look interested in why I'm there or in anything else, especially selling books, so I say "You're my last hope."

"Yeah, okay." It takes him a good few seconds to get around to saying "What?"

"You've got some books I want to buy."

"Yeah?" He comes to as much life as he's got and wanders into the shop to pick up books strewn over the floor. "There they are."

I think he's figured out which books I want and why until I realise he means everything in the shop. I'm heading for the shelf when I see *The Word*, *The Word*, *The Word*, *The Word* . . . "Where's *A Touch of Other*?" I nearly scream.

"Don't know it."

"Of course you do. Jess Kray's first novel and the two that go with it. He signed them all when you didn't want him to. You can't have sold them, crap like them."

"Can't I?" Kath scratches his head as if he's digging up thoughts. "No, I remember. He bought the lot. Must have been just about when *The Word* was due."

"You realise what he was up to, don't you?"

"Being kind. Felt guilty about leaving us with all those books after nobody came, so he bought them back when he could afford to. Wish we still had them. I've never even seen them offered for sale."

"That's because he doesn't want anyone to know he wrote them, don't you see? Otherwise even the world might wonder how someone like that could have written the thing he wants everyone to buy."

"You can't have read *The Word* if you say that. It doesn't matter what came before it, only what will happen when everyone's learned from it."

He must have stoned whatever brains he had out of his head. "I felt like you do about him," he's saying now, "but then I got to know him."

"You know him? You know where I can find him?"

"Got to know him in his book."

"But you've got the address where you sent him his books."

"Care of his publishers."

"He didn't even give you his address, and you think he's your friend?"

"He was moving. He's got nothing to hide, you have to believe that." Having to give me so many answers so fast seems to have used Kath up, then his face rouses itself. "If you want to get to know him as he is, he's supposed to be at Consummation."

"I've given up on fandom. The people I meet every day are bad enough."

Kath's turning over magazines on the counter like a cat trying to cover its turds. "There'll be readings from *The Word* for charity and a panel about it, and he's meant to be there. We'd go, only we've not long had a kid."

"Don't tell me there'll be someone growing up without *The Word*."

"No, we'd like her to see him one day. I was just telling you we can't afford to go." He shakes two handfuls of fanzines until a flyer drops out of one. "See, there he is."

The flyer is for Consummation, which is two weeks away in Birmingham, and it says the Sunday will be Jess Kray Day. I manage not to crumple much of it up. "Can I have this?"

"I thought you didn't want to know him."

"You've sold me." I shove the flyer into my pocket. "Thanks for giving me what I was looking for," I say, and leave him fading with his books.

I don't believe a whole sigh fie convention can be taken in by Kray. Fen are stupid, Sod knows, but in a different way—thinking they're less stupid than everyone else. I'll know what to do when I see them and him. The two weeks seem not so much to pass as not to be there at all. On the Friday morning I have a bath so I won't draw attention to myself until I want to. For the first time ever I don't hitch to a convention, I go by train to be in time to spy out the situation. Once I'm in my seat I stay there, because I've seen one woman reading *The Word* and I don't want to see how many other passengers are. I stare at streets of houses with steel shutters over the windows and rivers covered with chemicals and forests that children keep setting fire to, but I can feel Kray's words hatching in all the nodding heads around me.

The convention hotel is five minutes' walk from the station. After about ten beggars I pretend I'm alone in the street. The hotel is booked solid as a fan's cranium, and the hotel next to it, and I have to put up with one where the stairs lurch as if I'm drunk and my room smells of someone's raincoat and old cigarettes. It won't matter, because I'll be spending as much time with the fen as I can bear. I go to the convention hotel while it's daylight and there are police out of their vehicles. And the first thing the girl at the registration desk with a ring in her nose and six more in her ears says is "Have you got *The Word*?"

My face goes hard, but I manage to say "It's at home."

"If you'd like one to have with you, they're free with membership."

It'll be another that nobody else can read. I tell her my name's Jay Batt, and pin my badge on when she's written it, and squeeze the book in my right hand so hard I can almost feel the words mashing together. "Is he here yet?"

"He won't be."

"But he's why I'm here. I was promised he was coming."

She must think I sound the same kind of disappointed as her. "He said he would be when we wrote to him, only now he has to be in the film about him they'll be televising next month. Shall I tell you what he said? That now we've got *The Word* we don't need him."

I know that's garbage, but I'm not sure why. I bite my tongue so I won't yell, and when I see her sympathising with the tears in my eyes I limp off to the bar. It's already full of more people than seats, and I know most of them—I've written about them in my fanzines. I'm wondering how I can get close enough to find out what they really think about *The Word* when they start greeting me like an old friend. Two people have offered to buy me a drink before I realise why they're behaving like this—because I've got *The Word*.

I down the drinks, and more when they're offered, and make sure everyone knows I won't buy a round. I'm trying to infuriate someone as much as their forgiveness infuriates me, because then maybe they'll argue about Kray. But whatever I say about him and his lies they just look more understanding and wait patiently for me to understand. The room gets darker as my eyes fill up with the dirt and smoke in the air, and faces start to melt as if *The Word* has turned them into putty. Then I'm screaming at the committee members and digging my nails into the cover of the book. "Why would anyone be making a film about him? More likely he was afraid he'd meet someone here who knows what he wants us to forget he wrote."

"You mustn't say that. He sent us this, look, all about the film." The chairman takes a glossy brochure out of his brief-case. The sight of Kray grinning on the cover almost blinds me with rage, but I manage to read the name of the production company. "And they're going to do a live discussion with him after the broadcast," the chairman says.

I run after my balance back to my hotel. I can hear machine guns somewhere, and I have to ring the bell three times before the armed night porter lets me in, but they can't stop me now. I haul myself up to my room, snapping a banister in the process, and fall on the bed to let my headache come. Whenever it lessens I think of another bit of the letter I'm going to write. The night and the sounds of gunfire falter at last, and the room fades into some kind of reality. It's like being part of the cover of a book nobody wants to take out of a window, but they won't be able to ignore me much longer.

I write the letter and check out of the hotel, telling the receptionist I've been called away urgently, and fight my way through the pickpockets to the nearest post office, w431.

Here I get the address of the television channel. Posting the letter reminds me of going to church when I had to live with my parents, where they used to put things in your mouth in front of the altar. As soon as the letter is out of my hands I don't know if I feel empty or unburdened, and I can't remember exactly what I wrote.

I spend Sunday at home trying to remember. Did I really claim I was the first to spread the word about Kray? Did I really call myself Jude Carrot because I was afraid he'd remember the interview and tell the producer not to let me anywhere near? Won't he just say he's never heard of me? I can't think how that idea makes me feel. I left the other copy of *The Word* in my hotel room as if it was the Bible, and I have to stop myself from throwing the one under the bed out of the window to give them something to fight over besides the trash in the street.

On Monday I know the letter has arrived. Maybe it'll take a few hours to reach the producer of the discussion programme, since I didn't know his name. By Tuesday it must have got to him, and by Wednesday he should have written to me. But Thursday comes, and I watch the postman dodging in and out of his van while his partner rides shotgun, and there's no letter for me.

Twice I hear the phone in the hall start to ring, but it could just be army trucks shaking the house. I start trying to think of a letter I could write under another name, saying I know things about Kray nobody else does, only I can't think of a letter that's different enough. I go to bed to think, then I get up to, and keeping doing that takes care of Thursday and Friday morning. Then I hear the van screech to a halt just long enough for the postman to stick a letter through the door without getting out of his cabin, because presumably they can't afford to pay his partner any more, then it screeches away along the sidewalk. And when I look down the stairs I see the logo of the television company on the envelope.

I'd open it in the hall except I find I'm afraid to read what it says. I remember I'm naked and cover my peter with it while I run upstairs, though everyone in the house is scared to open their door if they hear anyone else. I lock all my locks and hook up the chains and wipe my hands on my behind so the envelope won't slip out of them, then I tear it almost in half and shake the letter flat.

Dear Mr "Carrot"
Jess Kray says

Suddenly my hands feel like gloves someone's just pulled their hands out of, and when I can see again I have to fetch the letter from under the bed. I'm already struggling to think of a different name to sign on the next letter I send, though since now I'll know who the producer is, should I phone them? I poke at my eyes until they focus enough that I can see her name is Tildy Bacon, then I make them see what she wrote.

> Dear Mr "Carrot"
> Jess Kray says he will look forward to seeing you and including you in our discussion on the 25th.

There's more about how they'll pay my expenses and where I'm to go, but I fall on the bed, because I've just discovered I don't know what to do after all. It doesn't matter, I'll know what to say when the cameras are on and the country's watching me. Only something's missing from that idea, and the absence keeps pecking at my head. It feels like an intruder in my room, one I can't see that won't leave me alone. Maybe I know what I'm trying not to think, but a week goes by before I realise: I can't be certain of exposing Kray unless I read *The Word*.

I spend a day telling myself I have to, and the next day I drag the book out of its hiding place and claw off the dusty cobwebs. I stare at the cover until it feels as if it's stuck behind my eyes, then I scream at myself to make me open it. As soon as I can see the print I start reading, but it feels as if Kray's words and the noises of marching drums and sirens and gunfire are merging into a substance that's filling up my head before I can stop it, and I have to shut the book. There's less than a week before I'm on television, and all I can think of that may work is being as far away from people as I can get when I read the book.

The next day is Sunday, which makes no difference, since there are as many people wandering around the countryside with nothing else to do any day of the week. I tear the covers off a Christ Will Rise pamphlet and wrap them round *The Word* before I head for Kings Cross, and I'm sure some of the people I avoid look at it to see if it's *The Word*. I thump on the steel shutter until the booking clerk sells me a ticket. While I'm waiting for the train I see through the reinforced glass of the bookstall that most of the newspapers are announcing a war that's just begun in Africa. I catch myself wondering if *The Word* has been translated in those countries yet, and then I imagine a world where there are no wars because everyone's too busy reading *The Word* and thinking about it and talking about it, and my fingernails start aching from gripping the book so I won't throw it under a train.

When my train leaves I'm almost alone on it, but I see more people than I expect in the streets. Quite a few seem to be gathering in a demolished church, and I see a whole crowd scattered over a park, being read to from a book—I can't decide whether it's black or white. All their faces are turned to the sun, as if they don't know they're being blinded. As the city falls away I'm sure I can feel all those minds clogged with Kray trying to drag mine back and having to let go like old tasteless chewing gum being pulled out of my head. Then there are only fields made up of lines waiting to be written on, and hedges blossoming with litter, and hours later mountains hack their way up through fields and forests as if the world is still crystallising. In the midst of the mountains I get off at a station that's no more than two empty platforms, and climb until I'm deep in a forest and nearly can't breathe for climbing. I sit on a fallen tree, and there's nothing to do except read. And I make myself open *The Word* and read as fast as I can.

I won't look up until I've finished. I can feel his words crowding into my head and breeding there, but I have to understand what he's put into the world before I confront him. The only sound is of me turning pages and ripping each one out as I finish it, but I sense the trees coming to read over my shoulder, and moss oozing down them to be closer to the book, and creatures running along branches until they're

above my head. I won't look, I only read faster, so fast that
the book is in my head before I know. However much there
is of it, I'm stronger—out here it's just me and the book. I
wonder suddenly if the pages may be impregnated with some
kind of drug, but if they are I've beaten it by throwing away
the pages, because you must have to be holding the whole
book for the drug to work. I've no idea how long I've been
reading the book aloud, but it doesn't matter if it helps me
see what Kray is up to. Though my throat is aching by the
time I've finished, I manage a laugh that makes the trees back
away. I fall back with my face to the clouds and try to think
what the book has told me that he wouldn't want anyone to
know.

My body's shaking inside and out, and I feel as if my
brain is too. There was something about panic in *The Word*,
but if I think of it, will that show me how the book is causing
it, or won't I be able to resist swallowing *The Word* as the
cure? I'm already remembering, and digging my fingernails
into my temples can't crush the thought. Kray says we'll all
experience a taste of the panic Christ experienced as we
approach the time when the world is changed. I feel the idea
cracking open in my brain, and as I fight it I see in a flash
what he was trying not to admit by phrasing it that way. He
wanted nobody to know that *he* is panicking—that he has
something to be afraid of.

I sit up and crouch around myself until I stop shaking,
then I go down through the forest. The glade papered with
The Word seems to have a meaning I no longer need to understand. Some of the pages look as if they're reverting to wood.
The night comes down the forest with me, and in a while a
train crawls out of it. I go home and lock myself in.

Now it takes me all my time to hold *The Word* still in my
head. The only other thing I need to be aware of is when the

television company sends me my train ticket, but everything around me seems on the point of making a move. Whenever I hear a car it sounds about to reveal it's a mail van. At least that helps me ignore my impression that all I can see of the world is poised to betray itself. If this is how having read *The Word* feels . . .

The next day the mail van screeches past my building, and the day after that. Suppose the letter to me has been stolen, or someone at the television company has stopped it from being sent? I'll pay my own fare and get into the discussion somehow. But the ticket finally arrives, which may mean they'll try and steal it from my room.

I sit with the ticket between my teeth and watch the street and listen for them setting up whatever they may use to smash my door in. Suppose the room itself is the trap? Or am I being made to think that so I'll be driven out of it? I wrap the ticket in some of a Christ Will Rise pamphlet so that the ink won't run when I take it with me to the bathroom, and on the last morning I have a long bath that feels like some kind of ritual. That would be a good time for them to come for me, but they don't, nor on my way to the station, though I'm sure I notice people looking at me as if they know something about me. For the first time since I can remember there are no sounds of violence in the streets, and that makes me feel there are about to be.

On the train I sit where I can watch the whole compartment, and see the other passengers pretending not to watch me. All the way to Hyde Park Corner I expect to be headed off. I'm trudging up the slope to the hotel when a limo pulls up in front of the glass doors and two minders climb out before Kray does. As he unbends he looks like a snake standing on its tail. I pretend to be interested in the window of a religious bookshop in case he tries to work on me before the world is watching. I see copies of *The Word* next to the Bible and the Koran, and Kray's reflection merging with his book as he goes into the hotel. He must have noticed me, so why is he leaving me alone? Because passiveness is the trick he's been playing on me ever since I read *The Word*—doing nothing so I'll be drawn toward him and his words. It's the trick he's been playing on the world.

Knowing that makes me impatient to finish. I wait until I see him arrive in the penthouse suite, then I check in. My room is more than twice the size of the one I left at home. The world is taking notice of me at last. I drink the liquor in the refrigerator while I have another bath, and ignore the ringing of the phone until I think there's only just time to get to the studio before the discussion starts.

A girl's face on the phone screen tells me my taxi's waiting. As soon as we're in it she wants to know everything about me, but I won't let her make me feel I don't know what I am. I shrug at her until she shuts up. There are no other cars on the road, and I wonder if there's a curfew or everyone's at home waiting for Kray and me.

Five minutes later the taxi races into the forecourt of the television studios. The girl with not much breath rushes me past a guard at the door and another one at a desk and down a corridor that looks as if it never ends. I think that's the trick they were keeping in store for me, but then she steers me left into a room, and I'm surrounded by voices and face to face with Kray.

There are about a dozen other people in the room. The remains of a buffet are on a table and scattered around on paper plates. A woman with eyes too big for her face says she's Tildy Bacon and hands me a glass of wine while a girl combs my hair and powders my face, and I feel as if they're acting out some ritual from *The Word*. Kray watches me as he talks and grins at some of his cronies, and once the girl has finished with me he puts a piece of cake on a plate and brings it over. "You must have something, Jeremy. You look as if you've been fasting for the occasion."

So does he. He looks thinner and older, as if he's put almost all of himself into his book, or is he trying to trick me into thinking he'll be easy to deal with? I take the plate and wash a bite of the cake down with some wine, and he gives me the grin. "It's nearly time."

Is he talking about the programme I can see behind him on a monitor next to a fax machine? Someone who might be a professor or a student is saying that nobody he's met has been unchanged by *The Word* and that he thinks it promises every reader the essential experience of their life. Kray's watching my face, but I won't let him see I know how much crap the screen is talking until we're on the air. Then Tildy Bacon says to everyone "Shall we go up? Bring your drinks."

As the girl who ought to learn how to breathe ushers people toward the corridor, Tildy Bacon steps in front of me and looks me in the face. So they've saved stopping me until the last possible moment. I'll wait until everyone else is out of the room, then I'll do whatever needs to be done to make certain she can't follow me and throw me off the air. But she says "We had to ask Jess how to bill you on screen since you weren't here."

If she thinks I'm going to ask what he said I was, she can go on thinking. "I'm sure he knows best," I tell her with a grin that may look like his for all I care, and dodge around her before she can delay me any further, and follow the procession along the corridor.

At first the setup in the studio looks perfect. The seven of us including Kray will sit on couches around a low table with glasses and a jug of water on it while Kray's minders have to stay on the far side of a window. Only I haven't managed to overtake the procession, so how can I get close to him? Then he says "Sit next to me, Jeremy," and pats a leather cushion, and before I have time to wonder what he's up to I've joined him.

Everyone else sitting down sounds like something leathery

stirring in its sleep. The programme about Kray is on a monitor in a corner of the studio. A priest says he believes the secret of *The Word* needs to be understood, then the credits are rolling and a woman who I hadn't even realised was going to run the discussion leans across the table and waits for a red light to signal her. Then she says "So, Jess Kray, what's your secret?"

He grins at her and the world. "If I have one, it must be in my book."

A man with holes in his purple face where spots were says "In other words, if you revealed the secret it wouldn't sell."

Is there actually someone here besides me who doesn't believe in *The Word*? Kray grins at him. "No, I'm saying the secret must be different for everyone. It isn't a question of commerce. In some parts of the world I'm giving the book away."

The holey man seems satisfied, but a woman with almost more hair on her upper lip than on her scalp says "To achieve what?"

"Peace?"

Good Sod, Kray really does believe his book can put a stop to wars. Or does he mean he won't be peaceful until the whole world has *The Word* inside them? The woman who was given the signal leans across the table again, reaching for Kray with her perfume and her glittering hands and her hair swaying like oil on water. She means to turn the show into a discussion, which will give him the chance not to be watched all the time by the camera. I'll say anything to bother him, even before I know what. "It's supposed to be . . ."

That heads her off, and everyone looks at me. Then I hear what I'm going to say—that the secret of *The Word* is supposed to be some kind of eternal life. But there is no secret in *The Word*, that's why I'm here.

"Jeremy?" Kray says.

I'm wondering if *The Word* has got inside me without

my knowing—if it was making me say what I nearly said and that's why he is encouraging me. He wants me to say that for him, and he's talking about peace, which I already knew was his weapon, and suddenly I see what everything has been about. It's as if a light is shining straight into my eyes, and I don't care if it blinds me. "He's supposed to be Christ," I shout.

There's some leathery movement, then someone I don't need to see says "All the characters are clearly aspects of him."

"We're talking about the narrator of *The Word*," the television woman explains to the camera, and joins in. "I took him to be some kind of prophet."

"Christ was a prophet," says a man who I can just about see is wearing a turban.

"Are we saying—" the television woman begins, but she can't protect Kray from me like that. "He knows I didn't mean anyone in his book," I shout. "I mean him."

The words are coming out faster than I can think, but they feel right. "If people don't believe in him, they won't believe in his book. And they won't believe in him unless he can save himself."

Ideas are fighting in my head as if *The Word* is trying to come clear. If Christ came back now, he'd have to die to make way for a religion that works better than his did, or would it be the opposite of Christ who'd try to stop all the violence and changes in the world? Either way . . . I'm going blind with panic, because I can feel Kray close to me, willing me to . . . He wants me to go on speaking while my words are out of control—because they're his, or because I won't be able to direct them at him? Then I realise how long he's been silent, and I think he wants me to speak to him so he can speak to me. Is the panic I'm suffering his? He's afraid—afraid of me, because I'm . . .

"I think it's time we moved on," the television woman

says, but she can't make anything happen now. I turn and look at him.

He's waiting for me. His grin is telling me to speak—to say whatever I have to say, because then he'll answer and all that the world will remember hearing is him. It's been that way ever since the world heard of him. I see that now, but he's let me come too close. As I open my mouth I duck my head toward him.

For a moment it seems I'm going to kiss him. I see his lips parting, and his tongue feeling his teeth, and the blood in his eyes, and the fear there at last. I duck lower and go for his throat. I know how to do it from biting my tongue, and now I don't need to restrain myself or let go. Someone is screaming, it sounds as if the world is, but it can't be Kray, because I've torn out his voice. I lift my head and spit it back into his face.

It doesn't blot out his eyes. They meet mine, and there's forgiveness in them, or something even worse—fulfilment? Then his head falls back, opening his throat so I'm afraid he'll try and talk through it, and he throws his arms wide for the cameras. That's all I see, because there's nothing in my eyes now except light. But it isn't over, because I can still taste his voice, like iron in my mouth.

Words are struggling to burst out of my head, and I don't know what they are. Any moment Kray's minders or someone will get hold of me, but if I can just . . . I bang my knees against the table to find it, and hear the glasses clash against the jug. I throw myself forward and find one, and a hand grabs my arm, but I wrench myself free and shove the glass against my teeth until it breaks. Now the light feels as if it's turning into pain which is turning into the world, but whose pain is it—Kray's or mine? Hands are pulling at me, and I've no more time to think. As I make myself chew and swallow, at least I'm sure I'll never say another word.

CHILIAD: A MEDITATION

CLIVE BARKER

PART TWO

A MOMENT AT THE RIVER'S HEART

Again, by the river: I dreamed a dream of the Coming. This is what I set down when I woke.

In the last dark days, I wrote, *even in the hours before everything changed forever, even in the moments that preceded the Moment, most of the people on the planet denied what they knew. They buried their attentions in a million trivial tasks. (Of course every task was trivial then, from the baking of bread to the dispensation of power: all of it would be as nothing very soon.)*

But the rest of the world was not so willful. Domestic animals for instance, even the loyalest, left their kennels and leapt their gates to go and sniff the open sky. Cattle in the slaughterhouse gave up their fear and lowed with pleasure, even as the fatal blow descended. Every bird fell silent, waiting for a finer music. Every raindrop twitched as it fell, eager to climb again, and have a glimpse of Heaven's bounty before the eyes of humankind.

The Pantheons made themselves apparent in the blink of an eye; perhaps less. At one instant the planet was a place of faith, doubt, and godlessness, the next there was room for none of these. Who needed faith when the senses confirmed all? As for doubt and godlessness, they were absurdities now that every deity that had ever appeared in human consciousness (and some several hundred thousand who had never made it) had manifested themselves. The Coming was indiscriminate; it made no distinction between great

CLIVE BARKER

divinities and small. There were vast and transformative powers abroad, deities that brought with them fleets of angelic vehicles and all manner of divine paraphernalia, but there were also threadbare local gods, guardians of painted rocks, spirits of bamboo groves; presences that healed sores and brought lovers, demons who haunted empty roads and forsaken hotels. A world of yearning and need was suddenly a place of surfeit; and the end of mankind began, for there was nothing left invisible, or unknowable, and therefore nothing left to hope for or desire.

That's what I wrote, sitting by the river, and conceived from this beginning a book about the days after the Moment; a book in which I would indulge my passion for deities. It would be, I decided, encyclopedic. I would create a pilgrim, after Bunyan, whose progress would not be marked by tests of faith and fortitude but by the horrors of certainty and the despair brought by limitless horizons. His excitement and his piety would quickly wither. He would sate his senses and his curiosity without fear of censure, and by degrees sink into a trough of complete indifference. I pictured him wandering through the city besieged by revelation. In the early hours, there would be packs of wild gods loose on the streets, howling their wisdom against the lightening sky. A few minutes after dawn the thoroughfares would be impassable, the number of people on the planet having swelled thanks to a universal state of resurrection. (There was a certain competitiveness among the deities as to who could raise the greatest number of dead souls; with all human graves empty, and all human ash recombined, the competitors were obliged to raise cows, and horses; soon it would be sheep and pigs; later, they would stoop to fowl.)

So the day would go, a chaos through which my bewildered pilgrim would make his weary way, his energies depleted wonderment by wonderment, glory by glory, until at last, on the outskirts of the city, he finds a hill, and lies down, closing his eyes against the thronged clouds. There is a pleasant darkness behind his lids, a restful absence. He wants to go into it forever. But how may he achieve such bliss? If he kills himself here on the hill, some eager messiah will surely find him, and raise him up like Lazarus. He must find a place to die where his corpse will not be discovered. Sighing, he gets to his feet and climbs to the crest of the hill. The landscape before him gives him no greater comfort than the city he has left. Every grove has its local god, every crossroads the same; every stump, every pebble. *Is there a mote of dust that some god or other does not exalt*, he wonders. *Is there any place he can be alone?* That becomes his pilgrimage then. With a heart unbearably heavy he goes on his way, looking for a place where resurrection will not find him.

It would not have made a good book, I think. It would have been a folly. Its best telling was in these paragraphs: they contain all the ironies a tome would have contained, and waste less ink. Now I'm free to turn my hand back to the death at the river.

ii

In my mind, the river runs both ways; but you know that. And I must commit myself to it, sooner or later, let it sweep me where it will. Perhaps I'll drown; perhaps I'll be pressed back against the shore. Perhaps I'll find love in the flood. Perhaps, from the rush of water, I will see the world as only saints see it. Until then — until I have the courage to go back into the tumult—I can only watch, and hope that I'll be able to finish what I began, though the beginning and the end may seem very much alike.

The man's name is Devlin Coombs, and he was until yesterday a married man of forty-one, happily unrenowned. He worked at a small insurance firm in the city, where he'd been a claims adjuster for a decade. Tuesdays and Thursdays he attended night school, studying ceramics. He has made three pots of which he could say: these I like. He has no children. He likes Beethoven and eel pie. At least, he did. He will not take pleasure in eel pie again; nor will he play a Beethoven sonata without weeping so uncontrollably he must turn it off. He will make no more pots; nor will he make love to Mary Elizabeth, for last night, his beloved wife's body was washed up by the river. It was the twenty-sixth of December, nineteen ninety-nine, five days before an auspicious day, five days before the millennium, when prophets of doom promise the end of the world. They were wrong by almost a week, Devlin thinks as he walks along the river: or else the world ended early, for what is the world worth without Mary Elizabeth?

All he could do now is mourn her, mourn her and wonder, while he mourned, how she had come to such an end. How was it possible that a woman of such upright morality, a woman who had never strayed from the path of the righteous, had lost her life to murder?

He had to identify the body, of course, and was not expecting from the police—for whom he had a nervous liberal's concealed contempt—any degree of delicacy in the business. He was right. There was none. He was brought in to a badly disinfected room and presented with the pitiful shape of her, laid out on a table of chipped white enamel. There was a sheet covering her from head to foot. He asked that it be taken off entirely. Here, at least, the detective showed some degree of empathy, telling him very quietly that he didn't feel this to be a wise idea.

"She's in a terrible way below the neck," the man said.

Devlin replied that he was ready for that. He wanted to see her all. And when the man drew back the sheet he did not regret his decision. She was indeed in *a terrible way*, her body horribly plowed. But the inertness of her bulk was more certain proof to him of her absence—the sense that she was gone, completely, or else she would not have allowed this wretched unveiling—that made the whole scene more acceptable. He would not know this woman again. All he could know now—the only mystery he could solve—was the identity of the man who had taken her life.

The police told him nothing—only reassured him that they knew their business, and that he could serve them best by first answering their questions, which he did, and then leaving them to work without demanding to know their progress every moment. This he found more difficult. Given that he was not a suspect (at the time of Mary Elizabeth's murder he had been a hundred miles away, helping his addled mother through the horrors of her third Christmas with Parkinson's disease; so she testified, though in truth she didn't know one day from the next) it followed that there were two classes of suspect. The first: somebody Mary Elizabeth knew—a friend, or a colleague at work. The second: a psychotic stranger whose path she had been unlucky enough to cross. The first was to Devlin's mind unlikely, even absurd. Mary Elizabeth had a small circle of friends, mostly women sliding into genteel middle age, and at work a few pleasant folks, most of whom he himself had met at company picnics and the like. There was not a one he would not have trusted. Which left his second hypothesis the only plausible explanation. His wife had met death by chance, because she had wandered its way. And with every hour the police delayed their pursuit of her murderer, asking asinine questions of men and women who were entirely blameless in the matter, the greater the chance that the guilty party would escape them, and forever. Unthinkable! that his beloved could be taken this way and the thief not be punished. But as the days went by (and the nights:

he didn't sleep, didn't even want to sleep, with the bed empty beside him), the more frustrated he became, and the more certain that if justice was to be served in this matter, he would have to be the man to mete it out.

iii

Devlin has a dentist whom he avoids visiting, but has recently become a near neighbor. He meets the man, one Edward Littlefield, as he goes to his car to drive down to the place where Mary Elizabeth was found. Littlefield's a wide faced, gap-toothed, pithy man, whose response to having one of the world's less glamorous professions is to ride it for all it's worth. But today he makes no jokes about oral hygiene. He's heard the news, of course, and remarks that he found Devlin's television interview the previous evening, complaining about the lack of police activity, very moving.

"You have to take these things into your own hands," he says, and explains that he speaks from experience. His son went missing when the boy was six, and was never found.

"To this day," Littlefield says, "I wish I'd trusted the police less and my instincts more. I could have found the kid myself if I hadn't just sat at home and believed every damn thing they were telling me." His gaze slides off down the street, as though even now he thinks he may see his son—gone now nineteen years—playing hide-and-seek between the sycamores. "My wife met a woman a couple of years ago who said she could have helped us, and I thought: dear God where were you when I needed you?"

"I'm sorry, I don't quite follow. Who was this woman?"

"My wife was the one who had the really involved conversations with her. I don't know—" He recalls his gaze from the distance and looks hard at Devlin. "—Are you a believer?" he asks softly.

"In what?"

"In that kind of thing. Paranormal stuff. Psychic phe-
nomena . . ."

"I don't know."

"But you'd be willing to give it a try?"

"Well the police are certainly no damn good to me. And
I'm afraid—" He breaks off, stares at the ground.

"Spit it out," Littlefield replies, as is his wont.

"I'm afraid if I don't find out who did it . . . I mean,
ever . . . I'll just go crazy."

Littlefield nods. Again, he's looking down the street. "I
know how that feels," he murmurs. "Not having a way to finish. Like a book with the last few pages missing. And you
know they'll always be missing. However hard you look;
however much you pray. I used to pray every night, as hard
as I knew how: *Dear God, tell me where my son is buried.*
You get to that point. Just tell me where he's buried."

Devlin keeps his silence a long moment, embarrassed by
Littlefield's vulnerability. If he could walk away at that
moment, he would do so, but he needs more information
from the man: the name of the psychic, and her whereabouts.
He doesn't have to ask. Littlefield needs only to glance back
at Devlin's face, and he has his wallet out, and a card from
the wallet, and he's scrawling a name and a number. "Funny,"
he says as he writes, "how you remember some telephone
numbers and not others. I could never remember my mother-
in-law's number; never; even though I must have dialed it
hundreds of times. But this"—he hands the card to Devlin—
"I remember this without ever having to think about it."

They part. Devlin doesn't pocket the card. He carries it
in his tightly knotted fist and calls the woman the moment he
gets home, though as soon as she picks up the phone and he
hears her voice it is as if she did the calling, and all he has
done is answered her summons.

———

So it is he comes to the unremarkable house in Camberwell, with its neat lawn and its blue door, and is invited into a place so utterly unlike its exterior it's as though he had stepped out of waking reality into a dream. His guide's name is Shirley Dunbar. She's fiftyish, recently blond, and might have been quite a beauty a hundred pounds ago. She has prepared a snack for them both: ham sandwiches, Christmas cake heavy with fruit and rum, and glasses of Scotch. Enjoy it, she says, as they sit in the dark parlor, its plaster walls covered with hundreds of small scraps of linen upon which incoherent signs are scrawled; this is the last you should eat or drink for twenty-four hours. You can have a little water, but nothing solid. You need to clean out your system before you go.

"Go where?" says Devlin.

"Back to see what happened," Shirley replies. She has made a mulch of cake and whiskey in her mouth, and savors it as she speaks. "You'll take the light and back you'll go."

"I thought you . . ."

"Me?"

". . . I thought that's what psychics do. You go . . . I don't know . . . to talk to your spirits or whatever."

"No, not me."

". . . but I don't . . ."

"What?"

"I don't know anything about any of this."

"You know your wife," Shirley replies. "I didn't. You saw her dead. I didn't. You've probably been to the place where she was found—"

"Yes."

"—I haven't. You see, I'm just here to facilitate."

"So you never . . . ?"

"Travel?"

"Yes."

"No. Not if I can help it. In my younger days, well, yes,

on occasion I'd go. I was more *interested* then, I suppose. I thought there was more to know than there was."

"More to know?"

"The grand scheme of things," Shirley replies, her pudgy hands describing a ragged circle in front of her. "But of course you learn . . ."

"What?"

"That there's nothing. There's only us wanting it, you know, and wanting isn't really enough, is it? I mean, in the end. It's just not enough."

Devlin's not certain how much of this he's really understanding, but he decides not to ask any more questions, which is fine by Shirley, who can pin thoughts together without need of prompting. She tells him, by way of a bewildering series of fragments, her life story. Born in Belfast, married at seventeen, lost all her children to disease; discovered her gifts when her husband (Mr. Dunbar she calls him throughout) ran away with "a lady-friend," and she was left in an empty house dallying with insanity. She has a gift, perhaps from her mother— a way of piercing the veil, as she puts it, that hangs between us and the dead. Once she'd grasped the nature of her talent, she says, there was no looking back. It was as if the woman she'd been until then simply evaporated. Indeed she keeps the name Dunbar—rather than reverting to her maiden name—as a way of reminding herself that she was once an ordinary married woman.

At last she comes to the crux of her monologue. "You'll be wondering," she says, "where all this is leading."

"Well . . ." Devlin begins.

"Trust's important," she replies. "I mean, here am I and here's you, and there's got to be trust hasn't there, when we've been brought together this way."

"You think we were brought together?"

"Oh, yes, you were *destined* to come here, Devlin," she tells him. Devlin wants to ask how this faith in predestination sits beside her dismissal of any grand scheme, but he decides not to break her flow, just lets her talk. "I've had things in this house . . ." she says, ". . . things you wouldn't find in Rome or Jerusalem. And you know, it's funny, I think they're better off here than they'd ever be in a fancy reliquary. Most holy things are humble at heart, aren't they? A nail, a lock of hair, a stone . . ." Her voice has become softer as she speaks of these treasures, and every last scrap of doubt has left Devlin's heart. He watches her whiskey-ruddied face, and knows this is no performance. She speaks of common scraps of matter raised by their association with the miraculous to a state of exaltation. *And if that's possible for a stone or a nail,* he thinks, *why not for a man?* And so thinking, feels the first trace of hope he's felt since he was told he'd lost his wife.

He cannot help speaking now; he feels empowered.

"I want to begin," he says. "Please. I want to begin."

"You've already begun, don't you see?" she says to him. "You began the moment you heard my name. But I want you to understand the consequences of this journey."

"I don't care."

"You should," she tells him sharply. "This isn't a matter of life and death. That'd be easy. No. This is . . . this is . . ."

". . . what?"

"It's hard to find the words," she replies. Then, after a pause to think them through, "I understand your grief, and I want to help soothe it, but there is only one object in this house that can truly aid you in your search. It's a flame."

"A flame?"

"Of sorts. You'll see for yourself. As I say, it's a flame. But . . . it's a lot more than that. It was brought here in the first year of my . . . what shall I call it? . . . my second life. The man who brought it wanted to be rid of it, and gave it to me."

"What does it do?"

"It will illuminate the way, back to your wife. Back to the moment when she died, if that's what you want to see."

"That's what I want to see."

"That and that alone?"

"Yes."

"You swear?"

"Yes."

"This is very important, Devlin."

"I don't see why."

"Well I'll tell you. Holy things have minds of their own. Unholy things the same. They have . . . *intentions*. Not all of them. Some of them are just what they seem to be. But this flame—"

"Intentions to do *what*?"

Shirley shrugs, pouring herself another ample whiskey. "I'm only warning you to be sure of what you want."

"I want to know who killed my wife," Devlin replies. "What could be plainer than that?"

iv

She tells him to return at dusk the following day. She tells him that what he wears should be cotton or silk, his shoes leather—no man-made materials. She repeats her instructions about not eating. He asks her what he should expect. She tells him she doesn't know. Every case is different, she says. This isn't an exact science, she says. We're dealing, she says, with the stuff of our souls, and only a fool would say they understood it. Then she tells him to leave, which he does, returned into the real world with his perception of things more than a little changed. As he drives home he has to stop a dozen times at least, because his mind simply drifts off. He finds himself wondering how much of the world around him is charged with significance. Is every inch of asphalt beneath the wheels of his car, every dead moth spattered on the window, a shard of some vaster mystery? Is there power in the dead matter of his fingernails, or the dried spittle at the corners of his mouth? If so, what a world this is; and how much, how very much, he wished he could tell Mary Elizabeth about it.

The next dusk he comes back to Shirley's house, as arranged. His stomach rumbles, his skin itches a little, he feels light-headed. He stands on the doorstep and talks to himself, say-ing: Be calm. You're the master of your body and your mind. This is what you wanted, after all. Be calm. Then he knocks on the door. It swings open at his touch, and he enters, calling Shirley's name. There's no reply, but nor does there need to be. He's only a yard down the hallway when he sees a flick-ering light from the living room, and knows that he is expected. He doesn't hesitate now, but goes into the parlor, a smile on his face. If Shirley is there to see the smile, she is not in sight of him, but then nothing draws his gaze other than the flame. It hovers in the air close to the hearth, giving off a sil-very light. As he approaches it he feels its touch on his face and hands; he turns up his palms and feels them pricked. Does he need to announce his desire? he wonders. No, no; the light knows. It's in his skull, brightening the darkness, comforting him.

He cups his hands around it, gently, just as he would if he were taking hold of a dandelion, or a butterfly. It responds to his care in kind: seeping into him through his pores. His flesh responds with shudders of pleasure, as though his sys-tem had been parched, and the light comes through its dusty channels like a long-delayed rain. Only when he has accus-tomed himself to its presence does the scouring power of its flow make itself known, and by then he's too exhilarated by the transformation he feels to care. That is its business, and he has no wish to deny it. Nor indeed would he be able. It has thrown off any pretense to gentility now, and comes full bore, piercing him, sluicing him, a spiritual emetic which leaves him shuddering where he stands.

And just as it seems his whole body will be washed to pieces, it stops its violent cleansing, is suddenly still in him.

He waits, expecting Shirley to appear and offer him some words of instruction. But she doesn't come. Ten minutes pass; fifteen, twenty; still he waits. At last he resigns himself to the fact that he's not going to get any guidance, from Shirley or anyone else. He's on his own in this endeavor.

"Well then . . ." he murmurs, almost as though he's expecting a dialogue with the light. "Shall we . . . ?"

He was going to say: Shall we go to the river? but he never finishes the sentence. The light shifts—he feels it move in him, momentously—and in a strange blur he passes out of the house into the street. He isn't aware of his limbs' motion; he isn't aware that he expends any effort whatsoever. He is simply transported, and on his way to realize his desires.

(Perhaps a word about Shirley is appropriate here. She is in the house that Devlin has just left, sprawled on the bathroom floor, where she has been incapacitated by a massive stroke. It will prove fatal in the next three hours. She will struggle to reach a phone, but fail. She will pray, but be granted no reprieve. At last, she will give thanks, lying in a pool of urine, her body dying around her, for a life lived with some measure of purpose. And as she gives thanks, she forgets herself; or at least she forgets her present condition. She's back on the streets of Belfast, at the age of nine. Blissful nine, innocent nine. Before she knew what sex was; before she lost faith with God and Father O'Connor, before her mother grew weary and white-haired. A summer's day, and she on Galway Street, wandering dreamily, smelling the green off the hills.

That's where she's living when she dies: in a moment

that she has not remembered for decades, but that surrounds her now like an embrace, and soothes her into death.)

V

Devlin finds himself beside the river. He does not remember passing through the streets to get here, though he assumes he must have done so. All he remembers is the calm, the blissful calm, being *in* and *of* the flame.

He knows the spot he's come to. It is several hundred yards upstream of the place where Mary Elizabeth's body was found, not far from the church, with its three glorious windows and its one of plain glass. He wonders if the speed of thought will take him the rest of the way to the murder site. But no, his body's apparently back under his own volition. He wills himself to walk, and his muscles oblige him, carrying him along the bank. And as he goes, the sky starts to brighten. *Dawn already?* he thinks. The night has barely begun. No, he sees, this isn't New Year's Day, dawning stride by stride; he's walking back into the afternoon in which Mary Elizabeth's life was lost.

A little girl runs past him, whooping. She makes no sign that he's visible to her, though perhaps she was too intent on her pursuit, or flight, to notice him. He watches her race away, her din receding. When he looks back along the bank his body starts to tremble, because there—less than thirty yards from him—is Mary Elizabeth. He had not anticipated the effect seeing her again would have upon him. His trembling is so violent it's almost like a fit; he has to will himself to stay on his feet. Tears come, and they carry refractions of the flame up out of his heart, blinding him momentarily before they spill down his cheeks.

Oh God; he hopes he can speak to her. Just a few words, nothing fancy, just to tell her how much she's loved.

But before he can get close enough to make an attempt,

he sees her turn; sees a man running between the trees in pursuit of her. *Oh Christ*, he thinks, *not so soon! Don't let it happen before I have a chance to—*

But *wait*. What's this? She's laughing at the man, not cowering in fear, and the expression on the stranger's face isn't one of malicious intent, but foolish. He crosses his eyes, he sticks out his tongue, all for her entertainment. And God knows, though it's a puerile exhibition, she's mightily amused. When he reaches her she doesn't push him away; she simply shakes her head, like a loving parent with an antic child. And that's not so far from the truth; her companion is half her age: a twenty-year-old at most, with the pimple scabs barely healed. Devlin thinks, vaguely, that she's spoken of him; pointed him out, perhaps, in a photograph of an office party. He isn't of consequence to her; or at least he's never had any suspicion that this might be so. Now he has reason to wonder, seeing the way she lets his hand stray to her shoulder, to her neck; oh now to her breast. She does not resist him; at least, not entirely. Again, there's that look of indulgence; a raised finger, a slight shake of the head, as if to say: don't be naughty; not here; not here. The attempt at discipline is ignored however; the lover capers in front of her, leering and caressing, blocking her way along the path.

She's dallying with death, Devlin knows. At some point along the way she's going to say or do something that irritates this youth, and the smiling will vanish and the capering will stop, and the bloodletting begin. She has pressed him aside now, so as to continue on her way, though she does so coquettishly. He walks beside her, whispering something that makes her blush, makes a gleam come into her eye. Devlin knows that twinkle. Time was he was the one who received it; and what a glorious gift it was, promising all kinds of intimacies. Now this damnable boy gets the look, and the promise, gets the kisses and the touches, gets the fucking, no doubt, when the teasing's over, gets her body under him in the backseat of his car—

"Oh God," Devlin murmurs.

And as he speaks she seems to hear him. At least she looks in his direction, and there's concern in her face.

"What is it?" her companion asks.

"I thought I heard . . ." She shakes her head, dismissing the thought. But even in the moment of dismissal she changes her mind. "He's here," she says.

"Who?"

"My husband."

"Don't be daft," the youth replies fondly, and to reassure her he kisses her on the lips. She doesn't object to his solace but kisses him back.

Oh God, Devlin sobs again, *Oh God*. This time, if Mary Elizabeth hears him, she makes no sign of it. She's allowed her lover to unbutton her coat, and he's fumbling down the front of her dress. Devlin is appalled: she's letting him tease her breast out into view, right here in the open. Her nipple is hard in the cold air; he warms it in his mouth, and she closes her eyes in delight at the sensation.

Oh you whore, Devlin thinks. *To do this, to cheat me of the love you owe me as a spouse—to turn your back in bed telling me it's not what you want anymore—when it is, it* is! *Look at you, bitch, with your hand on his trousers, with your tongue in his mouth!* Devlin feels sick to his stomach; he wants to look away, but he can't take his eyes off the scene. Surely they're not going to do it here and now; surely they're not so hot for one another they could fuck on the icy ground? The youth's whispering to her now, idly working her tit with his palm, and she's laughing, her cheeks flushed. How long since he saw that look on her face? Five years at least since she lay on the pillow all puffy with lust, all red and ripe and ready to receive him.

And never again. This is the last time he'll see her this way, forever and ever—

As his mind shapes this thought, some instinct tells him to look back over his shoulder. He does so, and sees there a second witness to his wife's infidelity. The mesh of undergrowth and the shadows of the trees keep the man's face from view, but there's something about the manner of his approach that makes Devlin believe he will know the voyeur when he comes into view. Devlin's suspicions, it seems, were twice misplaced: first in thinking Mary Elizabeth had died at the hand of a passing stranger, then ready to blame the youth at her side for the crime. *This* is the killer, here; Devlin's more certain of the fact by the moment. His heart quickens; his breath becomes ragged. Why does he feel such a terrible *excitement*? And then; and then . . .

. . . the leaves cease their concealment, the mesh of branches are divided, and there's the face of the man who will take Mary Elizabeth's life. At the sight of it he remembers how fine he felt, as he came between the trees, how righteous in his wrath, how strong, how joyful; yes, joyful, to have the doubts finally swept away, and the sight of her before him gasping as she was fingered.

He had put the deed out of his head completely once it was done; hidden himself from himself, so as not to lose the shreds of his sanity. But there's no denying it now.

I did this. I did this, I did this, I did this.

And all he can do is watch. All he wants to do is watch. He can't stop this scene being played out; it's already history. He came here only to discover the guilty party, and there he is, in all his vengeful glory, wielding the knife with such speed the lovers don't have time to run. He stabs the youth in the lower back, and down he goes. He's not dead, but he's too badly wounded to go very far. Then Devlin starts on Mary Elizabeth, who is sobbing that she's not to blame, not to blame; he took her by surprise—

Devlin simply says: *I've been watching you.* Then he cuts her, across the neck. It isn't a wound meant to kill.

Blood comes, of course, but only a little. He goes for the same place, to cut her again, but this time she puts up her arm to protect herself, and her hand is sliced, and gushes. She shrieks, and as if the sound were a cue, Devlin starts to slash and stab at her wildly.

Watching himself at work, Devlin remembers everything, his mind speeding ahead through the horrors to come. He will keep stabbing her long after she's fallen to the ground and has given up her pleas for help. He'll cut her breast. He'll open her blouse and doodle on her belly. He'll open his pants and try to urinate on her, but failing, he'll turn his attention to the lover, who has crawled a few yards from the murder site and there collapsed from blood loss. He is in a delirious state when Devlin gets to him; he looks up at his undoer and smiles, as though he's thinking he's in the crib, and this is his father, come to kiss him good-night. Devlin doesn't stab him, but moved by some perverse desire he picks the youth up in his arms and carries him down to the river. Even now, the lover doesn't understand his jeopardy. He continues to look up at Devlin dreamily, and is still doing so as Devlin drops him into the waters, which instantly close over his head. The youth has no strength in his limbs; he cannot even flail to keep himself afloat. Down and away he goes, lost to the sea.

Devlin watches himself return to his wife's body. His face is horribly slack; like the face of an imbecile. But hers is slacker still. Was she ever as lovely as he'd believed her to be? he wonders. There is no objective evidence. She always looked a little plain in photographs; almost as though she were rehearsing for the portraits that will soon be made here, while she lies in the grass. Nobody could see the luminosity that he'd seen in her (perhaps her young lover had seen it, too, but he wouldn't be writing any paeans to her beauty now); no, it would be a part of this mystery nobody would ever solve, because nobody living would know how it felt to be in her thrall.

It was that thought more than any other that troubled him. She was dead by his unruly hand, and that was terrible. But more terrible still, that nobody would understand her power.

Still hiding? he hears somebody say.

He holds his breath; looks around. There's nobody here but him, him and the dead.

Still he listens, and the voice comes again, up out of his own mouth. The words have light in them. *You can't blame her beauty*, he murmurs to himself. *You came here to understand. So look. Take the light with you and look.*

He doesn't need to ask where. There's only one place to seek the root of this unforgiving rage: in the soul of the man before him.

And so thinking, the light takes his phantom body across the grass to the spot where his bloody-handed other sits.

Ask your question, the light says, and dutifully he does so. *How did this begin?* he demands, as loudly as he can. The man makes no sign of having heard the question; but he draws a deep breath as he prepares to rise, and on the instant Devlin is gone, as if the inhalation was all the cue he needed to go into himself. The world vanishes, leaving him in darkness. It is a *pale* darkness, though such a thing should not be possible: its negritude a function more of its uncanny unfixedness than of its tone. There is nothing for the eye to hold on to, in any direction. Devlin does not panic, however. The light still bestows its calm upon his heart. Things will come clear, he thinks, if he will only be patient.

How long does he wait, suspended in this nowhere? It's impossible to say. But by and by the gray begins to coagulate in front of him, like a thing that was melted remembering its previous form, and gathering itself back into meaning. He sees before him a window, and through it a tree. He can smell spring now. He can feel the breeze that's gently stirring the blossom-laden branches moving against his face. Somewhere in the house behind him a door slams, but he doesn't turn to look. He knows what house this is, what window, what tree. He even knows what he will see when he goes to the window, though he has put the moment from his mind for more than thirty years.

I am me, he thinks. *I am in my memory.*

And what does he see looking down from the window through a mesh of branches and leaves? He sees a man and a woman, coupling, locked together in the most intimate fashion. The breeze rises; the canopy churns and eclipses the sight. He is frustrated; he wants to see more. He waits, and is granted another glimpse, and another, but he sees too little to answer his curiosity. He turns from the window and races through the house. All the windows are open, and everything the wind can find to move, it moves. Drapes gyrate, papers fly, a pot of geraniums is overturned. He's down at the back door now, looking out onto the dappled grass beneath the tree. There's his sister—thirteen years his senior—with her dress up almost over her face, so that the bottom half of her body, which is entirely unclothed, looks as though it's protruding from a lace-lined sack. She sobs and sighs, while a man the young Devlin does not know, his body entirely clothed (except for his phallus, which hangs out, half-aroused), fingers the tenderness between her splayed legs. Now the lover applies his mouth to that place, hooking his hands beneath the girl's knees and hoisting her feet off the ground so as to better devour her. She sobs more loudly, and calls his name. *Oh, Stephen*, she says, *that's so nice, oh yes, that's so nice.*

The boy Devlin can see more than he wants to see, but that doesn't mean he can look away. The pinkness of his sister, the wetness of his sister, the little knot of her anus, where her lover now applies his tongue; the little knots of her hands, as she squirms beneath him.

Could he run now? No; never. Even though he can feel in his belly the approaching disaster; though he can see, almost in slow motion, the frills of her dress riding down, like a dropped veil; even though he knows he will be seen here, seeing, and the consequences will be terrible, he cannot run from what is certain to happen.

And then it does. His sister's eyes come into view, first going to her devotee's face, and then, the instant after, to the face of her brother. She is crying out now, alerting Stephen to the presence of a spy, pushing him away as she flails to cover her nakedness.

The lover has risen, and his phallus wags before him like a fat, forbidding finger. He is at the boy in five or six strides, and starts to beat him so hard Devlin's on the ground in a few moments, puking as the world goes white. His sister's up now, her outrage at the presence of a witness turned to terror as the blows continue to rain down.

"*Don't kill him!*" she cries. "*Oh Stephen, no—*"

She's moving now to catch hold of her lover's arm, to check the fist before it cracks Devlin's skull like a tender egg, and for her troubles she earns a blow herself, hard, hard, across her face. It's followed by another, and another, which she answers with blows of her own, and curses, though when she spits them they come more blood than words. She falls to her knees, and seizes hold of Stephen's phallus, which is still hard. Does he fear she intends to tear it off? Or is he simply aroused to a new fever by her violence, and lets it erupt without care to the consequence? She cannot speak now; her face is too broken. And yet she holds on to his manhood, absurdly, while the blows break her further still.

And in the haze of his pain, Devlin feels the calm of the light come over him; feels the visitor he is slip out of the victim he once was, and move inexorably toward the man disfiguring his sister.

"*I want to go back to the river, please,*" he says to the

light, but he knows, even as he speaks, his journey has only just begun. He went in search of a guilty party, but having discovered his own culpability, the search cannot end there. If Devlin the man killed for the wounds Devlin the boy suffered, then what of the one who wounded him? Whence came *his* brutality?

And into Stephen's flesh he goes, like a candle flame at noon, invisible yet capable of igniting conflagrations.

vi

You know what happens next. The parable is perfectly transparent. But I have to tell you; I have to believe that my meaning resides not in the gross motion of the tale, but in the tics of syntax and cadence. If not, every story may be boiled down to a few charmless sentences; a sequence of causalities: this and this and this; then marriage, or death. There has to be more to the telling of stories, just as there must be more to our lives.

So now; Devlin is lodged in the memory of the man who brutalized him. And there he sees a dirty room, and a dirty bed. Somebody has shat on the bed, prodigiously, wiped excrement on the pillows, even on the wall against which the bed is pushed. The stench is ripe.

His borrowed gaze goes to the mirror, in which he sees reflected for an instant a man with a belt, who comes to the bed and pulls out from hiding beneath it a toddler of three or four, and starts to thrash the child without mercy. This is the Shitter, no doubt; his buttocks are caked with the stuff. But the punishment far exceeds the crime. In a few minutes the child's sobs rise to such a pitch Devlin-in-Stephen starts to scream hysterically. He instantly regrets his din. The shitting infant is cast aside, and the punishment comes Stephen's way instead: more blows, more cries.

And even in the heat of the assault, the calm of the light

comes again, and again Devlin's moving away, out of one memory into another; into the mind of the man with the belt. Is it all so simple then, he thinks as he goes: is it all only rage making itself over in its own image, down the generations? Is that the whole sorry story, forever and ever?

He's no longer in Stephen's head, but in the head of the man— is he a father, or a stepfather?—who beats him. He feels the man's heavy body around him, and heavy soul, and he sees before him not the wailing Stephen but a bare-chested boy, carrying a smile and a little knife. There is blood on the blade, and on its wielder's hand: the blood of the victim. And behind the boy with the knife, a cluster of grubby faces, enjoying the spectacle. This is what the man beating Stephen is remembering when he wields his belt: a time from childhood when the local bully entertained his cronies by pricking the defenseless boy. Devlin can hear the child's sobs; they are not so different from Stephen's, or his own.

I get the message, he says, hoping the light understands him. He doesn't need to follow the receding procession any further: the principle's perfectly clear. *Please*, he says, *you can let me go now*. But he's begun something he has no power to halt. He feels again the rush of his first inquiry, of his fierce desire to know who had taken love from him. It carries him forward, into the body of the youth before him. And there, with sickening inevitability, he finds the cruelty that made this soul brutal. A memory of the youth's mother, coming from the kitchen where she's been cutting meat, coming with the smell of dead flesh on her hands, and oh-so-casually cuffing him for some misdemeanor. It doesn't matter what. He gets half a hundred such blows from his mother every day; they don't leave bruises. But he hates her for the ease of her indifference. One day, he swears, he'll have the will to pick up the meat knife there on the counter, and stab her through her thoughtless heart—

Enough! Devlin cries again. But no, of course; he's

already slipping into the bloody-handed housewife, into this sad woman who thinks nothing of pain, given or received, who is dead to it, dead to it, watching her uncle skin an animal whose heart is still beating, and then smiling up at her with a look in his eyes she knows means he's aroused by his wretched work: by the agony of the animal, and the vulnerability of his little girl, not yet ten and sweeter naked even than the skinned body twitching on the rock. He will have his fingers in her very soon, and she will wish she were dead—

—and so does he, in the very moment of the deed. Wishes he were the dying animal, guiltless in its suffering, instead of the man he cannot help being, in all his wretchedness. He never sees himself more clearly than in the moment of violation, while she sobs for him to be quick, please Uncle, please Uncle—

—in his youth he knew a man of the cloth, who had told him that guilt and grief were as the salt of the soul, preserving us from the worm of contentment, and keeping us wholesome, so that God might devour us into paradise at the end of time. These words have haunted him, over the years: filled his head with images of his body laid on God's Table, along with all the other bodies of guilty souls like himself. And thinking of being devoured, he would be aroused, and in his arousal, think of children, and how he might bring them to that table with him, how he might have company on Judgment Day.

He sees the priest in his mind's eye now, as he steps away from the rock, leaving the raped girl to cover herself up. He sees tears rolling down the man's face. And the search goes on, into the priest's head; into a memory within a memory within a memory . . .

The priest had lost all hope of his own innocence during a little war, in Europe, in which he had fallen in love with a soldier. They had never touched, except to shake hands; nor even exchanged a word of affection. But the priest had been certain his tender feelings were reciprocated, and on the last day of the war he had gone to declare his feelings to the man. He found him, after much searching, among a heap of corpses. There was an old soldier rolling the bodies into a mass grave, and seeing the priest staring at his beloved's face, he asked: *Did you know this man?*

The priest had been ashamed of what he felt, and replied that no, he didn't know the man, he was merely meditating on the absolute authority of death. The gravedigger pretended to be convinced, but he was not. He hated priests—their cant, their smugness—and saw here an opportunity to discomfort the man before him. If it's inspiration you're looking for, he said, beckoning the priest closer to the soldier's corpse, then look no further than this, and so saying he uncovered the soldier's hips, which had been blown open to the shattered bone,

—and watching the priest reel and sicken and run howling from the sight, the gravedigger laughs, though there is no humor in his laughter.

He had loved deeply in his own youth, and lost the objects of his devotion: two sisters, with whom he had lived in godless bliss for five years, until a plague took them both, along with the six children they had given him, all in the space of a week.

And the plague had been spread to the women by a man who knew he was carrying death in his touch, and was passing it along even as he chucked the children under the chin and grazed the cheeks of the women with his thumb. He had got this plague in Africa, where he had gone as a mercenary, and had seen such cruelties visited upon innocents, and became so maddened by all he witnessed that he came to think of his plague-spreading as a kindness.

And so on; and on; mind within mind, harm within harm.

Devlin doesn't weep anymore. He is already inured against the harms that he's witnessing. He doesn't remember his purpose here; he doesn't even remember who he is. He only flies and flies, through a catalog of loss and cruelty, innocence punished and guilt rewarded, suffering unexplained, death undeserved. Sometimes he's in the body of a man, sometimes a woman, sometimes a child. He feels their forms changing around him, as the light carries him on down the line of deeds and doers. He vaguely grasps that this journey will deliver him at last into some primordial state: that he's journeying back to some first cause. But the notion is too difficult for him to hold on to for more than a moment; it's gone the next, and he's like a witless cargo dispatched into the past, his mind like a sleeper's mind, grasping only the vague forms of dreams.

vii

And on the riverbank, the birds grow silent. The cold air vibrates; it shakes silvery motes of frost from the tiniest blades of grass. Something is imminent.

The river is too mighty to be influenced, of course. It rushes on, its course unchanged. Some distance downstream of this spot, Shank is looking for the hillmen who he believes killed his beloved wife; in a matter of hours he will be dead himself, and in the river's heart, carried away. Now the shaking of things increases, and a form appears between the trees, lit by its own strange light.

Not far from the place, Oswald has come to fetch Agnes's body off the riverbank; and encounters there what he takes to be some kind of spirit. It isn't. It's just our poor, lost Devlin, wandering. He has come to the riverbank and seen the corpse there, and the sight has been enough to shake him back into some sense of his purpose. He remembers being in Shirley's house; he remembers the grief and incomprehenion that drove him there. And, of course, he remembers the deed that he had hidden from himself: his sweet Mary Elizabeth, bleeding before him.

Seeing this other woman—a more pitiful corpse (if that were possible) than that of his wife—lying in the mud, he is restored to a terrible sanity. That is to say: he is himself again. But he does not understand the symmetry of the events. He thinks he is seeing his own wife's corpse, somehow transformed. He goes to look at it more closely. No, this is not remotely his Mary Elizabeth.

Who is she? he asks the river. The river roars on, offering up no reply.

He turns his head away from the sight of her, and sees—there between the trees—a figure, dressed in animal skins, watching him. *Is this the murderer,* he wonders, *caught in the act of flight?* What a pitiful sight he is: a shadowy thing, that can never have peace.

And he starts to weep, thinking of that. Not of the man before him, who may not even be responsible, but of himself, who is lost on a search that has no conclusion, at least until he gets back to the first crime, to the Edenic sin: and how will he keep his sanity on a journey of that magnitude? Impossible.

He asks the man between the trees: *Who is she?* not really expecting a reply. He's not surprised then that the man takes flight and is gone, off between the trees, leaving Devlin alone beside the river, his heart too full for him to be able to shape questions. What is it full of? Oh, nothing pure, nothing that will bring the story to a nicely moral close. He does not feel a scouring remorse for what he will do a thousand years hence, on the bank of the river; he has not found a deeper comprehension of how the human heart works. He has only learned in his journey here what he already knew—that cruelty breeds cruelty. So what? So what if he was shaped by the hands of others to do harm with his own hands? There's no

beauty in such repetition, no deeper meaning. Shirley wa
right; there is no grand scheme.

So, where now, he wonders. Must he move on, and o
resigning himself to this terrible descent? He has no choice i
the matter, it seems. He is resigned to losing all meaning c
himself as he moves on, down the millennia, weaving throug
lives that are not his, and yet are, because he is their conse
quence: the grotesque summation of all their sufferings an
their harms.

If he could turn to me, if he could find me in my shac
by the river, what, I wonder, would he ask of me, who ha
control of his destiny?

I'm imagining him now, coming to the threshold, duck
ing his head under the mossy bough that makes the lintel c
the door, looking at me and saying: *Are you my maker*?

I tell him: *Yes, I am.*

You brought me here? he says.

I tell him: *Yes, I did.*

And where will I go now? he asks.

Well, I tell him. *The choices are simple. The river—*

—flows both ways, he says, a little irritably; *Yes, yes, s
I've heard. So it's either forward or back, that's what you'r
telling me.*

I shrug. *In short*, I say.

Well I like neither option, he replies. *If I go back, what
there for me? I give myself up to the police, claim insanit
and take my chances in the courts? Not a very attractiv
idea. And if I continue on my present path, I'll end up an ap
The first sinning ape, that's what I'll be. I don't like tho
either.*

So tell me what you want, I say to him.

*I want a way out, I want a chance at redemption.
want—*

He pauses in mid-sentence, looks back.

What is it? I ask him.

I heard—

What?

—somebody crying.

That's not so unusual, I tell him. *Maybe somebody in the river—*

Drowning, you mean?

It's happened, I reply.

And you just sit here? he says, making no attempt to disguise his disgust at my passivity.

Again, I shrug. *If they threw themselves in and then regret it, that's their problem,* I tell him.

But if it was an accident, he says; *if they were just walking by the river, and they lost their footing, and slipped, and didn't mean—* There are tears in his eyes now. *If they weren't able to control themselves—*

Like you? I say softly.

He glares at me. But the tears do not stop. They fill up his eyes, then spill down his cheeks. *I wish I could undo everything. I wish I could go to her grave and wake her up.*

I had a vision once—

Of what?

People living backwards. A man was digging these corpses out of the ground—

There's that cry again, he says, turning away from me. *Somebody's out there—*

Wait, I haven't finished telling you my vision.

Fuck your visions, he says; *they're no use to me now. You're as lost as I am.*

So saying, he leaves me in my hide, and the imagined conversation is at an end.

And yet I hear him still. Even though he was never with me, even though I have always been alone here at the river, waiting for a story to come and find me, I hear him out there, over the sound of the water.

Wait, he is saying. *Wait.*

Here's a new twist, I think to myself. The man acts a
though he has a measure of self-determination: as though h
can step away from me and still live, somehow. It's imposs
ble, of course. I conjured him in service of my story; he ca
have no existence beyond my dream of him; he can take n
journey that I do not first imagine.

And yet as I rise from my place in the shadows I know
am about to be proved wrong, and the thought exhilarate
me. Devlin has gone where I have not yet looked. All I ca
do is *follow*, strange though that may be.

I step out into the twilight, and look for him. There he is
not twenty yards from the hide, moving off between th
trees. The flame he carries flickers in him, spilling out upo
the grass, and the trunks of the trees, and the bare branche
over his head. I watch him, enchanted. So, too, does the ma
whose weeping called Devlin out here: Father Michael. H
kneels beside the body of Agnes, the blade with which he di
her such harm clutched in his hand. He has lifted up hi
robes, exposing his genitals. He intends, I think, to mutilat
himself here, beside her, to render his sex as unrecognizabl
as he did hers, so that when he's bled to death his body wi
look not unlike hers below the waist.

But the sight of Devlin puts such thoughts out of hi
head. He drops the knife, and his weeping ceases.

My Lord, he murmurs, meaning no profanity. The ma
moving between the trees toward him does indeed resem
ble his long-absent Saviour. The light that comes from hi
very substance; the sweet calm of his countenance; an
most of all, the way he reaches out toward Father Michael
as if to forgive what until this moment had seemed unfor
givable.

What should I do? Should I intervene to dissuade him o
his error? Tell him that the man from whom he is hoping t
receive forgiveness is just as guilty as he; just a sinner, lost i
time beside the river? No; that would be just another cruelty

add to the catalog; it would serve no purpose, except per-
ps to salve my envy at the comfort he feels.

I move a little closer, in the hope of hearing what passes
tween them, but I'm not quick enough. By the time I get
thin earshot they've already finished exchanging those few
rds they wished to say, and Father Michael is rising from
side Agnes's body, dropping the knife with which he was
ing to unman himself. He reaches toward his Redeemer,
d as he does so—tears of gratitude running down his
e—Devlin opens his arms. It isn't an embrace he offers;
's simply giving the repentant Father sight of the flame,
ich to my eyes at least seems to have taken up residence
Devlin's chest. It flutters to the rhythm of his heart, its
andescence being steadily pumped through his system. I
n see its spreading presence, even through the weave of
vlin's shirt and trousers: it's as though he's being con-
med by the flame from the inside out. I don't discard the
ssibility that this is indeed the case. Didn't Shirley observe
t holy things have intentions all their own?

Whatever the significance of this sight, it has entranced
ther Michael: no doubt it further reinforces his belief that
man before him is some divinity. He reaches out to touch
light-hearted Saviour, and as his fingers make contact the
me grows suddenly ambitious, and in a shocking moment
consumes the flesh and bone of Devlin Coombs entirely
ong with the clothes that covered that flesh and bone)
ving only a glorious filigree of light-filled veins standing
re, with a flaming heart at its core. Devlin makes no sound
he is burned away. It is as though the light has simply
alled the illusion of his substance into itself; as though he
d been the flame's invention all along, rather than mine.

(There's a thought: that the flame is all that exists here,
rest of us simply shadows it casts on a page, myself
luded. I thought I was indulging Devlin's delusions, let-
g him believe he was self-willed; but perhaps I am in my

turn indulged by the flame, which allows me to concea
omnipotence in a fiction.)

Father Michael has given up weeping; this is too tren
dous for tears. He watches, wearing a small smile, like
of an enchanted child, while the flame does what he
surely hoping it would do: it moves along his fingers,
into his own body. The pattern of veins that sketched the
of Devlin follows its maker, and goes where the flame g
Father Michael starts to say thank you, not once but ha
hundred times. Does he expect the fire to burn him out o
impure state? If so, he is disappointed. His body envelops
light, utterly, sealing it up. When it's gone into him the
nothing, not the least glimmer, to show that he has b
blessed by its presence. There is only the darkness of
wood, and the rushing of the river, and a woman, dead in
grass.

Father Michael doesn't look at her again. He walks
haps ninety yards from where she lies, finding a place wh
he has sight of the sky, and there he lies down himself, a
outstretched.

It's only after several hours that I realize what he inte
to do. He intends to do nothing, except to lie there in
grass and let his body die.

It is not a quick business, believe me. He stays alive
five days, lying in the same place, the stink of his evacuati
drawing the attention of wild animals, who are startled, w
they come too close, to realize this piece of human flesh
breathes.

On the second morning of his martyrdom, two men fi
the village come with Oswald and collect Agnes's bo
Plainly Oswald has warned them that this is a haunted pl
and they do not linger, but pick up the corpse and bea
away quickly. None of them sees Father Michael; nor doe
make any attempt to draw their attention.

The short hours of those first days of the year one th

and pass, and the long, cold nights, one of which brings a
light flurry of snow. I hear the priest's teeth chatter now and
then; and on the fourth night he slips into a delirious state, in
the throes of which he sometimes prays in Latin, sometimes
talks, as though to an invisible companion. More than once I
am tempted to go and sit beside him and listen. But I resist.
This is his time. He's earned his solitude.

Just before midnight, on January the fifth, his breathing
becomes quick and shallow, then it stops entirely. I feel
lonely, once he's gone, though I knew these men, this two-in-
one, less well than I had assumed. In fact, to be honest,
scarcely at all. Perhaps on reflection it's not loneliness I feel.
Perhaps it's envy, that they found one another, and redeemed
their souls with faith and flame and were so comforted by
that they believed they could die a wretched death and count
themselves blessed.

After a time, I go and watch the river.

And after another time, I set these last words down, lay
my notebook where I hope it may be found, and, discovering
a place where the waters are so tumultuous that there is little
chance I can resist them, I wade in.

I cannot tell you if John of the Desert, dressed in his coat
of goatskins, awaits me there, his hands spilling baptismal
water; or if Christopher the Giant will come to set me on his
shoulders, calling me Chylde; or if Christ may come, trout
leaping at His heavy hem, eager to strew their rainbows
before His pierced feet.

Or if I will be only carried away, looking through the
plain glass of my eyes, hoping to see before I drown sun,
moon, and stars hanging in the same firmament.

THE END

[an afterword]

BY DOUGLAS E. WINTER

Long ago, but not so far away, I edited an anthology of original stories called *Prime Evil*. The book was meant to celebrate that elusive fiction known as "horror" as it reached a publishing zenith in the 1980s. I thought of its contents as horror fiction for people who didn't read horror fiction: a showcase of name writers and quality prose that would remind readers of the grand literary tradition that was being trivialized by the idea of genre. My ambition was rewarded, and the book's success in the marketplace summoned an inevitable proposition from its publisher: the dreaded sequel.

I declined without hesitation. *Prime Evil II* seemed a contradiction in terms. There was much yet to say about horror, and the money was good; but by definition, the second in a series can merely replicate what has gone before it. There was also a grim irony: Revisiting the same territory would simply affirm the confines of genre that *Prime Evil* was intended to breach. A second volume seemed as vital as a seventh, or seventieth. What readers—and writers—needed was something new. I promised my publisher, and myself, that I could deliver something better than a sequel, and indeed, something unique.

The idea, when it came to me, was not entirely original. Every so often, when writers huddle together (usually in a bar), there is wild talk of collaboration and, on occasion, the outlandish possibility of a novel written by a group of bright talents.

Like others, I've wondered from time to time whether this idle conversation could be realized in print. There are precedents, including three novels produced in the 1930s by the "Detection Club," a conclave of British crime writers whose members included Anthony Berkeley, Agatha Christie, Milward Kennedy, and Dorothy L. Sayers. To celebrate an anniversary of *Fantasy Magazine*, Julius Schwartz conceived "The Challenge from Beyond" (September 1935), a pair of stories written "round robin" by such pulp fiction giants as Robert E. Howard, H. P. Lovecraft, A. Merritt, and E. E. "Doc" Smith. More recently, the saturnalian *Naked Came the Stranger* (1969) was penned by a pseudonymous cabal. But these texts were burdened by their very conceit, which forced writers to share characters, settings, plot, and—in pursuit of narrative cohesion—style. Vision and voice, the qualities that define our best writers, were subjugated to a common denominator.

A more tenuous group endeavor is the "shared world" anthology, in which individual stories are set in a fictional landscape with its own descriptive set of rules. These books are increasingly popular, but (as their name implies) dictate that writers share characters or settings, usually for the purpose of merchandising a popular comic book, television series, or film. Writers of imaginative fiction (save those who enjoy technical challenges or need the income) rarely find inspiration or create great fiction when bending their talents to the predefined needs of others. For similar reasons, writers sometimes opt out of vaguely collaborative "theme" anthologies, which tie stories together with a common, often slender, thread.

To bring the best and brightest of writers together, I needed a forum that would offer total creative freedom yet produce the narrative drive and thematic unity of a novel. For a time, I doubted that there was a solution.

Awakening one night in darkness, in the hammerlock of yssomnia, I found myself contemplating life in another ten ears, at the end of another decade—indeed, the end of a cenry—when I would reach an unimaginable fifty years of ge. Because I was born in 1950, my life has seemed meaured by the decade, and the year 2000 has held obvious sigificance for me; but I realized that this year was ripe with eaning for us all and that its passage should be memorialed in fiction.

In mathematical terms, the year 2000 marks the last year f the twentieth century (and not, as many believe, the first ear of the twenty-first). The number itself, with all those eroes, is daunting, especially following a year of triple ines. The way that we write, read, and perceive of years will e altered dramatically; but I doubt that the earth will shake, r the moon turn to blood. Although we have heard stories of illennial frenzy in the year 999, historians now discount the les of widespread panic that supposedly accompanied the lose of the first millennium.

The passage of a thousand years—a chiliad, as Clive arker observes—has particular significance for the hristian faith; but its meaning has been warped in errant vangelism such that many believe that the millennium is a arbinger of imminent destruction. In fact, the millennium voked in Chapter 20 of the *Apocalypse of St. John the ivine* occurs after the Tribulation; it is the thousand-year eign of Christ on earth, during which holiness will prevail efore the final Night of Judgment and the proverbial erfect Day.

The word *apocalypse* is likewise misunderstood to refer to verwhelming catastrophe, if not the end of the world. As the lternate title of St. John's delirious masterwork tells us, apoc-lypse—from the Greek *apokalyptein*, to uncover—actually eans revelation. Just as St. John's *Revelation* is the last book f the New Testament, the final years of a century—particularly those of a millennium—are latent with apocalypse. It is global anniversary and, inevitably, a time of summing up ar looking ahead. A time of revelations.

What better way to mark the close of the twentieth cen tury and the birth of the twenty-first, the end of the secon millennium and the start of the third, than through a sequenc of stories, one set in each decade of the past hundred years Here was a structure that allowed writers to work from the heart, yet through its chronological insistence would have the framework and continuity of a novel.

The result, the first "anthology/novel," was to be known a *Millennium*. For the next seven years, I learned the difficul of fulfilling its heady promise while living the life of the law In the process, my work came to the enthusiastic attention of HarperCollins, which became my new publisher. A televisio series co-opted my title, and I embraced a more meaningfu one: *Revelations*.

Despite my travels and travails, the writers who I asked t contribute responded with enthusiasm and energy, and stor by story we constructed the book. Their challenge, as writer of conscience, was to challenge our readers by creating enter tainment that engages the imagination and, in its be moments, offers precisely what our title promises: revela tions. You will find, I trust, that the writers who joined me o this journey have done just that.

There were no rules: the writers were given a choice c decades, the book's millennial title, and the rare opportunit to be expansive—to write without concern about page limit The stories, better described as short novels, were not writte in any particular order. No one saw what any other writer ha created, except for David J. Schow and Craig Spector, t whom I slipped F. Paul Wilson's "Aryans and Absinthe" afte reading the first draft of "Dismantling Fortress Architecture and recognizing the convergence of their tales. When the fina decade was completed, Clive Barker took on the dauntin

ask of creating a short novel that would "wrap around" the
entury and yet remain defiantly a fiction to be read on its
wn (and, in his hands, majestic) terms.

Although I invited writers who were known for their pen-
hant for the dark fantastic, not once did I use the word "hor-
or" in describing the book. That once-harmless sobriquet
ad become an epithet to some, a ghetto to many. Although
is a fine label for a sweeping literary tradition—try to name
great writer who has not produced a supernatural story—
horror" has been tainted by the clichéd, usually blackjack-
ted by-products of commercial publishing, most of them
bout vampires or serial killers (and sometimes both).

I wanted fiction that spoke to me with an original voice, that
ngaged me in a dialogue, and I chose the writers whose words
ad moved me, surprised me, remained vibrant in a time of rep-
tition and glut. I wanted assurance that the fiction nominally
nown as "horror" would survive into the twenty-first century;
nd I wanted *Revelations* to offer that assurance to readers.

In the final years of the nineteenth century, the Western
iterature of horror and the supernatural experienced a pro-
ound change. In the space of but a few years, an astonishing
umber of seminal works of horror were published, including
Robert Louis Stevenson's *The Strange Case of Dr. Jekyll and
Mr. Hyde* (1886); Oscar Wilde's *The Picture of Dorian Gray*
1891); Arthur Machen's *The Great God Pan* (1894); H. G.
Wells's *The Island of Doctor Moreau* (1896) and *War of the
Worlds* (1897–98); Bram Stoker's *Dracula* (1897); Henry
ames's *The Turn of the Screw* (1898); Arthur Conan Doyle's
The Hound of the Baskervilles (1901); W. W. Jacobs's "The
Monkey's Paw" (1902); and Joseph Conrad's *Heart of
Darkness* (1902). Although there are alternative explana-
ions—the imperial decline of the European states, the new
media (cheaply produced newspapers and books, through
which the written word obtained mass audiences for the first
ime in history)—it is tempting to consider the role that the

approach of double zeroes, the end of the century, played
the creative psyche.

The fin de siècle marked the transition of this literatu
from the gothic to the iconic. With the new century, and tl
advent of visual media (motion pictures and, later, com
books and television), the personification of horror in a visu
construct—the creature—became paramount. The aestheti
of seeing have dominated our popular culture ever sinc
spawning the "monster movies" of the fifties and the bloo
splattered special effects films of the eighties and nineties, 1
which optical illusion took primacy over plot—and, in tl
worst cases, the only human role was that of victim.

A deft morality play for television, Rod Serling's "Tl
Monsters Are Due on Maple Street" (*The Twilight Zon*
1960), warned of the dangers of seeking the monstrous i
skin other than our own. Just as Jane Austen's *Northang*
Abbey (1818) signaled the certain sunset of the gothic by cr
tiquing its preoccupation with the external, Serling's simp
scenario, in which everyday people hasten with McCarthyi
fervor to condemn each other as monsters, underscored tl
fragile reign of the creature. Horror, these writers remind u
is not the safe pretense of twisted houses or twisted bodies—
or even twisted minds. It is that which cannot be made safe—
evolving, ever-changing—because it is about our relentle
need to confront the unknown, the unknowable, and the emc
tion we experience while in its thrall.

Now we have seen the monsters—now that they hav
arrived on Maple Street—we have learned that certain trutl
They are us. Although we will no doubt endure, and occasior
ally enjoy, their reign for years to come, the success c
Christopher Pike and R. L. Stine in mediating the imagery c
monsters to young readers suggests that, as the Bible remind
us, there comes a time to put away childish things.

As creators and consumers of the dark fantastic, we fin
ourselves at a turning point not unlike that faced by the dream

ers and devotees who confronted the end of the nineteenth century. Perhaps the correlation is fortuitous, the product of social and technological forces that have no concern for calendars. But perhaps, just perhaps, there is something else at work, a metaphysical yearning as the clock counts down to the final minute of that hundredth year—to the end, and beginning, of a millennium—that tells us it is time to move on: to another horror, one that, like each new day, has unlimited possibilities.

Although each of the contributors to *Revelations* has my lasting gratitude for their remarkable efforts (and their patience), I must single out David J. Schow, who knows why, for the next round of black-and-tans; and Clive Barker, for being there, first and last and always.

The enthusiasm and encouragement of my original editor, Hilary Ross (whom I miss dearly), was matched and trumped by John Silbersack and Caitlin Blasdell of Harper-Collins U.S. and Jane Johnson of HarperCollins U.K. Each of them has my heartfelt thanks.

Revelations is one of the few books that has required a team of lawyers to see it into print, and I must acknowledge the work of Dan Brooks and Eamonn Foley of Layton, Brooks & Hecht in helping teach a certain someone a valuable lesson.

Thanks also to Peter Schneider, Walter Jon Williams, and Amy Stout for their honesty and integrity; to Michael Barry and William C. Winter for historical advice and assistance; to Steven Spruill for lunch; to Dr. Anton Trinidad for his words to the occasionally unwise; and, most of all, to my agent, Howard Morhaim, and my wife, Lynne, for standing by their man.

Douglas E. Winter
Detroit, Michigan, 1990–
Oakton, Virginia, 1997

THE CONTRIBUTORS

LIVE BARKER ("Chiliad: A Meditation"): Born October 5, 952, in Liverpool, England, Clive Barker began his career s a playwright and illustrator but took the publishing world y storm with his *Books of Blood*. His novels include *The amnation Game, Weaveworld, Imajica, Everville*, and *acrament*, as well as a book for young (and old) adults, *The hief of Always*. He has written and directed the motion pic- res *Hellraiser, Nightbreed*, and *Lord of Illusions*, and his twork has been exhibited at major American galleries. He ves in Beverly Hills, California. For more information, visit he *Web of Lost Souls* (http://www.clivebarker.com).

OPPY Z. BRITE ("Triads"): Born May 25, 1967, in New rleans, Louisiana, where she now lives, Poppy Z. Brite is a nique voice among a new generation of writers. She has ublished the novels *Lost Souls, Drawing Blood*, and *xquisite Corpse*. Her short stories and articles have ppeared in a diverse array of books and magazines, includ- g *Rage, Spin, Spy,* and *VLS*; some of them are collected in *ormwood* (also published as *Swamp Foetus*). She is editor f the *Love in Vein* anthologies, and she recently completed biography of Courtney Love. For more information, visit *andora Station* (http://www.negia.net/~pandora/).

AMSEY CAMPBELL ("The Word"): Born January 4, 946, in Liverpool, England, Ramsey Campbell completed s first collection of short stories, *The Inhabitant of the Lake*

and Less Welcome Tenants, at age sixteen. He has si
become one of the most widely published and honored w
ers of short fiction of our time, with more than two hund
stories and ten fiction collections to his credit. His fift
novels include, most recently, *The Long Lost, The One S
Place*, and *The House on Nazareth Hill*. He has edited s
eral anthologies, frequently writes criticism, and revie
motion pictures for BBC Radio Merseyside. He lives
Wallasey, England.

CHRISTA FAUST ("Triads"): Born June 21, 1969, in N
York City, Christa Faust worked for eight years as a prof
sional dominatrix before moving to Los Angeles, where s
traded in her whip to become a promising writer of inten
often darkly erotic, fiction. Her short stories have been p
lished in *Love in Vein, Hot Blood, Noirotica, Gargoyles,* a
Young Blood. She has starred in her own bondage video a
stalked runways modeling fetish designs; photographs
her have appeared in periodicals ranging from *Tattoo Sav*
and *Rage* to the *New York Times*. For more information, v
Pandora Station (http://www.negia.net/~pandora/).

CHARLES GRANT ("Riding the Black"): B
September 12, 1942, in Newark, New Jersey, Char
Grant served in Vietnam and the New Jersey school syst
before becoming a full-time writer. He has published m
than a hundred books, including pseudonymous excursic
into the realms of fantasy, humor, and romance, as well
twenty anthologies. His own stories have been showcas
in *A Glow of Candles, Tales from the Nightside*, and oth
collections. His novels include the Oxrun Station seri
the recent *Raven* and *Jackals*, and the Millennium Quart
whose initial volumes are *Symphony* and *In the Mood*.
lives in Newton, New Jersey.

OE R. LANSDALE ("The Big Blow"): Born October 28, 951, in Gladewater, Texas, Joe R. Lansdale is a lifelong res- dent of East Texas and has the accent to prove it. His talents pan the fields of mystery, suspense, fantasy, horror, adven- ure, and the western, and he has written over two hundred hort stories (which feature in seven collections), four tele- plays (including work on *Batman: The Animated Series*), and hree screenplays. He has also edited seven anthologies of iction and nonfiction. His novels include *Cold in July, Mucho Mojo, Bad Chili*, and a posthumous collaboration vith Edgar Rice Burroughs, *Tarzan's Lost Adventure*. He ives in Nagodoches, Texas.

ELIZABETH MASSIE ("Fixtures of Matchstick Men & oo"): Born September 6, 1953, in Waynesboro, Virginia, vhere she now lives, Elizabeth Massie has published short iction since 1984, with appearances in a variety of maga- zines and anthologies, including *Women of Darkness, Obsessions, A Whisper of Blood*, the *Borderlands* series, and he *Best New Horror* series. Her stories have been collected n *Southern Discomfort* and *Shadow Dreams,* and her first novel was *Sineater*. She has written for younger audiences in *American Chills: Ghost Harbor*, the *Daughters of Liberty* rilogy, and the teleplay for the Parents' Choice Award win- ing "Rhymes and Reasons."

RICHARD CHRISTIAN MATHESON ("Whatever"): Born October 14, 1953, in Santa Monica, California, Richard Christian Matheson survived writing and producing more han five hundred television episodes to become a leading Hollywood screenwriter with over fifteen original feature cripts, including the wickedly funny *Three O'Clock High*, to is credit. His short stories have appeared in *Penthouse, Twilight Zone, Omni*, and major anthologies, and many of hem are collected in *Scars and Other Distinguishing Marks*

and *Dystopia*. His debut novel was *Created By*. A drummer with the alternative rock band The Existers, he lives in Malibu.

DAVID MORRELL ("If I Should Die Before I Wake") Born April 24, 1943, in Kitchener, Ontario, David Morrell was a literature professor at the University of Iowa before resigning to write full-time. He is best known as the author of *First Blood* (which created the character Rambo) and a series of thrillers, including *The Brotherhood of the Rose* and, most recently, *Extreme Denial*; but his diverse writings have included a western, *Last Reveille*; a fantasy, *The Hundred-Year Christmas*; a horror novel, *The Totem*; and a compelling revery on the death of his teenage son, *Fireflies*. He lives in Santa Fe, New Mexico.

DAVID J. SCHOW ("Dismantling Fortress Architecture") Born July 13, 1955, in Marburg, West Germany, and imported to the U.S. (where he now lives in the Hollywood Hills), David J. Schow sortied into fiction and screenwriting in the 1980s, producing the collections *Seeing Red, Lost Angels,* and *Black Leather Required*, as well as the novels *The Kill Riff* and *The Shaft*. He edited *Silver Scream* and authored the *Outer Limits Companion*. His screen credits include *Leatherface: Texas Chainsaw Massacre III, The Crow*, and episodes of *Freddy's Nightmares, Tales from the Crypt, The Outer Limits, Perversions of Science*, and *The Hunger*.

CRAIG SPECTOR ("Dismantling Fortress Architecture") Born July 16, 1958, in Richmond, Virginia, Craig Spector is the co-author of six novels: *The Light at the End, The Cleanup, The Scream, Dead Lines, The Bridge,* and *Animals*. His short fiction has appeared in several magazines and anthologies, and he co-edited the *Book of the Dead* series. A graduate with honors of the Berklee College of Music in Boston, he is an accomplished songwriter and musician whose recordings include a soundtrack for *The Bridge*. He lives in Pasadena, California, where he is working on television and motion picture projects, as well as a new novel, *A Question of Will*. For more information, contact CraigS666@aol.com.

WHITLEY STRIEBER ("The Open Doors"): Born June 13, 1945, in San Antonio, Texas, where he lives today, Whitley Strieber has authored several novels of the dark fantastic, including *The Wolfen, The Hunger, The Night Church*, and *The Forbidden Zone*. With *War Day* and *Nature's End* (both written with James Kunetka) and *Majestic*, he turned to apocalyptic science fiction and political themes. His controversial *Communion: A True Story* offered disturbing accounts of his personal experiences with strange visitors, which were explored further in *Transformation* and *Breakthrough*. For more information, visit http://www.strieber.com.

F. PAUL WILSON ("Aryans and Absinthe"): Born May 17, 1946, in Jersey City, New Jersey, F. Paul Wilson began selling short fiction while a first-year medical student. He has since balanced careers as a physician and bestselling novelist, writing sixteen novels ranging from science fiction (*Healer, Wheels Within Wheels*) to the supernatural (*The Keep, The Tomb, Black Wind*) to his recent medical thrillers *The Select, Implant,* and *Deep as the Marrow*. Some of his short fiction is collected in *Soft & Others*. He has edited two anthologies and collaborated with Matthew J. Costello and Steven Spruill. He lives in southern New Jersey. For more information, visit http://www.siue.edu/~kcole/f.paul/f.paul.html.

DOUGLAS E. WINTER (editor): Born October 30, 1950, in St. Louis, Missouri, Douglas E. Winter is a partner of the law firm Bryan Cave LLP and is known for his critical writing on fiction and film, as well as his own short stories. He is a frequent contributor to major newspapers and magazines, and his eleven books include *Stephen King: The Art of Darkness, Faces of Fear, Prime Evil,* and a forthcoming biography/critique of Clive Barker. A trilogy of his short fiction is showcased in *American Zombie.* He lives in Oakton, Virginia, a distant suburb of Washington, D.C. For more information, contact OnEyeDog@aol.com.

And God shall wipe away all tears from their eyes;
and there shall be no more death,
neither sorrow, nor crying,
neither shall there be any more pain:
for the former have all passed away.

—Revelation 21:4

Explore the Many Worlds of

CLIVE BARKER

novels

There are more than 3.5 million copies of Clive Barker's novels in print from HarperPaperbacks.

SACRAMENT
EVERVILLE
THE GREAT AND SECRET SHOW
THE HELLBOUND HEART
IMAJICA (Volumes I and II)
IMAJICA (trade paperback coming soon)

plays

In addition to being an accomplished novelist, filmmaker, and artist, Clive Barker has also authored two stunning collections of original plays. Like his other works, their comedy is always tinged with darkness, and their tragedy is never far from wonderment.

INCARNATIONS
FORMS OF HEAVEN

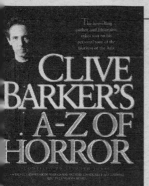